PHOENIX LEGACY

BOOK ONE

CAROL GIBBS

Printed in Australia

Cover by @lizzacreative

Images in this book are copyright approved for use by author

First printing: November 2025

Paperback ISBN 978-1-7643069-0-4

eBook ISBN 978-1-7643069-1-1

A catalogue record for this work is available from the National Library of Australia

Distributed by Lightning Source Global

DEDICATIONS

To my daughter for her inspiration, to my husband for his loving support and to my friends and family who read my work and motivated me to publish.

1

THE LEGACY

THE VAN SPLUTTERED as it pulled into the car park. As soon as Danika stepped out of her van she was met with the sounds of laughter and children playing. The small shopping precinct and green area outside the Hunter Valley Gardens was a buzzing hive of activity with holiday makers enjoying the area. Danika's mother had recommended the stop after seeing the gardens on a popular TV gardening show. Danika walked the short distance to the entry of the gardens and paid the entry fee, noting the big chunk it took out of her daily allocation of funds.

Grabbing the gardens map, Danika walked and studied it, deciding where in the stunning gardens and calming surrounds she wanted to see first. The pamphlet showed there were several gardens to view, however Danika was immediately drawn to the waterfall with its water splashing gently over granite rocks into a lake rimmed with conifers and roses with carefully pruned low bushes to give maximum view.

Mum would love this garden, thought Danika. *Well maybe not all the formal bits but this waterfall is so lovely. If I can just frame myself and the waterfall but then all these people get in the way.* Danika smiled at the other tourists enjoying the sunken garden and waited patiently for them to move out of her view to take a selfie just so she could prove to her mother that she was really enjoying her nomadic life.

'Would you like me to take your picture?' A voice from the side interrupted her thoughts. Danika looked around to see a tall, blonde and – she must admit – handsome man in sunglasses looking at her. Danika hesitated, not really wanting any interactions with anyone.

'I won't steal it.' He smiled a stunning set of teeth. A sense of foolishness washed through her, he didn't look like a thief or stalker.

'Thank you. It is rather lovely and my mother would enjoy seeing me in the shot so yes, thanks,' she said as she handed her phone over. Danika was not sure why she had brought her mother into this.

He took one picture and then offered to take another. 'One more, just to be sure,' he said.

She grinned at the phrase, which was the shot he took. It would be a more casual stance and expression than one she had planned as a selfie.

He handed the phone back to Danika but as she grabbed it their fingers touched. An electric shock raced through her, not like static but more an all over body shock. She looked away immediately. Mumbling a 'many thanks' she walked briskly past the stranger out of the gardens. Disregarding the fact that she had only seen half of the gardens and paid more than she could really afford for the privilege, she rushed to her van and, once inside, took the chance to look around. He hadn't followed her and she couldn't see him. She took a deep breath only then realising she had been holding it as she ran.

In the relative safety of her van, she rubbed her fingers where they had touched. Putting a hand on her side to half hug herself she resolved to shake off the experience and move on to the next winery she had been interested in, instead of going into the garden cellars. She chided herself for being so rattled by a touch and decided that she could always come back another day. Danika drove away in what she thought was the general direction to the next winery but a sense of direction was not always her best skill – it took a few extra turns and kilometres to get there. After parking and sorting her bag and money out Danika walked towards the cellar door but her hand paused on the handle as she recognised the man standing at the bar tasting wine.

Good grief, Danika thought but turned swiftly around. Getting back in her van she couldn't believe that she ran into – well, almost – the same man who probably thought she was crazy bolting away before. *I guess he is wine touring also*, Danika thought. *Well if he is here he won't be at the next winery.*

'Third time is a charm,' she murmured as she held a calming rose quartz crystal against her heart.

Cristian

Cristian knew he should be enjoying the beautiful gardens. Skilfully designed and meticulously maintained it could be argued it was art, though not the art he normally searched out. His family had said he needed to have some relaxation time, down time from the fast pace of his life for a little while. So here he was winery touring in the Hunter Valley, but it wasn't quite his style. Walking around the bend in the path he noticed a girl with long black hair trying to twist to frame herself in a selfie of the waterfall between other people walking past.

'Would you like me to take your picture?' he asked. As he moved closer he noticed her mesmerising green eyes. She paused for too long, she seemed to be having an internal argument.

'I won't steal it.' Cristian was quite amused at her pause.

'Thank you. It is rather lovely and my mother would enjoy seeing me in the shot so yes, thanks.' Cristian took her phone and framed her to the side of the waterfall. The water was mirrored in her eyes making them resemble deep pools of green. He took one shot then zoomed in and said, 'One more, just to be sure.' The girl gave a wry grin which he thought was perfect as he took another shot.

Handing the phone back, Cristian's fingers touched hers. An intense heat in his veins passed through his body. He could sense her heartbeat, he could smell her, every bit of her including the vanilla shampoo, and her citrus enhanced perfume. The fragrance of her skin slightly heated her unique essence. He was in shock.

The sound of others laughing nearby broke his trance and he was glad he had his sunglasses on so he didn't look like a zombie. He had no idea how long he had stood there but the girl was gone. Walking back to his car he noticed a colourful van leaving the car park and was certain it was her. She must think him crazy standing there like a statue. He remembered she had mumbled something as she walked away but couldn't recall what.

Back at his car he rubbed his fingers where they had touched and then ran his hands through his hair which felt like it was stiff and very sensitive. He looked in the mirror and was pleased to see his normal blonde hair. *I need a drink,* Cristian thought. Shaking his head, he turned out of the car park to go to a different winery to find something to drink tonight.

Cristian decided quickly on the wine he liked after tasting a few and bought one bottle to take and ordered a case to be delivered to his home. As he was paying he felt his hair standing on end and quickly looked around, feeling foolish at his rattled reaction. *So much for relaxing, time to go home I think.* Outside he thought he could smell that intense fragrance again. Surely he was being paranoid.

Driving away he decided he would just return to Sydney. There were plenty of orders to fill and research to be done on new works for his art gallery. He didn't need the rest his family suggested, he just needed to get back to work. He was about to call his gallery when impulse had him turning into another winery. He could not understand why he felt a need to be here. Pulling into the car park, suddenly there it was – the garish hand-painted van.

What is going on? he thought. *I don't understand this feeling.* He felt vaguely frightened by the intensity of his feelings – like a compulsion drawing him.

Walking across the lawns he couldn't see her but he could smell her. There, under the shade of a weeping willow she sat, her lunch just delivered. She had taken her thin flowing jacket off and slung it over her chair, heightening the fragrance of her unique essence on the breeze.

He didn't want to startle her so sat at a table a short distance away, curious to watch her and figure out this connection. He studied her smooth olive skin, the fine bones of her hands and her feet bare in thin strapped sandals. Then he felt her fear and realised she had seen him. Her green eyes were like pools of emerald sea, huge from terror. No, not terror, more like him – confusion. He moved to rise but she slightly shook her head and partly raised her hand to stop him. He sat back down not wanting to terrify her. She grabbed her bag and walked away from the table, leaving her meal and drink untouched.

Cristian sat where he was watching her go, wanting so much to follow her to understand this compulsion that was gripping him with every cell of his body. Seeing the fear in her eyes was all that stopped him moving until she was out of sight. He could not ignore the intense need not to harm her. Looking back to where she had sat, he noticed her jacket still slung over the chair. He walked slowly to control his desire to run and casually picked up the jacket as he walked back to his car. The feel of the thin fabric tingled against the skin of his hand. Cristian searched his mind and memories to try to understand what had happened. There had to be some deeper knowledge that had been forgotten to explain this. Carefully he folded the jacket and placed it in the glove box of his car.

He definitely needed to get back home. Returning to his hotel he packed his things and checked out early, waving off the receptionist's dialogue regarding refund policies and possible credits for a return trip. She was obviously concerned he did not like the venue. He just needed to be gone. Cristian thanked her for her concern and explained it was unavoidable family issues, smiling at her to allay her concerns.

Back in his car Cristian gripped the wheel and took several deep breaths. He had to calm down before he started to drive to make sure he stayed in the speed limit, he did not want to draw attention to himself. The desire to rush back home to find some meaning to today's encounter and these feelings was overwhelming. It would be a thoughtful few hours to get back to his family estate home in Glenbrook.

Danika

Danika had clutched the calming rose quartz crystal her mother had given her to her heart sitting in the car park before she drove off from the close encounter at the winery. Her mother had realised Danika needed to get away and had given her the crystal with instructions to hold it to her heart any time she needed to be calm and connect to her mother and family. Now was that time.

She had been enjoying her nomadic journey around Australia for the last couple of months after leaving her mother's home in Adelaide. Danika had been moving from free camp to camp, picking up work here and there. Finally free to move around after the months – years actually – of rolling lockdowns as the world was gripped by the pandemic.

Danika took a few calming breaths and drove on to the next winery hopefully to enjoy a relaxing lunch under the trees. Placing her thin jacket on the back of the chair the breeze felt like a massage to her soul. While waiting for the meal she had ordered she looked for the next place to camp and through the photos on her phone. Noticing the close-up the stranger had taken.

Before she could enjoy the meal that had arrived her skin began to tingle an inner vibration that felt like it went to her heart. Then she saw him a few tables away, staring at her feet it seemed. Tall, blonde and lithe he looked ready to pounce. Instinctively she raised her hand to stop him as she grabbed her bag and walked briskly away chanting a protective spell as she went.

She drove away, not sure of the direction. She needed distance from the stranger, from this unnerving feeling.

After driving for twenty minutes Danika pulled over to work out where she actually was and where to next. Not the coast it seemed, the east coast was experiencing massive flooding. Her options were now limited. She realised she needed to find somewhere calming eventually, settling for a national park. More driving and missed turns later she was setting herself up near a fire, placing her folding chair next to the van to enjoy the bush scenery. A nearby town she had driven through had a few notes in windows looking for staff. Danika decided she would explore the area more and perhaps get a few weeks work. She needed to recoup some funds after wasting money today on the gardens and an abandoned meal. The direction of her thoughts turning to the tall blonde stranger filled her with the tingling sensation she hoped to avoid.

Her phone rang, making her jump – her mother checking in on her day.

'Hi Mum,' Danika answered.

'Hi honey, are you okay?' asked her mother, concerned.

'Yes, fine, are you okay, Mum?' Danika asked, knowing what was coming.

'Well no, I'm not okay, I have been filled with dread all afternoon. What have you been doing, what happened today?' Danika's mother Selene was insistent. Danika should have expected this, she was used to her mother's psychic abilities.

'Nothing happened, Mum, just the normal crazy drivers and I feel like I'm getting a cold. And before you say anything, yes I will look after myself and yes I will take a test if it gets worse,' Danika said in her most exasperated voice that she could muster rather than dwell on her mother's intuition. 'Actually I'll send you some photos of the gardens I visited today. How did your market go yesterday?' Danika tried to deflect her mother's probing.

A favourite topic of Selene's was discussing her Tarot and palm reading stall at the local markets and how many crystals and herbs she had sold. She loved discussing the true believers and the sceptics who don't really believe but are still drawn to the hope of good fortune.

Danika let her mother talk about her trade all the while chanting silently a dampening ritual to prevent her mother from sensing her inner turmoil. Danika vowed not to hold the large pink crystal against her heart again if she did not want her mother to know her feelings. After thirty minutes, Danika was able to dissuade her mother from further enquiry and explained she needed to start a fire for warmth as a chill was descending.

Alone now, Danika could really work on her dampening ritual. To hold off those that could sense her feelings and whereabouts. To build a barrier of calm around herself and her van. She was surprised at how much she remembered from her grandmother's teachings so long ago – gentle encouraging teachings, not the more demanding style of her mother who assumed Danika would follow in her spiritual footsteps. Danika pulled from the herbs and essences in her packing. All were lovingly placed in a carved wooden box her grandmother had given her on her sixteenth birthday. Her grandmother had shown her so many wonderful visions and plays on potions and chants using herbs, candles and crystals. She'd explained the good, the bad and the evil to avoid, but in a generous and patient way. However, she had not explained how ill she was until no more could be done, her death coming shortly later. Danika had been heartbroken and at a loss to some extent ever since. Nearly twelve years since her grandmother's passing. She said she chose to go to the other side intact, not operated on for the cancer she succumbed to.

Holding a citrine crystal in one hand to clear her thoughts, Danika lovingly chose her few herbs to mix with a few drops of sandalwood essential oil into a paste. After starting a small fire Danika continued her chant and placed the paste on a small piece of wood to smoke and burn slowly, releasing the fragrance and healing properties.

As Danika looked into the gentle flames and allowed the smoke to drift over her and into her van she reflected on how strong all the women were in her family. She did not know who her father or grandfather was. As this was the way of the Carling women. Single and proud, each bearing only daughters continually for generations all the way back to their convict ancestor Jessica Carling, transported from England to Tasmania on the Phoenix in May 1822. *Nearly two hundred years it would be in May 2022*, Danika thought. The herbs and ritual to calm her mind and give her clarity was working. Something deep within told her she needed to go to the place where Jessica had arrived in Australia. Now she needed to make a new planned journey in a different direction.

Cristian

Cristian finally pulled into the long driveway leading to his home and began to feel more at ease. The drive back had been arduous as he was constantly replaying the events of the day, thinking about the girl and trying not to lose control over several hours. He remembered the look of her – her long black hair shining in the sun, the most stunning green eyes that you felt you could drown in. He remembered the look of her through the lens of her phone camera and wished it was his camera. Then the feel of her touch, the rush, the searing heat through his veins. The world just stopped. And then she was gone. But not the scent of her. He could still sense it in his nostrils like it had just happened and he didn't want it to go. He contemplated the insane demand of his body to pull over into the winery when he had already decided to go home. It was like the other unavoidable demand on his body that he had hated, loved, revelled in, and now finally – after twenty years – was at peace with: his true self, a man of two worlds.

There she'd been. It was almost like an invisible elastic joined them, pulling them together. He was scared, exhilarated, yet frightened of spooking her. Almost like a hunt, yet not. He'd only been able to study her for a few seconds before she sensed him. He remembered when their eyes met. They knew, but didn't understand, each other's feelings and fears. He'd let her go. It was the kindest thing he could do. He needed time to understand this. But he knew he needed to find the answers without his family knowing. Something in the pit of his stomach warned him that they would not understand. That they would stop him, stop her. What was it, he didn't understand, but by all the heavens he was going to find out.

Cristian drove past the house to park his car in the garage with several other vehicles, all with different purposes. He glanced at them, realising the divide between his family's wealth and that of the funny campervan. 'Why am I thinking about that?' he mused. It was like every part of his life was now a comparison to hers. 'I only met her for a few minutes.'

He grabbed his bags and moved out of the garage into the utility room next to the kitchen.

'Master Cristian, we weren't expecting you back so soon. Will you be staying for dinner?' Cristian had caught Ann by surprise coming through the utility room, though the ever-professional housekeeper didn't show it other than a slight rise to her eyebrow and a quick straightening of her apron.

'Yes, thank you, Ann. Is my mother in?' Cristian asked with an inwards chuckle to himself.

'Yes sir, would you like me to inform her you are back for dinner?'

'No thank you Ann, let's give her a surprise.' They both grinned at each other as they knew full well his mother would be aware of his return already. He pulled a bottle out of his bag and placed it on the work bench.

'Perhaps you could have this decanted to serve with the meal tonight?'

'Of course, sir, it will go very nicely with tonight's dinner.' Ann picked up the bottle to study the label of the Shiraz he had purchased earlier today.

'A fine vintage I'm sure. You do have a superb taste for a good bottle.'

Cristian gave her a quick nod as Ann turned to head back to her duties and he headed towards his rooms.

Once in his rooms Cristian found his thoughts moving yet again to the green-eyed woman that pervaded his every thought and movement. He knew, without knowing why, that he had to look through his research of the artefacts he had been gathering for years. His family history had long intrigued him however, since his father's tragic death fifteen years ago, he had turned to Robert, his uncle in Germany, for support to understand his family legacy. Robert and his mother were the ones who insisted he have a break from his research and art dealing after he had discussed his desire to trace the family line. They seemed keen to dissuade him from the endeavour. At least that was the vibe he was getting despite them thinking they had encouraged him for health reasons. With that in mind, Cristian had decided to keep this part of the research to himself. He was also certain that his mysterious green-eyed woman would remain a secret from them.

Cristian showered and dressed for the evening meal early so that he could use his laptop to review his previous work until dinner was called. The time slipped by in a blink before he heard a knock on his study door.

'Dinner will be in ten minutes, sir,' the kitchen hand called, he knew better than to open the door.

'Thank you, Ben,' Cristian called back and shut down his laptop.

Cristian moved swiftly through the house to the dining area to greet his mother who was already seated with her back stiffly upright yet fussing with the napkin in her lap.

'Hello, Mother, how are you?' He addressed his mother Elizabeth.

'Fine thank you, I had hoped you would be away longer. However, it will be nice to dine with you for a change.' She was clearly tempering her annoyance at her son's return, after only two days away.

Cristian poured them each a glass of wine, silence settling as they took their first sips.

'That is surprisingly enjoyable, should go well with the meal,' his mother remarked.

'So why did you return so early?' his mother asked between eating. 'I thought we agreed you would have a decent break from work to recoup and recharge after working so hard.'

'No actually we didn't agree, I just went because I was trying to stop you and Robert nagging me to slow down,' Cristian replied. 'Besides, I do feel refreshed and I think all I need is to go for a few decent runs and plan some buying trips now we can travel freely.'

Elizabeth looked at her watch for the date not the time. 'You know I don't like you running around the streets and you can't go away until after Easter.' A genuine concern had entered her voice.

Cristian continued his meal in silence remembering the horror of his father's death fifteen years earlier. He'd been hit by a truck as he ran out of the forest too close to the road and died instantly. The continuing nightmare of the investigation into why he was there, and the story of the driver seeing an animal not a man haunted them both.

'Don't worry, Mother, I am always careful where I run, wearing plenty of hi-vis.' He grinned at her. 'I am also well aware that Easter is only a few days away. Are you hoping for an Easter egg?'

Elizabeth was easily calmed by his humorous banter. He had become the 'man of the house' at only twenty-two when his father Henry was killed, stepping up to support her through their mutual loss and the harrowing coroner's investigation that followed Henry's death.

'This wine is perfect and Ann has outdone herself again,' his mother remarked, seemingly trying to lighten the mood they had both slipped into.

'I'm glad you like it, I have a case coming shortly,' Cristian informed her, then allowed them to continue to light dinner conversation.

'Have you decided what you will do this Easter? It is only five days away and I think the national parks may be very busy,' Elizabeth asked once they settled into the lounge after dinner with a stronger drink.

The estate backed onto the national park, their own estate being thirty hectares with large areas of managed forest where they maintained a small herd of fallow deer. It was the only home Cristian had ever known and he loved every inch of it. He ran through it regularly to clear his mind and stretch his muscles, often continuing into the national park for longer runs. He had noticed over the years more intrepid visitors to the national park venturing into the less accessible areas that he liked to frequent close to the estate. This recent increase in visitors certainly impinged his preferred private runs. He had mentioned this to his mother and now understood her concern regarding his current increasing need to run in the forest.

'I'll have a look tomorrow and let you know if I am staying on the estate.' Cristian finished his drink. 'I think I shall retire to my rooms and sort out a plan for the week.' Cristian rose and gave his mother a light kiss on the forehead. 'Good night, Mother.'

In his private rooms Cristian was torn between his need to understand the growing desire to find answers to his meeting with the green-eyed woman and a plan for the end of the lunar month for him that coincided with Easter, the biggest tourist season. The increase in celestial events had been widely advertised in the media and a growing suspicion that they may all be related was forming in his mind.

He started by reading through his emails and messages that he had ignored for the two short days he had been away. Many of the messages were from Robert, the most recent one insisting that they talk. Cristian suspected his mother had informed his uncle of his early return. Cristian certainly did not want to end this already difficult day with an argument with his uncle in Germany. He didn't know why Robert seemed to have so much sway over their family from afar. It was true that when his father was killed fifteen years prior Robert had immediately flown out to Australia to support him and his mother through the funeral and financial affairs and Cristian's induction as the head of the Australian side of the family. Robert had tried to persuade them to leave and join the rest of the extended family in Europe where they owned several large estates, chateau's and castles.

At a younger age, his uncle had left Australia as soon as he was old enough to join his cousins in Europe. Robert had been older than Cristian's father when their father had relocated them all to Australia in 1955 from England, selling the family estate before death duties could have devastated their wealth. At nine years of age, Robert never liked Australia and couldn't wait to leave and start his own line of the family in Europe.

Cristian's father in comparison loved the easy-going nature of Australia and its vast areas to be explored. He always thought his father – Cristian's grandfather – was very wise to use his portion of the wealth to purchase such a large parcel of land relatively close to Sydney. The area adjacent to the estate was declared the Blue Mountains National Park a few years later, preventing further development around their property. However now there seemed to be more people wanting to explore every part of the national park, some taking thoughtless risks because they believed they were entitled to explore and do whatever they wanted. This increased the number of people lost or injured in the area and increased the emergency services as well. It caused more people than Cristian liked near their home and grounds. Cristian stripped off the formal clothes he had worn to dinner and in more casual wear returned to his research, ignoring the messages.

Danika

The next morning, Danika started to plan her progress south towards Tasmania to arrive in May. She didn't want to rush straight there as she was keen to see some tourist areas along the east coast before taking the boat over to Tasmania, an experience that would be another first for her. With Easter coming up she knew that the regular parks would be full of holiday makers, so she planned to do a couple of days in Sydney mid-week after Easter at whatever backpackers she could get into. Then on to Canberra to see the galleries and library for a little research. A week later to make sure she was out of the forest at a beach to be able to really enjoy the planetary conjunction on the 27th, that should give her plenty of time to look around while motoring through coastal Victoria to Melbourne to meet the boat over to Tasmania.

Danika was feeling very proud of herself for being this organised. She was reluctant to spend anything on accommodation if possible as she was very comfortable in her little camper van but she was keen to book her passage.

Her phone rang, interrupting her passage planning. It was her mother again and she grimaced but answered it anyway.

'Hi, Mum.' Danika tried to sound pleased she had called.

'Hello, Danika, I haven't heard from you today.' Danika knew that meant her mother was trying to sense her, not a phone call. This was one of the major downfalls of having a witch for a mother, particularly a talented witch.

'I have been planning my trip, working out dates and places to see and stay. I thought I might head to Tasmania for a little bit.'

'What, now? It will be freezing, you don't like the cold, I thought you were going north.'

She sounds peeved and it isn't even her travel, Danika thought.

'I'm not going there for long, did you realise it will be two hundred years next month since our ancestors first came to Australia?'

'She was kidnapped; she didn't come here by choice,' her mother replied.

'Transported Mum, as many were back then even for trivial crimes.' Danika could hear her mother winding up. 'I know it was cruel, Mum, but I thought it would be the best place to get some history. I haven't been able to find any reference to her online.' Danika was now in full deflect mode. 'When did our family move to South Australia, do you know?'

'Well I believe it was around 1850, that was Emma, with her daughter – no, wait, I think her daughter was born here so maybe 1860, I'm not sure of the dates.'

'That is why I want to go there and maybe I can sort out a family tree for us, there seems to be a few gaps. Also, were they all as "in tune" as you and Grandma?'

'Who would know Danika, it's not like we advertise our talents.' They both laughed at that, because that was exactly what her mother and grandmother before her did. People never really believed it, a bit like being a magician. It was good to hear her mother laugh. She hadn't done that for quite a while after her grandmother had died. Danika herself still didn't laugh often, the loss had hit her hard. She had not realised how ill her grandmother had been, yet still strong enough to cast a spell to hide her illness right to the end.

No chance to say goodbye and then to have to clear out and sell her grandmother's home, finding no notes or farewells either. The loss had hit them hard. That was why Danika was so glad to have her grandmother's gift of the carved box of potion ingredients and crystals just a few days before her passing. She lovingly stroked the lid as she often did when thinking of her grandmother. The emotion must have been seeping through to her mother, her next words surprising Danika.

'I love you Danika, I only ever want you to be happy. So continue to enjoy your journey for now and hopefully you can find someone to share your life with soon.'

Ah there we go, thought Danika, *back to her ticking biological clock to bear a child*. Danika was now officially the oldest Carling woman not to bear a child in two hundred years. Luckily, her mother let it go for once.

'I love you too, Mum, now I better get some sleep. Tomorrow I am hoping to get a bit of work to build my savings up.'

Sleep was not fast coming with all her ideas rattling around in her head.

Danika woke early to get ready to cold canvas the local area for work. The trouble was that she really only wanted a week's work or two at most. Not many people wanted to trust someone for such a short time. She had seen several "help wanted" signs in shop windows in the small local towns, so she parked her van at one end of the main street and walked past each shop smiling as she went to get a feel for the needs of each place. On the way back she could feel a drawing in from one café located at the front of a house and walked in. It was obviously a busy spot as people were waiting and several tables had dishes left. Danika picked up a few pieces in stacks and moved to the back of the shop to grab a bottle of disinfectant spray and a cloth smiling at the shop owner as she went. The shop owner just smiled and silently mouthed a thank you.

Thirty minutes later there was a short break in customers and the owner finally looked at Danika. 'Who are you? Thank you so much. I'm Marge by the way.' Marge brushed a stray curl of her red hair back from her face where it had escaped the colourful scrunchy holding roughly the rest of her wild mop. Her freckled face was a little flushed. She wasn't tall but carried lots of energy and charm in her floral apron.

'My name is Danika and I am looking for just a week's work,' Danika said, smiling her winning smile.

'You are an angel, I was swamped. My other girl just rang in to say she was in isolation as her partner is unwell but she will be back next week.' Marge stood there shaking her head at the lucky chance, more strands of curls escaped.

'Well that sounds perfect if you are happy with my work,' Danika replied.

'Of course, your coffee making is excellent and you seem to be very organised and at ease in a kitchen, can you cook?' Marge sounded hopeful.

'I can, but I prefer to serve if that is okay?'

'Sure is. I prefer to cook and I have a style and system I like in my kitchens. I like to add those magic secret ingredients that keep them coming back.' Marge chuckled and winked.

'Sounds like a great plan then, looks like the next rush is on.' Danika nodded and served the next group who wanted cooked breakfasts, throwing a smile at Marge.

Several hours later as they were closing up, Marge was showing Danika the pack and closing routine and suggested for the week they could arrange some cash per day as wages. 'Are you okay to start at 7 am tomorrow?' Marge asked hopefully. 'Our tradies breakfast rush.'

'Sure, no problem,' answered Danika.

Danika asked if there was somewhere close she could park her van while she was working in town. Marge said she was happy for her to park in her garden and even offered her a key to the amenities at night. All seemed to be falling into place for each of them.

A few days later the Easter frenzy started as tourists filed into the area early to get a good spot to stay for the Easter period. The children enjoyed the hot cross buns that Marge made at this time of year and especially the free mini chocolate eggs.

Danika realised that Marge – who seemed to be about fifty years old and on her own – did not relax when she went next door to her house. Instead, that was when she started baking the lovely cakes that they sold in the café, and just for now the hot cross buns. Marge said that it was a labour of love, and that she felt it was her calling to share her love through food.

'This Friday and Sunday of Easter I open later at 9 am as no tradies and ANZAC day on the 25th, not until lunchtime.'

'I won't be here for ANZAC, sorry Marge,' Danika reminded her.

'Yes of course, one day and I already feel in my bones like you are going to stay.'

'Actually on Saturday afternoon I would like to drive somewhere quiet where I can see the full moon. To photograph it with no outside light,' Danika explained at Marge's enquiring expression.

'Hard to find a quiet spot but I know of an abandoned farm, I'll let the neighbour know you will be there that night if you like. I can draw you mud maps how to get there,' Marge offered.

The next couple of days Danika and Marge developed a great rhythm. Danika felt the love in everything Marge cooked, her special magic spices were actually her charms and the days went smoothly and quickly. Surprising how busy they were, so many keen to get out and about after so long locked up with the pandemic. Many customers even said they felt attracted to the café. So many positive vibes flowing, Danika soaked them all in and that gave her energy.

On the Sunday it would be nice to start a little later from a late night. As was the routine there on the Saturday there was a rush for breakfasts, a slight lull and then the lunch rush. Danika noticed a mother at a corner table with a young girl, possibly five years old, trying to explain they could only have one thing and they could share it. Danika brought over a warmed hot cross bun and a couple of mini chocolate eggs.

'Would you like this? It was a mixed-up order and I didn't want to bin it,' said Danika with her winning smile. The little girl was bouncing now.

'That would be lovely, thank you,' the mother said, gratefully. 'Can I order a small coffee and a hot chocolate also thank you?'

'Of course. With marshmallows? They are complimentary,' Danika suggested.

'Yes please,' the little girl answered. 'This is just the most wonderful day, Mummy.' The little girl hugged her mother.

Danika went off to make the order, adding a couple of mini cookies to the saucer of the drinks before returning to place the drinks and pausing to offer a card for the shop.

'Marge is looking for a casual employee urgently, I don't suppose you would be interested? Unfortunately it is only for the 9 am to 2 pm rush.' Danika handed the card over with Marge's personal phone number written on the back.

The young mother had tears welling and, clearing her throat, said, 'This is most kind, my name is Julie and this is Sarah.' The little girl was already engrossed in her marshmallow topped chocolate drink but looked up and smiled a milky smile. 'I shall definitely give her a call later,' continued Julie.

Danika smiled again and continued serving the other customers. After the pack and close for the shop, Danika had the directions on a mud map to find the abandoned farm. Carefully packing up her van she pulled out of Marge's garden and on to the road. After slowly following the directions she found a rusty farm gate and an overgrown track. Danika was careful to close the gate again after driving the van through. The track wound up through pasture to an old house that was slowly falling apart and becoming overgrown. It still showed signs of previous inhabitants with a line of agapanthus along the drive to the house, bulbs starting to show green shoots poking through the dried grass and the last autumn leaves of the fruit trees. The parrots had eaten most of the fruit, with just a few apple core skeletons left on the trees. Danika parked the van where she thought she could get the best view and remain level. The view was spectacular of rolling golden pastures showing the first new green grass sprouting after the rains with scrub in the distance and the blue hue of the distant mountains a frame to the late afternoon sky.

It seemed incongruous to Danika that such a wondrous view and once beautiful home had been abandoned. There were not even any signs that stock was using the land. With camera in hand, Danika walked around the buildings and once loved gardens taking several poignant shots of rusted metal lace work around the verandah, torn curtains on the inside of windows with still intact glass but peeling paint. Through the window of the kitchen Danika saw a set table with a cup and saucer, salt and pepper shakers and a magazine. It was as if they had just walked out and shut the door. She could not feel sadness though as she tried to be respectful of the previous owners and thought to understand the reason for the emptiness. She would ask Marge tomorrow. Moving around the sheds and back to the fruit trees she planned to capture the setting sun's rays on the autumn leaves.

The cool of the evening was starting to descend, inspiring Danika to get ready for the night sky. Inside her van Danika laid out a throw rug and put candles, matches and sprinklings of spices and oils. Rolling the rug up carefully, she climbed her little ladder on the side of her van up onto the roof. She laid out the rug again and placed the candles in a circle. From here she was able to take some spectacular panorama shots of the landscape and setting sun. Danika was not expecting to see the full moon until the early hours of the morning but that was not necessary for her to absorb the track of the stars.

Danika needed this boost to her inner strength, celestial movements and events were the most powerful for her to obtain this. The clear dark sky allowed her to focus on the stars and planets to absorb their energy. Danika had been sending out positive energy for the last few days in hopes of finding a replacement before she left on Tuesday. After meeting Julie and her daughter Sarah she knew that the plan had been successful, but it had taken a toll and she was keen to recoup and recharge.

Slowly chanting and lighting the candles Danika lovingly stroked her favourite crystals of jasper and moonstone as joy was one of the greatest powers she could harness. Looking up at the first stars she called their power into herself. Danika was oblivious of the cold as her body drew in the power of the celestial bodies like a battery on fast charge. She stayed like that for a couple of hours chanting and alternating between holding the crystals and lighting incense. Knowing she had several more hours before moonrise Danika chose to climb down and move into the van to make a hot drink before resuming her energy recharge. Warmed and relaxed, Danika set an alarm for 4 am and reclined to meditate and probably snooze.

Cristian

Between working at buying pieces for his gallery and fielding his mother's increasing anxiety about his health and upcoming Easter, Cristian ran. He ran in the morning, the evening and sometimes as a lunch break. All of which seemed to exasperate his mother more.

Running cleared his head while also giving him safe points of reference when he may not be able to completely know his surroundings. He often wondered if that may have been the problem when his father was killed as he was not keen to run as often as Cristian and Cristian had not been home that night. His father running alone had been something that had haunted him over the last fifteen years.

Cristian's research had at least found some references to green-eyed goblins that he believed may have been a side-step to discussing witches. Cristian could hardly discount any spiritual, psychic or supernatural reference considering his own experience. Another reference suggested a coven of green-eyed single woman that bore only girls, obviously men had to be involved but they seemed to be irrelevant. However that coven was in England over two hundred years ago and no other reference had been made to it since, a dead end.

Responding to an alarm he set to join his mother in her rooms, Cristian made sure to securely lock his laptop before preparing to go to dinner. Intense hunger hit him and he hoped for a hearty meal. Perhaps he should be a bit more respectful of his mother alone in this huge mausoleum of a house with him going off running and on trips so often that worried her.

Cristian left his own suite of rooms in the southern wing of the house, across from the entrance to the concert room and entertainment areas that had lain idle since his father's death and down to the northern wing which housed guest rooms and his mother's suite of rooms. He assumed they would be dining in her personal dining area and upon entering he could see a bottle of the wine he had delivered from the Hunter Valley, open to breathe before pouring. His mother entered the room in fairly casual clothing compared to her usual dining attire, looking a little frail. Cristian moved to kiss her gently on the cheek.

'How are you, Mother?'

Elizabeth looked a little flustered by his concern as they had not had friendly words of late.

'I'm fine, a little weary of avoiding fundraising events of late. Everyone seems to be in desperate need of support after the last two years and the recent floods.' She seemed thankful to take his arm as he led her to her chair and pulled it out for her to sit.

'How goes the research?' she ventured.

'Well, I have acquired several new pieces and found some buyers with particular needs and deep pockets.' They both grinned at that.

'The best kind of client for profits,' Elizabeth replied.

Cristian poured them both large glasses of the fine wine just as

Ben brought in a trolley carrying the meals under a lidded serving platter, useful to keep the food warm as it was quite a distance from the main kitchen. Ben lifted the lid to reveal charred rib-eye steaks with horseradish butter, a pasta bake and a small side salad.

'Pasta, Mother, I didn't think you liked it,' Cristian said, surprised at the choice.

'I know you do and you need the carbs with all the running you are doing.' For once his mother was not chastising him, well almost.

Ben left, quietly closing the door behind him.

'This tastes as good as it smells,' Cristian said after the first mouthful. They continued to quietly enjoy the food for several minutes.

'I wanted to discuss tomorrow with you.' His mother seemed ill at ease.

Cristian stopped eating and after a large drink of wine asked, 'What is there to discuss?' He could feel the hair rising on his neck.

'I don't think it is a good idea for you to go out tomorrow night. There will be a much more increased number of people in the area as it is Easter and everyone has been itching to get out and about. This week the estate staff have had to remove several would be campers from our land. So it isn't even safe for you to run in the estate. I think we need to employ some security.' Elizabeth was looking slightly flushed.

He could see the strain this had been on his mother and he had been so preoccupied he had been unaware of the trespassers.

'So what are you suggesting I do, Mother?' Cristian had some inkling but wanted to hear it aloud.

'Stay home.'

'You know I can't do that. You know it is impossible. You have lived with this for nearly forty years, Mother.' Cristian was trying to keep his agitation at bay but he had not run since last night and he could feel every muscle tightening.

'Yes I have lived with it for forty years and in that time twice your father also had to choose to stay home when he would rather be out there.' She nodded towards the garden. 'To keep the family legacy and the family safe. Now I am asking you to do the same. It will not be easy but I believe you can do it.'

Cristian could see his mother was tightly clasping her hands in her lap and the tension in her body was at breaking point.

'I'm sorry that this week has been so difficult for you, Mother. It is never my intention to impede your life. I could go away if I leave now.' The thought of the alternative was horrific and he had only heard once as a small child his father's sufferings in the bowels of the estate. He'd been too horrified at the time to actually ask about it.

'It is too late and you know it. You only have twenty-four hours now.' Elizabeth touched his hand gently. 'Eat, run and then tomorrow we must prepare for the legacy.'

The food and wine no longer tasted fine, more like cardboard, but he knew his mother was right. He had been oblivious of the danger looming at the gate so to speak and now would pay the price of his ignorance. He could see how upset his mother was and uncharacteristically gave her a gentle hug as they rose after the meal.

'It will be all right, Mother, it is only a short phase in life. I'll survive it.' Cristian tried to sound positive.

Back in his own rooms Cristian immediately began organising security for the borders of the grounds. At such short notice the price was exorbitant but necessary. He noticed an email ping from an encrypted information source he had been following previously. He hesitated to open it, not wanting to get involved with research again but this was too tempting. The mysterious author offered a picture attachment of a parchment from the 1600's plus a translation which referenced a curse against two supernatural beings. Not clearly defined as any more than he and she and they. It talked about the full moon and the stars being the power and the weakness. It really only created more questions in his mind that he did not have time to pursue now. Another email sat unopened from his uncle to go with the different message he had received, he guessed because of his mother's concerns. Another problem he did not want to take on at the moment. What he really wanted to do was run.

Out in the fresh evening air the rhythm of his footfalls started to calm his chaotic mind so that he could plan for the day and night ahead. He decided to run the boundary of the estate after his mother's revelation of trespassers. He noticed that the fence had been damaged in several places by falling limbs, land subsidence and human intervention. At those points Cristian could see evidence of camping attempts. All removed so far. Cristian noted a need to improve the fences as soon as possible. At over three kilometres, the boundary would probably take several weeks to complete. With a checklist to work through in his head Cristian completed his run up the main drive and in through the back of the house past the garage. He felt a drawing of senses towards his car and added one more item to his to do list.

Back in his rooms he took a long soak in the bath to improve his chance of sleeping. A couple of stiff drinks were sure to help also. Still, sleep was a long time coming. Fitful with dreams of the woman and their hands not just touching but clinging, joined actually becoming one. Both in pain and feeling loss yet unable to let go. He could feel her touch, smell her scent, sense her essence as well as he sensed his own. They clung to each other, staring into each other's eyes as if they could look into their souls. Then a sword pierced them both.

Cristian startled awake. Turning the light on he looked at his chest, expecting to see a wound, but there was nothing. Looking at his hand where it had been almost fused to hers, nothing. It had felt so real, the most vivid dream he had ever had. He was relieved it was just a dream. He took a few deep breaths to calm his heart but nothing could calm his mind, there was no returning to sleep now. He looked at the clock – 5 am – close enough to dawn. *No point lying here,* he thought and decided to dress and get on with his plans. First on the list was to look at the cellar tunnels.

Out of bounds to staff, any changes would be his to make. He went to the safe to retrieve the keys. It had been years since he had looked in there. There were several small boxes and some handwritten ledgers created pre-computers. His father's journal, which he had forgotten was in the safe, sat with its red bound leather, the family crest engraved into the front. He had never read it but supposed there may be some insight to what was ahead and decided to take it with him. At the back he found a metal box and in it were more than one set of keys – the cellar tunnel keys plus others he had not seen before. Taking just the cellar keys for now he determined he would ask his mother another time about the other keys. He locked the safe again, taking his father's journal to his study and locking it in the desk before venturing down to the cellar.

The cellar was located to the back of the main kitchen and housed several racks of wines. At the back of the cellar was a heavy wood and metal door with two metal bars across it, leading to the tunnels and locked with large bolts and padlocks. It took some time to unlock and move them all. Once open, a rush of musty air escaped. The light switches were on the outer wall and, when on, they lit both white and red globes. He turned off the red ones.

Before entering he went back and shut and locked the first cellar door so not to be disturbed. There were old spider webs in several places but less as he continued down steps into the main tunnel, which appeared to turn back under the house if his sense of direction was correct. Down more steps to another bolted heavy metal door, the same keys also unlocked this.

Inside smelt damp and mouldy and he could see the cell. The three walls of heavy stone and one of metal bars with a barred door created a space approximately four metres wide by six metres long. His heart was now racing as he took in the gravity of the situation he was facing. Inside the cell was rudimentary bedding on the floor. A stone bench of sorts protruded from one wall and next to that a stone sump. There were no windows, however there seemed to be an opening in the very high ceiling about thirty centimetres square.

Cristian opened the metal door to the cell and, stepping in, looked up at the opening. The ceiling was at least three metres high, even jumping he could not touch it. He stared up the opening, taking note to bring a torch back with him before he noticed a faint glow. The opening led up to the outside and what he could see was the beginnings of dawn. Time to get moving before anyone else got too interested in his actions.

He pulled the bedding out of the cell and pushed it to one side of the tunnel before he retraced his steps out of the tunnel, locking as he went back to the kitchen. He was surprised there was no Ann or Ben or obvious sign of them being there. Checking his watch it was now 6.30, normally the kitchen would be bustling. He checked the coffee maker, it was cold but next to it was a hand-written note from Ann on how to use it. So, they were not coming in. Mother must have given them the day off. He followed the instructions with a wry grin and then, looking in the fridge, saw several more notes attached to meals. This was a relief to be able to move about without having to explain his actions.

Cristian gathered a few cleaning tools and went back down to the tunnels to clear away the cobwebs and sweep out the cell, dragging the musty bedding all the way out into the garbage skip to replace it with something more appropriate. He found some long pruners and cut several eucalyptus and sandalwood branches from the estate forest, which he dragged back down into the cell. Hunting through the sheds, he found an old blanket used for moving furniture to throw over the branches. Stopping by the garage, Cristian moved to his car and took her jacket out of the glove box, instantly feeling his racing mind calm again. He decided to hide it in a pillowcase and hoped it survived the night.

Reasonably pleased with his efforts he made his way back to the kitchen where his mother was waiting for him. She was at the stove cooking a hearty breakfast.

'How are the preparations going?' Elizabeth ventured when they sat to eat.

'New territory, a bit daunting but as well as can be expected, I've organised security they should arrive around midday,' he replied between mouthfuls.

'I'm sorry, I don't like to go down the tunnel if I don't have to,' his mother apologised.

'No I don't think you should until you have to. Which I'm sorry you do have to. Because you have to lock up.' Cristian leant over and gently touched her hand.

'Yes of course, I have before. I have also suggested that the staff have tomorrow off and come in later on Monday after breakfast just to be sure. They are pleased to have a break to be with family over the weekend. They didn't seem surprised. I wonder that they may know something of the legacy,' Elizabeth pondered.

'I doubt it, they already know we are a strange lot, so nothing surprises them.' Cristian smiled at his mother to reassure her. 'Will you be alright on your own?'

'Of course, dear. I am often when you travel since your father died. Besides, the security will be out there at the boundary, when are they due to arrive?'

Looking at his watch it was not long till noon and he needed to get on with his plans. 'They should be arriving shortly, let me know when they are here and I'll take them through my expectations.' He looked at his watch again, a little agitated at his progress. 'I must get on if you don't mind, Mother?'

'Of course you must, leave this to me. It is actually strangely comforting to have something productive to do,' she replied.

It had felt good to have this casual talk with his mother. A rare thing since his father's death.

Cristian sprinted up to his rooms and retrieved his father's journal and a pillow, then stood still wondering what else he should take. Nothing else really mattered, he just needed to get through the next twenty-four hours.

The security arrived, five men to patrol the boundaries. Cristian explained that there were three kilometres of boundary but so far only about half was at risk of trespassers and showed them the particular fence breaks that were to be mended after the holiday period when he could get workmen in again. They suggested warning tape so that they could monitor if it was damaged or removed at any time. Cristian had already paid them half of their fee and hinted at bonuses with the other half tomorrow if no problems arise. He also made it clear that his mother would be in the house and not to call police without consulting her first.

Back in his rooms, Cristian opened the emails he had been avoiding from his uncle. The first one explaining about a prophecy they needed to discuss as soon as possible, preferably before today.

Well that's not happening now, thought Cristian. *If it was so important, why hadn't he rung?* Cristian knew he should have looked at all the messages on his phone he had been avoiding also. Scrolling through them, they ranged from the ones encouraging him to go away, then admonishing him for returning so soon, then the urgent plea to contact before today. It was too late to call as night was nearing for them in the northern hemisphere.

Cristian unlocked his desk and, taking his father's journal out, he started to skim through to a date before he was born. It looked like his father was only nineteen. February 1971. The journal mentioned Cristian's grandfather Jonathon, a blood moon, and a full eclipse of the moon and the fear of it. Cristian wondered why this had never been mentioned before.

I don't understand why father will not let me run with him tonight. He said I lack control in my run and the forces are too great tonight. What does that mean? Always these half-truths

and innuendos. Now he wants me to view the tunnels. I cannot
fathom his ways at present.

'Makes no sense to me either, Father, you never told me about this,' muttered Cristian.

I feel betrayed why did he not explain rather than coerce me to
that horror last night. I will never do that to another. Truth is
everything.

Cristian flicked further to a date when his own age would be around seven, a time he vaguely remembered his father in the tunnels. Just after his grandfather had died perhaps. He would need to check the dates another time.

I cannot bear to run without him tonight, my father had taught
me the control he said I lacked all those years ago. Locking me
in to protect me. Tonight I lock myself to protect my family.

I wish you had written more, Father. Cristian couldn't say much as he had never kept a journal at all. As much as he had a tenuous relationship with his uncle of late he now wanted answers, all of them. This secrecy was now a threat.

Cristian wanted to keep reading but knew he was avoiding going down to the tunnels again. A knock at his door interrupted him and he slipped the journal back into the desk. It could only be his mother.

'Yes, Mother, come in.'

The concern was clear on her face. 'It is almost sunset dear, is there anything I can do for you?'

'I am just going to bring some paper and a pencil just in case I feel the urge to draw.' He grabbed his drawing material. He had already changed into the running attire he normally chose.

They moved swiftly through the house and at the kitchen his

mother stopped to grab a plastic bottle of brown liquid she had prepared and handed it to Cristian.

'Whiskey, it helps.'

They continued down through the tunnels to the cell where he could see she had also placed a large section from one of the culled deer from the cool room.

'How do you do this, Mother? This legacy and its complications?' Cristian was overwhelmed with pride for his mother.

'Love, it is always love. One day you will love as I have, as your father did. He was my world.' Elizabeth hugged her son and, as he walked in with shaking hands, she closed and locked the cell door and walked away.

Cristian could hear a few minutes later her shutting and bolting the cellar door, then there was silence.

He could feel his skin starting to tense from anxiety at the unknown. He opened the bottle and took a large swig. Jameson's in a plastic bottle, his mother ever careful so glass wouldn't be broken. He smiled to himself and took another large drink. Sitting on the bench he looked to the paper and pencil and wondered why he had felt the urge to bring them. Then, he was drawing her. Well, parts of her anyway – her hand around the wine glass, her feet in the sandals, then the eyes. He had forgotten how much he enjoyed drawing. He'd set aside his own artwork to pursue others' art. He sketched for hours past dusk.

Too soon, he was fighting to stay in control. He drank more of the whiskey, now half gone. Putting the drawings under the branches he decided to lay down. Grabbing his pillow he breathed in the scent of her from the jacket hidden inside, which calmed him as much as it intensified his need to find her.

His breathing became more laboured and his body ached all over. Different he realised when fuelled by whiskey. Still he clutched the scent of her to him.

Cristian felt the familiar crave of his body to be released, felt his skin tightening and his body aching to run. Then his hand began to burn, a cold burn. He held it up to see it change to blue. The last he could remember was the scent of her and remembering her green eyes before the pain of his legacy was all consuming.

Danika

Danika woke to the persistent buzz of her alarm, smiling and stretching as she suspected her meditation would be more of a sleep. She loaded a few more candles in a bag and moved out of the van. The air, once very crisp now had dampness to it. The sky had changed as the progression of the stars around the earth moved on. She knew well it was the earth that moved not the stars but it was all part of the interpretation. Danika felt quite relaxed, as if the harmony had returned to her inner soul. Climbing up onto the roof again she could feel the dew had settled on the rug and candles. This would not dampen her spirits; she began to giggle at her thoughts.

Settled on the rug with her candles and incense lit, Danika began to draw the power of the new stars into herself making her tingle with anticipation of the power of the moon to come. She could see the faintest glow on the horizon. Then, the expected euphoria became something more intense. She held her arms to the sky, her hand began to tingle and then burn, a cold burn. Still she chanted her need to absorb the power of the moon as it rose in the night sky.

Danika chanted louder as she held her arms high gulping in huge lungful's of the cold night air. As she looked at her hand glowing blue in the night, all she could think of was his eyes, grey and deep like a well. She felt his pain and then it was gone, the connection broken.

2

THE RAPTURE

THE FIRST SOUND Cristian was aware of was the cellar door being unlocked, followed by footfalls coming along the tunnel. The red lights were on but he could see daylight coming down the opening in the roof. Cristian pulled the old blanket over his naked form and tried to acclimatise himself to the space. The carcass was ripped apart. The sump of water half empty. The bedding was strewn about yet the pillow was still intact. He looked up to see his mother holding a pile of clothing and the key.

'Are you alright, son?' Elizabeth asked with a waver in her voice.

'I think so. No broken bones.' He grimaced at his sore hands, as he looked at the marks on the stones and bars. Claw and teeth marks marred the surfaces. 'Are you going to let me out?'

'I checked on you at dawn a few hours ago but,' Elizabeth trailed off and started to cry.

'You shouldn't have done that, Mother, I wasn't myself. But I am now,' Cristian continued.

'Yes, I know, but you looked so much like Henry and I miss him so much.' Elizabeth began to weep.

'I never knew you had seen the legacy.' Cristian was shocked.

'Oh many times. He was so beautiful, I asked him to let me see him in the early days and then he was so trusting, never did I feel in danger. I just couldn't stand the pain, especially when he had to be in the cell, like you last night.' Elizabeth appeared to get herself under control and unlocked the door to place the clothes on the floor. Turning around and walking away, she added, 'Your uncle is expecting your call.'

Cristian dressed and, bringing the pillow with him, made his way up to the cellar where he bolted the door and turned off the lights. He did intend to clean up in there later but took precautions anyway.

He could smell cooked food and coffee percolating. Pouring a cup he noticed the time heading towards midday already. He chose a few items from the oven and sat to eat. His phone was pointedly placed on the kitchen table. He dialled to call his uncle.

'Hello Robert, it's Cristian. How can I help you?' Cristian waited for an angry response.

'Hello, Cristian, you have been hard to get. How was your night?' It was obvious Robert already knew.

'Cold and boring but otherwise fine.' Cristian was determined not to be baited into the move to Europe argument.

'I wanted to discuss with you an element to our history and legacy you may not be aware of.' Robert paused but Cristian was just waiting for the rest of the news.

'Our legacy is determined by the fact that the men of the family find their soul mate and imprint on them, as your father and I have, and continue the family line. You do not seem to be getting any closer to that important aspect of life but now we are at a critical stage in the legacy.'

'What critical stage? There are plenty of descendants on your side in Europe, why does it matter what I do?' Cristian was becoming annoyed, mostly because he was tired and wanted to go have a shower.

'There is a prophecy, that the legacy will be destroyed by another family line. A female line, of witches.' Cristian listened to his uncle's words and then began to laugh.

'This is no laughing matter Cristian, I am well aware of your research over the years into the family line. Surely this is no surprise and yet you laugh.'

'I have not been researching our family line in that way Robert. I research many supernatural mysteries, all so far dead ends. It never occurred to me that our own family had some mysterious prophecy of doom. Why are you telling me now and not before?'

'I had been worried it would be our line here in Europe, however we are all very well sorted with imprinted partners or the others too young to matter this year. This is the year it can happen, every two hundred years. There are many celestial events this year, including the blood moon next month in the northern hemisphere. As I said, that is not a problem for us. You need to find and imprint a partner before the prophecy can happen where you are.' Robert continued to emphasise the importance, 'You have a responsibility, Cristian, to protect your line of the legacy.'

'Well, Robert, this has been enlightening. Let me know if you have any other doomsday insights later but for now I'm going to get cleaned up, thank you.' Cristian hung up on his uncle before he could say anymore.

Shaking his head in disbelief, he went back down to the cell to clean it up before his shower. At least he didn't need to be worried about running into Ann or anyone else until tomorrow. Back in the cell he threw the ravaged carcass onto the blanket and then the branches to drag them out. Underneath were the drawings he had done the day before. Flicking through them he folded them up and forced them into his back pocket before dragging the blanket out all the way to the skip bin. He locked up as he went.

Cristian had been rocked by Robert's revelation but had tried to make it seem like it was trivial and of no interest while he spoke to him. He'd already found a few references going back hundreds of years of the legacy, a curse and a prophecy. Now, Robert was suggesting it was all intertwined and linked. He really was feeling disgusting and

wanted to clean up and rest. Tomorrow he would have a clearer mind
to tie his research together.

Danika

Danika was very grateful for the later start after the eventful night
before. It took quite a lot of time to get herself together and pack
away the damp rug and burned candles before slowly making her way
out of the farm and back to Marge's. Arriving just before dawn to
see the lights on in Marge's home kitchen, Danika walked in and,
as Marge looked up, she opened her arms to Danika. They hugged
without words. Marge poured a strong cup of tea for Danika and
herself and sat with her, waiting for her to say what she needed.

'What happened at that farm Marge? It seems lost in time,' Danika
asked, avoiding explaining her need for a hug.

'There were two generations who lived there. The last one, the
couple became quite elderly. They loved being there but their children
moved away, not interested in the farm. Unfortunately, the children
died in a plane crash on a holiday overseas before the parents. The
parents eventually went into a nursing home together a decade or so
ago and I believe they passed within days of each other a few years
ago. So it is just left. The town neighbours keep an eye on it to stop
any vandals.' Marge touched Danika's hand. 'Did something happen
there?'

'I thought it looked lonely, but not sad, like it was waiting for
someone to come back.' Danika smiled at Marge. 'The evening was
energising and surprising. I took several photos. But yes I am a bit
tired as it was a later moonrise. Thank you for the hug, now, what can
I do to help?'

'How about icing those cakes that have cooled over there, I'm just about to put the hot cross buns in the oven.' Marge pointed to the cakes cooling on the racks against the wall.

An hour later, several batches of buns were cooling on the racks and dozens of cakes were iced and ready to go into the café. Marge thanked Danika and suggested she make use of her bathroom before they opened up in an hour.

'You may get a call today from a lady, Julie, looking for work. I gave her your number,' Danika let Marge know before she went out to her van for supplies.

Marge just shook her head in amazement as Danika left.

The next two days in the cafe went well. Julie did contact Marge and came in to be shown the ropes and have a trial run for a couple of hours while her daughter Sarah sat in the corner with toys and snacks. With Sarah back at school on Tuesday and Marge's other worker also back on Tuesday, Julie would officially start and Danika would leave on the rest of her journey. All felt like it was falling into place. On Monday night Marge insisted on cooking Danika a meal as she would be leaving early in the morning. They chatted over a glass of wine while Marge still had to prepare a few cakes for the next day.

'So, what is your special superpower over people, Danika?' Marge asked.

'No different to yours actually. People love you and your friendly café with the amazing cakes. You have the same talent of spreading joy with your smile and food.' Danika easily side stepped the question.

'Oh I think it is more than that but thank you for the compliment. By the way, these are the details of that farm including the previous owners and the lawyers holding it until any relatives claim it.' Marge handed over a note with names and phone numbers and held her glass up in salute. 'I know I will have a full crew but I am still going to miss you.'

'Me too but I have a quest of sorts to follow, although I feel like I will be back this way some time.' Danika saluted also.

After they finished the meal and cleared away the dishes, they hugged again before Danika retreated to her van, intending to leave early in the morning.

Danika was grateful for her phone GPS to navigate the complicated highways and streets between Marge's home and the Sydney backpackers she was planning to stay at. After a few hours of stressful morning traffic and finally arriving at the hostel, she found out she could not park there, or it seemed at any hostel. It was, after all, the Sydney Easter show, they kept telling her. Everything was booked out everywhere no matter the price.

Okay, so maybe I will have to by-pass Sydney and come back another time, thought Danika, a little disappointed. Everything happens for a reason though. *Well I think I will just go view a couple of the icons just in case I don't get back and be done with it.*

Driving around the city was a nightmare but eventually she was able to get a park near the Clocktower Square and decided to walk around the area. The harbour with the bridge and the Opera House were breathtaking and she realised that she really needed to have planned better before coming here. Next time she would book a hotel. Danika took many photos and was planning to walk around to the Opera House when a need to change direction took hold of her. She felt the urge to have a cup of tea after her hours driving around and decided to treat herself in a café. There were several to choose from but, as often happened, one in particular called to her so that was going to be the best experience. Twenty minutes later she was settled at the window with her drink and a slice enjoying observing the flow of people around the Sydney Rocks area.

When the man from the Hunter Valley walked through the café door, Danika should have been surprised. Instead, she simply watched as he walked over and sat down with her, not asking for her permission.

Danika could see now how grey his eyes were, more like the silver of stainless-steel drawing her in as if they had known each other all their lives and longer. His hair, blonde like a surfer, bleached from the sun. He didn't look so tall sitting across from her but she could sense he had his legs tightly folded under the table. *Why am I even thinking about that?* she thought but couldn't speak, only stare.

Cristian

Cristian couldn't believe she was there in front of him, not in a dream or running away. Her eyes were like a bottomless pool, drawing him to want to drown in them, the flawless pale olive skin and jet-black hair seemed like fiction. *Why don't you talk man?* he thought in stunned silence.

The waitress interrupted their intense eye lock, asking Cristian for an order. He ordered coffee just so she would leave.

'I didn't think I would ever see you again,' Cristian said as if they knew one another well.

'Nor I, but here we are,' the woman answered. 'My name is Danika.'

'Yes, sorry, my name is Cristian.' They didn't shake hands, each seemingly reluctant to touch. 'What is this Danika, why are we drawn to each other? This is no coincidence.'

'I actually have no idea. This has never happened to me before. I feel like we have known each other a lifetime, Cristian,' she confessed.

'I think we should go somewhere more private to talk. If you agree, my apartment is in walking distance,' he suggested.

His drink arrived in a to-go cup which he hadn't realised he had requested. They left with the waitress clearing the table ready for the others waiting to be seated. He mused at the fact that they had each easily had a seat and received their drinks. *Was the world serving them as a priority? Where is this thinking going?* He felt quite removed from the actual real life they were walking through. As she followed him almost by his side up the several levels to his penthouse apartment without speaking, he mused that she was following a stranger to an unknown private space and yet he sensed she was not afraid. It seemed they both needed to understand this connection they had.

As they entered the building, Danika began to softly chant beside him, all the way through the elevator and up to the door. Cristian didn't ask what it was she was chanting, or why her hands spread slightly in front of her as if preventing something invisible from touching her. But it felt important.

Cristian could not believe she was here, no research needed. As if that invisible elastic had pulled them together again. No longer strangers, but what were they? At his door, her whispering stopped as he ushered her in.

Cristian was mildly nervous at how she would judge his private world and wondered why. It had never bothered him before. Although few had ever been here, he preferred to keep it to himself.

The apartment had many artefact pieces as well as art on the walls. Not quite cluttered but busy in an eclectic yet ordered way. He watched her silently moving slowly into the large open area he used as his lounge and general living space. He noted her reaction and avoidance of some pieces, felt her general fear towards some of the pieces, and thought he would have them removed. Then as she moved to look at the view of the Opera House from his window, she seemed to admire his favourite artefact of bloodstone. It's rough base was set into a carved blackwood stand, and the top had been smoothed to a football shape. The piece always gave him renewed strength, cleared his thoughts and seemed to keep the darker ones at bay. He often wondered what it would look like in pure moonlight, but here in the city that was not possible.

'I have something for you,' Cristian said as he moved away from the window to his bags, still yet to be unpacked. Unzipping the side pocket he pulled out the pillowcase that held Danika's jacket inside. He took the jacket out, walked back over to the window and handed it to her.

'Oh, you found it.' She looked at him for a moment, then revised her comment. 'Took it.' Her head tilted at that realisation. 'It was my grandmother's. I called the winery, they searched for it.'

'Yes I took it. I couldn't help it. I had to connect with you.' Cristian stumbled over his explanation. 'It helped me. The night I…' He held it for her to take.

As Danika moved to take the offered jacket, she instead wrapped both her hands around his, clasping their hands together. The jacket fluttered to the floor, their eyes transfixed. Cristian felt he could see into her soul, feeling it all.

Cristian grasped Danika's hands as if he had no will power to do anything else. He felt her drawing all his energy, his memories, his soul, out with those mesmerising eyes and the soft yet firm touch of her hands. A warmth spread through his body then a heat he recognised and feared. *The legacy*, he thought. *This can't happen. Not now, not here.* The calming of her chanting brought him back down, cooling his core and making him more aware of his surroundings that had completely disappeared for the moment, or the hour… He couldn't tell how long they had stood there together. He knew he had been breathing rapidly and deeply, yet now his breaths were calmer and returned to normal. Still they held hands as if glued together, she continued to chant though shaking as if she had exerted a large amount of effort.

Danika

At his apartment Danika recognised the wealth with the stunning views of the harbour despite the mildly threating vibes of the art pieces. Then he was handing her the missing, no, taken, jacket.

Danika felt the rush as soon as they held hands and looked into the depths of his eyes now seeming to be dark grey almost black as the pupils enlarged. The visions rushed into her mind like a movie on fast forward. The pain and fear, she had felt it before the night of the full moon. The anguish and then release and intense tiredness. As soon as it started she had begun a protecting spell for herself and Cristian included, dampening the intense black thoughts, calming them to a level so they could both return to now. She could feel herself shaking from the effort. They both looked down at where they were holding their hands and slowly released them. Danika wavered slightly and he steadied her, holding her arm.

'I think you should sit down.' He showed her to one of the two seats near the window obviously placed to enjoy the view. 'I'll get you a drink,' he offered as if not really sure what drink that would be.

'Here, it's a tea of sorts. I think we need it.' Danika passed him the little cloth pouch from the bag she still had slung over her shoulder. He made up the dried mix and handed a cup of the brew to Danika and then sat with one himself on the other chair.

'What just happened, Cristian?' Danika asked as she sipped the hot brew.

Cristian

Cristian was sceptical but sipped the brew and felt an inner strength returning, it felt similar to the emotions experienced by his bloodstone connection. He could not discount the mystical effect Danika was having on him, he wanted to tell her everything.

'I think we imprinted. Actually, I know we did, as if I have always known it yet just learned it today.' Cristian looked at her, appealing to her to understand. 'And you are a witch, am I correct?' Not an accusation, more an enquiry.

'Imprinting, and that means what? Yes, I am a witch, but what are you? A demon? Not a warlock, but something I am not supposed to be connected to, yet now we are. I need more answers than that we "imprinted" on each other.' Danika gulped down the tea in one go.

'No, I'm not a demon. Well, maybe, depends on your definition I suppose.' He began to explain but, looking at her impatient expression, blurted out, 'I'm a werewolf, it's a legacy not a turning.' As if she would understand the comparison. When Danika didn't display shock, his interest increased.

'I felt you that night, during the full moon. It was harrowing. All those feelings and emotions rushed into me, I was almost overwhelmed by them. Your pain made me cry. My hand where we touched it turned blue in the moonlight. I felt that you were sad.' Danika was crying at the memory. 'I don't understand how we were so connected then.'

'I'm sorry that you went through that. I was forced into a difficult situation and I felt calmed by your jacket. The sense and smell of you on it helped me through the transition. My hand was blue also until my memory faded,' he explained. 'I don't remember my actions and experiences when I have transitioned.'

'That makes sense now, my grandmother was a very talented witch and she must have placed a connection spell on the jacket. So that I would choose it and ultimately you connected also.' Danika was deep in thought. 'A werewolf, right, so they are real then. What do you mean a legacy not a turning?'

'I was born to it. Occasionally by accident a person is bitten and the poisonous effect turns them insane, like rabies but a bit more violent. It never ends well. I usually make sure I am safe to transition away from people so accidents don't happen, in forests mostly. But I was distracted this lunar cycle and had to make other... arrangements.' He trailed off not wanting to explain all the details.

'You locked yourself up, didn't you? How awful, that was what I could feel, the anguish that you couldn't run. I felt your confusion at the walls and then fear. It was right here,' Danika cried and touched her chest.

'Can you read my thoughts now?' He wanted so much to hug her and wipe away those tears.

'No, not really, just some of the more intense or deep emotions. Not really memories either, more like visions of your memories. Snippets that make little sense at the time until there is context.' Danika wiped her tears with the back of her hand. 'What does this imprinting mean? Are we going to be psychically linked forever now as we go about our lives?' Before he could answer, Danika continued on, as if she'd heard some answers already from him somehow. 'Whoa, let's just back up here a bit. You mean we are now together? As in forever together, like a couple.' Before he could explain or calm her down she had stood up and moved away from him and then started to laugh. Holding her hands over her face she laughed even harder. He was beginning to think she was becoming hysterical.

'Oh my heavens and stars that is just priceless. Selene said I had to find a mate.' Danika began to laugh more.

'Who is Selene?' Cristian asked, a bit suspicious about the word 'mate.'

'My mother, she is concerned my biological clock is winding down and I have to continue the line. We don't have partners, just sperm donors. I had no father, no grandfather, not even any siblings.' Danika's words were blunt but Cristian could sense her desire to hit back, not directed at Cristian seemingly but at her whole life.

'My family is the same, demanding I had to imprint now or the world was going to come to an end.' The words were out before he could filter them, he realised his mistake as soon as he looked at her. 'It's not like that, not desperation as in any woman will do.' He was floundering now. 'I can't control who it is going to be, well… not really, I don't think.' She must think he was some kind of a stalker.

'So you mean there is no book on this.' Danika nodded towards the extensive literature in the bookcase that took up half of one wall. 'It's okay Cristian, I know this is a connection planned by the universe, not something either of us had control over. There is a much bigger event happening than either of us could have planned, I can just feel it. I know you are not a stalker.'

Cristian was relieved she didn't think he was a stalker but was now certain she was reading his mind.

'I think we need to sit down and try to work out where to from now and perhaps compare notes, so to speak.' Cristian was actually not sure what the next move was and was hoping Danika had suggestions. This was definitely new territory for him. He had always felt alone but now with this connection he wanted her there in every aspect of his life.

Danika looked at the clock on the wall, hours had passed since coming to the Rocks. 'Oh bloody hell, I'll have a ticket, I have to go. I have to find somewhere else to park. I have to find somewhere to...' She trailed off in her thoughts.

'You can come here, I have parking space underneath the building. We can sort it out just for today if you like. We have a lot to discuss.' Cristian smiled at her.

'Okay, I suppose you are right, not sure my van will fit though.'

'It will be fine, I'll come with you and show you how to get in and where to park.'

They walked side by side and found Danika's van with two tickets on the wiper. She removed them and stuffed them in her copious patchwork bag. Unlocking the van from the passenger's side, Danika removed several bags of stuff that Cristian could not fathom and placed them in the back of the van. She dusted crumbs off the seat.

'Sorry, normally only me in here,' Danika apologised as she moved around to the driver's side. As Cristian managed to get his huge frame into the small space, he realised that she had nowhere to put her bag, which he assumed would normally live on the seat he now occupied. After putting on the seat belt he offered to hold it for her and she relinquished it into his lap.

'Good grief, what have you got in here, it weighs a ton?' Cristian smiled but didn't look.

'Oh this and that, runes, potions, crystals, herbs like wolfsbane.' She grinned broadly at him.

'Very funny, it's a myth, you know? Same as vervain. But it is poison, to everyone, not just me,' he replied.

'Oh no, there aren't vampires as well are there?' Danika asked, genuine concern evidence on her expression.

'Not that I know of, but nothing would surprise me at the moment.'

After they'd parked beneath Cristian's apartment, Danika stuffed a couple of books and an old charm box into a huge bag already filled with candles and incense. Danika paused, as if considering what else she needed.

'It is easy to come back down and get more, whenever you like.'

'Yes, of course. I'm sorry, actually I think I need to soak. Clear my head.' She nodded her head.

'Do you mean in a bath?' Cristian was really not sure where this was going.

'Oh no, sorry, soak in smoke, as in burning incense.' Cristian could feel her exasperation as Danika explained while they made their way back up in the lift.

'I draw my power from the celestial bodies, mostly at night when I can focus on them with a clear sky. I am feeling drained and I can't use them now or probably not tonight in the city but I can summon the energy of a flame and the smoke as it releases to the air. All hocus pocus stuff most people glaze over about.'

He opened the door for her and replied, 'No problem, all fine with me. I'm pretty open to anything today.'

Back in the apartment he showed her around the three bedrooms, one of which was obviously his and the other two guest rooms, then the two bathrooms. He pointed at the bath which made her smile. He led her into the large kitchen and dining area that he barely used, followed by the large study filled with more manuscripts, artefacts and general office equipment. There were two balconies total, each designed to provide exceptional views. Danika didn't appear to have the energy to marvel at them as they passed them.

'What do you do for a living, Cristian?'

'Well, mostly I work as an art dealer, my gallery is not far from here. My plan had been to be there this week. My work takes me away overseas a fair bit also.' It felt very strange to Cristian to just be so honest and open with Danika. He never could be with anyone, always something had to be kept back and hidden. It was a freedom he had only dreamed of. 'What about you?'

'Currently I'm between jobs. I just finished a week in a café not far from our last meeting. I prefer to work mostly in service industries where I can see and touch people. So I can draw energy from joy and can pass positive energy out as needed. Not that my mother knows this, she thinks I am a fairly weak witch. It serves me well that she doesn't know.' Danika paused before gushing, 'Oh my heavens, did I just say that?' She grimaced at Cristian. 'It is like we have been hit with a truth stick at least around each other, hopefully not everyone else.' Danika shook her head.

'Ditto,' Cristian agreed. 'Where would you like to do your soaking? I can move furniture if you need.' Cristian felt quite at ease that she was in his personal space and he was happy to accommodate her literally and figuratively.

'Would it be alright if I used one of the guest bedrooms?' He nodded and helped her move her heavy bags into the larger of the rooms, then left her to sort herself out.

Cristian unpacked his own bags and contacted the gallery to explain he wouldn't be in after all today. They forwarded a few messages of clients looking for items, plus one from the Art Gallery of New South Wales that invited him to a private viewing of new pieces as he was a major sponsor. He marked the date in his calendar and was checking a few other messages on his laptop when he heard

Danika moving around the kitchen. She was opening cupboards and drawers.

'Were you looking for anything in particular?' He smiled at the consternation on her face.

'Healthy food and drinks. Not much to choose from.' Danika had a flush about her face and extra energy.

'I can have something delivered or we can go out if you like?' Cristian suggested.

'No problems, I have lots in the van, I'll just go down and get it, make us a meal. We really need to talk more.' Danika held out her hand for the pass key. 'Key please.' He handed it over and she breezed out.

Something in his new knowledge of her told him it was unlikely she was going to be cooking meat. He was beginning to realise he was quite hungry and needing protein so, despite her food plans, Cristian rang the nearby deli that he had an arrangement with to deliver groceries on short notice. They were always obliging as he paid them very well. A quick call to them would help fill his stocks up again.

Cristian was beginning to think he should check on her when she came bustling through the door carrying several very full, large, colourful bags. He helped her immediately to carry them into the kitchen. As the contents spilled out there were many different food items but also cooking utensils and more personal items.

'I am astonished all this fit in your van. I do have cooking utensils,' he offered.

'I know, but I get used to these ones and I was guessing I'm cooking so I just thought be prepared. I don't cook meat though, not that I'm vegan but I'm no good at it. Same with fish so I tend to stick mostly to vegetables and lentils etcetera, so it probably looks like I'm vegan. Plus, it's hard to store it in the van. My fridge is tiny.'

'I suppose you like lots of meat? That's bad of me. I'm not judging.'

'Yes I eat a lot of meat but also other carbs especially before and after the legacy,' Cristian explained.

When everything had been put away, Danika set about preparing a meal.

'Why do you call what happens to you "the legacy"?' Danika asked. Cristian offered her a drink of white or red wine as he settled in to watch her work. Danika accepted white wine.

'I actually don't know why, we just always have. In my lifetime anyway and as far as I know back to my grandfather's. That is part of my research, well the private side, not for the gallery,' he explained. 'I think it is as good as any term. What else could we call it? The change, the damning, the curse.' Cristian's mood was starting to become melancholy.

'Is it a curse for you?' Danika asked, her concern of his change of mood evident. He knew she would be feeling the anguish coming from him.

'I didn't think so at first. I thought it was exhilarating, a gift, a special secret society. Very stimulating as a youth but then my father was killed and it all changed. This time it was horrific.' Cristian gulped his wine down at the fresh distressing memory and then felt it fading as warmth started flowing into him.

Danika was hugging him, tightly, her head against his chest and whispering words he didn't understand but each one seemed to pull more pain out of him. He hadn't seen her move so quickly to hug him. She wouldn't let him go despite his hands on her arms trying to move her away. He was worried at how much energy she was using on him now. As the feeling of calm washed over him he released his grip and let the calm fill him. He kissed the top of her head and moved his arms around her in a gentle embrace. Danika looked up at him with a dreamy expression, her eyes dark green like a forest. He was heady with the intoxication of the blissful feelings she had given him and felt a need to kiss her.

The thought was interrupted by the entry buzzer. Instead he kissed the top of her head again and released her, going to check the intercom.

A few minutes later the deli delivery person was handing over several bags of goods. Cristian thanked him and handed over the payment. He placed the bags on the kitchen counter and then went back to give Danika a bear-like hug.

'Thank you, are you alright? I could feel how much of your energy you were giving me.' Cristian was so surprised at how at ease he felt, as if he had been holding his breath for a very long time until now.

'There you go, your gratitude gives me some back, it all works out in the end. Now, I don't know about you but I am ravenous.'

Through dinner, their discussions remained light, focusing on different foods they would and wouldn't eat and the merits of sustainable agriculture and complimentary farming.

Both seemed to be avoiding the feelings they had when they were hugging. Cristian loaded all the dishes in the dishwasher and helped clean up the kitchen. It was getting dark outside as they moved back into the lounge to relax. Danika chose a single chair and curled her legs under her skirt. Cristian sat opposite her on the couch, his long legs stretched out.

'Where to from here then Cristian? I'm not ready to settle down, I am traveling on a quest, a search for answers about my ancestor who came from England two hundred years ago. I also feel like I need time to wrap my head around today,' Danika blurted out.

'I was doing my own researching. I thought all my searchings were coming to a point actually. I have wanted answers about my family for years. Why are we the only ones, all descended from one line that I am struggling to trace back beyond about four hundred years. Usually nobility has good history lines but it gets a bit murky then. I have a few new leads and lots of theories, but I've been trying to put it all together between lunar cycles and work commitments.'

'Do you have to work?' At Cristian's smile, Danika continued, 'No really, I don't know what wealthy people do, never really had much to do with them other than as a waitress. Our family always worked to keep a roof over our heads, but the work we chose was never lucrative, just sustainable. Each of us – my mother and grandmother at least – had different driving forces. For my mother it is spiritual forces, afterlife, animals and the general universe. For my grandmother it was more nature, plants, the land, the earth itself, gravity. It is hard to describe. With me it is celestial and the emotions that people exude, the vibes so to speak. I don't think I have ever discussed our talents with anyone other than my family. And we just "get it" so no description needed. I think though in this time frame we are lucky.'

'How so?' Cristian was really enjoying watching her as she talked about herself and her family, so at ease.

'Well as a whole we– as in witches, gypsies, sorceress' – have been maligned or blamed for the crazy actions of others. Historically ostracised, beaten, hung or burned out of fear. Fear that we knew too much or could influence outcomes. Put men's power at risk. Now though in an age of enlightenment everyone wants to have a dabble whether they have any true talent or not so they seek our guidance, information and knowledge. We are accepted.'

'So you could probably make money out of that and live more comfortable?' Cristian was trying to understand her point of view.

'Well there's the rub. Those that are the players, think they have the gift or really want others to think they have the gift. They make the money because they are not living the truth. Whereas we have the gifts and if they are really truly discovered then the fear and suspicion starts again, or ridicule or condemnation. They fear that our gift can influence and be more powerful than they want. It is a dilemma. So we keep to ourselves, mostly hide our true talents or only let it out while others are not watching. You didn't answer my question.'

'No, I probably don't have to work. I could live off the various investments we have. I certainly don't have a nine to five life. But I like the thrill of the chase. Looking for treasure, whether it is a fine piece of art or an answer to a mystery or closing a lucrative deal. It gives me a reason to get up and it makes us a lot of money.' Cristian laughed. 'You know, that word is taboo in our family, we don't discuss our wealth, it is deemed unseemly and crass. The life I and my family have to lead to hide the truth and still live costs money and a lot of it. Why did you come to Sydney, Danika? The city doesn't really seem to fit you. If you don't mind me asking?' asked Cristian.

'No, it doesn't fit me as you correctly pointed out. I have a rough plan of travel and thought I would do the icons at least once on my way south. Then when I got here there was no accommodation, or at least none I could park at so I was planning on leaving. Except I had to take the iconic photos before going and so here we are,' Danika ended as she held her hands up a little exasperated. 'Do you think I would be able to see stars out there?' Danika pointed at the balcony now that it was dark outside.

'Not very likely. The city is too well lit and it may also be a bit overcast. But we can go have a look,' replied Cristian.

Moving over to the large glass sliding door he opened it for her and a rush of cool air flooded in, bringing the smell of the harbour and the city with it.

'Ooooh yes!' Danika threw her arms up as the cold air rushed over her. 'So invigorating.'

Cristian smiled at her enthusiasm. He pressed his remote and the lights inside turned off to create a little more darkness for her. They could just see the faint glow through the clouds of the moon that was waning from the full moon from two days ago. Danika began to chant quietly and Cristian was sure he could see an aura forming around her. He felt like his heart was expanding and filling his lungs with energised oxygen. The temptation to howl was growing inside him and the realisation of it felt ridiculous so he moved back inside, leaving her to enjoy her celestial soaking.

A few minutes later she came back in almost bouncing at each step with a very broad smile on her face.

'So when you change, it is just the one night, not the one leading up to it or after it? Sorry I am just so intrigued,' Danika apologised. 'And how do you travel and cope in other countries?'

Cristian offered her a soda water, he guessed she didn't want alcohol. She enthusiastically accepted.

'We fly, in planes, usually our own over the last two years,' he explained. 'We keep our travel short and, if it goes over the lunar cycle, we make sure we are somewhere safe at one of our estates.'

'One of your estates?' Danika mulled over that. 'How many do you have?'

'As a family at least one in each major country. Only the one here in Sydney which is getting a bit difficult to keep prying eyes from.' He was thinking about the first time he had needed to lock himself up, just two days ago. 'We have many in Europe as they were acquired centuries ago.'

'Wow that must be so difficult for you. What happened two nights ago? Something horrible, I felt it.' Danika teared up as she seemed to recall the memory.

'It is alright Danika, I survived. A bit like locking a dog up when you are trying to keep them out of trouble.' He realised she was not joking, that she really felt sorry for him.

'What are you going to do next time? I almost couldn't believe the pain you went through and then the fear and disbelief of being caged.'

'Occasionally I go bush here in Australia or I make sure I am near one of the estates when I am overseas. The timing was just really off with it being Easter, too many people around and I hadn't realised how unsecured my estate had become here. I am getting that sorted now,' he explained.

'Well at least we have a few weeks to work on that to keep you safe,' Danika said, naturally referring to them as 'we', entrenching themselves together. She put her hand over her mouth and continued, 'Oh my heavens, I am so sorry, that sounded very controlling.'

'Interesting as you not long ago said you were on a quest and had a life of your own.' Cristian grinned broadly. He was amazed how much he was enjoying her thoughts.

'What quest is this you spoke of anyway, I am intrigued,' Cristian asked.

'I just realised recently that it is two hundred years next month since my ancestor landed in Australia from England. We don't have any proof and there is a lot of history unknown, only the story passed down through the family. And then there is this.' Danika pulled her medallion out from her clothing and held it up for Cristian to see. The dark metal circle about the size of a 50-cent coin hung on a leather thong. He could see it was ancient metal, probably bronze. It spun slightly to show both sides, on one side was a Druid Triquetra and on the other a crude Celtic Lleuad Blaidd – the symbol of the moon cycle and a stylised wolf face. Cristian recognised the symbols immediately from his research and without thinking or asking he reached out to grasp it.

The images flashed in his head rapidly and filled his body and soul. Images similar to those before and after the legacy. Images of riding, running, pain and deep sorrow then more of intense anger and hatred and others so distorted and horrific it took his breath away and shocked him to let go.

He became aware of Danika leaning on his chest, he realised he was on the floor. She was white as a sheet and looking as shocked as he felt. He tried to get up but she held him down, easily it seemed.

'Stay still, I thought you had died. You went as stiff as a board and fell down ripping the medallion from my neck after you brought me down on top of you. I couldn't get the medallion from your grasp. Those thoughts, I couldn't understand.' She pushed up and ran away from him.

Cristian managed to push himself up to sitting, his head pounding, and he heard Danika retching in the bathroom. He realised she must have seen the images through him also. Images of people, mostly women, being tortured and burned. He wondered from how long ago the images had come from, it felt like a very long time ago. He saw the medallion on the floor and decided it was best to let Danika retrieve it. He went to see if she was alright. Without any confirmation he knew those images were of her ancestors.

In the bathroom she sat on the floor, weeping. Her face wet where she had splashed water on herself. He wasn't sure that she would want him there but she looked at him and held up her arms. He picked her up, feeling the buzz between them, this time it was not exhilarating but was deeply sad. He carried her to the guest bedroom and laid her on the bed. As he moved to stand straight she grasped his hand, so he laid down next to her spooning her in a hug while she wept. He whispered soothing words to her and stroked her hair and eventually her breathing returned to normal.

He handed her the tissue box and after a couple of minutes she croakily said, 'Let's not do that again.' They both sat up knowing she meant the medallion, not the spooning.

'I think I'll make us another of those teas of yours,' Cristian said, 'followed by a chaser at least for me.' Danika nodded her head.

Cristian was pouring hot water over the tea in two mugs with two glasses of spirits next to them as Danika walked slowly into the room. She looked at the medallion with the broken leather thong on the floor and picked it up by the thong before gingerly touching the medallion. She brought it over to the kitchen counter and placed it with the Lleuad Blaidd symbol facing up. Danika sipped the tea slowly as they both stared at the medallion, then looked at each other.

'That has been in my family as long as I have known. Passed down to each generation either as they came of age or had a child, whichever came first. But I have never really paid attention to the symbols that much. It has been against my skin for nine years giving me strength and never have I felt anything other than positive energy. Do you know what that is?' she asked him, pointing at the symbol.

'It's a Celtic symbol of Lleuad Blaidd, the Wolf and Moon. But it is very crude and worn so much that the features are not clear.' With the spoon in his hand he pointed to the semi circles indicative of the moon around the edge, 'Crescent moons,' then he pointed to the face in the centre, 'the wolf head.'

'Huh, I always thought it was just a long-nosed person. What is it made of and how old do you think it is?' Danika asked as she gingerly turned it over. 'This one I know, the symbol for all that we draw from in the unbroken circle and triangle.'

'The Triquetra. It is probably bronze and, at a guess, probably four hundred or more years old.' Cristian knew the Lleuad Blaidd well as it appeared on many of their family heirlooms, gifts given to each other, not to be shared to others. 'Just another guess but I think it holds the memories of the wearer, or at least fragments of them. The strongest ones, perhaps.'

'There have been many generations, at least nine besides me that I know of since my ancestor came to Australia. I have no idea how many or how far back before that. But I am certain we need to find out.' Danika began to shake again and grabbed the glass and downed the drink in one, using the fire of the fine scotch whiskey to warm her and calm her shakes.

'I agree, that medallion may be part of the key to my history and possibly yours. Our lines are linked I am sure of it. What I saw and felt was engrained in our lives. As if we were cursed and now it needs to come to a conclusion.' Cristian realised the enormity of what he was suggesting but equally that it was absolutely necessary, as if this were what he had been waiting to do all his life. 'Did you want to talk about what we saw in the visions?' Cristian didn't want to but thought he should offer.

'No, I don't think I could or should now. They were from another time not to be dissected or reviewed. Perhaps a guide later but not now.'

Cristian was glad Danika did not want to go through those memories again, however he was certain they would need to at some stage. He poured them both another shot of Jameson's whiskey and then placed out a small tray of chocolates.

'Now you're talking my language,' Danika said as she placed a large ornate chocolate delicacy completely in her mouth. Cristian smiled as he watched her go into raptures as she ate. She barely finished chewing before saying, 'Oh my heavens and stars that is awesome.' She washed it down with a sip of the whiskey.

Cristian did the same, nodding in agreement. Danika grabbed the medallion and placed it in her pocket, then they sat back where they had been before the experience. Sipping the last of the whiskey, they were both in their own thoughts until Danika jumped up and went back over to the balcony to grab the last of the moonlight. Cristian watched her from the bloodstone as she held her arms up to draw the strength of the few brightest stars into her. He held both of his hands on the bloodstone to calm his thoughts while he watched her. He so desperately wanted to kiss her it was making his blood race and the hair on his neck stiffen. He knew now was not the time despite his urges.

'I think I shall go lay down now if that is alright, I am quite exhausted.' Danika interrupted his reverie.

Cristian turned to look at her, knowing she had used her energy to calm his sensual thoughts. 'Yes, of course. There are towels and supplies in the bathroom if you don't have your own. I hope you can get some rest. I'm going to go over some notes and turn in myself.' He held up one of his books.

'Thanks. Well, goodnight Cristian.' Danika turned and went back to the room where he had laid her on the bed.

Cristian enjoyed hearing her say his name. From her lips it sounded so different to that spoken by any other. Like a caress of his mind and body. *Good grief man, get it together,* he chided in his thoughts and turned off the room lights as he went into his own bedroom.

Cristian had really wanted to talk to Danika more, all night but he could sense she needed space physically and mentally from him, from the whole enormity of the change in their lives. He knew also that he had no hope of sleep in his current state of mind. He sat at his desk to take notes of the day, trying to record all that he could remember using single words rather than phrases where the images were distorted. The experience with the medallion was most vivid and disturbing because it did not just show Danika's family memories but also a glimpse of his ancestors and their part in those memories and horrors. He wondered if Danika realised that or had the imagery been enough to horrify and haunt her without the connection.

When he thought on that further, Cristian realised she had known that and he felt a deep emotion of pride in Danika that she had not blamed him for any of what she saw. He had thought to look through more of his notes and tie in the images to his research but then felt calm come over him as if he really needed to sleep. Guessing Danika was sending out those thoughts he took the hint and decided to take a shower before turning in. The warm water was soothing and his thoughts turned to running. He had missed his morning run the last two days and decided he would set an alarm to go out early. After preparing for bed he opened his door to get a drink of water and the faint scent of incense came from the other bedroom. He noticed Danika had removed some of the items from her room to the corridor and made a mental note to remove them and the other offending items tomorrow. He may even take Danika to the gallery to let her choose a few pieces in exchange. Taking in a few deep breaths of the incense he returned to his rooms and fell into a deep sleep surprisingly quickly.

Danika

Danika knew that they needed to discuss the day and the future but she just needed some space. She had been enjoying the solitude of the last few months and now she was facing a life never alone and was not certain she could do that. She looked about the room more critically. Certainly not her taste and there was the odd creepy vibe with some of the artefacts that were meant to be arty and stimulating no doubt. She moved a few out into the corridor then cleansed the others of the previous owner's ill will. Setting up her candles safely on the dressing table she lit them and some incense to start a deep cleansing ritual. She emptied the contents of her bags onto the bed to sort out a few clothes and find her runes and crystals, talking to them as she went to re-establish their place in the world. She placed them around the room and the adjoining bathroom as she chanted.

There was no balcony for this room but she was able to tie back the curtains and open the window wide, deeply breathing in the cool night air briefly, closing it to a narrow gap again before it threatened to blow out the candles. Her grandmother's potion box she placed with the candles on the dressing table then changed her mind and put it on the bed next to where she was going to sleep. Finally pleased with the vibe of the room Danika prepared to have a shower before going to bed. The bathroom was compact yet well laid out and unadorned, thankfully. As Danika undressed she looked critically at herself in the full-length mirror, not something she had done in many years. Her vivid green eyes stared back at her, not all the Carling women had them but her grandmother did and a few others she had told Danika one time when she had been picked on at school. She had told Danika that she was rare and beautiful and destined for great things. She guessed she looked okay – all soft lines not trim or muscular like someone who worked out regularly, which she definitely did not. Her Triquetra tattoo on her side always linked her to her lineage.

The faint green mark on her chest where her medallion had sat against her skin reminded her of it in her pocket. She took the medallion out and placed it on the vanity so she would remember to fix the leather cord. Finally, she stepped into the shower and let the warm water flow over her longer than she normally would. Once out of the shower, she dried her long, wet hair and then dressed in the robe on the back of the door. Taking a seat on the bed Danika sorted out her things for the next day and realised she really needed to sort out her van also. *Tomorrow is soon enough,* she thought. With her hand on her grandmother's box she drifted off into a peaceful sleep.

3

THE JOURNAL

CRISTIAN WAS WOKEN by his 5.30 am alarm, amazed that he had slept so soundly and dream free, a rarity for him. Quickly turning off the alarm so as not to disturb Danika he put on running attire and, leaving a short note on the kitchen counter with the spare key, he left for his run.

Outside, the city was well awake. *Did it ever sleep?* Cristian doubted it. But now it was abuzz with the early risers like him out for a run before work or going about the business of their lives. The sun had not risen yet though the lights everywhere created a constant glow so it was easy to run anywhere. After an hour, the sun became visible and Cristian thought it best to return to his apartment to make sure Danika was alright. The need to do this gave him a boost in his step. He liked feeling responsible for her. He entered the building by the car park to check out the cardboard skip bin for any boxes finding a couple of suitable ones to pack up some artefacts. Walking past Danika's van he smiled at the artwork on it and wondered if she had done it herself.

Inside his apartment he placed a few items from the lounge in one box and then moved to the pile on the floor outside the room Danika was in. Trying to remove them quietly so he did not disturb her, he bumped the door accidentally that had not been fully closed. In the dim light he could see her wrapped in the white robe from the bathroom laying on the bed with her black hair streaming across the white towel. The robe had parted and he could see the line of one breast and the length of one leg almost to her hip. His blood pumped hot and fast and he felt the hairs on his neck rising.

Danika moved and the robe parted more to expose a central naked view that nearly made him drop the box he held. He moved swiftly away, placing the box on a table and going into his rooms to take a cold shower. Looking at his image in the mirror on the way through he could see his eyes had deepened and gold flecks had appeared. Similar to the transition, he had never had that reaction to any other liaison he had with a woman. Not that he had those very often. The cold shower helped the intense emotions subside a little.

This could be a problem, he thought.

Danika

Danika woke feeling very refreshed, stretching out her arms to her fingers above her head and then her legs down to her toes. She realised she had fallen asleep in the robe she had put on and had come open as she slept. The bedroom door was ajar and Danika pulled the robe back around her before going to close it so she could get dressed. She noticed the items she had placed in the corridor had been removed. *Hmm did he cop a look?* she wondered. *Of course he did.*

Dressed and feeling hungry, Danika moved to the kitchen where she saw his note and the spare key.

Spare key is for you to come and go as you please. I am just heading out for a short run, see you for breakfast.

She knew he was back as she could hear and sense him.

Danika placed the key in her pocket next to the medallion she'd taken again from the vanity, reminding her she needed to get the cord fixed. Looking through the fridge she decided on eggy bread. Most called it French toast but she preferred it simple. She was just debating if she should knock on Cristian's door once she had finished when he came out.

'That all smells wonderful.' Cristian noted her efforts. 'I'll make some coffee. Did you want some?'

'No thanks, I have tea,' she said as he approached her to get to the coffee and she moved away to take out the hot food. 'I'll just put this on the table.' She moved, keeping the oven door then the plates of food between them. She could feel the heat rising in her cheeks and was glad to be moving away. Placing the plates on the table she went back for her tea just as he looked back at her with his cup of coffee. She nearly dropped the cup. He smelled delicious of sandalwood and patchouli and looked so handsome, his blonde hair freshly washed and damp. For the first time, she noticed his grey eyes with their dark pools and flecks of gold.

Quickly turning away to go sit down she tried to bring herself back to normality. She really was hungry but the mouthful she took served also to keep her from focusing on him as he moved to sit opposite her.

'Are you alright?' Cristian asked. His eyes settled on the flush of her cheeks and Danika could feel similar emotions invading his mind through their new, unknown connection.

'No, not really,' Danika said, taking another bite. 'What is this?' She started fanning herself with a napkin to cool her burning cheeks, which really was not working.

'It's the rapture. It happens after imprinting,' he explained, continuing to eat as if he could ease her discomfort.

'The rapture… Well, how long does it last? I can't think straight.' Danika could feel the warm spreading through her, down to her chest and lower.

'While we are this close it will last until we marry and consummate the marriage.' Cristian was holding the edge of the table, seeming to also struggle with the feelings.

Danika almost choked on her food. Glaring at him she said, 'I can't marry you.' She shook her head at his sorrow. 'No, I mean, I can't marry anyone, not just you. We can't – I can't – we never do.' She thought of the wasted years in a pointless, loveless relationship with a friend briefly turned lover that slipped into a monotonous existence. She had finally ended it last year, going their separate ways gratefully.

She blew out a big breath, trying to ease her panic, and held up her hand to stop him getting up before going over to the sliding door to open it to the balcony. Taking in deep breaths she stood there looking back at him.

'Sorry I was a bit overwhelmed there, not prepared. I can fix that now that I know. Phew that was intense,' Danika said, looking at her plate of food on the table. 'And I'm still hungry. Please eat if you can.' She laughed.

'Oh I can eat no problems, it has your scent all over it,' Cristian said. He smiled between each mouthful. It only served to make an ordinary breakfast erotic and Danika was not sure eggy bread would ever seem the same again.

Still standing with the fresh air at her back Danika tried to come to terms with what he had said. 'So, we now have a dilemma then, Cristian, because of a curse, prophecy, your legacy, whatever it all means. My family has a curse that says that Carling woman – as in me – cannot love a man and marry him – as in you – or we lose our talent, craft, gift. You get the picture.' She stared at him enjoying all the food at the table other than her slice on her plate. 'Now, you are saying this "rapture" will last until we marry and do the thing. What if we go our separate ways, or don't marry. What then?'

'To be honest, I'm not sure. I don't think that has ever happened. Well, not for the last several generations that I am aware of anyway. Is it really a curse? Has it been put to the test? Would it be so terrible if you married and things changed?' At her pained look he retracted what he said, 'Yes of course it would. It is your essence then, you wouldn't be you?'

Danika could sense his sorrow again. 'To be honest sometimes I am so lonely feeling like a part of me is incomplete and angry that I am reminded of this curse by my family. I would like to marry and have more than one daughter or a son, a whole football team even. But I'm scared of what it would do to my mother, she would never forgive me.'

'I'd like to have a daughter,' Cristian said almost wistfully. 'There are only sons in the family. So much testosterone at family gatherings it is a wonder the wives can cope with it.' He laughed cheerlessly.

Not quite ready to have that level of conversation with Cristian, Danika switched topics. 'So what was the plan for today? Because I have to spend a bit of time preparing to calm our emotions down so we can sort out a few things.' Danika gave him a warning look to not touch her food as he cleared away the other things from the table.

'Apart from sorting out a curse and prophecy and a life together forever and planning a research trip, I thought I could take you to my gallery. We could take back the offending pieces and let you pick some that you like.' Cristian smiled at her as he pointedly left her plate alone.

'That would be nice, the gallery bit anyway.' Danika acknowledged his kindness, 'Thanks for removing those other pieces I left in the corridor.' They met each other's gazes, immediately thinking about the sight he would have had through the crack in the door. 'Stop it! Right, okay, I'm going to my room to get some protection.' Danika sprinted through, grabbing her slice of eggy bread on the way to her bedroom.

Behind the securely closed and locked door she sighed and took a bite of the bread. After thirty minutes she had several crystals and runes loaded with as much power as she could muster from the burning candles and the sunlight through the window. Coming out, she noticed two boxes of artefacts at the door. The combined negative energy was nearly overwhelming. Sensing her discomfort, Cristian quickly pushed them out the door until they left.

'Sorry about that. You will have to tell me sometime what is in them.' Cristian sounded concerned but curious also.

'Thanks, I have a few pieces here. You need to wear this one around your neck and these in your trouser pockets.' Danika place them on the table and moved back. Cristian moved over to collect them as instructed and she moved a little further away. 'I have a few of my own already in place.'

Once Cristian had fixed the crystal around his neck, Danika felt his calmness washing through their connection. The two crystals placed in his pocket completed the triangle to centre him. 'Okay, so best that we go in separate cars to the gallery rather than you trying to travel with that lot.' Cristian gestured towards the door. 'You can follow me. It isn't too far but the roads are a bit tricky in the CBD.' He paused for a moment before adding, 'By the way, I have been invited to the New South Wales Gallery on Friday and wondered if you would like to accompany me. It is a meet and greet of the benefactors of the gallery. You get to have private viewings if you like.'

'Um, I suppose so. Can we talk about this later because I need to be some places next week and I need some more supplies to keep up the protection?' Danika did a circle in in the air with her hand directed at Cristian.

'Of course, we do need to talk later. I'll take the boxes down and let you know when it is safe to come down.' Cristian left for his car, taking the two boxes precariously stacked together with him.

Danika felt the pull subside as he left. Even with the protection of her spells and crystals it was still there just lingering. She went back to the bedroom and made sure she had her purse and keys and her grandmother's potion box. Putting on a gaudy cardigan she decided she could probably go down to the cars now. Pulling the door closed behind her she saw the lift door open and Cristian walk out.

'You go down, I forgot my phone. I think we should exchange phone numbers,' he said as he watched her step aside for him.

'Good idea, then we can talk from a distance,' Danika replied raising her eyebrows. 'I'll head down. Rainbow needs to warm up. My van,' she added at his questioning look.

Danika was glad to be traveling in the lift alone and in the van to have some distance. Maybe they could sort out some kind of schedule apart and still work together on the research. That sounded okay in her head but when she said it out loud to test it out it seemed ridiculous. At the van Danika stowed her bag and started it up with a bit of prayer to the heavens that it would start. Thankfully successful on the second try, she was just getting it warmed up as Cristian came back down and started his car which, of course, started first time. He backed out and moved off to wait for her to do the same. Rainbow stalled as she was backing out. *Not warm enough girl*, Danika thought and gave her a few gentle revs, then they were on the way, Danika hoping that didn't happen again at an intersection.

Cristian was considerate and careful to make sure he did not lose her through the busy streets to his gallery, and Danika could tell he was taking the easier rather than quickest route to get there. He paused out the front of the gallery, making sure she spotted the parking space in front before he drove around to the back. Danika pulled into the parking spot, grateful to be out of the traffic. She waited at the car until Cristian came out the front door to get her. She guessed he was dropping the boxes off out through the back.

Inside was amazing. The building went up and back further than it appeared from the front. With pieces hanging from the ceiling as well as filling the walls and half the floor space it was very impressive.

Cristian introduced Danika to his staff. The receptionist and the two curators quickly said hello but went back to work as there were already a few customers looking around and discussing pieces. Cristian showed her around and was about to take her out the back when she put her hand up to her mouth and shook her head. Quickly turning away from the doorway she looked at him, sure she was failing at keeping her fear hidden from her expression.

'You have some seriously evil pieces out there, I don't know how you can't feel that.'

'Sorry, I source pieces from lots of ancient relics so we can only guess at the story behind them unless the curators can find the history. You could be invaluable in the research.'

'Not likely. The best I could offer would be happy, not happy and evil.' She managed a smile as they moved away from the evil pieces and found their way to others. 'On that note, these are happy and lovely.' Danika pointed towards the stand of handmade jewellery with iconic themes.

'We put them in for the lookers who want to feel they have bought something they could afford while in here. They sell surprisingly well, made by local rural First Nations artists,' Cristian explained. 'Anything else you think would be suitable as a replacement in the apartment?'

'No, sorry, I think some of the large pieces are nice but too big. Oh, that piece is nice, can I hold it?' Danika pointed at a bronze statue of a cat in play mode sitting on the floor by the door.

'That's our doorstop when we are loading pieces in and out the front door,' the receptionist pointed out as Cristian picked it up to hand it to Danika.

'This is filled with love.' She hugged it to her. 'The lady who made this loved this cat and loved watching it play. When the cat died she made this piece and then didn't make any more as she was sad. But this is full of love. You should take this home.' Danika handed it back to Cristian who was looking at the scowling receptionist.

'I will take this home. Just find something else heavy to put there.'

Danika sat down on a central padded bench and looked up to the ceiling. 'Up there you will find another piece that you should have.' Cristian looked up also.

'Which one?'

'You can't see it. It is in the ceiling. The people that lived here many years ago left some things up there. Worth looking at I think. Good luck getting to them though.' Danika pointed to where she thought they were.

'I'll get the guys on to it after closing.' Danika felt a swell of happiness as Cristian didn't doubt her in the slightest, seeming to only focus on the logistics of accessing the roof.

'I think I would like to go somewhere to get some supplies now. Would you like to meet back at the apartment?' Danika said, no longer interested in being in the gallery with so many false and unhappy vibes.

'If you like. I have a bit of business here, I'll message you later.' Remembering they hadn't exchanged numbers, they quickly did so before Cristian walked her out to the van and watched her drive off, his feeling of loss trailing after her as she drove.

Danika left the gallery but only moved to the next available parking space. She didn't want to be seen trying to get her thoughts back together. The latent evil she felt in the gallery had been overpowering and she wondered how they all could be in there with it. It had taken all her energy to focus on the few good vibes emanating from the jewellery and the cat statue. She did wonder what his staff might find tonight in the ceiling as there were many varied feelings up there.

When she had gathered her thoughts, Danika searched for places that might sell the psychic items she was looking for. She looked at each name and location until she was sure she had the correct one. Not the closest but hopefully the most honest. Danika started the GPS locator and moved off to find the store.

Cristian

Out the back Cristian stood still to see if he could sense what Danika had. He had to admit there was a hum about the place, almost like a deep motor he had never realised before. After discussing with the curators about the possibility of getting into the ceiling they pointed to a trap door at the top of the racks that they thought might go through to the front ceiling area. They found a suitable ladder and secured it so Cristian could get up to the trap door in the roof. It took some time to get the old frozen hinges and latch to move but once started he was determined to get it open. He had taken his jacket off and replaced it with a dust coat, hat and goggles as protection for when he was able to open the trap door.

Sure enough there was a century of dirt and dust that filtered down as the door swung upwards into the ceiling space. He came down to extend the ladder into the opening and then with torch in hand went back up. The space was not quite big enough for him to stand up in at the highest point but he was able to stoop to look around. There were a few planks across the beams to walk on so he wouldn't go through the ceiling. Shining the torch around, he noticed a few boxes stacked up towards the front of the building where Danika had pointed.

Cristian made his way carefully towards them, finding four old tea chests. It was too difficult to look in them here so he pushed them one at a time towards the trap door. His curators helped him make up a pulley around the beams to lower each one down.

The first one had books, photos and journals from the late 1800's into 1900's. The second chest had some pieces of China, ornaments typical of the era. The last two had pieces related to travel around the world in that time. Some of the pieces were tourist objects, some actual artefacts that looked to be from Egypt and China, including a small, heavily carved, wooden box possibly used for tea. Inside was tissue paper around a broach of many tiny cut gems in black and green formed into the shape of the Triquetra.

This was intriguing to say the least, he thought as he placed it in his pocket. He arranged for the curators to photograph and document everything. It was late in the afternoon when his receptionist handed him the boxed-up cat and said she had found out about the artist. She handed him a document she had put together of the history.

'Seems your friend was correct. The cat is the last piece the artist Maude Brooks made, lost to history until now. It is probably quite valuable and we were using it as a door weight.' She shook her head.

Once he'd packed the items up and driven home, Cristian was glad to be back at the apartment to get out of his filthy clothes. The dust coat and hat only helped a little. He made a mental note to have a vacuum cleaning agency come and clear out the roof cavity. Leaving the statue on the table still in the box with the notes he went into his rooms to strip off and get the dust showered off. He pulled the trinket box out of his trouser pocket with the runes and placed them and the one from his neck on the dresser. Cristian didn't hear Danika come back so when he came out of the shower he decided he should send her a message saying he was home. He walked out with just a towel around him to get his phone from the jacket he left on the lounge.

Danika

Danika thought the store had the right feel about it when she pulled up outside. Not in a busy shopping centre but in an old-fashioned corner block of shops from decades before with a community op shop next to it. Danika loved it already before going through the door. Inside, the scents of the herbs, spices and oils were so uplifting it was just what she needed. They had some of the more unusual essential oils that she had run out of in her grandmother's potion box as well as some lovely spice mixes for making soaps or for cooking. Danika felt a bit like a child in a lolly shop.

She had placed many and varied items in her basket when she

noticed the rack of clothes at the back of the shop. They were lovely and felt both exotic and magical. Danika was thinking about Cristian's invitation for Friday and knew she didn't really have anything nice enough for such an event. She picked out a dark purple velvet dress with a plunging backline with crossover ribbons and handkerchief hem embroidered with black silk thread and glass beads across the bodice and hemline. It was too beautiful to go past so she tried it on and the storekeeper said it was perfect for her. Danika also bought some black cord to fix her medallion and took a card so that she could call to check on available supplies to have them forwarded to wherever she ended up. Danika was feeling very happy with all her purchases despite really dipping into her savings while she placed them in the van.

The community op shop was still open so, loving to browse and get a bargain, Danika went in. The scent of old clothes and lives mixed with lavender, bay and rosemary to keep away moths was very comforting. She chatted with the ladies helping to put out donations and talked about her purchase from next door. One lady pointed out that she had just unpacked a lovely black velvet shawl if Danika was interested. She definitely was interested and thought it would go perfectly with her dress. Then the ladies were on a mission to find her shoes and jewellery. They all were laughing at some of the funny shoes and jewellery they found and eventually all concerned wanted Danika to do a fashion show of all the different pieces together. She laughingly agreed to this with the lady from the spiritual shop next door coming in also for a quick look. They all oohed and aahed at her which made her feel very special and, for the first time in months, she missed her mother Selene.

When it was finally time to make her way back to the apartment she found herself hugging all the ladies to absorb and share the good vibes of the day. They all stood and waved her off. Danika returned to the apartment, burdened by the bags in her hands as Cristian walked out from his rooms in just a towel. She froze, staring at him.

'Retail therapy I see,' Cristian said. Danika was overwhelmed by the feeling of the rapture rising within him.

'You need to go get your protection and calm down Cristian,' Danika said, firmly, seeing his eyes changing. The fine hairs on his chest were standing up as well as his manhood. She dropped the bags and was already chanting as she held her hands up in front of her.

He stood there staring at her actions then looked down. 'Oh God, I'm so sorry.' Turning on his heel, he hurried back to his rooms.

Danika picked up her bags again and took them to her bedroom to unpack. She shut and locked the door, leaning against it to get her breath and calm her mind. She sorted her purchases how she liked with a plan to hopefully help Cristian's urges. Nearly finished, she could hear Cristian moving around the lounge and then music playing.

She came out and saw he had unpacked the cat statue and placed it prominently for her to see. Next to it were some notes which she picked up and read. 'So what I felt was correct then,' she said.

'Yes I think my receptionist is a bit in awe of you.' Cristian seemed relieved Danika didn't make a comment about his loss of control, eager instead to talk about the statue. 'By the way, I went into the roof from the back area and found four tea chests with personal items from a family at the turn of the previous century. My curators are cataloguing it now as there are hundreds of photos and other items.' Placing the trinket box on the counter he added, 'I found this and I thought you might like it.'

Danika picked up the trinket box and could feel the strength coming from it already. Inside in the original tissue paper that was falling apart in her fingers was nestled a stunning broach of tiny black and green gems studded in what appeared to be silver in the shape of the Triquetra. The love and power in this piece was significant and her tears involuntarily flowed.

'This was what I could feel. The love in this is outstanding. These gems I think are onyx and jade. Not sure of the metal, probably silver. This has been made with love and given with love to one who understood and perhaps used the craft. This is too much, Cristian, it is superb.'

'It is yours to keep. A small token for the incredible and very valuable finds you made today. Finds that made me realise I need to move away from the type of artefacts I have been acquiring and move more towards the ones you have found,' Cristian said with certainty.

'Now, I have something to give you.' Danika pulled the medallion from her neck. Cristian backed up. 'I think I can give you mental protection so that if you are hit by the urges of the rapture again you can calm it down. You do not need to hold this. Do you trust me?'

'What kind of mental protection, hypnosis?' he guessed as she projected her thoughts at him.

'Yes with a suggestion. Do you trust me?' Danika was in his head already.

'Yes, I trust you.' Cristian was already entranced by the hypnosis, having been focussing on the medallion.

It took Danika a lot of energy and patience to place the suggestions in Cristian's head. She used a mixture of reactions to his emotions, some words he would hear and the scent of an unusual essence oil, Tulsi, which Danika made sure she had on her. Creating suggestions from words and scents was relatively easy but for emotions proved difficult because the emotion has to be stimulated for the suggestion to be associated with it. Danika could only achieve this by removing the protective runes from Cristian to stimulate the rapture. It was invasive and dangerous and she felt guilty at this violation but knew they could not have a repeat of the accident this afternoon.

Leaving Cristian in a semi-conscious state, Danika turned down the lights and went out on the balcony to absorb as much energy as she could from the stars and the moonrise. She was exhausted and wanted to sleep. Finally complete, she brought him out of the trance with a calming, happy thought and a suggestion he may be hungry and want to cook. Cristian looked at her feeling very refreshed. 'You said you had something for me,' Cristian asked, oblivious to the last hour of hypnosis.

'Silly I know but I couldn't resist it at a community op shop today.' Danika held up a toy stuffed wolf and laughed. Cristian laughed in turn, taking it from her and pretending to hug it.

'I'm starving; I think I will cook that steak. Are you interested in anything, my turn to cook?' he asked, moving over to the fridge.

'Perhaps later, I think I need to lie down.' Danika went to lie down on the bed in her room and quickly fell asleep.

Danika woke, realising she had collapsed on the bed in her clothes. Turning the bedside light on, she saw the clock on the wall – six o'clock. It was still dark and she was not sure if it was night or morning. Looking at her phone confirmed it was morning. Danika decided it was time to get herself sorted, to form a real plan for today, tomorrow and next week. But first, she wanted a shower.

As the water poured over her she briefly went through the day, trying not to dwell on the incident when she came home. Incident… *Well, what else was she going to call it?* she wondered. The sexual tension was there for her also, her protection spells were for her as much as for Cristian. She felt herself wondering what was under that towel and then shook her head and realised being naked in a shower thinking about him was very dangerous. *Move on, Danika,* she chided herself, *make a list.* Danika was not good with lists but she really felt she needed one. Dressed and feeling hungry the kitchen was the next point on the 'plan'.

In a search through drawers and cupboards she found post it notes and cereal. With a hot cup of tea and a huge bowl of cereal she was now armed with a pen and making notes, sticking them across the counter in a swirling pattern, her kind of list. It was well and truly daylight outside and she could hear and feel the thrum of the morning traffic. Taking the remains of her cereal she sat out on the balcony with her feet curled up under her skirt and absorbed some of the sunshine on the harbour. It truly was a beautiful sight. She had a strong desire to get out of the city though and on the road again. She needed a forest, a beach and no traffic. *Yes, almost time to move on,* she thought. *I really want to go to the art gallery night though.* She felt his presence before she felt the warm air from the door sliding open.

'Good morning,' Danika spoke first. 'How did you sleep?'

'Better than usual, I'm guessing you have dampened some of my more intense thoughts,' Cristian replied as he sipped his coffee.

'Hmm, yes I had to, but you did agree at the time.' She turned to look at him, glad she had spread some of the protection to herself. With the sun on his blonde hair and face, making his grey eyes very pale almost like mirrors, he was stunning.

'I saw your notes; apparently you need to call your mum. Also something about the beach.' Cristian moved back inside as Danika rose to come in also.

'We talk often and I have broken the link she had put on me so she could trace my thoughts. I know she would be suspicious of that. Besides, I feel a need to talk to her.' Danika moved to her notes to read them over, noticing she had written 'call Mum' more than she had realised.

'Are you going to tell her about us?' Cristian asked, watching her closely.

'No, what would I say anyway? I still can't get my head around the "us" part myself. I have things I want to do – need to do – and originally they did not include anyone else.' She looked up at him. 'But now I know they do. Are you prepared to come on my quest? Because I have to do it and something in my soul tells me you have to be part of it also.'

'Yes. That is the short answer, but I think you are correct. I wrote a list last night also. Not as pretty as yours but strangely enough a similar theme.' Cristian briefly left the room to bring back the list he had written, placing it on the counter so Danika could read it.

Top of the list was arranging sale of the gallery art. Cristian looked at her notes and, grabbing the one with sad faces in a stylised but obvious drawing of his gallery, placed it next to the first item on the list.

'I have decided to sell off most of the gallery artefacts and move to a different theme of history and art, hopefully with your help.' Danika was a bit shocked by that change of ideas. She had never considered doing any other job than the casual ones she had been doing. 'Your thoughts on that would be good.' He was waiting for her response.

'I have to admit that the negative energy there was very overwhelming so it was difficult to enjoy it until I found those few pieces. There may have been more but I couldn't sense them.' Danika was apologising for her part in the change of his gallery theme. She touched the broach which she had pinned to her black and green top today.

Looking back at his list, one item was the function at the New South Wales Art Gallery tomorrow. She picked her note with the smiling faces and placed it next to the list item.

'I'm surprised you think everyone will be smiling there,' Cristian commented.

'Oh that is not the guests at the function,' Danika explained. 'That is the ladies that sold me my outfit yesterday, they were so lovely.' Danika smiled at the happy thoughts that oozed from them all as they waved her off.

'Of course, silly of me,' Cristian said. She jokingly punched his arm.

His next on the list was 'Coast?'. Cristian pointed to it and asked, 'You said something about needing to be at the coast next week?' Danika picked the note with the planets and waves and 27 April written on it, placing it next to that list item.

'I need to be where I can see the planetary alignment on the 27th of April next week. I thought somewhere on the coast south of here because I thought I would have been on my way south by now,' Danika explained without looking at him.

Next on his list was census search. Danika looked at it and asked, 'What is that about?'

'I was thinking about the different options to tracing your ancestry. Census' were started in Australia in 1828, firstly in New South Wales before it went national, but prior to that each state had what they termed musters. They could be very useful for our search. There are passenger lists too,' Cristian explained.

'I know my ancestor Jessica arrived in 1822 and then we have a verbal record of her descendants. My mother thinks they moved from Tasmania to South Australia in about 1860. The problem is we don't really know anything about the period between 1822 and 1860. Or in fact, the period before 1822 when she was in England,' Danika explained. 'I just know that in that missing history is the key to the curse and prophecy and your legacy.'

Danika picked out a couple more post it notes, one with her Triquetra symbol and another with a masted ship and put them next to the census comment.

'Perhaps you should write down your verbal history so I and others can help trace your family lineage,' Cristian suggested. Danika nodded at the sense of that.

Next on Cristian's list was 'Father's Journal'. When Danika pointed at that he elaborated.

'I found a journal in my father's safe at the back. Not sure why I hadn't bothered to look at it before. It may have some interesting insights. I haven't had time to read it yet.'

Cristian picked up the note with multiple dollar signs.

'What are these representing?' he asked.

'Oh I need to get some work after the alignment to pay for my journey south and the ferry to Tasmania,' she explained.

'Ferry? Have you booked it?' Danika felt a strong surge of protection rise from Cristian before her protection spell dampened the urge. Cristian sighed deeply and Danika felt a wave of sadness for having control over his emotions.

'Yes I have booked it for the 12th. That gives me a week before the anniversary of Jessica's arrival. It also gives me time to get some work and travel not too quick to Melbourne.'

'I can't go on the ferry so I will fly there and meet you. Also you know I will make sure you are financially safe.' Cristian seemed to not want to say those words.

'Why can't you go on the ferry?' Danika had so much more to say and ask. She was feeling very forced but that was the first she blurted out.

'It is the confinement with no way to escape. No cruises either. I can do short trips, I have been sailing. I didn't particularly like it though. Also I never plan trips within days of the legacy in case something delays it. I can't chance being stuck somewhere where I can't be away from people before and during the change,' he explained, continuing with, 'I can sense you are not happy with my suggestion of meeting you, and picking up the tab so to speak.'

'No, part of me really is not happy at that but another part is enjoying having a companion to share my time and quest with someone who is very understanding and supportive and apparently rich.' She smiled and continued, 'I do need my own money though and when I work it is not just the financial gain. I get energy from the interactions with others. I need to be around other people. When is the next lunar phase? Let me think, it will be after that.' Before she could calculate it in her head Cristian intervened.

'The 16th and in the northern hemisphere it will be a blood moon.' Cristian paused, seemingly lost in thought. 'I think you need to meet my mother.'

'What!' Danika was completely thrown at this change of direction of thought. 'How were you planning on introducing me as your 'mate'? I'm not ready for that at all. No, no, not at all.' Danika backed away from him.

'Not today, but soon. I would like to meet your mother also. In the meantime I'll get a map up on the computer and try to help you plan your journey.'

Danika could sense that Cristian was struggling with the protection charm and fighting it. She worried how long it would hold for each of them.

Danika remembered the road atlas her mother had given her, knowing what a terrible sense of direction her daughter had. 'I have a road atlas in the van. I'm going to get it.' With that she grabbed the keys Cristian had given her and went down to the car park while Cristian went into his study to look up destinations.

In the lift and journey to her van Danika thought about Cristian's revelation of meeting his mother. It just did not feel right. She had only known him a few days. She wasn't sure of the future with him, or their future together. It was far too difficult to come to terms with yet. Sat in her van with the road atlas on her lap she decided to call her mother. In this space if her mother could connect with her at least she would not sense Cristian. Her mother picked up after several rings, answering a little breathlessly.

'Hello Danika, lovely to hear from you. How is the trip going? I have been flat out getting ready for this weekend of markets, it's a long weekend you know? Where are you now?' Selene, as usual, commandeered the conversation before it had even started.

'Hello, Mother. I'm in Sydney but not for long as it is too expensive. I took a few iconic photos though which I will send you. I forgot about the long weekend, I'm glad you have a few markets.'

'Have you been able to get any work?' Selene was already sounding distracted.

'Mum, I was wondering if you could send me a list of our family, back to Jessica and any dates you know. I thought I might look through the census to trace any gaps in the family.' Danika thought she would run with Cristian's plan of attack.

'I'm a bit busy now Danika, I'll see what I can do later and text it to you. I don't think the census will help though, the women tried to stay hidden mostly until more recently. But good luck with your search. I really must go I have candles to dip. Love you darling.' Selene was ready to hang up.

'Love you too, Mum, I'll send the photos as a reminder for the list. Bye.'

Danika knew her mother had already hung up on her last words. Danika felt a bit deflated as she really wanted to talk to her, but in reality, she didn't know exactly what about. It wasn't like she could explain the situation with Cristian, her mother would have a fit. As she sat in her rainbow van, as cramped as it was, she realised after just two days she was missing being on the road with Rainbow as her trusted home on wheels. It was her space, not shared with a stranger, now her apparent soul mate.

She put her hands over her face and then flopped back onto the bed, the atlas falling to the floor. What was she going to do about this situation? *Do you truly want to end your solitary nomadic life for this dangerous complicated situation?* The thought of him was starting to arouse her senses – the way he looked this morning with the sun highlighting his hair and face. His chiselled features and the shine of the individual hairs on his face. Her thoughts turned to last night when he had come out of his rooms in just a towel. In that brief view she had taken in his muscled arms and legs, lithe not heavy, the fine blonde hairs across his chest. Her thoughts ran on to the view of his arousal. She could feel her blood pulsing and her breath getting faster. She suddenly became aware of where her thoughts had drifted and she sat bolt upright, pushing her hands into her pockets where she grasped her crystals and chanted a calming verse. Once she thought her pulse was under control again, she picked up the road atlas and, after locking her van, slowly went back up the apartment by the stairs not the lift.

'Are you okay?' Cristian asked when she finally entered the apartment, the concern clear on his face.

'Sure am, I just climbed the stairs. I really need to do some exercise, walking or such. I am a bit weary of sitting about I think.' Danika tried to cover her slip in control.

'I could show you some good places to run if you like?' Excitement radiated from Cristian with his question, the thought of them running together seemingly something that brought him a lot of happiness. A moment later, sadness swiftly followed. Danika could feel Cristian's emotions, despite the dampening chants.

There was still so much they hadn't spoken about before, so much of each other's lives they didn't know, but Danika could feel the direction of Cristian's thoughts. Flashes of a man, older than Cristian though similar in appearance, exchanged between them and Danika knew this must be his father.

'I feel a connection to my grandmother whenever I use my herbs. I was much closer to her than my mother, and when she died she kept her illness a secret. I was devastated, losing someone that close.' She offered this piece of her life in hopes that it prompted his own, sensing that he needed to talk about the sadness he was feeling.

Cristian walked over to the lounge and sat down, putting his face in his hands briefly to gather his thoughts. Danika sat opposite him, knowing she had prompted the right pathway to encourage him to speak.

'I was away in South America buying artefacts when I was twenty-two. I thought I was so clever and bullet proof. It was the lunar cycle of the full moon but I wasn't concerned because I had a jungle to enjoy. My father and I had been running together each full moon since my coming of age at sixteen. We would run the estate at first, then moved into the national forest a few times when we had confirmed it was clear of people. He must have decided to run where the estate and the edge of the park meet the night he died. We worked out through different witness statements that he must have been harassed by dogs and lost his bearings. He ran onto a road and was hit by a truck.'

Cristian was staring into space. Danika was quietly weeping at his pain as he continued, 'They said he must have died instantly. At his death he changed back to his human form and was naked. The inquest into his death was gruelling. The police and media wanted to know why he was naked running around the streets. The truck driver insisted it was a big dog he hit. My mother was alone to deal with it until I could get back a few days later and we both had to field a lot of questions. We prefer our privacy which was destroyed at that time.' Danika so wanted to hug his pain away but knew that would be their undoing so she just hugged her knees as the tears rolled down her cheeks.

'My father and I were very close even before the legacy but when I came of age and changed for the first time with my father by my side it was as if finally I had someone to share my strange life with. I lost that with his death fifteen years ago, until this month and when I met you actually.' Cristian now turned his full gaze at Danika. 'I love my mother but never thought she really understood me until this last full moon when she had to help me. I now know differently. That was why I thought you would appreciate speaking with her.'

'I rang my mother when I went down to the van before,' Danika admitted. 'As usual she was very focussed on her particular needs and life choices. I think that was why I was so close to my grandmother. I'm sure she knew I had more skills than my mother gave me credit for. I only have that jacket you found and her potion box to remember her by and of course all her training. She hinted that something special was going to happen to me but didn't have time to tell me anymore. That was twelve years ago and I have felt alone ever since, until now. That is why I am not going to tell her about you until the last possible moment.'

'When my mother told his brother Robert, my uncle, he flew out to Australia from his home in Germany. He never understood our desire to stay here. He still doesn't. He is older than my father and had memories of England and Europe and never liked Australia. He flew to his cousins as soon as he was old enough to leave. I think my grandfather was very disappointed, he had hoped that there would be a grand family tree established here. I only knew my grandfather when I was younger and he died before I came of age. A heart attack, which is very unusual for our family, generally – accidents aside – we live long lives apparently. I think he may have indulged too heavily in all life could offer. He truly loved the opportunities and lack of formalities here in Australia. He was great fun,' Cristian explained.

'My grandmother may have been similar, much easier going than my mother. Learning the craft was done with fun instead of how my mother taught, who took it all very seriously.' Danika was smiling at the memories now. 'So here we are Cristian, reminiscing about dead relatives who may or may not have held the key to our current predicament. Where to from here?'

'Where to indeed? I have a calendar here for you to help map out your travel plans. It was a freebie from the local grocer you met the other day. Do you have your maps?' Danika felt Cristian's eagerness to change the subject.

'Yes, this map shows the east coast south of Sydney and a few different possible spots for viewing the planetary alignment. I like the look of this one.' Danika was pointing to a coastal tourist area with a peninsular called Sussex inlet. 'It seems to have views from several directions and nice beaches I hope,' Danika said as she was pointing to a free campsite on the coast.

'Canberra is not too far from there. You could do some research of your ancestors through passenger lists and census' perhaps,' Cristian suggested.

'I actually asked my mum about a list of ancestors today but she seemed to think they would have avoided any official contact. So I'm not so sure we are going to find anything that way. Although Canberra was one of those places I would like to visit, perhaps after the alignment.' With that thought Danika started making notes on the calendar that Cristian had given her. Tomorrow the gallery event. Monday – ANZAC, Wednesday – planets and beach. She flipped the page to May and wrote on the 12th 'Ferry'.

'I'm surprised you would want to be around people for ANZAC, isn't that a lot of sorrow?' asked Cristian.

'Oh no, actually maybe a little sorrow but mostly pride, very deep patriotism, kindness and pride. It is very powerful,' she explained. 'I usually try to find a small RSL to go to and help out. I can absorb the wonderful emotions and spread them around. I spotted one near where I was shopping yesterday.'

'So based on your planning you will have about two weeks to work and travel between the coast, Canberra and get to the ferry. Does that sound correct?' Cristian was taking notes.

'I guess you are right. Why?' Danika could sense he had a plan.

'I can get you work at the Australian National Gallery in Canberra in the café or the shop if you want. I can pull a few strings so to speak. That way we could research as well as meet your desire to earn your way.'

Danika was so surprised at this suggestion she just stood, staring at the notes for a little while to gather her thoughts.

'I know you are trying to be helpful but I have to do this myself. I need to feel the vibe of a place before I work there. Sorry.' Danika was feeling a bit pushed into his way of thinking. 'Can we agree that after tomorrow night I am going to start travelling south down the coast for now and maybe we can meet up in Tasmania either when I get there or after the full moon when you can travel?'

'I'm sensing that you think we can go our separate ways for a while. I am not trying to push you but I know you can feel the pull, even through all your chants and charms. You do know that we have to resolve the imprinting and rapture? We could just do away with it all and succumb to our needs.' When Cristian moved towards her, Danika began to chant, the scent of the spell washing over them. He stepped back and looked at his hands, the veins standing out. He sighed deeply and then nodded his head.

'Okay I get what you are trying to point out so deliberately. What did you do, remove some of the protection to make a point?'

'No, I didn't have to. It isn't strong enough today. I just have to ramp it up a bit while we are working so close together. After tomorrow I will need to take a break, get some distance so we can work together another day.' Danika was trying not to sound angry at him as she was well aware this attraction was difficult for them both. 'Actually I think I might go for a walk and come back to this a bit later.' Danika left the room to gather her bag and a jacket before leaving.

Cristian

Cristian stood out on the balcony and watched her go. She was wearing the brightly coloured jacket from their first meeting over her black and green cheesecloth top and black billowing pants. She reminded him of a tropical bird as she rapidly walked away. The temptation to run after her was almost overpowering but then it dampened, though not quite as fully as before. He had to admit that Danika was correct – the protection was dulling. What would happen if it were gone completely? Cristian was very concerned that he wouldn't be able to contain the rapture. The thought of scaring or hurting Danika was like a cold shower.

He decided he would turn to his father's journal to hopefully give him some understanding and guidance. Cristian retrieved the journal from his desk and sat to thumb through it to look at the dates first. He was looking for the entries prior to his father meeting his mother but then changed his mind to read it from the beginning. The first entry was just before his father's sixteenth birthday in 1968.

Father has said it would be good to write a journal of such a momentous change to my life and be able to look back on it. I am so scared. I wish Robert was here, I don't understand why he had to leave. Now I only have Father, I don't remember Mother. At least Robert has that, not that he ever spoke about her. Father said he will be with me every minute for the legacy and that it gets easier each time. I wish he had let me watch but he said it was too dangerous. He says these things but does not explain.

The next entry came after his sixteenth birthday.

It's not fair, this is horrible, why are we cursed with this? It was disgusting to lose control. Father said he ran with me. I don't remember anything other than the pain and the humiliation of waking naked. Why hadn't Robert warned me?

Cristian remembered his first time being very frightening but not with the disgust his father did. Perhaps having his mother to help before and after was the difference. His grandmother had died back in England, maybe that was why his grandfather moved. So many questions still. He noticed the next entry was many years later.

1982. Robert continues to harass Father to move us to Europe. Banging on about suitable mates for me, I feel like he talks about me as a stud bull. He doesn't trust my judgement. Father misses Mother terribly and is happy for me to take my time finding the right girl.

1983. Happy new year, happy me, happy Father, not so happy Robert, who cares. Elizabeth is beautiful, intelligent and mine. I'm sure the universe controls this, having her turn up at the staff post-Christmas pool party as young Ann's friend. What a shock to us both when we imprinted at the pool house of all places. Lucky it wasn't the pool, we could have drowned. She understands me like no other and is not scared in the least. We can't wait to be married, she has no close family. Poor girl, only a few more days. Lucky she doesn't live here, I wouldn't be able to keep my hands off her. The last change was so different

I could feel where she had touched me. I can't wait for the next one after we have married and consummated the connection. First time I have ever wanted it.

His father had drawn hearts and smiley faces at this entry which made Cristian smile, not a side of his father he had expected. Well at least he had mentioned the rapture effect briefly. So, he had felt the effect of them touching, no mention of blue hands though.

February 1983. My darling Elizabeth has encouraged me to write in my journal. I want to write everything and then nothing. It has been over a month since we married. Our wedding night was so unexpected as if we were one. I felt like I could have gone through the change with her, as if my blood was her blood. We understood each other's needs without speaking yet we talked and touched every part of each other. Her hair is so soft. She told me what I look like after the change, she said she was drawing a picture for me to see soon. I have told her no photographs though which she completely agrees.

April 1983. Our lives will be complete before the end of the year as we are expecting our son in November. My darling Liz is a little sad that she can never have a girl. I wish I could give her what she wants but this bloody curse hangs over us. I can't risk her safety during the change so hide myself away in the forest each time now.

November 1983. I had thought watching Liz growing our son and his not so little kicks was the most magical thing but nothing compares to having him here where we can hold and love him together. I didn't think she could spread her love so far but it actually grew. She still loves me just as much and now our son Cristian also. How amazing she is. I can hardly get any

Cristian thought he needed to ask his mother if she still had the picture she was drawing of his father. He remembered his father insisting he watch the change before he had to go through it himself, thinking it would help him understand and not be so frightened. That had just made his first change more terrifying. Although his father had looked magnificent, with his hair long and dark grey shining in the moonlight. He thought he would not do that to his son though.

Immediately a picture of Danika being pregnant filled his mind followed by an image of what looked like their wedding night. What wedding night? *Good heavens man, get it back together,* he chided himself. He turned back to taking notes. He needed to talk to his mother, understanding now that a little distance from Danika was better for her. He really did want to please her and let her make her own decisions. That his father saw the negatives in their lives as he had himself, especially after being locked in the cellar, surprised him. Cristian continued to read the journal. There were a few gushing baby entries which he flicked past until he reached a sombre one.

*December 1990. My poor dear Liz cannot stand another loss.
I cannot put her through that again. This will be a sad Christmas for us all. Father dying after his heart attack, now another
miscarriage, another girl. To hear her crying is unbearable. We
thought perhaps another boy would be possible, brothers like
myself and Robert but I cannot risk her mind if she lost another
baby. Cristian will be enough for us to love and enjoy, watching
him grow and succeed.*

This entry really shocked Cristian. He had been oblivious as a child that his parents went through that sorrow. He was heartbroken when his grandfather had died when he was only seven years old and remembered them helping him through that grief while they kept their own to themselves. Another side to his mother he had not appreciated.

September 1999. Where has the time gone? Cristian will be 16 soon. I am going to sit him down and explain the change in as much detail as possible. He also needs to see it so that he can fully understand that, as awful as it looks, he will survive it.

Cristian had forgotten that 'talk' with his father in the study. At first thinking it was some ruse to scare him, the more he spoke of the family legacy and the change, Cristian had realised he thought of it as a curse, a dreadful affliction that he had to face, but not alone. *Funny how the specifics melt away over the years until you are reminded of them,* he thought.

November 24th 1999. My marvellous son who I would die for is now cursed also. I tried to hold my change as long as possible to talk him through the pain of his own change and watched him writhing in agony. Nobody, no parent should have to endure this curse. I shall encourage him not to have children to break this horrendous cycle. Perhaps he could pursue the prophecy. Vague as it is I know Robert knows more than he will tell. Cristian is so very clever he will be starting university next year, ahead of his peers. I am so proud of him.

Finally something useful. Robert, I should have known that he would know something, Cristian thought. Cristian had been through the change hundreds of times now but thought back to that first one. His father had shown him his own change twice which was terrifying yet fascinating at the same time out in the estate woods. Then, the night of his sixteenth birthday happened to be a full moon starting before dark. His father had been able to hold it off while he talked Cristian through the searing heat of his racing heart. Every hair on his body had felt like needles digging into his skin. His father had encouraged him to strip off his clothes. Every one of his bones seemed to break and he fell to the ground. Cristian remembered hearing his father's voice and felt the touch of his hand and then no other memory until he woke the next morning with his mother crying over him in his bed. His father must have carried him there. They had helped him into the shower, his father holding him up in the stream of water to get him clean. He had felt exhausted and he slept the whole day.

So, Father didn't want the legacy to continue for me, that was why he and Mother never encouraged me to meet a girl. Unlike Robert, Cristian was well aware of the European side of the family, all happy to increase and spread their wealth to purchase larger estates. Cristian sensed that with the increase in the public curiosity and every man and his dog buying drones that it was only a matter of time before their secret would be discovered. There were so many more journalists and interested parties in Europe with the war in Ukraine and the refugees from it at present also.

March 2004. Cristian's graduation day. My darling Liz and I were so proud of him working through a double degree in record time for his age. He has had so many job offers which weigh heavy on our hearts as he cannot accept them, always having the needs of the legacy hanging over him. He hopes to visit the digs he has been invited to though in England and South America as he searches for anything regarding the super-natural forces that run our lives. He looked so grown up in his graduation silks – the first in our family to do so.

Cristian looked up from the journal to the photograph on the shelf in his study of the three of them on his graduation day all smiling broadly, a tear in his mother's eyes. So many memories flooded back to him. His parents so supportive of his achievements and encouraging him to travel to pursue his dreams yet worried if he did not take care each full moon. It must have been a double-edged sword for them. If he had not been so determined to follow his own needs he would have been home and his father would not have died the following year. Cristian realised that was a dangerous path of thought to go down and went back to the journal.

He had drawn a pine tree and gift box at the end.

Cristian sat at his desk with tears streaming down his face, realising this was the last entry his father had written. He hadn't cried over his father's death until now. He had had to remain strong for his mother and to stand up to the forceful demands of his uncle expecting them to sell up and leave Australia, angry at the death of his younger brother and Cristian's trips around the world. Then the police and coroners investigations going on for so long. There had been no time for tears then. He put his head in his hands with his elbows on the desk briefly and let the tears out.

When the tears ran dry he regained his composure, walking away from the journal and his notes to get a drink.

On the counter was still the unresolved list comparison and left over post it notes. The 'call Mum' ones were scrunched up. Left over were a few scribbles of signs, not actual words but the Triquetra and what looked like a rubbing of the medallion? He realised that the Lleuad Blaidd was a raised symbol but the Triquetra was engraved or scratched into it on the other side.

Cristian felt his hunger as he searched for a cool drink in the fridge, noting the time was past breakfast and lunch. He hadn't realised how long he had been reading and going down memory lane until now. This meant that Danika had been away for many hours, he wasn't sure he was concerned or just very intensely curious. He had to give her space and also be sure he could remain objective and settle with her need to have space from him. After making some sandwiches he decided to send details to his curators of the pieces he wanted to sell as soon as possible. That seemed the best use of his time for now other than scouring the city for Danika or sending her the hundred messages he felt like doing.

Many hours later he was reaching to turn on the desk lamp when he noticed that the sun was setting. Still Danika was not back. Now he was getting worried and relented to call her on the pretext of what meal to plan. He only got her voice mail and left a message but also sent a text as well. After what seemed hours but was only minutes, Danika sent a reply text explaining she had been in a cinema with her phone turned off but would be back shortly once she found a taxi. Cristian offered to pick her up to save her money if she let him know where she was. He stood out on the balcony with the cooling sea air blowing over him in case he could see her. She sent no reply but twenty minutes later he saw a taxi pull up, before she stepped out, laughing with the driver. His senses immediately ramped up, emotions of protection and need flooding over him.

Cristian wanted to meet her at the door and know everything she had done today – what she saw and felt – however, he stayed out on the balcony knowing that it would just be too overbearing. He was concerned he would scare her away. He felt at a loss what the best way forward was. He knew what he wanted and wanted it with every fibre of his being but he knew Danika was frightened of the effect on herself and her mother. Would they be responsible for some cataclysmic change in their world? So he sat on the balcony waiting to see if she would come to him instead.

Danika

As the driver pulled away Danika looked up and saw him in the dull light of the streetlights and the inside lights. Her pulse increased and she realised she was pleased to see him there. Turning away, Danika went into the building through the front doors, using the stairs to go up rather than the lift. It had been good to use up some energy today and exercise latent muscles.

Danika was not trying to avoid him but she had been going through all the events and feelings of the last couple of weeks. The one major overwhelming feeling was that she just did not want to be alone anymore. Sitting in a cinema watching a children's movie, actually mostly just absorbing the love and laughter in the dark had made that become a more concise thought, along with the longing for a child or lots of them. She really wanted to be a mother and could almost feel the swelling in her breasts at the thought. It took her the whole movie to really absorb these feelings and decide on a way forward with her needs, Cristian's needs and their future together. Her confused thoughts seemed to have clarity at last. As the credits of the movie and the lights came up she noticed the missed call and Cristian's text message. This definitely was the right decision; she hoped he felt the same. Danika walked out to the balcony and picked a neutral topic.

'How was your day?' she asked while Cristian continued to sit.

'Enlightening, I read my father's journal. I think you might like to read it also. How was your day?' he replied. Danika could tell he was fighting to keep his tone casual but felt through their connection the feeling of his stomach starting to turn.

'Good, enlightening also. Cristian?' At the sound of his name he stood up. 'I think we should get married as soon as possible,' Danika said quickly and then released her breath.

'What changed your mind? Are you sure? Did you drop your protection?'

Danika turned round to go inside again, holding out her hand for him to follow. As they moved inside together, he grasped her hand and warmth and a light hum buzzed through their fingers.

'I realised today I don't want to be alone. I want to be with you forever. I want a family, not just a female line of single women. I don't know that I can say this is love that we feel between us but it is the best feeling I have ever had. I needed the distance today to understand that.' Danika watched him, taking in the fine blonde stubble that had grown since yesterday and his grey eyes that now looked like clouds and dark pupils intensely watching her she reached up to touch his face and feel his rough cheek.

'I was reading Dad's journal and all I could think of was that I wanted to share my life with you as he did with my mother but I was prepared to give you as much time as you needed because I was so worried I would scare you off with my uncontrolled rapture. I was ready to put distance between us rather than lose you. You truly are very beautiful you know, not just on the outside. I can feel your true kind soul. Are you really sure you want to marry and quickly?'

'I don't know how quickly we can marry, I don't know how it works but I just have this deep feeling that we need to before the next full moon in three weeks' time. I am not talking about the rapture; this is a deep spiritual knowledge. Also we need to do it without family because I am also certain they would stop it. Do you trust me?' Danika took her hand from Cristian's cheek and grasped his other hand.

'Last time you said those words you were hypnotising me.' Cristian smiled broadly at her, his trust obvious. 'Well I happen to know the rules in Australia are that it will take about thirty days to get approval except in special circumstances. Or we can marry overseas if you have a passport. In New Zealand it is only a three day wait. I think I can get something arranged here through my lawyer in that time. Do you trust me?' Cristian gently squeezed her hands.

'I trust you completely. I think my passport has expired but you give me access to whoever we need to talk to and I can help the process so to speak. Can we sit down? I want to explain today.' Danika gently pulled on his hands to move over to the couch. She sat on his lap with his arm around her, their bodies together casting warmth now. 'I was in the cinema and there were so many families enjoying the movie, chatting and laughing. I was absorbing it all and sending happiness to any of them that were a bit upset and the joy in the room was breathtaking. I realised that I had never had that and never would if I didn't break the cycle, no matter what the cost was. The myth of our family line is that the woman can never love a man and marry or we will lose our craft. Well I don't believe that but even if it is true I can live with that. There is only my mother now so I would have to live with that consequence.'

'I am going to call my lawyer James shortly but I found out today that my father wanted an end to the legacy because they desperately wanted a daughter. Our prophecy is around marrying right or the legacy could end. I don't know why they think it is so important. They are wealthy despite it and every year it is harder to conceal it. I don't know if our actions would affect the extended family or just us. I could certainly be happy if I never change again.' Cristian had been winding Danika's long hair around his fingers and watching it slip through as he spoke. 'Do you think it would be safe for us to kiss?' His fingers moved to her neck and under her chin.

'Only one way to find out.' Danika looked deep into his eyes and could see the gold flecks now in the grey. She put her hand around his neck and felt the hairs at the back of his neck standing up. Danika tilted her head slightly, her eyelids lowering. Cristian slowly lowered his face until his lips gently touched hers, the tingle immediate between them. He moved back slightly but she followed him to press a little firmer on his lips then pulled away.

'Okay that was nice in a fizzy kind of way, is it usually like that for you?' Danika was staring at his lips.

'No, never, not that there have been many kisses to compare it to. Shall we try that again?' he asked with a wry grin.

'Yes, but only kissing okay?' Danika was concerned they might both lose control. Her concern was warranted. The next kiss was firmer and then his arms tightened around her as she gripped his neck to pull his mouth down harder to her. The kiss became deeper and more urgent until he pulled away and pushed her slightly away. Danika went to move on his lap slightly to see him better and he shook his head.

'Don't move okay.' Danika wasn't sure if this was some sort of werewolf thing before she realised how aroused he was and stayed very still.

'Are you alright?' She was very concerned that neither of them could control the next action.

'I'm far from alright but I am determined that we shall marry first. Next time maybe not a lap dance.' He leant down and kissed the top of her head and then lifted her completely off his lap and placed her on a chair and strode out of the room to his own bedroom.

Danika was feeling pretty aroused also and hugged herself, rocking slightly while blowing out a sigh. She could hear his shower going.

I need to direct this somewhere else, she thought and decided to make a meal. She was chopping vegetables when Cristian returned to the room, his hair dripping sometime later. He watched her intensely as she quickly and precisely prepared the dinner.

Placing the meals on the table feeling a bit flushed she said, 'Bon appetite.'

'This looks and smells awesome. Are you feeling okay though?' he asked taking a first mouthful. The chilli almost overpowered the taste. 'Hmm spicy.' He sipped his water.

Danika took a mouthful. 'Yep just how I like it.'

After a while Danika could feel her flush subsiding.

'Better?' he asked, and Danika nodded.

'This has been one hell of a day, don't you think?'

'Sure has been. So if you have the papers we need and you are still serious about marriage, we are on for next week. I had a reply from my lawyer James.' Cristian showed Danika the message. Reading the details from his lawyer, Danika visualised it against their calendar of commitments.

She met his grey gaze to show she was determined. 'What do I need? And where would we go to do it? That would be the day of the planetary alignment. Could we still get to the coast before nightfall?' Danika asked.

'It is a long drive but we could be there before dark. Would you be happy for me to book something?' he asked.

Danika surprised him with a hug. 'Thank you.' She kissed him on the cheek quickly and then added, 'I'm just going down to Rainbow to get those papers. I can take her, can't I? Well, I'm going to anyway.'

In the van Danika found the papers she needed and, in an old, battered suitcase, a few special items for the days ahead. Tidying the van for the trip her excitement was building and she wondered how they would get through the next five days.

Danika took her suitcase into the bedroom and sensed Cristian in his study.

'I was thinking about selling off a lot of the artefacts. I have pictures if they are not too distressing to view,' Cristian said as she entered.

'We could look for new items over the weekend. I think it would be good to get a new perspective,' Danika agreed, handing him her papers as she came around the desk to look over his shoulder at the screen. She sucked in a deep breath at the sight of the artefact on the screen.

'That one definitely to go then. Are you going to be okay doing this?' Cristian asked as he reacted to her tension at the bad energy of the piece on screen.

'Definitely, I want to see them gone so I can enjoy the gallery space with you. Okay, so if I put my hand on your shoulder and just squeeze when it has to go then I can focus on protecting myself.' Danika was determined to help however she could to get rid of those horrid items.

'Sure but let me know when you have had enough.'

At almost midnight Cristian called a halt to the culling. They had sorted over a hundred items to be culled with a few to be kept.

Danika protested against stopping, saying she could continue but they both knew her strength was drained.

Pleased to be able to help Cristian sort out some of his artefacts, it still took a toll. The pieces she identified as needing to go were quite evil and full of hate. Her barriers had started to slip when Cristian called a halt which she was relieved for despite wanting to continue.

A feeling of lightness overcame her, and she wondered if she had fainted before she realised he was carrying her. She laid her head against his chest and closed her eyes. The breeze tickled her face, cool and full of the smells of the sea and the city. He had taken her out to the balcony. It was just what she needed. Music and laughter sounded in the distance and she drew what she could from that as the stars were well shrouded in cloud. Cristian brought her a tea and a candle in a glass to stop it blowing out, placing them both on a little table next to her. His thoughtfulness filled her with happiness and she reached for his hand to draw in more.

'Thank you, this was just what I needed.' Danika released his hand and waved her own over the flame before sipping her tea.

'That is definitely enough for tonight, it is nearly midnight,' Cristian stated firmly. 'I noticed a few items didn't go on the cull list yet they looked similar. Can you explain them?'

'Most of what we culled was about power or hatred. Some were used to murder.' Danika shivered at the thought. 'But some were used in ceremonies for marriage and birth, never being used for evil at any time. I think I will go to bed now, I feel a little tired.'

Cristian offered to carry her again. Danika smiled and said she thought she could manage. She knew he watched her carefully until she was in her room. Once there, Danika realised how exhausted she was and could barely stand. She pushed the suitcase to the side and crawled under the quilt without undressing. Her last thought before drifting off was the kindness of Cristian and how he cared for her and how much she loved that feeling.

Cristian

Cristian marvelled at her humility and kindness. He knew how hard it was for her to see and feel the items he had not known were evil. He'd started to feel the change in her soul before she squeezed his shoulder on each piece, predicting more easily which pieces to cull. He'd been able to scroll past them before they affected her too deeply.

Out on the balcony Cristian had felt not just Danika's touch but the pulse of strength moving between them. Not drained but shared. It was very humbling that she wanted to take that from him, knowing the risk of an uncontrolled connection he tried to keep it just to build her strength again.

Once Danika was in her room he locked the balcony, planning on retiring himself. Yet he could not get passed the thoughts and feelings of Danika as they worked together and the sharing of energy, an unexpected thrill that he could do that. He decided to go back to the cull list and get the items up for sale. He sent emails and messages to his staff to warn them of the items being listed for sale. Before he closed his laptop he noticed there was already some interest in the items he listed. Pleased with his efforts and feeling a little less euphoric he retired to his bed, noting it was not long until dawn.

4

ART

THE SOUND OF a siren broke into Danika's conscience followed by the other sounds of a busy harbour city muted through the windows. Feeling constrained when she went to move she realised she was still fully clothed under the quilt. *At least I kicked off my shoes,* she thought. She had slept very soundly and felt quite refreshed. The clock to her surprise showed mid-morning. She needed to get out of her clothes and into a shower was her first thought even before thinking about Cristian or food or the day ahead. The warm water streaming over her from head to toe was very relaxing and she spent longer than usual enjoying it.

Slowly the thoughts of Cristian last night and their connection while working came to the fore. Their connection had been refining over the days they had been together. The thoughts weren't initially intense but slowly the rapture sensuality crept back in. It was so lovely to be sharing thoughts and feelings with him, the experience giving her an all over tingling. Danika looked at the runes and crystals sitting on the vanity that she had been loading with protection over the last few days and decided to try being around him without them. She wondered if she should remove the hypnotic suggestions from

Cristian, she felt they were slipping after their kissing experience anyway.

Looking at her fairly limited clothing options she gathered a few items to wash then remembered she hadn't dealt with the sheets from the van. She pulled on just a t-shirt and harem pants. Opening the suitcase she had brought up from the van, Danika pulled out a white silk and lace top her mother had bought her and a tie dyed white and emerald-green handkerchief hemmed skirt both of which were very pretty but not practical for her travel in a van. Shaking them out she hung them in the bathroom to steam the creases out later. Soft white embroidered ballet style shoes would complete the look. In a satin pouch were a few jewellery pieces that she liked but rarely wore and a hair comb in black plastic studded with silvery fake gems in the shape of a bird. She could use that tonight to hold some of her hair up. In a little box sat a fine silver and freshwater pearl necklace and earring set she had bought in an op shop when she had started her trip because it had been made with love and she could feel it.

Yes, she thought, *that would be nice on Wednesday, our wedding day.* She felt her face flush at the thought and a little ripple of excitement went through her. Before she could dwell on anything else there was a knock on her door.

'Just a minute,' she called out and threw a cover over the things on the bed before going to the door.

'Are you alright? I could hear you moving around and I thought I felt a bit of a tingle, this is all a bit new to me,' Cristian asked, trying to look past her as she pulled the door to.

'Yes fine, just sorting a few bits and pieces out. Gee, it is later than I thought. When are we going out later?' Danika replied as she moved towards the laundry to sort out the sheets into the dryer.

'We have to leave about 4.30 pm so everyone can be seated by 5 pm for some formalities before the dinner,' Cristian answered as he looked at her wet hair. 'What has changed Danika? I feel you, did you do some new spell?' Cristian put his hand on her arm and rose his eyebrows. Danika could feel his excitement.

'Actually the opposite, I decided to not continue the protection. I only have my medallion on and I was thinking about removing the hypnotic suggestion. We are managing our time together well at the moment anyway.' She looked at the hand on her arm and placed her hand over the top of his. 'I think that is why you can feel the connection more. Do you think we can cope over the next five days?'

'If we take it slowly and perhaps keep busy like you suggested it should fly past. I might go sort out some brunch and leave you to whatever it is you are doing.' He nodded towards her room.

'Thanks. I'll be there shortly.' Danika was a bit in awe that they were agreeing so much and wondered if it would last after the wedding.

Sheets in the dryer, more clothes in the washer and the special items put out of sight, Danika moved towards the delicious aromas coming from the kitchen. Laid out on the table were fruits and sliced avocados. As Cristian opened the oven she saw a stack of pancakes and one of bacon and eggs. Danika moved the plunger coffee on the side over to the table with cups and sugar.

'This all looks wonderful and enough for a huge family.' Danika sat down as Cristian had indicated.

'I like to cook to relax but small is not my style. It is nice to cook for someone. Back home we have a cook, Ann, who is lovely but we rarely get to do anything in her kitchen.' Cristian sat down to dish up a plateful for himself.

'Do you have many staff at your home and do they know about your legacy?' Danika asked between mouthfuls and groans of enjoyment.

'We have three permanent employees which is less than we used to have before Dad died. They are from one family. Ann is the cook and Mother's helper; Ben the housekeeper, butler and general all-rounder; Mark the grounds and herdsman. Plus a couple of casual staff when needed by the others. We trust them,' Cristian explained before stopping to pour coffees. 'Nothing has ever been said but they know we are a bit strange and we pay very well so they don't ask questions. They have been with us as a continuing family staff since Grandfather came here in the fifties.'

'I sent copies of your identity to my lawyer last night which he has already acknowledged and put into action. Also the culling list we worked on last night I have priced them all and put them up for sale. As of this morning about half were already sold. My gallery staff are certainly working for their money this week.' Cristian sat back from eating. 'I think they are all glad to see the back of the pieces I am selling. Strange that they never mentioned it before you visited. They can't wait to set up some new displays.'

Danika leaned back also letting the food settle. 'It is surprising what people will put up with until they are given a better option. I'm glad I could help everyone be happier. On that note, are you ready to be free of my protections?'

'Yes I trust you and hope you trust me.' Cristian looked straight at her. Danika stood up and held out her hand. They moved together to his blood stone.

Danika asked for the runes he had around his neck and in his pockets and sensed he felt the hum as soon as they were removed. She held up her medallion which he looked at but didn't touch it this time. 'Do you trust me?'

Cristian

Cristian looked down to see he had both hands on the bloodstone and Danika standing out on the balcony. *How did she get out there so quickly?* he wondered before realising she must have hypnotised him again and he had no memory of it. He felt very different. Not a calm hum and easy thoughts. He felt like he did after a big run, hyped up and muscles burning. He really wanted to get out and run, wanted to go and grab her and kiss her until she was out of breath. He could feel the arousal and nothing to dampen it down. But he stood his ground with his hands on the stone and made his breathing calm down himself with no help from other means. Removing his hands he felt the full force of the rapture until he could lower his breathing again. He remembered the entry in his father's journal. But he did not want to send Danika away or go himself. They would just have to deal with it.

Cristian opened the sliding door and looked out without going out. 'How are you feeling?'

'I'm fine, how are you is more to the point?' Danika replied.

'Tonight we will be putting it to the test. We can leave anytime if we need to though. I have a reputation of being aloof and strange on my side.' Cristian grinned to ease the tension. 'I'm going to spend a couple of hours checking out the sales reports before getting ready. Is there anything you want to do?' He was trying to sound more under control than he felt.

'Actually there is, if you seriously want to do some searching for gallery items this weekend I might scope out some places to check out,' Danika explained, holding up her phone.

'Okay I'll check how you are going at about 4 pm. I'll just be in my study.' Cristian smiled but felt anything but at ease as he left the room for his study, closing the door and leaning against it. All he could think of was covering every inch of Danika with kisses. *Okay, well now I know what the protection was holding back.* The small amount of separation was helping. He opened his laptop to start work.

Danika

Danika was very impressed at how well Cristian hid the effect of the protection being removed. He really was determined to keep himself under control. She was not so sure she could despite her confident sounding 'I'm fine' comment. She could just keep picturing ripping his shirt open and more. Shaking her head she went back out to the balcony to sit with her phone and search for various types of second-hand dealers including charity shops.

It will be interesting to take Cristian around those charity shops tomorrow, she thought then remembered only a few dealers will be open Sunday and even less on ANZAC day afternoon, if any at all.

Luckily Danika had put an alarm on her phone because she had become more engrossed searching for possible sites to purchase items than she realised until the alarm sounded. She was giving herself an hour to get ready but doubted she needed that long. Leaving the list of places to visit over the weekend on the kitchen counter she grabbed her now dry clothes and retreated to her room, locking the door.

Danika pampered herself with moisturiser and changed into her new dress, tying the crossover ribbons tight across her back. She rarely put her hair up but decided to braid each side at the temple towards the back of her head and used the encrusted hair comb to hold it in place. This style showed off her ears and the length of her neck so her jewellery should show well. Looking at her meagre supply of makeup that she rarely wore she applied a light touch and purple eye shadow before she decided less was more and stopped before overdoing it. Her naturally dark lips only needed a little shine. She enjoyed putting the jewellery and shoes on that the lovely ladies found for her remembering and feeling the joy of that day. Grabbing the wrap and her little black bag for her phone she walked to the lounge just as Cristian was coming from his bedroom in his black tuxedo, white shirt and dark purple straight tie holding a dark purple kerchief.

They both stood still staring at one another across the room for a few seconds until Cristian moved towards Danika and said, 'You are stunning.'

'Thank you, you scrub up well yourself.' As she looked at him, his tuxedo hugging every part of him, and then down to his very shiny leather dress shoes she held out her hand and he passed her the kerchief which she carefully folded before gently pushing it into his jacket pocket. 'This is a lucky guess for colour coordination.'

Danika knew he could feel the warmth of her fingers even through the fabric. She turned around and heard him suck in his breath at the sight of her bare back to her waist. Danika took the wrap that was draped over her arm and pulled it around her back.

'You might have to wear that all night if I am going to stay at this function,' Cristian said with a wry grin. She held out the Triquetra broach so he could pin it to her wrap. His fingers barely touched her skin as he made sure he did not prick her with the pin. 'I like your hair like that, I can see more of your neck.' He gave her skin the slightest of brushes as he moved his hands away and cleared his throat. 'We had better go before we don't go at all.'

In the confines of the lift the fragrance of her perfume was evident. 'That is a most unusual perfume,' Cristian commented.

'It is essential oil with a mixture of rosemary, thyme, sage and oregano plus a little jasmine so I don't smell like an Italian restaurant. It is to protect me from any malicious or evil feelings in the gallery,' Danika explained. 'It's not too much is it?'

'Oh no, you smell delicious,' Cristian confirmed. Thankful it was a short ride to the basement Danika was grateful he helped her into the Austin Martin making sure none of her dress would be caught in the door before closing it.

They were directed to a reserved parking space when they arrived, the front lined with onlookers and photographers trying to get exclusive pictures. Danika hadn't expected that. She was beginning to get more than a little nervous.

'Are you alright?' Cristian asked, meeting her gaze.

'I had no idea this was such a big event. I feel a little out of my depth and under dressed.' Danika was clutching her bag in her lap.

'Believe me, you look stunning. The journo's just try to grab any photo opportunity of the wealthy end of town. They don't know who I am so I usually slip past them. We can go in through the service entrance from here, no photographers at all.' Cristian grabbed her hand from her lap. The hum of their connection was immediate. He lifted her hand to his lips and gently kissed it, then placed it back in her lap all the while staring into the depths of her eyes.

'Thank you for bringing me back down from fear to intense arousal,' Danika said with a smile. 'Definitely need to get out before this goes any further.'

Taking the lift to the reception area closed to the public now they waited to be directed. As they were entering what looked like another exhibition room Cristian handed the doorman a card.

The doorman announced, 'Mr Cristian Blakesley and Miss Danika Carling.' She felt like all eyes were on her. They accepted a glass of champagne each although neither drank from them. Cristian steered her towards a quieter space. Danika was getting her bearings to hopefully breathe properly again and began to sidle towards a small painting on the wall. Danika saw and felt his question for her change of position.

'This one is happy. So I can absorb some of it. I can't get any good feelings from these other people yet,' Danika said nervously.

Cristian caught the eye of a lady in a cacophony of colours and layers and nodded to her. She made her way through the now milling crowd of dozens of people.

'Hello Juliet, may I introduce you to my new consultant Danika Carling? Danika this is Juliet Meyers, one of my best customers.' The women each held out a hand and Danika felt the strength in Juliet's enthusiastic handshake.

'Pleased to meet you Danika, we don't see Cristian at these functions very often. Consultant hey, so are you responsible for

Cristian selling off half his collection?' Before Danika could think of a reply, Juliet had turned to Cristian. 'So, what are you up to my boy, making room for some new collection? I'd like first viewing of course.' She smiled broadly and with a knowing wink was off again to talk to someone else.

'So, I'm a consultant now?' Danika watched the retreating figure of Juliet winding her way through the crowd chatting.

'Well, that is what Juliet will be telling everyone. Saves us having to meet them all and explain. She is better than social media for spreading the word.'

'Will we have to go to these events often?' Danika asked. She felt Cristian's excitement rise at her question before he calmed it down.

'Not if I can help it. Oh, I can see we are being ushered in to our seats,' he replied then joined the line to be allocated their table.

As the night progressed Danika began to relax and was able to absorb some of the laughter and good will in the room, even directing a little towards another nervous person she felt at the next table. Being able to share the good vibes helped to make her feel more at ease. A few speeches were made and thanks given to the patrons, Cristian had acknowledged with a nod when his name was called. The formalities now over, the guests were invited to view the new exhibition before it was due to be opened.

'Did you want to look around Danika?' Cristian asked as he held her hand. She shook her head slightly in reply. Cristian very deftly said his goodbyes, moving them towards the doors to leave. Danika stood at his side smiling as he shook many hands. Juliet spotted them on their trek towards escape.

'Cristian just words before you go please.' Juliet placed a hand on his arm but looked at Danika. 'You must give me a clue to the new collection my dear and when I can get a private viewing.'

Danika gently removed Juliet's hand from Cristian's arm to shake it and said, 'You will be the first to know.' Her eyes now a vivid forest green. Juliet took a step back and released Danika's hand.

'Thank you, have a good night,' Juliet said as she moved off towards the others going into the exhibition. Danika felt Cristian's eyes on her as she whispered a chant. They proceeded uninterrupted to the lift.

'I don't know what you did then but I don't think I have ever seen Juliet lost for words.'

'I just made a suggestion that she would be much happier with the others. Also I thought I would clear a path for us to leave.' Danika smiled at Cristian.

Once in the car Cristian turned to Danika. 'I hope that wasn't too difficult for you. I'm sorry, I forgot about the photographers, I usually ignore them. We don't have to do this again if you don't want to.'

'Actually after the initial shock and trepidation I began to enjoy it a little. There were so many interesting vibes going on. Juliet is rather lovely in a flamboyant way. I could see you needed to network and you managed it vicariously through her. That was very clever of you.'

'Well selling off so much of the collection was bound to get tongues wagging. I don't like attention for obvious reasons. Now let's go home I need to get this monkey suit off,' Cristian exclaimed, starting the car.

Once they were back at the apartment Cristian asked, 'Would you like to select a drink while I get into something less formal?'

'Sure. I might do the same first.' Danika went to her room to change before realising she couldn't reach the knot that had tightened on the straps across her back. She went back out to the lounge to wait for Cristian who was walking out as he was pulling on a t-shirt, his track pants around his hips showing a fine track of blonde hairs. He looked at her questionably.

'I um, can't seem to get my dress undone.' Danika turned her back to him showing her bare back but for the two ribbons crisscrossing.

Cristian

Cristian took a deep breath trying to steady his hands. He was trying not to damage the dress as he carefully prised the tight double knot apart. His fingers moved up and down her smooth skin, torturous for them both. He pulled the ribbons apart and the fabric slipped off her shoulders slightly. Danika turned back to face him and leaned against him, wrapping her arms around his neck to kiss him.

Cristian automatically put his arms around her, sliding his hands across her bare back and under the fabric of her dress. He could feel her breasts pressing against his torso and was immediately aroused. As the kiss deepened, he moved one arm from her back up to her neck under her hair. The other hand he slid further under the dress around to her midriff. A shock zapped at his fingertips that reverberated through his whole body and he startled away abruptly.

Danika still had a dreamy look on her face, her lips pouting and rosy when he pulled away.

'What the hell was that?' Cristian asked. 'Was that your medallion I touched?'

'No, it is here at the front under my dress. I… Oh no, I wonder.' Danika touched her side. 'Here?' she asked looking at him. He nodded back at her.

'Why, what is there?' he asked, wondering if they would ever be able to get together physically.

'My tattoo of the Triquetra, I didn't realise it had any power. I bet my mother had something to do with that. She was with me when I got it.' Danika shook her head. 'I'm so sorry I had no idea. I am getting a bit fed up with all these barriers. It's only a little tattoo,' Danika said, as if trying to cajole Cristian to try again.

'I think that, as much as I really want to romance and seduce you till you beg for more, I can wait till we are married and we can explore all the possibilities then.' Cristian turned towards the cupboard to get a drink. 'I really do need one of these now.' He held up the bottle in offer to Danika who nodded but left the room to change.

Cristian made himself a drink and left a drink on the bench for

Danika before retreating to the balcony. Danika joined him a few minutes later, holding the drink and dressed in her regular attire, taking a seat in the other chair.

'Did you mean what you said tonight, about me being your consultant or was that just for show?' Danika asked then took a sip of the scotch.

This was not the question he was expecting but he preferred that line of thought. 'I was trying to think of the best way to introduce you and really it seemed the most logical. I really do value your input with the collection and the change of direction I would like it to go.' He glanced over at her silhouette in the dark. 'Is it a problem?'

'Not at all, I am flattered and excited. It feels like a real job but still using my craft. I have to ask though,' she looked directly at him, 'what is the pay like?'

Cristian laughed and nodded at her question. 'Well actually I was thinking more along the line of a partnership which means you get half the profits after salaries.'

Danika seemed to choke at his answer, surprise evident through her raised brows. 'Oh my heavens and stars, are you serious? Everyone will think I'm a gold digger or something. Maybe just a regular wage to begin with would be better.'

'It is nobody's business but ours what we do.'

Danika yawned. 'I think that scotch has gone to my head. I'm going to turn in and set an alarm to get going early tomorrow. Lots of shopping to do!' she reminded him. She stood and leaned over to give him a quick kiss as he looked up at her. 'I really did enjoy tonight and I know we will tomorrow.'

Cristian was surprised at how easy that brief intimacy had his heart racing yet again but he was determined not to race after her. He sat quietly sipping his drink and thinking about the night at the event. He had alternated between being thrilled that Danika was admired by everyone in the room and wanting to rip out the hearts of the men who appeared, to him at least, to be leering at her. She is beautiful and tonight she seemed to glow when she was absorbing the 'good vibes' as she put it and then passing them back where needed. He had not seen her craft before other than the intense protection spells and it left him even more in awe of her. He could see now what she meant by her power being a perceived threat and needing to be hidden.

Danika

Danika was trying not to get overly excited but the combination of trying something new and being with Cristian was making that difficult. She decided to take her herbal tea out to the balcony to view the harbour. The cool morning air was just what she needed. Last night she had considered getting another scotch to really help her sleep after Cristian's bold statement that they were going to be partner's. She had laid awake thinking on what that might mean for far too long. Could she really be an art consultant for a living or was he just being kind?

I guess we shall find out today and I shall find out if I like it, Danika thought. She could sense that Cristian was up and moving about so, after taking a few deep breaths, she went back inside to sort out a plan for the day.

'Good morning, how did you sleep?' Cristian asked as he poured a cup of the coffee Danika had ready for him. 'I could sense you were still awake when I was in the study.'

'Despite being tired I was a bit keyed up from the event and a new venture. That partnership bombshell was a bit much to take in. I had to get up and meditate in the end and all was good after that. I've already been down and given Rainbow a quick warm up she can be a bit sluggish in a cold morning especially if she hasn't been driven every day. I packed a bit of fruit and some water in the van if we get peckish.'

'We're taking Rainbow?' Cristian asked, raising a brow.

'She has more space, and you need to get used to driving her compared to that fancy Martin of yours!'

Cristian laughed.

'Don't laugh at me, I'm new at this.'

'I am not laughing at you; I am enjoying your enthusiasm. You know the sale doesn't start until 9 am and should only take a little while to get there?' Cristian was grinning as he spoke.

'I know what the advertising said but I just have this feeling we need to be there at 8.15, I can't explain why. Can we do that? We can cruise past and even park a little away. I'm sure we can kill a bit of time if I'm wrong.' Danika was hoping he understood.

'I am not going to question your information sources and I believe in you completely. We are up anyway. I can also call Paul, one of the curators, to bring a van if there are any large pieces needing to be collected later today. Maybe you should eat something to steady your nerves. My father took me on my first buying venture when I was twenty-one. I remember how enthusiastic I was and my father trying to explain how not to show that enthusiasm or I would end up paying more. Just a hint for today.'

'Believe me, I will be quite under control when I get there that is why I am releasing the energy now. Do you have an umbrella? We are going to need it this afternoon. I have one but it is very colourful, you might like something more subdued,' Danika asked.

'Are you weather forecasting now or more premonitions?'

'The *forecast* was for possible showers in the mountains this afternoon so I am just being prepared. I have my poncho packed and my umbrella is already in the van.' Danika checked her pockets to make sure she had the right crystals then decided she wanted to change her tote bag.

Cristian

Cristian watched in amusement at her preparations but took her advice and went looking for his umbrella. He had to admit to himself that her enthusiasm was rubbing off on him. It had been a long time since he had done this kind of ad hoc searching for gallery items. Not really since his father died. He had switched to prearranged scheduled buying trips or online purchases after a period of very little buying at all. He noticed the list of places to visit on his desk, and briefly looking at it, slipped it into his pocket. The first address of the deceased estate was vaguely familiar but he couldn't quite remember why.

Jacket and umbrella in hand he went back to the lounge just in time to see Danika putting away the uneaten foods and bouncing as she went. *Yep she is bouncing,* he thought and a wave of emotion washed over him. Happiness mostly but definitely a deeper sense of joy and love pouring out of her which almost took him off guard.

'I have some cash here for you to put in your purse.' He thought he had best say something rather than stare at her.

'You don't need to give me money I have my own,' Danika answered, he sensed with pride.

'This is not for you as such. This is business money for sales today in case they only want cash.' Cristian held out several hundred dollars for her.

'Oh of course, I am definitely an amateur at this. I usually shop in op shops and garage sales using coins.' Danika took out her battered purse to try to stuff all the notes in it. 'I don't think I have ever carried this much money.' She put the bulging purse back in her tote bag.

'What is your registration number for the tolls?' Cristian asked, creating a new account on his phone so they would be paid automatically. He plugged in the registration she recited. 'Okay, that's all done and the account backdated to cover your fees over the last couple of weeks.'

'I'm very green to these city customs. We don't have tolls in South Australia, yet anyway. Thank you.'

'I'm going down to Rainbow and check the seat is okay,' she said as she picked up the keys and her tote bag. Cristian noticed some of her enthusiasm was wanning but saw no reason as to why.

'We can go now anyway, you never know how busy it will be on a Saturday morning to Manly.' Cristian had a niggling memory float past as he said the destination.

It took a little while to get settled in the van with his long legs and warming up the engine again. He could see that Danika had decluttered everywhere and cleaned through the van. She explained that the light on the dash was not a warning it was a faulty light. Cristian made a mental note to book the van in for a thorough service as soon as possible. Once on the road he was getting used to the change in vision in the mirrors compared to Martin.

Good grief, he even mentally called his car Martin, he thought.

Pulling up just on 8.15, Cristian recognised the house immediately as his mind raced back to a family visit here what must have been when he was about twenty years of age and just thinking about art collecting. The people were old friends of his mother's family. Sadness filled him at the realisation that they must have passed away. As they were getting out of the van an older lady was being assisted down the front steps to a waiting car. She looked up to see Cristian and waved her hand and stopped walking.

'Master Cristian Blakesley is that you?' she asked with fondness in her expression.

'Yes, Mrs Walton. How are you?' Cristian came closer to see she had aged considerably from the vibrant woman of that visit so long ago.

'I was sorry to hear about your father Cristian and that I couldn't get to the funeral. I was caring for my James by then. He has passed now. Are you here for the sale? You should go in now and see if there is anything you would like.' Mrs Walton turned to her carer and said, 'Go tell them Cristian can have first viewing and choice please dear. I'm alright here while you do.' She held her hand out for Cristian to support her. 'Who is this delightful girl, Cristian?'

'Mrs Walton, this is Danika, my new consultant.' Cristian turned to Danika to see a tear forming in her eyes.

Danika held out her hand to Mrs Walton and as they touched she was pulled into an embrace. Danika whispered in her ear and then Mrs Walton touched her face and said, 'Congratulations on your new life with Cristian, he is a wonderful, caring boy. I'm sorry but I have to go now it is too painful to stay. I am so pleased you are both here and can take some of my memories with you.' She patted Danika's hand and then took the arm of the carer who had returned to help her into the car.

As the car left a man ushered them into the house and closed the door saying, 'This is a bit unexpected, there had been no arrangement for a previewing. Our client's wishes are utmost though.'

Cristian looked at Danika who now had many tears and asked, 'Do you still want to do this?' As she nodded he added, 'Okay so just nod your head or say yes and we will take it alright?' Danika nodded her head.

They walked slowly through each of the many rooms that were stuffed full of antiques and art. Danika touched some pieces while others she stood in front of and let the tears roll. The agent was walking behind them putting sold stickers on the pieces they chose. Up in one of the bedrooms Danika first went over to the window and looked out to the coast.

'She liked to stand here and watch the boats. Especially when she couldn't leave the house anymore. There is more in the attic that has not been sorted yet. I think we should arrange to come back, but I need to leave now.' Cristian could see that her face was pale and that she no longer wanted to be there so let her walk past him while he spoke to the agent.

Once they were safely tucked back into Rainbow and out of ear shot of any others, he asked if she was alright. Danika nodded so he pulled out of the space, moved to another quieter road and pulled up.

'Okay, are you able to tell me what happened now?' Cristian knew a lot had gone on over the last forty-five minutes they were there that she couldn't say at the time.

'Did you feel anything in there, Cristian? I was so overwhelmed at first by the grief but it fell away to reveal the love and happiness. Mrs Walton is a marvellous woman with a secret that was eating her away. I felt her secret in the last bedroom. She believes she doesn't deserve to live. She is so wrong but grief can make you blind sometimes.' She was crying again.

'Yes, I felt the happiness. I remember being there when my father and her husband were alive. The ladies drank cocktails and the men told jokes out the back around a barbeque that they burnt. Everyone laughed and Mrs Walton brought out the alternative dinner already prepared. They talked about their travels and purchases and steered me to the best places for bargains. Later they danced to old songs played on vinyl. It was the only time I went there, unfortunately being young and preoccupied I didn't value those experiences enough until they were gone. What was her secret?' Cristian enjoyed reliving that memory more than he realised. It had been a time when everything felt normal.

'She let her husband die,' Danika said it between tears.

Cristian was shocked. 'What do you mean?'

'He was sick. I don't know what with, but he wanted to die. He asked her to do it. She didn't but agreed to stop all his medication that was keeping him alive. It was horrific for her but she loved him so much she couldn't go against his wishes. But she blames herself. I told her he was happy and waiting for her when the time was right.' Danika sighed deeply.

'You knew she was going to be leaving this morning, didn't you?' Cristian was still shocked by her revelation.

'Not as such but it was like the universe was urging me to go there when I saw the ad and then to be there early. I couldn't understand why. I'm glad we did so I could talk to her, it would be nice to meet her again under better circumstances,' Danika said, wiping away the last of her tears.

'I hope the rest of the day is not as gruelling for you. We could just go relax somewhere if you prefer.' Cristian was concerned at the intense effect this meeting had on Danika and he wanted to protect her.

'No, it will be fun I'm sure, but that meeting had to happen for you also I think. How many pieces did we select in the end?' Danika was now back to the task of stocking the gallery.

'About fifty so far, but perhaps more once they catalogue the attic, which they didn't know about until you pointed it out. This is turning out to be one of your tricks.' He smiled at her and grabbed her hand. 'You were amazing in there today. I think the agent was in awe of your choices without looking at them. As was I, you have a great sense for good pieces.'

'I was channelling Mrs Walton and her husband. They were the pieces they wanted us to take.' Danika squeezed his hand and looked directly at him. 'The next place will probably surprise you but I think we might find a bargain.'

It was after lunchtime by the time they had visited a garden nursery closing down, a garage sale and a church charity sale. Despite his reservations, the back of Rainbow was now filled with a variety of unusual pieces that Danika had negotiated down to very profitable prices. They also had a few bags of plants, vegetables, a cake and a dozen eggs. For lunch they found a little bakery before heading to a park down by the Nepean River to eat at the picnic tables. It didn't take long for a few birds to gather waiting for scraps. Danika spoke with them as if they understood and they did seem to wait patiently as she suggested.

Cristian had never experienced such a strange yet fun day.

'How did you know there would be items we would want when you picked the places we went to today?' Cristian was trying to understand her particular talent for finding the right piece for the right price.

'I didn't know what would be there but I projected to the universe the type of things I am looking for. Not specific but just the feel of them and then wait for the answer.' She shrugged her shoulders as if it was so simple. 'How do you pick the pieces for your gallery?'

'Usually research and a few good contacts and then I fall back on gut feeling I guess. Until recently I have been looking for and leaning towards more overseas pieces that had a more mystical history, obviously without realising their malevolent nature.' Cristian also shrugged. 'It is getting on a bit. Where to next? It seems to be getting very dull now.' Cristian looked at the clouds building up.

'Towards Katoomba, there is a little art gallery halfway there. We had best go if we want to catch them before they close.' Danika threw the crumbs to the birds and placed the rubbish in the bin before heading back to the van.

'Katoomba, that is quite a drive. Will Rainbow make it?' Cristian had only been there once a long time ago as a child and had not been keen on the road.

'We shall find out. We don't have to go, there is always another day,' Danika said as if sensing the reservations Cristian had.

'No, all good, let's get going.' Cristian started up Rainbow and plugged in the new GPS destination. It took them straight down the road he didn't ever want to go on again. The road had definitely been upgraded since he was a child and Rainbow was running surprisingly well for the steep and winding road. He concentrated so much with the amount of traffic he didn't notice how long they had travelled until the GPS was telling them they were nearly at their destination. The driveway was a bit overgrown and the fencing was starting to fall down. Yet there was a faded sign for a gallery, he wondered if it was actually open. With the rain now starting they made good use of their respective umbrellas.

There was only one other car there when they pulled in. Through the trees the view was stunning. Danika pointed to a statue hidden in the undergrowth. Cristian took a couple of pictures and sent them back to his curator.

Inside there were several other large pieces by the same artist from decades before and a few smaller pieces that looked less talented and more recent. The whole building seemed extremely run down as if it could just fall off the cliff. He felt sad seeing what would have been a thriving business at some point in this state. Danika put on her winning smile and was complimenting the lady on some of the smaller pieces. Before long, the lady, who introduced herself as Janet, had told her the history of the gallery, explaining how she needed to sell and that a developer wanted it for an astronomical price but she couldn't leave her beloved pieces behind to be bulldozed. So, here she still was. She really did want to move and her children wanted her to move but no one wanted the art pieces.

'How much would you take for all of your wonderful art?' Danika asked. Cristian had received a report back from his curator and could see where Danika was going with her conversation. The question stumped Janet at first but then, likely thinking no one would buy the lot, she gave a price that Cristian decided was reasonable and he could turn a profit to the right crowd. He nodded at Danika.

'We would like to buy it all. We can give you a deposit today and our details so that we can organise collecting it all as soon as possible if that is acceptable.' Danika spoke slowly and smiled gently at the owner's shock. Janet clutched Danika's hand and started to cry.

'Thank you so much. You have saved my life today, are you some kind of angel? I can't wait to call my children and let them know.' Danika gave her a hug and then they exchanged details and Danika paid a substantial deposit with the gallery credit card. Janet insisted they take whatever they wanted right now, with the van free to come later to collect the pieces. Danika picked up an angel and Cristian selected a dog, both from her earlier, more stylised, work.

The trip down the mountain and back to the apartment was long and slow in the rain and dusk. Cristian was focused on the road and Danika didn't distract him with talking. They were both glad to pull into the underground park well after dark. Collecting the perishable goods only they locked up and made their way up in the lift, too tired to even strike up a conversation.

Danika collapsed on the couch, kicking off her shoes. Cristian dropped the keys on the table and made his way to his bedroom.

Danika

Leaning her head back with her eyes closed, she dozed until she felt Cristian kissing her forehead. Her eyes shot open as he stood up and told her he had ordered food to be delivered. Danika realised that they had hardly eaten all day. Cristian had changed into a loose top and track pants with bare feet.

'I don't know if we are going to be able to fit anything else in the gallery if we go to that clearance sale tomorrow,' Cristian commented as he took a seat across from her.

'I think you could be right. We still have to empty Rainbow tomorrow and organise when the rest can be collected in between getting married and then going off on my quest. It is going to be hectic at the very least.' Danika blew out an exaggerated sigh while smiling at him. 'I had a great time today, even if I am completely exhausted and ridiculously hungry.'

'I actually have another storehouse that I might send Janet's work to, especially the outside pieces which I think might need some restoration. She used to be very well known thirty years ago. It was a shame to see her distressed today. You did a good thing.' Cristian was glad Danika's universal answer had guided them there.

'Is it usually this hectic? When you're buying and selling?' Danika wasn't sure she could keep up the pace.

'Good heavens no, this you have brought on yourself.' He reached his foot over to tap on hers. 'I usually do all the buying and the staff do the selling. So if I don't go on a buying trip they only have what they prepare and sort for display to sell.'

The access bell rang and Cristian buzzed the delivery person up. The delicious aromas coming from two bags filled the room as he placed out several boxes of food.

'I wasn't certain of your tastes so I have probably over ordered. We have Korean and Indian. And mango lassi.' He held up the drinks.

'Wonderful.' Danika deeply breathed in the aromas.

'I'd like to take the things we have in Rainbow to the gallery tomorrow if we can. I can check how the vibe is going there as well,' Danika suggested.

'Of course, I'll drive Martin and you follow in case I need to stay there and sort out pickups and so on, just in case you may not want to hang around,' Cristian suggested.

Danika tried to stretch out a few knots in her neck and back from the long day.

'Would you like to run a bath? It might help soothe out the kinks. Lots of bath stuff Mother bought for show, should be used.'

'You read my mind. I haven't had the opportunity for a nice soaking bath since I left Adelaide months ago. Long showers can be great but not the same,' Danika said wistfully. 'Thank you.'

Danika walked through Cristian's bedroom to his bathroom which she had only glanced at a few days ago. The bath was a huge corner spa. Pouring a few bath crystals in and a little bath gel ran the water, checking the temperature with her hand. A vanilla and sandalwood fragrance filled the room. Walking back to her room to gather some personal items she passed the study where Cristian was now on the phone and looking at his laptop. Gathering up a change of clothes, toiletries and hair ties it all felt quite natural until she walked back to his bathroom and started to lock the door.

Why was she locking the door? He knew she was in there, she completely trusted he would respect her privacy. Was it a barrier she needed? In a few days' time they would be married. No barriers then, they would be here in his rooms together.

Undressed and with her long locks pulled into two messy buns that reminded her comically of Minnie Mouse, she smiled at her reflection in the mirror. Once settled in the water she turned on the jets which were surprisingly loud. It was amazing and she settled in for a long soak. Closing her eyes, the sounds seemed to melt away.

Her thoughts went back to their impending marriage. Where would they live? Here she guessed, but maybe at his estate. *Oh my heavens and stars, an estate and he is wealthy and now wants to share it with me. It all seemed very strange*, she thought. To have been a single nomadic witch earning just enough to get by last week to now being an art buyer funded by her husband-to-be. There were so many details that had not been considered or discussed, such as when were they going to tell their mothers.

She had thoroughly enjoyed the hunt for items today and helping out two ladies that needed their help was rewarding. But now she really wanted to get back to some of her original plans. She hoped she could still enjoy the Celestial events she had looked forward to and her quest that seemed to be on the back burner. Her thoughts moved on to tomorrow and going back to the gallery to drop off the items in the van. Then what was she going to do? Perhaps she could still go to the farm clearance anyway. After all, the universe had given her a guide to go there. Her nose itched and she took her hand out of the water to brush it and felt something across her face. She opened her eyes and was confronted with a wall of bubbles.

Danika squealed without thought trying to find the off button for the spa and standing up. The door opened with Cristian looking very worried until he saw Danika standing almost hidden in a mountain of bubbles.

'Are you alright?' He was clearly trying not to laugh.

'I didn't know this would happen, I've never used a spa before. Stop laughing it's not funny, how do I get rid of all this? Hand me a towel please,' Danika said with indignation.

Cristian pretended to cover his eyes with one hand as he passed her a large bath towel. Danika tried to wrap it round herself without too many bubbles included and then Cristian held out his hand so she could safely get out of the spa.

'Thank you, you can go now so I can get dressed and deal with this lot,' Danika said waving a hand at the bubble mountain.

'It is best to do it before you put dry clothes on. Just pull out the plug and I'll help. I have to say, you are very entertaining,' Cristian said as she bent down to pull out the plug.

'Oh, stop it. Get out you're no help at all.' Danika laughed. She picked up a mass of bubbles and threw it his direction but they drifted slowly, more like a cloud.

'I will go; there is a limit to my gentlemanly control. Call if you need anything.' He left still with a huge smile on his face.

'Are you okay?' Cristian asked from the chair he was sitting on near the window when Danika emerged.

'Good grief, Cristian, you scared me.' Danika jumped at his voice. 'Yes I'm okay. I'm going to get my moisturiser which is cheaper than your fancy one but it helps to bust the bubbles with your hands.' She continued to her room.

Cristian went into his bathroom and could see that the bubbles had reduced but were now spread across the floor also like a mist in a cheap horror movie. He went to the laundry to get a mop and bucket. Danika came out of her room, dressed now with a tub of moisturiser. Between the two of them the bathroom was cleaned up in ten minutes.

'So much for a relaxing bath. What a mess that turned into. I'm so sorry,' Danika apologised as she collected all her clothes and toiletries. 'Are you sure you want to marry such a klutz?'

'In a heartbeat.' Cristian grabbed her shoulders and kissed her hard, nearly causing her to drop all she was holding. 'Now best go to bed before I throw you on mine.'

Danika did a little sprint out of the room then continued walking to her own saying, 'Good night, Cristian.'

Her thoughts drifted to Cristian's warning of throwing her on his bed and straight away she was aroused and having to admonish herself that she wouldn't sleep if she kept on with those thoughts. She just really wanted the wedding day to hurry up but for now she was going to get what sleep she could.

5

JESSICA

D ANIKA WOKE HOLDING her medallion. Looking down at it and then around, her surroundings were a cramped dark area that smelled of the sea. She couldn't stand up. Letting go of the medallion, the view changed to a damp forest. She fell to the ground and looked up to see a hand held out to her, a dark hand. Taking it, she looked into the kind face of a woman with dark skin and curling hair wrapped in animal skins. Danika tried to talk but the vision changed again. The same women, helping her give birth in a stone hut. The vision melded into a view of the women working together cooking a meal, the child crawling. They exchanged items, a stone which looked like a rune and a stick.

Danika felt something heavy and she couldn't breathe. She was hitting a man with the stick. An older woman looked on. The stick flew past her head to stick in a tree and the woman disappeared, along with everything else. Remaining was just a field and a knocking sound that she couldn't tell where it came from.

'Danika, are you awake?' Cristian was knocking on the door.

Danika quietly called back to say she was as she settled out of her dream. The dream felt important but she had no idea why. Dressing slowly, she tried to remember the bits of the dream as she came out to the lounge.

'I've boiled the kettle if you want tea?' Cristian looked at her concentrating face. 'Problems?'

'I had a dream that I was trying to decipher. I think it was my family from a long time ago maybe a hundred years or more. Just flashes and images, I could feel the weight of a man. It was awful. I think she killed him.' Cristian went to her and pulled her into a hug. She leant her head on his chest.

'I knew it wasn't real but I felt I was there with them. I could feel her fear and desperation then her gratitude and love when she gave birth. But then I felt a different woman and the horror and anger of a man trying to rape her, it was horrific.' Danika shivered and Cristian held her tighter. Eventually Danika pulled away slightly and looked up at him. 'I think it might have been Jessica.' Danika stepped back so she didn't harm him and pulled out the medallion. 'I felt it through this. I think it was reminding me I need to find answers but in my soul I know it is not just for me. It is for us.'

'That's a lot to take in. Did you still want to come to the gallery today or do we need to do something else to help you?' Cristian asked.

'This is our quest now, not just mine. I just feel it so deeply. But having said that I'm not planning on rushing off anywhere until we can plan together,' Danika confirmed. 'So I'm thinking carry on as planned at least for the next few days.'

An hour later they were both pulling up to the back of the gallery to unload Rainbow. Paul, one of the curators, was there to meet them. Danika cautiously walked towards the loading dock waiting to see what vibes were coming out. She could still feel a few odd pieces but definitely better than last time. Paul showed her the now catalogued and photographed pieces from the attic that she had 'found' last time. She loved seeing the old photos with the fashions of years past. Noting that none of them smiled unlike today's photos. There were a few little trinket pieces including a tiny Faberge egg that was in the box where

Cristian had found the Triquetra brooch. Paul showed it to Cristian to explain it was the only valuable piece out of the four boxes.

'Actually, Paul, I think it is all valuable you just need to find the right audience,' Danika said smiling. 'Do we know who the people in the photos are? They may have relatives that would be interested,' Danika said, picking up one of the framed photos.

'Not so far. Even the journal doesn't have full names so it's a bit hard to trace.'

Danika turned over the photo. 'Have you looked behind this photo? It may have a clue.' She handed it back to Paul who carefully opened up the back on the bench and separated the back from the front. Between the layers was the dated invoice from the photographic studio with the names and ages of the people in the photo.

Paul looked directly at Danika. 'You are very intuitive, perhaps you should do my job.'

'Thank you. I think I prefer the hunt for items. I'm so glad you do this important part of the business, I would get too distracted. I think I might just walk around the stock and gallery for a little bit, Cristian.'

'Absolutely, let me know if you have any thoughts on any of what is left. It is looking a bit empty at the moment.'

Moving into the front of the building with the main gallery open to the public she noticed that many larger pieces were gone and others rearranged to fill the gaps. The receptionist came over and greeted Danika by name introducing herself, 'Hello Danika, I don't think we were introduced properly the other day. I'm Adrienne, everyone calls me Rene though. I believe you instigated the sell off the other day. Thank you, they were weird feeling pieces. I can't wait to see what comes in this week, are we going to do a proper open of the new collection?'

'I'm glad it is gone also. I think you will like selling the new pieces. Yes, we probably could do an open,' Danika answered a bit distracted. Having seen what she needed, Danika left, going back out through the storeroom to say goodbye.

'I was thinking I will go to that farm clearance after all,' Danika said when she found a break in people needing Cristian. 'If you are going to be awhile we can meet up somewhere or back at the apartment, if that's okay?'

'Of course, as long as you don't mind going alone. Just call if you find anything big. Do you need the company card or more cash? Message me when you want to meet, okay?' Cristian seemed to acknowledge Danika needed a little space today. She nodded and wandered over to her van to go, pausing briefly to look back at Cristian deep in conversation with Paul again.

Danika checked the address of the farm from her notes. It was lucky it was a late auction being a Sunday, she was sure she would be able to get there for a quick viewing before the auction started. The drive away from Sydney felt refreshing and she knew it was time to move on. Rather than continue those thoughts she concentrated on the heavy traffic of weekend travellers all glad to be able to move about freely again no doubt. After an hour she was pulling off the highway to a narrow road that shortly went to gravel and then down the rutted driveway to a farm with many four-wheel drive vehicles lined up ready for the clearance auction. Rainbow certainly made a statement in amongst them.

The crowd was mostly men with only a couple of women. Danika walked past all the farm machinery and the flotsam of farm life set out in piles with a lot number on each ready for the auction. Moving past the sheds, she didn't feel any connection until she got closer to the house where she started to feel the pull. The inside of the house was off limits to the crowd but under the verandah were many piles of personal items, white goods and furniture, even some clothes. It was a little sad to know it would all go today for whatever someone was prepared to pay. Danika could feel the pull getting much stronger as she moved towards trestles set up with kitchenware, ornaments and a few paintings. Still she could not see what was calling to her. Eventually at one table she found a collection that looked like souvenirs including old calendars all bundled as one lot. Lying on the table almost hidden was the stick she had seen in her dream. This was why she needed to be here. The number on the lot meant it would be near the end of the auction so she would just have to wait. The urge to pick it up was very strong but she did not want to draw attention to it.

An agent approached Danika so she could register as a bidder. He gave her a number to use when bidding. As she had never been to an auction before Danika decided to watch it from the beginning to get a feel for it. The auction started a short time later and at first Danika found it hard to keep up with the bids from the farmers. After several lots though, she was definitely getting the hang of it. By the time they were nearing the household lots several of the farmers were no longer bidding and were making plans to take the items they were successful with. The anticipation was building for Danika and she was worried she would not get what she wanted.

When the lot of the clothing was next she could sense no one was interested so she thought she would give it a go. They could be donated back to a charity. Only one other lady seemed interested however Danika easily out bid her. Danika tried not to cheer at her accomplishment.

Finally, a few minutes later, the lot she was waiting for was next. Her stomach had started to churn at the thought of not acquiring it. She had nothing to worry about as no one else was interested at all. She could have bid very little and won it but she knew the money was for someone who needed it so she bid one hundred dollars which really surprised those that were still there. She didn't care that they probably thought her to be a kook but she was just grateful to be able to get it all.

After paying for her purchases she then took her receipts and went back to her van to wait her turn to pick up the items. It was nearly an hour before she was able to drive up to the house and load everything into Rainbow, including the clothes rack which she hadn't realised was included. It was a bit difficult to manoeuvre until she realised it came apart. Purposely she loaded all the souvenirs except the stick into the back before picking it up using a cloth, not daring to touch it directly.

Straight away she could feel the connection. It took all her willpower to put it in the front seat and drive away. Danika found a small pull off further down the road to be able to examine the stick closer. It was obviously an item made by a First Nations artist. About sixty centimetres long with burnt markings all around, along one end was the stylised Triquetra. This made no sense to her. Why would a Western mystic symbol be on an Indigenous artefact? She decided to take the chance to hold it in her bare hand. The pull was there but not as strong as she expected. Still, she was glad she had it.

Now what am I going to do with this lot? she thought as she looked back at her full van. She decided to drive over to the op shop next to the store that she had bought her dress at. Perhaps they had a donation bin or a phone number she could call. The address was still in the memory of her GPS so off she went on another trek, feeling pleased to be on the road doing something positive.

Once Danika pulled up at the little block of shops she realised being a Sunday no one would be around. She got out and checked for any contact details. In the window of the op shop the only number was for business hours only. She was trying to decide what to do next when the lady from the dress shop pulled up behind her.

'Hello, I remember you, how did your dinner go? Was the dress a hit?' she asked.

'Oh, hi. Yes, thank you, it was a great night. Do you know if there is a donation bin I can leave some clothes and things in for the ladies?' Danika replied.

'How much have you got? I could probably put it out the back until Tuesday when they are open again.'

Danika opened the van to show the lady what she had. 'I went to an auction to get one thing but ended up with this lot as a practice,' she said with a wry smile.

'That is quite a lot, hang on I've got one of their phone numbers I'll just check.'

Fifteen minutes later one of the volunteers was there opening the op shop and all three loaded the items all the way to the back so they could be sorted. Many thanks were said all around and Danika was on her way again having gained lots of positive vibes.

As she was heading back to the apartment she saw an old jewellers. Closed now, but she felt the need to pull up outside anyway. She checked the opening hours and their phone number, glancing at the few items they had left in the window displays while closed including a tray with a few silver rings. It occurred to her that on Wednesday they would need rings. They hadn't talked about that or very much about the day at all.

By the time Danika was pulling into the underground car park at the apartment it was late in the afternoon but Cristian's car was not there. With the stick and her bag she made her way up and, as she did, the feel of the force in the stick became stronger. Intrigued, she wondered what it was connecting to. Inside she walked around with the stick like a divining rod, eventually getting to her room and her grandmother's potion box. This just made for more questions in her mind. She put them on the table to discuss with Cristian once he was back.

She was making dinner when she heard Cristian's key in the lock. The sight of him coming through the door lifted her spirits and the tingle of her senses was almost addictive. She smiled broadly at him before informing him tea was in the oven.

'How was the sale?' Cristian asked. Danika sensed his own feeling of exhilaration and could tell it came from feeling the hum of their connection.

'Interesting. Hopefully I am not directed to one again but I bought a rack of clothes, some paintings and souvenirs and that.' Danika pointed over to the table. Cristian moved towards the stick to have a better look. 'I wouldn't pick it up though. There is definitely a family connection, my family that I still have to work out. It seems to be connected to my grandmothers potion box.'

'It looks like a message stick and it looks old. But what is that? Is that Triquetra?' Cristian was as intrigued as Danika was. 'That is very out of place.' After a moment, he turned back to her and said, 'A rack of clothes, did you need them?'

'No. I had never been to an auction before and I watched for nearly an hour and then thought I'd have to give it a go as a practice before I bought what I wanted.' Danika pointed at the message stick. 'So I decided at least if I bought the rack of clothes it could be donated. The lot that the message stick was in included a flotsam of art works, ornaments and other stuff. I have already taken it all to my favourite little op shop today, I didn't think it was any value to the gallery. How did you go today?'

'We have organised that the works from Mrs Walton will be collected on Tuesday morning and brought directly to the gallery. The pieces at Janet Wells' gallery will take longer as most the outside ones will go to a separate storage unit for restoration. The better, earlier pieces that were not outside will come into the gallery stores for sorting and most of the more recent pieces will be sold online. It is likely to take most of the week just to remove them and weeks to sort. We have hired two extra hands for as long as needed and Paul is going to oversee it all until you and I are back. He is more animated than I have seen him in a long time, as are Rene and Tony, the other curator you didn't meet. Your effect on so many people's lives this week is extraordinary.' He moved over to her and pulled her into a soft hug.

When dinner buzzed, they sat down together, a glass of wine poured in front of each of them.

'It has been a bit full on this week. Really I will be pleased to have a break for a couple of days,' Cristian said as they ate.

'Actually I wanted to talk about that.'

Cristian looked up, concern written across his expression.

'I don't have cold feet but we haven't discussed anything. The where, when, how of the marriage ceremony. Where to afterwards? And then after that, do we come back here? Is this where we are going to live? When are we going to tell our mothers? I have lots of questions.' Danika sighed.

'All very valid questions. Some I have answers to, some I don't because it has to be mutual,' Cristian replied.

'My lawyer sent me some details today. He has assured me that all will be okay for us to marry officially on Wednesday in a civil service at their chambers. The time is up to us anytime between 10 am and 2 pm. The ceremony will be performed by a celebrant. He has a generic script that we can add to if we wish, I have a copy for you to view.'

'That sounds very well organised. Do we need witnesses and rings or swear on a bible or something? I have no idea how this works other than a few movies I have watched.' Danika was unsure how she felt about just being a spectator almost to her own wedding.

'There will be plenty of people at the chambers who can be witnesses. Rings were something that I thought about and wondered if you would like to shop for them together on Tuesday?'

'I found a jeweller today I'd like to look at. You know me and the feel of a place. If that's okay with you?' Danika asked cautiously, wondering if Cristian had some large family jewellers he normally went to.

'That sounds fine. I don't know my way around jewellers at all. I usually give pieces of art as gifts. If we go first thing then it would give us the option to look elsewhere if we had to. Would you be happy with an early ceremony because I don't know about you but I think it would be hard to wait until later? Then we can leave on our honeymoon,' Cristian suggested.

'Oh, honeymoon. That's not something I thought I would ever hear. Now I am getting nervous I have to admit. Have you organised that? We are still going to Sussex inlet? I feel a bit useless. Don't most brides do all the organising? Oh my heavens and stars I just said bride.' Danika covered her face with her hands.

'Yes, we are going to Sussex inlet. I have booked accommodation for a few nights there. Are you really okay? You seem like this is overwhelming you. What do you want to do?'

'I don't know, I just want the mystery to be ended I think. The mystery of being married, the mystery of our connection and the mystery of our history. So yes, the sooner we finalise everything the better. Am I making sense?' Danika reached over to hold Cristian's hand.

'Let's just take a few breaths, finish what we want here and then move on to the next mystery over there.' Cristian nodded towards the table with the message stick.

A short time later they were both staring down at the two objects – the message stick and the potion box. Danika picked up the message stick.

'I feel a bit of a pull on my senses when I pick this up. Closer to the potion box and the pull gets stronger. Do you want to test touching me to see if you feel it?' Danika held out her other hand which Cristian took in his. With the connection between them open, Danika felt as Cristian did, feeling the hum of their connection but also more. It felt like a pushing away from her. He held on tighter. Danika moved it towards the potion box and the feeling became much stronger.

'It feels like it is pushing me away.' Cristian explained, the grip on her hand tightening.

Danika put the message stick down and picked up the potion box. 'I think I'll take the contents out and see if it is them or the box.' Danika carefully took all the bottles of essential oils, crystals and herbs out and placed them on the table away from the stick or the box. Then she picked up the stick again and moved it towards the contents with no change. As she moved it towards the box the pull became stronger.

'Okay, so it is the box,' Danika confirmed. She put down the message stick and picked up the box, examining it all over. She had not looked at it this closely since she was given it by her grandmother when she was sixteen. 'I can only sense the love in this, nothing like the message stick was indicating. Are you game?' Danika held it out to Cristian to look at.

Cristian touched the box gingerly and then grabbed it. 'No problem so far,' he confirmed. 'This doesn't look really old, maybe fifty years old would be my guess.' He handed the box back to Danika. She held it in one hand and went to pick up the message stick. Cristian put a hand on her arm first then she reached out and grabbed the message stick.

Danika felt the intense connection immediately. She started to see images in her head similar to the dream she had but with even more emotions attached to each image. The image of the older woman looking over the girl started and straight away she feared for Cristian but could not warn him as she was locked in the vision. She felt the weight of the man and then she changed her view to be the older woman holding an axe. Danika tried hard to push Cristian off or drop the message stick but it was all so quick and then there was blackness.

Danika woke on the floor saying his name. 'Cristian? Where are you, Cristian?' She sat up and saw he was on the floor also, unconscious. She crawled over to him and checked he was breathing and a wave of relief washed over her. She touched his face. 'Cristian, wake up please.' Danika started crying. 'Please, Cristian, I'm sorry.' She leant down and kissed him. He stirred and moved his arm to touch her. With her help he sat up.

'Are you alright, did it knock you down also? I could feel a lot of images as a third person looking through a haze. What did you see?'

'The same as my dream but much clearer and more like I was actually there. I was the girl one minute and then Jessica the next. I'm sure it was Jessica. I knew what was coming and I was really worried for you.' They both managed to stand up and then Danika noticed the potion box broken on the floor. As she picked it up the bottom dropped out of it and a piece of linen dropped to the floor. As Cristian reached for it Danika stopped him. 'Wait.'

Picking up the cloth she felt the power of many souls coming from it. She wavered slightly from the force but then was able to centre it to herself. She turned to Cristian to explain but the shock on his face stopped her.

'Your eyes,' Cristian said. 'They are completely black.'

'There are many souls in this, I don't know why I haven't felt them before. My ancestors have each touched this. Perhaps I needed the message stick to release them.'

'Danika your eyes and voice… it's as if they are all trying to speak at once. Can you put it down Danika?'

Danika moved to the table and carefully laid it out to show writing of what looked like many names. Once she stopped touching it the link was broken. Danika wavered but grabbed the edge of the table not to fall. She looked around at Cristian who looked very worried.

'I'm alright. The link is broken,' she said quietly. Cristian came to her and hugged her.

'I was so worried, you looked and sounded so different. Like several people at once. Who are they?' Cristian pointed at the names roughly written on the linen with ink. Several by a different hand it seemed.

'I think we need more light, some of it is very faded.' Danika was trying to read it without touching it again while Cristian went into his study to get a desk lamp. He also brought back a pen, paper and a magnifying glass.

Once well-lit, Cristian started taking photos of the linen in total and as close as he could magnified before they started to examine it themselves closely. 'I'll read out the names. The first list seems to be by the same hand.' Danika had the magnifying glass and was trying to find the best distance to read the names. 'Okay, first one is Bronwyn, it looks like a Triquetra next to her name. Then Mary, Anne, Jane, Alice, Mary, Sarah, and Emma. Oh, my mother spoke of her the other day. Then Isobel, Jessica – she has a Triquetra next to her name also – and Amelia.'

Danika looked at Cristian. 'These are my ancestors, no dates though. So I'm not sure how far back this goes and if they are a lineage of single woman or sisters, but I know Jessica's name.' Danika tried to read the line at the top which was more faded and a bit damaged as the edge was frayed. 'I think it reads "Never forget your past". My mother used to chant names at me trying to make me remember them. I hated it and didn't want anything to do with it. I wish I had remembered now.' Danika leant over to read the other names.

'This part has been damaged by a spill of some kind.' She leaned closer to smell it. 'I think some of the oils may have leached into it. That is probably my fault; I didn't know this was in the box,' Danika continued after adjusting the lamp to focus more on the last corner. 'Okay, so the last name in that writing was Amelia, then we have Emma again in a different hand, then Helen, Rose, and Celeste. It's hard to read, the next ones Isabelle I think.' Danika stood up straight and looked at Cristian, her eyes were filling with tears. Cristian let her come into his arms.

After a minute of him holding her while gently stroking her hair and whispering calming words he handed her his handkerchief to wipe her eyes. Danika looked up at him to explain.

'The next one is my grandmother Naomi and I think that she wrote it. The other two are probably my mother and me but it is very hard to read. The ink seems to have bled out into the oil stain.' Danika tried again and then turned back to Cristian. 'I don't understand why she never told me this was in the box when she gave it to me. Obviously my mother never knew about it either otherwise the responsibility of it would have been drummed into me.'

'Perhaps your grandmother thought she had more time to explain.' Cristian tried to focus on the corner of the linen with the magnifying glass. Then he took his phone camera again and magnified it for the photo. He opened the shot up on his phone and zoomed it further out. 'Look at this Danika.'

Danika looked at the phone screen and faintly she could see her name in the brown stain and next to it was a Triquetra symbol like the ones next to Jessica and Bronwyn's names.

'This just gives me more questions. What does the message stick have to do with this list of names and why on earth was it at a farm clearance sale?' Danika shook her head.

'You said it was in a lot of souvenirs so maybe the owners bought it on a trip. Perhaps we could ask them where they bought it,' Cristian suggested.

'I don't think so. It was a deceased estate clearance. I found out while I was packing it into the van. There was a person there who appeared to be a relative though. Do you think we might be able to contact through the agent. I have their name on the receipt?' Danika was a little more hopeful.

'I can follow that,' Cristian said.

'I need to put this somewhere safe, but the box is broken now.'

'I have an idea, give me a minute.' Cristian went off to his study and came back with a frame. In it was an award behind glass. Pulling it apart, he said, 'I think it will fit in here and be safer for either of us to pick up perhaps.'

Danika carefully laid the cloth record into the frame and put it back together. She had felt the power of the ancestors as soon as she picked it up but she was ready for it that time. Once it was fully encased in the frame the connection was gone. Danika held it up to show Cristian. 'It should be safe for you to hold now.'

'I think it can be repaired. I can organise that if you want?'

'Thank you, I'd like that.' Danika moved into the kitchen and found a plastic container she thought she could use and placed the contents from the potion box into it. 'This will do for now.' Danika put it down and turned to Cristian.

'We seem to be lurching from one immense mystical event to another while we are together, Cristian. I feel we need to think about what we know of our ancestors and what the curse and prophecy really mean to us. This has to end if we are to have a life together.'

Danika felt Cristian's concern at her profound statement so she grasped his hand to give a comforting squeeze. They moved over to the couch to sit together in comfort.

'I know that my uncle knows something but I don't trust him if he knew about us. Call it a gut feeling. I can try talking to my mother in case she has any insight at all. I am determined that we don't contact either of them until after Wednesday though.' Cristian gently squeezed Danika's hand.

'Gut feeling?'

Cristian nodded at Danika's question.

'I understand what you mean. I feel the same way about Selene. She is so anti-men and we have had a very uncomfortable relationship since my grandmother died. Not that it was great before that. She used to go on about not marrying and that it was for the best. She knew I wasn't in love with Eric so she never worried about him but she kept on about my biological clock.'

'Eric?' Danika could feel Cristian's protective emotions.

'Eric was a past friend who I shared a house with for quite a while. One drunken night we hooked up. Big mistake. We were definitely not compatible and it just made the accommodation arrangement uncomfortable but each of us didn't have much ambition to change the situation until a few months ago. That's when I decided to pack up and go on my working holiday trip around Australia.' Danika could feel Cristian calming down.

'I remember once Selene going on about how Carling woman can't love a man or marry because we would lose our talent, craft, power, whatever you want to call it.' Danika shrugged her shoulders. 'I wonder if it wasn't just a self-perpetuating myth but there are no men in the histories, not even the names of the biological fathers. Only ever female births. I don't know if they never conceive males as no one ever talked about it.'

'I didn't know there was anything else besides our werewolf curse until I read my father's journal and found they only sire boys. Any female pregnancies seem to abort. He and my mother were very distraught about that.' Danika could feel his pain. 'Also Robert going on about a prophecy and the blood moon.'

'That's this year,' Danika confirmed.

'Yes, apparently next month in the Northern hemisphere and here in the Southern hemisphere in November. I checked it out also.' Cristian looked at her and then said, 'We need to find out what this prophecy and curse and myths all have in common particularly with us.'

'Do you think we could end it?' Danika asked, feeling a mixture of apprehension and excitement. 'I would love to have a tribe of kids – boys and girls – all enjoying being in a big family. I have been very lonely most my life despite having Selene.' Danika hadn't realised she had started to cry until Cristian was wiping away her tears.

'I understand how you feel. I was very close to my father. When he died I had no one really to turn to. My mother was grief stricken and I had no friends. It is a bit difficult and dangerous to explain my monthly changes to anyone.' Cristian turned to Danika. 'I wouldn't miss this curse every month. Robert seems to think it is the key to our existence but I disagree.'

'Is it very terrible? I remember what I felt when we connected last full moon. It felt so painful and something else, confusion.' Danika held his hand again.

'I have a need to run regularly which incidentally hasn't been so profound since you have been in my life.' He squeezed her hand. 'I actually need to run to keep fit to cope with the change. I get very restless which is a warning so I try to be somewhere private and outside where I will be able to run. Then I undress. Because clothes will all get ripped or is a constraint if I don't. Then the pain starts as the bones change and weirdly the hair spiking is like needles and my teeth ache. By about that time I lose sense of who I am and don't know where I am. After that I don't know anything until I wake up the next day naked hopefully near where it all started with no memory of what

I did.' Danika had hold of his hand but had moved it almost into a hug against her face.

'I watched my father change for the first time just before I was coming of age. It was the most terrifying thing I had ever seen. It was so much worse than any horror movie because we were living it. The way he contorted and writhed in pain was horrific. When it ended there stood this magnificent beast, larger than a regular wolf, the fur was so amazing with the mane standing proud. I didn't fear him though, I could tell he knew who I was and then he was gone, running away into the estate forest.' Cristian looked straight at Danika. 'I do not want a child of mine to go through that. Robert might think it is a rite of passage or some path to fortune. That's why they call it the legacy but I see it as a curse.'

'My life is a doddle compared to that. Although never truly being able to share my skills openly is a shame so I do it in secret and vicariously through others making them feel lucky and hopeful briefly. Being here with you is the happiest I have ever been, I don't want that to be at risk. So we are in agreement that we are going to smash this curse as soon as we can I'm guessing?' Cristian pulled her hand up to his lips and kissed her fingers.

'Absolutely. But now for bed.' At Danika's raised eyebrows he clarified, 'Our individual beds.' Cristian kissed her quickly and stood to help her up. 'We have an early morning with the ANZAC service, don't forget to set an alarm.'

Danika woke to the alarm and was very pleased not to have been plagued by strange dreams. Dressing quickly she grabbed her coat and bag and went out to the lounge. She couldn't hear any movement or notice lights on at Cristian's end of the apartment. She decided to knock on his bedroom door. Still no response. With the hall light on she opened his door and could see he was in bed but seemed to be dreaming as he was making gibberish sounds and jerky movements. Danika tried to shake him awake as this did not look like a good dream. Cristian yelled out and almost hit her as he flung his arm out.

Now he was awake and blinking at the light streaming over him from the hall.

'Oh sorry, I didn't hit you, did I?' he mumbled with sleepy lips. 'I forgot to set my alarm.'

'No, I dodge well. I'll let you sort yourself out.' She turned on his bedside lamp for him as he rubbed his eyes. Danika made up two water bottles for them to take with them to the dawn service. Twenty minutes later they were out on the path making their way to the Cenotaph.

The crisp harbour air and the brisk walk were invigorating and as they became closer other walkers were joining the path to the dawn service. Danika absorbed the patriotic spirit of those around them. The excitement mixed with pride and the sense of being a part of something special. Despite the early hour and chill there were old and young in the crowd forming in relative silence where only whispers disturbed the hallowed air of the morning. Many wore medals, those of their relatives and some their own. Nearly all had a poppy or badge on their jackets or coats. Danika suddenly remembered and reached into her pocket for two badges for legacy and soldier on charities and handed one to Cristian.

She whispered, 'I got them from the ladies selling them at the op shop the other day.' They each pinned them to their coats. Over the next couple of hours they were humbled by the large and respectful crowd, including the children, waiting for the dawn and listening to the actions of the catafalque party and musicians playing, "The Ode" and "The Last Post". It was all very moving. They waited until all the different dignitaries laid the wreaths and, like the rest of the crowd, slowly moved away.

It was still quite early in the morning and the area was buzzing with people looking for breakfast and warm drinks. Cristian suggested they continue their walk toward the gardens. Danika was enjoying the day immensely and the breakfast and coffee at the botanic gardens continued the positive vibes.

Cristian showed Danika many of the different flower and fern houses and eventually after several hours they walked towards the harbour. Making their way round to the harbour view lawn, Danika took several photos before they rested on a bench to watch the boats and the tourists.

'It is lovely here. The view is stunning.' Danika had not realised that this lovely green space was in the middle of such a large city.

'Do you think you could live here?' Cristian asked.

'I guess I could, at least to begin with, we will have a lifetime to decide.' Danika smiled at him. 'I saw a place recently that I thought was so lovely with room for a large family to grow and run around. A farm that had been filled with love but was now abandoned and slowly falling apart. South of the Hunter Valley, one day I would like to spend some time in a place like that.'

'Who owns it?'

'My last employer gave me the details, not that I knew what I was going to do with them, I have them in the van I think,' Danika replied. 'I was there during the full moon. Sat on top of Rainbow calling to the moon and stars and channelling you as it turned out. By the way, what were you dreaming this morning when you nearly clocked me?'

'Just battling demons, imaginary ones threatening you. I was going to kill them when you woke me.' Danika saw the image of a man flash through their connection, and her instinct told her this was Cristian's uncle.

'Do you battle demons in your dreams often?' Danika sensed he was not telling her everything.

'No, but sometimes after the change I dream what I think must have been my experiences as the wolf. I dream of the hunt, the chase and the kill which is gruesome yet satisfying. That is a horror in itself. As my human self I couldn't kill anything.' Cristian was looking away to the harbour view rather than at Danika. She reached for his hand again.

They sat in silence for a short while watching the families walking with prams and playing with their children. They were both deep in their own thoughts yet sharing the feel of their dreams of a family. So many were stopping to take a selfie with their phones with the iconic backdrop of the Harbour Bridge and Opera house. Danika looked at Cristian.

'Come on, let's be tourists.' Danika stood up still holding his hand to drag him over to the path for a photo.

'I don't do photos,' Cristian protested.

'Well get used to it, we are going to do lots from now on,' Danika insisted. Cristian didn't deny her exuberance. They stood at the wall of the path like so many other couples had and took photos of themselves with the Sydney skyline and harbour as a backdrop.

'This is how we met; remember me trying to take a selfie?' Danika asked.

'Yes and I wished I had those photos I took of you,' Cristian confessed.

'Easy done,' Danika said as she forwarded the two photos from their first meeting day to him.

Cristian replied with the photo he had just taken of them. 'Now I feel suitably like a tourist. Shall we carry on?'

The rest of the day was spent walking around more of the gardens and then on to Circular Quay. They finally wound their way back to the apartment late in the afternoon.

Both were happy to sit out on the balcony with a cool drink enjoying the last of the daylight.

'I don't think I have walked that much in a long time. I am pleasantly tired. I have had a wonderful day.' It felt like the beginning of her new life that she would be sharing with Cristian every day. 'I've been thinking.'

'That sounds ominous.'

'About the future… the far future, but more about the immediate future. Apart from Wednesday I still need to find out about my past ancestors and so do you. So do you know your family tree?' Danika asked seriously.

'How is that immediate future? Just trying to clarify where this is going,' Cristian said.

'You mentioned about searching census and passenger lists of convict boats and so forth. Did you think we should go to Canberra still? I'm just trying to work out taking Rainbow and the ferry I have booked to Tasmania. It all kind of changes once we are married,' Danika said it in a rush.

'Changes in what way? You still want to do the searching and we both want to find out about how to break the curse. I'm just wondering what you are trying to get to? Is it the logistics?'

'I don't want to be apart. Not in a needy way, well… maybe a little. I mean, I think we should remain as close as possible until we find the answer. As in, not me on a cruise and you somewhere else. But I don't know how to sort it out. Also what is going to happen at the next full moon? Where do we have to be? I have so many questions all bubbling to the surface now.' Danika was getting agitated. 'I think I might need to meditate for a while.'

'That was a change of pace from "I've had a wonderful day". Is this pre-marriage jitters perhaps? Firstly, I don't want to be apart either. Secondly, yes we can go to Canberra if you like, lots of info is online as well. Thirdly, you can still send Rainbow on the ferry but not cross yourself and we can fly over together. As for the full moon I would rather be somewhere private. I can look for a few alternatives both here on the mainland and in Tasmania. Home would be best though, as in the estate. How would you feel about being there?' Cristian was watching the play of thoughts across Danika's face in the failing light.

'That was another question I had. When do we meet our respective mothers? I think for safety, and because this will be my first time watching and being part of your legacy, that it would be best where you are safest so it makes sense to be your home.' Danika was starting to shake a little, not entirely from the chill wind.

'I think we should go in to finish this conversation, you're shivering.' Inside they sat on the couch and Cristian grabbed her hands, his warm over her cold ones. He started rubbing them, concern evident in his eyes.

'At the end of this week, if you are ready, I can introduce you to my mother Elizabeth. You can decide when and where we let your mother know. I believe once you meet Mother and talk to her about the legacy you will feel less anxious. I should really go back to the estate in the next week to check on the progress of the new fencing and gate anyway.' Danika nodded along as he spoke.

'Friday night I'll call my mother on a video chat before we go see yours, if that is okay? She will be out all weekend like this last weekend doing markets and I don't want her to feel she was not first to know if you get my drift, she will know!' Danika was feeling warmer and calmer. 'Sorry about the rant I think I was so determined to enjoy the day that I bottled it all up.'

'Why don't you have some meditation time out while I make us some dinner?' Cristian gave Danika a quick kiss and stood up.

'Thanks. You're a keeper as they say.' Danika returned his kiss lightly and went to her room.

The bombardment of questions in her head was still happening and she knew she needed to quieten them down. Gathering her treasured pieces and candles, she set up a meditation circle.

Danika spent more time meditating than she intended, a testament to her need. The incense finished, the candles well burned down and her legs becoming numb, she came out of the trance to smell instead a delicious savoury aroma. Her stomach rumbled as a reaction.

In the kitchen Cristian had set out bowls and bread with a pot of soup simmering on the stove. Danika lifted the lid to see and smell a delicious looking chicken and vegetable soup. As she replaced the lid Cristian came out of his study.

'Ready to eat now?' asked Cristian.

'I sure am. This smells delicious, sorry to keep you waiting,' Danika apologised.

'Not a worry, it was best left to simmer longer. I have plenty of work to catch up on also,' Cristian explained as he came over to dish up their meal.

'Do you need any help with the work? I'm not sure what I could do but I suppose I should understand more of the whole business. I've never had to know much more than my own needs.' Danika stopped to enjoy the food. They were both quiet for some time before Cristian answered.

'You do need to know the business as you will be a partner but I think we can get to the finer points of it next week. For now I'll just say that the business is actually several. The art dealership is separate to the gallery. There is a company that buys and sells real estate including some that are leased. Also there is a separate investment portfolio. The estate is actually in Mother's name so that it is not at risk from the businesses and company. I pay her to live there and I am the sole heir, so far. Personally, I also own this apartment, some real estate overseas, some money in the bank and my car,' Cristian said this all matter of factually.

Danika had stopped eating and was staring at him, shocked.

'I had no idea. I can't be a partner to all that, it is way too much. I thought it was just the art gallery and that was too much. I am never going to get my head around all that.' Danika was losing her appetite.

'You don't have to, that is why we have accountants and lawyers. I inherited most of it when my father died. Then I have built on it. Until we can get all the papers sorted out I want to give you some money of your own. We can set up a new bank account for you or I can just deposit it in your current account.'

'I think I need to meditate again. Can this wait for now? I'm feeling a bit overwhelmed.' Danika couldn't finish her meal and started to clear it away.

'Of course, I hadn't meant to scare you. A discussion to have later with the accountant I think.' Danika felt Cristian's concern, feeling the direction of his thoughts mentally kicking himself for being so blunt.

Danika went to her room to get her keys. 'I'm just getting something out of the van.' Then she left the apartment.

Down at the van Danika found the piece of paper Marge had given her with the farm agent details. She got in the back and sat on the bed to think about what Cristian had just told her. She pulled the quilt around herself and contemplated the enormity of the change to her life.

I'm going to get married and spend the rest of my life with Cristian and not alone, big positive there. I could possibly be a mum one day, huge positive. I would have a new job as an art dealer, big positive as long as there is plenty of people contact. I'm going to be a partner in a massive business and company, not such a positive because although there would be all those people to run it, I would need to know that everyone was happy and no one was being disadvantaged or it would be too much for me to bear. Definitely not a positive. Would I have to attend functions and meetings? I don't have the right clothes. I've never worried about that before, she thought. *Danika get a hold of yourself, one day at a time. Tomorrow buying rings, the next day married and starting the honeymoon. That is enough to focus on for now. I'd better sort my clothes out. Right Danika move your bum.*

Cristian

Cristian was relieved to hear the key in the door. He was beginning to think she may stay down there or even drive off.

'These are the details I was talking about for that farm.' Danika handed him a piece of paper with an address and some contact details. She briefly went into her room and came out with her bank account details. 'This is my bank account. I think I will go to bed it has been a long day.' Without another word Danika retreated to the bedroom.

'Goodnight Danika.'

Cristian was concerned how quiet she was but could also sense she was calm and very tired. Looking at the details she had given him he went to his study. The first thing he did was transfer several thousand to her account with a weekly direct deposit set up. He then sent a message to his lawyer to look into the property managed by the agents before sitting down to research whatever he could find about it.

The satellite image was stunning. He could see why Danika was so attracted to it. The whole property included many hundreds of acres of natural woodland as well as a creek and cleared grassland around the house and outbuildings. Trying to do a street view was difficult but he could get a sense that the view from the house would be down the valley to see the sunrise and moonrise. He continued to look till he thought he had found the little town she must have worked in and a street view showed him the bakery and other small shops. He felt pleased with himself to have found something that related to Danika's life before today. He knew very little about it, he realised. She was not big on sharing very much like himself. They were strangely very much alike. Yawning understandably considering they were up before 4 am he closed the laptop before going to bed, falling asleep quickly.

Danika

Danika sat up as soon as the alarm went off. She knew that she was overly excited but rather than dampen it down she decided to use it to get as much done as she could before bombarding Cristian with her emotions. Consequently she had sorted her clothes and half packed them for tomorrow, about three times before deciding to have a shower and check that the creases had fallen from her wedding outfit. She practiced a few different hair styles deciding on tomorrows outfit and changing to a simple braid for today. Satisfied there was no more to do in the bedroom she slipped out, closing the door behind her. It was only 8 am.

At the dining room table she looked down at the things they had left there. The message stick, framed ancestry list and her grandmothers broken potion box and the contents unceremoniously in a plastic box. What to do with them? Cristian came from his room just at that point.

'Good morning.' Cristian had a winning smile as he said it. 'Are you trying to decide what to do with them?'

'Yes I kind of want them out of sight so they don't spoil the mood so to speak.' Danika was frowning as she spoke. 'I really want the box repaired as soon as possible though because I think I want it with me on our trip.' Danika turned pleading eyes at Cristian.

'Well I think you could move those two items into the third bedroom.' He pointed at the message stick and frame. 'And we can take the box with us today because I have two ideas about it.'

'I forgot about the other bedroom. Yes, that is a great idea. What are your two ideas about this?' She pointed to the box.

'Take it with us to the jeweller you mentioned. If he can't fix it today I am sure Paul could.' Cristian moved over to Danika and put his arm around her shoulders as they both looked down at the items. 'I have a cardboard carton that it should fit in to take it today.'

Danika turned around into his arms and hugged him while muffled speaking to his chest. 'You have no idea how much it means to me to have someone to share my thoughts with.'

Cristian kissed the top of her head, his protective emotions washing over her, combined with a feeling of pride. 'Okay let's get this done because otherwise I might not be able to stop seducing you.' He hugged her tighter and then tried to release her.

Danika held on tighter and, standing on her toes, leaned up to kiss him. Danika felt like they were immersed in a pool of love, drowning yet not needing air. She hadn't realised he had lifted her up to the table until she was wrapping her legs around his waist. They were each pushing aside clothing to kiss from their necks slowly further down as her hands slid down the skin of his torso to his waist then Danika pushed her hand on his chest and warned, 'No!'

Cristian stopped immediately.

'You nearly touched the medallion. I don't want to hurt you,' Danika said as Cristian placed his hands on the table either side of her as she pulled her top back together.

He kissed the top of her head again and moved away to sort out his unbuttoned shirt and adjust himself. 'Sorry about that.'

'Don't apologise I shouldn't have started it. I'm a bit excited today,' Danika apologised herself. 'Roll on tomorrow.'

Danika slipped off the table and picked up the message stick first, taking it to the other room before coming back for the frame separately to prevent any problems. Cristian had brought back the cardboard carton for Danika to place the potion box in. He then moved into the kitchen to make coffee and a tea for Danika.

Danika sat at the counter to watch him. Still a little euphoric from the kissing at the table she could feel her breath increasing as she stared at his muscles moving under his shirt, the heat rising up her neck and down to her stomach to her…

'Stop it Danika, I can feel that from here,' Cristian said with his head bowed, his hands gripping the bench.

'Oh my heavens and stars I am so sorry. This day is going to be too hard, pardon the pun if I don't get this under control.' Danika slid off the stool and went back to her bedroom to calm herself down. Danika sat on the floor and, holding her calming crystals, chanted to herself, projecting it into the runes in her lap. Once satisfied she was calmer she came out to find her drink on the counter and no sign of Cristian. He had made her a tea using her own herbs. The love for him swelled in her heart but not the sexual desire thankfully.

Cristian came out in different clothes, his hair still a little wet. 'Take two. Are you okay now?'

'I'm so sorry it was very remiss of me, I had been using my excited energy to get a lot done quickly and meant to dampen it before coming out but I forgot. Have it sorted now,' Danika explained and was holding the runes up to show him. 'Would you like one of these to get through the day?' He nodded but let her put them down on the counter. 'Thank you for my tea.'

'Did you have that address of the jeweller? I thought we could go in my car, better for early morning city traffic,' Cristian suggested. Danika nodded her head and pulled out the paper scrap she had written the address on the other day. Cristian picked up the runes and placed one in each pocket of his trousers yet again.

An hour and some bad peak-hour traffic later, they opened the jeweller's door, the bell attached to the door tinkling, making them both smile. The smell of the old building added to the masses of old displays almost to the ceiling made Danika sure this was the right place to be. The man that came out from the back was tall with greying hair wearing glasses with a jeweller's glass attached and a big friendly smile. Danika felt at ease immediately.

'Good morning, how can I help you?'

'Good morning. We are looking for wedding rings perhaps with a difference,' Cristian replied, looking at Danika who quietly nodded.

'Were you after yellow, white gold or silver, with stones or plain?' The shop owner – Gerry based on his name tag – seemed to notice they had no idea what they were doing, his expression a gentle smile.

'White gold maybe, with stones perhaps,' Danika answered. 'But not the usual style.'

'How about I get a few trays for you to look at and we will get your ring size as well. Try these on until they feel okay.' Gerry placed two sets of ring sizes out, one for Cristian and a smaller set for Danika to try, while he gathered a few trays from the counters and one from the window display.

'Were you after wedding bands and an engagement ring for the lady, Sir?'

'Oh sorry, I'm Cristian and this is Danika. I think wedding bands and I would like to look at the other rings also, thanks,' Cristian replied. Danika was feeling a little giggly and tried to contain it.

'Have you decided which ring feels comfortable, Danika?' Gerry asked after Danika had tried on a couple. Danika pointed to the size which Gerry noted down.

She was scanning the tray of wedding bands that were nice but fairly plain. Cristian was doing the same with the tray of men's wedding bands. They tried a couple of the more ornate ones from the trays but put them back. Neither of them seemed to like any of the styles that were before them.

'I have many more to show you. Let me move these and I shall get a few more.'

Cristian grabbed Danika's hand and said, 'It's fine, he has a lot to choose from.'

Danika smiled at him and slipped out her hand to move around the displays, her hands out in front of her, trying to feel for the right one. She moved around the shop stopping at one display and pointing to a tray. Gerry had been watching her and pulled the tray out. Danika then stared out to the back.

'Do you have more in your safe still?' Danika asked.

'Yes, a few trays of older rings and ones that were ordered and not collected and a few that were pawned.' He placed the tray Danika had selected and one other on the counter as he went back to his safe to get the oddments trays.

Danika was more interested in the silver rings that seemed to have more style and patterns to the plain wedding rings. Cristian also preferred the more unusual. Most were a little large for Danika's fine hands.

As Gerry placed the two trays of very unusual rings down they both reached for rings. Cristian grabbed a dark metal ring with a pattern of the changing moon stamped around it. As he put it on it looked like a good fit.

'That is titanium so cannot be adjusted. How does it feel?' Gerry asked.

'Perfect,' Cristian confirmed. 'Do you have a chain to match? Sometimes I will have to take it off.' Danika felt nothing but love as Cristian kept his gaze fixed on her, the emotion of the moment overwhelming them both.

'I think I might.' Gerry went off to get the chain tray.

As Danika tried on a few rings she spotted a set of two rings intertwined in white gold. The wide band was studded with diamonds and emeralds in a swirl like a river with the main ring a large oval emerald surrounded by diamonds. They matched her eyes perfectly. They created quite a chunky look but were small in size. As Danika slipped them onto her finger they felt like they were hugging her as she went.

'Do you like them?' Cristian asked and Danika could only nod as she stared down at her hand and touched the stones.

Gerry returned, saying, 'Those were a commission set from twenty or more years ago. They were never collected but with so many stones they are difficult to resize. How do they feel?'

'They feel very good, still have a little room to slide them over my knuckle. I think these are the ones.'

'There were also earrings and a necklace to match. I always hoped they would come back, they only paid a deposit,' Gerry informed them.

'Do you still have that set?' asked Cristian.

'Yes I'll get them. Most people baulk at the price of true emeralds. So I haven't put them out in a long while.'

The earrings and necklace was a perfect match to the ring. The earrings were a droplet style of an oval emerald surrounded by diamonds, as was the necklace. The price was still displayed in the box which made Danika gasp and pull her hand back from touching them.

Cristian grabbed her hand again and said, 'Don't look at the price, that is not important.' He looked at Gerry and confirmed, 'We will take it all, thanks.'

'Did you still want a chain? This one is titanium also, a bit chunky for most people as well as the price.' Gerry was pointing to a heavy darker metal chain with large parrot clasp.

'Yes that will be perfect.' Cristian then looked at Danika and asked, 'What about something for Selene and Elizabeth?'

'What a wonderful idea. Yes Mother's Day is next month.' Danika took off the rings and handed them to Gerry to pack up with the rest of what they had chosen. She wandered the displays again to choose something for the mothers. 'A brooch I think for them each. What do you think, Cristian?'

'Sounds good, you choose. Elizabeth's favourite colour is red.'

'Good and Selene's is blue.' Danika chose a large silver brooch studded with turquoise with a pentagram base for Selene and a small yellow gold brooch of a bird with a ruby body and diamond eyes. 'Hopefully they like these.' Cristian looked over her shoulder and nodded his approval.

'I knew this was where we needed to be today. Oh I almost forgot the box.' Danika had placed the carton on the floor while they were looking at jewellery. Now, picking it up, she looked at Gerry and asked, 'Is there any way you could mend this for me? I dropped it.'

'Let me have a look. That is lovely and I'm guessing very sentimental. Now okay, I see. Yes, I think I could push this back in here and with a little glue and a tack here. I might have some little brass screws to fix the hinges. When did you want it?'

'Later today if possible we are getting married tomorrow.' Danika glanced at Cristian.

'I think I can manage that but best to not use it until tomorrow to let the glue set. Perhaps after lunch and I can polish and pack all these other items for you to collect then if you like?'

Cristian pulled out his wallet and settled up with Gerry who refused to take anything for the box repairs.

'I see you are parked across the road in front of the florist. Faye has lovely flowers, tell her I sent you she may give you a discount.' Gerry smiled the suggestion as he completed the transaction and wrote out a guarantee for the jewellery, handing it to Cristian.

'Thank you, we will be back this afternoon.' Cristian shook Gerry's hand.

Cristian ushered Danika out into the cool air compared to the warm shop, grasping her hand to walk across the busy road. The florist now had a few buckets of flowers out the front and a couple of pot plants. Cristian opened the door for Danika to go in and the bell on the door tinkled. She looked at him and smiled. 'I love these older shops.'

Inside, the lady, Faye, was busy making up posies.

'Hello, be with you shortly.' She pulled the tape around the stems tight then placed them in the fridge behind her.

'How can I help you?' Faye beamed a huge smile. 'I saw you go into Gerry's.'

'Yes, Gerry said we should say he sent us but truly we were coming here anyway. We are getting married tomorrow and I was looking for something. Not so much a bouquet though, it is rather informal.'

Danika turned to Cristian for guidance but he just shrugged and said, 'I'm leaving this to you.' He gave her a peck on the cheek before he moved away to look at some of the plants by the window.

'What colour are you wearing?' Faye asked. Danika looked across at Cristian again who appeared to be preoccupied.

'White and green,' Danika whispered.

Faye grasped a few stems from the fridge and mocked up a little spray on the counter to show her. 'If I put some ribbons here and here you can wear it like a sleeve on your non-writing arm like this.' Danika held out her right arm as Faye roughly showed her what it might look like. 'Then when you put your hands in front for photos it looks a bit like a bouquet but you don't have to hold it all the time.'

'You are brilliant I love that idea.' Danika was amazed how intuitive Faye was.

Faye reached round for more little green pompom style flowers. 'A few of these to add the green. I can do this for your fiancé as a buttonhole.' Faye picked up two smaller stems to show Danika. 'And what about your hair?'

'I was going to braid the top a bit like a crown and have some on my neck.' Danika glanced at Cristian again who was picking up pots and putting them down again.

Faye pulled out a box of tiny imitation flowers on wire stems. 'Would you like a few of these to put in the braid?' Danika could only nod as tears were beginning to flow.

Faye grasped her hand. 'Getting a bit overwhelming, is it?'

Danika nodded and whispered, 'I never thought I would ever marry.' Faye squeezed her hand. Danika wiped her tears hopefully before Cristian could see them.

'Well I think we have it all sorted then. So would you like to collect them this afternoon?' Faye asked. 'You can pay then once you are satisfied.'

'That would be lovely. We have to come back at 2 pm to see Gerry,' Danika confirmed.

Seeing that as his queue Cristian came up to the counter and added, 'I would like to take two of those 'never fail' plants and two matching pots when we come back also if you could pack them up, thank you.'

They thanked her and Cristian held the door of the shop for Danika and then the car door also for her to get in.

'Any ideas where you want to go now we have several hours to kill?' Cristian asked.

'No I don't really know my way around. Perhaps where we can sit and have a drink. Can I leave that to your judgement?' Danika was feeling a little drained after the emotional roller coaster so far today. Cristian nodded and continued to drive.

Cristian

Cristian had felt all the gambit of emotions spilling from Danika today as well as hearing most of her whispers, one of the perks of the legacy. It took all his willpower not to hug her to soothe her in the shops but he realised she needed to make these decisions herself.

They drove over the bridge and he sensed Danika's change of emotion at the sites as they came to a coffee place on the coast near Kirribilli. Once seated Danika seemed to relax and look at the view. Cristian had stopped to order with the waitress as Danika had been shown to the table.

'This is lovely thank you. I think I've used up my decision making today.' Danika reached over to Cristian's hand.

He held it tightly and, looking at her rather than the scenery, said, 'I felt you today, you were sad quite often and I was struggling not to whisk you away from your fears. It was difficult. I'm not sure these damn stones were helping.' Cristian tapped his pocket.

'I'm sorry, I only tried to keep the libido at bay not all emotions. I'm just missing my grandmother and I guess to some extent my mother. Not the one I have but the mother I wish I had who would be happy for me and helping with the arrangements.' Danika looked at Cristian. 'I'm normally much stronger than this I'm not sure where all this is coming from.' She waved at her face as she felt the tears again.

'Well you made lots of decisions on the run so to speak and I'm proud of you for finding two amazing shops.' Cristian squeezed her hand and let go just as their coffees arrived shortly followed by hearty meals.

Taking their time after the meal they walked along the foreshore and, yet again, Danika took a few photos. Turning to Cristian she asked if anyone would take photos of them tomorrow.

'No reason why we can't get someone to do that, I guess, using these.' Cristian held up his phone.

'Just that Faye the florist mentioned it and I realised you have no photos at the apartment. Do you have them at home, as in the estate?' Danika enquired.

'A few photos in albums, none on show. Mother finds it too difficult to see Father in a photo.' Cristian looked at Danika. 'What about your family?'

'The same actually, just a few in an album, none on display. Obviously no photos of the fathers. I don't even know if the women knew who they were. One of the sides to my family I hated when I went to other people's houses with photos everywhere.' Danika was feeling sad again Cristian could feel it.

'We can change that from now on. I feel a selfie coming on.' Cristian poked her in the ribs to make her smile and then they posed, badly, for a selfie, laughing at the result.

'Shall we go? I might stop by the gallery to see how the pickups have been going. Then back to the jewellers and florist,' Cristian suggested, putting his arm around her shoulders.

The long detour to the gallery killed the time needed and Cristian was able to look over the Walton collection now there in full. Some of the Janet Wells pieces had arrived also. They all agreed that an official opening of the collection was in order and that they could have it ready for a Saturday opening in a week's time. He reminded the staff he would be unavailable for the rest of the week other than very urgent matters only by text at first.

He watched Danika talking with Rene again about plans for the opening invitations. She wanted Mrs Walton and Janet Wells to be invited to the opening but for them and Juliet to be invited to a private showing the night before. As she discussed catering and set up for the opening again he couldn't keep from thinking that she was perfect as both a consultant and partner.

Danika

Driving back to the jewellers Danika was talking non-stop about the plans for the opening and having Mrs Walton, Janet and Juliet at the viewing the night before. Turning to Cristian she asked, 'I'm not overstepping you or her or anybody am I? It's just that it felt right and I want this to go well. My first ever event and…' Cristian grabbed her hand while they were stopped at the lights.

'You are doing a fantastic job but you need to calm down a bit. We can talk more once I'm not driving.' Cristian looked at her briefly before focusing on the traffic again. A few minutes later they pulled up outside the florist again.

Inside Danika's excitement changed to delight as Faye showed her the spray of white and green flowers for her arm tied neatly with two elastic white satin ribbons that could slip over her arm. She tried it on and it fit perfectly. Danika showed it to Cristian who was impressed by the result. Faye showed him the buttonhole she had made to match. Danika noted his surprise and sensed a ripple of excitement from him. With the little box of hair ornaments, Faye put them in a larger box with instructions to keep them in the fridge until they needed them tomorrow. Faye wished them all the best for the day. Cristian paid for the flowers and plants which they loaded carefully into the back seat of the car before walking across to the jeweller.

As the happy sound of the doorbell tinkled Gerry came out to meet them carrying Danika's potion box. As he placed it on the counter for her to see the tears started to fall. The box was back together and looked better than before as Gerry had given it a clean and light polish also. He showed her the new brass hinges. Danika ran her hands over it with love and thanked him between tears. Gerry carefully placed it in the carton they had brought it in. Danika was so thankful that she had her grandmothers gift back in one piece again. Gerry placed several red velvet boxes on the counter to show them the polished rings, necklace and earrings for Danika and the ring and chain set for Cristian. The brooches he had wrapped in gift paper with bows. Danika could hardly speak through the tears so Cristian was left to thank Gerry and shake his hand. Gerry congratulated them and wished them well for tomorrow. With the jewellery in a bag and Danika carrying the carton they left to negotiate the busy road.

Danika kept the carton on her lap as they left the curb and headed back to the apartment. Sitting with her hand pressed against the box the tears flowing freely. Cristian continued driving in silence until he pulled into the park of the apartment at which point Danika had managed to get her emotions a little under control. Turning to her, he brushed her face with his hand.

'How about we take the lighter pieces up now and I'll come back for the plants in a little while.' She nodded, feeling a little drained from the raft of emotions that had run through her today.

Cristian helped her out of the car so that she could hold the carton. Then, with the bag and the flower box in hand, they went up to the apartment. Inside Cristian cleared a shelf in the fridge to fit the flower box. Danika had taken the potion box from the carton and was placing the bottles of oils and other items back into the box. Cristian took out the velvet boxes and placed them on the table. Finally Danika was able to speak.

'Thank you so much for leaving me to sort out my crazy emotions. I hadn't realised how much today had affected me until it all spilled out.' Danika hugged him.

Cristian held her lightly for a minute then slowly moved away so he could look at her tear-streaked face.

'I have to thank you for the flowers and the jewellery today.' Danika raised her brows questioningly at him as he continued, 'I have barrelled on with the technical plans for this wedding, the forms and such, without once considering how special tomorrow is for both of us and I'm sorry for that.'

'I could have stopped you and said more if it had been a top priority but I have to say it is all new to me as not a tradition in my family so I had nothing to base it on. Today and the enormity of it and then when those lovely strangers wished us well I felt weirdly lonely,' Danika tried to explain without upsetting Cristian but she saw him stiffen. 'Believe me when I say I am more than happy to spend the rest of my life with you, it was the old loneliness of no extended family to share these momentous events with.'

'I haven't even checked if you have an outfit or anything. I feel very obtuse.' Cristian was shaking his head.

'I'm all set. What about you?' Danika didn't want to give away what she would be wearing until tomorrow.

'I must admit to not giving it much thought until now. As I said, very remiss of me. I will be ready though.' Cristian laughed as if to try to alleviate Danika's concerns. 'While I am in compliment mode, you seem to be taking on your partnership responsibilities well. I noticed when you were talking with Rene earlier.' Danika felt humbled by the compliment, she hadn't noticed he was watching and then felt bad she hadn't discussed with him first.

'Thank you, I have surprised myself. Many years in hospitality I suppose. I've never been the organiser before but it felt good to have the ideas and be able to initiate them. Is it alright to get that involved?' Danika did not want to get off side of anyone.

'Heavens yes. I don't think Rene wants the full responsibility and really there isn't anyone else anymore to plan something on this scale. My first grand opening Mother planned before Father died. Since then we have not done much in the way of events more just individual invites.'

'I have a few ideas I might run past you so I can send a message to Rene to order some things while we are away.' Danika was getting more excited about the opening to draw herself away from the thoughts of tomorrow.

'I trust you completely and give you free rein Danika. Enjoy yourself.'

'I might get some notes down then if that's okay? Then I can send them to Rene, I'll feel much better knowing I have given her some guidance. Would you have a note pad I can use?' Danika suggested.

Cristian left her to her thoughts and plans when he gave her some stationary that she may need for her planning.

Cristian

Cristian felt ashamed he hadn't thought to ask Danika earlier if she was prepared to her satisfaction for tomorrow. So many things not discussed yet she seemed comfortable and excited at the little they accomplished today, as was he. Yet again her intuition and selections seemed to just fall into place. He wondered if he could be that intuitive. A suit and tie chosen, Cristian decided to get back to his emails.

Many of the emails were dealers fishing for a hint of the new collection. He noted down the names of the ones he did and didn't want invited for next week's opening. He also noted an email from Robert that he knew he needed to open. His uncle was warning him that he was coming to visit immediately after the lunar cycle. Expected arrival 18th May. Cristian swore under his breath as he knew he couldn't put him off. He also noticed that his uncle had copied his mother into the message. Perhaps she had not seen it yet as it was only sent today. He knew she would want to discuss Robert's visit. Cristian sent his mother a quick text pointing out Robert's visit and explaining that he was unavailable until the weekend but that they could discuss then. Looking out the window he noticed it had darkened while he was engrossed in work. He could not hear Danika but could sense her which made him smile, the connection was comforting.

Danika was still writing notes for the running plan of the opening plus the positions for pieces in the gallery. She had about a dozen drawings and lists laid out in front of her when Cristian came out of his study to check on her. She looked up and smiled at him, he could feel how happy she was.

'How is it going?' Her style was very different to his own, much more visual and tactile.

'Really well, I think Rene will be glad when I stop texting her and sending photos of my ideas though. Just have to confirm the guest list with you and it's pretty much sorted.' Danika stretched as she spoke and the last couple of words were muffled in a yawn.

'I've just sent her a who's who and who's not list so that is sorted as well.' Cristian rubbed Danika's shoulders to which she moaned in enjoyment. 'Happy if I order a food delivery for dinner?'

'Mmm please, a vegan salad for me, not sure what you were thinking.' Danika was enjoying the neck rub which was heading down her back now.

'Okay I'll see what I can do.' Cristian stopped the back rub before it became too difficult to stop. He then rang his favourite delivery people before helping Danika tidy away her plans.

'Tomorrow I'll drive us in my car to the chambers and then we can come back and swap vehicles for the drive down the coast if that is okay with you?' Cristian suggested with the city traffic in mind driving Danika's van.

'Great idea so I can pack Rainbow tonight then we will be good to go tomorrow.'

'Yes I suppose we should.' Cristian was about to follow Danika to her room with the pile of papers when she stopped him and took them from him.

'Secret bride business, thanks anyway.' Danika grinned at him.

By the time Danika was satisfied with the items packed into Rainbow for them both it was getting late but she was still keyed up. Cristian had been watching her racing back and forth tidying and changing her mind on some items. He noted she must have made a dozen trips down to the van although she seemed happy. As she stood in the lounge mentally assessing her packing Cristian handed her one of her calming teas and started to direct her out to the balcony.

'Thank you, I need this.' She placed her drink down and stood at the rail lifting her arms to the sky and breathed in deeply.

'If you aren't going to stop now I'll leave you to lock up and I'll see you in the morning?' Cristian stood up, kissed her on the cheek and went to his rooms.

Cristian couldn't believe how quickly he had gone from amusement watching Danika racing about with packing to concern for her to stop then almost immediately to desire to take her to bed right now. *One more day*, he thought. Then they would be married.

6

THE WEDDING

DANIKA WOKE BEFORE the alarm she set for 6.30 am as she thought she might. It took a long time to sleep last night, eventually she had to meditate to calm her mind after dwelling on the momentous occasion that this wedding would be. She would be the first in her family to marry at all let alone a werewolf and for him the first of his family to marry a witch. Now here she was on her wedding day sitting up in bed contemplating her first move.

An hour into her getting ready, Cristian knocked on her door to tell her he had made her a hot drink and left it at the door.

Her quick heart jump that he might come in was replaced by a warm feeling of gratitude.

'Thank you,' she yelled from the bathroom. When she thought she could move without losing her place braiding her hair, she carefully opened the door a fraction and took the now lukewarm drink and the biscuits he had left with it. She sipped the drink before going back to the task of completing her complicated braid.

Cristian woke to his 7.30 am alarm pleased he hadn't had any nightmarish dreams. No dreams at all actually. At first he could not hear Danika and wondered if he should wake her so he listened at her door and could hear movement in the bathroom. He felt a bit at odds whether to bother her or not. Finally deciding to at least make her a hot drink and leave it at the door. He doubted she would want anything to eat as he could sense her emotions from here.

After another hour he was as spruced up as he intended and was standing at the table wondering what to do next when Danika yelled out if he could bring her jewellery. So the conversation was through a closed door.

With her hair finally done, Danika realised that she'd left the necklace and earrings in the lounge the night prior. She called to Cristian through the door, not wanting to reveal anything until she was ready.

Cristian dutifully passed her the closed box through a tiny crack in the door.

With everything adorned, Danika instructed him to go to his study and wait. When she heard him retreat to the study she finally cracked her own door and retrieved the flowers from the fridge.

'Okay, you can come out now.' Standing in the lounge, Danika waited for Cristian to see her for the first time on her wedding day in her complete outfit looking her best, she hoped. She was proud of her outfit but stood with trepidation of Cristian's reaction.

Cristian

As Cristian walked down the hall he finally saw Danika standing there, glowing like an angel. Her hair was braided into a crown laced with tiny white flowers, the braids like a veil down her neck joining impossibly together in a loop with more tiny flowers. Her white silk and lace top flowed loose over the top of her long white and green skirt with its handkerchief hem showing her thin ankles and white embroidered slippers. The necklace and earrings were a perfect complement to the outfit. The flower sleeve, unique and beautiful, gave her a serene angelic stance. He wasn't sure if she even had makeup on, her face looked so natural and beautiful.

'I feel like I am looking at an angel. You are so beautiful and precious, I don't feel worthy to see you, let alone touch you.' Cristian couldn't move as if it would break the spell of Danika's angelic appearance.

'Don't you dare make me cry. I didn't think you were going to say anything and then you said too much. I wish my mother could see me.'

'She will, because we will have many photos starting with now.' Cristian took several of Danika from several angles, including close ups of her hair.

'How did you know to pick green?' Danika asked as she lightly touched his kerchief, matching somehow perfectly to the green in Danika's.

'An educated guess.' At Danika's quizzical look he admitted, 'I heard what you said in the florist. Wolfie hearing.' He tapped his ear which had her laughing.

'I'm guessing I should carry the rings. Did you want to wear the large one now or at the ceremony?' Cristian was trying to slip them in his jacket pocket to see how they fit.

'Yes, I suppose I could.' Danika slipped the emerald ring onto her finger.

Danika went back to get one of her tote bags so she could carry the original papers just in case, the ring boxes and her phone. They were a little early but neither could stand waiting any longer.

'Oh wait, wait, and your buttonhole, we nearly forgot.' She grabbed it out of the box and carefully put it in his buttonhole and pinned it in place. Danika was focused on getting it straight as Cristian stood still, taking in the beauty of her hair, her skin and the fragrance of jasmine delicately pervading from her. He could see closely the dozens of tiny flowers she had woven into her braids and was astounded she was able to do it herself.

'Your hair is amazing, it must have taken hours. How did you see what you were doing behind you?'

'Years of practice with my grandmother's help many years ago. I haven't done it for a long time, I wasn't sure I would remember,' Danika admitted. 'Thank you.'

At James' office they had made the effort to clear the conference room and put flowers in which Cristian was very grateful for Danika's sake. James had organised a celebrant to perform the ceremony so he could be one of the witnesses and his secretary Mary was the other. The ceremony was pleasant and relatively brief, mostly about the legal aspect of commitment and respect.

Danika glowed as the ceremony progressed and their eagerness filled the connection between them. So much expectation for this moment and the ceremony itself felt like it was flying by. Cristian felt only love as he stared at Danika's eyes, unable to stop looking at them. Then he was reaching for the rings from his jacket. He repeated his vows and slipped the ring onto Danika's hand to match the engagement ring.

When Danika repeated her vows, she nearly dropped his ring before pushing it firmly on to his finger. Cristian couldn't keep himself from smiling at her nerves.

'You may now kiss your bride,' the celebrant said.

The room almost faded away as Cristian gently kissed her. When it went on a little longer, James cleared his throat and they pulled apart with a guilty grin.

'Just a few formalities and signatures to get through,' the celebrant told them. James took some photos of them standing together with the flowers as a backdrop and then signing the papers, the same as any other wedding. James congratulated them and offered them a drink but they declined saying they had a long drive ahead of them. He slapped Cristian on the back and shook his hand, then handed him a bottle of a very fine scotch whiskey. Mary complimented Danika on her hair and outfit and then handed her a lovely box of chocolates. Cristian whispered in James' ear so as they went out he offered to take more photos of them coming down the lovely staircase. Mary threw a few rose petals at them as a surprise which made them laugh, all of which James managed to get photos of. Many more thanks all round and they were leaving.

It all seemed a blur. One minute they had been going in the building and what seemed only a few minutes later they were leaving. It had actually been nearly an hour.

Cristian helped Danika into his car to make sure she and her dress were safe then headed back towards their apartment. Danika was sitting very still staring ahead as Cristian drove and he was wondering what she was thinking.

Out of the blue she asked, 'What do you think if I changed my name?' Danika looked directly at him.

Cristian was silent as he felt the weight of the question.

'To Mrs Blakesley. Would that be weird with your mother?' Danika explained. 'I suppose I would have to change lots of things, my licence and well lots.' Danika petered off.

Cristian didn't think he could feel happier than he did when they were finally married but this was more than he could ever hope for. It had never occurred to him that his wife, especially Danika, would be a Blakesley. Ignorance on his part. His reply was measured while he was driving.

'I would be honoured to have my wife be Mrs Blakesley, but it is entirely your choice. Changing your details I can help you through after our honeymoon.'

Danika giggled. 'Honeymoon, Mrs Danika Blakesley.' Danika giggled again looking at the ring on her left hand then pinched her cheek. 'Ow, I just needed to make sure I wasn't dreaming.'

Cristian could barely contain himself. He felt his jaw tighten, the tightness of his suit against his arms and chest as he gripped the wheel harder. He could barely even keep his breathing under control.

Blood rushed lower and through their connection Cristian could tell as Danika noticed his physical reaction to his attraction. As he felt her body react to his, he moved his hand from the gear stick to hers and squeezed it hard.

'Don't or I'll have a crash.' Cristian wasn't looking at her he was trying hard to keep control of himself and the car.

He heard Danika's breathing quicken beside him, followed by her own attempt to intentionally get it under control.

'I'm sorry about that, I don't have any dampening on me, it didn't go with the outfit.' She placed her hands over her face and laughed hard at that.

'Neither did I. The stones in my pockets made me look like I was at half-mast.' Cristian was laughing as well now. He was relieved to be pulling into the car park at the apartment.

'We have to make a decision before we go up. Is the trip down to Sussex inlet for tonight most important or not?' Danika seemed to understand the gravity of his question. She took a deep breath and her silence showed she was thinking it through.

'Yes, it is. I really want to start our honeymoon there. So we probably should load up the dampening protection until we get there.' Disappointment and understanding flooded him. He could barely keep his eyes from her.

'Okay, that is the plan then. It's going to be a bloody hard three-hour drive wife of mine.' Cristian grasped her hand and kissed it. 'You go up first, I will follow. I don't trust myself in that lift with you.'

Cristian barely made it into his bedroom without going straight to Danika. He changed out of his suit into jeans and a t-shirt and jacket, placing the stones in his pockets and trying to get his emotions under control. He stood still staring at the bed.

Just as well I love you Danika to put up with this torture, he thought. Turning away, he made sure he put his phone, wallet and keys into his jacket before coming out of the room. They each walked down the respective halls towards each other. Danika spoke first.

'I'm ready to go but first I want to say that I am so very happy to be your wife and that I know how lucky I am to have you as my husband. Thank you for putting up with me and understanding that I need to go where we are today. I love you.' Danika's eyes were tearing up. The weight of her declaration of love hit him, the words spoken aloud for the first time.

'I love you too, Danika. I thought at first that all of my emotions were being driven by some mystical legacy but I know that I love your quirks, humour, strength and empathy. You are so very beautiful inside and out. I am happy, well, probably more resigned to this road trip because it is important to you, so it is to me. No promises at control once we get there though.' Cristian smiled at her. 'Now if you think you have all you need, let's get on the road.'

They managed the lift together this time as they felt the dampening control in place. Rainbow started beautifully which surprised Danika, who commented on the lack of annoying light on the dashboard. Cristian had organised a mechanic while they were out yesterday to pick it up and do a full service as a surprise. He owned up to it there as they sat listening to Rainbow's gentle hum.

'She's so quiet,' Danika commented.

'Yes everyone should be healthy and happy for a road trip,' Cristian confirmed, feeling much safer driving the van today.

The drive to Sussex inlet was interesting as they were roads they hadn't been on before yet all either of them could think about was getting there. They didn't stop, not even for food. For the whole two hours and forty minutes they kept their conversation to safe topics, before finally pulling up outside a two-story villa overlooking the water. The gardens were lush and beautiful. Danika was breathing in the ocean air as Cristian found the lock box for the keys to get in. They quickly moved their luggage and other items from the van into the villa. A large welcoming hamper sat on the kitchen bench with complimentary champagne which Danika immediately moved to put in the fridge which was stacked with food.

As she stood from the fridge Cristian grasped her in an embrace, kissing her. She was quick to respond, matching his urgency and running her hand through his hair. After a few minutes they pulled apart both flushed with desire. Danika's eyes were deep pools of emerald-green. He could not contain his desire any longer. Holding her hand he led her up the stairs.

Cristian could not keep from kissing her again as they climbed the stairs to the master bedroom, less urgently but deliberately kissing her mouth and neck as his hands were stroking her back. Danika was returning his kisses, sliding her hands up inside his jacket and over his shoulders to make the jacket fall to the ground. Her hands went to the buckle of his trousers trying to get it undone. He helped her and then stepped out of his shoes and jeans. His arousal was obvious. Cristian started to lift the hem of her top to pull it over her head but Danika warned him to pause while she took off the medallion and then her top.

Cristian stood staring at Danika's breasts peaking from her white lace bra. She had placed a large bandage on her side over her tattoo. He bent down to kiss her breasts one at a time holding her arching back in one hand as he ran his hand over the lace of her bra to arouse her nipples with the other. Danika slipped her hands under her waist band and pushed her skirt to pool on the floor. She stood there in her bra and g string as Cristian's hand on her back now moved down to her buttock to stroke and grasp the soft mound in his fingers. He continued his onslaught of kisses on her breasts and neck.

Danika's hands were trying to get his t-shirt off unsuccessfully. He sensed her frustration and stopped briefly to pull the t-shirt over his head. While he did, Danika undid her bra and let it fall to the floor. Cristian gasped and then bent down to suck her nipples into his mouth one at a time. Danika moaned with delight. Trying to lean into his body, she slid her hands inside his jocks and grasped his buttocks. He stopped his sucking and stood more erect, leaning his manhood into her navel. Danika pulled the front of his jocks to release his erection then downwards so his jocks came down for him to step out of. Cristian moved his hand to her crotch and felt the dampness of her arousal. He rubbed the lace fabric to feel her getting wetter. Danika's knees buckled. Picking her up he laid her on the bed.

Continuing his stroking between her legs he pushed the fabric aside and rubbed her clitoris before slipping his fingers into her wet, hot vagina. He felt the pulsing of her orgasm as he moved his fingers rapidly in and out. Danika arched against him, her arms clinging to him as the waves of her orgasm overtook her. Cristian pulled her soaked panties down her legs, kissing her breast and stomach as he went. Danika grasped his erection which made him stop as he doubted he could control himself with her hand rubbing up and down, her finger brushing the tip of his penis. She looked directly into his now gold flecked eyes to let him know she was determined to have him. She lifted one leg up and around his legs and leaned her wetness into him while directing his penis toward her desire.

'I want you inside me,' Danika demanded. Cristian moved his body between her legs, his arms either side of her as he arched up to see her. His erection was touching her wet vagina as she arched up to meet him. He slowly slid into her soft warm embrace and stopped, his buttocks tense as he regained control, trying to make the experience last for them both. Danika however had other ideas as she both arched and pressed her hands on his buttocks. He growled and then was moving in and out rapidly as Danika met every thrust with equal force until he could feel her orgasm starting again. He thrust slower and deeper until she was writhing and let himself release at the same time. They both yelled each other's names on the final thrust.

Cristian lay on top of Danika with his weight still on his elbows. Her legs had relaxed their grip as had her hands until he went to move out and off her. She held him there as another wave of orgasm came over her. He could feel every pulse and slowly rolled on to his back holding her in place. She came with him and was then on her knees sitting on him as her orgasm continued to build. She wriggled around with her head thrown back and he watched the ecstasy moving through her body and face. His hands moved up from her hips to her breast to massage them, pressing her nipples between his fingers and thumbs.

His erection quickly returned. Danika moved up and down, taking the full length inside her. Her hands were on his stomach and she moved one down to where he was inside her, grasping him with her fingers as she pulled up and down. Cristian pulled her down to his chest and held her tight as he released again. Once their breathing had returned to normal he rolled Danika to the side and slipped out of her, both of them shivering at the sensation.

They lay together like that for several minutes before Cristian brushed her face with his hand. Kissing her, he whispered his love for her. Danika returned his kisses and words of adoration as they slowly explored each other's skin with their hands now that the feeling of urgency had passed.

Eventually, Cristian got up and moved to the bathroom to wrap a towel around him to go shut the blinds properly.

'I'll get us some water.' Returning shortly after with two glasses of water, Danika had pulled back the cover and slipped under the sheet. There were several little flowers strewn across the bed and on the floor from her hair. Cristian offered to help her take her hair out. He sat on the bed and Danika sat between his legs as he pulled the remaining flowers out, placing them on the bedside table and then started to undo each of the braids. Usually straight and gleaming black it was now fuller and wavy like a mermaid as he brushed it out between his fingers. He brushed it aside and kissed the back of her neck as he slid his hands around to grasp her breasts. Danika wriggled back to rub his penis with her buttocks making it rise up again.

One hand moved from her breast down to where she was still wet and he pushed his finger in without hesitation. Danika writhed and moaned again. He could feel she was close to orgasm as Danika turned around to sit in his lap and guide him into her. They both sat still for a few seconds then Danika rocked back and forth as she pulled her legs tighter around his back. He nibbled her nipples and then he was kissing her, his tongue moving in and out of her mouth as she rocked until they both released again together, clinging to each other.

Danika

Danika looked past him to the window and Cristian followed her gaze to see that it had become dark outside. With one cheeky last thrust she slipped off him and stood up.

'I have some planets to view tonight remember. Can we get back to this later?' She turned to go and he smacked her lightly on the bottom as she wiggled it at him. She went into the bathroom and turned on the showers, it was a double.

'Not too much later. I think we could both use some energy replacement though,' he replied. He brought their toiletry bags into the bathroom and stepped into the shower with her. They soaped each other up but tried to avoid getting more involved for now, laughing as they each teased one another.

Once dried Danika slipped on a dress only so that she was decent enough to move around if anyone could see her. Cristian pulled on track pants and the t-shirt from earlier. Opening the blinds, Danika went out on to the balcony. The sea breeze was lovely if a little cool. It was quite dark with the waning moon so several stars were visible. Out the back of the villa were lawns that lead down to the water line and in the dim light the outline of a small mooring jetty was visible.

Finding the bag with her candles and incense from the pile of other bags, Danika moved out the back to view the jetty and look up at the sky. The celestial forces were filling her soul. She nearly cried as she had been prepared for her craft to be gone after marrying Cristian. Perhaps it was all a cruel hoax.

She sensed Cristian come out. 'It is beautiful,' he remarked as he looked up at the stars. 'Do you have time to eat, if you want to that is?'

'Yes I'm starving I'll set up and then come in to eat,' she answered.

Cristian kissed her once more, leaving her to fill up her energy from the celestial event. Instead, he went to prepare a meal as Danika set up her rug and candles and incense on the jetty. The location was perfect especially as the other villas appeared empty.

By the time he had dinner ready, Danika was just coming back inside the villa.

'This is lovely, Cristian, thank you for finding it for us.' He was flipping half an omelette on each plate and tipping ready prepared salad next to it. A simple setting on the table with condiments completed the meal.

They ate faster than usual, realising how hungry they both were as they really hadn't eaten all day.

'I could feel the stars. I worried it would be gone,' Danika said.

Cristian looked at her quizzically and asked, 'Wasn't that why we are here?'

'Yes, but I thought maybe I wouldn't because of the curse and myth about not loving or marrying a man. Well I love you, we married and definitely consummated our marriage and I don't feel any different. In a witchy way that is. I definitely feel different,' she clarified. 'Did it feel like the first time for you? I suppose not, you probably have been with lots of women.' Danika didn't think she would ever feel jealous, but there it was all of a sudden.

'Yes and yes.' Danika frowned at his answer. 'Yes, it felt like the first time because it was. The first with you, the first with my imprinted mate and actually the first in a very long time. Yes, I have been with other women when I was much younger but it was more about carnal desire which was disrespectful to the women so I stopped,' he explained. 'And what about you? I'm not your first, am I?'

'No, but I am ashamed to say it was a drunken mistake that I can hardly remember nearly a decade ago. So to me you are my first, especially first werewolf.' She grinned at him when he growled.

'Well not really, I am human. You can't go near me when I change,' Cristian said in a wistful way.

'You do change a little, you know. Your hair gets stiffer and thicker and your eyes change to have gold flecks when you are aroused. Apart from the growling,' Danika informed him. 'It is a huge turn on.'

Danika could sense he had not ever realised that this was now their very special secret.

'I saw you glowing today. Your energy and love was an aura around you, it was so magical and special, I hope you never lose your powers.' Cristian stood up and kissed her before clearing the table. 'So go get some energy so we can burn it off again.'

Getting her medallion, Danika went out to the jetty again using her phone torch. Lighting some candles and incense, she carefully sat in the circle to finish lighting the rest. At first she held her crystals, to clear a spiritual path then started to call to the stars and the planets for energy and guidance. The candle flames flared higher. Cristian watched her from the dark having turned all but one small light off.

Danika chanted a wellbeing chant for them both asking for fertility and the blessing of the universe. As she held her arms up her aura was glowing again. She asked for an answer to reveal itself to release the curse. She could feel a heat in her stomach where Cristian had been and was concerned that had never happened before but she continued. She thanked the universe for guidance and destiny. She had a flash of Cristian hurt and the shock had her stop chanting and yell out.

Cristian

Cristian watched as her beautiful aura of green and blue suddenly turned red. Danika cried out in pain and he was moving towards her instantly, there in a flash and picking her up. Ignoring the candles he kicked over into the water. She clung to him weeping. He took her inside to sit cradling her.

'Are you hurt?' he asked desperately.

'No you are. You may be. I don't know it was awful.' She buried her head in his chest as she hugged him.

'I was watching you as you called to the stars. Your aura was magnificent bright green like your eyes and then blue like when our hands glowed last full moon. Then I could feel your pain here.' He placed his hand below her navel as the aura became red.

'I was drawing the energy from the celestial bodies. It was very potent, as if they were offering more if I asked. So I did. I asked for health, fertility and wellbeing for us both. Then when I asked for an answer to reveal itself I felt a heat here.' She placed her hand over Cristian's, still on her stomach. 'I've never felt anything like that before, it was frightening. I was trying to thank the universe to break the connection when I saw a vision, just a flash of you lying hurt, us hurt. It was so quick and there was a face I didn't recognise but I think you did. Then you had me. Thank you.'

'Perhaps the stars and planets are not happy with us?' Cristian had to voice his fear.

'No, I don't think so, they gave me all I asked. I think they were trying to help, to warn. I want to go out again, not to ask for anything, just to absorb energy, come with me.'

Cristian was sceptical and was not happy that anything could harm her but an idea was coming to him. It seemed a little like his own nightmare experience not that long ago.

'I'm not letting go of you. Do we have to be over the water?' He was looking at her eyes as he held her, feeling her heartbeat and emotions.

'No, not over water but I will get the candles and rug,' she confirmed.

Together they gathered all but those Cristian had knocked into the water and set the rug on the grass closer to the villa with a wider circle. Sitting cross legged opposite each other, Danika took off the medallion and placed it between them, not touching either. She held his hands before she gently called to the stars. Cristian could feel the gravity sway through her and was surprised how benign it felt. She moved their hands closer to the medallion without touching it, still calmly absorbing the energy. They could both feel the negative energy trying to push him away. Danika held his hands harder to keep just above the medallion. It felt like magnets that were in opposition. She slowly moved their hands away then unlinked hands.

'You could feel that, couldn't you?' Danika asked Cristian.

'Yes, I was getting a bit worried when we were hovering over the medallion pushing me away,' he confirmed, staring at it.

'I don't think it is just you, I think it is the link we have and I am positive we will be the answer, the two of us. But there must be another artefact to link to this.' She pointed at the medallion. 'Did you feel the push away like an opposing magnet?'

'We are not going down a path of hunting for artefacts, that's how I ended up with all those evil pieces we just sold off.' Cristian had been doing this for many years and knew it was a dangerous and malevolent path. 'We have to go about this a different way. Not now though. Now we are going to continue our honeymoon and no more spiritual or mystical labyrinth,' Cristian insisted.

'Yes you are right but I am so happy to know this, that 'us' is all meant to be, I am certain.' Despite the seriousness of the night, Cristian could feel Danika's happiness. They gathered up all her pieces and rug and went inside.

After closing the doors and curtains he went to the fridge and pulled out the champagne and strawberries. Pouring two glasses he held up his and toasted, 'To us, for a long, happy and fruitful life.'

Danika chinked her glass against his. 'To us.' Danika opened up her gift of chocolates from Mary. As they drank and reflected, Cristian remembered his camera. Both looked through the shots he and James had taken this morning that seemed longer ago. They flicked through the photos more than once.

'Let's head back up,' Cristian said, collecting the bottle and strawberries to take also. Danika picked up the chocolates and the two glasses, following him up the stairs.

Placing the glasses down for Cristian to refill she pulled the dress off over her head. She looked so different with her hair fluffy and wavy, the bandage still in place. She swayed to imaginary music as she held her glass and sipped. Cristian dipped a strawberry in his champagne and wiped it on one of her breasts to then lick it off again. Danika stepped back as he went to do it again. 'No fair, you too,' she said.

Cristian put his drink and strawberry down and peeled off his clothes. Dipping a strawberry in her drink she did the same to Cristian's stomach. The cold liquid made him suck in his stomach and breath. She tipped some of the champagne over his erection before, looking him in the eyes, she got down on her knees and began to lick off the liquid. Danika looked up at him again and took a mouth full of drink. Without swallowing it she grabbed his shaft and quickly sucked the head into her mouth. The cool of the champagne was as much of a shock as her actions. He couldn't believe the erotic desire that was spilling from Danika into him wanting more. He gently put his hand under her chin and lifted her head away and helped her up. She had such a wicked look on her face as she brushed her hand over him and walked seductively to the bed. The view of her rear swaying was getting too much. She took a large strawberry to her mouth and sucked it like she had sucked him. He took her glass from her, placing it on the bedside table and then poured a little of his own in her navel. Getting on the bed with her, he slowly licked up the liquid that had started to flow towards her already wet nest. He continued to move down, licking and sucking as he went. She was writhing. As an orgasm was building he would stop and blow on the wet trail to cool it down and start again.

She cried out for more, for him to stop, to never stop. She was seemingly delirious, pleading for him to take her. On another gasping plea he took her with one massive thrust. She screamed his name and with her arms flung above her head her hips bucked with the force of her orgasm. He let her have it all without moving and as he felt her convulsions slowing down he started to move slowly in and out, getting faster and stronger, bringing on her orgasm again as he too convulsed.

They lay intertwined, the stickiness of the champagne gluing their torsos together. Cristian pulled out of her making her tremble as the heightened nerves of her clitoris were rubbed. He suggested they shower off the champagne but Danika was making more moves to go again. It was becoming clear to Cristian that she was tipsy. He looked at her pouting lips when he side stepped her grabbing him and asked, 'Do you always react like this with champagne?'

'It's the bubbles. Gets me into trouble. But it doesn't matter now.' It might have made sense to her but Cristian wasn't one for taking advantage of inebriated women, including his wife.

He walked her into the shower and turned it on. 'Come on, help soap my back.' She turned and backed up to him. The temptation was great but so was his respect for her. He did soap her up but then pushed her under the stream of water to wash it off. He washed off the stickiness from himself without letting her grab him again. Once he was satisfied she was clean he turned off the water and wrapped a towel around her and then one around her head as best he could. Cristian directed her back to the bed to wait while he dried and dressed himself.

Back in the bedroom Danika had curled up on the bed and drifted off to sleep. He smiled at the various sides of her he had seen and explored today and decided not to give her champagne again. He picked up the debris of their love making and wiped spilled liquid and discarded berries off the tiles. He took the glasses and bottle down to the kitchen. With a final tidy of the rug and candles, he went back up to make Danika more comfortable out of the wet towels before pulling the cover over her as she slept. He left the light on in the bathroom in case she woke disoriented. Cristian undressed and slipped in next to her, gently kissing her cheek. He laid his hand on her hip and drifted to sleep also.

7

MOTHERS

DANIKA WOKE AND took a little while to orient herself in time and place. She could hear birds and smell the sea. It didn't feel like Sydney though as no traffic. She slid her hand across the sheets under the cover and it felt warm. She sat up and realised she was in the villa and Cristian was not in bed.

Her Cristian, her husband Cristian. She smiled at the thought. Where was he? She was trying to remember the last thing from last night. The memories came flooding back and she put her hands to her cheeks, mortified. She buried her face in the cover in her lap and screamed. *How can I face him? What will he think of me?* She could hear him moving around downstairs. She didn't even know what time it was.

She lifted the cover to see she was naked, well of course, but clean also. Did he shower her? Her hair was not as wavy and felt a little damp so that would be yes. The room looked very tidy and cleaned up, even their pile of bags seemed to be gone. She took a chance, looked in the drawers and found her clothes. She dressed in a fresh skirt and top with underwear and slipped on her sandals that were neatly placed next to the bed. Finally finding a clock, it read 10 am. Good grief, she never slept that late. After going to the bathroom and cleaning her teeth she felt she could finally face him to apologise.

As she came down the stairs Cristian called out.

'Good morning gorgeous, finally awake. Would you like a hot tea?'

'Yes, thank you. Sorry I slept in, did you have plans today?' Danika was not sure what to say to him as she walked over to the counter in the kitchen.

'No, none at all, but walking the beach might be nice. We are here to relax don't you think?' he responded.

Danika took the tea and sipped it, looking into his stunning silver-grey eyes. When he looked back at her she blurted out, 'I'm so sorry, you must be so disappointed in me. I…' He came swiftly around to put his finger on her mouth to stop her.

'You have nothing to apologise for whatsoever. I should apologise for not realising sooner that you were not yourself, I feel like I took advantage of you.' Cristian was serious in his apology she realised, but she snorted a laugh.

'Took advantage? Good grief, the little I remember I threw myself at you in the most suggestive way. You have nothing to apologise for.' She couldn't believe his statement.

'That's the point Danika. "What little you remember" means you were in no state to make decisions.' He was deadly serious. 'So how about we agree no more champagne fuelled bedroom sessions?'

'Agreed, but I don't feel any better, I can't remember much past bringing the drinks and stuff up to the bedroom. Fill me in?' Danika didn't like not knowing.

'Not at the moment. How about we have a late breakfast and go for a walk?'

After their breakfast they walked out along the road towards the sound of the waves. A few photos later with the wind on their faces they walked along the beach picking up a few pieces to look at and place them back down. With a driftwood stick Danika drew patterns in the sand watching the waves wash them away. Then she drew the Triquetra in one line.

'You were very pleased with our spiritual circle last night and I could feel most of it but not so sure what you were happy about in particular.' Cristian watched her drawing more symbols higher above the water line.

'The Triquetra symbol has been in our family as long as we know. The medallion has it and we use it from time to time. My mother has it on her business cards. But it is very common so we didn't give it that much credit of power. But this,' she had drawn a simple representation of the Lleuad Blaidd, 'you told me is your family symbol. I didn't understand exactly what it was and it is hard to see on the medallion as it's very worn. Put the two together and they are our families intertwined over the centuries. We were always meant to meet, the universe decided it.'

'I think the Triquetra symbol was added to the medallion. Because it is scratched into it whereas the Lleuad Blaidd was stamped onto the metal. It is very old, as in centuries, perhaps the first connection between our families,' Cristian agreed.

'Yes, I think it has a twin that we need to find, like two magnets. Not sure how we find it because my family only has this and now the linen list that goes back to Jessica. There must be more somewhere. What about your family?' Danika's words were being muted by the wind.

'I don't think there is anything here in Australia but I will look through what I can back at the estate. It is more likely to be in the Europe side, there are many dozens of them spread over a few countries. Although they must be looking to their future with the threat of war. The only one I have any contact with is my uncle, Robert. He is a bit intense. What is it Danika?' Cristian asked, as if he sensed the tension that came over her at the mention of his uncle.

'I think we should go back to the villa to talk out of the wind. But can we take a photo first?' Danika was smiling but she could tell Cristian felt the barrier she'd put up.

'Of course, for the album.' Cristian took out his phone and, turning into the wind so her hair was clear of her face, he took a picture of them with the beach in the background. They walked back slowly. Danika picked up one shell and put it in her pocket.

Back at the villa they tipped the loose sand from their shoes and brushed off their feet to walk in barefoot. Danika noticed the folded blanket with the remnants of the spiritual circle last night sitting on top she hadn't seen earlier. She took the candles and set them on a plate on the occasional table to light them. She spoke a few words over them as she moved her hands above them. She motioned for them both to sit on the couch.

'That is just to calm the spirits while we talk,' Danika explained. 'They hold the remnants from last night. When I asked you out on the beach about your family you spoke of your uncle and his image flashed in your mind of course.'

'That's who you saw last night, wasn't it?'

'Yes and I think you did also, some other time. Was it a dream? It was such a quick flash of shock, fear and recognition all at once in a split second it is hard to recreate it.' Danika was trying to remember without the fear.

'It was a nightmare that I dismissed before I knew that everything is connected,' Cristian explained. Danika caught a glimpse of the nightmare through their connection.

'Yes, that is a similar image to last night. I'm guessing he is not going to be pleased with our union then. I'm hoping these images are symbolic and not a true premonition.' Danika voiced the fear they both had growing at the imagery.

'I'll never let him hurt you.' Danika watched as his eyes changed darker with the gold flecks and even his features slightly shifted. She grasped his hand and placed her hand behind his head, feeling the hairs stiffening. He looked into her eyes.

'Have you ever changed outside of the lunar cycle?' Danika asked, as she felt him calming.

'No, why, what did you feel?'

'You were changing right then, your eyes and hair and I think your jaw a little. Has this not happened before?' It concerned her if he was unaware of this happening. 'Did you feel it?'

'I have spent my life controlling my emotions. It was drummed into me by my father and before that my grandfather. The aim was always to direct any anger in other ways. I have never felt rage before. When Father died it was more a despair than rage. Perhaps that is a trigger that they were aware of but didn't share the details.' Cristian was shaking his head. 'There is so much I feel that I should have known and no one has bothered to tell me. I want to know everything. Our children are not going to be left in the dark like I was.'

Danika felt his protective anger rising again. The candles were flickering and Danika could feel the last of last night's celestial energy going with them. She knew she had more candles in the van.

'I'm going to get some more candles out of Rainbow. Just in case we want them later for ambiance.' Grabbing the keys to go out to the van Cristian followed, watching her rummaging under the bed for more candles.

'How did you fit in here to sleep?' He was looking sceptically at the bed and all the windows.

'Oh it is easy, and you get used to it. Watch this.' Danika then proceeded to undo and spread the curtains to cover all the windows and block off the front seats. Then she crawled on to the bed and lay down. 'See, all private and cosy. Plenty of room for one anyway.' She patted the bed. Cristian got in the van properly and close the door. He was too tall to stand up completely. 'Well that is a problem for you I guess.' He pulled the curtain across and then sat on the bed looking around at the floral curtains.

'It feels like a floral coffin.' He grinned at her.

'Don't be unkind, Rainbow has been my companion for many happy months.' Danika pretend punched his arm. He lay down next to her but his feet hung over the edge.

'We could only do this if we are spooned against one another, I don't think I can even turn over.' He was showing her what he meant and she was laughing as he tickled her, the tickling soon changing to more of an exploration.

Hours later they were redressing and getting the van tidy again before bringing the candles back into the villa. The light was fading as a few clouds were building up to block out the late sun. Cristian checked the weather forecast. 'Looks like we may have rain overnight, so no stars and planet watching I think. Plenty of games in that cabinet in the lounge to choose or there is always bedroom games.'

Later that night once they had finished dinner they settled in for a game of cards. Their previous conversation about family had become the elephant in the room, Danika thought with a grin at the image of one standing in a corner.

Cristian finished clearing away the plates and pans into the dishwasher then turned to her and asked, 'Why are you thinking about an elephant?'

'I can't believe how in tune you are now, is that part of the legacy?' Danika asked looking at him intently.

'I guess it is. My parents neglected to share any of that with me and it wasn't clear in my father's journal. I have no idea what the others experience. You didn't answer my question.'

'Oh, I was thinking that not talking about our families was the elephant in the room. But here we are talking about them so the elephant can toddle off.'

'Robert has said he is coming to Australia after the next lunar cycle,' Cristian told her. Danika's fear spiked immediately.

'How long have you known that?'

'A few days, I didn't want to spoil our wedding day and actually had not thought about him until today. As I have said we have a strained relationship,' Cristian admitted.

'Can you explain to me how many there are in your family?' Danika asked, trying to get an understanding of the family dynamics.

Cristian walked over to the table and, using the pack of cards, placed two kings with queens next to them, a jack for one king and two jacks under the other, then two jokers and ones under the jacks. Then an ace above them all.

'The ace is my grandfather, kings are my father and Robert, jack is me. Those jacks are Robert's sons and those jokers are their sons and think one has some kids. Robert is older than my father and a bit more prolific.'

'So you have two cousins and two second cousins? I'm trying to see where the dozens come from?' Danika couldn't see what he had meant before.

'That's because that is only my grandfather's line. There were many others before, we were just the last on the English line and Grandfather chose Australia. All the others moved to European countries decades, some centuries, ago. I'm not sure how many, only a few have a second son though. Most are one son families,' he explained further.

'Okay, so you are only replacing yourself unless you have a second son. Are there no daughters ever?' Danika was trying to work out how many there could be.

'None that survive as far as I know. That is another aspect of the legacy slash curse,' Cristian stated. 'What about your blood line?'

'Just me, my mother isn't having more children. All the women only have one. I don't know why,' Danika explained. 'If I don't have children the line dies. Why is your uncle so adamant about who and when you marry? What is your uncle so afraid of if you didn't marry? There must be something he knows. Does he have the history or relics of your past?' Danika was trying to form an idea.

'Possibly, he is living in the castle of one of the ancestors from a couple of hundred years ago. What were you thinking? The twin to the medallion perhaps? Problem is we can't ask him outright and I think he is very powerful within the family.'

'Do you have any connection with the extended family? Someone who you could trust?' Danika felt that this was the correct direction.

'I'll have to check out a few things. I think my mother is a possible source of information. Are you still alright to visit her this weekend?'

The idea of meeting Cristian's mother reminded Danika that they needed to also meet hers, which made Danika tense.

'Yes actually, I am looking forward to it in a slightly terrified way,' Danika admitted. Cristian laughed out loud. 'I am more fearful of talking to my mother because I feel I have to tell her first on a timeline basis, just in case they ever talk to each other. And besides, I can't lie.'

'When do you have to call her?'

'Tomorrow because she will be busy getting ready for the weekend market trade and I can keep the conversation brief.' Danika put her hands to her cheeks, feeling their heat and knowing she was blushing. 'I can't believe I am avoiding my own mother.'

Danika got up and walked to the window, it was dark now outside and when she opened the door slightly she could smell rain. She walked outside to the edge of the patio and could see the fine rain gleaming in the light. She reached out her hands so that they were getting damp and then held them to her face. She repeated that a couple more times as well as holding them to her throat and chest.

Cristian had been watching her and Danika heard his thoughts wondering why she didn't just stand in the rain.

'Because I don't want to get my clothes wet,' Danika called over her shoulder.

Cristian smiled at her response to his non-question. She felt his love and awe, heard the way his thoughts turned to feeling grateful for her. She moved to him quickly, sliding into his arms and kissing him. 'I love you too,' she said between kisses. He picked her up in his arms and walked out into the rain making her squeal with the cold and then laugh as he spun around a few times before going back under the cover of the balcony.

'Tomorrow we are going shopping,' he announced.

'We are? For what? More gallery items?' Danika was sceptical.

'No, we are shopping for the most ridiculous tourist mementoes we can find to give to people. Once they know it was our honeymoon they will have to keep them.' His wicked grin had her very excited at letting her silly side out.

'I love those souvenirs but could never justify the expense, oh goody.' Danika jumped around like a child, not entirely pretending. 'We have to go to lots of shops to share the love around.'

'Sure thing, as many as you like.'

Danika moved over to the hamper and started pulling bits out to look at them. 'Oh I think this should have been in the fridge.' She held up a little pot of pate.

'Pate, Peter that's his name,' Cristian said suddenly. 'My cousin, dozens of times removed Peter. They sort of pronounce it Pater. I spoke to him a long time ago when my father died, he was a bit scathing of the family back then not sure now.'

'That's great, I hope you can contact him when we get back, I'm still throwing this out though.' Danika dumped the pot of pate in the bin.

Cristian

Changing into dry clothes, the sound of music playing downstairs caught Cristian's attention. When he re-entered the living space there was only one light on over the table and several candles burning with the light background music playing. Danika had cards on the table set up for poker and a couple of sodas poured beside the remains of the box of chocolates and the box of matches.

'I found the CD player and a few discs. I poured us some sodas if you want.' Danika seemed to be skirting something. She was shuffling the cards again as Cristian sat down opposite her.

'I was thinking we could use these matches as chips and chocolates as a prize for winning hands. Loser takes off an item of clothes,' Danika said it all so innocently.

'Oh really. So strip poker then? Are we playing draw or hold 'em?' Cristian smiled at Danika's puzzled look. 'Have you played poker before?'

'Sort of, a long time ago. You have to get two of a kind or something like that.'

'Yes, something like that. More of the same is good or a run of same cards like jack, queen, king works also. I'm sure you will pick it up as we go.' Cristian sensed she had not been serious about winning at first. 'We can play a practice hand first.'

It didn't take long for Danika's hidden competitive side to emerge, Cristian noted, finding it very amusing. She definitely did not have a poker face though, with her grinning and frowning as the play went on. A few hands in and Cristian was sitting in his jeans with his t-shirt and socks discarded. Danika had the hint of chocolate around her lips and only her jacket and a top in the pile. She still had a camisole and skirt and whatever other layer she had pulled on while upstairs.

'I believe this game may have been loaded to your advantage wifey,' Cristian observed as he looked at his cards and made a bet. He won the hand and she stood up and slipped off her skirt to show black lace knickers, adding it to the pile before sitting down again.

'Are you blocking your thoughts?' Danika looked him in the eye.

'That's your trick not mine I just focus on the cards. Maybe not my cards but…' He left the sentence unfinished as he grinned at her.

Danika made a pretend annoyed face at him and dealt the hand again as she watched him slowly eating a chocolate.

Danika lost again and slowly pulled the camisole over her head to reveal the matching black bra. Just then the music stopped so she went over to choose another CD of classical music. Cristian had watched her deliberately swaying her hips as she walked across the room to the CD player. Her choice of classical music was a surprise.

Cristian shuffled and dealt the cards as he struggled to concentrate when he could see Danika wriggling about as she reached over to place matches in the pile. He felt himself stiffen. He lost the hand. Standing up, he undid his belt and took off his jeans carefully, folding them before placing them on top of the other clothes. His erection was obvious.

Danika had been about to eat a chocolate but now just stared at him. Her hands were shaking slightly as she shuffled and dealt the hand. Cristian could feel Danika thought she had a great hand and could see her hands shaking but he won with a flush.

Danika stood up to undo her bra but her fingers were trembling with the intensity of excitement. Cristian came around to help her undo her bra. Then he lifted her up to sit on the table and that was the end to the card game. Kissing, they each tasted the chocolates they had eaten. The music playing was complicated yet beautiful and was building to a crescendo. Cristian picked Danika up with her legs wrapped around him and walked over to the couch. They moved to the music and matched their love making to the beat until the crescendo. Lying in each other's arms as their breathing returned to normal, Cristian pulled the throw rug that was draped across the couch over them as they lay quietly listening to the rest of the CD until the end. Cristian rose moving around the room blowing out the candles and turning off the light as Danika watched, until they both walked up the stairs naked to the bedroom.

The next morning, Cristian came down with his hair still a little wet to see Danika making breakfast. He was holding a fresh bandage. 'Did you mean to put this on? Would you like a hand with it?' Danika had been replacing the bandage over her tattoo several times as needed to prevent Cristian getting a nasty shock.

'No, I am going to try leaving it off as long as possible. They are starting to affect my skin.' She lifted her top to show him the red mark forming around the tattoo. 'I'll talk to Selene about it this evening when I call,' Danika explained.

It upset him that he had not sensed her discomfort and that she had not shared it with him during the last two days, too preoccupied with his own desires and needs.

'My desires and needs also Cristian, don't blame yourself,' Danika said, sensing his thoughts.

'Not fair Danika, you have been closing off your thoughts and then you read mine like a book. Please don't hide your health and needs from me.' Cristian gently chastised her as he pulled her into a hug.

'You're right, I'm sorry I'm not used to sharing every tiny bit of myself with anyone,' Danika clarified.

'Same for me. Now let's work out where we are going first.' Cristian had the information book left in the accommodation spread out to see what was in the town or region.

The rest of the day they spent as tourists. Taking photos of the beautiful scenery and walking from shop to shop browsing and buying fun souvenir pieces. Cristian booked them in for dinner at the tavern that night. Danika needed to call her mother before then and suggested they went back to the villa for her to change for the evening and call Selene. Cristian could feel her tension rising. Once they were inside with their purchases Cristian suggested she make it a video call as that would be much more personal. Danika explained she was not sure she could do that on her phone.

'Use mine. Just send her a warning text first or she will think it is a scam from an unknown number.' They sat on the couch as Danika sent the text message. Selene responded and they called her. Danika made sure to only show her face at first.

'Hi, Mum. How are you?' Danika could not hide the nervousness in her voice.

'I'm good, busy for tomorrow as usual. How is the trip going? I haven't heard from you for a while.' Selene's phrasing suggested she was suspicious of the call.

'Really good. I want you to meet someone.' Danika expanded the view out to include Cristian sitting next to her. 'This is Cristian.'

'Hello Selene, I'm pleased to meet you.' Cristian put on his winning smile. Selene did not say anything yet so Danika continued.

'Mother, Cristian and I are married. We married two days ago in Sydney.' Selene's expression was dead pan, as if she was staring at nothing.

'Danika we need to talk in private,' Selene said very stiffly.

'No, Mother, no private talks. We love each other, we are married and I am now living and working in Sydney,' Danika said forcefully. 'We would prefer your acceptance but are continuing our lives even if you don't, you just won't see us again.' Cristian held Danika's shaking hand.

'I hope you know what you are doing. Cristian, are you aware of Danika's history?' The way Selene said that as if it was something to be ashamed of had his hackles rising in defence of her. Danika now squeezed his hand.

'Selene, I am well aware of Danika's amazing personality and skills. We share everything and she knows my life and has accepted me also.' Cristian was trying to keep his speech tempered.

'Are you not travelling anymore if you are working? I thought you were tracing our family history.' Selene was obviously still not accepting what they were saying.

'Yes, we will be investigating that and Cristian's own family. I am working in Cristian's art gallery as a consultant. We are free to move around as we need to. We plan to come to South Australia at some point.' This was new information to Cristian but he fully supported it and rubbed his thumb on her hand to let her know.

'I don't think you have a future in this relationship and you will realise that as you investigate your history. I can't accept what you have done Danika, I don't think you understand the implications either Cristian.' Selene was visibly angry at this point.

'You are wrong, Selene. We were destined to be together to break the curse and the prophecy from our ancestors and we are going to do it together with or without your help.' Cristian was not going to be polite and sidestep their lives to her anymore. He saw the shock on her face. 'Danika and I will be raising a family together and we would be pleased if you would want to be a part of that.'

'I don't want to discuss this anymore. Goodbye.' Selene broke the connection. Cristian could feel the tight emotions draining from Danika as she started crying. He pulled her into his arms and let her sob on his shoulder. Cristian could sense the tears were not sadness but more a relief.

'That could have been so much worse. You shocked her but I think she will come round once she thinks about it.' Danika wiped her eyes and smiled at him. 'One down, two to go.' Then she started laughing.

'I think you may want to wash your face before we go out.' Looking at her tear-stained face he kissed her wet cheek.

When Danika still had not returned downstairs a short while later, Cristian went up to find her. She was trying to navigate the necklace clasp with all her hair in the way as Cristian came looking for her. He took over the task. Pushing her hair to one side, he kissed her neck and then turned her back to look in the mirror.

'You are stunning. Everyone will be amazed how I managed to have you marry me.'

'Thank you for everything. You managed that conversation so well.' Danika turned back around and stood on toes to kiss him.

'Now let's go to dinner, I'm famished. If I don't get food I'll start eating you.' Cristian raised his eyebrows as he looked at her pointedly.

'Now that's all I'm going to think of over dinner.' Danika punched his arm.

'I hope so.'

At the tavern, Cristian was right. Everyone was looking at Danika. He hadn't thought it was possible but she seemed to be getting more beautiful with every day.

After deciding on the meal and ordering a drink, Danika only wanting water, they glanced around them, several people averted their gaze.

'I told you everyone would be looking at you,' Cristian told her.

'It's the bling. You have no idea how many of the woman are staring at you.' He felt an intense surge of love through their connection. He picked up her hand and kissed it.

'By the way, I messaged my mother that I was coming home tomorrow for dinner with a lady guest. She acknowledged the message and asked dietary needs. I said not red meat. I would think that she and the staff will now be in a tizz,' he explained.

'Oh why did you say that, I do eat meat sometimes? Don't you have guests at the estate often?' Danika asked.

'No, Robert has been the only visitor since Father died. Our diet is usually very heavily rare red meat including home grown venison.' Cristian watched as Danika put her hand to her mouth. 'See what I mean, best to give you some distance from that for now.' She nodded.

'Is it alright for us to stay there, as a couple I mean?'

'I have my own wing of several rooms so yes we will be fine. When we get back to the apartment we can change cars and wardrobe if that is agreeable with you,' Cristian asked just as the first course arrived. Danika fell into a silence and Cristian detected a brief glimpse of her feelings.

'Are you missing home?'

'No, not really. I hadn't lived there properly for several years but I underestimated how beautiful it is. The property is in the Adelaide Hills, many acres that have been in the family for as long as anyone knows. The house is in a shocking state though. A patchwork of generations of ideas. My mother has lived there alone since I moved out so she is very defensive anytime I mentioned maintenance and so on.'

'Some time we will be able to visit and win your mother over and perhaps help stabilise it for the future. We can remind her little feet will be running there,' Cristian reminded her.

Danika looked like she was going to cry. 'Don't do that, those men will think I upset you and will be defending your honour.' Cristian nodded towards the men at the bar making Danika laugh and the tears abated.

The waitress refilled their glasses before returning with their meals. Cristian had a huge, rare steak, and Danika a chicken caesar salad.

'You've missed big steaks since we have been together, haven't you? And what about running. You said you need to do that also.' Danika's brows expressed her worry.

'I have missed meat and runs before depending on where I was, I am looking after my needs. But I probably will run at the estate. Are you going to be able to be without your chants for a couple of days?' Cristian suspected she would not use them at the estate out of respect.

'I'm never far from the energy of the universe so it will be fine,' Danika clarified.

The waitress came over and asked if their meals were alright. 'Is this a special occasion?'

Cristian replied for them both as he grasped Danika's hand, looking into her eyes before answering. 'Our honeymoon, we have enjoyed looking around this delightful area.'

'Congratulations, I love your jewellery.' The waitress directed her comment to Danika.

'Thank you.' Danika pulled her gaze away from Cristian to look at the waitress.

Shortly after the waitress returned with a large chocolate and strawberry dessert with two spoons to their table and explained, 'Compliments of the chef for your honeymoon.'

'How lovely. Please thank everyone for a wonderful meal.'

Ready to leave Cristian went to pay and a couple of the men at the bar congratulated him and shook his hand. Back at the table he pulled Danika's chair out and helped her with her jacket, As they left some of the other diners cheered them out.

'Did you pay them to do that?' Danika joked outside.

'No but I did leave them a big tip.' Cristian helped her into Rainbow and as they drove off they both laughed till they nearly cried. What a contrast to everything else her jewellery was worth more than Rainbow.

Cristian was out on the balcony although it was quite cool with a row of candles and incense on foil to stop the mess. Danika's rug was laid out with cushions, ready for her. Danika joined him, turning off the light and taking off her jewellery and outer clothes before coming out in her underwear to sit on a cushion. She began a chant and a wave of warmth rushed over them. He took off most of his clothes also, relying on her power to keep them warm.

Sitting opposite one another as Danika continued to call the power of the universe down to them and through the flames, she started to move her hands over Cristian's knees and legs then up his arms. Cristian was doing the same to her. He could see the red marks on her side where the bandage had been over the tattoo. Danika rose up on her knees and encouraged Cristian to do the same. Their body warmth felt by them both. Even as they touched she continued to chant. The slow rub of her hands over his skin was very erotic. He was careful not to touch her side as he rubbed his hands over her. They hugged and kissed for quite some time until he wanted to take her inside.

Instead Danika pulled him down on the cushions as they continued their exploration of each other with feather light fingers including through their hair and across their face. Danika rolled on top of him and lay there without moving. Still she chanted quiet words. He felt warm all over as she slowly slid him into her. He wasn't sure how she managed that but it felt amazing. She leaned back as she brought her legs either side, bringing him into a sitting position. They each had bent knees. She sat very still and continued to chant. They were completely joined as one, skin to skin, thoughts as one calm yet euphoric.

She stopped chanting and just said one word: 'Now.'

His mind and body felt like they were exploding as one. He clung to her for support until the convulsions subsided. They sat still, joined for a long time as the candles burned out and the cold started to touch them. Carefully with her hands on his shoulders Danika stood straight up. The rush of cool air on their wet bodies was invigorating. She walked inside and Cristian followed, taking her to bed.

Cristian woke at first light with Danika nestled into him, her back to his front spooning with his leg over hers. Despite desire already aroused he thought they needed to move or they would be late. Cristian kissed her and went into the bathroom to shower.

They had been alone for two days but now Danika noticed someone walking from the next villa. Cristian came out of the bathroom when finished to see Danika standing naked at the window peering past the curtain.

'Are you contemplating flashing that person?' Danika jumped at his words, she was so focused on looking outside.

'You scared me,' she said as she turned around with her clothes in her hand. 'No, I was just looking at what we need to clean up.'

'I'll do it, you had better get dressed before I can't control myself,' Cristian responded at the sight of her.

She snuck past him towards the bathroom to quickly shower and dress.

'Danika focus on something else,' Cristian called to her, still sensing the direction of her thoughts about their last love making.

'Sorry.'

Danika

The trip back to Sydney was much more leisurely with an earlier start and not sexually driven. Stopping briefly for breakfast takeaway, they were able to look around more at the scenery which was beautiful apart from the traffic and suburbs as they got closer to the city. Danika was surprised how keen she was to get back to the city and was thinking about the event next week which she was really looking forward to. Finally, they pulled into the underground car park four hours later.

It took a couple of trips to unload Rainbow and they were standing looking at the piles of bags on the lounge floor. Danika picked up the souvenir bags to spread them on the table to find the ones for Elizabeth and the staff. Cristian was already taking clothes to the laundry and grabbed Danika's bags to put them in his bedroom. Danika turned to see him do that and a little thrill went through her. She followed him down to his room.

'I thought you might want your things in here now,' Cristian suggested.

'I hadn't thought about it to be honest, but yes if there is room I would really like that,' Danika replied smiling. Cristian showed her half the wardrobe was empty and he had a few drawers available as well.

'I'll go get the rest so I can work out what to take for the weekend.' Danika quickly walked to the room she had been using for the last week.

When they had finished repacking their bags, Cristian hugged her. 'Are you okay with us rushing off as soon as we are back?'

'Absolutely. Your mother needs to meet me. Meet us as a couple and hopefully she will be able to give us some guidance also.' Danika hugged him back. 'I won't lie, I am a bit nervous about making the right impression. I am still coming to terms with living with wealth.'

Danika could feel his surprise. 'I didn't mean to intimidate you. It is just the way we live.'

'I know, I understand. But my life has always been frugal and living from one week to the next which I am very used to so I am not looking for sympathy. I have spent the last week seeing what money can buy and not in a material way. It buys speed as in no waiting and people pleased to help, to give their time when money is not an issue. It is just different. I will still love going to op shops.' Danika was trying to explain her nerves.

'I would not want you any other way and having watched you work last weekend there was more than money involved. You have the flare for whatever you put your mind to including the event next week. I love everything about you.' Cristian kissed her lightly. 'Are we ready to go now?'

'Yes definitely. I'll take the prices off the gifts on the way. Don't want to be rude.' Danika laughed as they gathered everything to make one trip down to the car. 'How long will it take to get there?'

'About an hour if there are no delays. So hopefully just after three, time to orient yourself before dinner,' Cristian confirmed.

Cristian

Danika was settled in the car with the souvenirs on her lap with gift bags. Cristian drove the Martin down roads he had many times but this time it felt very different with Danika by his side. She was busy pulling off stickers and making sure each one went in the correct bag before placing them behind her and focussing on the road. As they slowed down in front of the estate large metal gate Cristian pushed the remote gate opener.

'Hollingrove. Is that name significant?' Danika asked. Danika pointed out the name on one of the side pillars.

'Yes, it was the name of the manor that belonged to the family in England that Grandfather sold to come here.' Cristian had never really thought that much about it before.

'How long did your family own the manor?' Danika asked.

'Over four hundred years, I believe. They had other estates in Wales that were older I think. Not something I bothered to find out about because we live here.' He could sense from Danika that he may have to be bothered about it.

Cristian drove the car slowly through the gates and up the drive so that Danika could take in as much as possible before he pulled around into the garage. 'I'll get Ben to bring our bags to my rooms. Just grab what you need for now.' Danika had her tote bag and the souvenirs as they left the garage and entered through the main foyer of the house. Ben was there to meet them. Cristian asked him to get their bags from the car and take them to his rooms. 'Ben, this is Danika, our guest for the weekend.'

'Please to meet you, Miss. Your mother asked me to tell you she is in the sitting room.' Ben bowed to them.

Danika looked at Cristian when Ben bowed. As they walked through the foyer to the sitting room he informed Danika that Ben didn't normally bow.

Cristian held the door open so they could both go through. His mother was sitting in an armchair near the fireplace. She stood as they entered. 'Hello, Cristian, and who is this?'

'Mother may I introduce Danika. My wife.' Cristian expected his mother to be shocked but not to stare for a long time. 'Mother, you're staring. Did you hear me?'

'Hello, Mrs Blakesley, I'm Danika. I'm very pleased to meet you.' Danika looked at Cristian who touched his mother on the arm to break her uncomfortable stare.

'Green eyes. Oh my please forgive my rudeness, Cristian you should have warned me. Please call me Elizabeth, my dear.' Elizabeth held out her hand to Danika. As they clasped hands Elizabeth looked into her eyes again. 'We have much to talk about.' She sat down.

'Please sit. Not you Cristian, I haven't forgiven you yet. Why did

you keep this a secret? And for how long have you kept it a secret?'
Elizabeth could not stop staring at Danika who was trying to smile.
Cristian could feel her sending calming vibes to Elizabeth.

'We met at a winery when I was there a few weeks ago. Then again
in Sydney after the cycle. It was love at first sight as you would know.
We married on Wednesday and now we are here.' Cristian gave her
the short version.

'I see. Well, you still could have warned me. I could have helped.'
Elizabeth was thinking about her own wedding rushed with few
people there.

'We have pictures if you would like to look at them, only on the
phone screen though for now,' Danika offered, holding her hand out
for Cristian's phone. Kneeling next to her, Danika showed Elizabeth
the photos. For a few minutes the two of them talked about the dress,
his suit, the flowers and her hair just like any two women would over
a wedding. Then his mother noticed the rings.

'They are exquisite, did you pick them Cristian?'

'We picked them together, Elizabeth. There is an earring and
necklace set that matches,' Danika explained. Elizabeth noticed
Cristian's ring also.

'Show me what you have there,' Elizabeth demanded. 'How is that
going to work for you?'

Cristian walked over to his mother and showed her his ring. 'I
have a matching chain to keep it safe when I need to.' He slipped the
chain out from his shirt to show her.

'Alright, you can sit,' Elizabeth allowed. 'But I am still not happy
with you. Don't tell Robert until we can be sure.'

'Sure of what, Mother?' Cristian looked at his mother who was
now holding Danika's hand.

'We never had the chance to tell you and I have not been myself for
a long while. There is a prophecy that the single men can never marry
a green-eyed girl. Your father and grandfather thought it was just a
scary story. But Robert, now he is different. He believes all the myths

and lords it over everyone,' Elizabeth said, still holding Danika's hand as if it was a lifeline.

'Danika and I are trying to find out about the prophecy and the curse,' Cristian started to explain, which had his mother's attention. 'Danika's family also has a prophecy and curse. We think they are linked.'

'I have some documents and journals that you may both be interested in reading from your grandfather, Cristian. But for now I think you should help your wife to become accustomed to her new home.'

Danika shook her head slightly as he was about to tell his mother they were not staying.

'That would be very helpful, Mother. I will show Danika around. Starting with Ann who will be eagerly awaiting no doubt.' Cristian stood and went over to his mother to give her a kiss on the cheek.

'Elizabeth, Cristian picked this souvenir of our honeymoon for you.' Danika held out a little paper gift bag. Inside was a snow dome sort of ornament with a photo of the inlet at the back and a floating dolphin inside, bobbing on imaginary waves. It had a message 'Greetings from Sussex Inlet'. Cristian almost winced at her as she had done all the gift picking.

'Very thoughtful of you, Son. It will have pride of place in my rooms.' Elizabeth watched as the dolphin moved as she tipped it. They all smiled at the joke.

Cristian showed Danika out of the sitting room and past the library and dining room which he briefly opened the doors to show her.

Next he took her to the kitchen to meet Ann. As they walked in, both Ben and Mark the groundsman stopped talking.

'Good, you are all here, that makes it easier to introduce you to Danika, my wife.' Cristian enjoyed saying that as Danika stepped forward to hold out her hand when Cristian introduced her to each of them.

They were very polite to not stare for too long at her eyes or her rings, a sign of their competence as staff. Danika was smiling broadly as she said how pleased she was to meet them. She handed them each a gift bag to express how happy they were to all be part of the family so to speak. The three were quite taken aback, clearly not expecting gifts.

'From our honeymoon at Sussex Inlet,' Danika explained. Ann's was a large fridge magnet of a psychedelic pattern with a message 'We went crazy at Sussex Inlet'. She walked over and placed it in the centre of the fridge door which otherwise was blank. Ben's gift was a nodding silly fluffy bird over a glass that you put water in to make it nod with a similar message and Mark's was another magnet on a piece of wood with a cartoon fisherman and fish looking happy to be caught. They said their thanks and laughed at the gifts as Danika and Cristian had hoped.

Ann apologised that Master Cristian had not given them much notice or explanation and she hoped her stay would be pleasant. Also that dinner would be at six. Cristian then continued to show Danika around some more areas, including pointing towards the back of the house to where the staff area and utilities were without going that way.

'Do the staff live here?'

'Yes and no. They have rooms for themselves if they chose to stay but they also have their own homes to go to. They usually have weekends off, particularly Sunday.'

'Oh no, we have interrupted their family time coming on a weekend,' Danika said with concern.

'Believe me, they all couldn't wait to meet you. Besides, they will have plenty of other days off instead, we like to keep them happy to work here,' Cristian explained.

Back out in the foyer he motioned towards the north wing as the area where his mother lived downstairs. Cristian guided Danika up the central staircase that dominated the foyer to the next floor.

'This is the south wing where we have our rooms in. The north wing upstairs is not used except at the back where Ben has his room. The sitting room and study at the front, then this is the bedroom.' Cristian noted that Ann must have instructed Ben to make a few quick changes while they were speaking to his mother. His normally male dominant room now had a different, less masculine, cover and more pillows. Flowers filled the vases and, when he looked in his wardrobe, sure enough a space had been made for Danika's clothes.

'That was lovely and thoughtful of them to change things. Is that fine with you?' Danika asked, clearly picking up on the changes as well.

'These are our rooms now, so change whatever you like. Except no floral please.' Cristian really felt like he wanted to throw her on the bed and block out the world.

He looked at her as the intense feeling came over him. Danika moved to him and said, 'Tonight we can, but for now we need to unpack and you need to show me a bit more.' He felt her sending calming thoughts. 'There is a lot of testosterone in here, Cristian, you are tapping into it. Shall we move to another room?'

He nodded and they went on to the next area of more bedrooms and bathrooms. He pointed to Ben's rooms and then back to the unused area. Opening the double doors of the very large room, he turned on the lights to show that it had a small stage in the corner. It smelled very musty and old, the room dark as the curtains were closed.

'When was this last used?' Danika enquired.

'My parents wedding, I think, or maybe something after that but before I have memories. It has a small kitchen and bar area through that door and another bedroom unused except when Robert visits.'

'Is there an attic?' Danika asked.

'Yes but I don't think anything is stored there. Can you feel anything?' Cristian had been pleased that Danika had not felt anything malevolent when she entered his home.

'No, just checking.' She smiled at him. 'I'm pleased too, I like your home.' They moved back towards his rooms.

'Have these always been your rooms?'

'Our rooms now, but no, they were my grandfathers until he died and then when I was branching out into business I moved in here from down the hall. I didn't change much, just the bed, so his personality is in everything.' Cristian could sense Danika's apprehension and that she was trying to hide it.

'In here there is a nice view of the gardens and forest I will show you tomorrow.' Cristian guided her to his sitting room used as a study.

Danika was looking around the room and touching pieces as she made her way to the window.

'Both your grandfather and father stood in here as they mourned by themselves. Not just the losses of people but also the loss of freedom because of the legacy, their curse. This room is quite sad.' Danika had lost her smile and wandered out of the room to the balcony doors. 'Do these open?'

'They should.' Cristian turned the locks and opened the doors with a push. 'They get the full force of the weather, I think they need some maintenance.' Cristian was looking at the peeling paint on the outside. There was evidence of moss on the stone paving. Danika stood and breathed the chilling air as it faced east.

'I like this balcony. I could sit out here at night to enjoy the stars and moon.' Danika held her hands out.

Cristian was very pleased to hear Danika talking about living here. He had become worried at her reaction to their rooms. 'Would you like to help redecorate our rooms? We can move furniture into other rooms and get new or you may like pieces from other rooms. It is up to you.'

'Are you sure? You have known me for five minutes so to speak and now you are suggesting changing decades of your history.'

'My mother changed everything in their wing once she was here so she will probably expect it and will be happy if you are,' Cristian said, sensing Danika's thoughts fretting over his mother's approval. Cristian moved to stand behind her and hugged her as they watched the light fading, the mountains casting a shadow even though the sun had not set.

'We had better change for dinner I think. Ann will be keen to see if you like her food,' Cristian elaborated.

'Is it formal or neat casual?'

'As it is a special dinner perhaps a bit more formal. Are you alright with that? It isn't a rule, you can do your own thing.' Cristian did not want her to feel ill at ease.

'Okay, let's do this. I need your help though.' Danika pulled out the purple dress with the ribbons that had tangled after the gallery showing.

Just before six o'clock Cristian in a suit walked down the stairs with Danika on his arm wearing the purple dress with the emerald and diamond jewellery. Her hair was partly up but her back was not bare this time. Danika had one of Cristian's black kerchiefs tucked in and held in place by the ribbons tied tight. It looked like it was meant to be there and was more modest.

Elizabeth was coming from her rooms as they were coming down the stairs. 'Is that the necklace you spoke of Danika? It is stunning, as are you.'

'Thank you, yes it is,' Danika replied. 'Your dress is lovely, Elizabeth, the colour matches your blue eyes.'

'It is nice to have another lady in the house. Ann is wonderful but it is not quite the same.' Danika had felt her pride and then pleasure at the compliment.

Once in the dining room Cristian helped his mother sit before helping Danika. The table was set for three but still close together at one end. Ben came in to offer wine to everyone. Danika declined and asked if there was any soda water perhaps. Ben was quick to retrieve some from the small bar fridge in the corner.

'Not a wine drinker my dear?' Elizabeth asked Danika as they ate the first course.

'I have been known to drink it on occasion but recently had an experience that I don't want to repeat,' Danika said as she licked sauce from her fingers. Cristian grinned at her, which Danika noticed, switching instead to wiping her fingers on her napkin.

'Mother, Danika and I were discussing redecorating the south wing. At least our rooms, what are your thoughts?' Cristian just threw it out there and now Danika felt under scrutiny.

'Very good plan. It hasn't been changed since the house was built back in 1955. Except your bed I think Cristian but that must be twenty years ago so definitely about time. You must come visit my rooms in the north wing Danika, it might give you some ideas. Mind you, that was a few decades ago since I did a makeover.' Elizabeth seemed interested in any new changes. 'Actually we should sell off some of those big pieces up there rather than store them. Cristian told me that you have been consulting with him in the gallery. Do you have experience in that field?' Elizabeth enquired as Ben removed their plates.

'Actually no, I hadn't, but it seems I might have a knack for it,' Danika replied.

'Excellent, I never liked those dreary pieces you had filled the gallery with Cristian. That was why I stopped going in,' Elizabeth stated. 'I am keen to see the new collection. Are you responsible for it Danika?'

'Why didn't anyone tell me about their thoughts on the artefacts? Thankfully, Danika did. Yes, Danika bought or selected most of the pieces. Some were from the Walton's, do you remember them, Mother?'

'Yes, I remember them. It was awful when her husband became ill just before,' Elizabeth paused not mentioning his father's passing.

'Mrs Walton was selling off everything in the house and we were able to talk to her before the sale. She said to pass on her apologies for your loss back then. Mr Walton has passed also,' Cristian continued. 'Danika has invited her and a few select others to a private showing the night before we open the new collection. Would you like to come then also?'

'Thank you, that is very sympathetic of you, Danika.' Elizabeth reached across until she could touch her hand. 'I'm not good in crowds anymore.'

Ben brought in the next course he announced as baked salmon, before serving them the meal on the table with a selection of both vegetables and salad.

'I think Ann is cracking out her best recipes tonight. I've never heard them announced before.' Cristian was finding it very amusing.

'Behave yourself, Cristian. Ann has been stifled by our poor diet,' Elizabeth admonished him.

'I thought it would be nice to show Danika around the estate tomorrow. Perhaps we can do that early and then Danika can visit you in your rooms after,' Cristian suggested.

'What about you, Danika, is that what you would like to do?' Elizabeth asked her directly.

'I'm pretty open to anything actually, I'm on a fairly steep learning curve here. I would like to talk to you about our plans tomorrow though. I saw the ballroom upstairs this afternoon, it is quite the party area. I suppose it was a nice place to dance once.'

'Our family by nature does not encourage visitors but occasionally in the past we held events. My wedding was small but festive and we used it then. The last time was for the welcoming of Cristian into the family. Others would do that at a christening but we don't share that belief so it was a party of welcome. Many more turned up for that as we had time to send invitations.' Elizabeth seemed to be remembering the event.

Ben came in to take their plates and asked if they would like to change the wine to accompany the dessert. He also addressed Danika directly to ask if she would like a mocktail.

Danika thanked him, saying it sounded lovely. Danika looked at Cristian who was grinning broadly again. 'What is so funny tonight?'

'We normally have one course and one wine. You are definitely being treated like the princess you are tonight.' Cristian was enjoying it all very much but put on a more sober face when Ben returned with Danika's drink of two colours in a cocktail glass with fruit and mint. Ben brought new glasses for the others and poured Tokay.

Taking a sip Danika said, 'This is delicious; it is a dessert on its own.'

The panacotta desserts with fresh berries complimented their drinks.

'I'm going to have to lift my game from stir-fries when we are back home I think.' Danika was savouring every mouthful of both the dessert and mocktail.

'When were you planning on returning to Sydney?' Elizabeth asked with her head bowed, focusing on her dessert. There was a disappointment to her tone, and Danika frowned, sensing it also.

'We have to leave early Monday for now, Mother, because we have a lot to do for the launch of the new collection. Then...' Cristian started to say but Danika interrupted.

'Then we plan to be back here as soon and often as we can. After this week we should be able to let you know our plans.' Danika was looking at Elizabeth until she looked up. 'We will see you on Friday at the pre-launch though, won't we?'

'Yes, you will. Please let me know if you need any help with anything,' Elizabeth said. 'I might retire and leave you two to enjoy the rest of the evening.'

Cristian rose to assist his mother to rise and kissed her on the cheek. 'Goodnight, Mother.'

Elizabeth reached to touch his cheek. 'I am so pleased for you both.' Looking at Danika she added, 'Goodnight, Danika.'

'Goodnight, Elizabeth, I look forward to our talk tomorrow.' Danika started to rise but Elizabeth waved a hand for her to stay seated. Danika had felt Elizabeth's whirlwind of emotions and sent calming thoughts to her.

As soon as Elizabeth had left the room, Ben came in to take away the remains of the meal.

'Thank you, Ben. Would you ask Ann to come in so we can thank her also please?'

Cristian could not stop thinking how much he loved his mother and Danika tonight. Looking across to Danika, he knew she was definitely exuding positive vibes to all.

Ann came in wiping her hand on her apron, looking a little flushed with Ben standing behind her.

'Ann, I just wanted to say how wonderful the meal was tonight. I felt very privileged and spoiled. That mocktail was a bit special.' Danika smiled broadly. 'Please don't think you need to do that every meal though, I might burst at the seams.'

'You're very welcome, Mrs Blakesley, it was a joy to cook something different.' Ann glanced at Cristian as if not to offend him.

'I enjoyed it all of course, Ann, your cooking would match any chef.' Cristian was sincere is his praise.

'Would either of you like a coffee or aperitif to finish the meal?' Ben asked.

'Coffee would be very nice unless you had chai tea by any chance?' Danika asked and saw Ann beam. 'And please, call me Danika, at least when it is just us.'

'I'll have the dram, thanks Ben.' Cristian was still amused at the play between the staff and Danika. As they left to get the drinks Danika kicked him under the table.

'You have been a bit of brat tonight.' Danika was referring to his thoughts more than his actions.

'I just find it amusing and charming that they turned on such a different and delicious meal for you.' Cristian rubbed his kicked foot against hers. 'Perhaps I need punishing.'

The mental image he projected had Danika gasping. She glared at him as Ben came in with their drinks on a tray. The tea smelled divine. It had been several days since Danika had had a real brewed tea. The first she poured from the pot she drank quickly and was about to pour another when the images Cristian was sending stopped her in her tracks.

'I think it is time for us to retire, Mrs Blakesley,' Cristian said. Cristian's eyes had changed, she knew that look and she bet his hair had too. Her fingers were itching to find out.

'Yes, I think you may be right. You obviously can't behave yourself anymore,' Danika admonished.

Cristian quickly came around to help Danika rise from her seat but she avoided his attempt to kiss her. 'Not yet buddy.' As they left the room and made their way up the stairs Danika made it clear that she did not want him to touch her. Once they were in the room Cristian closed and locked the door.

'What are you up to, Danika?' Cristian again tried to touch her which she avoided.

'You were very naughty tonight and for that you do need punishing.' Danika was trying to sound stern. 'So sit down there and do as you are told.' Danika pointed at the blanket box at the end of the bed.

'Or what?' Cristian replied but sat where he was told anyway.

'Or I will remove privileges.' Danika stood in front then turned her back to him. 'Now no groping, just undo the ribbons please.' He did as he was told. Danika turned back round to face him but just out of reach. Slowly she pulled one shoulder of the dress down and then the next so that it clung at her breasts then let it all drop to the floor. Stepping back, she stood in her black lace underwear and shoes. She picked up the dress and walked over to place it over a chair keeping his black kerchief in her hand. Danika walked back to stand in front of him. He was starting to loosen his belt when she stopped him. 'Oh no, you don't get to do that yet.'

His arousal was nearly painful.

Danika held the kerchief up to her breasts then turned around for him to undo the clips. She turned back to facing him and, still holding the kerchief with one hand, slipped one arm out and then swapped to take the other out, letting the bra slip to the floor, her breasts still covered with his black kerchief.

Cristian was now more than uncomfortable. He was hot in his suit and very constricted. He felt like he was in a vice. As she chanted he felt her thoughts hold him sitting down. Standing before him with her fingers holding the kerchief in place she suddenly raised her arms above her head. His gaze focused on her arms going up then he realised she had let go of the kerchief halfway to flutter past her bare breasts. He thought he was either going to faint or explode from the heat. His jaw tightened and he gritted his teeth as she turned again and bent over to retrieve the kerchief. With her legs splayed she had pulled the edges of her knickers together to form a g string. He so wanted to grab her but felt forced to resist. She then drew the kerchief over herself turning to face him as she waved it near enough to his face for him to get the full scent of her, then slowly pulled down her knickers and stepped out of them, taking her shoes off as she went. Walking to the bed, she threw off the cover and lay down.

'Your turn to show me what you've got,' Danika instructed. The thought of a slow deliberate undress to taunt her passed his mind in a nanosecond quickly followed by the fastest undress he had ever done. He was sure he ripped some seams and definitely popped a couple of buttons. He nearly exploded when he released his erection and had to pause briefly to gain control.

Danika released the bond she had on him not to touch. Before she could say anything he was there with her, joining and then they were together, reaching the peak as one.

After their breathing returned to normal she mumbled against his shoulder, 'Consider yourself punished.'

He laughed and the movement made their nerves where they were joined tingle. He brushed the hair from her face and slowly, methodically, worked them both up to ecstasy again.

8

THE QUEST

D ANIKA WOKE REALISING she was alone immediately as they had been entwined all night until they both drifted to sleep. She reached out to feel the sheet near her. It was only slightly warm. She rolled on to her belly to feel the last of his heat before stretching out like a cat. She sat up to sense if he was in the rooms at all. She couldn't hear him and searched by feel and just had the slightest hint of him breathing heavy. Was that a ghost of a feeling from last night? No, it was getting closer. Piecing together that he was running, was pleased that he was. It had been too long since his last run. Getting up, she could still see their clothes strewn around the room, which she gathered as she went heading to the bathroom. She noticed that a few buttons were missing from his suit vest and his shirt. A quick shower later and she was wrapped in his robe, kneeling on the floor trying to find the buttons. Cristian found her in this position when he walked in.

'Is everything alright?'

'I was trying to find the missing buttons that someone recklessly ripped off last night.' She sat on her haunches to look up at him. He was in his running gear and very sweaty. The scent was strangely alluring. She turned away to curb her thoughts. Danika wanted to get on with the day, not return to bed. At least, not yet.

Cristian went into the bathroom shower, saying as he went, 'I have arranged a tour of the estate after breakfast.'

Getting up, she dressed quickly, offering him his robe without going into the steamy room. 'I'm heading downstairs,' she called as she slipped her phone into her pocket.

Instead of going down the stairs though Danika did a quick look into the rooms without a private sign on them. The furnishings under dust cloths were much the same as their rooms just a little smaller. As she opened the room held for Robert the malevolence nearly knocked her over. She didn't have her barriers up and felt the full force. She was just pulling the door to as Cristian was by her side. 'Don't go in there.' He pulled her back.

'I don't know why I didn't feel that earlier, I would never have opened the door otherwise. When did you say he was coming? I think I need to be well prepared.' A ripple of repulsion went through her.

'Not for a couple of weeks at least, after the lunar cycle.' Cristian moved her away. 'I thought you were going downstairs.'

'I was, then I thought I should check out the furniture in each room before in case there was anything useful to my ideas. There isn't, as it is much the same,' Danika concluded. She took a deep breath before going downstairs with Cristian to have breakfast.

In the dining room were dishes with lids on the buffet plus both coffee and tea urns. Danika looked in each dish until she was sure what she wanted. 'This is excessive for just us. I like that we help ourselves though,' she said choosing pancakes and toppings.

'The staff will have breakfast after us, not much will go to waste as there are chickens as well as the deer,' Cristian explained as he loaded his plate up after building an appetite from running.

Danika made them each drinks. 'So where are we looking this morning?' Danika asked before starting her food.

'I have arranged to use the gator to drive around rather than walking. We can get around more that way,' Cristian explained between eating.

'What is a gator?' Danika had visions of an alligator that she felt were possibly inaccurate.

'It is a four wheeled buggy, very stable and fast. Mark uses it mostly moving stuff around the estate. Very useful.'

'I don't have to learn to drive it, do I?' Danika was beginning to wonder what other new things she had to learn about being in this family. 'I don't think I'm dressed for this,' she said, looking down at her skirt and sandals.

'No you don't, but you can if you want. I haven't used it for quite a while. You get to wear a helmet as a precaution but really it is like being in an open car, much safer than a quad bike.'

Cristian finished his food watching Danika stew on something, then asked, 'Why are you so uptight? I can feel there is more than one thing. You are safe, I won't let anything happen to you.'

'I don't understand why I didn't sense that room. What else am I missing? I'm worried I may be losing my touch, my craft.' She had thought it wouldn't matter because she loved Cristian but facing the reality that she may lose her skill, her craft, was very different.

'This house is full of good feelings that probably overwhelmed the one bad one. Don't let it worry you. You were pretty on form last night; I knew what you were doing.' He smiled knowingly at her.

'Okay well I'll give this tour a go as long as the tour guide has lots of good stories. I dislike tours where you just get driven around looking at the scenery,' Danika joked.

'Come on, Mrs, let's get on with the tour then.' Cristian showed Danika out through the foyer and garage the way they had come in the previous day, continuing on to the sheds next to the stables. Cristian spoke with Mark and then offered Danika a helmet. She took it but had no idea how to get it on. She watched Cristian then tried to move it over her head until he assisted her get it on. With all her hair it was snug. Her face felt weird as the sides and face plate wrapped around her head. Cristian helped her into the gator and strapped her in. She felt like she was going on a show ride. She had only done that once.

Cristian was talking to her but she couldn't hear properly. He reached over and adjusted something on the side of the helmet. 'Can you hear me now?' There was a headphone in the helmet and obviously a microphone also.

'Yes I can,' she replied, glad for the connection. When Cristian started the gator she jumped so he slowly and carefully pulled away from the sheds and started the tour around the estate. He explained that they no longer had horses, it was something his grandfather had wanted to keep and his father had used them until his grandfather died. Now the stables are used for storage and when any deer need attending or separating.

Cristian proceeded to drive around some of the fence line which had been recently replaced with a much larger, stronger security fence. He explained that the previous poor fencing was one of the main reasons he had needed the cell two weeks ago. Danika remembered the fear and pain he had felt back then, hoping that would never happen again. She was fascinated by the deer pens and thought that the stags were magnificent. The rock cliff at the back of the estate was spectacular and the gardens at the side of the house were amazing also. Danika had a few ideas for changes in the gardens that may be nice as she went but kept them to herself for now. Round the back of the house they passed the chicken coop and noticed they were enjoying the last of the breakfast. Cristian confirmed that most of the eggs used in the kitchen were from their own chickens. Danika loved the idea of the recycling. Finally they were back at the work shed to drop off the gator back to Mark. Cristian helped Danika get out of the gator and take the helmet off, her hair going everywhere. They had gone so slow she wondered why she had needed the helmet.

'The helmets were because you may have got brave and wanted to go faster,' Cristian explained without her asking. As they walked away from the shed he pointed out that their mental connection was still strong.

'I think I will go freshen up before meeting Elizabeth,' Danika decided as they made their way back into the house. Cristian followed her up to their rooms as he wanted to go through a few more things in the study he explained. Danika went into the bathroom to wash her hands and brushed her hair, then went to her tote bag and pulled out her medallion. She was putting it on as Cristian came back in.

'I didn't think you were going to wear that anymore.' Danika could sense his concern at the barrier of the medallion.

'I just have a theory I wanted to try out.' She walked out of their rooms and could feel Robert's room immediately. She turned back to Cristian. 'This intensifies my ability to feel the different vibes. So it is one part of my craft. I hadn't taken it off in so many years for this long I didn't know. Don't worry, it will come off tonight.' She tucked it under her top before leaning in for a kiss.

Despite the door being open Ben gently tapped on the door frame. 'Excuse me, ma'am, Mrs Blakesley would like you to join her for tea in her rooms. I can show you the way.' Ben then stepped back to wait for Danika to be ready.

'I'll meet you back here later.' Danika kissed Cristian again and then followed Ben down the stairs across the foyer to the north wing. The room overlooking the gardens at the front of the house was the sitting room for Elizabeth where a table of tea and delicacies had been set up. Elizabeth was sitting in an armchair next to the fireplace staring into the flames. Ben left the room closing the doors.

'Good morning, Elizabeth, thank you for inviting me for tea.' Danika stood near the table looking over at Elizabeth deep in thought.

'Hello my dear. Danika would you like to pour tea and sit over here to talk?' Elizabeth was still a little distracted by her thoughts, Danika sensed, as she made drinks for them both. Sitting opposite Elizabeth they sipped their drinks for a few minutes.

'I enjoyed a tour around the estate with Cristian this morning,' Danika said to break the silence.

'Henry and I thought we had plenty of time to tell Cristian what to expect when finding his love and the future. But we were wrong and then I couldn't tell him anything I was so overtaken by grief.' Elizabeth looked at Danika. 'It must have been a shock for you both.'

'We were a bit surprised. It took a bit of patience and understanding but we were able to get there in the end.' Danika was not sure how much to share of their connection.

'The joining of hearts and minds is all consuming and when that link is broken it is unbearable. Some of the family members have not survived it. Cristian's grandfather left England after his wife died to try to move on from his grief.' Elizabeth was looking into the flames again. 'My Henry was the kind one who followed his father's philosophies of empathy and providing for others less fortunate whenever they could. Robert always resented being dragged to Australia away from his cousins that he liked to get into mischief with. He couldn't wait to leave and did once he was eighteen. He was not kind, even as a child apparently. He never came back until Henry died and then it was only to try to convince us to move to Europe. Why would we do that and be lorded over by him?' Elizabeth obviously needed to get that off her mind. 'I'm sorry Danika I should not air our dirty laundry but I think you need to be well informed before Robert gets here.'

Danika decided to take a chance with Elizabeth to share what she and Cristian had discovered so far.

'Elizabeth, Cristian and I have the connection you speak of but it is more than that. We believe we may be linked to the original curse. The source of the prophecy and myths that each of our families hold on to.' Danika waited for Elizabeth to really take that in.

'What myths and prophecies does your family hold?' Elizabeth asked.

Danika felt she was not sceptical but more not wanting to build hope. Danika could feel her interest. 'My family, the Carling's, are a line of woman that never love or marry and can only bear one female child at each generation. Our line came to Australia as a transported woman in 1822 from England. The myth is if we love and marry we will lose our craft.' Danika took a big risk now. She could see and feel that Elizabeth was very interested to hear more. 'We are a family of witches.' Danika waited to see how Elizabeth would react to what she had said and saw one tear escape and fall down Elizabeth's cheek. 'You're not surprised, are you?'

'I thought this would never happen. I only have handed down tales from Jonathon, Cristian's grandfather.' Elizabeth was so filled with relief and hope Danika could feel. 'What have you found out so far?'

'Well I was a bit reticent to say too much to begin with but I can feel that you can take it. I was a bit economical with the truth about our connection before. It was cataclysmic actually. There are a number of mystical and physical barriers that we have had to overcome to complete the imprinting, rapture and finally our marriage.' Danika pulled out her medallion. 'This is one of the barriers, it has been in my family as long as I know. Cristian cannot touch it.' Danika moved closer and took it off so that Elizabeth could see it.

'It's the family symbol the Lleuad Blaidd,' Elizabeth commented. 'It is very faint but I can see it. What is this symbol?' Elizabeth asked as she turned it over to see the other side.

'The Triquetra is the symbol for my family.' Danika was watching and still trying to sense Elizabeth's thoughts. 'We didn't realise that was a wolf's face with the moons. Our family is a bit disjointed, I know very little of the true history. Cristian and I were going to try to trace it back. We just feel that we are going to be the ones to end the legacy that haunts the men of your family.'

'Has your marriage changed anything that you are aware of so far?'

'No I still have my craft and I suspect Cristian will still experience the change at the next full moon.' Danika was herself swaying between hope and disappointment. 'I have been driven to find artefacts related to us. I found two in the last week that were very strong and knocked us both over, literally. The thing is that we do not want Robert to know any of this. I can't do anything about my eye colour but we can keep everything else from him. Are you up for that?' Danika asked as she held Elizabeth's hands.

'Absolutely. I think Jonathon and Henry wanted the legacy to end and spoke of a family myth that it could end with a green-eyed girl but no other detail. The old historical papers and artefacts going back to the 1600's are all with Robert. They were passed down the line going to Europe hundreds of years ago and he has just ended up with them through inheritance. They were sure he knew the answer but was so driven by power and greed. They believed he was certain that if the legacy ended so would their wealth. They didn't trust Robert.' Danika could feel the fear Elizabeth had for Robert.

'Jonathon left his wealth and this house to Henry, not Robert the eldest, because he knew he would have just thrown us out,' Elizabeth stated. 'Robert wasn't happy about that.'

'We will get through this as a family, Elizabeth. Cristian thinks there might be other family members who feel the same way his father did. He is going to try to contact a Peter I think.'

'I have heard rumours of unhappy and scared family members. One of them is Peter's mother I believe,' Elizabeth confirmed. 'It is getting more dangerous for them all as the world is closing in, especially in Europe with the Ukraine war. It is getting harder to keep their legacy a secret. I think they are all a bit scared of Robert though.'

'Have you ever discussed this with Cristian before? I think he has been trying to discover things on his own.' Danika realised how alone Cristian had been.

'No, I didn't know where to start or if he was even interested. It was as if life stopped for me with Henry's death. I'm so sorry.'

'Well this has all been a real revelation. I think we need another cup of tea and then a change of topic perhaps?' Danika thought they both needed something else to focus on.

Danika moved the tray closer and poured more drinks from the heated pot and passed the delicacies for Elizabeth to choose some. 'You need a pick me up.' Danika tried to send positive energy her way. Elizabeth thanked her and did take a small cake.

'Now, I wanted to talk to you about redecorating as I remember you suggested I look around your rooms. From what I can see here they are much brighter at least than upstairs.'

'Yes it is all very dull and masculine up there. It must be a bit overwhelming for you.' Elizabeth was at least now turning her thoughts elsewhere. They spent the next hour talking about different decorating ideas, including a family portrait wall, and Danika wondered how many photos Elizabeth had that could be added to the wall.

'I'll have to have a look through the albums. We have not been much for displaying anything really. Would you like to look at one of the albums of Cristian?' Elizabeth was warming to the idea of a photos wall, Danika could feel it.

The first few baby photos included Henry and Danika touched Elizabeth's hand to give her strength. There were a few more milestone moments, lost teeth, first day of school and learning to ride. Danika soon realised it was Elizabeth behind the camera.

'You have an excellent eye for a shot Elizabeth, these are wonderful.' Danika was enjoying seeing the child side of Cristian immensely. 'He was very cute.'

'He was our joy. We were very proud of his achievements, I still am.' Elizabeth was showing signs of weariness after such an emotional awakening.

'If you don't mind, I think I will go check what Cristian is up to. Will we see you for dinner again tonight? We will have to leave early tomorrow and might miss you.'

'Yes I think I will, maybe not so formal tonight though.' Elizabeth smiled and was happy to take Danika's hand again before she left.

Danika had so much to tell Cristian about her conversation with his mother. Also an idea was forming regarding photos and she was hoping he could help. As she made her way from the north wing she was feeling a bit peckish after not really eating what had been on the tea table and wondered if there was anything to snack on down in the kitchen. She crossed the foyer rather than up the stairs and continued on to the kitchen where she found Ann rolling pastry.

'Hello Ann, you look busy. Would I be able to find a light snack for lunch?' Danika wondered what delicacy Ann was putting together.

'Yes of course, ma'am, I can make you a salad or sandwiches or something else if you like.' Ann was wiping her floured hands on her apron, a different one since last night.

'I don't want to bother you. I think I can make something up for us if you don't mind me getting into your fridge.' Danika was still feeling her way with the norms of the household.

'You help yourself by all means. Actually, I can ask you now, I was planning to make beef wellington for Mrs Blakesley and the master. Is that something you would eat? I have chicken as an alternative.'

'I've always wanted to try beef wellington. Perhaps a small serve with lots of vegetables would be very nice.' Danika genuinely didn't mind eating well made meat dishes. Danika had found some items to make up salad sandwiches and was putting them together when Cristian came in. Danika sensed Cristian enjoying the domestic scene making her smile.

'I hope you like ham and salad sandwiches with a pickle of course.' Danika put one on a plate for him to sit at the kitchen table and handed him a glass of fruit juice. She sat with her cheese salad sandwich opposite him.

'Ann you will have to pack us something to take back to Sydney with us tomorrow until we can get back here again. We are going to be very busy this week.' Cristian was smiling as he ate the last crumb.

'I'll see what I can do, Master Cristian.' Danika put their dishes in the washer and followed Cristian out to go towards the library. Once inside Danika told Cristian about her meeting with his mother today.

'Your mother has been very informative today about your family history. I told her about us leaving out some of the more graphic bits.'

'How did she take that?'

'Surprisingly well, pleased actually. She had heard about the family prophecy from your grandfather and possibly some information from your cousin's mother. She seemed to think there may be some support from that sector. They don't like Robert's power and control.' Danika thought about their discussion. 'I think you should talk to her. She is apologetic at being a bit absent but also very lonely.'

'In depth conversations have been off the table since Father died. It is hard to break that habit.'

'Well, you just have to do it. We have to be united in this quest to be successful,' Danika said with more force than she had shown since coming to the estate. 'Bringing our finds here when we come next will help also I think.'

'Were you thinking of setting up base here now rather than the apartment?'

'Yes, if that is alright. Because it is private here in a different way, private from the public. Besides, I have lots of decorating ideas to share with you and your mother if she agrees.' Danika was glad that Elizabeth was supportive of the change to their rooms but it was still her house.

'It is my house actually. Father left it to me as is the tradition of the Blakesley line. I just signed it over to her for legal reasons. I am her sole beneficiary but it keeps it away from Robert. Mother has many other investments Father left to her. So I'm pretty open to whatever you want to do other than pink or floral. Also we have to be conscious of the lunar cycle for workmen coming to the estate. At least for now. I have some information I need to show you once we go upstairs.'

'Okay, that's good, because I have another idea that I need help from you with, a family photos wall. Are you able to download the photos we took on our cameras and print off some for me please? I have to buy lots of frames and I thought we could give Elizabeth the nicest one of our wedding day,' Danika said it in a rush hoping Cristian agreed because he only had the one photo of his graduation at the apartment. She could feel him considering that.

'I think Mother might have some photos of us from a long time ago if you are interested in going back that far. What about your family, do you have photos?'

Danika had been trying to follow Cristian's thoughts and his question threw her off slightly. She realised that her family were really no different in their secretive attitudes and no display of history in photos. 'I think there would be a few at Mum's house, some awful school photos as I remember. We need to plan a trip over there.' Danika felt a wave of wanting to see her mother, which really surprised her yet pleased her also.

'Well, we can get the photos off the phones first and go from there. If we go back up to the study I can print them also. We need to try to lock in some travel dates around Robert's visit also,' Cristian reminded her.

They made their way up to the study where Cristian had been trying to find anything from his cousin Peter and had come across a couple of emails from an unknown source of bphowl that had gone to junk but were titled unlike a scam. He had not opened them yet, wanting to talk to Danika first. Now she was in the study he explained what he had found and for them to look together. The first he opened titled 'one of the twins' showed one photo of their family symbol on an old horse ornament. It was very clear and similar to Danika's medallion except for the wider edge. They wondered if her medallion had been ground down to be easier to wear. The next photo was of the other side with the Triquetra engraved as on Danika's, also very clear.

'Oh my heavens it is the same as mine.' Danika put her hand to her mouth. 'Who is this bphowl and how does he know about our theory of twins?'

'I am not certain, but there is an older one from a couple of weeks ago titled "them". Cristian opened it and it was another photo, hard to see as it appeared to be taken in a very dark situation. It looked a bit like a manuscript or a page in a large book. He tried to zoom it to read better but that just made it blurrier. 'I'm going to print it so we can use a magnifying glass instead.' He was downloading the photos from the cameras at the same time.

'That seems to have come out alright when it isn't zoomed on the computer.' Cristian looked critically at the photo with a magnifying glass. 'It appears to be a list of names below a statement regarding an event with other names. The writing and wording is difficult to read in the first part and changes down the list. Does that look like Cristian to you?' he asked Danika, pointing to the last name on the list, handing her the magnifying glass.

'Yes it does a bit. Did you have an ancestor with the same name?' Danika was looking more at the top of the photo. 'Write this as I spell it out. I'm trying to match it to other letters.'

'B, r, o, n, w, y, n. I think that it is Bronwyn. Is that an S or a C?' Danika handed back the glass.

'C I think. That word looks a bit like witch.' Cristian was reading ahead and suddenly moved it away from her view. But he couldn't hide his thoughts quick enough and Danika heard what he speculated in his mind.

'We don't know what this is Danika, I would like to get it to a calligraphy expert to decipher it correctly. Let's not jump to any conclusions.' Cristian was clearing his mind as much as possible.

'It is very kind of you to try to hide this from me but I've already seen it as it happened remember?' Danika was trying not to relive the event of horror she saw at the apartment. 'They burned them as witches, didn't they? But not all of them, someone got away and cursed them. When do you think this was?'

'Mother might know which ancestor I was named after. Most of the new descendants are named after an ancestor. Not all, but most. So we might be able to work out a year.' Danika sensed as Cristian was overwhelmed with a feeling of guilt, his thoughts turning to the awful acts against the witches.

'This is not your fault Cristian. None of us are responsible for our ancestor's actions. What we can do is try to put it to rights.' Danika had not said anything about Bronwyn but it was obvious that she and the others were her ancestors. 'Who found this document and from where? We need to know more about the actual curse that they cast. I have no way of recreating it to break it without that knowledge. I don't even know if I could.' Danika felt she was going to fall down from the weight of this new information and moved to sit quickly.

Cristian went to her, bending down to his haunches to be able to look at her. 'I'm sorry you are going through this. I should never have opened those messages while we were here. It is a miracle you are alive and a descendant, they may have all died. I don't know who sent the emails but I can guess. I'm not sure who he is referring to with his title "them", whether it's my family or yours. I think we need to move away from then and them and try to get back to here and now.'

Cristian closed his email and brought up the photos he had loaded, the first one was of Danika at the Hunter Valley gardens, the day they met. The next was the close-up he had taken, he hit print. There were plenty of tourist shots of Sydney and then the one they took together at the botanical gardens, he printed that also. Cristian moved to the side so Danika had a good view of the photos he was scrolling through. James had taken so many photos of their wedding day which was thoughtful of him. Danika chose a few to print, one she printed twice so that they could give it to Elizabeth. Looking at the wedding photos, the love in their eyes was obvious and she remembered the feelings of the day. Slowly her mixed emotions settled. She picked up the photos they had printed and was pleased with their choices. Cristian offered her a manila folder to put them in so they could take them to be framed. In another folder he placed the print of the document and the photos of the horse medal. He packed them in a brief case to take back to Sydney.

While Cristian was finishing up in the study Danika decided to go back into their bathroom to have a shower. She had a feeling of filth on her skin that needed to be washed away before she could face Elizabeth. Cristian came into the bathroom shortly later as Danika sat on the floor of the shower, letting the water stream over her head. He slipped off his shoes and stepped in to the shower, lifting her into a hug with the water running over them both. He told her how much he loved her and how proud he was of her. Eventually Cristian turned off the tap and they helped one another off with the wet clothes to then wrap in the robes.

It was nearly time for dinner so Cristian helped Danika brush and dry her wet mass of hair in slow methodical actions while she sat on a chair. The feel of his hands on her head and shoulders as he brushed and held the dryer was very therapeutic and calming. They were finally dressed again just as Ben knocked on the door to warn them of dinner to be served shortly.

Going to her bag Danika found one of her crystals to put in her pocket and then focused on the few nice touches that Ann and Ben had put in the room to absorb the good feelings. Her harmony level was still a little behind but she was getting there. Leaning into her, Cristian told her again how much he loved her and, holding hands, they went down to dinner.

Elizabeth was already sitting at the table with a small pile of photos on top of a book. Red wine was decanted on the table for Cristian and Elizabeth and a bottle of Perrier for Danika. Elizabeth showed the photos to Danika and asked if Cristian would be able to make them larger to be framed. There was one of Jonathon, Henry and Elizabeth on what must have been their wedding day. Another photo was of them and Cristian as a baby.

'These are wonderful I hadn't noticed these in the album today,' Danika said as she admired them.

'They are from a different album,' Elizabeth explained. 'And this is for you Cristian. I had forgotten about it. It is a journal of your grandfather's. I haven't looked at it but it may be interesting to you.' Cristian thanked her. They each put their little gifts off to the side just as Ben brought their main meals of beef wellington in. Cooked to perfection as expected Danika's portion was much smaller with more vegetables for which she was grateful. They were all enjoying the meal too much to talk until finished. Then Cristian enquired about who he was named after as he knew that most of the Blakesley men were named after others.

'When your father and I were trying to think of a name for you, we wanted a name different to all the rest of the family but couldn't decide. Your grandfather suggested your name and it seemed so different we fell in love with it. He then told us it was still a family name but from many generations ago from an ancestor born two hundred years before.' Danika sensed Elizabeth was enjoying the memory. 'By the way I've started up a contact again with Ingrid, she is Peter's mother. It is all a bit cryptic so I am sure something is going on. I will try calling this week, she was very pleased I contacted.'

'That is very useful, Mother I have received two emails from an unknown source which I think might be Peter using an alias.' Cristian stopped when Ben brought in the desserts.

After the meal they all settled in the sitting room where Ben had already started the fire. Danika was amazed at how quickly he acted on the merest suggestion and wondered how in tune he was.

'Well, Mother, what did you mean by the cryptic conversation with Aunt Ingrid?'

'Well, we started off talking about family health as you do. Very non-committal, but then she was talking about weather as if it was of vital importance, also mentioning the war. I think she was actually talking about Robert. Well that is my theory anyway, so I am going to call her and hopefully we can talk in less riddles. What about these emails you have?'

'No explanation, just photos of artefacts the first was of a bronze horse medal like they used to wear on the saddles and bridles it had the family symbol on it. Very old it is similar to Danika's medallion but in better shape but it also had the symbol of her family on the back,' Cristian explained as Danika took off the medallion again to remind Elizabeth of it. Danika was sending him warning thoughts not to go too far with the other photo description.

'The other message was a photo of an old manuscript or page from a book it is hard to tell. There were a lot of names on it including the last one being Cristian but it wasn't a good photo so a bit difficult to decipher much else.' Cristian was watching his mother closely. Danika was trying to feel her thoughts also.

'Jonathon, your grandfather knew he was ill, his heart was failing. He didn't think he would survive another change. He said a few things to me that did not really make much sense at the time but now it does. He particularly wanted your father and me to keep you away from Robert, even back then. His own son and he didn't trust him.' Elizabeth paused as if trying to remember all that Jonathon had told her. 'He had said something about deserving the curse for the atrocity and that they had missed the opportunity to break it. That you Cristian may be their last hope.' Elizabeth looked at her son with love and concern. 'You were just a little boy and I thought he has a bit delirious or affected by his illness.'

'You and Father never said any of this to me.'

'Jonathon only said it to me. If your father was given the same speech he never told me as I did not tell him. Your father was devastated when Jonathon died. He felt the weight of the responsibility to protect you and our life here without the support of the rest of the family overseas. I think we became a bit insular.' Cristian moved to hold his mother's hand in reassurance.

'It seems that we will all be busy this week now. The gallery collections launch, Danika's renovation plans and now a cataclysm to research. Do keep me up to date please.' Elizabeth was showing signs of tiredness.

'That reminds me, Elizabeth, I completely forgot to talk to you about the guest list for the launch. Can I send you the list to look over and see if we missed anyone that should be there?' Danika was keen to keep her involved in everything. It was definitely improving her general mental health, she thought. She sent the list on her phone to Elizabeth's number.

'Of course and for now I think I shall leave you two and wish you well for the week. I won't see you to say goodbye in the morning, so have a safe drive.' Cristian helped his mother rise and gave her a hug and kiss, whispering his love to her.

Danika was going to shake Elizabeth's hand but was also pulled into a hug. 'Goodnight, dear. I'll let you know about the list once I see it.' She waved off any assistance back to her rooms.

After Elizabeth left, Danika looked at Cristian and said, 'This has all been a revelation to you also. I am so proud of how well you are handling the whole situation.' She sat down on the couch so he could join her if he wanted. Cristian sat next to her and held her hand.

'Thank you, darling. I have to say that there is a simmering anger though. I was taught by Father and Grandfather that controlling the anger was essential. I thought it was just good manners but I suspect that there is more to it. You mentioned about the little changes you have noticed. I have felt it also but didn't realise it was an actual physical change until you said. To say I am worried about that is an understatement.' Danika could see and feel his love and fear all at the same time. She was still glowing from him calling her darling though.

'I should never have pushed you that much last night, I'm sorry.' Danika was beginning to think she may have been playing with fire if she read his thoughts properly.

'Oh no, don't hold back my love. That is vastly different than anger. Our love is ours and unique, not to be sullied by my family history or this damned legacy.' Cristian moved from love to anger in a flash and Danika could feel the change coming from him. She pressed his hand and felt his blood rate slow and noticed the hairs on his scalp loosen again.

'Well I think I need to pack and sort out our things so we can get an early start and then turn in. I'm feeling a bit wrung out now.' Danika was feeling tired after another day of so many new things and a roller coaster of emotions yet again. Danika was craving a little bored monotony. Cristian squeezed her hand and then let her go.

'I'll be up shortly to help.'

Cristian

Cristian was only ten minutes behind her and yet she was fast asleep and he intended to leave her that way. He pulled out his mother's photos again and, going into his study, scanned them and printed them larger to match the other photos. He also went back to his emails and replied to bphowl with 'must talk'. Closing everything down again he came back to the bedroom to see Danika had not moved and was deep in sleep. Undressing he slipped into bed, careful not to disturb her and lay next to her without touching. She arched closer to his warmth in her sleep and they ended up spooning. A little distracting at first but sleep claimed him also.

Danika

In the morning Danika slipped out of bed careful not to disturb him. She really did want to start early to leave so, dressing in the bathroom, she looked at her face, it looked the same and yet she felt different. It had been a confronting weekend. Cristian was still asleep and she thought she would leave him for a few minutes longer as he had a long drive and decided to go down to the kitchen to grab a quick drink before they left.

Cristian was up and nearly dressed as she walked in with the drink. They quickly prepared and carried their items downstairs, grabbing a hamper from Ann who stopped them before they exited through the garage. Danika mused about fitting her van in the garage or whether to keep it at all.

As the gates closed behind them, Danika felt she was leaving home and shared that with Cristian, who touched her on the knee before continuing.

As they drove, Danika madly wrote notes in the diary of a 'to do' list that seemed to go on to the bottom of the page. Some she discussed, others were just mind maps as she called them, complete with her usual little drawings of arrows, stars and smiles. She flipped through a few pages and added notes for the coming days and weeks and even dog eared one page for extra attention.

'What is that for?' Cristian asked as he was stopped at the lights.

'Full moon. We have to decide where we will be. Not today though, too much to do today.' Danika was wondering if she had loaded up today too much.

Cristian just nodded at that statement as he concentrated until the next opportunity he asked, 'What are your plans looking like for tomorrow? Would you have time to go back into James' chambers with me?' Cristian briefly looked at Danika before driving on.

'Tomorrow was mostly today's spill over so should be easy to juggle around. Why do we need to do that? Is it to do with the speed marriage?' She was grinning at the image.

'Yes and no. Now that we are Mr and Mrs, something that is up to you is changing your name. But you will need to apply to change your name and I'm guessing you will have to do it through South Australia because that is where you were born, isn't it? So there will be a few things to then change name on after that. Mainly I want to get started on the wills and division of assets.'

'Wills, assets, good grief, we haven't been married a week yet.' Danika was feeling a bit surprised at the rush.

'James has been at me for a while to get my will in order so now is the perfect timing. Besides, you need to know all that we have, it isn't just the estate and gallery. James will have the full list. Do you have a will at all?' Cristian was very firmly fixed in this so Danika knew she could not sway him.

'No I don't have much so couldn't see the point of it.' Danika was yet again astonished between her previous simple and meagre lifestyle compared to her new massively busy and complicated one. She didn't pull her thoughts back quick enough.

'If you want to sell everything and move to a deserted island with me tomorrow it can be arranged.'

'As lovely as that sounds, my love, I am determined we will sort out this damned mess our ancestors started and then we can revisit that idea.' Danika sent him a kiss image.

They were both pleased to be pulling into the apartment car park in better time than expected for a Monday peak hour trek. Lugging all their bags and the hamper into the lift to get it up in one go. Once they were in the apartment they both dropped everything and just took a breath and hugged.

'I love you,' Danika said kissing him.

'I love you too.' Both hugged again and then got back to sorting out what they needed to do.

Danika was relieved to know she didn't need to worry about cleaning and they could leave for the gallery. At the gallery they met with Paul and Rene out the back. They announced that they were now married and that Danika was a full partner with all the privileges and responsibilities that entailed. After congratulations were said she handed them more of the silly souvenirs. Danika had already noticed the black cloths over the windows and signs saying new collection coming soon with the website for peek preview. She liked the mystery of it.

Danika was ticking off items on her to do list rapidly as they worked through the logistics of the displays and general theme of the collection. When the restored pieces arrived a new thought of showing before and after came to her as a possible extension to the gallery. Cristian could feel her energy waning and suggested a quick break for everyone to enjoy the hamper from Ann. After, when they were back to work Danika was moving around the gallery chalking lines and with her hands outstretched.

Cristian moved beside her to ask if she was using her craft to which she burst out laughing and hugged him. 'No darling, checking there is enough space to walk between the displays. Probably a bit amateurish but it made sense to me.' Cristian kissed her and was glad to see her humour back again. The rest of the day seemed to pass in minutes and they were surprised to see from the back dock that night was falling. They decided it was better to come back refreshed than continue with the gallery setup any longer.

Once they were back in the apartment Danika didn't think twice before she stripped off and stood in the shower to let the warm water wash away the grime of the day. Cristian joined her shortly after as they mutually enjoyed the warm water and soaped one another's backs. Before the cleaning could turn to anything else, the entrance buzzer sounded. Cristian quickly wiped most water off and, wrapping a robe around him, went to answer. Danika followed shortly after with a robe around her and her wet hair in a towel, to find Cristian laying out their dinner, newly delivered. She thought she was too tired to eat then surprised herself how hungry she was.

After, Danika sat on the bed with a drier and brush, not wanting to sleep with wet hair. Drying her long, thick hair each day would be too much effort, Danika thought, and decided to braid it in future with a scarf over while they were working on the gallery set up. Cristian saw her eyes drooping as she held the drier and took over finishing it off for her as he had done before. Satisfied her hair was dry enough for

her to lie down, he helped her out of the robe and slipped her under
the covers to sleep.

Cristian

Robert's face was in front of him. He was in wolf form but Cristian
knew it was him. He stood between Robert and Danika and was
calmly warning he would kill him first before he would let him harm
her until Robert lunged then he was there also as a wolf determined
to protect her and kill Robert. He heard Danika screaming, yelling
his name.

Suddenly he realised it wasn't a dream and that Danika's screaming
was real.

'Cristian wake up, wake up, let me go.' Danika had hold of his arm
and was trying to prize it off. The bed clothes were long gone and he
looked down at his arm as the last remnants of his fur were going. He
sat up and saw the fear on Danika's face as she jumped up out of the
bed and stood there looking at him wide eyed. On her stomach were
a few red marks.

'You changed in your sleep. Has that happened before?'

'I'm sorry. Are you alright? No, you're not, are you? Let me see.'
Cristian was trying to understand what had just happened but as he
moved to get closer to her, she backed away.

Danika

'Cristian, answer me? What just happened? I woke to your growls in my ear and a pain in my stomach where you were holding me so tight. I couldn't read your thoughts though, you had started the change.' Danika had started to shake, either from shock or from standing naked in the cool air of the morning, perhaps both. Then she was getting glimpses of his human thoughts.

'Robert, of course I should have known. Did you know you could change outside of the lunar cycle?' Danika could now sense he had not known that which relieved her and frightened her in equal amounts. She sensed he was ashamed and horrified now of what had happened. His next thought to protect her by distancing himself she vehemently denied.

'No, you are not going to hide from me, so don't even go there.' Danika was grabbing clothes to put on to hide the welts and feel more in charge.

Cristian ran his hands though his hair which was now back to normal. 'I can't put you at risk if I can't control myself. I could have killed you, or worse.'

'You were not trying to hurt me, you were protecting me. It was just a very big shock wake up. What is worse than death though?' As she asked, the mental image he showed soon had her stomach churning. 'Okay, I get it, but no you are not distancing yourself from me and that is final. We can manage this.' Danika was trying to project positive vibes despite a ripple of fear still at the edges.

Cristian's alarm on his phone started. Danika looked at him and said, 'Don't need that, we had wolf alarm.' She smiled broadly at him as she looked at what she had grabbed randomly to wear and threw it down to decide on different clothes. 'Come on I refuse to let this ruin our life.' Danika was sending bucket loads of positive and happy vibes at Cristian so that he eventually laughed more at her efforts than anything.

'What are you doing? You have been going through all your clothes and discarding them.' Danika sent the feeling of desire towards Cristian, who quickly took up the opportunity to kiss her and take her back to bed.

Eventually they had sorted out their needs and were on their way to James' chambers. Cristian was holding her hand between driving and they were both much calmer and ready for the day. Danika had braided her hair up and had a scarf around her neck, ready to put over her head later, wearing trousers and shoes rather than her usual skirt and sandals, ready for more work at the gallery.

The paperwork and legal aspect of a name change and signing over the assets took longer than expected. The wills were drafted from a fairly standard format, that was all getting a bit too emotional for Danika. James tried to spin the simple "just in case" excuse and "you have plenty of time to refine it later once you have kids" to ease her fear of tragedy. James confirmed he would forward all the copies of the papers through email for them to view in case they wanted to make changes but otherwise they were all legal as of now.

Danika could feel Cristian's relief that she would be financially safe in the event of his death, not realising it was no relief to her as it meant he would not be with her. She was looking forward to getting to the gallery to get her mind off of sombre thoughts.

The next few days seemed to fly past. The work at the gallery progressed well, with everyone pleased of the results by Friday morning. The website teasers had generated an overwhelming response, forcing Cristian to admit security would be needed for the launch. Rene sent out reminders to invited guests to bring their invitations for security purposes and that a valet service would be available due to parking distance issues. Danika's head was spinning as she thought about the NSW Gallery event they had gone to. Rene explained that they had been contacted by a few journalists to do a short story and was wondering who to accept.

Both Cristian and Danika felt concern about Robert knowing they were married and decided that keeping that part a secret was paramount. They were well aware of how quickly news could travel around the internet. He instructed the staff to keep it a secret as not all overseas relatives had been advised. He quickly sent a message to his mother and James also. At home in the apartment the tension built each night as Cristian was obviously not certain of sleeping near Danika in case of a repeat of the legacy incident. Danika had made it clear that she had put plenty of protection in place, yet he was sceptical. More than once, Danika found him asleep on the couch.

'After the launch we are going back to the estate, aren't we?' Danika asked him when they were alone.

'Yes if you like, that was what you had said to Mother, wasn't it?'

'Good, I'll make sure I pack for it. Was your mother staying with us at the apartment tonight?'

'No, Mark is her chauffeur tonight and is taking her back. Mother sent Ann and Ben away for a couple of days to make up for last weekend. They will be there Sunday again though,' he replied.

Danika was nodding but she was also shielding her thoughts. She knew Cristian could tell but before he could ask about it Paul was asking him about security for the back dock area.

Although Cristian and Danika had suggested that Paul and Rene did not necessarily need to be there, they were just as keen to see the first reactions to the major changes they had made. They all ended up waiting with bated breath for the first person to arrive. The security camera showed Mark pulling around the back with Elizabeth. Cristian went to meet them. Next to arrive a short time later was Juliet Meyers, Danika met her at the front door. The black screens were still on the windows and a temporary one had been placed just inside so that no casual lookers could see in.

'Hello, Juliet, pleased to see you again.' Danika extended her hand which Juliet took in a quick firm shake before almost barrelling past her to go inside.

'Hello again, Danika, let's see what all the fuss is about,' she replied, as obviously the response online was no mystery to her.

Juliet stood still once she was past the screen and looked around in surprise. The art gallery starkness was gone. In the centre was a plinth with Maude Brooks' cat statue pride of place with a cat toy strategically placed as if it was playing. Against the walls were a mixture of seats, designed to make you feel as if you wanted to sit in them with tables or stools, lamp stands and art on the walls. A couple of rugs also added to the homey feel. The theme changed as you moved around and looked back as well. At one end were some of Janet Wells' works, as if they were in a garden setting with scenery projected on a large wall screen. Danika handed Juliet a small handheld mirror to view the photos and art that lined the higher walls and roof without needing to crane her neck.

Juliet had been quiet for a minute or two before expressing her surprise and delight at the change of gallery.

As Danika handed her a catalogue she said, 'This is exclusive though, Juliet, so not for sharing until after the launch, please.'

Cristian was coming in with his mother just as Juliet had come in and stood speechless briefly just inside the gallery. The second time Danika had been able to do that, this time without witchcraft.

'Hello, Juliet, glad you could make it. May I introduce my mother Elizabeth?' Cristian shook Juliet's hand and then let the two women speak briefly as he looked at Danika and smiled, sending congratulatory thoughts her way.

Elizabeth turned to Danika. 'My word. What a difference Danika, you have obviously all been working very hard this week.' Danika guided her around the displays and handed her a mirror also. She was explaining the ideas when Rene had noticed more arrivals and met them at the door. Mrs Walton was being assisted out of a car so Danika went to meet her and make sure she could manage the step. Elizabeth came over and they were both hugging and crying together at lost loves. Danika suggested they sit on the two-seater couch together so they could talk while she got them a cup of tea.

Slightly later, Danika made her way to the front of the gallery and saw Janet Wells sitting in her car at the end of the street. She could feel the woman's nerves from where she stood, so she performed a comforting chant. Cristian came out at that moment to join her.

'She's very nervous, I'm trying to encourage her. She made it this far,' Danika said quietly, knowing he would still hear. He went back inside so as not to put her off. Danika was sending out a stream of happy thoughts towards Janet.

Before long, Danika was showing Janet into the gallery. Cristian took his cue from her to keep Juliet busy at least until Janet was a little more settled. She spotted her art in the projected garden first and was quite emotional. There was more in the window hidden by the screens for now with a water feature that Danika turned on to show her, explaining it would look better from outside once the screens were down. Finally she was able to take in the rest of the gallery. Danika handed her a mirror to view the ceiling display then went back to speak to Mrs Walton and Elizabeth.

'Are you ladies ready to look through the rest of the gallery and studio?' Danika helped Mrs Walton to her feet and then she was pleased to just take Elizabeth's arm as they wandered around, looking at the displays and discussing old times. After, Danika went back over to Janet to see how she was going.

'Thank you for inviting me, I nearly didn't come. I'm so glad I did. You have been very kind to make such a feature of my work. I'm living with my family now, it is wonderful to have the grandchildren around me. I've started teaching them to draw and sculpt. We are planning a holiday away together, something I couldn't do before, all thanks to you.' Janet touched Danika's arm.

'Well, thank you actually, for letting us buy your collection. Our curators have found new ways to restore the work sympathetically. If you would like to come out to the back studio you can see what I mean.' Danika knew that Janet really only came to see her own works even though she had given her a catalogue and offered her the mirror. She took her out to the studio as Juliet was coming back with Cristian who was offering her some of the snacks and drinks back in the gallery. Danika stopped to introduce them.

'Juliet, can I introduce you to one of our featured artists. Janet

Wells makes the wonderful sculptures out the front besides the ones out here.' Juliet beamed at Janet as she had already picked a couple for her own garden.

'I've already put my name on the bidding list for some of your work, lovely to meet you in the flesh.' Juliet held out her hand for the obligatory hard quick handshake.

Cristian nodded he would keep an eye on them so Danika could get back to the other ladies who were now sitting down again talking with Paul about the work to put the collection together.

'Elizabeth and I have decided to catch up next week thanks to you. You and Cristian seem to be very close. Is that more than work?' Mrs Walton asked smiling.

'You never know what a spring wind will bring.' Danika smiled back.

After an hour Mrs Walton and Janet were both ready to leave so Cristian and Danika made sure they got to their cars safely and wished them well. Inside, Juliet was making her last choices and commandeered Cristian to try to find out more details of future works from him. Danika passed them out to the studio where she found a group with Paul and Rene talking to Mark who had come in to check on Elizabeth and was having some supper and drink also. Cristian locked the front door and turned off the outside light after Juliet had left, joining the group to discuss how it all went.

Danika could feel all the positive vibes spilling from everyone. Mark was having a quick look around, explaining that he was not much for art or galleries but was still impressed. They all started an informal debrief about what did and didn't work to prepare for the next night. 'Thank you for keeping Juliet entertained tonight,' Danika said quietly to Cristian, seated beside him.

'I believe she thinks she has an exclusive first buy at the whole collection. I didn't tell her that the online bidding and sale room doesn't open until the launch time tomorrow.' Cristian smiled at them all.

Elizabeth motioned to Mark who came over to escort her to the car. 'I think I shall take my leave now. Congratulations everyone, it all looks wonderful and in such an amazing timeframe. You should all be very proud of yourselves.' Elizabeth held her hand out to Danika who kissed her on the cheek and then Cristian was also hugging her.

'Thank you, Mother.'

'I actually wouldn't mind a couple of those statues in our gardens if you have any left after the launch.' With that comment she then went with Mark out to the back car park.

'I'll clear up here if you two would like to go now, thank you so much for all your work and input. Get some rest, we'll see you back here about 10 am, no need for an earlier start. I think we will be busy tomorrow night,' Danika said to Rene and Paul. She thanked them and sent gratitude thoughts to them both.

As Danika was packing down and flicking off more lights, she bumped straight into Cristian. Unusual for her, she was normally very aware of his presence. Cristian grabbed her arms before she lost balance and gave her a quick kiss.

'Well done, Mrs Blakesley, you should be proud,' Cristian said, letting her go.

'Thank you Mr Blakesley, I didn't do it alone. How did I miss you?'

'You didn't miss me, I was a bit sneaky. I used the legacy,' Cristian admitted. 'I have a theory that I can turn it on with practice. It includes super-fast movement.'

'I'm not sure how I feel about that. Why do you want to do it, is there a purpose or a plan?' Danika moved away from hugging him and was feeling a bit uneasy at his easy attitude.

'Yes, there is a purpose. To make sure I have all the weapons in the arsenal so to speak. My plan is that I don't get on the back foot when I meet with Robert.'

'I'm disappointed you didn't discuss this with me first, because I know this is about me and protecting me.' Danika was not sure if she would have agreed or not but that choice was taken from her.

'Let's talk about this more back at home, I'll help close up.'

The ride home was quiet with them both containing their thoughts.

Danika knew Cristian had blocked his thoughts as she had also for the first time. She could feel an argument coming on. It would be their first and it saddened her greatly. She understood in his mind being prepared made sense, but for her it meant he was planning to expose himself in the worse possible way in his bid to protect her. Maybe she didn't need protection, he had not considered that. Her mind then moved to the type of protection she was going to need; might require some practice herself. That thought bubbled around in her head until they arrived at the apartment.

They unpacked the car and took the lift up to the apartment in silence, each in their own thoughts, still not sharing them. As they shut the door and put things down they looked at each other and, going into their arms, opened up completely.

'I'm sorry, I love you and I believe in you. I know you are doing this for me, for us. I'm sorry I doubted you,' Danika blurted it all out at his chest as she started crying.

'I love you and I was wrong not to say anything to you first. I believe in you but I am just so scared that I might fail you and not be able to protect you,' Cristian said to the top of her head. He leant back to see her face, swiping away her tears. 'No need to cry, we will work through this together.'

'That was our first argument it was horrible. I don't ever want to do that again.' Danika couldn't stop crying. 'I'm scared too, but I've kept busy trying not to think about it.' She moved away to get a tissue to wipe her eyes and nose. 'I don't want you to sleep on the couch again. I'm lonely and I said I never wanted to be lonely again.' Another wave of sobbing overtook her.

Cristian picked her up and moved to the couch to hold her until she had stopped crying. It took quite a while before she was able to calm, but he spoke to her in soothing tones the whole time, telling her how much he loved her and promising he would not sleep on the couch again. She was quiet for a while, processing her thoughts.

She squeezed his hand and asked, 'So, what can you do by choice using the legacy then?' Curiosity had got the better of her.

'Well, you already know I have good hearing, I can turn it up a bit more.' He demonstrated this by going in the bathroom and closing both doors, having instructed her to whisper something he would not expect while keeping her thoughts closed off also.

Her whisper had him by her side in a flash. She looked at him and said, 'Did I just experience two of your wolfie skills then?'

'Are you sure? How do you know?' Cristian asked, ignoring her question and focusing on her whisper.

'I am fairly sure,' Danika admitted. 'But a pregnancy test won't work for another week. I just can feel it. I asked the universe for fertility and that's what I got.' Danika was smiling at him as he was now more concerned than ever.

'Another week, but that will be the lunar cycle.'

'Show me more if you are game. I need to understand this also.'

Moving over to his blood stone. Cristian put one hand on it to keep himself centred and then thought of the dream that had him changing the other night. A growl escaped first and then his lips pulled back to reveal lengthened teeth. His hair on his head and face became long and thick, and then just before it went any further he broke the thought and placed his other hand on the blood stone to calm down. His hand was nearly a paw.

Danika was mesmerised by what she saw. It all only took a minute or two as did the change back. 'That must hurt.' That was all she could think of at first.

'Yes it does, but I can cope when it is gradual. A full fast change would be debilitating and I'm not sure if I can direct myself yet. As in, can my human thoughts rule my lupus mind?' Going over to the cabinet he poured himself a whiskey to swill around his mouth and swallow it.

'I can't control it on a full moon. Something I read in Father's journal about holding it as long as possible gave me the idea about having some control. I knew my hair became stiff at times of great emotion but until you said about what you had witnessed I hadn't realised how much it may be possible to change without the moon. So I have been practicing my control.' He was watching Danika to see her reaction as she stared at him.

'You closed your thoughts again. Why?' Danika was still grappling with this new information.

'The image I projected for myself to practice is not one I want you to see and you didn't need to feel the pain I was experiencing.'

'I don't want you to do that anymore please. Your practicing has to be mine also. I need to learn how to cope with your change otherwise the next one could be too much of a shock.'

When Cristian reluctantly agreed, Danika excused herself to do some meditation on the balcony. Afterwards, Cristian handed her a cup of tea to warm back up and together they prepared for sleep. Her mind was a whirl of thoughts, but she appreciated the time to try to grasp them slowly.

Cristian

Cristian had watched her slow walk to the bed and the pink marks where he had scratched her were still visible on her stomach. Strain was still evident on her face which made him worry about her. Even more now she thought they were going to have a baby. A baby. He was now at odds. She was so beautiful he wanted to make love to her but was worried about the baby. What did he need to do? He remembered his father's journal again. His father had only mentioned the lunar change as dangerous, no other time. Perhaps he should ask his mother or get Danika to. He looked across to her and could sense she was asleep. He didn't want to disturb her but had promised not to sleep away from her. Turning off all but the bathroom light, he placed a pillow between them and crawled into bed with his back to her.

9

THE LAUNCH

CRISTIAN WOKE FEELING very warm and realised that Danika had rolled over at some time during the night, removing the pillow barrier and now had her head against his back, her arm draped over his torso and one leg over his. It was agony waking aroused and, not wanting to be that way, he tried to disengage her to go have a shower. She was having none of that, holding him firm she mumbled something at his back. He didn't dare turn over and confirm his desire. Too late. Her hand move downwards but he grabbed it to stop her. Now she was no longer mumbling.

'What is the problem? We have time.' She sat upright, her breasts clear to see. 'Oh no you don't. You are not pushing me away because of some misguided fear of hurting me or this.' Danika touched her stomach.

'We don't know. I could hurt you if we get too energetic or I start to change.' He was definitely bewildered, not wanting to be aroused but staring at her naked breasts. He could see she was angry.

'So, is this going to be our second argument in less than twenty-four hours? Women have been having babies for millions of years and being pregnant does not stop them having sex.' She held up her hand as he was about to point out the difference of their situation.

'No, I refuse to believe that the Blakesley woman go into some sort of hibernation from sex during pregnancy because of the legacy. I'm going to ask Elizabeth when we see her.' Danika now stood out of bed, anger flooding their connection, and stormed into the bathroom and slammed the door.

Cristian had been going from concern to apology and, now watching and feeling Danika get angry, standing there naked and so indignant, he was ready to burst. He leaped out of bed and was bursting through the bathroom door in seconds. She was stood at the vanity, shocked at his entrance and then they were in each other's arms, no apologies from either of them as they grasped and nipped at each other. Cristian lifted Danika onto the vanity so she could wrap her legs around him, both climaxing in seconds.

'I like this make up sex,' Danika said into his chest. They both laughed and then Cristian looked over to the door.

'I think I broke the door.' They laughed more.

'Can we please now agree it is business as usual on the home front? Full disclosure, no holding back without consultation?' Danika asked as they separated.

'That sounds very businesslike, but yes I agree,' Cristian said and kissed her before helping her down.

After a playful shower together they were dressing and discussing the upcoming day's plans and the launch in the late afternoon. Breakfast was leisurely and large as they were both very hungry and guessing they may not eat much later. They could both feel the tension and secrets had gone and they were now working as one again.

It was just after 10 am when they pulled into the back dock area of the gallery. Paul's car was pulled in tight to the fence to allow as much room as possible for the caterers vehicles and Cristian did the same.

Danika was very pleased with the way the day was going despite the bumpy beginning. They laughingly did a practice walk through all together to see how a group of people navigated the area and made a small change to the position of items that may be jostled and damaged, otherwise it all seemed to work well. Checking the website and emails they seemed to have a 90% acceptance from the invitations which is normally unheard of. Hopefully they could accommodate everyone all at the same time. Danika suggested a quick change in the office and kitchenette area so they could make more room for the caterers and give a bit more room in the studio. Paul also suggested he could move the no go area barriers back another metre. None of them expected to be doing these last-minute changes but all went well.

Rene offered to walk down to the nearby café to get them all drinks rather than mess up the kitchen and Paul quickly offered to help carry them. Danika watched them go, thinking how wonderful it was that they were enjoying each other's company. She took the opportunity to sit down and look at the work they had all put in. Cristian came to sit with her also.

'This is probably the only break we will get until it is all over. I have to say that for a beginner at art dealing and events you have certainly come to this like a fish to water. I am so proud of you.' Cristian held her hand. 'Paul and Rene and the others are happier also.'

'Thank you for saying that. I could never have predicted this change in my life, but now I am here I couldn't imagine doing anything else. Keep an eye on me tonight in case I get intoxicated from the vibes.' She smiled at him at the joke when he thought she was serious briefly.

'I know I had Paul put up no photography signs but I might just take our own later on just for the record. You could send some to your mother,' Cristian suggested.

'Yes I might. I am really looking forward to this being over now strangely.' Danika was trying not to get too excited and spread her energy over the night. She grasped her crystal and whispered a little to calm her nerves. Cristian rubbed her other hand to share his calm thoughts with her, making her smile.

When Paul and Rene returned Danika spotted them let go of their hands. Everyone enjoyed the coffee break just before the caterers and security turned up. Then they seemed to be busy right up to the open.

Danika decided to take five minutes to check her hair and clothes and then sneaked a peak out at the crowd growing outside. The road seemed congested even with the excellent efforts of the valets. She hoped no one complained. Then it was time for her and Cristian to greet the crowd before letting them in.

Danika was pleased Cristian greeted them introducing Danika as the main art consultant which made her blush. Then they were filtered in to view the collection.

All four answered questions, steered people to different displays and assisted both caterers and security questions as needed. Juliet was there again to see the response and note who was there. She was very complimentary and generally helped also. Danika was very grateful and made sure she knew that her expertise was valued.

When it was time for the speeches Cristian yet again took the lead, introducing Paul and Rene and thanking the other staff responsible for the displays. Lastly pointing out that the collection would not have been possible without Danika's intuitive eye. Everyone clapped and the staff cheered, making Danika feel very emotional. The hours passed in a blur and before they knew it they were showing the last person out and the caterers were stacking their trays into the vans. Security had not had any problems more than the temporary traffic block that cleared quickly once a couple of them helped the valets get the cars to the leased parking. Overall a fantastic collection launch.

Danika remembered that she had wanted some photos and had Paul, Rene and Cristian stand in different places so she could take photos, then they insisted that she had a photo also. Paul openly held Rene's hand as they left, Danika happily noted. The ride from the gallery to the apartment was a relief to be able to sit down. Despite being very tired Danika was still going through the running of the day and night hoping everyone was happy.

'You do know you can't please everyone all the time?' Cristian had parked and looked at her in the passenger seat. 'I think you did an amazing job of being the ambassador for the gallery and an amateur art dealer that seemed to surprise the professionals with your passion and descriptions of the pieces.'

'Thank you darling, I am pleased with how it all went. Believe me, no one was more surprised than me how well it went. I kept thinking someone would think I was a fraud. Weren't the staff all amazing tonight?' Danika was mentally hugging herself.

'That's because you picked them all except Paul and Rene, but even they have come alive since you came on the scene.' Cristian held her hand and said, 'Come on love let's get you upstairs and into bed.' At Danika's image of exhausted love making he added, 'That was not my plan but if you want to?' He left the question open and then they were making their way up to the apartment.

Late the next morning they woke together, both eager to get back to Hollingrove after the hectic week leading up to the launch. They both wanted the space and calm of the estate.

Pulling up to the gates Danika felt the stress of the city fall off her shoulders. As they drove up the drive Danika was sure the front of the house looked different but couldn't quite pick it. Ben met them in the garage to take their bags up to their room and the empty hamper to the kitchen, directing them to go into the dining room where lunch was waiting for them.

Ann was bringing in a jug of juice as they came into the dining room adding it to the other covered dishes on the buffet.

'Welcome home Master Cristian and Ms Danika. Mrs Blakesley will be joining you shortly but asked that you start without her.' Ann was smiling broadly.

The selection as usual was large and delicious. Danika enjoyed seeing all the fruits and salads with Cristian filling up on sliders and sweet potato chips. Danika was considering a slider also as Cristian was enjoying his so much when Elizabeth came in.

'Hello, you two, you look hungry,' she noted their full plates smiling.

'We missed dinner last night and breakfast this morning. We couldn't wait to get here,' Danika admitted rapidly before sitting down to start on her full plate.

'I'm glad you waited, Ann's food is much healthier than take away. How did it go last night? Have you seen the reviews?'

'Reviews? What reviews?' Danika stopped eating as Elizabeth handed them the newspaper turned to a journalist's review of the launch. 'Did you know he was there?'

Cristian looked at the name. 'I know him as a dealer, I didn't know he also had a column in a newspaper.' The photo showed all four of them standing in front of the collection but it was obvious that Cristian had his arm around Danika. 'There was a ban on photography, this was obviously a sneak view between people.' The only good outcome was the colour of Danika's eyes did not show, they looked like they were black.

'The review was very complimentary and at least they spelt everyone's names correctly. Hopefully this does not rate overseas.' Elizabeth was trying to be positive.

'I refuse to be afraid of a maybe and someone I have never met. It was a great night and I am going to finish my lunch.' Danika was trying to be brave as she stabbed a piece of fruit. Inside she was trembling and Cristian could feel it.

'Before we forget, happy Mother's Day Elizabeth.' Danika put a small, wrapped box on the table in front of Elizabeth.

Cristian stood up and gave his mother a kiss on the cheek. 'Happy Mother's Day.'

'Oh, I had no idea. I don't follow those event style traditions,' Elizabeth said but Danika could feel how happy she was as she unwrapped her brooch and was very taken by it. 'It's lovely, thank you both.' She pinned it to her top for them to see.

'Elizabeth, I've had an idea about the renovations.' Danika was determined to carry on as planned. 'I thought I might repurpose what we already have and paint it a different colour. That seems to be the current theme in furniture. It seems a waste to discard it and buy new, less sturdy furniture.'

After lunch, Danika asked to join Elizabeth in the north wing while Cristian agreed to amuse himself.

'Have a seat by the fire my dear, now what did you want to discuss?' Elizabeth sat opposite her.

'I'm going to leap straight in because I don't know how else to do it.' Danika took a deep breath. 'Did Henry change at all outside of the full moon?'

Shock covered Elizabeth's features before she slowly nodded. 'Yes, when he was particularly emotional. Anger was the worst and fear. Then sometimes when we… well I'm guessing that is why you are asking?'

'Yes. But could he control it, as in turn it on and off?' Danika wanted to know more, not sure how personal she should get. This was Cristian she would be talking about, to his mother.

'He started to think he could and was planning to practice with Cristian before he had his accident. He had said that he was positive that Robert was doing it regularly but it is dangerous if there are any non-werewolf people exposed to it. Did something happen?'

Danika weighed up how much she should say. 'Cristian wants to practice. I noticed a slight change and then there was a little incident while he was dreaming. He thinks he needs to have all the weapons in the armoury when he encounters Robert.' She hoped Elizabeth would understand.

'Did he hurt you, by accident?' Elizabeth asked, very concerned.

'Not really, just trying to protect me against an imaginary threat.' Danika didn't want Elizabeth to worry any more than she had to. 'But it meant he was scared to be near me for a few days. Did Henry keep away from you when you were pregnant for instance?'

'Only close to the full moon he kept well away. Are you trying for a baby?'

'Not trying, more like not *not* trying if you get my drift.' Danika started to laugh. 'Thank you for helping and I know this is very personal. I may need to ask more if that is okay, after all my mother only has experience with a girl.'

'When are you going to introduce Cristian to your mother?'

'We did a video chat just before we visited you. It didn't go well unfortunately but hopefully we can visit shortly and win her over with our love and happiness.' Danika realised she hadn't told Elizabeth anything of her life. 'My mother is a witch also as were all my female ancestors. We don't know our fathers as they never identify them or have them in their lives. In the past we all only have girls so it is going to be interesting if we have a boy.'

'Where does your family live?'

'There is only my mother Selene now. My grandmother passed away twelve years ago, she was my mentor. My mother is a bit intense. She owns a rural property in South Australia in the Adelaide Hills. It has been in the family for about a hundred and fifty years I think. It is rather beautiful, a bit too much for her to look after alone but she is fiercely independent.'

'That must be very difficult for her alone. Would she accept your help if you gave it?'

'I guess we will find out. I'd like to repair her house or build a new one.' Danika didn't want to pursue that today so changed the topic. 'Anyway, getting back to my decorating ideas. I plan to paint the furniture cream probably with black features like the handles. Also changing the rugs and curtains for new lighter ones. Then removing the heavy wallpapers for either paint or lighter paper. I might need a team of helpers though. I would love your input with the colours.'

'You need to remember to take before and after photos too,' Elizabeth reminded her.

They were both glad to finish the conversation on a lighter note.

Upstairs Danika was just about to go into the bedroom when she heard Cristian in the study. Going in to check on him, he was downloading and printing more photos from the launch party. He smiled as Danika entered. 'Hello you, how did the talk with Mother go?'

'Did you hear any of it?' Danika sensed he had.

'A bit, not all. It seemed rude to eavesdrop so I focused on something else. Actually I have something to show you.' Cristian stood up and came around to Danika. 'Come this way.' He led her out again to the hall and across to the balcony where he opened the door smoothly and showed her out. Outside the balcony was now clean and tidy with a new paint job.

'Oh thank you, I thought it looked different from the brief view I had when we arrived, this is wonderful.' Danika was already planning to come out tonight.

'You can decorate here also, chairs, plants, whatever you want.' Cristian was glad she was pleased. 'I have downloaded the photos from the launch would you like to see them? You can choose any you want to print.'

Going back into the study they were looking at the photos together, commenting on some of the ones he had taken without people knowing; they were some of the best. 'You have your mother's keen eye for a shot. I would like that one of the four of us you had James take for the studio. I think your mother wants to tell you something about an email perhaps, I couldn't grasp all of her thoughts.' Danika thought Elizabeth needed to tell him something alone. 'We had a good talk and I feel I could ask her anything about the legacy from her perspective. We probably need to read your grandfather's journal also.'

Cristian stood up to hug her and gave her a kiss. 'Are you happy, Danika? We haven't left on the quest you wanted or planned any travel. Did you still want to leave this week?'

Danika kissed him back before replying. 'My plans, our plans, seemed to have been set aside I agree but I still think we are being driven by the universal forces. So I am going with the flow so to speak while we work it out. I still would like to go to Tasmania after Robert's visit if we could and then perhaps to visit my mother.'

'Of course if you are happy to wait that long. I thought it would be a good idea to completely relocate here also from the apartment. I mean, bringing the artefacts and your van. How do you feel about that?' Cristian suggested. 'That way we could offer Robert the apartment rather than staying here if needed.'

'I understand your thinking and yes I don't want him here if possible or anywhere near us but I know he is still your family.' Danika's aversion to Robert, a man she had never met, seemed to be getting stronger by the day. Cristian hugged her tighter. 'Can we leave it a few days before we go back to Sydney. I would like to recuperate and enjoy walking around the estate?'

'Yes definitely, I need to run regularly this week ready for Monday's full moon. Which I should point out is during the day which gets a bit complicated. I'm sorry my darling.' Cristian moved her so he could look at her face. Danika was instantly worried and confused.

'What do you do when there is a daytime full moon?' Danika was struggling to get her head around the implications.

'Usually I make sure I am somewhere very isolated. I had thought we would be near Canberra and I would head for the forests, not that it is as easy to hide anywhere now during the day. I prefer somewhere I have been before so there is no confusion.' He was trying to sound positive. 'I'll have a look around and if nothing becomes obvious I'll go to the cell again. We just have to send all the staff home.'

'You don't want to do that though, do you?' Danika looked at him. 'So that's it, we have to organise a safe place for you as a priority. Please, I need to know you are going to be safe.'

'I will, don't worry. Now I will go down and see Mother about these emails and leave you to unpack if that is alright?' He kissed her and then went down to speak to his mother.

Danika was realising how her connection and marriage to Cristian had now put him at risk. He had not planned his lunar cycle and was not going to be where he needed. She didn't understand why he hadn't said anything sooner and let her plan the collection launch.

She would research forests if she knew what she was looking at or for. The sooner this curse was broken the better.

Cristian

Cristian knocked on his mother's door and waited for her to call him in. 'Hello Mother, I thought I would come to see if you had heard any more from the family overseas.'

'Yes, I didn't want to bring it up when you first arrived but we probably should address it sooner than later.' Elizabeth went to her desk drawer and pulled out some emails she had printed. 'These are from Ingrid, your distant aunt, mother of Peter who came as the European representative when your father died.' She handed them to Cristian who scanned them quickly.

'So they have been searching for a cure from the curse also?' Cristian was not really surprised. 'She thinks they will all die out if they are discovered. Is this all you have so far, Mother? I wonder how many are for a cure and how many are not? It would be nice to know what we are up against.'

'You don't think they would come after you or anything, do you? Ingrid seemed very scared by the tone of her message but determined at the same time. It seems several of the young wives have become rebellious at not being able to have girls and the travel restrictions over the last two years of the pandemic and now they are restricted because of the legacy. I noticed Ingrid does not call it a legacy anymore.' Elizabeth had read more between the lines than Cristian had noticed.

'I will read Grandfather's journal tonight, perhaps he has some insights. I found Father's journal in the safe a couple of weeks ago and found it insightful for my experience with Danika.' Cristian watched his mother for a reaction, she seemed as if she was waiting for more.

'He said that you had drawn him in the change, did you keep the drawings?'

'Oh yes, of course I did. I couldn't photograph him so it would be the only memory I had of him that way.' Cristian sensed his mother was stronger than recently, he was very proud of her resilience.

'Would it be all right if I saw your drawings? I remember clearly what he looked like when he showed me before I came of age. But a drawing would be different.' Cristian wasn't sure if she would agree.

'Just a moment.' Elizabeth went out of her drawing room and into her personal rooms to return with a satin covered pouch file and handed it to him.

Inside were several drawings of parts and of his whole body from different angles. It was obvious they were drawn with love. Cristian was amazed at the talented artist that she was and wondered why she had not drawn more. As he looked through more there were drawings of a baby and a boy obviously him. 'These are wonderful Mother, you are very talented. Would it be all right to show Danika?'

Elizabeth hesitated and left the room to come back with another drawing. She handed it to him. 'Yes you can and this one I drew last month after seeing you. You can give this to Danika. She is a lovely girl Cristian, I am so glad she is here with you. So glad we are going to be a family. I will do anything to keep us all safe.'

'Danika does not want Robert to stay here and neither do I. We are clearing the apartment this week as an alternative for him.' Cristian was pleased to see his mother nodding her head. 'We have to research more and I may have to use the cell again because it is a daylight full moon on the 16th with a partial eclipse and too hard to find a suitable location.'

'Oh Cristian that is hard for you again already. I'll have to give the staff the day off.'

Cristian took the satin pouch with him back to Danika to look at with the precious gift from his mother. As he was making his way up the stairs he could hear sounds of furniture being moved. Then he was next to her, stopping what she was doing.

'What are you doing? You shouldn't be lifting anything heavy.' Cristian put a hand on her hold on the cupboard in the next room.

'I didn't hear you coming. I'm alright just trying out an idea.'

'What is your idea?' Cristian couldn't believe how worried he already was of their yet unknown unborn child.

'Oh sweetheart, I'm all right.' She hugged him. 'Well I want to renovate and we don't want Robert here, am I right?'

'Yes okay, and?' Cristian hadn't joined the dots yet.

'So if I start then we have our excuse why he cannot come here. Besides I could get some colour charts for our rooms and a nursery.' He kissed her hard at that statement.

'Well, what are you trying to do in here?' Cristian thought it just looked like the other spare rooms.

'I was going to put most of this furniture in the one Robert used. I know I can't move it all that way alone but I was testing how heavy it was. Sorry I scared you.' Danika then put on a please help face. 'But as yet I can't go in his room. Could you and I'll look through the door?'

'Okay, come on then,' Cristian said.

He had dropped the pouch on the sprint to Danika and now picked it up and put it on the cupboard before they both walked across the landing to the spare bedroom Robert had used in the past. Danika stood back, holding her crystal in one hand and medallion in the other as Cristian opened the door. The push back was noticeable but bearable.

'Did he leave anything in there that seems specific?' Danika asked.

Cristian started opening drawers first, even looking under the paper drawer liners. He went through the wardrobe and the bedside tables but found nothing, then looked under the bed. Moving the mattress to look at the base he still didn't find anything unusual.

'Can you narrow it down?' Cristian suggested.

Danika moved in closer and held her hands out, the crystal in one and closed her eyes to focus, pointing. Cristian followed where she pointed to a picture on the wall. Just a print of a European scene, similar to where Robert lived. Cristian lifted it off the wall and brought it closer, making Danika back up. Instead he put it on the bed to look at it. Turning it over there was an envelope attached to the back of the picture. It felt like a heavy metal object was inside. He took it off and went to come out but Danika held him back.

'That's it, don't bring it out we need to look at it first and then I can cleanse it hopefully.' Danika held her hand up, chanting to protect herself.

Cristian opened the envelope and tipped out the flat metal object. It was a bronze horse brass with the Lleuad Blaidd on one side and the Triquetra on the other.

'Why would he bring that here? When was he here last? I don't understand. I never thought it would feel evil. I thought it was part of the twins with mine.' She held up her medallion and Cristian sensed the moment the vision took her over, feeling as anger and hatred swam around her.

'He came here late last year, the first chance of travel. He said to support us but it was more to harass us to sell up and come to Europe, even England he had said would be better. We didn't agree. He left and didn't want to come back until now.' Cristian looked at it. It looked exactly like the photo he had received except for one thing. 'Danika can you go get the photos that Peter sent please. They are in the briefcase in the study.'

She quickly brought them back. Cristian looked at them carefully and compared the horse bronze. 'It is not the same one. The photos show some wearing of the back as if it had rubbed the edges. This one the engraved Triquetra appears new.'

'It's a fake, but why? That is why it feels so evil.' Danika and Cristian came to the same thought together. 'Insurance in case we worked it out and he wanted to stop the process.'

'Can you render it safe? Then we can put it back so he doesn't know.' Cristian was asking a lot of Danika but it was for their future, the future of their family.

'I can try but I am going to need some strong magic to break it. He has accessed the dark side of magic to create this. He had help.' Danika had only heard of this but never experienced dark magic. 'Leave it in there for now and I will have to work on a spell and come back to it.'

Cristian placed it back in the envelope and left it on the bed, closing the door behind him.

'What did you have when you came up here?' Danika asked.

'Something Mother gave me. We should look at it together.' Cristian retrieved the pouch and they both went into the sitting room, sitting on the couch together to view the contents. 'Mother gave me printouts of emails from my distant aunt Ingrid, the mother of Peter who sent the photos.' He handed them to her to read.

'She is scared and it seems the others are also angry and scared, which is understandable. The world is closing in on them. If any of them were caught it would be unimaginable. That was what Mother thought. I also asked her about the drawings of Father. She let me borrow these to show you.' Cristian slid the older drawings his mother had made out of the pouch of his father and him over the years, many years ago.

Danika held them with reverence. The artistry *was* stunning. She had captured the essence of each subject, the first few of the specifics. One of a paw, an ear, a face and then the whole body standing proud.

'These are stunning Cristian. Your mother is very talented.' Danika turned over another and then there were the baby ones. Danika began to shed a few tears. 'These are better than the photos, so much love.'

Lastly he handed her another drawing. 'She is giving this one to you.' The subject was a wolf lying down with its head across an outstretched paw, appearing to be asleep. The fur had been drawn lighter than the others. Cristian could feel the course of Danika's changing emotions.

'This is you, isn't it? When was this?' The answer came before he could say. 'Last month, I can feel it. Elizabeth has not lost her talent for drawing; I do hope she continues to draw. What a precious gift.' She reached out for his hand. 'How did it feel for you seeing this?'

'I'll admit, a bit strange. I had remembered how Father looked the couple of times I saw him before I came of age but I have never seen myself. I had a vague memory of a reflection in water once when I was overseas but it was in a dream so a bit hard to hold on to it in waking thoughts.'

'It is such a shame these can't be part of the photo wall, but the baby ones can. I will ask Elizabeth later. For now we can lock these all away.' Danika handed the pouch back to Cristian, plus the emails and the drawing of him separately, which he stopped to look at again. 'After dinner I would like to spend some time out on the balcony absorbing strength from the stars to try to work out a plan to neutralise that dark magic.'

Later that night, they had a leisurely dinner with Elizabeth chatting about some of the finer details of the launch.

'Thank you for sharing your drawings with us. They are wonderful, you are very talented. I would like to display two of the baby ones of Cristian if that would be alright.'

'I would like that. What about you, Son, how do you feel about that?' Elizabeth looked at Cristian who was patiently listening.

'You know me Mother, not one for showing myself to the world especially as a baby but I have to admit your drawings are extremely good. So it is more about your talent than the subject.' Cristian reached for his mother's hand as reassurance.

After dinner, Cristian carried a tray of coffee and tea upstairs where they situated by the fire in the sitting room, the journals placed in front of them. As Cristian handed his father's journal to Danika he warned her that it may be difficult for her to read so he wouldn't mind if she needed to leave it.

'Thank you darling, I will take it carefully.'

As expected Danika felt all the emotions of his father's entries. Cristian tried touching her hand to dampen them a little so he could focus on his grandfather's journal. His grandfather had written many more entries than his father had. He tried to skim through most of them. They started in England with his coming of age. A few entries about travel during the war. Cristian wondered how the family had hid their legacy during that time. Then meeting his wife Jane. Their joy of a child, which would have been Robert. Some comments about worry over his wife as his own father had been. Then the joy of another boy, Cristian realised that was his father. Several entries regarding the arms race and concerns over the opinions of some of the European family. It had been a difficult and dangerous time for them all during the war. Most had gone to Switzerland or Sweden to avoid the conflict. The next entries were hard to read regarding a horror year for Jonathon as his own father was killed, in a hunting accident said the official report. Shortly followed by the death of his wife Jane to suicide at the depression of losing yet another baby girl.

Suddenly Danika was hugging him and crying. They had each reached a similar point in the journals.

'Do you want to stop reading?' Cristian was hugging her, trying to soothe her thoughts.

'Yes and no. It is nice to know that you get your wonderful nature from your father and, I can feel through you, from your grandfather also. I think it is good that we know the history.' Danika wiped her tears. 'So Robert was how old when your father was born?'

'Six by my calculations. Then it looks like it was only two years later that my grandmother took her own life. Father was only two, no wonder he never knew his mother.' Cristian could understand the grief of his grandfather now to lose his father and his wife then have two boys to look after while still dealing with the legacy. 'He must have sold up not long after that because they were here by 1955, that is the date on the front of the house.'

'How on earth did he look after two children on his own while he built this house, still dealing with the legacy?'

'I have yet to read that part if he wrote about it. Do you want a break? You wanted to meditate and enjoy the night as I remember.' Cristian was very concerned knowing the next few entries regarding his own coming of age may be difficult for her to read.

'I think you are right. I need a break but if you want to keep reading that is fine. I can distance myself from your thoughts while I meditate.' Danika kissed Cristian and went to gather a few pieces to take out on to the newly refurbished balcony.

Once Cristian could feel that Danika was settled and their link was closed off he started to read the journal again.

I don't think I would have coped if Sonya had not come over from Sweden to help with the boys. Her own boys are old enough to look after themselves. Robert has taken to her and keeps asking to go back with her when she leaves. He was always jealous of his baby brother Henry and blames him for his mother's death. It doesn't matter how many times I and Sonya try to explain it. I think we need to leave here.

Cristian realised now the background to Robert's thoughts, jealousy and resentment.

My enquiries regarding suitable large properties in Australia have been fruitful. The purchase of the scrub (as they call it down under) farm in New South Wales is nearly complete. Hollingrove will be sold in the coming months. A new beginning for my boys I hope.

Cristian wondered if his grandfather had taken any photos of the original property.

Robert is being very difficult as he doesn't want to leave England and wants to go with Sonya. It may have been a mistake to let her take the boys back to Sweden for a few weeks while I organised the clearing of the estate. Robert likes his cousins and their rough and wild ways. I hope moving away to a wilder land will change his attitude.

Cristian could hear Danika calling to the celestial bodies for strength and guidance.

The flight to Australia, the colloquially named kangaroo route, was long and arduous with little Henry who suffered with ear pain and boredom on the plane. The hostesses were wonderful with him though. Robert seemed to enjoy it more playing chess with another passenger and reading his comic books. Arriving in Australia four days later despite the heat was a blessing. I am glad I chose to stay in a hotel for a couple of days before going out to the farm.

Cristian could not imagine four days flying. What a change to today.

The last month has been challenging and hectic. I was lucky enough to find a wonderful family to help at the farm. Just in the nick of time, a nanny for the boys as well as a cook and farm help. The house is rudimentary but clean. Robert hates it because of the dirt, the flies and the smell, he says it smells different. He is right, the gum trees have a different aroma to the green fields and oaks we left behind. Henry seems to love the space to run around. The Norton family dote on Henry and try to engage with Robert. Building work on the new house starts next week. I hope to incorporate the stone from Hollingrove in it when the rest of our things arrive on the cargo boat.

What stone, Grandfather? Cristian wondered. He couldn't remember seeing or being told about any special stone from their past.

School has finished for the summer here, so different to England. The Norton family said that despite the heat they still make a traditional Christmas lunch just with seafood as well. The area for the house has been cleared and the foundations have been laid. Digging out the extensive cellar was considered strange by the builders but I am paying them enough not to argue. The works stop for two weeks over the Christmas and new year builders break, so we have constructed a fence around it as I am worried about the boys falling in. After the rations in England the bounty of food here is incredible.

It felt like a history lesson reading the insight into his grandfather's arrival to Australia. He listened for Danika and thought it sounded like she was packing up her things. He marked the page with a bookmark and closed the journal.

Danika came in looking serene with a glow about her. Cristian was very pleased to see her more herself after the last week. She put her rug and basket of candles and crystals down and came to his outstretched arms. They stood hugging for a few minutes then they opened their thoughts again to each other. As the mutual suggestion and agreement washed over them they turned off the lights in the sitting room and walked into their bedroom.

They woke late wrapped in each other's arms. After their slow and deliberate ministering of each other's needs and wants last night they slept long and deeply together. Dream free also which Danika said she had instigated as with the emotions of the day she felt it would be a risk.

They took a leisurely shower together and Cristian put his running gear on, knowing he would shower again after. Danika dressed in her more colourful clothes with plans to spend time in the gardens and talking to Mark about her proposed plans. Cristian said he would eat after his run. Taking the tray from last night with her Danika decided to go see what was on offer for the day down in the kitchen.

Danika was finishing the last of her waffles with berries and yoghurt as Cristian came through the kitchen. He grabbed a piece off her plate and grinned at her pulled face.

'I can dish you some up, Master Cristian,' Ann offered as Danika slapped his hand before he took her last piece.

'I would love that after my shower, thank you Ann.' Kissing Danika before he went he pinched one of the strawberries she had left and ran out the door.

Danika

Danika found her notebook and felt pen plus hat and sunglasses and made her way back down to the gardens. She could see that they had perhaps been a bit lusher and more laid out in years gone by but were now restricted to a smaller area within Elizabeth's view from the north wing downstairs windows. Danika realised she needed to find plants that were water wise during the summer. It seemed strange that at the moment lack of water was not an issue with the past floods in some areas. Danika hoped that in future they would be able to invite people for social events, not just the workers, and wanted the entrance and turn around at the front to be more welcoming than the expanse of gravel. Danika drew little plans, different on several pages.

Moving on to the established gardens with their roses and hedges it was all very formal but colourless during the winter months. She made notes about researching winter flowering plants, perhaps bulbs. She could see the statues which could use the touch of the curators, like Janet's artwork, to tidy them up. She remembered there was a piece to come here that Elizabeth had requested. More notes.

The water feature was looking a bit tired as it hadn't been turned on for a while. She walked around it then stopped as she felt a pull she couldn't quite understand. It felt like the pull of her own family pieces, that soft intangible connection that she took for granted. She leaned closer and still couldn't work out what it was and then she noticed a block of stone that didn't match the rest. It was halfway up the plinth that held the little cherub that would normally spout water. She thought she could see a mark on it and ended up getting into the dry trough for a closer look. She was so shocked by what she saw she had to sit down on the edge of the trough as she stared at the stone.

Then Cristian was there with her, checking she was alright. 'Danika are you alright? What happened?' He was looking at her face staring at the fountain and she raised her arm to point. He followed her direction and looked closer at the stone.

'That must be the stone Grandfather brought from England. Fancy him choosing that one.'

Cristian turned to look at Danika who was drawing the symbol as she had many times before, the Triquetra. He squatted down to have a closer look.

'There is something else, initials perhaps on the opposite corner. PC, probably the builder. I have no idea how old that would be the estate was built centuries ago apparently.'

'Sorry, I didn't mean to scare you, it was just such a shock. I felt this pull like I do with my own pieces or my mother's, like a family connection and then I felt a mild form of that as I got closer. I need to touch it.' Danika stood up and leaned closer with her hand outstretched. As she touched it the pull felt a little stronger but different like something of her mother's but not the same. 'I think this may have been something of my family, it is very faint.'

'Were any of your ancestors female builders?' Cristian stood up and helped her out of the water feature.

'I don't know because I don't know anything of the English connection. I don't think any question is silly at this point. If this was done by a male ancestor it must have been before the curse. There have been no males since then as far as I know from what Grandma and Mother have told me. Why did he choose to bring this one I wonder?' Danika was feeling like they needed to explore the English connection more. 'I feel like our connection is more than imprinting. More than that horror we felt. As we find one thing another question comes up.'

'I'm not sure. Perhaps he has written more in further journal entries. He wrote a lot more than Father did. Are you finished out here now or did you have more you wanted to do?'

'I wanted to do more but I think I might just come back up and do some plant research, feeling a little rattled at the moment.' Danika thought she wanted to write a list of things to follow up and then speak with Elizabeth and Mark.

Cristian walked back with Danika to the house as she pointed out some of her ideas. By the time she was back to look on the internet she was feeling less rattled. The rest of the day, Cristian read through more of his grandfather's journal while Danika researched appropriate plants for her plans, drawing some of her ideas on larger paper for Elizabeth to see and hopefully Mark to be able to help.

'The stone was part of the renovations in the 1600's. Apparently one wall was incomplete and patched up for no reason known and it had fallen into disrepair and been pushed aside. Grandfather literally just picks up one piece as a memento as he was leaving.' Cristian eventually found another reference to the stone being put in the water feature. 'Also his great, great uncle, Henry, who Father was named after, moved to Germany in the early 19th century, taking a lot of artefacts with him to the current castle where most of the history of the family has been kept. He makes mention of Robert being very enamoured of the history and maintaining the legacy at all costs.'

'He mentions the Norton's being invaluable a few times also and that he felt like they had a sixth sense about his needs.' Cristian was paraphrasing as he skimmed entries.

'Who are the Norton's?' Danika looked up from her sketches.

'Ann, Ben and Mark now but we had more here apparently in earlier days.' Cristian looked up at Danika. 'Have you ever felt anything from them? Do you get senses from others like you?'

'I can sense when people have a little talent that they are oblivious of but so far I have never met another like myself or my family. I even went to a few psychic fairs to try to find anyone like me.' Danika had a wistful feeling come over her. 'Unless they know how to keep it hidden. Ann and Ben I think are just very intuitive which is a rare talent. We haven't talked about Monday, are you going to try to get away or stay here?' Danika had been avoiding the question and wondered if he had given it any thought.

'I would rather be around and prepare for Robert's arrival so I will stay home. I can use the cellar again because of the timing. We have to send the staff away for Sunday and Monday.' Cristian was resolute about it. Danika could still feel his dislike of the process.

'I can help with whatever needs to be done.' Danika didn't know what that meant but she was determined she was not going to leave him.

'You can't be near me during the change it is too dangerous.'

'How does it work when it is a daytime full moon?'

'It is difficult and dangerous because it is unpredictable. Normally it is only at nightfall so you can prepare but daytime I can feel the pull yet seem to be able to hold the change until the night. As long as there are no high emotions involved.' Cristian remembered a couple of close encounters overseas and, with their connection open, Danika saw them as well. 'Last month the late moon meant I was slow to recover and Mother saw me, hence the drawing,' Cristian explained.

'Oh, I wondered about that. It is a miracle you all survive these monthly tests.' Danika was really beginning to understand the weight of the legacy.

'I think that was the point. We weren't supposed to. It was after all a curse. Obviously the survivors were more tenacious. Possibly because of their wealth and land holding they could hide. I never thought about Grandfather and how he coped moving to Australia with two children on his own. I have a newfound greater respect for him.' Cristian was putting out so much pride that Danika absorbed the feelings.

'What do you think about going back to the apartment tomorrow to gather our belongings to bring here?' Danika felt she needed all the pieces together. 'Including Rainbow so I might have to go talk to Mark about garaging.'

'If you like I have a message from James to collect some papers also so we can get a few things done in one trip.'

'Good. Well I might go find Mark and talk cars and gardens then.' Danika kissed Cristian before leaving, taking her drawn plans with her.

Danika found Mark in the stables making up some plant stakes with a few seedlings in a box next to them.

'Hello, Mark. What have you got there?' Danika was very interested in anything plant wise.

'Winter seedlings for the vegetable garden. Peas, beans cabbage, broccoli and a few others. Time to pull out the summer crops. Is there something I can help you with Mrs Blakesley?' Mark had stopped what he was doing to give her his full attention.

'I can't get used to that name, please call me Danika. Yes I have a few ideas for the garden to the side of the house and plans for the drive for another time. I wanted to touch base and get your opinion on them. Also, more importantly, I am bringing my camper van back tomorrow and wondered how we can fit it in the garage with the other vehicles?'

'Well the garage is the priority then so let's go have a look shall we. Danika, how big is your van?' They walked together over to the garage as Danika was trying to give him hand signal measurements.

Mark pointed out that one of the vehicles rarely used had been Cristian's grandfather's car. He pulled the dust cover off to show a pristine looking FJ Holden sedan. He thought they could probably move it around to park the estate car next to it, that would give more room for the van at the end.

Danika couldn't stop looking at the car and running her hand over it, the joy and fun times seemed to ooze from it. Her eyes were gleaming with unshed tears of joy as she turned back to Mark. 'She is so beautiful and much loved.' She had forgotten who she spoke with, then pulled herself together. 'Does it still run?'

'I turn it over every so often and make sure nothing gums up but it is up on blocks. Wouldn't take much to change that and move her.'

'Perhaps it would be better if I park my van next to her so that the estate car is still easy to get to. I don't think I will be using my van much in future but I am still a bit attached to it, if you know what I mean?' Danika was glad she could sense that he did. 'Would it help if Cristian came down to help with this?' Danika had already been sending thoughts to Cristian anyway as soon as the car was unveiled. He walked in before Mark could answer.

'Hello, you two, what have we here? I wondered where you were.' Cristian covered her summons.

'Hello, Master Cristian, we were just talking about moving cars to get Danika's van in,' Mark replied. Danika had to dampen Cristian's reaction to him using her first name, admitting she asked him to.

'I haven't seen this beauty for a while. You keep it immaculate Mark. Does she still turn over?'

Mark walked over to the key safe and brought out the keys, handing them to Cristian to try it. 'You can get in carefully as it is still on blocks,' Mark warned.

Cristian climbed in carefully, his fondness from memories seeping through to Danika, and turned the key. It started straight away. He looked at Mark, knowing he was the one looking after this precious car.

'Sounds good Mark, well done.' He revved it a little and then turned it off before getting out and handing the keys back to Mark.

Cristian and Mark spent a while sorting the car out while Danika went out to watch the chickens out the back and have a better look out that way. The utility side of the house, some of the structures of the chicken house and covered walkway looked very large and sturdy, almost like parts of a bigger building. Danika went over to an ornate wooden post and held it. She could feel the different lives that had touched this post including Cristian.

She felt him behind her.

'Was this something else before it was a chicken coop?'

'I believe it was recycled from the old farmhouse that was here, like the walkway to the clothesline. There may still be some of the posts and other wood up in the stable loft. Grandfather liked to keep what could be reused.'

'Have you told Robert that he can't stay here yet?' Danika asked as they returned to their rooms a few hours later, having completed their plans for the garden adjustments with Mark. They'd even found piles of the reclaimed wood and organised for a rotunda to be built where they or Elizabeth could spend time enjoying the gardens.

'Yes, he hasn't replied but he has read the message,' Cristian confirmed.

'I am going to call my mother tonight to ask her about the dark magic and if she knows of others like us.' Danika decided she needed to render that bronze piece in the other room harmless.

'Okay, whatever you feel comfortable with. Are you going to let her know we plan to visit?'

'Yes I should. At least that way I will know if we can or not.'

Cristian

The next day they arrived at the apartment before ten o'clock. It took longer than expected to load everything into the two vehicles. Making sure the blood stone was not going to fall or be knocked was a puzzle until they decided to sit it in the passenger seat with the seat belt and lots of packing around it. The plants went in the van also. The last to go down were the artefacts that Danika took on her own to put in the van, wrapping them in towels. She was pleased that her bouquet had dried nicely as had the lapel pin she hoped to display in a shadow box.

Cristian made sure they had removed all that was important to them each, then decided to wipe all trace of being there on all surfaces, such was his apprehension regarding Robert. Danika checked the laundry and bathrooms again to be sure and helped him wipe down all the surfaces there also. Then out to the balconies to do the same. The clearing was tinged with sadness as this was the place that they imprinted and got to know each other and loved. She was realistic though knowing this was necessary.

Danika said goodbye in her own way, spreading good thoughts throughout the apartment before leaving with Cristian as he locked up. Cristian went off to see James his lawyer and Danika made her way slowly back to the estate, making one short stop on the way.

As she pulled up to the gates of Hollingrove on her own for the first time she had a moment of pause until she remembered she had the electronic pass Cristian had given her in her bag. *I really need to get a different bag,* she thought as she searched the copious tote.

Once inside the gates she slowly approached the garage, deciding how to back in when Mark hailed her down.

'Would you like me to back in the garage for you?' he suggested.

'Yes please Mark, I would hate to scrape anything on the way.'

With Mark's help, and eventually Ben and Ann's, they got the van unloaded and all the items stowed into new locations inside Danika's and Cristian's rooms. With all four of them working together it was finished in no time definitely quicker than it took to load it all at the apartment.

By the time she had finally put things away in an orderly fashion Cristian was arriving back. She looked at the two artefacts and decided to put them in the next bedroom while she considered their use along with the dried flowers yet to be placed in a suitable display box.

Ben appeared with more clothes of Cristian's. After putting away the first round of their clothes by herself, Danika accepted Ben's help to put them away. Cristian was behind him bringing up the laptop and other office supplies, sitting on top was his graduation photo. In his hand was a cotton sack which held money from the apartment safe. He looked across to the window where his bloodstone had been placed with the two plants in their display pots either side of the window. He had a rush of feeling very pleased to be home. Danika felt it as well.

'Ben put them there for you,' Danika confirmed. Cristian in turn thanked him for his help as Danika had done. 'Is there much more to bring up?'

'Just a few toiletries and personal items I can bring them up.' Cristian looked at her. 'Are you okay? You look a bit tired.'

'A bit yes but I expected this to be a busy day moving so much in one go.' Ben was still in their room putting away the last of Cristian's suits. Danika felt a little buzz from him and pushed it back in a very light way. After he left saying dinner would still be at six if they wanted to come to the dining room. Danika whispered to Cristian what she had felt.

'I don't think they can hear us. What do you mean you felt a buzz?'

'I went into the kitchen earlier to thank Ann for accepting our left-over foods and she was so pleased we had moved here the emotion she let out was like a little buzz. Different to the emotions I sense from others more like what I feel from Selene or even you. I just felt that from Ben.' She nodded at Cristian as the penny dropped. 'I said I wondered if they had the talent. I'm not sure if they know though.'

Finishing up a few points, Danika and Cristian decided to freshen up. The warm water and gentle massage from Cristian as he spread soap over her was definitely invigorating. When dinner approached, they headed downstairs to join Elizabeth who spoke passionately about the garden changes already under way. Danika was pleased Elizabeth had gone outside to have a look.

'By the way I have given the staff a few days off from Sunday to Tuesday and once you can be sure when you are going on holiday those weeks also.'

'Did you have plans for that time, Mother?' Cristian asked.

'Yes. Monday I am going to visit Jean Walton. We have been in contact since the pre-launch and I thought I would stay in town for a show. I might also go away for the two weeks. Still debating that one.' Danika could feel that the thought of travel was daunting to Elizabeth as it had been so long since she had.

'That sounds nice Elizabeth. Where were you thinking of going?' Danika was trying to send encouraging thoughts to her.

'I have a cousin in New Zealand that I have been a pen pal to for many years. Our plans to meet up were stalled by the pandemic but I think now is a good time.'

'Will there be someone to watch over the estate animals?' Danika was concerned if they were all going to be away.

'Yes, Mark's family help out from time to time here so they will fill in.' Elizabeth smiled as Ben took their bowls before bringing the next course.

'I'm going to get a start on the up cycling of some of the cupboards this week to see how it goes. When we put a few of the items from the apartment upstairs I could see my ideas fitting in,' Danika remarked.

'I'm pleased to hear that my dear. I look forward to the finished style.' Elizabeth was now preoccupied thinking about her trip. Danika was pleased and passed it on to Cristian that Elizabeth was taking the leap to get out more.

They continued the light banter over the remainder of the meal and all retired early for the night. Danika remembered see wanted to call Selene and, despite being tired, she knew it was important so settled in their sitting room with the crystal her mother had given her and several calming candles lit to make the call. Cristian kept his distance so she could concentrate. It took a few rings before her mother answered. Danika wondered if it was because she hadn't wanted to take the call.

'Hello Danika,' Selene answered with some scepticism.

'Hello, Mum. How are you?' Danika held the crystal to her heart.

'I'm well, how are you? Is everything alright?' Danika then knew her mother was picking up her feelings.

'I'm very well thanks. But I have a few questions that perhaps only you can help with.' Danika hoped this would intrigue her mother.

'Oh, really. What about?' Danika could sense the scepticism in her voice again. She felt now some truths were important.

'I have been researching a little of our family line. Did you know Grandma had a list of the Australian line of our family?' Danika asked hopefully.

'Well we all know that Danika. It is recited at each generation, you should remember that.'

'Yes I do remember, but an actual handwritten on linen by the ancestors list is what I mean.' Danika could feel this shocked Selene.

'No, I didn't. Where is this list?'

'It was hidden in Grandma's potion box that she gave me, I only found it recently by accident. It is very powerful I could feel the touch of them all, except you and me.' Danika hoped this intrigued Selene enough to answer more questions. She had gone quiet.

'We were thinking of coming to visit next month. I could bring it to show you.' Her mother was still silent. 'I have another question. A bit random but do you know of any others like us?'

'You mean not our family but with the craft?' Selene was interested again. 'Why?'

'Yes, because I found something that seems to have been loaded with dark magic and I was wondering how to cleanse it?' Danika was taking a leap of faith now.

'I have heard rumours of others overseas. Roma or Gypsies and I have felt a few people with light talent but I have never actually met anyone. Why do you need to cleanse it? Why can't you get rid of it?'

'I just can't at the moment but it is important that it is cleansed. Would you know how?' Danika was still hopeful.

'Is it general to anyone or is it aimed at you Danika?' Selene was picking up her daughter's fear.

'Aimed at me, that is why I need to cleanse it.' Danika held the crystal tighter. 'Can you help?'

There was another long pause while her mother thought about it.

'You are going to need to protect yourself and have someone on hand to stop it if it gets out of hand. Can that husband of yours help?'

Cristian had been listening from the other room not wanting to interfere but sent Danika strong reassurance of his support now.

'Yes he will definitely be with me. What sort of protection are we talking about here Mother?' Danika hoped she had enough of what she needed on hand.

'You have to gather items of love and strength of your own. Call to the energy that works best for you and if you can stay in contact with me and I can help guide you through it.'

'Thank you Mother, I really need your help. I use the celestial bodies as my energy source. If I get it all ready could we do this tomorrow night?' Danika wanted it done before Robert's visit.

'Yes that will give me time to get ready. Shall we say seven o'clock your time? Can you send me a picture of the item so I can picture it in my plans?'

'That sounds great and yes I will send photos but I have to warn you it is a fake replica of the twin to the medallion.' Danika had to warn her mother before she sent any photos.

'I see. Well that is interesting and concerning all at the same time. Call me if you need to otherwise we will connect again tomorrow night. By the way, thank you for the gift in the mail. The brooch was unexpected and very nice. I love you Danika.'

'I love you too Mother and thank you so much. Good night.' Danika was crying now.

'It will be alright Nika sleep well.' Selene sent all the love she could towards her daughter.

Selene's use of her pet name for her daughter made Danika cry more, she hadn't heard her use it in many years.

Cristian was there hugging her as soon as Danika ended the call. He pulled her up onto his lap as he sat with her on the couch. Once she had finished her need to cry for all the years of lost words and thoughts with her mother he asked for her phone so he could go take the photos she needed to send. Wiping her tears away before kissing her lightly he then went to take the photos they needed. He thought the envelope smelled of something and brought it back for Danika but she couldn't touch it so he tried to send the thought of the smell to her.

'It's nutmeg,' Danika said. 'Harmless in small doses which is how most of us use it but very dangerous in large doses. Whoever did this is using it a lot for it to be infused in the envelope. This is good to know, I'll let Mother know also.'

'Okay, well I'm learning something every day,' Cristian replied.

Danika sent off the photos with the new information of the smell of nutmeg also. Selene replied as Danika had said, 'Good to know.'

'Well wifey, this husband of yours thinks you need to come to bed and rest.' Cristian was sending loving but firm thoughts to her.

'Sorry about her comment earlier but it was actually a big step for her to acknowledge you at all. Yes I need sleep now that is for sure.' Danika walked into the bedroom as Cristian turned off lights and came to bed also, making sure she was comfortable with a glass of water beside her. He then slid in beside her to cradle her with love and peaceful thoughts until they fell asleep.

10

FULL MOON

THEY SPENT THE first half of the day running around to home depot stores, collecting supplies for the projects Danika had in mind around the house. Working with Mark and his cousin Dean, the arrangements for a rotunda in the gardens had been made as well as the restoration of an old pool Ann made mention to Danika that she hadn't previously seen. She kept herself busy but it wasn't until after finishing her lunch that Danika found her erratic thoughts were calming at last.

'I feel like my thoughts and body have been a little hysterical lately. So much I want to do but over the top is the need to find answers to questions that keep building up. Plus there are the two scary points coming up.'

'And those two scary things are what?'

'How I am going to react to the legacy and Robert's visit.' Danika felt bad saying it because she really did love Cristian but she was scared it wouldn't show when he changed.

'You don't have to watch, I sent Mother away last time. In fact you shouldn't watch. As for Robert he would not be stupid enough to make any dangerous play while he is here.'

'I will be there with you. I am not leaving you and don't bother arguing about it. It is better that you guide me than push me away.' Danika's resolve was final. Cristian nodded, obviously not happy but relenting to Danika's wishes.

'I really will need your help tonight. I don't know how it will go. I've never come across dark magic before.'

'As you said to me, I will be there with you. I am not leaving you to do this alone.' Cristian held her hand.

As the day ended, the staff of the estate left, Danika watching them from the balcony. She gathered her meditation rug and candles, moving the chairs and small table to one side of the balcony she then lay out the rug and started to form a circle large enough for them both to sit while chanting protection spells over each piece. The runes and crystals she placed in a smaller circle in the middle with a metal tray she had brought up from the kitchen and some smaller metal bowls to burn various items in if necessary. The apprehension Danika had felt earlier had now been replaced by resolve as she used her craft more so her confidence increased. She realised how she had missed not using it daily and was determined to exercise it at every opportunity from now on.

Cristian was coming up the stairs as Danika came from the balcony to bring more to the meditation area. 'I've just come from Mother after showing her one of the gallery statues. We talked briefly about your plan for tonight and she gave me this photo of Robert in case you need it to focus.' Cristian handed Danika a small photo of Robert from a previous visit.

'Thank you, this will help I am sure.' Danika placed it on the tray with a bowl on top so it didn't blow away for now and then placed nutmeg in one bowl, mace in another and then her own concoction of herbs and oils as instructed by Selene in a message earlier.

Cristian made sure there was water on hand and a bucket of sand just in case. He stood behind Danika when she called Selene a little before the agreed time on a video call. The greetings over, Danika showed Selene what she had gathered and Selene said she had found out little of specific witches outside of a small cohort exploring the dark craft in Europe. She said there were plenty of small troupes around but as far as she knew they were underground, not even practicing as she did in a 'hidden in plain sight' way. The ladies were ready as dusk had fallen where Danika was and the sun was still to set where Selene was. Cristian went to get the horse bronze.

As he approached with it to place it on the metal tray the malevolent force was palpable. Danika had her mother's crystal at her heart so Selene felt it also. Danika could sense Cristian's feeling to protect, so strong he was struggling to control. His features shifted slightly, his intense emotions sparking a slight change. It was just as well Selene was not seeing that. As instructed, he placed the photo of Robert on top and then poured first the nutmeg and then the mace. He sat down opposite Danika, taking the phone from her so he could show Selene clearly her daughter and what was going on without seeing that his face was now more wolf than human. Danika only saw him with love.

They both started chanting as they linked together to remove evil and negative thoughts as Danika dripped essential oils over the top. Selene drew strength from the setting sun and Danika from the stars. Mentally she projected to Cristian to light the oils with a candle. He pressed his mind and soul to Danika for added strength. The oils bubbled and ignited the spices, the smoke was black and swirled in a spiral upwards. Still they chanted until the flames died down. Danika carefully held her hand above the ashes, it felt neutral. Cristian brushed aside the ashes using a leather glove to reveal the horse bronze. It needed a clean but otherwise seemed unharmed. Danika held her hand above it, still fine. She risked a light touch. All was okay. She breathed a sigh of relief.

'Thank you, Mother, I think we did it.' Danika was very grateful. She could see her mother did not seem as happy.

'Do you want to explain to me what he is now? I felt it as he was trying to help you. You were still open to me.' Selene had felt the strangeness of Cristian's wolf form without seeing it. He was back to normal again as he turned the phone image to himself to address her directly.

'We were hoping to explain this when we visited in a few weeks' time Selene, better face to face.' Now Danika was standing in front of him so that they were together in the screen. She held his other hand for support. 'I am a descendant of the family cursed by your family we believe for the atrocity committed hundreds of years ago. Danika and I are destined to break the curse.' There it was, all said and out in the open. Well not quite all.

To her credit Selene was taking it in her stride. Danika could feel more support from her mother than negative vibes. 'So what is the curse for you Cristian?' It was the first time she had addressed him without rancour. Danika squeezed his hand.

'I am a werewolf, my male family are werewolves.'

'It may have been useful to know that before we started this show tonight.' Selene actually smiled. 'So you are different to your uncle then?'

'Yes very different. There is a growing cohort of my relatives that want an end to this curse. My uncle considers it a legacy. He thinks his wealth and power comes from it. His followers are becoming the minority we believe,' Cristian replied.

'What of you Nika? Do you think breaking this curse will rob us of our craft like the myth says?' Danika sensed Selene's happiness to see how in love her daughter was and no longer feeling alone.

'Honestly Mother, I don't know, but other people have the craft and are not our family. Why not us? If we lose it though so that our future children can have normal lives finding and loving a partner is that not a better outcome after all these years?' Danika had her hand still in Cristian's and the other pressing the pink quartz crystal to her heart for her mother to feel.

'Yes you are right Nika. Your grandmother hinted that you were going to do special things, I think she was right. When were you planning on visiting?'

'We have to wait until after my uncle leaves then we were planning on going to Hobart for Danika to trace Jessica's arrival. Then on to you,' Cristian explained.

'Would you mind if I met you in Hobart? I am feeling more that Danika and I need to find this answer together with you.' The suggestion made Danika feel pleased.

'We think that is a great idea,' Cristian said. 'We can book all the flights, yours as well, once we are certain Robert is leaving if that is alright with you?'

'That is a plan then, please keep in touch with me. I always have my phone on me even when I am at markets. Good night to you both.' Selene ended the call.

Danika turned round and gave Cristian such a long tight hug. She couldn't keep from crying. He let her get it out. 'Are you okay now?' he asked after a while.

'You have no idea how long I have waited for a connection like that with my mother. It was as if she has been holding her breath all this time and finally she can see an end to her loneliness. She never told me and it is all thanks to you.' Danika reached up to kiss him.

Cristian suggested Danika replenish her energy while he cleaned up the horse bronze and return it to the hiding place. The night had gone better than hoped for and they both gladly tidied and then prepared for bed. Danika still had so much running through her mind including all their plans for the future. Cristian tried to bring her back to one thought at a time eventually making her sit on the bed while he massaged her shoulders to release the tension that had built up. The massage eventually becoming wider spread he found another way to keep her mind off her enormous to do list.

The next few days seemed to go by in a blur as building and renovation plans were worked out and started on the pool and rotunda. At night they both researched as much as possible regarding prison ships arrivals, passenger lists and anything else on the internet regarding Danika's ancestors. Danika had to agree with her mother that her family had avoided detection over the years, only finding any kind of census in the last fifty years. They went through news reports in Tasmania and had their first break through regarding an arrest for murder and a court case in 1858. It was the first mention of Jessica Carling, not in a way Danika was happy to see. At least now she knew she wasn't a ghost and they could perhaps find out more in Tasmania as there was only the one reference. Danika remembered the vision she had between the women.

'I'm not sure that Jessica was the one to kill that man. Perhaps she took the blame.' Danika had been making many notes in a separate book of what they knew for sure and the artefacts involved, trying to find a pattern.

When Sunday came, they prepared for the staff to go away for three days. Ann had left a list of suggested meals plus lots of delicious baked goods. She'd left a note about the venison leg that they may want to defrost today to have tomorrow. Danika showed Cristian the note.

'She knows I don't eat venison, why would she suggest it?' Danika had the penny drop as soon as she finished speaking. 'It's for you, isn't it? I thought they didn't know.'

'They don't, she just knows I like it and they will be away.' Despite his words, Danika could see the confusion on Cristian's expression.

Elizabeth caught up with them in the kitchen to let them know she was leaving shortly when her taxi arrived and wished them all the best. Hugging Danika she said, 'You can get through this, you are stronger than you realise.' Danika hugged her back.

'Thank you. Enjoy your visit to Mrs Walton.'

After she left Danika looked at Cristian and asked, 'What do we need to do next?'

'I'll show you the cellar.' Cristian handed her a torch just in case and then showed her the large, bolted door and the light switches in the tunnel. 'Once I change it is easier on my eyes if it is just the red lights.' Danika nodded her head. Once they were at the cell area the magnitude of the situation really came home to her.

'Last time I cut a few branches to put in here so I wasn't on the cold stone. I think I shall do that again. I have to bring some water also.' Cristian was watching Danika as she stared at the cell. He unlocked the cell and walked inside. Danika walked over to the doorway and then inside she looked up at the opening in the roof letting light in. She noticed all the scratches on the walls and bite marks on the bars. She was starting to shake but Cristian grasped her arms and made her look at him.

'You don't have to do this or be here during the change, I told you that, but I need you to lock me in and lock and bar the cellar door, that is all.' Cristian was trying to reach out to her senses also but her mind was still and not open. She looked directly at him and then the resolve came back.

'I'm sorry, I'm alright now. So let's get on with this and be ready for tomorrow.' Danika was in control again. 'Branches, maybe a blanket, water, the venison. Anything else?'

'Loose clothes until I can go up to have a shower. There is a trolley I used last time to bring things in and then out again when I cleaned it up.'

'Okay, well we can start with the branches, as in soft leafy ones I am guessing.' Danika nodded her head to clear what she wanted to bring for herself also.

Cristian started up the gator as he pointed out they could travel over a larger area easily and went around, picking the softest parts to prune off of the trees on the forested area.

It didn't take long to gather all they needed and take it down to the cell. Danika took a kitchen chair, a small table and bucket of water down while Cristian was outside. She intended to sit there with him for as long as possible. By midday they had done as much as needed. Cristian encouraged Danika to trial leaving and made her shut and lock the door and the cellar door so he was sure she knew how to do it. After that they sat in the kitchen and enjoyed a hot drink and some of the lovely pastries Ann had made while they were fresh.

'What time do we need to be down there tomorrow?' Danika was trying to plan it in her head. 'How long will you need to be there?'

'Midday at the latest, earlier is better so there is no accident. The end will be obvious as I will be back to normal. Daytime full moons are always difficult to know and, add a partial eclipse as well, there is no telling how long. I'm sorry I can't be more specific.' Cristian was feeling a mixture of emotions. Embarrassment, sadness, tinged with fear followed by anger. Danika sent a wave of calmness towards him. 'Thank you.'

'We are in this together, I love you. Don't be embarrassed by something that is beyond your control.' Danika lay a hand on his where he gripped the table.

With the cell prepared, they spent the remainder of the day working on Danika's photo wall, framing enlarged photos and others holding collages of their memories so far. The excitement kept Danika's mind from the weight of the next day, passing the time pleasantly with Cristian.

'Why don't you enjoy some celestial energy while I sort out a meal? I'll come get you in a little while.' Cristian kissed her before going downstairs.

Danika was grateful for the suggestion and went out to the balcony to draw in some energy from the stars. She could see the moon was nearly full which had her heart racing again. It took some time to bring it back down.

'Better?' Cristian asked as he came to get her some time later.

'Yes thank you, dinner looks nice and I'm famished,' she replied after a long kiss.

They discussed travel ideas and general renovation works, both avoiding the topic of tomorrow. After clearing up they both decided to go up to their rooms. Danika suggested having a bath, without the bubbles this time. Lying together in the warm water to soap and rinse each other they became more interested in getting out and on to the bed, with towels and robes loosely wrapped around them. It was more of a wrestling match which had them both laughing until the erotic senses took over. Neither could sleep thinking about the coming day so to take their mind off it they each started new and wonderful love making.

Eventually they drifted off in each other's arms only to be woken a few hours later by Cristian's alarm. He switched it off quickly to say he was going for a run. Danika stayed in bed briefly then decided to wash and go down to the kitchen to make coffee for him and a tea for herself.

Curiosity got the better of her and, having been shown their security room the day prior filled with screens showing cameras of the entire property, she looked at the security monitors and caught glimpses of him running the boundary. She wasn't sure what he would want to eat so decided to wait till he came in. She sat sipping her tea and waited. He came in breathing heavy.

'Would you like anything to eat? I brewed coffee.' Danika was feeling very aroused as she felt his increased tension similar to the rapture.

'Just coffee thanks.' She knew her heightened emotions would be feeding through to Cristian. 'You need to dial that down Danika you are reacting to my heightened senses, we don't want me changing too soon.'

'Sorry I didn't realise, first time and all.' Danika stood away with her arms out in front and chanted a dampening spell. They both felt much calmer. 'Well there you go, now we know your change can affect me also.' She poured him a coffee and another tea for herself then sat down opposite him.

'You should eat, I generally don't a few hours before but I need drinks. I need to take that leg down,' Cristian said, indicating the leg of venison Ann had prepared for him. 'Normally I hunt. When I can have the space for the legacy to run in the wild I hunt down something. Most of the time I don't know what unless I wake with it near me. So I will need to have something to attack even though it isn't a true hunt.'

'That makes sense, no different to any other animal in the wild. Don't be ashamed to give me details, the more I know the easier it is to understand.' Danika was sending love to him so he knew she was truthful in her opinion. 'Let's hope we don't have to use the cell in future, but for now we will make the best of it.' She reached out to hold his hand. She felt his gratitude and love that she was there and she sent him love and support. 'I'll make myself some breakfast while you sort what you want to take down with you.' He nodded and kissed her before going up to their rooms.

Cristian

After showering he dressed in loose clothes and went back down to see Danika was clearing away after breakfast. Cristian picked up the venison and went down to the cell to place it in the corner furthest away from Danika's chair. He was still not happy that she was insisting on being there. As he was not certain of his actions during and after the change he would be horrified if she was revolted by anything he did. He knew there was no point arguing with her though, her mind was set. When he came back to the kitchen she was not there and he searched for her feel realising she was out the back with the chickens. He found her talking to them as she threw out some scraps and grain to them then checking for eggs, thanking them for the few she found. They watched her entranced, only eating once she left.

'Are you channelling to them now?' Cristian was intrigued.

'Yes a little. I don't use it often, mostly animals are just lovely and do their own thing. I stopped a bull chasing me once when I took a wrong turn in a paddock. Then it was very useful.' Danika smiled at the memory.

'Do we need to feed the deer?'

'Probably not. Mark would have made sure they had plenty but we can check their water if you like.' Cristian was now more intrigued if she had the same effect on the deer.

'I am not going to make them do tricks you know?'

They checked the water and decided to top it up anyway as they were there. They could see there were several bales of lucerne for them, plenty for several days. A couple of young bucks thought they would jostle at each other around the females. Danika gave it a try and managed to get them to part and go eat in separate directions.

'Time for those fellows to be separated out of the herd by the looks of it. I saw what you did.' Cristian found it fascinating as she made it look like it was their own decision.

'It is their own decision I just suggest to them it is the best option.' Danika confirmed his thoughts.

Cristian watched the deer eating and then a hawk overhead startled them. The does did a sprint to the other end of the field. He felt himself wanting to run after them and was now feeling very wound up and said he needed to go in. They made their way down to the tunnels, Cristian went in the cell pulling the door closed behind him. Danika just stood and stared at him. 'Lock the door Danika.' He looked straight at her sending encouragement. 'There is a hook above your chair to hang it on.'

Danika moved slowly and, while looking straight at him, turned the heavy key in the lock, turning round to hang it where instructed. She sat down and pulled out yesterday's newspaper she had found in the kitchen and started to read the news articles out loud.

'You don't have to amuse me darling I am used to this.' Cristian smiled at her flowery narration. Then he went quiet as she continued to read. She stopped at one point to take a drink when she noticed he had his eyes closed until he said, 'What happened next?'

'I thought you were asleep.' Danika continued reading the lengthy article till its conclusion.

Danika

She looked at her watch. It was nearly time for the full moon. She turned to the puzzles and asked him questions to see if he could concentrate. He answered the first few and then she saw him breathing heavier and could feel a change in his mind. He took all of his clothes off and pushed them through the bars. Then he took his wedding ring off and put it on the chain around his neck, the weight pulling it down to the middle of his chest. Standing their naked he was magnificent.

He looked straight at her and said, 'Whatever you think of doing, do not under any circumstance put your hand near me. If I bite you by accident it will kill you.' His hair began to change. Danika could sense he was trying so hard not to yell out from the pain. He crouched to the floor, watching Danika through the pain.

Danika watched her love, her soul mate, going through the most horrendous pain. The only thing she knew she could do was give him love and try to ease his pain, real and emotional at knowing she was watching. He crouched on the ground as the hair grew and his face changed like it had at the cleansing but more. His head was now completely covered in hair with the ears growing long above his head and his mouth changing to a snout. He yelled out which turned to a growl.

She felt his human mind was slipping away so she called to him before it did. 'I love you Cristian and always will.' His arms and legs changed and covered in fur, his hands turned to paws with long nails and he then writhed as his back arched and changed, longer, with the tail seeming to be the last to grow. He was biting at his own paws and yelping now. When the change appeared to be complete he stood on all fours and howled. The sound reverberated around the tunnel and was so loud she covered her ears with her hands.

He paced the cell, pushing his head against the bars and sniffing all he could reach. She thought he was so beautiful. He was huge. She had seen a wolf at a zoo and he appeared to be much larger by at least 50%. The fur was blonde like his human hair with areas of dark tints across the hackles and the edges of his ears. His chest was paler, not quite white. He was sniffing the air from the hole in the ceiling and as the natural light shone on his fur it seemed to almost glow.

She called his name and he looked at her but she felt no recognition, just a response to a sound.

What did you think was going to happen Danika? she thought. She continued to sit on the chair and watch as he moved around the cell, several times sniffing and pulling at the bedding with his teeth and paws. At one stage he leaped up on his back legs to stand against the bars. His front legs reaching up, he sniffed all the stone looking for a way out. He seemed to stand about eight feet high at full stretch. His underside was paler also. The temptation to touch him was strong but she remembered his words and knew it wasn't just about her anymore, there was also their child to consider. With that thought in mind she decided to leave him briefly while she gathered a few more supplies for herself. Before going she carefully picked up his clothes while he was at the other side of the cell and folded them up near her collection of things.

Back in the bedroom she grabbed one of the kits from her tote that she had bought the other day and went to the bathroom. She set the timer on her phone and then gathered a warmer jumper and a couple of throw rugs and a pillow. Changing her shoes for her ugg boots as she knew it was just going to get colder down there. The timer on her phone went off. She looked at the test kit and yelped with glee. She knew she was pregnant but just needed confirmation. She took a photo of it to show Cristian.

With her bedding under her arm she skipped down the stairs. She pulled the outdoor cushions off the patio chairs out the back and added them to the bedding on the trolley. In the cupboards were pastries and she made herself a thermos of hot tea. Before going down to the tunnels again she made sure that all the doors were locked. She felt she was set and then went through the process of going through the cellar door to the tunnels.

She heard him growling at her approach so she spoke to him with her voice and mind to let him know who she was and he seemed to calm down. He was watching her closely as she prepared all her pieces, talking to him as she went. She laid out the chair cushions about an arm's length away from the bars and put her pillow down with the throw rugs. She could see he had drunk some water from the sump as the droplets glistened on his chin. 'Boy have I got some good news for you when you are back.' He shook his head and she felt a few drops of the water hit her making her giggle.

'Well I might join you in a drink also.' Danika sat down and poured herself a tea using the thermos cup lid. 'Now where were we with this puzzle?' After a few hours of reading the paper, doing puzzles and just talking about plans for the nursery, Danika was getting very tired. They hadn't slept very well the night before, she thought about some of their love making which was pleasant but pointless as she looked at him lying on the floor. At last he had stopped his pacing. There was little light coming down the air hole now. She walked back to the cellar door and, making sure all the locks were in place, she turned on the red lights and the white lights off. She walked back to see him standing watching her return.

'It's okay Cristian, I said I wouldn't leave you and I meant it.' Danika crouched down and then tried to get comfortable on the cushions on the floor, pulling the rugs over her. She watched him walk over the brush and blankets bedding and lay down also. She continued to talk to him until finally she fell asleep.

His howl startled her awake yet again. Light was coming down the hole and she wasn't sure if that meant night or day. She looked at her phone. Okay, so only eight o'clock.

'Crikey Cristian you scared the wits out of me.' She watched him pacing again. He started clawing at the bars and was about to bite them when she tried to stop him with her mind and words. 'You are going to hurt yourself like that my love. Maybe you need to eat.' She tried to portray the meat in the corner. Finally he stopped worrying at the bars and walked over to the venison, sniffing it first then pawing at it and then grabbing it to carry over to the bedding to lay down and bite at it. He tore large pieces out of the leg to chew it up, using his paws to hold it in place. The whole process fascinated her. She had never had a pet of any kind and did not get the chance to watch a predatory animal feed in real life, only the little she had seen on TV. She resumed her seat on the chair and pulled out a few of the pastries to eat while she watched him gnawing at the meat. She was cold and wondered how he felt, pulling on her extra jumper. She pulled out the front of the jumper and said, 'I wonder if this will stretch enough to cover a growing baby?'

He looked up briefly with meat all over the fur of his face and paws then went back to eating. 'Yep you're right, I should just buy a new one. I was going to buy more clothes, now I have another reason to. I might even drag you along. Surely you can put up with a couple of hours of ladies clothes shopping after this night my love. If you can refrain from howling I think I might try sleeping again.' She lay down again, looking at him and sending calming thoughts that had her falling asleep fairly quickly.

Sometime later, a gentle squeeze to her hand woke her back up. She opened her eyes to see Cristian laying against the bars, his arm stretched out and linked to hers.

'Hello, darling, are you alright?' she said it groggily with sleep still in her mind. Still sitting on the makeshift bed she reached for his clothes for him to put on.

'Have you been here all night?' Cristian pulled on the track pants and hooded top.

'Yes, apart from one small trip for extra supplies.' She was standing now, trying to get the kinks from her cold bones and reached up to get the key to let him out.

'Why didn't you wake me when you saw I had changed?' He was pulling on his runners.

'I didn't know you had until now. Sorry, I fell asleep.' Danika was wondering why he was asking that and then she felt his confusion.

'Why was I holding your hand then?'

'Your leg was sticking out through the bars and I just had to touch you.' Danika was not sorry. The connection was wonderful when she did and she refused to apologise. 'You're not allowed to be mad at me today.' She pulled her phone out of her pocket and showed him the photo.

He stared at it for a little while until he understood what he was looking at and then he was lifting her up and trying to kiss her but she was pulling away.

'Oops sorry I'll go have a shower then we will get back to this.' Cristian helped her gather up bits and pieces and put them on the trolley to take back out. Once they were out he sprinted up to their rooms while Danika sorted out what she could in the kitchen and pulled the trolley outside to deal with later. He was back still dripping a few minutes later lifting her up to kiss her. She was laughing as he wanted to touch her stomach and talk to it.

'I don't think it has ears yet darling.' Danika was laughing more because it tickled. 'I think it is my turn to shower now.' Suddenly he had lifted her in his arms and was carrying her up the stairs. In the bathroom it looked like a disaster area, strewn clothes and towels and steam dripping everywhere.

'I'm going to tidy up while you shower and be back soon.' Cristian kissed her hard and was sprinting away again. She could feel how elated he was, it was just oozing from him. She couldn't get the smile off her face as she felt his happy thoughts and love even from a distance. She looked out the bedroom window when she heard a bang, it was Cristian loading rubbish into the skip bin and returning the trolley. Danika realised how hungry she was after only eating a few pastries last night. *Cristian must be hungry also*, she thought.

Halfway down the stairs, she ran into Cristian returning.

'Breakfast or bed?' she asked.

He made the decision quickly, picking her up and sprinting to the bed then carefully laying her down. He lay beside her and placed his face on her stomach, kissing her and then lightly rubbing the area making her wriggle because it tickled. 'I only hoped before now that it is definite. I am happier than I thought was possible.' Danika was rubbing her fingers through his still damp hair.

'This is what you look like only all over.' She rubbed his ears. 'The tufts and your nose are a bit darker and this,' she ran her hand over his chest and downwards, 'was much lighter, almost white.' He had rolled on to his side with her hand on his stomach. He moved his hand from her stomach to pull her hand down to his crotch.

'What about here?' He wasn't joking, he really wanted to know, she could feel his thoughts.

'Well when you stood up on hind quarters at the bars I must admit I got an eyeful.' She closed her eyes briefly at the memory and tried to show it to him. 'You are magnificent. It was pretty furry but huge like the rest of you as if you were wearing a mohair genital jumper. I'm sorry I am not trying to be flippant.'

'It is weird I'm jealous of myself of you spending a night admiring another male other than me.' Cristian shook his head. 'I might need a therapist to work out that one.' Then he leaned over and kissed her stomach again, running his hand over her stomach and then pushing it under the line of her pants. As he leaned into a deep kiss Danika straddled him and just sat until she could feel herself rising to orgasm.

She knew he wanted her to move but she was determined for him to feel it all. She felt the orgasm coming and let the spasms roll on and on, only moving slightly to keep it going longer. Cristian was shaking as he also exploded.

'You keep surprising me. I want to spend the day in bed with you but I think we might both need some sustenance.'

After they had stuffed themselves with Ann's wonderful, packed meals and rehydrated, they curled up in the sitting room.

'When is Robert due to arrive?' Danika asked.

'He has just sent his itinerary. Looks like he arrives in Sydney about 8 pm tomorrow night. With customs and other issues he will probably stay at the apartment or in a hotel and want to visit Thursday morning.' Danika was pleased to have another day before his arrival. 'I was checking my messages and mail, I have one from James regarding that property you liked near the Hunter Valley. It will officially be ours early next month.'

Danika stood looking at him, shocked. 'As in you and me, not the company? Our own family property?'

'I guess so, if that is how you want to think of it. I see it more as a holiday retreat. It is a fair way from our businesses. It was actually really easy. The extended family were not interested in keeping it but needed a push, a large financial push helped. Also James let it slip that a young newly married couple wanted it just like their grand uncle and aunt had been. They agreed to a quick settlement.'

'Can we go there after Tasmania once we can get the keys?' Danika was emotional as she remembered how wonderful it felt. 'I could drop in on Marge and the girls.'

'Of course, we can take Rainbow because we will probably be camping,' Cristian suggested. Danika was nodding because she couldn't speak. She threw her arms around his neck and kissed him.

'Thank you, I love you.' He pulled her on to his lap.

'I looked it up on the internet, here let me show you, I like it. Also it is a very large property, much bigger than this one.' Still sitting on his lap he showed her the size of the property taking in a large area of forest that was edged with more mountainous forest, not likely to ever be developed. 'Here is the creek and I can't quite get the angle but I gathered from the house you would look down the valley at the rising sun and therefore moon. Excellent star gazing I would think. There are a couple of photos of the sheds and inside the house. I asked the real estate agent to take them.' He scrolled through them for her.

'Yes that was what I could see from the window, as if they had just walked out one day. So I am thinking that some of the excess furniture here may go perfectly in there.' She smiled.

She put her hands on her cheeks. 'Oh my so many projects to work on. Maybe I am an art consultant come renovator now.' Danika was not overwhelmed more overjoyed. 'I hope we can leave on our trip soon so I can get the information we need. How marvellous would it be to be able to travel without worrying about the lunar cycle.' She was scrolling back and forth through the few photos available plus the satellite search. 'I suppose I should know how much we paid for this?'

'About twenty percent over market value for the area land value only. I suspect they thought it would be demolished. I know it won't be though, will it?' She was zooming in on each little item in the photos.

'I could show you Mum's place.' Danika changed the satellite image to the area in the hills above Adelaide where her family had lived for about 150 years.

Cristian was quite surprised how much land was involved. The street view wasn't helpful because the buildings were too far away from the street. But even the satellite image showed the mish mash of different rooves. No garden but several fruit trees and poor fencing. 'Looks like your mum could really use some help there.'

'Yes she could use help. Each year the costs get higher and the last two years of only a few markets have not helped. Although she has embraced online sales with some success. Go Mum.' Now that the negative attitude by both of them had been removed she could value her mother's achievements all on her own.

'Do you think we can plan to leave on Sunday for Hobart and have Mum meet us on the Monday? That way she still has the weekend markets,' Danika asked.

'Yes that should be fine,' Cristian said. 'I'll just book the flights and then you can let her know.' Cristian was so used to planning trips it just rolled on so easily and thirty minutes later he was giving Danika the flight details for her mother and letting her know the flight plans for themselves and house where they were going to stay. 'I haven't booked the return flights yet, I figured it will depend on what we find.'

Finally, Danika thought, *We are back on track for my quest, our quest.*

'I'm going to call Mum to make sure she gets the details as well as sending them.'

The call was short but congenial. Danika had the distinct feeling someone else was there with her mother but she never said anything. Selene said she was pleased to get another market in and wondered if she could be back on the Friday night for the next markets? All felt like it was falling into place as they hung up happily.

'Do you think we should wait to tell the mothers of our news?' Danika asked, returning to Cristian, her hand protectively to her stomach.

'I would be happy to tell them as soon as we see them because I don't know if I can hide my joy.'

'Elizabeth will be back after breakfast, we could tell her then. I think it would be good that she knows before Robert arrives. I'd like to tell Selene face to face.' Danika was smiling at his thoughts of a little girl. 'You know it could be a boy.'

'Either way as long as it is healthy is all I want.' Cristian leaned over to kiss her. 'All the others will be back tomorrow so let's make sure we have not left any mess about. Then I'm going to see if I can get the old BBQ started.'

Once they were both satisfied the cell and tunnels were now clean and tidy they turned off the lights and bolted the door. 'I hope you never have to go in there again.' Danika had been distressed by his anguish of the change and his confinement and had needed to use a lot of her power to calm him and take some of the pain. She forgot to hide that as she relived some of it.

'Thank you, I thought it was easier this time, but please don't do that again it might harm the baby.' Cristian was firm in his words and thoughts. 'I have done this a lot of times, I can cope with it.'

'We are one now so it is shared. No matter how you look at it I feel your pain also so if I can relieve it at all it helps me also.' Danika was equally firm. She walked into the kitchen to plan the food to take outside. 'Come on, you have meat to cremate.'

'Oh ye of little faith in my barbequing abilities.' Cristian found the tools he needed and a lighter.

Danika made up a simple salad and cut up onions for the BBQ. As she went outside the smell of heat and smoke drifted by.

'Are you ready for these now?' she asked, watching his dealing with the smoke problem.

'Just about, I'm using some flavoured wood in a smoke box to flavour the meat, I hope.'

Danika smiled and went back for the salad and drinks.

She sat and watched Cristian cook and chatted about ideas for this area and possibly a pool house.

'I don't mean it all has to happen straight away, we have a lifetime to enjoy this home. I just like to share my ideas.'

Cristian was listening while he was focused on not burning anything. 'I like all your plans, somewhere in the next month though we will need to find a few more pieces of art because the pieces you found are mostly sold or pre-ordered once they are available.' Danika was surprised how he knew. 'Message from Paul and Rene.' He held up his phone. 'These are done, plates please.' Cristian dished up the shish kebabs for Danika then the huge steak on to his plate. After eating, they relaxed briefly until the cold was settling on them and then took all the tools and leftovers back to the kitchen.

'I am really tired and want to be my best for the coming days. I'm going to go up to bed.' Danika could feel he was also ready for bed but in a different way. She smiled and felt him mentally hug her goodnight. She kissed him and made her way upstairs. Setting an early alarm she crawled under the covers and fell asleep almost immediately. She only stirred as he came to bed a few hours later hugging her back to a deep sleep.

11

FAMILY

Danika's five o'clock alarm woke them both. The idea of staying in bed was potent but brief as they each had early morning plans. Kissing good morning had to suffice until later. Cristian dressed for running and Danika dressed in many colours, pulling on ugg boots, comfortable and ready for action with her hair tied up in a ponytail.

Only a few minutes later as Danika was sorting her washing, Ann and Ben arrived. Ben swooped in and took over organising the clothes in preparation for their leaving on Sunday, and Danika still struggled to get used to someone else doing her washing for her.

'Ann is just boiling the kettle if you would like a cup of tea,' Ben suggested, as Danika idled hesitantly.

In the kitchen Danika sat down at the table and said good morning to Ann. The realities of her new life was slapping her again.

Ann placed the cup of Chai tea down for her and said, 'Good morning ma'am, it's nice to be back.'

'Ann I come from a very different background to this and sometimes I get a bit mixed up between my responsibilities and crossing into yours.' Danika looked straight at Ann. 'I hope you feel free to remind me if I am getting it wrong.'

'There is no wrong way ma'am. You have a busy life now working and planning your redecorating, we are more than pleased to be here to make that all run smoothly for you. If you want to do any of our jobs that is fine but I don't think we can do yours.' Ann smiled as she was sorting out the coffee percolator.

Danika nodded. Ann was so lovely. 'Thank you for all the food and instructions you left for us, Ann. It was very nice and perfectly timed. Did you enjoy your weekend?'

'I'm pleased you enjoyed your time alone. Yes, our family was able to all get together at once for a change. Usually one of them is off doing something.' Ann put sugar in a cup and was pouring the coffee just as Cristian came in the back door. 'Good morning, Master Cristian.' She handed him the coffee.

'Good morning. You're an angel, Ann, thank you.' Cristian sipped at the drink. Ann had prepared Cristian's drink without knowing he was coming and Ben had been by her side as she needed him in the laundry. They definitely had the sight she was positive.

As Ann set about making them breakfast and Cristian ran upstairs to shower, Danika couldn't help but pry. 'Your family has a long history with the Blakesley family, Ann. Have you always lived in Australia?' Danika's curiosity was increasing about the Norton connection.

'I believe our family came out from Europe about 1930 to avoid the persecution of the Romani. Many of them dispersed around that time. Some didn't get away before the war broke out unfortunately and we lost touch with them. We all have stayed mostly around the Sydney and outskirts area. Mostly in service – maids, butlers, gardeners and so on. When Master Cristian's grandfather arrived he needed all the help he could get. We just stayed on, now into a third generation here.' Ann was working as she spoke almost as an automatic action. Danika watched her hands moving like a ballet across several cooking utensils.

'I love seeing an expert at work. I can cook but not to your level of volume and expertise.' Danika was genuinely impressed.

'You're very kind. It is my job of course but it is nice to be complimented.' Ann was just putting the last waffles on a plate as Cristian came back into the kitchen. Then there were plates of protein, bowls of fruit, tubs of yoghurt and so many sauces – savoury and sweet – to choose from. They each helped themselves and sat to eat as Ann served them their drinks of choice.

Danika ate mostly fruit as she didn't feel so hungry. 'I think I need to walk some of this off. I might go see what Mark is up to and discuss some other ideas we had,' she said, like Cristian was part of the planning process.

He laughed and said, 'All your ideas, my love.'

The reinstating of the pool and building of the rotunda was moving along as Mark's cousin had brought more workers with him. Danika found Mark was overseeing their access to the gardens and use of estate resources. 'Good morning Mark, how is it going?'

'Quite well ma'am. We are hoping there are no major holes or cracks in the pool. We will have a fence up around it once it is exposed. The foundations for the rotunda should go in today. Was there something else you wanted to discuss?'

'Yes I believe there may have been a pool house at one stage, I'm not sure where that was, I can't see it anywhere and a BBQ area would be useful also.' Danika was looking around towards the house.

'It was before my time here but I asked my uncle about it, he said it was off the back of the house. The amenities were basically incorporated into the back of the house and are now the downstairs amenities just over there.' He pointed to the corner that had appeared to be part of the original design but she could see now was slightly different in brick colour. 'We could reinstate the outside entrance fairly easily and have an open-air covered area if that would be what you are looking for, including a BBQ area. I saw that you used the BBQ yesterday. Not such a great area for you.'

'Well, that sounds easier than I expected. Would it be alright if

I look at those amenities?' Danika didn't want to barge in on what might be the staff private area.

'Of course. It actually could use a refurbishment as it was installed with the house and then just basically adjusted back years ago.' Mark showed her through the back entry she had not gone through before. The original workmanship was excellent but it was very dated now. She pulled out her phone and took several photos so she could research a reno plan.

Danika thanked Mark for his guidance and decided to continue back up to her room via the back stairs. Certainly a different view of the upper level. It was dark and gloomy. Better lighting would be a good start.

As Danika walked past the rooms on the northern side she looked at all the trims. They were well cared for but the overall feel was darkness. She thought she must ask Ben how he perceived it. As she crossed the landing she saw a taxi pull up with Ben there to assist Elizabeth and her bags. She thought Cristian and she should pay Elizabeth a visit once she was settled back in her rooms.

Danika found Cristian at his laptop in the sitting room. She took in the whole scene as one and was thinking about rearranging it all. Cristian turned around from his concentration to look at her. 'More decorating ideas, darling?'

'I think we need to rearrange the layout once we decorate. I would like to hide the office area.' Danika was planning in her head as she slowly looked back and forth across the room. 'I think screens would be fine for now.'

'We have plenty of other rooms I can move all this to if you want more room in here.'

'Mm yes, I know, but I think we will be using a few of them in future.' Danika touched her belly.

Ben appeared at that point and knocked at the open door. They both looked around. 'Mrs Blakesley wondered if you would both join her for morning tea in her rooms.'

'Thank you Ben, we shall be down shortly.' Danika answered for them both.

Before going downstairs Danika went into the music room and retrieved the photo frame of their wedding day for Elizabeth. Ben greeted them at the door as he came with the trolley of tea and coffee pots and a tray of sandwiches and cakes. Elizabeth was already seated by the fire. Danika could feel that she was more relaxed but happy to be home. Ben retreated to leave them alone, closing the door behind him.

'Good morning, Mother.' Cristian was the first to speak as he leaned down to kiss her cheek then sat on the couch so that Danika could join him.

'Good morning, Elizabeth,' Danika said as she sat down.

'Good morning to you both, you look well.' Elizabeth did not ask directly how Cristian's change had been for them.

Danika was struggling to contain her excitement for their announcement. Cristian held her hand and gave her calming thoughts.

'Thank you for asking us here. We have something for you.' Danika handed Elizabeth the framed photo of their wedding day. A close-up of them smiling and looking at one another that James had taken. 'We thought you may like this one.'

Elizabeth was thrilled. 'Oh how thoughtful of you, this shows how happy and in love you are. I shall put it on the mantel so I can look at it often.'

'We have some news for you also, Mother.' Cristian wanted to be the one to tell her. Danika was squeezing his hand. 'We are going to have a baby.'

Elizabeth had several emotions run through her all at once and Danika felt them all. Thrill, pride concern, hope then a big dose of love. Elizabeth started to cry.

'Oh my, silly old woman, I am so very pleased for you both.' Elizabeth reached for her handkerchief to wipe her eyes. Then stood up so that she could hug them each individually.

Danika was crying tears of happiness also. 'We wanted you to know as soon as possible. I will tell my mother when I see her.'

'Oh my, I am very privileged to be the first.' She pointed to the trolley. 'We must celebrate with a cup of tea.' They all laughed at that. 'When will you be seeing your mother, dear?'

'We wanted to tell you that also. We are leaving Sunday for Hobart and Selene will meet us on the Monday there so Danika and I can tell her face to face.' Cristian was holding his mother's hand as he spoke. Danika smiled directly at her, absorbing all the love she was giving out, then turned to pour them drinks.

'I have a bit to tell you as well.' Elizabeth accepted the cup of tea from Danika. 'I had a lovely time in Sydney. I spent a couple of days with Jean Walton. Oh the memories we had to share, lots of laughs and lots of tears. We definitely both needed that. Apparently Danika had surprised the sale agents at her insight to the items in the attic when you visited. Well there was a huge amount of extra art and artefacts up there plus many personal items, photos and such.' Elizabeth took a sip of her tea and thanked Danika for the plate of food. 'Well, apart from the personal items, Jean would like to donate all of the rest to you both as a wedding gift. Not to keep, she made it very clear that she did not expect that you would want to, but for the gallery.'

Both Cristian and Danika were stunned. 'That is so generous and a lovely surprise.' Danika spoke first.

'Jean said that first morning seeing you both and something you said to her, Danika, had brought her out of a deep pit of grief.' Danika could feel gratitude from Elizabeth as she remembered the change she felt after meeting her and then love and understanding from Cristian who knew of Jean's grief. 'Apparently the agents just want to know where to send it all.'

'I'll give you the address of the storage and restoration sheds so it can be itemised and sorted.' Cristian sent his mother a text message with the details that she could pass on. 'Just get them to let us know when to expect the delivery. We are going to be away for a few weeks.'

Danika handed Cristian coffee and a pile of sandwiches which he started on straight away. He was hungrier than usual and she had sensed it. Then she sat with her own drink.

'To family,' Elizabeth said. 'Our new growing one especially.' They held up their cups in a comical salute.

'We hope to trace some of my family in Hobart with my mother. She needs to get away for a change. I have recently reconnected with her so I am looking forward to it.' Danika was feeling quite emotional.

'You are bound to want to be near your mother at this time Danika. You must invite her here when it is convenient.' Elizabeth put down her cup. 'Anyway, how is the renovation plan going? There seems to be a lot of activity happening.'

'We are trying to reinstate the pool. The builders seem to think it is in surprisingly good shape. Something needed to be done to make the area safe anyway.' Danika thought she would tell Elizabeth one thing at a time.

'We had a lot of fun out there in the earlier days. It was where your father and I fell in love.' Elizabeth was looking directly at Cristian. 'Do you remember the pool?'

'Yes, vaguely, but I think it was boarded up after Grandfather's death.'

'It had been there for nearly fifty years and was at that point of needing something done. Your father didn't want to spend the time or money repairing it completely but equally missed his father so much he didn't want to destroy it, if that makes sense. Then there was no reason to have the pool house either.'

'Yes that is another part to be addressed as well as a BBQ area.' Danika decided to keep the rotunda a surprise still at this stage. 'I don't suppose you have been upstairs recently. I have upcycled a couple of cupboards and plan to do more now I am happy with the results. The rear of the wings is very dark and gloomy, I was thinking of trying to lighten them up and put better lighting in. Then of course there is the nursery to decorate now also.' Danika was feeling very happy at that thought.

'Don't let her overdo it, Cristian. I can see she is set to be involved with everything,' Elizabeth said with concern.

'Don't worry I will keep an eye on her.'

'I'm right here you know. Besides he just bought me – I mean us – a holiday retreat that I now need to get renovated also.'

'Have you indeed, where is that?' Elizabeth asked.

'Up near the Hunter Valley, southwest of Newcastle. It is a beautiful area. An abandoned farm I spotted in my travels. Once it is more habitable we should all have a holiday there.' Danika thought it sounded reasonable but now she sensed Elizabeth was very worried, remembering the trauma she had been through losing several pregnancies seemed to be fresh in her mind. 'I'll be fine Elizabeth. I won't risk this baby for a bit of renovation. I will be delegating.'

'That is good to hear, make sure you eat plenty. Little and often or the dreaded morning sickness might get you.'

'I think this baby talk is my exit cue. I will go have a chat with the builders and Mark. I'll see you at dinner, Mother.' Cristian kissed his mother on the cheek before putting his hand on Danika's shoulder. 'Stay, chat and eat some more.' He grinned at her.

Danika did take a sandwich as instructed without eating it and poured more tea for them each.

'You mentioned before that you were going to go away when we did, are you still planning that?' Danika asked.

'Yes, I was waiting to see how long Robert would be here but I guess you know if you are going away on Sunday.'

'Well, we don't actually know his plans. Cristian said he never stays long so as we have not invited him to stay here we have made our own plans,' Danika explained. 'We are hoping he gets the message that he isn't actually welcome anymore. The new security helps.' Danika was still feeling very nervous of the interaction with him tomorrow.

'When does he arrive?'

'Late tonight apparently. Cristian has given him access to the apartment if he wants while he is in Australia then has suggested that he comes for lunch here tomorrow. Cristian has booked a table for us for dinner in Sydney if you would like to join us.' Danika could feel Elizabeth's mixed emotions.

'I think the more united front we project the better. I think there may be some dangerous feelings between Cristian and his uncle now so I may be of assistance calming that tension down.'

'Thank you, I appreciate your support. I have to admit to being more than a little nervous.' Danika was most concerned about Cristian changing if he was enraged or protective. 'I have to tell you about that item Robert had left here as a trap loaded with dark magic. Cristian told you about it I think. Before he had any idea I existed Robert must have left it at his last visit. My mother and I have removed the threat but not the item. While we were creating a spell over it Cristian was there to protect me and he partially changed because he could feel the threat to me through our connection.'

'I see. Well that is interesting. Robert hasn't been here for quite a while, so at some stage he believed that Cristian was going to meet the one that could break the curse and he planted the trap. That means he believes it is possible.' Elizabeth was emotional, not from fear but relief. Danika could feel that Elizabeth was now much stronger knowing this. 'I think I need to contact Ingrid again, especially while he is out of the country. I know this sounds strange but we need to create the illusion that you are not pregnant I was thinking we can have Ben serve you mock drinks. How do you feel about that?'

'I can see where you are coming from but not sure about while we are out.'

'Leave it to me.'

Danika eventually left and found Cristian out the back discussing plans with Mark and his cousin. All seemed in agreement about something and a little reserved once they saw her but she couldn't sense why.

'Everything alright, love?' Cristian asked and the other men turned from their conversation.

'Yes, just a little weary. I'm going upstairs. I was wondering about emails from family.' Danika was sending thoughts of Peter and his mother to Cristian.

'I'll come up with you.' He turned back to the guys. 'All good fellas, I'll chat with you before end of day.' They all nodded in agreement and then he was escorting her back into the house via the back door.

'See what I mean about it being dark and gloomy.' Danika pointed out to Cristian as they walked up the rear stairs.

'Yes I do. Now what has gone on with Mother while I was out there?'

'I told her about the horse brass trap and sorting it out. She made a really valid point we may have missed. Well more than one actually.' They entered the sitting room and closed the doors behind them.

'Robert hasn't been here in a long time yet he set a trap basically for me not knowing I actually existed. So that means he has foresight, or someone who can see the future, or he has the details of the curse and how to break it. Maybe all three.' Danika felt better sharing this with Cristian. He came and hugged her, willing his love and strength into her, she clung to him. 'Thank you, I needed that.' He kissed her several times and then broke off to prevent them taking it further, giving her a sly smile.

'Was that all of Mother's valid points?' Cristian moved them over to the couch to sit.

'She thought I should give him the illusion I was drinking alcohol, as in not pregnant.' Danika looked at him while he digested that.

'I think that if we don't give him any idea that is not such a bad plan. But how are you going to do that when we go to dinner?'

'Apparently your mother said she would handle it. I invited her for support,' Danika confirmed. 'She said she is going to contact Ingrid while Robert is out of the country.'

'I might try Peter as well. I shall ask him some more direct questions such as does he have the horse bronze and the manuscript or just the photos.'

'I'm going to go meditate for a little while in the bedroom down the hall where it is a bit quieter.' Danika was not feeling very positive and she needed to change that. She picked up her potion box and favourite rug and bag of crystals and candles.

Cristian

Cristian could feel Danika's concerns and was worried about her. The increase in worry he could feel from her was all regarding Robert. He could sense she had accepted his own particular issues but now she was having a baby that must be an extra concern, just as it was for him.

He spent the next few hours connecting with Peter and his mother Ingrid using the secure email. The information confirmed Peter actually had access to both the horse bronze and the manuscript but that they were hidden from Robert. Peter also confirmed that Robert had been using a person who practiced dark magic. Peter said that Robert regularly made a complete change to terrorise the family members that he felt were not taking care to protect 'the brand' so to speak. There were several family members who had died, some by their own means, others possibly by Robert or his henchmen. Peter admitted that his own wife had struggled with the fact that their one son would have to go through the legacy in a couple of years. She had given up trying for more children after several miscarriages of girls.

The same as Mother, Cristian thought.

Robert had threatened Peter's wife to keep quiet as she actually was no longer required. He said that the problem was that the ability to buy property that was safe from view had become impossible in

Europe now with the movement of refugees from the Ukraine war and everyone having drones these days. The few safe properties were owned by Robert's group. He said one family had moved to Canada and they thought they had been successful in acquiring a property but there was no real income or work to be had so it wasn't a viable option for a larger group to go. In general they felt their days were numbered and Robert didn't care.

Cristian discussed his own problems regarding safe access and using the cell twice in a row. He did explain he had just purchased a large property with an inaccessible forest perfect for his needs and he hoped to use it next lunar cycle. He made an offer for Peter and his family to visit if they wanted. Mostly he had hopes that within the year he could find a cure. He didn't want to elaborate regarding the way he was going to do that or that he was married with Danika. He trusted Peter but not someone else listening or watching. Peter said he would support him in whatever endeavour he had to end the nightmare that was their lives.

Cristian checked the time and thought he should make sure Danika was okay. He could only feel a dull mist of calm so assumed she was still meditating. He needed to check she had been drinking water. The first bedroom next to theirs was empty so he continued to the last one which was very gloomy at this point with no natural light and inadequate artificial light, as she had said. Danika had pulled the curtains wide and pinned them back to get more light in and was sitting on the bed, her candles in their trays around the bed. Incense had burned down and the fumes filled the room. She looked asleep. He pushed at her mind several times and eventually she smiled and then opened her eyes.

'I wasn't sleeping,' Danika disputed. 'This room had slightly more light and space and was a bit musty so the incense will help.'

'Fair enough. I thought you may want to freshen up before dinner,' Cristian answered. She put out the candles with a wave of her hand and left the remaining items.

'You spoke with Peter?'

'By email, but we were both online so it was a fairly quick to and fro,' Cristian confirmed. 'It will be interesting what contact Mother has with Ingrid.'

They walked back to their bedroom. 'I think I shall shower before changing, I need the extra massaging.' Once she was undressing to shower, Cristian came in to massage her back while she was in the shower.

'I could massage the rest as well if you like?' He was sending images to her making her smile.

'As lovely as those images are I really just want to get to dinner and then go to bed. I haven't done much but I feel really tired,' Danika admitted.

'Of course darling, are you sure you are up to going down? We could have something sent up.' Cristian worried about her.

'Yes I am determined to continue on. I can sleep afterwards.' Danika smiled at him. He placed the big robe around her and rubbed her dry. Then he started to brush her hair that nearly sent her to sleep. He helped her dress and did her hair up in a large braid and pinned it in a roll for her.

'You're good at that. Good practice if we have a girl.'

After speaking with Peter, sadness came over him. He couldn't imagine the horror of losing babies because they were girls. He was careful to keep that from Danika.

He changed his wet clothes and then made sure he was holding her arm as they walked downstairs. They were the first in the dining room. Ben came in and offered Danika a couple of drinks to try that were zero alcohol but looked like wine.

As he poured her a full glass Elizabeth came in.

'Good evening everyone. How is the non-wine?' Elizabeth seemed very upbeat. Ben poured Cristian and Elizabeth a different white wine.

'Surprisingly good,' Danika agreed. 'Is that the plan for tomorrow night?'

'In a sense yes. That way you feel part of the table group. How goes the other plans for your trip?'

'The flights to Hobart and accommodation is all sorted. We thought we would leave the tour and return plans a bit open, depending on what we find,' Cristian answered. 'Selene – Danika's mother – may only be there during the week as she has weekend commitments. We hope to visit her in South Australia before returning.'

'That sounds quite an itinerary. Don't burn yourself out, my dear.' Elizabeth put a hand on Danika's.

Ben returned with the mains, checked they were all fine for drinks and returned to the kitchen.

Cristian eyed Danika, knowing she should be eating but she simply pushed her food around in a disinterested state. She looked exhausted. After a moment, Danika pushed her plate away.

'Please excuse me, but I think I need to lay down.' She had gone white and, as she tried to rise, Cristian was there grabbing her before she fell.

Danika

She could sense there were a lot of voices and a feeling of movement. The next she knew she was being spoken to by a different voice and felt a hand on her wrist.

'Hello, Danika. Back with us again. My name is Dr Davis.' He was holding her wrist and taking her pulse. 'I'm just going to take your blood pressure.'

She felt the band around her arm tightening. She tried to sit up but he encouraged her to keep still. Her senses were finally coming back and she could feel worry and fear coming from several directions but not from Dr Davis.

'I'm going to take a blood sample. How are you with needles?' he asked as he swabbed her arm. All she could manage was a nod. She felt Cristian's hand in hers as he squeezed it so she looked to him and finally could feel all his fears. 'Also we need to do a Covid test and a swab to be sure to rule out any other issues. That's all for now.' Dr Davis placed a bandage on the extraction point and folded her arm over to tighten it. 'Leave that on for thirty minutes.' He helped her sit up a little as Cristian placed more pillows behind her.

'Now Danika, you gave your family a scare tonight. You obviously already know you are pregnant so you need to be more in tune with your body's needs. More fluid, especially water. You are a bit dehydrated at the moment. A lot more foods with high iron content. I shall write down a couple of supplements to help that for now. Your body is working pretty hard to adjust to its new role making a baby so be kind to yourself at least in the first trimester. Sleep often but exercise as well. I shall email you some suggestions and get my office to call you with your results. We need to book you in for an ultrasound in a few weeks' time.' His timer for the Covid test went off. 'All clear. Now, do you have any questions?'

'Is our baby alright? I haven't hurt it, have I?' Danika was teary.

'Your baby is probably fine, it is you that needs a bit of TLC. Come and see me in a few weeks' time. Cristian can organise that for you, can't you?' Dr Davis directed his question at Cristian. He nodded briefly looking away from her. 'These are the supplements you need to get.' Dr Davis wrote a couple of items down and handed it to Cristian. 'Make sure she eats tonight.'

'Will it be alright if I fly and travel? We were going on a holiday this week.' Danika was able to rally more as she sipped the water.

'Absolutely, as long as you are not hiking or doing extreme sports. Just follow a healthy diet and drink more water.' Dr Davis stood up and put his things in his bag to leave.

'Right then, if there are no other questions I shall go. Elizabeth it was lovely to see you again. I am guessing I shall see you all a bit more now.' He was smiling broadly.

As he left the room Elizabeth went with him. 'Thank you so much Michael I'm sorry we pulled you away from your dinner and your family. Is she really alright?'

Elizabeth returned shortly after as Cristian had pulled Danika into his arms, her tears leaking into his shoulder as he spoke gentle calming words to her and stroked her hair.

Cristian gave Danika tissues to wipe her tears. 'Thank you for getting Dr Davis here so quickly. I almost remember his face, you must have known him for quite a while.'

'Yes, he had been my doctor through my younger years and occasionally lately. Now it seems he may be in contact more often. As long as you are happy with that of course, Danika.'

'I feel a bit of a fool at the moment not listening to my body or even researching what I should be doing while I am pregnant. I just thought nature took its own course.' Danika looked annoyed at herself.

'No harm done, darling, other than scaring the wits out of the whole household. All will be fine again by tomorrow. We can cancel our meeting and look after you.' Cristian was determined not to put Danika in any jeopardy.

'No please, don't cancel. I'll be fine, I'm sure.' Ann came by, dropping off some food and hovering worriedly around Danika for a moment longer than normal. When she stopped fussing around her and left, Elizabeth also pushed to stand.

'I shall leave you two also. Call me if you need anything.' Elizabeth went out, closing the door as she went.

Cristian was watching her eat until she stopped and said, 'Please don't watch me. Besides you probably didn't get to finish your dinner either, did you?' He stood up and pulled a chair closer to sit on.

'No, but I can get something shortly from the kitchen. I'm so sorry I didn't read all the signs that you were not well. I'll keep a better eye on you in future.' Cristian was feeling very guilty that he had not looked after her better.

'This is all on me you know, thinking I was invincible. I just completely forgot to drink properly and I thought I was eating okay. But now I think about it I skipped a few meals and there was a lack of iron in most of it. This is delicious as usual from Ann.' Danika was trying to eat and talk but now focused on eating, sending thoughts to Cristian instead.

'Robert's plane is due to touch down shortly. After customs he will probably get a taxi to the apartment as offered or a hotel. I don't know and truly I am not concerned either. I'm sure he will message that he has arrived,' Cristian replied to her mental question.

Danika wiped her mouth and sighed at how good the sandwich had tasted. Cristian sent her drinking thoughts. 'Okay, let me get my breath.' She took a long drink of juice followed by a sip of water. 'I'm guessing I'm going to have several watch dogs looking over me from now on.' She picked up a chocolate and savoured it.

'Most probably, I think I'm going to get a scolding from Ann when I go down. They both rallied around so well they really are like part of the family. Mother called Dr Davis, Ben made sure the gate was open and all the lights were on, Ann found the drinking bottle for you to sip on and cleared up the table.' He had forgotten to close that thought off, the image replaying of Danika's falling and pulling most of the meals and drinks in disarray.

'Oh no, I'm so sorry to cause all the fuss.' Danika washed another chocolate down with water. She tried to move the bed tray and Cristian was up helping her remove the tray. A knock sounded at the door.

'Stay there, don't get up yet,' Cristian said to her as she was swinging her legs off the bed. 'Come in.'

'Good evening, sir, I have the things the doctor recommended.' Ben placed the bag of items on the cupboard and took the tray from Cristian. 'Good evening ma'am.'

'Thank you Ben, I am very grateful for all you have done tonight.'

'Always a pleasure ma'am,' Ben said as if it was an everyday occurrence and then left them alone.

Cristian came over with the bag. It held so many bottles and packets and a big bottle of coconut water. He tipped them out for her to see. 'Looks like he got a few extra things, these are the supplements you have to start now.' He handed her a folic and an iron capsule.

She took them dutifully and then said, 'I really need to get up now I have had about a litre of liquid.' He helped her to make sure she wasn't woozy again then stood just outside the bathroom.

'I'll help you undress,' Cristian said firmly with stronger thoughts so she knew not to argue. Once he was satisfied she was comfortable back under the covers he tidied up the array of packets of healthy iron laden snacks, ginger lollies and the electrolyte coconut water onto the bathroom cupboard.

'I'm feeling wide awake now,' Danika complained as he made it clear she was not getting up again tonight.

'I'll get you the laptop to view in bed. But if you are determined to be part of the meetings with Robert tomorrow you need to fully recover.'

'I liked that Dr Davis. I could feel how attached he is to this family. I hadn't thought about the fact that I would have to do medical stuff. A bit naïve, I guess,' Danika admitted.

'It is very early days It's new to me also.' Cristian brought her the electronic notebook which had a tray to sit on. 'This one is better for when you are laying down. I'm heading downstairs, here's your phone and I can hear you also remember.' Then he leaned down to kiss her.

In the kitchen Ann was cutting a sandwich in half to put on a plate as he walked in. 'Would you like a sandwich, Master Cristian?' She pushed the plate towards him.

'Thank you Ann. For this and everything tonight.' He sat at the kitchen table and was about to eat when the vision of Danika fainting in the dining room came to his mind. He ran his hand across his eyes. Ann came around the counter and laid a hand on his shoulder.

'She will be fine I'm sure, Master Cristian. Don't you worry, we will all look out for her.' He placed his own hand on Ann's. He realised that the family he didn't think he had was here all along. 'Eat up then, don't go wasting my food.' It was an old joke when he had been a wiry run about child.

He ate in silence enjoying the sounds and view of Ann tidying her kitchen and humming to herself.

His phone beeping had him check it immediately in case it was Danika but it was his uncle announcing he had arrived but stuck in customs, so he would go to the apartment eventually and come to the estate in the morning. Cristian sent a reply to advise when he leaves the apartment tomorrow. Cristian checked the time, nearly nine p.m.

'Thank you Ann, that was delicious as usual.' He took the remains of his coffee up with him to check on Danika who was asleep. He took the notebook from her lap and pulled the covers over her. He looked at the internet browser she was on regarding what to expect while pregnant. He sat down and continued reading what she had found before he logged into his email to check any further updates from Peter. There was one warning that Robert may not be traveling alone as no one had seen one of his sons since Robert had left. He looked across at Danika sleeping and could feel his protective forces emerging with a tingling down his spine. Taking a few deep breaths he calmed himself again.

He had meant to talk with his mother tonight about the emails but had not had the opportunity. He took a chance to send her a message to see is she was still awake to talk. She was and was keen to talk. He was confident Danika was resting peacefully before he went down to his mother's rooms with his laptop to show her the emails.

'How is Danika now?' Elizabeth asked.

'Sleeping. I think she believed she could continue on doing whatever she wanted without listening to her body. She knows better now. I will not let that happen again,' he confirmed.

Cristian brought his mother up to date. Elizabeth was not

surprised by Peter's comments regarding the family as she said Ingrid had hinted at some of it. The warning that someone else may be with Robert this trip was a surprise.

'Ingrid described the person she believed to be the one practicing dark magic that had befriended Robert. As if it was some abhorrent liaison on that persons part wanting to be a werewolf and trying to find a way to be. She said it was sickening. She said Rasputin came to mind when she was trying to describe him. Ingrid wasn't certain what his name was or where he had come from, only having seen him in the background hanging in the shadows at Robert's castle. Ingrid believed that they were each feeding off the worst aspects of their personalities and that Robert had become much more dangerous now,' Elizabeth explained.

This worried Cristian greatly. Robert had not said his reason for visiting and had obviously assumed he would be welcome and be able to stay at Hollingrove so that would have been his first annoyance. He had not mentioned anyone travelling with him. Hopefully it was just a concern, not a reality.

'Can Danika protect herself from any influences Robert may have acquired?' Elizabeth asked.

'Danika is such a gentle and kind soul. In the past all she did was absorbing happiness and share it back to people. Her energy source is mostly celestial bodies, so nighttime is best for her. She can load various energies into crystals and runes to use and candles help. In the short time I have known her the strength of her craft has increased as she practices it more. The medallion she wears is her greatest strength but she has found a few other pieces lately. She has recently reconnected with her mother and the two of them are very strong.' Cristian was glad to have finally shared that with his mother.

'Our imprinting is one connection we have but we can actually read each other's minds. She is better at it than me and we can each close thoughts off. Did you have that connection with father?' Cristian had never asked direct questions of their relationship before.

'When we imprinted it was such a revelation to be in tune with another person. Once we married and were living together the intensity reduced but we always had a mental connection knowing where each other was and our emotions, but not specific thoughts. When he died that connection broke and it was as if half my mind was gone, besides the heartbreaking grief of losing the man I loved. Hence I struggled to continue until Danika arrived. Did you know she helped my grief? I still miss your father terribly but the desire to end the pain finally has gone. She did the same for Jean Walton.' Cristian could sense how cathartic it was for Elizabeth to finally say this out loud. 'Danika is indeed a kind soul but I believe she would use her strength to protect her family. We need to make sure we are there to back her up.'

'Yes, we will be. I should get back to her and make sure she has a good night's sleep.' Cristian touched his mother's hand before kissing her. 'Good night, Mother.'

'Good night, Cristian. I love you and am so proud of you both.'

Back in his rooms Danika had barely moved, just slumped down a little lower. As he went to pull the covers up again he noticed she was holding her medallion. He wasn't sure that was a good thing but didn't want to disturb her.

He undressed and carefully got into bed, trying not to disturb her. Searching her thoughts they seemed very calm and non-specific, so not dreaming. That was a relief. He eventually drifted off to sleep himself.

Pain woke him, followed by the realisation he was pinned down. His arms were pinned to his sides by Danika as she mumbled and warned him to 'be still I've got you'. But she was not awake and the visions were assailing him faster than he could grasp. The pain in his chest was taking his breath away.

'He's gone, you're safe,' she mumbled more and then let go.

He was able to move her off and the medallion went with her and so did the pain. It was first light so he shook her awake. 'Wake up Danika.'

She looked at him through glassy eyes. 'You're safe now, stay with me.'

'Danika wake up.' He shook her again.

'What happened, was he here?' She was awake and looking around now, realising she was in bed. Her medallion had left a burn mark on his torso. 'Are you alright?' Cristian moved away before she could touch the mark.

'Tell me what was happening just now, while you can still remember it.' Cristian was adamant.

'Robert was searching for us. It was like a labyrinth we were in, he was using magic to find us but I was using magic to hide us. I think the labyrinth was symbolic not real. He was carrying a spear to impale us on it. That was what I thought anyway from perhaps something he had said earlier in the dream. The magic he used was not his own, it was as if it was from an extended arm that he was directing. But he couldn't find us in time, as in the time frame was wrong. He was on one plane and we were on another watching him. That's all I can remember.' She looked at his burn. 'I can heal that, please let me.'

She put her medallion away and then Cristian hugged her. 'I love you darling, I would never knowingly hurt you,' Danika said. He could tell she was mortified that she had burnt him with her medallion.

'I love you too and I trust you. Do you think there is something pushing these dreams?' Cristian was thinking of his conversations last night.

'What are you not telling me?' She moved out of his arms.

'I'm not hiding anything; this came out while you were sleeping.' Cristian brought her up to date on the emails he and his mother had received.

'That is disturbing and sickening at the same time. This dystopian ideal he is forming is becoming clearer. He has to be stopped.' Danika definitely felt stronger today. 'Let me look at that burn.' Her strong thought brooked no argument so he showed her. She took one of her potion bottles and spoke a few words over it before jabbing a tiny bit on the burn then she blew on it. The pain stopped immediately and the redness was going.

'You could make a fortune from that,' Cristian commented as he looked at the mark disappearing.

'Only works if I do a spell and blow on it, not so convenient.' Danika kissed him and made her way to choose clothes and have a shower. She was sipping the coconut water as she went. She read the different bottles and packets and took one of each folic and iron capsules. Then scooped them into the top draw of the vanity saying, 'I think these are best out of sight.'

She slipped the medallion off and then headed towards the shower. She turned and held her hand out to him.

Later, both dry and dressed, they headed down for breakfast holding hands. The choices for breakfast were all higher iron content foods. Elizabeth followed them in as they were choosing their foods.

'Good morning, Mother,' Cristian greeted her before sitting down with his breakfast.

'Good morning to you both. Danika you are looking more refreshed,' Elizabeth replied.

'Thank you yes, definitely firing on all cylinders now.' She smiled. 'Thank you for introducing me to Dr Davis, he made me feel at ease and safe.' She sat also with a huge bowl of food.

Elizabeth was more sparing with her choices but poured a large coffee.

'Cristian, do we have any idea when Robert is likely to turn up?' Elizabeth sipped her coffee as if it was very welcome. Danika could feel she had not slept well and she passed that on to Cristian.

'No and hopefully he does as I asked and warns us when he is coming. The gates will be open anyway because there will be a lot of workers here today. Mark sent me a message that the builders needed to be here today as they had other work they are doing next week.'

Cristian was pleased to have a larger audience actually. Danika agreed as she focused on her food.

'Are you ready to meet him Danika? Do you have all the resources you need?'

'I am ready, thank you. Did you know some of the herbs and plants in your garden have very useful healing properties. I gathered a few recently. Cristian might remember me using them at the art gala we went to,' Danika answered.

'Yes I remember, you smelled delicious.' He smiled at the memory of her.

'Now we just need to be sure the testosterone levels don't get too high,' Danika pointed out. They all mulled over that for a while knowing what she meant. 'I can hear the builders arriving.' Danika was referring to her feelings rather than sounds but Cristian could definitely hear them.

'I'm full to bust with this food. I think I shall go get ready early then I can focus on the day to go have a chat with the guys.'

'I won't be far behind you. I'll let you know Mother if I hear from Robert.' Cristian finished his coffee and waited until Danika was out of hearing, he closed his thoughts. 'She is much stronger today but we had a moment this morning when she was dreaming – a premonition of sorts – that Robert was going to pursue us in the future. I'm sure he doesn't know of her yet.'

'It is important that we never let him get her alone.' Elizabeth's resolve was apparent.

'Agreed. Now I will go see how she is going.'

Cristian found Danika in the bathroom building up her protection with the herbs and oils she put together and pouring them into a small vial. The remains she rubbed on her inner elbows, temple and chest. Then, slipping off her shoes, she rubbed it on the soles of her feet. She had swapped her trousers for a dark green layered skirt with pockets. She spoke to her crystals and runes before placing them in the pockets and made sure her medallion was hidden.

'I love watching you work.' He could feel the push from the magic she had surrounded herself with. 'I can feel that. Does that mean I am being pushed away?'

'Not you, just your thoughts. Anything malicious so if you are thinking of him that could be why.'

Just then his phone pinged, looking at it confirmed his uncle had said he was just on his way to Hollingrove. 'If the traffic isn't too heavy he should be here in about an hour.' He sent a message to his mother. He then went into the study to pick up the internal phone to advise Ben also. 'Okay, well everyone will know now. Did you want to go down to talk to the men?'

'Yes I do, I'll just get my jacket and sunglasses.' Danika remembered to take her water bottle also.

Between the conversations with the builders and Mark over plans for the coming weeks and into the future the time went quickly and Cristian suggested they move towards the house to greet Robert. Ben had seen the gate security camera show Robert slowing down. The fencing and security would be new to him. Cristian and Danika waited on the top step and Elizabeth and Ben joined them a moment later. Robert pulled up on his own in what would have been a hire car. They waited until Robert was approaching them at the bottom before Cristian greeted him.

'Hello, Robert, how was your trip?' Cristian did not welcome him or extend his hand until Robert started up the stairs. Cristian had to put his stamp on his territory. They shook hands very briefly.

'Long and uncomfortable. Good to see you, Cristian,' Robert replied with some hesitation.

'Hello, Robert,' Elizabeth said, but did not extend a hand.

'I would like to introduce you to my wife, Danika Blakesley.' Cristian made a point of letting Robert know she was definitely part of the family.

Danika still had her sunglasses on and did not extend a hand either. 'Hello, Robert.'

'Well, this is a surprise that you kept from me. Hello, Danika.' Before he could extend a hand the builders came noisily around the house. Then equally noisily apologised for their ruckus.

'Please come in,' Elizabeth said and turned her back on him to walk in the open door Ben held for them. Danika followed with Cristian behind and Robert at the rear besides Ben closing the front doors.

Elizabeth went into the sitting room with the others following and sat down, indicating for everyone else to. Danika took off her sunglasses and sat next to Cristian on the couch with Robert taking one of the other chairs. She was furthest from him.

'You didn't mention why you were coming to visit, Robert,' Elizabeth said, showing her strength in holding the conversation.

'Well, it was to discuss Cristian's future as he had not responded to my messages but I can see he has moved on since our last discussion.' Robert looked at Danika holding Cristian's hand and looking down. Then she turned and looked straight at him. Cristian could see the impact her emerald-green eyes had on Robert, as if they pushed him back in his seat.

'Yes, Danika and I met on that holiday you insisted I went on. So our lucky meeting is almost down to you Robert.' Cristian was not holding back the satire of that statement.

Danika could feel the confusion coming from Robert as if he was questioning his own beliefs. She shared her insight with Cristian who was pleased to know his uncle was not at ease.

Ben came in to break the tension and asked if they would like tea or coffee served in the sitting room. Elizabeth again took the lead.

'Yes, thank you Ben, just the drinks.' Then she turned to Robert. 'You did not want anything before lunch, did you Robert?' He just shook his head as Ben left.

'While you are here you will be able to see the changes we are making to Hollingrove. And the gallery is doing very well, thanks to Danika.' Cristian turned to her to smile encouragement as much as rub it in Robert's nose.

'So is that your trade Danika – art?'

'I have a few strings to my bow and a flare for picking good art pieces it seems.' Danika was using a lot of power to keep Robert unsettled, Cristian could feel her energy being sapped. He squeezed her hand and moved slightly to break the eye contact she had, sending her a thought to save her energy. Ben brought the trolley of drinks in and stayed to make them each a drink.

Her thank you to Ben was more than just receiving the drink he passed her. He winked as he was turned away from Robert. Once all the others had drinks Ben left the room.

'I noticed the changes to the fencing and the security when I arrived.' Robert was not usually one for small talk. Cristian knew this meant he was still rattled.

'Yes we have had several incidents of curious people coming onto the estate. We value our assets and our privacy. The gates are usually closed but with the builders here today it seemed easier to leave them open. Ben keeps an eye on the security cameras.'

'I was shown an article about the gallery the other day. A launch of new items, was it?' Robert clearly wanted them to know he was watching.

'Yes the gallery had become a bit stale. Thankfully Danika was able to find just the right trend needed to give it a fresh feel. It has been very successful, hasn't it dear?' Cristian was trying to give her lots of his energy.

'You're too generous, but yes it looks like I need to source more on our holiday now darling.'

'Yes, you wouldn't know, but we have planned an extended holiday from Sunday as our honeymoon was too brief before the launch.' Cristian understood Danika's desire for Robert to realise they expected him gone before then. 'I have tentatively booked us a table for dinner tonight in Sydney if you are interested Robert.' That made it clear they were not planning on entertaining him here at Hollingrove.

'Would you like to see the works in the garden, Robert? You may remember in the early days when there was a pool. It is the plan to reinstate it.' Elizabeth was again taking charge of the proceedings making it clear they should move on. She stood up as if to usher them out.

Danika went out with Cristian holding her hand towards the front door again. 'It is best this way, the back is quite busy with building implements,' Danika explained without looking at Robert. The men were singing as they worked and Cristian felt Danika absorbing the good feeling from that. With her sunglasses on again she was running her hand over the plants as she went. As they moved closer, the gravel paths were covered in planks to make it easier for the builders to walk and push the barrows over.

Robert didn't seem interested at all that was happening but was being mildly polite following them. Until they reached the pool, now empty of debris and the first coats of blue sealer applied. 'I remember playing in there with Henry as a boy on those stinking hot summers,' Robert said, then seemed surprised to have spoken the memory. Cristian knew Danika was pushing that one out. Elizabeth and Cristian turned to look at him having not ever heard him speak of any happy memories of being in Australia.

'We are all looking forward to the summer now,' Danika continued the thought.

Danika communicated to Cristian that she could sense Robert trying to push away any happy memories he had when he was here and thought what a sad person he was.

'You seem to have several projects happening at the same time and you said something about renovations inside.' Robert was fishing.

'Availability of the builders at the moment is the main reason,' Cristian explained. 'We also want to lighten up the dark areas upstairs.'

'I would like to see that,' Robert said but Danika sensed he was lying and had an ulterior motive. They headed to the back door to go upstairs. Elizabeth deferred to go back to her rooms rather than using the stairs. As they started up the stairs behind the men Danika sent an urgent thought to Cristian that she hadn't cleared away her candles in the back bedroom and to steer Robert the other way. Cristian drew Robert the other way as Danika scooped up the candles in her rug and dropped them down the laundry chute.

'What is all this?' Robert said of the mixture of photos and frames as Danika caught back up with them. Danika explained that she planned to make a photo wall of the family but was still gathering photos.

'Don't bother looking for mine, I do not want to be on your photo wall.' Roberts's true character was returning.

'No problem, I'll bypass them then,' Danika said, not giving his comments the time of day.

'You seem to have entrenched yourself and your ideas very quickly here. What else are you planning to change?' Robert said sarcastically. Cristian was getting angry and Danika sent calming thoughts, reminding him that he was baiting him.

'Well we think we will gut that room.' Danika pointed at the room he had used in the past. 'To use it as a gaming and media room, aren't we, Cristian? After all it is not needed as a bedroom anymore.'

Ben appeared. 'Excuse me ma'am, there is a call for you from the gallery. They were not able to reach you on your cell phone.'

'I need to take this, please excuse me.' Danika went into the study to pick up the call.

Cristian was furious with the rudeness of his uncle directed at Danika. 'I see you haven't lost your touch to be brusque and rude.' Cristian wanted him gone but knew it needed to be done more delicately.

'You are letting her run your life.'

'My relationship with my wife is none of your business, just as the disregard you have of your wife and family is none of mine.' Cristian could feel his hairs tighten. He warned Danika not to come out.

Robert had clearly had enough of this impudence. 'I cannot see anything to keep me here any longer I shall leave you to your grand plans for the estate but I will meet you for dinner tonight. Send me the details and add one, I have Karl traveling with me. He had business in Sydney.'

'I'll see you out.' Cristian sent more thoughts to Danika to stay where she was.

Cristian watched Robert leave, waiting until the gates shut behind him. He walked back in to be met by Elizabeth and Danika. 'He won't be coming back here. But he has agreed to meet tonight, for some reason bringing Karl with him, so Peter was right.' They moved into the sitting room to continue their discussion.

'Who is Karl?' Danika asked.

'His son, I'm not sure if I met him but from what Peter has said he is like his father.' Cristian was not pleased that the group would now be uneven.

'He was rattled today, he will be looking to regroup so to speak.' Danika looked at Elizabeth and said, 'I caught a few of his emotions rather than thoughts. He actually was surprised that he had any happy memories here. There is definitely a more reasonable side to Robert that he is trying to hide.'

'Do you think he is being coerced?'

'I don't know having not known him before today. However I wonder that his severe attitude may have been enhanced by other forces. Whether that was by his choice or he has been coerced, we may never know.' Danika was trying to evaluate her limited connection with Robert. 'He is a misogynist though, that was obvious. He didn't like me talking back to him.'

'Or me holding any part of the conversation, he hasn't seen that since Henry died.' Danika reached over to touch her hand.

'You definitely shocked him.' Danika smiled at Elizabeth.

'The call I had was from Paul regarding the extra items from Mrs Walton. I said I would go to the warehouse tomorrow to view them. I thought best to before we go away. Would you like to come also, Elizabeth, in case there was anything you would like?' Danika suggested.

'I can take you both in the estate car. I have some business to sort as well,' Cristian explained. 'We will use it tonight also. I need to change the booking and let Robert know where so I shall excuse myself to sort that out.' Cristian stood and leaned over to kiss his mother. 'You did very well today.' Cristian and Danika were proud of Elizabeth's fortitude.

'I might go ask Ann to change lunch to in our rooms if that suits you. I have some things to follow up as well,' Danika suggested.

When Danika returned upstairs having sorted out the arrangements, Cristian was on the computer trying to contact Peter. The time frame for Germany was wrong, he would probably be asleep at present. Danika was starting to feel a bit weary after the adrenalin high of the last few hours. Cristian felt it and was taking the bundle from her and making her lay down.

'Rest now. There is nothing you have to do but build your strength for later.' He passed her the water bottle to make sure she was having enough. She nodded, smiling, and let him spoil her.

Danika

Danika stirred as the sound of voices next door in the sitting room filtered through. She had napped for an hour and felt more refreshed. The voice was Ben delivering the lunch, and the smell of the soup had her appetite up.

They spent the early afternoon looking up details of Hobart to get their mind off Robert. About the prisoners and various work they had. Some of the articles were a bit harrowing. It looked like it was such a hard life in a new land, especially for any women. The First

Nation peoples were treated abysmally also. Danika was beginning to wonder how she was ever going to find the truth of her ancestors.

The whole day was unsettling, Danika thought. The interaction with Robert had been better, yet worse than she expected. He didn't rage, which was good, but she knew it wasn't the last they would see of him. After all, why would he still want dinner with them unless it was to try to gain the upper hand again. Where did Karl fit in with all this? Danika decided she needed to go for a walk around the gardens and absorb some of the beauty and perhaps some of the good spirits of the builders. She took scissors with her also to cut some lavender. She kissed Cristian, who was back on the laptop, before she went downstairs.

Ben caught up with her fifteen minutes later and offered to put the flowers in a vase, explaining that Mrs Blakesley would like to see her. Danika entered Elizabeth's sitting room and was called through to her bedroom.

'Cristian mentioned you wanted to improve your wardrobe now you are a little more corporate than traveller. Also that you apparently like op shops. So I was wondering if you would like to look through some clothes before I send them to one,' Elizabeth asked in one breath. This was not what Danika had expected but could feel the love from Elizabeth.

'That would be lovely, thank you.'

'Some may be a bit dated, I was quite slight in my youth and there are a couple of maternity outfits also.' Elizabeth was showing Danika the pieces she had put out on the bed for Danika to look through. Danika was drawn to a stunning red three-quarter jacket with a wide lapel. Then so many other beautiful outfits. After an hour Elizabeth had reminisced when she had worn them going to functions with Henry. They both needed this break from worry and had some laughs as well. After the pile was sorted in to keep and to go as well as Danika trying a few on to confirm they fit she decided she may go up to get ready for tonight.

When she returned to their rooms, Cristian explained that he had just received a response from Peter regarding Karl and Danika's thoughts about influencers and Ingrid's Rasputin comment. Peter confirmed that Karl was the one that found the person Peter believed had been introduced to Robert. Since then, Robert and Karl had become harder and darker in their thoughts towards other family members. For some reason the other person could not leave the country. Peter was going to try and find out why and what his background was but they had limited knowledge of him. Claus was all they knew for now.

'So as usual we have more questions than answers,' Danika said. 'I think I shall start my preparations for tonight.' Danika made sure she reapplied her evil warding off oil again before tying her medallion around her waist. Then she worked on her hair braids, keeping her hair off of her face to show off her jewellery and fine neck. The length of her hair still flowed down her back. The simple lines of her little black dress enhanced her jewellery. Black tights and black high heel shoes made her look very elegant. She pinned the Triquetra broach Cristian had given her to the lapel of the red jacket. Danika placed protection charms on the broach and the crystals in the pockets of her jacket and in her little bag which she would keep with her. She asked Cristian to see if he could sense the baby. He confirmed that the medallion hid it completely. Before she went into the bathroom to apply her makeup Cristian kissed her soundly.

'I love you. I love your strength and kindness,' he said between kisses.

'I love you too and feel blessed by the heavens to have this family now.' She meant Ann and the others also. Cristian agreed.

Ben had brought the estate car round to the front for them and informed them that all the workers were gone for the day and he would set the security behind him as he left.

Despite some traffic congestion they were at the restaurant before seven p.m. and before Robert. None of them wanted to drink alcohol tonight, preferring to keep their wits about them. Elizabeth had arranged that zero alcohol beer and wine would be available. They had their drinks served before Robert and Karl came in. Danika had her jacket off and placed on the high back of her chair. The waitress showed the men to their table and took orders for drinks from them. Danika could feel the waitress was not comfortable around them and wondered what they had said to her. They were obviously not concerned about drinking and ordered Jägermeister.

Robert introduced Karl to Elizabeth and Danika as his 'sister-in-law and Cristian's wife.' Cristian vaguely remembered Karl from a visit to Germany twenty years ago. He must have been about fifteen years older than Cristian. From Cristian's memories, Danika could see he had changed and become heavier set, as if he used weights. Elizabeth felt a little intimidated by him so Danika shared some strength with her. Karl spoke some broken English to them and German to his father which was rude on purpose. Cristian said he knew that he spoke better English than that. Cristian asked Karl about the business he had in Australia. He said it was real estate development, which seemed more than unusual to be doing that from Europe. Cristian guessed that was more likely a ruse.

Karl then asked Cristian, 'Why did you sell off the best gallery pieces so cheap?' They had obviously been watching the online sales of the gallery.

'They had stagnated and we have a new more successful collection now,' Cristian responded.

'I have seen this. Not to my liking now.' Karl was obviously baiting them as his father had.

'So did you buy any of the preferred pieces while they were cheap Karl?' Danika asked. Karl turned to her with a sneer. She could feel the disdain coming from him because she spoke to him at all. She could feel Cristian getting angry and lay her hand on his leg.

'I don't waste money on art when there is land to own,' Karl eventually answered.

The male waiter came to their table to ask if they were ready to order. Danika realised the girl waitress did not want to come back to their table.

The men ordered large, rare steaks and the women ordered fish and salad. Then all ordered more drinks.

'Father said you are leaving on a holiday. Where are you going, somewhere warm maybe?' Karl was obviously going to hold court tonight.

'South, we have much history to view and Danika's family to visit.' Cristian was deliberately nonspecific also.

'Colder, so do you ski? Do you have snow in this country?' Karl said it with further disdain.

'We are not going for the skiing, although it will be good later in the season. Yes we have extensive snow fields that we may visit in a couple of months.' Cristian was trying to pull the conversation his way.

'My father told me about the work at your house, Aunt Elizabeth. Is that something you are happy about?' Karl was insinuating that she had no control over her own home. He really liked to pit a person against one another, that was obvious.

'I most certainly am, it is about time to bring that old home into the twenty-first century.' Elizabeth smiled at him.

'If I come back again I would like to see this estate that copies the English much more admired manor by name only.' Karl held up his glass to get the attention of the waiter.

The meals came out at that point by the female waitress. Karl leered at her and nearly touched her but Cristian moved his arm in the way, creating a smirk from him.

The waiter brought Karl and Robert another drink. The others declined, not needing more. The food was cooked to perfection yet Karl and Robert both had to comment that in Germany it would be served with more accompaniments. There was no pleasing either of them tonight. After they had finished the meal Robert and Karl said that they should continue drinking liqueurs. Their rudeness was bound to deteriorate further with the drinks they were having.

'We have a long drive back, so no thank you. I am ready to take Mother and Danika home now.' Cristian called for the bill. 'Do you need me to get you a taxi?' Danika felt both Robert and Karl taking offence at that suggestion.

'Of course not, this has been nothing. You are all weak in this country.' Karl swept his hand over the glasses.

Cristian put his card on the bill for the waiter to take away and then stood to get the chair for Danika and help her on with her coat. Karl sneered at Cristian's action and then Cristian helped his mother the same.

'Goodbye Robert, goodbye Karl,' Cristian said making it obvious he meant that to be the end of it. Then, as he showed the ladies towards the door, he met the waiter returning his card and had a quiet word with him. Karl was watching.

Once he was sure that the women were settled in the car he took them towards the harbour. He felt they both needed to appreciate some pleasant views before returning home. As he pulled the car to a stop they all sighed.

'I'm glad that is over and I hope we never see them again,' Danika said what they all felt.

'It seems Karl is worse than his father. I didn't think that was possible,' Elizabeth commented. 'What did you say to the waiter?'

'I told him to not worry if they stopped serving them and feel at ease to call the police if they get too obnoxious,' Cristian answered. 'I hope they don't have trouble with them.'

'I think I shall get out and speak to the stars if I can see them.' Danika stepped out and felt the cool air on her face. She took her shoes off so she could feel the gravity of the earth and held her arms up and spoke to the night sky. She felt refreshed and shared some of it with Elizabeth who was watching her and a little over to Cristian who came and hugged her. Eventually he walked over to the car again with Danika. When he was back in the car he thanked his mother for bringing him up in a loving household. Elizabeth was very moved by that and shed a happy tear.

'Well ladies I should get you home now if you are ready.' But before he started the car he had a phone call from a number he didn't recognise.

'Hello, my name is Senior Constable Marsh. Who am I speaking to?'

'I am Cristian Blakesley. How can I help you, Senior Constable?' Cristian was concerned about the restaurant owners. Danika could feel his concern.

'Do you own the apartment at Harbourside, sir?'

'Yes, is there a problem?'

'Have you allowed your family to stay there tonight?'

'Yes, my uncle Robert is staying there and his son Karl may also be there. Is there a problem?' Cristian repeated his question.

'Are you able to meet us there, sir, now?'

'Yes I have not left Sydney yet. I can be there in ten or fifteen minutes.' Cristian realised the senior constable was not going to answer his enquiries.

'Something has happened at the apartment I have to go there. I'm sorry you will have to stay in the car while I sort this.' Cristian apologised to them and was trying to sound like it was a small thing but Danika could sense his trepidation.

Cristian

He parked just out of sight of the apartment not wanting Elizabeth or Danika to see anything that may be distressing. There was a police car parked on the road with lights going and, as he walked towards the building, he noticed another in the parking lot looking at the car Robert had driven earlier.

Inside the building in the lift it smelled very rank and he wondered what had been spilled. At the apartment the door was open and what he saw inside shocked and disgusted him. The police officer at the door noted his reaction. Inside his uncle and cousin sat as if they could get up at any time, but it was obvious the other two police were warning them to sit where they were. In here also was the same smell and now he realised what it was. The furniture was wrecked and had several tear marks across the cushions, the walls also were marked by scratches. He could see marks on the carpet.

'We received a report from neighbours and passersby of loud noises and what appeared to be an injured dog howling. We attended to find these two naked at that point yelling at each other. No dog was found.' The senior constable was reading from his report book. 'Was this the condition you left the apartment in last time you saw it?'

'No.' Cristian was staring at his relatives and was working hard to control his anger which seemed to amuse them. He kept his view of the apartment from Danika. Danika could obviously feel his anger because he could feel her calming him.

'Do you want to lodge a complaint? In which case we will take them in for questioning.' Cristian sensed the senior constable would definitely like to take them in. However Cristian just wanted them gone.

'No, thank you, Senior Constable.' Cristian was still staring at them. 'I believe they are leaving on the next plane out of Sydney.'

'There is also the case of possible drink driving,' the police officer said.

'I'm sure that the work that is going to be for you tonight on just a possibility and that these people will be leaving the country as soon as possible would not be the best use of your valuable time.'

The senior constable showed Cristian out of the apartment. 'I can see sir that you have a family domestic problem here and as long as we are not called back here or anywhere else to do with them I am going to let this go. Am I right that you would prefer them to leave as soon as possible?'

'Indeed. I shall make sure they leave on the next plane I can get.' Cristian could not believe how disgusting they had been. The police left and he walked back into the apartment.

'You are packing and going to the airport now and getting the first flight out of Sydney. I don't care where you go as long as you leave tonight and do not return. Otherwise, I will make a formal complaint and confirm you drove drunk then watch them see your real self while locked up.' Cristian was still keeping his voice under control despite wanting to scream at them. 'I will order a taxi for you.' Cristian walked out of the apartment. He sent a message to Danika what he was doing but not why.

Obviously the threat of possibly being locked up for the lunar cycle was enough to get them moving and they were packed and bringing their bags out at about the time that the taxi arrived. The stink in the lift from their scent marking was disgusting. He saw them into the taxi and asked for the keys for the hire car which they said were upstairs. Then they were leaving. Cristian walked back to his car.

'What happened?' Danika asked as she got out of the car to join Cristian.

'They defiled the apartment. I shall say no more.' He shook his head at the image while trying to hide it from her. 'I have to go back up there to get the keys for the hire car to sort that out. You can't come with me. Are you both alright to stay here a bit longer?' Danika and Elizabeth agreed although Danika wanted to help.

Cristian returned to the apartment and retrieved the keys from the main bedroom cupboard, putting them in his pocket. That room was also destroyed and stunk. He then went to the laundry to get cleaning items to clean the lift. As he walked past the room that had been Danika's, the mess was the same in there. Not the last bedroom though. He did the best he could to make the lift smell better then tossed out the cloths. He would have to contact his cleaners and pay them a lot to deal with this. He locked up and went down to check the hire car. It was not damaged thankfully. He checked the boot and found a satchel of papers which made him swear, hoping they would not come back for them. He locked it and went back to his own car with the satchel.

As he started the car he apologised for the later night. Danika laid her hand on his, asking if he wanted to talk about it. He declined but handed her the satchel, asking her to look through it to see if they were likely to want it back. In it were various real estate details and pictures. All larger areas of land with forest. Danika described it to Cristian who was interested but not concerned. He doubted they would find anywhere they considered suitable as he had looked a few times himself. The land he had just purchased thanks to Danika finding it was a rarity. He sent those thoughts to Danika to allay her fears. Elizabeth was very tired and eventually drifted to sleep as Cristian was driving. It worried him to keep his mother out this late under very stressful circumstances. He realised Danika had been sending calming thoughts to her until she drifted to sleep.

'Thank you for helping Mother tonight.' Cristian was aware how much Danika had bolstered his mother. 'This whole episode must have been very confronting for both of you.'

'I sensed the intention from them both was to intimidate us in various ways. The fact that all three of us were in some way "one upping" them all day was infuriating to them. They probably are not used to that.' Danika was trying to reread the thoughts and senses she had gleaned from them today and tonight. She held up the satchel. 'This is no doubt part of that intimidation.'

'They risk a lot to come back near us or to Australia at all. I won't hesitate to have them charged with the damage. They would lawyer up and get out of it but they would be stuck sorting it out and timing is everything, as you know.' Cristian was focusing on the driving rather than looking at Danika. 'I have to warn Peter and his family.'

'What did they do at the apartment?' Cristian knew she could sense his holding those thoughts very tightly away from her.

'Trying to make a point in their drunken way, I will deal with it tomorrow when we come back and you are at the warehouse. I have to check that the restaurant owners were not affected as well.' The repercussions of their actions could have been huge. They had certainly let themselves go in a foreign country. Hopefully they would realise their mistake when they sobered up.

The remainder of the ride home was in silence. At the gate Cristian had to turn off the security to enter before restoring it again. He was glad to have that safeguard in place. He parked at the front so that they could escort his mother to her rooms. She had luckily stirred when they stopped at the gate so it was easier to get her out. Danika walked with her and made sure she was settled.

Cristian had parked the car back in the garage while she was with Elizabeth and met her as she was coming from Elizabeth's wing. He made sure all was locked and secure before going up with Danika who let him know that Elizabeth had requested to stay home the following day. It was well after midnight and it felt that it had been several days, not just one. Danika made for the bathroom while Cristian went to contact Peter to warn him of the events tonight. He felt like the disgusting scent was in his nostrils and stripped off his suit and other clothes to go to the laundry, walking naked towards the bathroom. He found Danika trying to undo the medallion around her waist, otherwise naked also. She smelled him and felt his arousal. Finally freeing the knot of the medallion she pushed him into the shower that had been running while she had grappled with the knot. She took a loofa and soap and washed him. He realised she could smell him. 'I'm sorry I brought that stink with me.' Cristian was getting angry again at what they had inflicted on his family.

'It's okay, they're gone and so will the smell.' She leaned against him and they hugged under the running water, absorbing their love for each other.

12

HERITAGE

THE NEXT TWO days went fast and without incident. Cristian organised the stripping and cleaning of the apartment. The damaged furniture and carpets were removed, the walls were due to be repaired and he would have new carpet installed and furniture delivered by the time they returned from their holiday. Peter had confirmed that Robert and Karl were back and full of scathing comments of Australia and of them saying they were backward and impotent, a waste of their time and energy. Cristian was relieved to hear that. He decided to now let Peter know that he was married to Danika and what had gone on in the time Robert and Karl were in Australia. He said he would let the rest of the 'on board' family know.

They said their goodbyes and well wishes to Elizabeth and saw her into the taxi that was taking her to the airport, pleased that she would be catching up with her extended family in New Zealand after so many years apart. 'That will be us tomorrow.' Danika was getting excited by it all.

They headed back inside to eat and talk with Ann, who offered Danika fruit salad once she had cleared her plate. She was looking at Cristian's food as if she could eat more. Now that she was eating properly, her appetite felt like it had grown out of control. She took a big gulp of her juice to try and kerb it.

'How are the travel plans going?' Ann was making small talk as she checked through the fridge to clear it out.

'We have our flights and accommodation I believe. I am learning about both because it is new to me,' Danika admitted.

'So never flown before?' Ann asked.

'No, this will be my first so good that it is a short one.' The day went slowly as Danika couldn't stop herself from expressing her excitement. Eventually though, after a restless night's sleep from the excitement, their alarm woke them the next day and they set about their travel plans.

Getting to the airport and going through the check in and security was exciting but stressful, especially when Danika's medallion set off the metal detector. Cristian showed her to the Qantas lounge as a member so she could have breakfast in peace and calm down.

Cristian was loving feeling and seeing her child-like fascination and joy of this new experience. He was hoping the actual flight was fun for her also but for now he just wanted her to eat and drink as she had been too wound up back home. They had been lucky that the check in had gone smoothly and now had plenty of time before the boarding would be called.

After eating Danika had finally calmed her senses. She had 'felt' the room and spread some of her abundance of joy to a few wary travellers. She had been listening for the different flight information and watching the screen for their flight yet she still jumped when boarding was announced. He held her hand all the way on to the plane and had made sure she had the window seat when they booked. He explained to her where she needed to put her bag and how to use the seat belt. All he could see past the mask they'd still kept to wearing in public after Covid were the enormous pools of vivid green of her eyes taking everything in. She absorbed every word of the flight attendant speech as they taxied before take-off. Then she was transfixed looking out the window and clutching his hand as they left the ground. He could feel her heart racing. The view of the clouds was her undoing and tears started welling and soaking into her mask. She sent thoughts of how beautiful it all was to Cristian and her extreme gratitude for him being there to share this with her.

When the short flight was over and they were loading their bags into the hire car, they followed the GPS to the house Cristian had booked for their stay before she could take everything in. The house was a better option than a hotel room, especially with Selene arriving tomorrow. The view of the water reminded her of Sydney but here the atmosphere was calmer. Danika cleared the top of a cabinet in the lounge of the display items and placed the message stick, linen ancestor list and potion box on top one at a time. Cristian handed her a tea and made her sit down with a snack, he had felt her energy waning.

'I sense you are disappointed, about what?' He sat down next to her.

'I don't know. I think that I thought there would be some revelation here, some feeling to show me the next step. Silly really, hopefully it won't be a wasted trip for Mum.' Danika was looking into her cup.

'Seeing you and hearing our news will not be a wasted trip for her. Besides, you have only been here five minutes in the scheme of things. Some history research after we pick up Selene will probably turn something up,' Cristian encouraged.

'Once Mum is here we will have to go shopping for herbs and candles seeing as we couldn't bring any with us.' Danika was leaning heavy on him. He took her tea and put it down and suggested she have a nap to recharge her energy. She nodded and went in the bedroom to lay down, pulling a blanket over her.

After a refreshing nap, some food and a long shower, they settled down together on the couch.

'While you were sleeping I looked up some details of early Hobart. There is quite a lot on the net but we may be able to get some hard copy information at museums and the info centre. In the 1800's the ships docked at Sullivan's Cove, which is basically the main wharf now. Looks like they often sat offshore for days before unloading the convicts or free immigrants to their respective destinations.' Cristian watched her start eating before he continued. 'Your ancestors name was not on any passenger lists that I could find. They are all very well documented. The free immigrants included both full fare paid and bonded immigrants, mostly women. Do you think she could have been one of them?'

'I don't know, but the family verbal history that my mother is adamant about was that she was kidnapped. But you know, hundreds of years and Chinese whispers, who knows the real story,' Danika replied.

'Once your mother is here you can search together, perhaps museums first and that news report we saw,' Cristian suggested. 'Would you like to sit outside to see the stars tonight? It is very cold but there is a heater out there.'

'Yes, I might, at least for a little while.' Cristian went out to the patio to start the gas heater, taking a couple of blankets outside as well as her rug and some cushions. Danika set herself up with the rug and the cushions then sat with the blankets around her as she channelled the celestial energy. After a short time Cristian could feel that she was getting less from it than trying to stay warm so he intervened and carried her inside.

'Thank you, that did help. I think I shall just retire and be better tomorrow.' Danika wanted to be as energised as possible to meet her mother. While she slept Cristian continued searching for any details he could of the murder charge of Jessica Carling.

Danika

Danika woke alone and looked for Cristian by thought and couldn't locate him. She got up and found a note that he was running. She made herself a tea and took it into the bathroom as she showered and dressed. Finally feeling more normal, Danika decided to look through the supplies, finding an instant pancake mix in a bottle and bacon and eggs to start with. She was busy making pancakes and adding them to the other foods in the oven when Cristian returned. His face flushed from the cold but smiling and please to see Danika she could feel. 'Good morning, that smells awesome.' He kissed her cheek and his face felt like ice.

'Oh my heavens you feel like a freezer.' Danika jolted.

'I'll go shower, only be a few minutes.' Then he dashed off. Danika was smiling but could still feel the spot of cold on her face.

Once she heard the shower turn off she put the eggs on and started the coffee machine. Handing him a coffee as he came in and dishing up a pile of food for him and a couple of pancakes for herself.

'You need protein. What else are you having?' Cristian was adamant.

'Okay, I will have an egg.' She placed an egg off to the side of the pancakes. 'It doesn't go with the berries though.' She piled strawberries on top with yoghurt.

They sat eating with him watching to make sure she did eat the egg. He was sending her loving thoughts and how worried he had been again yesterday. She relented and understood she needed to be more mindful of her needs.

As she finished she said, 'I love that we can thought talk and eat at the same time, I wonder if we will lose that.' Danika looked at him as she sipped her tea. 'Your mother said that she and your father were connected but not on our level of thought transfer.'

'If we do then it is because we have broken the curse and it would be worth it. We would have to get used to talking more. I did a fair bit of research last night and have found a couple more references to your family in news reports from the state library. I worked backwards from that first one we found.'

'September 1858, unholy alliance of women found. Missing man, John Walsh, had told a friend he was going to visit the women. Walsh's friend confirmed he was drunk and had no good in his heart. The unholy alliance of women denies seeing Walsh. A search is ongoing.'

'What does unholy alliance of women mean, a coven?' Danika asked, her mind spinning on the thought.

'I looked it up, they mean homosexual,' Cristian explained. Danika was shocked and had not expected that.

'I had never thought about any of my family being gay. Do you think they actually were or just branded with that because there were no men around?'

'October 1858. Missing man found murdered. Missing man John Walsh has been found murdered in bushland. Police search for several female suspects from den of unholy alliance.'

'So now it is a den. I wonder how many women lived there.' Danika knew probably at least three.

'October 1858. Woman charged with murder. Jessica Carling was charged with the murder of John Walsh while police still look for her daughter and granddaughter who may be witnesses or perpetrators also. November 1858. Death by misadventure. The true events of the death of John Walsh are not known as several women may have been involved. Judge Rhodes has sentenced the remaining woman, Jessica Carling, to the workhouse for her part in disposing of the body of John Walsh. It is likely she will see her days out there. That was all I found, no mention of other names. Perhaps we should look for them?' Cristian suggested. 'Did you bring the handwritten list?' Danika was deep in thought.

'Yes, but I remember after Jessica was Amelia and then Emma. Mother said Emma was the one to go to South Australia but no mention of Amelia. Poor Jessica, how awful to lose her family because of that horrid man.' Danika was very upset now.

'How old would she have been if she was a grandmother?' Cristian wondered.

'Well if she arrived in 1822 maybe a late teen or in her twenties. Then thirty-six years later, maybe in her mid-fifties.' Danika sensed his thoughts. 'Did they keep death records from the workhouse I wonder?'

'I didn't mean to upset you but I thought it was important to move on this, now we can hopefully trace more while we are here.'

'Yes, you're right, it just feels like yesterday reading this after feeling what I did – we did.' There was so much she had to tell her mother.

'Yes, there is much to tell her and ask her. She will be arriving in about an hour so we can,' Cristian confirmed, looking at his watch as he tidied the kitchen so Danika could focus on getting ready to meet her mother. She wore her grandmother's jacket over warmer clothing.

Standing waiting for her mother was very stressful but Danika was grateful that she actually could. Not that long before, they would have had to wait outside the airport. Wearing a mask was a small thing compared to seeing a loved one arrive. Then she saw her in her many layers of blue for the cold. She couldn't contain herself any longer and ran up to Selene who opened her arms. They both clung to each other, Danika crying and Selene comforting her. Selene finally looked over to Cristian who was giving them space physically and emotionally. He was smiling broadly at the love pouring from them both. Selene held Danika away from her, then looked back to Cristian.

Danika knew what her mother was asking and said, 'Yes we are having a baby.'

Danika was overwhelmed with the love and joy of her announcement. Selene turned to Cristian and said, 'Blue floral case.' Cristian turned to get Selene's bag from the luggage carousel. Danika and Selene slowly followed him. It didn't take long to get the case and move towards the car. Danika and Selene sat together in the back so they could keep their connection. At the holiday home, Cristian carried Selene's case into the other bigger bedroom while Danika showed her in. Taking off her coat, Selene was wearing the broach they had sent her.

'So, let's have a good look at you then,' Selene said to Cristian. She meant more than looking with her eyes. As she held out her hands, Cristian put his out for her to grasp. Danika sensed as her mother probed into Cristian's mind, knowing it would have been disconcerting if he had never felt it before. He opened his mind for her to see he was hiding nothing. Selene dropped her hands as she had seen the pain and fear of the change and realised it was not a privileged power in Cristian's mind.

'Are congratulations in order for you both then? Are you both happy?'

'Yes, we are,' they said in unison. Danika hugged Cristian.

'We wanted to wait to tell you in person, it was only confirmed on Monday,' Danika said.

Selene noticed the items Danika had laid out on the cupboard. Her mother's potion box that Danika now owned was looking very polished and neat. She held her hand above the message stick and then the framed linen list.

'They are the pieces that I get a strong impression from, when I hold them, of a particular event here in Tasmania that happened to Jessica and her daughter and granddaughter. The linen list is in the frame so we can hold it safely. Cristian found some news articles about them last night.'

Cristian offered to make them tea while they discussed their findings for Selene to get caught up on all they knew and suspected so far.

'Well you certainly have found and experienced many aspects to this curse. What are you hoping to achieve and when?' Selene asked with reservation. Cristian spoke up then.

'We want to end the curse to the Blakesley family and the Carling women. Which would mean the current and future Carling women can experience love and have as many children – girls and boys – as they want. While the Blakesley family would no longer have to live through the werewolf horror and could have female children.' Danika was nodding in agreement.

'The prophecy is that the Carling line will lose their craft if they love and marry. What about your family?'

'Our prophecy is that if we marry a green-eyed woman we will lose our power and wealth. So that prophecy hasn't happened either,' Cristian confirmed. 'Not that I consider disfigurement every full moon any kind of power.'

Selene nodded. 'So the prophecies may be more symbolic than actual.'

'Yes that is what we are thinking. It certainly rattled Cristian's uncle when he saw me though.' Danika was pleased he had been rattled, but nothing else about her contact with Robert.

'We need to find the wording of the curse or at the least the intent to break it. I'm not sure how you are going to do that.'

'Those items over there showed me Jessica's experience here in Tasmania in flashes. We need to find some way of going back all the way to Bronwyn. I think that was who it started with. But I don't know how to get back that far other than this.' Danika held up the medallion. 'Cristian also has a picture of a manuscript that may be a record of the original event.'

'Do you have the pictures with you?' Selene asked.

'Yes, I'll get them.' Cristian went to their room to retrieve the pictures and the framed photo of their wedding day.

He handed Selene their wedding photo. 'We thought you may like this.'

'You look beautiful, Nika, your hair is amazing.' Danika sensed her mother's sadness that she had not been there to see it.

'We have many more photos to show you on our phones. It was a simple ceremony, no guests.' Danika felt she needed to explain that.

'I'd like to see them later.' Selene continued to look at the framed photo and then took it to her room.

Cristian laid out the photos from the manila folder on the table for Selene to view. He had thought to bring the magnifying glass also. Selene returned a few minutes later. It was obvious she had been crying.

'Has Danika explained that we have slightly different strengths with our craft?' Selene asked.

'Only a little. I have watched Danika and felt her strengths firsthand, they have been increasing,' Cristian confirmed with pride.

'I wondered if you had been keeping that from me Nika.' Selene looked at Danika who was a little humbled by her scrutiny. 'My strength is the afterlife although, like Nika, I can sense the here and now also and perform the charms which are useful for my business. I may be able to get back to the original event but I will need more than one thing as a reference from then. Actually the more links the better.'

'I only have the medallion. I don't think that linen goes back that far. That was why we were hoping to get the twin of the medallion. Jessica must have known the history, I think she wrote the linen list. Well that's my hunch actually,' Danika explained. 'Did you want to try a calling later?'

'Yes I think a test of these items would be a good idea. Get a feel for where to from here so to speak. You feel tired though Nika.'

'Yes, she needs to sit and drink and have at least a snack to keep her strength up.' Cristian was directing Danika to sit while he went into the kitchen.

'How long has this been going on? Have you seen a doctor?' Selene came over to sit next to her and hold her hand.

'I am just a little anaemic and low on iron. So I am taking supplements and have to eat more often I am told. And drink more water.' Danika was trying to hide the fact that she had fainted last week and been weak again yesterday.

Cristian handed her another tea and some protein bars. He had noticed she was getting weaker and now worried it was the baby that was the issue. He didn't hide his thoughts quickly enough.

'I'm fine, I just got excited about Mum arriving and forgot to have a snack. Don't blame the baby.' Danika glared at Cristian. Selene put her hand on Danika's stomach.

'When do you see the doctor again?' Selene asked, trying to stay neutral in her thoughts.

'Next month. A couple of weeks I think. Why?' Danika was getting a little worried at her mother's attention.

'Good, hopefully for an ultrasound to confirm my theory.' Selene looked between them both. 'I had no problem carrying you, Mother had no problem carrying me. Strong as horses actually but you aren't and I think I know why. I think you are having twins.'

Danika held her hand out for Cristian who was there in a flash and then he was placing his hand where Selene's had been while he looked at Danika. 'Are you certain, Mother?' Danika asked with a tear in her eye.

'Fairly certain. I am guessing that Cristian could try listening later. Most of this is too early for technology but our senses are a bit better in tune.' Selene was looking at them both. 'It answers why you are affected more than usual. So consider that you are now growing two and need more of everything. Especially if we are to work on this curse together you need to be at your peak, so look after yourself. Perhaps go have a rest and we can come back to this.'

'That's a good idea.' Without asking, Cristian picked Danika up and took her to their room with her bottle of water and snack.

He placed her on the bed and really wanted to try listening but was waiting for her permission. She lay down and pulled her top up and her skirt down. Cristian placed his ear to her stomach.

'There's lots of gurgling.' This made her smile. He moved his head slightly and concentrated. Besides Danika's obvious strong heartbeat resonating Cristian took a breath and held it, slowing his own heartbeat. He heard a faint rapid heartbeat that seemed to be echoing then, concentrating more, it was two very faint but two slightly off beat to one another. He turned his head to kiss her belly twice. Then they were both crying and hugging.

'Oh my heavens, I'm going to be huge.' She put her hands to her now hot cheeks and started to laugh. 'Can you send Mum in, please?'

Cristian did so and remained in the other room to give them their privacy.

Danika held out her arms for her mother to come to her. They hugged for quite a while then Danika looked at Selene and said, 'I need you to fix something for me – this.' Danika pulled her top up from the side to show her tattoo. 'It zaps him every time he touches it.'

'Oh, I'm sorry, I forgot about that. I thought you would have realised a lot sooner than this, it was just to slow things down when you were so young.' Selene held her hand to it and whispered a few words. 'That should have fixed it.'

'Well this has been quite a meeting, I'm still in disbelief. He was already worried about me now he will be having palpitations.' Then she smiled.

'He can hear you, can't he?' Selene realised. 'Can he hear me?'

'Yes, he tones it up or down though otherwise he would be bombarded. You know that vibe from your markets. How are they going by the way? You haven't said much about them,' Danika asked.

'Actually, they are going really well. That was why I didn't want to miss any. I have started sharing my space with a potter, we save money and our style compliments one another and we can take turns looking after it all.' Selene decided she needed to be honest about the arrangement, Danika sensed her hesitation. 'He is very good, quite the artist. He is looking after things for me while I'm gone. His name is Clay. Well, Barclay actually, but everyone calls him Clay, bit of a joke really as a potter.' Danika could sense her mother really liked Clay.

'Oh you have to tell me more.' Danika was intrigued. 'So is that plant pots or art pottery?' Selene got out her phone and showed Danika a few of his pieces. They ranged from large sculptures to small, easy to sell pieces for the markets. Danika was very impressed. 'They are amazing.'

'Yes, I think so, but it is hard to sell the larger pieces as you can imagine. They are the ones he loves to make though the small ones are for income.'

'I look forward to seeing it. Well I'm feeling on top of the world at the moment. I think we could plan a calling if you want Mum.' Danika wanted to get on with things so her mother could go back to her friend.

Cristian put his head in and asked, 'What is a calling and is it dangerous?' Danika could feel all his heightened senses of protection ramping up and warned him, looking at his eyes.

'Like a séance but not so open, calling a particular past life or lives. I have to get a feel for these people first though.' Selene meant the artefacts and what Danika had experienced.

They set up the message stick and the linen ancestor list from its frame on the table then Danika handed the medallion to her mother to wear. 'I'm going to film you, Mum, and I'll intervene if it doesn't look safe.'

Selene picked up the message stick to have a close look at it then put it down and picked up the list. She had been talking as she did this but her voice had not changed like it had with Danika. Selene tried picking up both the stick and the list. Danika sensed as she tried calling to Bronwyn who they believed to be the connection to the start of the curses. Nothing came of it despite trying several different methods. They all realised it needed to be Danika. Selene handed the medallion back.

'You need to film this darling.' She was sending Cristian reassuring thoughts. 'I think we will hold this together Mum.'

They sat opposite each other at first, picking up the message stick each at different ends. The buzz was stronger this time. They each took an end of the ancestor list. Danika knew the visions she'd seen the first time were flowing through to her mother. Selene called on Bronwyn but still the visions were of Jessica. First came a scene of many ships and a name – Phoenix, then an image of Jessica hiding and, more clearly, her dragging herself out of water at night into the scrub. They were cold and shivering, feeling Jessica getting colder. A hand pulled her up – a black hand, that of another woman – and words they didn't understand.

Then came the pain of childbirth. Selene recognised it and calmed Danika so she wouldn't fear it. Some images of a baby then a child – happy images of a love between Jessica and the other woman. Sadness and anger then joy at helping to deliver Mary's baby. They realised that was the name given to the Aboriginal woman. Hard times for the four and hiding Mary and her child when the Black Line came to round them up. Jessica seemed to be working in a dairy and Mary was the one she came home to looking after the two baby girls. Jessica was writing on a piece of white cloth and reciting the names to her baby and Mary.

'It was meant to be me I think, but I was scared and I couldn't be with a man, I'm so sorry. He loved me that Cristian, but his father stopped it. I'm so sorry Amelia,' Danika said.

Danika was struggling to continue so her mother brought them back and pulled the stick from her grasp to break the link. Danika was crying for Jessica and because of her.

Cristian nearly dropped the phone he was recording on when he heard his name from Danika but not her voice. Selene moved the artefacts away from Danika and Cristian while he made sure she was alright.

'I'm positive she had the chance to end this with your namesake back two hundred years ago but she was scared and because she thought she could never be the link with him because she was gay. She mentioned his father not him. I wonder if he ever wrote anything about the meeting.' Danika was trying to be analytical but knew Cristian could feel how much it upset her when she felt his name and slightly his image.

'There seems to be a barrier to going back further to England, probably because the only connection there will be this medallion and we need more than one connection. Although the name of the ship was a new vision,' Selene explained. 'I think we need candles and incense, so need to put them on the to do list for tomorrow.'

'Did you know Jessica was gay, Mum? Do you know if any of the other women were? That could have brought the whole line to an end.' Danika had never considered that.

'I didn't know about Jessica but your great grandmother Isabelle was gay I think. She always had a lady as her companion. I wouldn't be surprised to hear if the women in our line who didn't want to be with men had been forced to.'

'When I had the first images of those thoughts they were so fast I couldn't grasp them but Jessica and Mary exchanged loved pieces. So Jessica had the message stick and Mary a rune. I wonder what happened to it.' Danika yet again had so many questions and she was disappointed she had never heard from the agents at the farm clearance all those weeks ago.

'How about you two watch what I recorded while I make us some dinner. Selene, is there anything you can't eat?' Cristian asked.

'Not can't, but prefer not to eat meat,' Selene explained. 'Sort of vegetarian, eggs are good.'

'Easy peasy.' Cristian smiled as he passed them his phone to replay the images.

The ladies sat watching the replay a few times, stopping it at different points to discuss how it felt. Danika was enjoying being so in tune with her mother and being able to share in her craft. At about the time they had watched it enough Cristian was ready to plate up the food.

With Cristians encouragement to rug up Danika and her mother headed outside to enjoy the night.

It was very fresh but Danika could see a couple of stars and called the forces to herself. Selene watched on as daytime was her preference. 'He loves you very much and he is just a good person, I can feel it,' Selene said when she thought Danika was finished.

Danika knew this but to hear it from her mother was very special. 'Yes, he is, his parents loved him and showed him empathy over power was the correct way to live. I think he will make a wonderful father. I know it is difficult with your markets but I would love it if you could come visit us sometime. I think you would like his mother, Elizabeth.' Her teeth were chattering and Cristian was sending her strong messages to come inside or he would come get her at the same time as her mother was ushering her in. He met her with a big bear hug and rubbed her hands to warm up. 'Wow it is so much colder here than Sydney.'

'I think I shall go unpack and rest for tomorrow, if that is okay with you two.' Selene kissed her daughter and smiled at Cristian.

They sat talking for a little while, mostly in silent thoughts as they could hear Selene on her phone. Danika relayed her thoughts about her mother's connection with Clay. She was well warmed up now and threw off the rug. 'I have something to show you actually,' she said, suggesting they go to the bedroom.

As she closed the door she took off her top clothes quickly and said, 'I asked her to fix this.' She pointed at the tattoo. 'Want to give it a shot?'

Gingerly, Cristian touched the tattoo and then rubbed it and finally kissed it. *Hallelujah*, was his thought, making Danika laugh. 'I just have to avoid that now,' he said pointing to the medallion.

'Oh sorry forgot it was there.' She took it off and placed it on the dresser. 'I think I will get ready for bed. I know it is really early but I feel like we are going to need to go to the museums tomorrow and I need to rest.' Cristian kissed her and had a quick rub of the tattoo again then left her to rest.

Cristian

Cristian went back out to check his emails and do more research if he could. He was just about to sit down with his electronic notebook when he felt his phone buzz, a number he didn't recognise. He went outside to take it. It was the family from the farm clearance, he'd messaged them earlier after Danika's thought to contact them. They were very nice and had been surprised at the interest. Cristian asked a few questions wishing Danika was awake but knew she was sleeping. The most interesting connection was they had moved from Tasmania. He got their previous address, thanked them and expressed his sympathy at their loss. His research was then in a different direction.

Cristian retired a few hours later with Danika sleeping peacefully on her side away from him. He left her to sleep but then woke to the realisation she was gone and the bed felt cold. Pulling on track pants, he found her kneeling in the lounge talking in a different voice. Selene was watching and held up a hand, an indication to stay quiet.

'My love, my baby, I'm sorry I couldn't save you.' Her hands were moving as if to cover something and she was holding the medallion in one hand. She mimicked picking up something small and kissing it. 'I gave this to thee to keep my love, from my family to yours forever.' Then more actions as if picking up heavy things and putting them down. Then she collapsed. Cristian grabbed her in an embrace and Selene found a blanket to put over her as she stirred. 'She buried her love and their baby.' Danika was crying in sobs. Selene took the medallion from her loose hand.

Cristian carried her to the couch and used soothing words and stroked her hair as he had so many other times until the sobs calmed. He looked at Selene, 'What happened?'

'I heard her talking in that other voice and came out just a few minutes before you.'

'I'm sorry, I'm alright now. It was just a lot of sorrow all at once.' Danika kissed Cristian then looked at her mother. 'Jessica buried Mary and one of her babies. They must have been sick I think. Jessica put the rune she gave Mary in the grave. I'm sure the rune goes back to Bronwyn.'

Cristian still cradled her on his lap on the couch. 'I may have some information about that, I had a call late last night from the family of the clearance sale where you found the message stick. The parents used to own land here. It was generational and they had found pieces in a little crumbled stone hut and kept them, including the message stick. For some reason they kept it when they moved to New South Wales.'

'Do you know where the property is? Could we go there?' Danika was hopeful.

'Yes, I know where it is. It is up for sale again, empty by the looks of it. I've sent an email to the real estate agent for a viewing. Just waiting for a reply now.' Cristian was relieved she was feeling better but worried at the effect of this on her and the babies. Danika touched his face to reassure him.

'I'm okay darling, this is good news. The sooner this is sorted the better for us all. I just need to get more comfortable now.' She was sending him thoughts she needed to shower. Cristian let her up.

'I'll put the kettle on,' Selene said.

Danika

Selene was brewing a pot of tea as Danika came out of her bedroom. She poured one for Danika and herself.

'That smells good, Mum, I really need a cuppa. Cristian will probably have a coffee,' Danika said as she sipped the drink. 'He'll be out shortly.'

'Okay, do you want to explain now what happened in more details?' Selene asked.

'I'm here so we can both hear.' Cristian entered the room and kissed Danika's cheek as Selene handed him a coffee.

'I was dreaming as you can guess. Jessica and Mary were living together and Mary appeared to be looking after the two children while Jessica worked. She had to hide more than once from soldiers looking for the blacks, her words and thoughts not mine.' Danika sipped more and closed her eyes to bring back the thoughts again. 'One of the times Mary and her baby – perhaps another baby it is hard to tell – must have become sick. They didn't recover, especially as Jessica had to keep going to work at the dairy. Jessica buried them not far from the hut and covered the grave with rocks and placed the rune she had given Mary in the rocks. She was heartbroken and at a loss because she had her own child Amelia to care for and try to work. The timeframe is hard to work out. That was when I woke up.'

'I'm going to get dressed and we can plan our day out then.' Selene left them for her own room.

'I'm glad this is moving ahead love, but not the toll it is taking on you. We are not going out unless you have breakfast and I feel like you are strong enough, don't bother arguing about that.' Cristian was full of support and love but was very determined also.

'Yes, you are completely right and I am not going to argue. How lucky are we to live in this age and not in hers?' She held his hand and sent him love and contrition for worrying him. 'The universe is trying to help us I'm sure.'

When Selene came back out she offered to make breakfast then looked through the supplies on hand. They all enjoyed a simple but filling breakfast and talked about the future plans for Hollingrove and the new property in the New South Wales hinterlands. Selene talked about the Adelaide Hills property and her disappointment at not being able to bring it back to a better level although Clay had offered to help. Both Danika and Cristian were sending thoughts to one another, wanting to help. 'We would like to come visit from here, if that is okay with you,' Danika asked, sending loving vibes to her mother. 'During the week so we don't interfere with your market trade.'

'Yes I would like that but unfortunately you will have to stay somewhere else,' Selene apologised.

'That is very easy. Danika can work out the closest bed and breakfast to you,' Cristian confirmed. 'In the meantime, would you like to look at this property I have asked to view?'

'Yes we would.' Danika and Selene both watched as Cristian showed them the satellite view as much as possible. They agreed there were several spots where there seemed to be rock outcrops or piles of rocks but lots of scrub also.

'I think we might need some boots or good shoes to look around those areas,' Selene observed. 'Hopefully they let us look around that much.'

'I can make sure that they do. Cristian can keep them busy also can't you darling.' They were both grinning at one another as they passed thoughts between them.

While they were still viewing the property a message came up saying Cristian had an email from the agents. 'Okay ladies, we are on for a midday viewing. How does that sound?'

Everyone was very pleased to achieve something so soon. 'Great we can get a few supplies first and plan to go to the museum perhaps later today or tomorrow.'

After shopping for candles, incense, tea and boots with Cristian driving them around without complaint they were pulling up to a hillside acreage that did not have a for sale sign, hoping they had the correct property. Eventually another car pulled up with a fellow, changing his shoes for boots to unlock the gate and show them in. They both pulled their cars in and up to the house. They asked about any heritage structures, even crumbling ones. The agent wasn't certain but told them what he knew and that by law he had to inform them of ancient burial grounds from past pioneers and pointed to the general area. Cristian asked about the house and had the agent show him while the ladies walked hand in hand towards the burial grounds. Nothing there other than past immigrant owners but they took photos of the headstones in case it would be important.

Danika suggested moving to where she had a faint sense. She

pulled out the message stick she had hidden in her coat and they felt a stronger pull together. They checked that the agent was still with Cristian and continued towards overgrown areas that lead into a slight forested area. Danika was sending updates to Cristian as they explored. After pushing through the worst of the bushes they came to a more open area with a collapsed wall. They could both feel the connection but it was just a pile of stones. They tried to navigate around the pile but it was covered in thick bushes. Danika decided to stand still and focus more, using the message stick like a divining rod. With one hand on the medallion and Selene holding the message stick they were directed up a slight rise. There was another pile of rocks. Placing their hands on them they felt the strong buzz. Carefully moving one stone at a time they found the rune – a smoothed pale grey stone, the mark scratched on one side was the Triquetra. Carefully they replaced the stones and thanked Mary for looking after the rune and for loving Jessica. Danika let Cristian know they had the rune.

They then had to retrace their steps and make it look like they had been looking through the out sheds. They walked up to the house and looked through very quickly. The view was lovely and Danika wondered why it hadn't been snapped up. The agent explained everyone so far had not been keen on the graves. They thanked him for his time and went back to the car.

Back at the car they changed out of their boots and moved away from the property. 'It seems a shame that no one wants that property. I fear developers will just bulldoze it all for a housing development if it isn't sold to a farmer soon.' Danika was feeling protective of Mary's grave and where her ancestor had eked out a life with her. She didn't know about the other graves. 'I took photos of the other graves in case it is relevant for our search for Jessica.' Cristian was sending her calming thoughts that it could be sorted and not to stress.

They went on to have lunch and wander into the library, realising the museum was not where the records were kept. The few newspaper references Cristian had found gave them a fairly easy starting point to find out more. It seemed that Jessica had been sent to the Cascades Female Factory that had been changed to a prison while the case was determined. Her employers had given her a glowing reference and several other witnesses had backed up her account of the drunken man bragging about going to attack the women. As her daughter and granddaughter were nowhere to be found and it was determined Jessica herself was not fit enough to have killed the man she was released and the case was closed. It was assumed to be self-defence by one of the others. Danika and Selene were shocked and relieved but also sad that Jessica no longer had her girls with her to take care of her.

'So, did Amelia and Emma flee to South Australia then?' Danika wondered why they had not gone back to be with Jessica.

'I think so. I didn't know they fled but just that they went there. South Australia advertised for workers from all fields of work back then,' Selene confirmed. 'Once they settled at the property I have a fairly good record of history there.'

'How did women manage to buy land back then Selene?'

'Oh, they didn't. They inherited it. It was left to Emma and her daughter Helen by the man they worked for. He was quite elderly and on his own, no other family. They had been looking after him and the property from when Amelia and Emma were first employed there. He may have been Helen's father but not certain. So our family has been there ever since. I will be the last.' Danika touched her hand in support and apology. 'It is okay, Nika, your nan moved away and had her own place many years ago. She wasn't interested in the farm. I'm just a bit too attached to it to let go yet.'

Danika's energy was flagging and Cristian gave her a mental push that it was time to go back and rest. She agreed and, holding her mother's hand, passed on she was ready to go. Back at the holiday rental Cristian, with Selene's support, insisted that Danika rest on the couch with a blanket so she was still around them but resting.

'Hopefully that is the end to visits from Jessica now that we have solved that mystery. I think it is best you do not wear the medallion tonight Nika, you need to have a good rest. We can plan a calling for tomorrow evening if you are determined.' She held her hand out and Danika took off the medallion and handed her the rune as well. Selene placed them over with the other artefacts.

Danika was pleased that Jessica was not convicted of murder but very sad she was separated from her family and wondered what happened to her. She was looking through her photos of the gravestones and was trying to zoom in to view them better. 'Can I download this to the notebook with a larger screen? I can't read it all properly.' Danika handed her phone to Cristian.

After a short while he handed her the notebook to view the photos larger. 'Look at this. I've seen those names before. Weren't they the family that gave Jessica a reference of support?' Danika scrolled through to where Cristian had taken a photo of the news reports they found at the library. 'Yes they are, so that is where she worked.' She was looking closer and turning the screen, it was zoomed as far as possible so Cristian handed her the magnifying glass. 'Look at this.' She pointed at a small stone off to the side of the other graves. Cristian had a look and passed it to Selene to look also.

'I think that says Jessica. I can't read the date.' Selene was amazed that she would be there and have a stone, albeit small. Danika was sending pleading thoughts to Cristian who had already messaged the agent which he confirmed to her. Selene and Danika hugged and, with a few tears, they chatted about what they had achieved and what they hoped to achieve while holding hands.

Cristian

Cristian left them to have their discussions and made them tea before looking up a few places to send out for dinner later. Danika did well to stay awake and chatting for as long as she did but eventually admitted she needed to go to bed. Cristian made sure she was alright and then came back out to talk to Selene.

'Do you have unlimited money? You seem able to act on her every whim.'

'Not unlimited by any stretch, but I have a reasonable back up. Any real estate I buy is usually an investment of some kind. Generally I don't lose on it. As for whims, well, I like to make Danika happy and if the tables were turned and I had just found the last resting place of a relative I would want it protected also.' Cristian did not feel like Selene was being rude, just curious. 'I would look at preservation of the relevant sites and probably leasing the property as a whole or in sections. The property north of Sydney is for our rest and enjoyment away from the city with privacy. The renovations at the estate are long overdue, it took Danika to see the need and potential. She is very insightful and the change to the people she comes in contact with also is quite magical.' Cristian knew he was probably sounding like he was boasting but it was all true.

'I have to admit that I never realised the extent of Danika's talent and insight until we contacted over that video call. I thought it was me bolstering her. I know different now. Her grandmother used to say to me that she was destined for something great when the time was right. I will try to shield and help her where I can,' Selene reassured him.

'Thank you, Selene. I believe we are both destined to break the curse to our two families, I just hope there isn't too high a price for that. I worry now with the babies it will be too much for her.' Cristian was glad to be able to say that out loud.

'It is important that she keep up with her doctor appointments and understand the messages her body is giving her.'

Cristian remembered seeing her faint which was traumatic enough. He was keen that didn't happen again. 'I am trying to keep her on track with that but I fear she feels like I am nagging her. I was such an independent entity until I met her and now I can't imagine life without her. Thank you for listening to me Selene.'

'I think I might move these items,' she pointed at the artefacts, 'into my room tonight to make sure she isn't attracted to them if she gets up or has a dream.' Selene picked up the items one at a time to move them onto the dresser in her room.

'Tomorrow I think some actual site seeing might be in order,' Cristian suggested to Selene.

As she came back from moving the last item Selene agreed. 'That would be nice. I think I shall retire and meditate for a while. Goodnight, Cristian.'

'Goodnight, Selene and thank you.'

Cristian made a coffee and sat to check his emails and follow up on the Tasmanian property. Finally the stress of the very long day was easing and he was able to go to bed where Danika was sleeping soundly. She snuggled into him as he carefully lay beside her.

The next day Cristian drove them all around the views, including a fish farm and tasty produce. By the end of the day they were glad to be back to put their feet up. The cold wind had made their cheeks rosy and left them feeling pleasantly tired. They sat and reviewed each other's photos and Selene sent a message to Clay to show him what they were doing.

'Does Clay know about your craft Selene?' Cristian wondered how close they were.

'I think he suspects but has been too polite to ask. He has a cat.' They both looked at her, wondering what the connection was to this information. 'Apparently she doesn't like people but she likes me. We have never had pets as you know Nika, but I find I enjoy her attention.'

'Why haven't we had pets?' Danika asked.

'We suffer too much when we lose them. Also animals were to be useful back in the day so it paid not to become attached to them. What of your family Cristian, do you have pets?' Selene asked.

'Not pets, we have a herd of deer and some chickens for recycling food waste and the eggs. I never really asked but I suspected it was because of the legacy they wouldn't get on well with the change.' Cristian had not thought about this aspect of their lives since he was a boy and his school friends talked of their pets. Danika agreed with him having had the same experience at school. 'As a boy I wondered a couple of times what it would be like to have a dog.'

Selene offered to make a simple pasta dinner and they quietly enjoyed the night listening to music and chatting. As they relaxed, Cristian and Danika sharing thoughts as they had grown accustomed to doing, he felt the moment Danika caught a glimpse into her mother's relaxed mind and heard something that caught her attention.

'What are you hiding, Mother?' Danika grabbed her mother's hand quickly. 'You tried a calling on your own last night, didn't you?'

'It won't work. We need a third piece if we are to get back to Bronwyn. The three points of the Triquetra, we only have two. That was all I was testing, you didn't need to be involved.'

Danika didn't know whether to be annoyed her mother had tried this dangerous connection alone or pleased that there was no point to try it herself.

'Exactly and that's why I did it.' Selene answered her unspoken comment. Cristian was being an observer of a silent conversation and Danika was trying to bring him up to speed. They both realised the possible third piece at the same time.

'We may know of a third piece back at the estate, a piece of stone from the original Hollingrove manor where the curse originated,' Cristian explained aloud to bring the conversation to the fore. 'My grandfather brought it all the way out to Australia and incorporated it into a water feature. Danika felt the connection.'

'Well we will have to plan the best time to tackle this together then, but it won't be anytime soon.' Danika had to agree.

'Tomorrow I think more tourist activity would be good, then I leave the next morning,' Selene said, shifting the topic of conversation.

'That sounds like a great idea, but we have to call into the real estate agent first thing. The owners have accepted my email offer.' Cristian showed Danika the message he had received while they were talking. Danika hugged him.

'Thank you, Cristian.'

After another full day of exploring they decided on dinner out for their last night together. The arrangements had been made for the purchase of the property which probably could be completed quickly as it was vacant. Selene packed away her few purchases ready to leave the next morning. The time had gone so fast but they had achieved so much. Cristian had already changed their flights and booked accommodation in South Australia from Monday for a few days before returning to Sydney.

'It's a shame to waste the five extra days we had here. Can we offer it to anyone?' Danika didn't like waste at any time.

'I'll have a word to the owners if you like when I call them.' Cristian was not surprised by her suggestion. Feeling her thoughts and knowing she generally knew something he didn't he called straight away. He put the call on speaker so she could hear. Sure enough a family that was coming for their granddaughter's wedding had nowhere they could afford to stay individually and had asked the owners about the property only just that day but had been told it was booked. She thanked them for the generous offer.

'I needed that. Being able to absorb and share has been a bit lacking in the last couple of days,' Danika explained. 'Not your fault just happens sometimes.'

All too soon Danika was farewelling her mother at the airport knowing they would be following her in a few days. As a surprise, Cristian took her to a children's movie complete with popcorn and an ice-cream. He was pleased to see her happy and absorbing all the joy and laughter and found himself laughing also. He could see her glowing in the dark and hoped it was just his excellent eyesight and not that others could see her. He held her hand and sensed her pure joy and thanks for the treat.

Danika

As they came out of the theatre Danika asked if they could go look at the property again as she wasn't sure when she would be back. They pulled up outside the real estate agency, who was happy to give them a key as the large deposit Cristian had paid had cleared and said to keep it. The day had been clear but cold. At the gate they both changed into boots that were still in the boot of the car. Danika opened the gate for him to drive through but decided to walk towards the gravesite rather than up to the house. She bent over to clear away the grass from the little stone on the side and could more clearly make out the name. The surname was visible now the grass was gone – Jessica Carling 1865. Danika had no idea how old she was, only that she had a daughter and granddaughter in 1858. She guessed maybe sixty. She took a photo to send to her mother. Cristian had parked the car and came down to see the gravesite that he hadn't seen before.

'They must have valued her to pay to have a stone carved for her. And put it next to them,' he observed. 'Where was the other site you found?' Danika showed him through the bushes that she and her mother had pushed through a few days ago. He could see the pile of stones on the slight rise and the pile behind them where they had found the grave of Mary from her vision. He walked around the large pile that was probably the hut, it went further behind a large sprawling bush which he broke through to show her some of the walls were still in place. He pointed out the line of the walls. 'We could probably have them rebuilt as walls to see if there was anything inside another time. After all she must have lived here until her passing.' The thought pleased Danika.

'Thank you. I know it can wait for a little while but yes I would like to reinstate it and make more of the two grave sites. I have just realised I never asked about your father and grandfather. Where are they buried?' Danika felt bad she had never given them a thought until now.

'They are not buried. They were cremated as is our tradition which is more important in this generation of DNA testing. Their ashes were scattered around the estate which were their wishes. What about your family?' Cristian wondered about Danika's ancestors in South Australia.

'We have a small family plot on the farm but it got too difficult to get permission for burials so Grandma and I think her mother were both cremated and scattered on the farm. It is amazing how similar our families are.' Danika felt they were almost in parallel.

'Did you want to look at anything else? It is getting very dull now and might rain. We should probably leave.' Cristian was worried they would get stuck if it was too muddy.

'No, I was not interested in the house as such but it is nice. Just not a priority today.' Danika agreed it was time to go. She walked back to the gate so she could close it after Cristian drove through.

Back at the holiday rental they washed off the boots and decided to leave them for whoever would like to use them as they didn't need to take them in their packing.

'I think I shall pack the case with the artefacts now. They are in Mum's room still and I don't want to forget them.' Danika realised they had bought candles and incense also and hadn't used them. Perhaps she still would and placed them on the lounge sideboard. She took the large pieces one at a time to her luggage on the bed and then put her medallion on, feeling the familiar hum from it. When she picked up the rune she felt the connection and agreed with her mother that there seemed to be something missing. She took it to the luggage and wrapped it before placing it in her potion box. She decided to take the medallion off for now and placed it in the potion box also. She covered them all over and closed the bag.

After dinner they both decided that bed was a good option and lay talking for quite some time about the day and the next two before their thoughts moved into a more intimate direction. Danika laughed as he kept touching her tattoo carefully to make sure it didn't zap him again.

Cristian

Cristian was up early and left Danika to sleep as he researched a plan for the two days they had left. Sensing her stirring and wondering where he was he sent her thoughts of a hot tea. As she wandered out with a blanket wrapped around her to perch on the couch he asked if she was up for a drive.

'Sure, I feel very refreshed and fulfilled.' Danika smiled inwardly, thoughts shared between them of their slow, delightful embraces the night before, and thought how it could be nice to stay in bed also.

'Your choice my love, but we leave Monday morning and I was thinking of a drive to Bruny Island today. There is a ferry across that we can take the car.' Cristian assured her he would be fine on a short trip when she was concerned.

'That sounds nice. I should have a shower and get a move on then.' She took her tea and, dragging the blanket, went back into the bedroom. While she was in the shower he packed the small travel case for an overnight stay just in case. Then it was his turn to shower and he instructed her to eat as he wasn't sure where the next opportunity would be. Before long they were driving down the coast admiring the beautiful scenery then lining up to go on the ferry. Cristian could feel her excitement and he was glad he had suggested the trip.

They had realised quickly that there was more to do than they could fit in on this trip. After buying whiskey, cheese and honey and enjoying the amazing views despite the cold wind, Christian asked her if she would like to stay overnight for a special surprise he had for her. After lunch they booked in to a very secluded cabin. Cristian unpacked the small case, showing her the candles and incense if she wanted them. They still had time to drive around more but Danika preferred to just walk the path to the beach and enjoy some quiet time. She knew there was still some little thing he was hiding but didn't press him on it.

As the sun was setting, Cristian lit the gas heater on the patio so they could sit outside to wait for the stars to show. A few clouds were drifting by and he hoped for a clear night for her. She set up her candles in a ring to sit and enjoy the few stars that shone so beautifully here with no other light around. He left her to absorb while he sat watching and sipping a whiskey bought earlier. It was very dark now and getting colder. He slowly pushed his thoughts at Danika to open her eyes. The spectacle before her was breathtaking. The Southern Lights – Aurora Australis.

'Oh my heavens, that is so beautiful.' He could feel her absorbing the joy and wonderment. 'Thank you, you kept this a secret.' She had tears in her eyes.

'I didn't want to get your hopes up in case we didn't see them.' He came over and helped her up from her cold, cross-legged position and they hugged, wrapped in a blanket, to watch the dance and play of the lights. Cristian tried to take a picture but knew even his good camera phone was not going to do it justice. She laughed at his next thought.

'Yes, a selfie is definitely in order.' Danika had an aura about her that was in tune with the lights as they turned their backs to try a selfie. Not too bad, and lots of fun. As much as they kept wanting to just sit and view the lights it was very cold so they packed up the candles and gas heater and moved inside to have a few snacks from their purchases and view a little of the lights with the cabin lights off, just one candle on a plate burning. Finally the clouds were blocking the view and they decided being in bed was the warmest place.

They were up early enough to do a little more sight-seeing before catching the ferry back and settle into repacking everything and tidying up to leave the Hobart holiday house in the morning. Danika had found great solace in coming to the place where her ancestor had landed in Australia and being able to protect Jessica, Mary and her baby's resting place. They would come back again but possibly not for quite a while.

The next day was a whirlwind to pack and tidy for the next people and hand back the rental before flying out to Adelaide then collecting another rental car and finding the new accommodation in the Adelaide Hills. Cristian was concerned that Danika still ate and drank enough to not get too tired before going to her mother's property. They were invited for dinner there but Danika wanted to go early so it was still light enough for Cristian to see the slopes and trees. She was too keyed up to take a nap as Cristian had suggested.

'I'm fine. I need to get there and meet Clay now. I think there is more of a connection than a shared market stall.' Danika said she would drive so Cristian could look around and not have to take directions.

As they pulled up the long driveway, Cristian noted that the fences were not in good order but the scenery was beautiful with large gum trees and many bushes on the steeper slopes. The house was not visible until nearly right up to it. With no clearings and much leaf litter across the roof he could see it was a fire risk which Danika confirmed she had worried about for a long time. The original stone structure could be seen with several add-ons over the years in various stages of disrepair. Many different coloured paints had been used on the woodwork. There were lots of wind chimes around the verandah and hanging from the lower branches of the nearby trees. Her mother came out as they pulled up. They could see a van parked around the side next to Selene's station wagon. On the verandah were a few cane and wooden chairs with cushions and knitted throw rugs as well as many and varied ornaments. It was all colourful and busy yet not actually cluttered.

'Welcome to my home. Cristian, this is Clay,' Selene said as a stocky dark greying haired man with rugged features came out of the house behind her. His smile was genuine and broad. He held out his hand to shake Cristian's.

'Pleased to meet you, and you must be Danika. You look as lovely as your mother.' He turned to Danika and shook her hand also.

'Thank you and good to meet you also, Clay.' Danika turned around to point at some pieces of pottery on the verandah. 'Are these your work, Clay?' He nodded. 'They are very good.'

'Thank you, you are very kind.' Clay appeared happy but embarrassed at the accolade.

'Come in and have a drink, unless you want to walk around now,' Selene asked.

'Yes, a walk would be good. We have been sitting for a long time today. Is the path still okay to walk up the hill?' Danika asked her mother.

'Yes, Clay helped me clear it not that long ago so we could sit up there. Are you okay to climb up there?' Selene was asking of Danika.

'Of course I am. There is a great view of the whole property from up that hill.' Danika pointed to the closest slope with a walking path just in view. Cristian knew better than to argue with her and knew he could carry her if needed.

The trek up the path didn't take long but had them all but Cristian breathing hard at the top. The path was indeed in better shape than the last time Danika had walked it nearly a year ago. At the top there was now a bench to sit on which Danika took advantage of. Clay had made a pottery compass and cemented it on the ground which Danika and Cristian both thought was a great idea.

Selene was describing the boundaries by landmarks around them and explained it was fenced on the flatter sections but not the slopes as it had been too hard to maintain. 'We don't run any grazing animals here other than the native ones that come and go as they like.' She then pointed to a small group of kangaroos that had come out to graze now in the shadows. Up this high they could see the sun still although most of the property was in shadow from the higher slopes.

They carefully made their way back down to the house where Clay started a fire in the hearth for them as it was getting a bit colder. Inside Danika commented to Cristian that that her mother had moved a lot of things around and it was less cluttered. More new items of cushions and curtains were on show as well as more pottery. She was not sure if it was their visit or Clay's influence but it looked more positive than when she had left. The colour theme was more blues and greens, less hectic rainbow. With all the wood cleaned and polished it was very welcoming. The fragrance of herbs and baking was delicious.

'Not as cold as Tasmania though,' Selene agreed. Selene made them coffee and tea. 'It isn't even winter there yet.'

'Yes I have become accustomed to the warmer weather near Sydney, I have to admit,' Danika agreed.

'Your property is very impressive Selene it must be difficult for you to keep up with the maintenance on your own.' Cristian genuinely enjoyed looking around. The size of the gum trees most impressed him.

'It certainly has been. Clay has generously helped me lately to get ready for winter. Cleaning gutters and cutting wood. I'll have to show you the garden another time out the back. We have planted herbs and edibles and a few flowers to enjoy.' Selene turned her eyes to Clay with more than thanks in the look. 'I hope quiche and salad is okay. I have been baking more recently so there is dessert.'

'Well it all smells pretty good.' Cristian was looking at the candles on many surfaces, some lit. 'Are those candles your creations, Selene?'

'Yes the big ones are hard to sell though. Most people don't understand the work involved they just see the price, so I often end up using them myself,' Selene explained.

'I can see where Danika's eye for art comes from. You are all very talented. I appreciate that skill, not a skill I have,' Cristian admitted. 'So I am very happy to be the one that buys those pieces that others pass over because of the price.'

'Good for you mate, we need more like you coming to the markets,' Clay pointed out. 'Mind you I generally don't transport my big pieces anymore. Too heavy and easy to damage but I always take the portfolio with me, just in case.'

'I'd like to see it sometime. We are looking for more pieces for the gallery and for the gardens at the estate.' Cristian thought this could be useful to them all.

'Mum showed me a couple of photos of your bigger pieces. I think they are amazing. We recently bought an entire collection from a retired sculptor with great success on sales. I would like to see your collection also,' Danika said.

'Let's eat, shall we?' Selene intervened. 'Nika, can you help me?'

Danika

Danika knew her mother wanted to talk to her so she followed her to the kitchen at the back of the house.

'It is nice what you are doing for Clay, but please don't get his hopes up.' Selene was right into the point straight away as she placed out plates to dish up.

'We aren't Mum, we genuinely are interested and needing to get more works all the time. You showed me his works remember and you seem to have it everywhere.' Danika noted the plates were probably his. She turned one over and saw his mark. 'You are very defensive of him, is he more than a friend?' Danika caught a glimpse of her mother's emotion before she could hide it. 'He is, or you want him to be.'

'I wish he could be but I have been too frightened to let him get close because of the curse. He is very patient with me considering I probably seem like a nut case.'

'Have you told him?'

'Not in so many words then he would be convinced I'm a nut case. No, just said it was a family problem without really explaining. I guess that's worse.'

Danika helped take the plates of food to the dining area which in the past had been more storage than eating and was now well laid out and tidy. After the meal Clay and Cristian settled in by the fire sipping a fine scotch Clay offered him while Selene and Danika cleared away the dishes.

'They seem to be getting on well,' Selene noted with a relief in her tone.

'Yes, they are both fairly easy-going men. So what is Clay's story then?' Danika was hoping her mother was safe and not going to be upset in the future.

'The short version is that Clay was a soldier from his teens and had more than a few bad experiences as you can imagine. He married but children didn't eventuate then his wife became sick and died. He threw himself back into work with the army to cope and saw more death. He was in a raid where his mates died, he was injured and was medically discharged. He took up pottery as a therapy but turns out he had an aptitude for it and here we are.' Selene obviously knew more but did not want to explain his private life in any more details.

'So he is hesitant as well, you are both well suited to be good friends. When did you meet?' Danika couldn't remember him when she had left only five months before.

'We met at the markets once they finally opened again late last year but only combined stalls and started seeing one another outside the markets about two months ago.' Selene was truly happy, Danika could feel it.

'This food is too good Selene you're going to make me fat,' Clay said to her easily with a broad smile.

'This is delicious Selene rivals Ann's cooking.' Cristian smiled at Danika.

'Who's Ann?' Selene asked.

'Ann is our cook who is more family than staff at home,' Cristian explained.

'I had a cook for twenty years in the army it didn't taste like this,' Clay joked making them laugh.

After dessert, they arranged to go see Clay's workshop the next day before coming back to look around the gardens as Selene had suggested. Cristian offered to take them out for dinner the next night. Cristian was concerned although it was not late that it had been a long day and Danika should rest. Selene agreed. As they left Danika was sure she saw Clay hold Selene's hand in the rear-view mirror and was pleased.

Danika drove very slow and carefully down the drive as kangaroos were common at night and sure enough they waited for a couple to move out of the way before getting finally to the road. The trip to their bed and breakfast was only a few minutes which Danika was glad of as she had to admit the long day was catching up with her. She was even too tired to have a cup of tea so Cristian made sure she was settled in bed before leaving her to sleep.

They woke to a quiet white blanket of fog on the world as they enjoyed the breakfast left for them. Danika told Cristian what her mother had said about Clay last night and how she felt he has a kind soul. Cristian agreed and mentioned Clay said he was enjoying helping Selene around the farm with maintenance and growing vegetables.

'The inside is a lot neater and user friendly since the last time I was there. Mum really likes him, I'm sensing not just as a friend. I saw them holding hands as we left.' Danika was smiling at the thought. 'I didn't have any men in my life and now I might have two.' Danika moved around to hug Cristian as she was feeling so happy about how their lives were progressing. 'Shall we get ready to go meet them at

Clay's home?' She sent him a thought that they could shower together to speed it up which had him laughing at the image.

'That definitely will not be quicker.' Cristian picked her up to take her to get ready.

A couple of hours later they were pulling up outside the home that was very neat with paving and artificial grass. The only break in the solid paving held a large white fountain in the middle. It appeared to be one of Clay's pieces of a stylised fairy, all soft features and edges. It was very lovely.

Clay came out to meet them and show them through his home. Cristian had noted several camera's as they approached and security lights. Clay explained he had previously had trouble with vandals and theft of his works from the front yard hence why it looked so bleak and the tall ironwork fence. 'It feels a bit of a prison now, that's why I like working at Selene's farm. There's so much more space and positive vibes. Anyway, this is my humble abode.' Clay showed them through the simple home that was fairly sparse of furniture, just the most necessary. It was very tidy and clean as he lead them out to his workshops. The kilns were in the middle with a clay working area, the drying racks, cooling racks and the biggest shed with his finished collection. It was very full. 'I am building up my pieces now while it is quieter so I am ready for the spring and summer markets but I am running out of space. I think I need to build a few more racks.'

'Can we see your bigger pieces or your portfolio if we can't get to them?' Cristian asked. 'We saw your fountain out the front. Is it a one off?'

'Yes it was a prototype. It turned out to be very difficult and not cost-effective time wise to reproduce. I would have to charge so much no one would be interested. She is rather beautiful though.'

'I really like it, if you ever were interested in making another I would pay whatever you needed for it.' Cristian was very interested. He sent Danika a vision that it reminded him of her aura.

'Well if you don't mind the tight spaces I can show you through behind the racks to my other large pieces.'

Cristian and Danika fell in love with a dozen of his large more conceptual pieces. 'The glazes are such works of art besides the formwork; they are very intriguing and beautiful. How long does it take to make something this large?' Danika was looking at a piece nearly as tall as her.

'That piece took about six months but some others only a couple of months. I don't make the big pieces anymore because I have so many and no sales over the pandemic. I'm not so good at online selling. Selene got on to it last year and did reasonably well she said. Transport is the killer for pricing.' Danika could sense Clay getting a bit sad about his situation but not wanting to portray it. 'Would you like to see my other smaller pieces?'

'Yes, thank you, that would be great.' Danika was sending thoughts to Cristian that they should buy most of the big pieces, he agreed. 'I noticed a few of your pieces at Mum's. I really liked the bowls.'

Clay handed Cristian the portfolio he had asked to look at while Danika was looking at some of the medium and smaller pieces. He said he had been trying a new line of animals but was still trying to work out the fastest way to make them to keep the price down. He showed Danika the iconic Australian animals' ones that he had glazed and a few still in the raw clay form that he was trying out. He explained he had had a few requests for eagles, bears and wolves. Besides elephants and lions some were too difficult. Danika picked up a wolf and turned it around. 'This is very good Clay, I would buy this glazed.'

'Thank you. I had a request for black but I prefer the lighter colours that bring out the lines better.' Clay was looking at another he had.

'I prefer the lighter colours also but if you have an order I guess you go with that,' Danika agreed.

'I have a firing cooling at the moment, I can show you in about half an hour.' They continued looking and being informed of the processes and timelines by Clay before he took them in for a mug of tea just as Selene arrived to join them. The mugs were obviously his work also. Cristian brought the portfolio with him, handing it to Danika to look through as they sat at the table with their drinks.

'Clay I am interested in buying your bigger pieces and probably some of the smaller ones also. How would you feel about that?' Cristian asked on Danika's thought.

'How many were you interested in?'

'Actually all of them. So long as you understand that we would be selling them from the studio at a higher price. I say that in case you see them listed in our catalogue.' Cristian went on, 'We pay you what you want and cover the transport costs but then increase the price to make a profit. Would you be agreeable with that?'

Clay was overwhelmed, Danika could feel it. Both her and Selene sent out calming, encouraging thoughts to him.

'Well this is certainly a surprise. Would you be expecting me to make more?'

'That would be up to you. We are still currently showcasing a local sculpture for the next month or so but then we could showcase your work which would give it a fairly wide exposure so you may get enquiries and more orders. It would be up to you how many or any orders you take. Or we can keep it more ad hoc, buying what we like from you at different times.'

'Okay, well you can buy what you like mate, cash is good.'

After an hour of selection and transport arrangements, they headed back to Selene's farm. Danika could see the changes and repairs that Clay had been making and he was discussing some of it with Cristian. Out the back the once bare ground leading to paddocks was now neat rows of raised beds with a variety of vegetables and herbs. Clay explained the summer ones were due to be pulled out to make way for more winter vegetables. They had planted a few fruit trees as well in a square with fencing and netting to keep the birds away. Clay said he was worried about the state of the roof and gutters though, especially as a wetter winter was predicted.

'Selene would like to make an extension out here also for when you visit as a family. She told me you were expecting, I hope that was alright.' Clay was showing them the proposed extension area.

'Yes we are and it would be wonderful to stay here as a family in future. We have a fantastic family that help us with all our renovations, I wonder if they have any relatives here in South Australia we could ask just for a quote?' Danika suggested to Cristian.

'This house has good bones, it would take well to being re-roofed and a tasteful extension.' Clay obviously appreciated the house more than Danika had. She had to agree that it felt happier and more of a home than previously. 'Were you planning on showing Cris any tourist sites?' Clay had shortened Cristian's name and Danika had never heard him addressed that way. Cristian's thoughts assured her it was okay, that was what he was called when he was at school.

'I hadn't thought about it, but yes I probably should. By the way, Cristian booked our dinner at the Stirling Hotel tonight for six pm. Have you been there before?'

'No we haven't but I have always wanted to go so that will be nice.' Selene thanked them. 'Would you like some sandwiches on the verandah for lunch? The birds will line up for scraps.'

'I forgot about them, so you still feed them?' Danika remembered throwing her crusts to the birds and watching them squabble when she was younger until she taught them to behave.

'Yes and they could use your manners training.' Selene walked into the house. 'You can help me Nika.'

Danika heard the exchange between the two men through Cristian's sharing, as they headed inside to make food. 'Our girls are pretty special aren't they Cris?' Clay asked.

'Yes they are Clay, we are lucky. So Selene is your girl then?' Cristian asked.

'I'd like to think so but she is a bit shy of men so I'm giving her plenty of space and time to come to that understanding. Yours was a bit more whirlwind I guess.'

'You could say that.'

In the kitchen Danika looked at her mother and said, 'You have to tell him. He really likes you and I know you like him. Before this relationship gets full on he needs to know the truth about you, about us.'

'I know I should I just don't want to lose him,' Selene admitted.

'You need to have more faith in him, Mum.' Danika just knew Clay would love her anyway.

'I made some sandwiches earlier so let's just take these out. You take them, I'll bring a tray of drinks.' Selene was pushing Danika mentally out.

They settled on the verandah, enjoying the view, and the birds started to flock in the trees and on the ground with a couple of cheeky ones on the railing chirping at them. Danika stood up and with a flick of her hand told them to join their friends and wait. They did as they were told and, as a reward, Danika threw a few crumbs. She looked at the shy ones in the trees and called them down to eat a little away from the others and then gave them a few crumbs also.

'There's a cocky with an injured foot that I try to feed but the others get to the food first. He is just up there.' Selene pointed to a white corella sitting in the tree watching the others eat.

'You lot wait a bit. Now come on my pretty it is your turn.' Danika swayed her arm back and forth as she sang a little tune to encourage the corella down to the rail. She placed some seeds from her bread on the rail. Her other hand she held up to stop the cheeky birds coming back. Eventually the corella came down but still away from her. She cooed and encouraged and the bird walked with a limp closer. It was eating the seeds and Danika could see it had some twine stuck around its foot tight. She let her mother know and, as she kept the bird occupied, Selene brought clippers and eucalyptus oil and more seed. Between them cooing and talking to the bird they were able to cut the twine and dab the foot with the oil as they fed it. 'Now that must feel better my love. Come back tomorrow for more food.'

The bird walked slowly to the end of the rail and flapped back into the tree. Danika scattered the seed for the other birds. The men had been enthralled yet quiet watching the whole event. Cristian wondered what Clay would make of it.

'Like mother like daughter, both angels.' Clay spoke with pride.

'Well you know how to compliment a girl,' Selene said over the noise of the competing birds. 'Danika I forgot to say among the other items we found when we were sorting storage was some family photos. Would you like to see them?'

They spent the next hour looking through dozens of photos Danika had never seen before of her ancestors. One was of them in white at a cheese factory. A couple outside this house standing on the verandah with the original owner that left the house to them standing next to them. Then more recent school photos over the past sixty or so years. They recognised some of the changes to the buildings which dated when that happened. Then Danika was trying to push away a photo of herself as a child but Cristian spotted it. She was probably about three with her hair in two buns on top of her head like ears with her bright green eyes and a huge smile.

'This reminds me of something. I would like this one,' Cristian said remembering her accident with the bubbles.

'Take any you want to copy and return them. Danika said she was making a photo wall, I think that is a great idea. I should do something similar.' Selene gave them a big envelope to put them in.

'We could get them copied tomorrow when we are out being tourists,' Danika said. 'But for now I think we might go back and sort out a few things before dinner, if you don't mind?'

The next three days were spent viewing iconic sites around Adelaide. Cristian liked the beaches as they were quieter than Sydney and safer. He remarked how much easier the traffic was while Danika did most of the driving so he could look around and she knew the roads without a GPS. One day, although windy, they drove to a coastal town to go across to a granite island and walk around. They were simple and enjoyable days with meals at Selene's farm at night. The transport had been arranged for Clay's artworks to the Sydney warehouse in two weeks' time so they had time to box them up. The last evening sitting in the lounge at Selene's farm they were feeling very relaxed. Danika sat next to Cristian on the couch watching the flames in the fireplace.

'It is a shame you couldn't stay longer, perhaps next time you will be able to see the markets as well,' Clay commented. He and Selene had been packing their cars all day in readiness for tomorrow's market while Danika and Cristian had been touring.

'Yes it has been a rush but I have a doctor's appointment and we have to make plans for the arrival of your works. Also I would like to visit the property we bought in more detail before the weather gets too wintery.' Danika smiled at her to do list that she only gave them a précis of. Cristian squeezed her hand to make her calm and not get too wound up of things to do when they were back.

'You sound very busy, I hope you don't overdo it,' Selene said.

'I'll make sure she doesn't. As will everyone around her once they know she needs to take it easy.' Cristian was giving her a mild warning.

'Oh good grief, I'm right here you know and I was walking kilometres only yesterday all over an island with no problems, give me credit you lot.' Danika was worried she was going to be treated like an invalid once she was back in Sydney. 'Thank you for such a lovely stay, Mum and Clay, and good luck with the markets this weekend. The weather seems to be getting a bit more cold and wet. We won't see you in the morning of course.'

They stood up to leave and as Danika hugged her mother she felt her put a barrier up regarding her thoughts and wondered why. They said their goodbyes and, with Cristian driving, went back to their holiday stay.

'Mum was hiding something from me any time we touched, that is when I can read her the easiest and she knows it,' Danika commented once they were inside.

'Everyone has secrets Danika. She has only just opened up about her relationship with Clay, she is going to be a grandmother and you are leaving. She has many emotions to contain.' Cristian was trying to be reasonable to Danika.

'You're probably right. I will be glad to be home and not live out of a suitcase for a little bit,' she said as she was repacking yet again to fit her few pottery items she had from Clay safely.

'We don't have to go up to the property if you don't want to.' He could feel her answer before he finished the sentence. 'Okay so we do have to but we need to be prepared that it is probably unliveable.' Then he had a flash of Rainbow. 'I can't sleep in that.'

'I know she isn't any good for us both to sleep in but I have thoughts about that. We could camp inside the house. But I can use her to transport cleaning stuff and a blow-up mattress and other stuff.' Danika was trying to make it sound sensible. 'Besides, if all else fails we could find a place like this to stay and I can just be in Rainbow for the full moon.' She could feel him about to disagree. 'We can work out the finer details once we are there and can get inside the house. For now I think I just need to lie down and try to clear my mind, do you think you could help with that?' Danika held out her hand and was sending thoughts of lying together.

It was just as well they had set alarms to leave as they both slept soundly in one another's arms. Before long they were ready and leaving to go to the airport, although Cristian had made Danika eat and take her supplements before he would let her out the door knowing she would forget otherwise in the excitement to get home.

Several hours later they were arriving back at Hollingrove in a taxi to almost a fanfare of greeting from Elizabeth and the staff. Danika could feel the joy and relief that they were back safe at home again and that they had much to show them. Ben and Mark took their bags up to their rooms while Ann offered them tea and some of her biscuits in the sitting room where a fire was blazing.

'Everyone seems very excited Elizabeth, it is nice to be home,' Danika noted as Ann left the room.

'Yes they are a bit. They want to show you what they have been doing while we have all been away. I only got back myself yesterday.' Elizabeth was smiling openly. 'It was a lovely visit but I am glad to be home also.'

'Yes we will have to exchange travel stories another time. I thought they were supposed to be on holiday while we were away,' Danika asked now concerned that the staff hadn't had any holidays.

'I did also so we will have to sort that out another time.'

'Well we had better let them show us their surprise before they burst. I can feel it from here.' Danika smiled and shared some of it to Cristian.

They stood up and barely opened the door before they were greeted by Ben who asked if it would be alright for them to follow him so he could show them the progress in the gardens.

They went from the front door around to the side gardens. The first thing they noticed was the rotunda. It was beautiful. They walked straight over to it. The gardens had been well tidied and paving slabs replaced the gravel. In the rotunda were bench seats and cushions. With the mini hedge around the outside it looked like it had always been there. Painted to match the house, Danika noticed the finials that looked perfect. Elizabeth and Danika went inside to sit and look over the garden. Danika could feel tears forming but Cristian warned her to look around as there was more they wanted to show her.

'This is so wonderful Mark, Ben and Ann.' She could see Ann behind them and could feel Ann may have helped with the decorating. Then she looked across to the pool area. She could feel the love coming from them. Danika stood up and walked over towards the pool which was gleaming in the wintery sun. It looked brand new with the modern paving and stylish grasses. Elizabeth touched her hand to show her the Janet Wells sculpture that had also been installed near the pool.

'Oh that is perfect.' Danika realised she wasn't speaking enough just sending her thoughts and feelings to everyone. 'I can't get over how much you have all managed to get done in such a short time. It is wonderful and beautiful and actually I am lost for words. Thank you all so much, my wonderful extended family.' Now she couldn't contain her tears any longer. They went over to the pool house area and Mark showed them how the protective blinds came down and showed Cristian the new BBQ area. They shook hands on a job well done. Danika tried out the view from the seats across the pool.

Mark was explaining the filtration and pool cover to Cristian while Ann leaned into Danika and said, 'I think Ben has more to show you.' Ben was standing to the side, smiling at Danika and Cristian's reaction to the changes.

'Ann has hinted you have another surprise for us Ben,' Danika asked as she watched Cristian lean down and test the temperature of the water. He sent her a thought that it wasn't freezing cold.

'In your own time, ma'am, something inside.'

'Well I need to know now, let's have a look.' Ben showed Danika and Elizabeth around the back which looked a little different with the extended pool house roof offering cover all the way to the back door and amenities. 'This has come together really well, I am in awe that this was completed in a couple of weeks.'

Ben showed her inside. No longer a dark recess but now a bright well-lit welcoming entrance. The stairs well-lit showed gleaming polished wood rails and what appeared to be new carpet on the steps. The walls were painted up to the hall where new lighter wallpaper was installed. It was a pattern Danika had showed an interest into Mark weeks ago. Elizabeth had stayed downstairs so Danika came back down. 'Is this new carpet?'

'No it just wasn't used much and a good clean has brought it back to new.' Ben and Ann were proud of the work they had done inside the house Danika could feel it.

'Well I think we should celebrate. What about a BBQ pool side tomorrow with your families, including Dean. I know he must have worked like a Trojan.' Danika was sending this thought to Cristian who agreed. 'Before it gets too cool to be out there, can I leave it to you all to sort out invites and such?'

13

LUNAR HAVEN

THE POOL SIDE BBQ had been a huge success with over a dozen people, including Paul and Rene who had never been to Hollingrove before but had arranged the sculpture delivery. Dean's children braved the cool weather and christened the pool much to everyone's delight. Danika showed Paul and Rene some of Clay's artwork that would be arriving in a few weeks plus the two little pieces she had brought back. Dean suggested a distant family member in Adelaide that could take a look at Selene's house for an extension, while Dean himself offered to have a look at the new property when they were ready. The buzz of the group gave Danika so much energy and joy Cristian could see her glowing confirmation that she needed to be around people more often.

The next day Danika had her initial appointment with Doctor Michael.

'Good to see you looking well, Danika. How have you been?' Michael asked. Danika could feel his reservation.

'Pretty good actually. Those supplements help and I have several people making sure I eat and drink enough.' She held Cristian's hand and shared her thoughts that the doctor was being careful in his dialogue.

'Good news. Well I want to get you in for an ultrasound in the next few weeks as an initial check and then again at about thirteen to fifteen weeks to check progress of the baby,' Michael said. 'I have the results of your blood tests, I ordered a DNA test also just as a precaution. Your parents, Cristian, had a few issues that I am not sure if you were aware of.'

'I didn't know you were doing that. But yes, I had recently discovered Mother had some miscarriages when she was young.' Cristian was concerned, his thoughts wondering if lupine showed up in DNA.

'So, Danika, your iron level was low but that was no surprise. Sugars were good and all else seemed fine. The DNA test showed a surprise. I compared it to your father's record, Cristian, that I still had and there was a very distant link.' Michael was letting that sink in.

'What sort of link?' Cristian was convinced the lupine must have been identified.

'From what my pathology researchers have said, perhaps ten or even twenty generations or more ago your two families were related,' Michael explained. 'Nothing to worry about, unless there was some history of genetic problems on both sides. It was just curiosity really. Do either of you know about your ancient ancestors?' Michael asked. Danika could read the shock in Cristian's expression as easily as she knew he would be reading it on hers. 'I didn't mean to worry you; it honestly wouldn't make any difference. It is not like you are cousins.'

'Well, wow… That was not something we were expecting to hear today,' Danika spoke when Cristian was finding it too difficult to. She could feel his relief now overlaid with a different worry and disbelief. 'Doctor, I know this may seem odd, but at the first ultrasound would they be able to detect if I am carrying twins?'

'Do you think that is possible? Is there a history of twins in your family?'

'No, no history of twins just a feeling. Strange I know,' Danika answered as she held tight onto Cristian's hand.

'I am not surprised by any mother's intuition anymore. We can schedule the ultrasound at ten weeks to be sure to get a good view. Then again, as I said, at fifteen weeks to make sure of growth and progression. So, with that in mind, it will not be detrimental to increase your supplements and I would recommend five small meals or three with two snacks. Increase water intake at least until the first ultrasound. It is only a couple of weeks and you can reduce if it is no longer necessary. If you get any morning sickness it may be harder to maintain enough intake so get back to me if that becomes an issue.' He wrote her a few notes regarding help with morning sickness. 'I will send you the date of the ultrasound and a follow up appointment with me for the results.'

Outside they were sitting in the car without moving when they looked at one another and hugged. 'Who do you think it was?' Cristian asked.

'It had to be Bronwyn or earlier, because after that there was only girls.' Danika was stunned.

'What about the men before the curse?' Cristian was unsure if there had been females born to his family before then.

'I think my line were never more than poor workers so it was unlikely that the men had their way with any woman from your family, if you get my drift?' Danika said. 'So we are linked by blood as well albeit very ancient bloodlines. Our children will be the first combination again in hundreds of years.'

'Yes, did you pick up that Dr Michael was not just intrigued but worried about us?'

'Yes, he tried to pass it off as nothing but I know he was concerned. Especially when I asked about twins. I think we should be very positive when we get back. Elizabeth and the others don't need to be worrying unnecessarily.' Danika was determined to not let concerns rule their lives. 'We can still go to the property at the end of the week.'

'Okay, but I am taking my car also and Rainbow can stay there as our backup.' Danika had to agree.

The next few days passed smoothly, without saying much to Ann and the others. When the day came that they were headed to their new property, Danika was glad to be following Cristian there as she knew she would have been lost otherwise. Leaving early in the morning they were unlocking the gate before noon after Danika had to stop twice for comfort and a snack.

The grass was greener and taller from the wet weather than she remembered. Danika showed where she had parked just a couple of months before to watch the full moon as they moved to the front door to go inside. Cristian handed her the key to open it herself. The house smelled old and dusty but not damp. The furniture was still there as it was left from years before. In the lounge, magazines were stacked next to an armchair beside the fireplace as if someone would come sit there again. Doilies and tablecloths were on most surfaces to protect and decorate with precious items in a glass cabinet. Opposite was a dining room that was sparse and appeared unused. The kitchen that Danika had viewed through the closed window, though dusty, felt like someone would come through the door and prepare a meal at any moment. Cristian cautiously opened the fridge which had been cleared out and cleaned with a newspaper to keep the door slightly ajar.

'Do you think it would work?' Danika was curious.

'Perhaps but I wouldn't want to rely on it. The electricity is connected but I was told not to put it on as they said someone should be present in case there were any wires that were broken. I will go turn it on, we may get lights at least.'

When Cristian came back, he tried the lights and several came on. Danika tried the kitchen light but it didn't work. Cristian took out the globe, searched for a replacement in the drawers and tried again. Sure enough, it worked. They continued finding different useful things throughout the house. The taps didn't work so Cristian checked to see if the water was on as he had requested but it seemed only the tanks were connected to the main house and they were rusted and dry. Eventually he found where the water came onto the property but for some reason was not connected to the main house but perhaps to the wet area extension. He was able to flush the lines and get some water to take into the house in a large pan. Danika had found an old vacuum cleaner which surprised her when it actually started up.

In the wet area of laundry, bathroom and toilet the water was connected thankfully. After a bit more looking through the house they went out to the sheds which were a museum of finds that would take them months to sort out. They decided that after Danika cleaned in the lounge area they would set up the blow-up mattress and may even be able to have a fire if the chimney was not blocked. Danika worked on making sure they had a bed and that the toilet could be used, then she brought a few supplies inside to try out the kitchen. They agreed it was too dangerous to use the gas stove and relied on her electric kettle for a hot drink. Cristian found a small wood supply and tried the chimney with paper first to make sure it was not blocked. A short time later he had a small fire going which instantly changed the feel of the room.

'I think we shall have dinner at the pub tonight,' Cristian suggested.

'Yes and breakfast at Marge's café,' Danika agreed. 'I might be able to get more set up tomorrow but for now we can have some of the food Ann packed for us.' They carried the fridge in but realised there was only one power point in the house besides the kitchen and, not wanting to overload it, set up the fridge in the laundry.

'It looks like although they could have easily had more power and water here they just never bothered. It isn't that long ago that they lived here.' Danika knew this meant a lot more wiring work to be done. They were sitting on the camp chairs on the wonky verandah out the front looking down the valley as they ate the sandwiches and drank fruit juice. The view was stunning looking across the vast paddock of grass down the valley to where she knew the sun and moon rose each day. To one side were the driveway and more paddocks down to the road and to the other side was a steep ridge leading up to higher craggy mountains covered in native scrub.

'There is one external power point in the fuse box if you want to drive Rainbow around there and connect to the power for your fridge and anything else you may want in there,' Cristian suggested. 'Tomorrow I want to look around the property further, out to the fences and the forest to get an idea where I can run. This is very beautiful and calming Danika. I'm so glad you found it.' Danika felt as privileged as Cristian to be able to own this property.

'Thank you I just felt it was meant to be. I might walk around some also. You know, we could use a gator here,' Danika commented making Cristian laugh at the idea but nodding agreement.

'Righto.'

After moving Rainbow around beside the fuse box and connecting to power Danika used the kettle to heat up water to clean and worked her way around the kitchen until she was happy it was dust free and disinfected. Cristian was checking the outside for repairs he suspected but would get Dean to arrange someone to come and do a full renovation inspection. It was in surprisingly good shape.

'Do you want to clean up before we go out? I can organise a bath for you,' Cristian asked as he watched her trying to clean the windows.

'Oh yes I probably should. How were you going to heat the water, by the kettle?' Danika asked.

'Yes and a few pots of water on the gas ring and fire,' Cristian explained. 'A bit laborious but fun also I guess, having to think it through on a simpler level.'

'Yep camping of a sort.' Danika smiled enjoying his new thoughts. Danika put the kettle on and then helped Cristian light the gas ring in Rainbow to boil a pan of water. He put another older pan of water next to the wood fire to heat also. 'Did you have a look at the hot water heater?'

'Yes it is empty of water I think so it can't be turned on. After all this time it is unlikely to work. We need to get another one,' Cristian explained. 'The house is in better condition than I expected though. If it wasn't we would be staying at a bed and breakfast, that may have been a better idea anyway.'

'Ah but then we wouldn't be having all this fun.' Danika had to laugh.

After an hour and many laughs they had both used the few centimetres of warm water in the bath to clean up to go to dinner and were back fairly quickly tired. They stoked the lounge fire and settled on the blow-up mattress with the bedding from Rainbow. The humour of the situation turned to cuddles and surprisingly good sleep.

They woke early but Danika knew Marge opened later on a Sunday so they sat out the front in blankets to watch the sunrise with a hot drink. 'I think we should give this a name. I thought of Haven,' Cristian suggested. 'Any ideas?'

'I'm rubbing off on you. Well I found it because of the moon so what about Lunar Haven?' Danika shared her thought.

Cristian nodded. 'I like that.'

Cristian pulled out his phone as it buzzed. 'Dean said he feels like taking a drive up here today with the kids for a look. He should be here by ten.' At Danika's puzzled look he added, 'I contacted him yesterday when I was looking around and suggested today or Wednesday.'

'Great, I'll tidy up a bit before we go for breakfast and bring back some snacks for them from Marge's,' Danika said with a smile, glad to have a plan. Cristian mentally reminded her not to overdo it. 'Well you better help then.'

They moved the blow-up bed to on top of the old bed in one of the rooms and made sure the wet areas were accessible for anyone and moved the dining chairs out to the verandah. Once they were ready they left in Cristian's car for the café.

After greetings and hugs, they were enjoying a huge breakfast with a box of cakes to take back with them sitting on the table. Marge wanted to sit with them but it was too busy and they promised to come back in the afternoon after close so they could talk. Danika ate till she felt she would bust; the food was so good. With a few cool drinks as well they left with a quick wave and were back at Lunar Haven a few minutes before Dean and his two children and Mark showed up. Dean's wife was happy to have a day to herself she had said so Mark asked to tag along.

The children ran around wanting to look at everything within minutes and yelling and whooping it up as they went. Danika loved the sound and was enjoying and absorbing the happy vibes. The men walked around more slowly discussing Cristian's ideas and Dean's suggestions focusing mostly on the house. Dean even got up in the loft to have a look at the roof structure which he found to be in surprisingly good condition. After an hour they were sitting on the verandah watching the children kicking a football in the paddock discussing a plan of attack for the neediest points first.

'You could use a gator out here,' Mark suggested. 'Do you know if the tractor works?'

'Not sure about the tractor, I could get a mechanic out to look at it another time. Yes a gator is probably a good investment. It is a big area I haven't walked it yet.'

'We could drive in the truck.' Dean pointed to his dual cab RAM.

With the kids yipping and wriggling, the three men and the children went for a drive around the property. Danika said she would wait for another time to do that. Danika could sense that Cristian was enjoying the male connection. He had so few opportunities for that. The same could be said for Danika who had limited female connections until more recently. So much had changed for them both in a short time. An hour later Cristian was sending her a warning they were on the way back. Danika had the cakes and drinks ready for them all as they pulled up and the children jumped out of the car, running around again until they saw the cakes. Then they stood relatively politely waiting for permission to have some.

They all sat and looked out at the view as they discussed the merits of the space and view. Then they all looked around inside room by room with Dean taking more notes on what Danika was hoping to achieve. They agreed that power and hot water was the priority. By mid-afternoon Dean was trying to round up the children to go. Danika handed him the box of the remaining cakes as a travel incentive. As they left, the quiet was only broken by the birds that were gathering in the bare fruit trees. Danika threw a few crumbs out for them and sat and watched as the birds decided if they wanted them or not. Cristian sat next to her and held her hand. She was still remembering how wonderful the sound of the children was.

'This is going to be a wonderful holiday home for the whole family.' Cristian voiced their thoughts.

'Yes so much space, how was the survey of the property?' Danika had only had glimpses of his thoughts.

'Really good I couldn't see any other buildings of neighbours at all. Perhaps up on the ridge you will but I wasn't exploring that while the kids were here. I found a little waterfall and creek that you may like to look at tomorrow. I think it is too late now. Dean and Mark were very impressed that you found this place. He made a few suggestions I hadn't considered around more room for our extended family to stay in the future.' Cristian pointed upwards.

'Oh really, like a second story?' Danika had not considered that.

'No, he said there is plenty of space up there with the pitch of the roof to put dormer windows looking towards the ridge just for bedrooms,' Cristian explained. They sat quietly in their own thoughts for a while and then noticed the kangaroos moving into the bottom of the paddock to feed. Cristian could see them better and counted at least a dozen and described them to Danika who could only see the heads of the bigger ones. Danika felt his mood turning a little sombre but he was hiding his thoughts. She guessed anyway.

'Are you worried about the full moon?' Danika had to ask. He couldn't hide his emotions from her even if he could his thoughts.

'I can't control what happens in the change and I have no memory of it. I may injure or kill an animal. I would rather you never knew that.' Cristian's actions worried him more and more. There wasn't really anything Danika could say to allay his fears or encourage him so she decided to stay silent and just send him her feelings of love and support. 'When were we going back to see Marge? I thought we could get dinner at the pub again, I need meat.'

'Soon probably, she will be closing now.' Danika was looking forward to speaking to Marge more leisurely. 'I'll just freshen up I think before we leave.'

As they pulled up outside the café they could see the lights were off and Danika directed them around to the side door to Marge's home. She insisted they stay for dinner so they could talk more as she had a leg of lamb cooking. Marge didn't seem at all surprised that Danika was married or that they bought the farm.

'It will be such a wonderful holiday home for you and your family.' Marge was encouraging. 'And I get to see more of you. Did you see Julie and Sarah? They are so much a part of the family now it is wonderful. That was such a great thing you did.' Danika showed Marge a few photos of the wedding which had her crying and then some of the gallery and artworks. 'Next time you come this way you should look at the printed silks one of our locals makes. Something to consider in the future anyway.'

After a few hours and loaded up with more cakes in another box they left. As they pulled up the driveway of the farm the headlights showed a mob of kangaroos in the paddock closer to the house that watched their progress until the car stopped and then loped a little further away. There seemed to be about twenty of them including mothers with joeys. Danika could feel Cristian's concern again. This was meant to be a happy safe place for his lunar change but he was worried he would spoil it for Danika.

It was cold in the house so Cristian started the fire again before they moved the mattress back into the lounge. Danika decided she needed to take his mind off his concerns and it didn't take long to get his thoughts on to other things as she undressed in front of the fire. They both agreed they needed to get a proper bed there for the next visit.

In the morning Danika was attempting again to heat up large amounts of water for a bath of sorts. The humour was wearing off, especially in the cold of the morning. Once they were both dressed and well fed they set out to walk over to the ridge where Cristian had seen the waterfall and creek. It was very serene and lovely. The sound of the water trickling down the ridge was all they could hear, although Cristian pointed up to show her different birds he had heard. They walked along the creek that seemed to disappear under rocks at different points. They could see what looked like animal tracks where there were pools of water. Cristian decided to climb up at one point to see how far he could view but did not want Danika to follow. She waited while looking more at the undergrowth and ended up startling the mob that were resting under the bushes. They only moved a few metres away as she talked to them to calm them down. She worried also about their safety but was careful to keep that thought closed off to Cristian.

Walking back to the waterfall, she let Cristian know that was where she was. Sitting on a rock she thought it would be nice to have a bench here to sit on and meditate. She closed her eyes and focused on feeling the sway of life around her and the feeling of the gravity of the earth. She could feel different small animals moving around the rocks and bushes, mostly lizards. She felt Cristian getting closer, having climbed across the ridge face until he was nearer the waterfall and looking for a way down. It was bit too slippery so he instead walked out to the edge of a rock overhang and jumped. Danika heard and felt him do this and it made her gasp. It must have been ten metres or more that he jumped but he did land safely and made his way to her.

'I'm okay, I was very careful. It was just a bit quicker than climbing all the way back down.' Cristian tried to calm her. 'I found a cave up there, not high enough to stand in and it only goes back about two metres, but I think a few animals may have sheltered in there at different times.' He tried to send her images of what he saw. Then handed her his camera to see the few photos he had taken including a couple of the house.

'This is great as a before reference before the upgrades.' Danika explained her thoughts about this spot being a meditation place and what she had felt before his leap.

'The forest behind the house was too rocky and dense for us to explore with Dean's car but we could walk back that direction if you like. How are you feeling?'

'Really good and pleased to be exercising a bit more, let's go.' Danika smiled at his worry.

Danika agreed it would be easy to get lost without Cristian's great sense of direction as even a few metres in the scrub and the house and paddock were not visible and there were no high points of reference. Cristian showed her obvious animal paths, probably kangaroos and other small marsupials, and then he held her back as he looked closer and sniffed the air. He pointed to paw prints.

'Could be a wild dog or a dingo. Not so likely a single dingo on its own though. These are fresh so we will have to watch out at night.' This spooked Danika a little as it was difficult to look more than a couple of metres around. Cristian directed them out of the forest and it was only a short distance before the buildings came into view again.

Danika hadn't looked closely through the sheds with the others and now as she went, she marvelled at the old-style tools and unknown objects all kept in a type of system and order. There was even an old horse buggy in one corner. Danika imagined so many years of happy times as the owners had carefully looked after everything maintaining a very simple life.

'I'm sure someone could use these tools, or maybe they could become garden art. I don't want to just throw them out. Perhaps Marge knows someone local, I can ask next time we are there. After lunch I think I might try to make some changes in the bedroom.'

Later with Cristian doing most of it they moved the old double bed into the next bedroom and Danika cleaned away dust and cobwebs before they moved the blow-up mattress into that room. She felt a lethargy overwhelm her just as Cristian was about to order her to stop. She decided a nap was in order but set her alarm so she didn't sleep too long. Cristian spent the time bringing in more wood and putting together a makeshift grill plate. When he sensed Danika stirring he put the kettle on for a cup of tea, the cold was already creeping in despite the late sun. She gladly sat in front of the fire as he handed her a hot tea.

'I see you have been busy, what are your plans with that?' Danika pointed at the grill plate.

'Toasted sandwiches, warmed apple pie and whatever else we think of,' Cristian answered which made her smile. 'Dean sent a message that he has arranged an electrician to come here Wednesday mid-morning to do an assessment he was just checking we would still be here. I said we would wait until he is finished before we leave. Is that okay with you?'

She nodded and sent a yes thought also. 'He is a fast worker, well the whole Norton clan is.'

'Yes they are and hopefully next time we are here it will be more liveable,' Cristian expressed as he was working out what to attempt to cook first.

'I think I shouldn't have insisted we stay here until tomorrow. Sorry about that.' Danika had to agree it had not been the best use of their time.

'It hasn't been that bad and it will make us appreciate the improvements more. You could still go to a BnB tomorrow and I can catch up with you.' He had barely finished the sentence when she was mentally disagreeing before she could get the words out.

'Absolutely not I am going to be here with you, where I should be. I want to see you free to run not like it was last month.' Danika's throat caught and she started to cry on the last words. 'You cannot send me away.' She realised she had not let him know that before.

'You kept that from me all this time.' Cristian moved to hug her. 'I told you not to watch and not to be there and this was why. You cannot be near me at the change especially if I am free to move around you. The babies' safety is paramount.' He was sending her very firm thoughts bordering on an order.

She nodded and said, 'I know but I sort of have an idea. I thought maybe tomorrow early I could go buy night vision glasses at the sport and hunting store to watch from afar.'

'You could do that but I doubt you will see much from these windows.' His pointed remark made it obvious he did not want her to leave the house tomorrow night. 'Now back to our gourmet dinner.'

Later they agreed the attempts for dinner were sometimes better and sometimes worse than hoped but it gave them a laugh. Not much in the way of phone connection either as they were too far from Wi-Fi or towers. They flicked through some old magazines briefly before deciding bed was the natural option.

The next day, besides getting the night vision glasses and a good torch, they also bought a few things Danika could eat without cooking. Cristian was not eating now as was typical for the prelude to the change. Once they were back Cristian moved his ring to the chain just in case he forgot later. They had locked the gate as well to make sure they were not disturbed. Danika set her rug up on the porch with candles to catch the first stars before she would have to go in for the moonrise. Cristian wasn't keen on this stating that sometimes the change could start before the moon was visible. She promised to go in if that happened.

The day seemed to drag on. They talked about possible changes and colours and drew a few drawings. Eventually they decided to sit on the porch and wait until Danika was due to eat and Cristian insisted she did even though he was not hungry.

The light was fading and as the first star twinkled Danika pulled whatever she could from it and the others as they started to appear. Not long after, Cristian sat upright, catching Danika's focus.

'Go inside now Danika.' She did as she was told and shut the door, watching as he carefully took off his clothes and laid them on a chair. It was fully dark so Danika watched through the night vision glasses, having turned off all the lights. She had the torch in her pocket. She sent whatever calming helpful thoughts she could to him until he no longer returned her thoughts. His head and legs were now fully formed and, same as last time, the tail was the last to grow.

Cristian didn't howl. Instead, he ran off out of her sight. She ran to other windows and still could not see him but she could almost tell where he was as she had charmed the chain around his neck. This was the first time she had tried it out and it was only letting her know a rough direction. She sat near the fire and eventually noticed the full moon on the horizon, just as Cristian let out a howl from the direction of the ridge. She went out and pulled the energy from the moon briefly then went back inside to the dying fire again.

She must have drifted off to sleep as she was woken by an awful noise of barks and yelps. Grabbing the night vision glasses she tried desperately to work out what was happening but could not make anything out. She sensed he was in the paddock and wondered if he had chased the kangaroos. Again the noises that sounded like two animals fighting sounded. It was blood curdling and she was terrified Cristian was in danger. She cried, the not knowing was definitely worse. She tried to rest with a blanket over her in the lounge chair, she couldn't go lay down in the cold bed.

She heard birds and realised dawn was not far away. Danika made a cup of tea but, as she did so, her stomach heaved and she only just made it to the toilet in time. Still her stomach felt queasy and she remembered the ginger sweets in Rainbow. Checking for Cristian, she couldn't feel anything and with the night vision glasses she checked around and couldn't see him anywhere. Carefully she went out to go to Rainbow and the waves of nausea overtook her again. She doubled up and dropped to her knees, heaving like her stomach wanted to run away from her.

She smelt him before she saw him. She kept as still as her treacherous stomach would let her, yet she did not fear him. He came closer and stood next to her. As she was overcome again by retching he leaned against her. Finally she thought she could stand and she carefully reached up to put her hand on him. Stickiness coated her hand. It smelled like blood and her stomach threatened to heave again. The first faint glow showed him looking straight into her eyes, his head at her chest height. She could see the blood clearly now.

Cristian changed back, much quicker and looking much less painful. He was awake but only just, the tears to his skin obvious around his shoulders and arms. She tried to support him but he pushed her off and said 'No' the only way he could, with his mind. Cristian staggered to the water outlet and turned it on to wash the dirt and blood off him. Danika brought a blanket to wrap around him. He accepted her help to get him inside. She wanted to ask so much but knew he would say what he could when he could. She ran to get the first aid kit from Rainbow, grabbing the ginger as she went.

'Why were you outside?' Cristian asked with a rasping voice. She could feel he was angry at her.

'Well furry you was nicer to me. I was ill and trying to get to Rainbow. He stood over me to protect me.' Danika was a little indignant but very worried also. 'Do you know what happened?'

'Not really, why were you sick?' He was struggling to stay awake.

'Morning sickness I think.' She held up the ginger lozenge which she put in her mouth. 'It was relentless and unavoidable. Let me look at those wounds.' Danika methodically put antiseptic and bandages on the lacerations. Despite the pain, Cristian dozed off and Danika left him to clean up the mess of blood and get some clothes for him. She made a warm drink and he was stirring as she brought them to him.

'Thank you for your help but you didn't listen to me again Danika. What you see may seem fascinating but it is so very dangerous. Once I can, I shall go check if I left an animal in pain and deal with it. You will not come with me.' Cristian was tired but very succinct in his wording. He sipped the warm tea and dressed, taking his time to get his shoes on then walked out of the back of the house, picking up a shovel as he went. He was gone nearly an hour. She had watched him walk down the paddock to where a few crows and a hawk were hovering around but lost sight of him.

As he came back he was sending her reassuring thoughts that all was well but did not let her see what he had found.

'I heard horrible noises last night and stayed in the house. You were right, I couldn't see anything with the glasses. I was so scared for you.' Danika was trying to keep from crying.

'It was that wild dog that we saw the tracks for. I think it attacked the kangaroos then killed a small one and I must have fought and killed it.' Cristian was feeling all the bruises and rips from the fight but could not actually remember it. To allay her thoughts he added, 'The bite marks on the kangaroo were much smaller than the ones I made on the dog. I buried them both. I didn't know I would protect them and you as it turned out. I'm sorry I was angry at you earlier. How are you feeling now, have you eaten?'

'I'm fine. Better than you for once. I had some toast, cooked in Rainbow while you were out. Are you going to be okay driving back later?'

'Yes I think we both want to get home now. We will leave as soon as the electrician is gone. I should go unlock the gate.' He moved over to drive to the gate and back rather than walk.

'I'll pack up what we have to so we can put it in Martin.' Danika thought he should eat and rest but left him to make that decision himself.

The trip back after the electrician left was longer than it should be because they had to stop several times due to Danika's nausea. It gave

Cristian the chance to walk around and keep awake also. She sent Ann a message that they were both okay but very tired and would just retire to their rooms once they were back. She also thanked her for the ginger. That way no one would bother them too much. They were greeted by Ben who took their bags and Ann who informed them hot drinks and food were in their rooms and then they were left to go upstairs.

Cristian flopped on the bed where Danika threw a cover over him. She tried some of the chamomile tea and water crackers before enjoying the first proper hot shower in days. Once done, she joined him on the bed with a different blanket over herself.

The next day Danika looked at Cristian's wounds and was worried some should be stitched and cleaned better than she was able to at the farm. Cristian reminded her it would be difficult to explain. She disagreed as it was obviously a dog attack but she offered an alternative that he couldn't discount.

'Like the burn you had from the medallion I can heal it but I need to stitch it first. I can reduce the pain as I do it.' She was sending him stern thoughts and then added, 'Or I could tell Ann.' She used the warning he had on her not that long ago. He nodded and she found the items she needed while he had a very quick shower and, in a towel in the bathroom where the light was brightest, she started. It took nearly an hour for her to complete it to her satisfaction and she knew he felt each stitch even if she was able to reduce the intensity of the pain. He didn't flinch but they both seemed thankful when it was done. She had been so focused on the job it wasn't until she let her guard down that she started to cry. Cristian sent her thoughts of tea and breakfast which left her stomach heaving again.

Over the next few weeks Danika learned to live with the nausea in the morning. She ate better from noon until later than usual to keep her intake in line. She focused on getting the furniture renovated to the colours she liked and picking a few pieces to go to Lunar Haven. Cristian made sure the gallery was running well and that there were still enough pieces to entice buyers from the large store of items in the warehouse as well as managing the renovations at Lunar Haven. Dean had sent them a few progress photos. Most of the furniture had gone to charity with some of the unwanted shed items sold online.

Danika's ultrasound appointment date arrived and they both felt like they had been holding their breath all this time. Lucky it was in the afternoon as she thought no way she would have kept down all the water she had to drink in the morning. Dr Michael Davis greeted them in his rooms and showed Danika where she could change into a gown. Her belly was still small but obvious now at ten weeks. She lay on the bed and the doctor warned her it would be a little cold. It didn't take long to confirm two babies. She was holding tight on to Cristian's hand but was still concerned as the doctor continued to take measurements and apologised for the pressure on her as he moved the scope around. 'I'm getting measurements that will give us a basis to start from to make sure growth is as expected. Sorry it is taking so long, a few more bits to count and measure.'

'Is it too soon to know the gender of them?' Danika had to ask as so much was at stake.

'Yes sorry, we will do another ultrasound in five weeks to compare these results but it is unlikely we will know then either. That is enough prodding for now if you want to get cleaned up and dressed and come into the office Danika. Take your time, Cristian you can come in now.' Danika sent him a thought to tell her everything the doctor said to him but then she was keen to get to the toilet and get the rest of the gel off her stomach.

Cristian

Cristian followed Dr Michael into his office and sat with some trepidation as to what he would say.

'Is Danika worried she will have the same problems your mother had?' Dr Michael was quick to ask.

'Partly I suppose, but also her family has only had girls for quite a long time so either of us will be pleased whatever gender they are.' Cristian decided partial truth was safer. He relayed this to Danika who was dressing at record speed. The doctor waited patiently until Danika had finished and arrived.

'I can say all looks well for now at ten weeks, they are a good size. As I said, fifteen weeks will be another good test of their growth. How is the morning sickness going?' Dr Michael was keeping it all very positive as usual. Yet again Danika could feel he was holding something back and pushed him to say more with her thoughts.

'Was there anything else you have determined?' Cristian asked for her.

'It is very early and the view is not clear but having seen a few twin pregnancies in my day it appears that they are fraternal.' At their confused look he added, 'Not identical. So from two eggs being fertilised not a single egg splitting. This does not mean it is safer or not, just an observation.'

Once they were in the car after they finished up, they smiled at each other, sharing happy thoughts. Without saying it they knew this meant there was a chance of a boy and a girl, although two of either would be amazing also. They had to kiss and hug despite the gear lever. 'Now we can confirm with our mothers,' Danika commented. Cristian agreed.

The phone call to Selene was a formality as she already knew but it was polite to confirm. They talked about how things were going with Danika and the renovations here and as it turned out at Selene's. Then it was time to tell Elizabeth, who was shocked and delighted at the same time to hear they were having twins, tinged with concern for Danika to not do too much.

They planned their next trip in a week to Lunar Haven to be basically overnight, only to check the renovations so far and let

Cristian run through the change. Danika wanted to move Rainbow also as she was concerned about the torrential rains again but Cristian had already organised that with Dean having given him the keys when he had mentioned it wasn't good to leave their van out in the weather. So many warnings of flooding expected had Danika getting very concerned. Their properties were safe but so many other people were likely not to be safe. They checked all the staff would be alright.

As the date to travel became closer Cristian was not keen for Danika to travel with him in the pouring rain. Dean had confirmed the roof and verandah were safe with no leaks and the hundreds of tons of gravel laid on the drive now made it safer to get to the house. Danika argued these points but still he worried if the power went out or something else happened while he couldn't protect her.

'It's only one night and we have better torches now. I am less safe if I am worrying about you from afar.' Danika continued to state her case. He gave up arguing.

The drive up to Lunar Haven was slow due to the number of detours for flooding and road damage. They didn't need to stop as often thankfully as the morning sickness was not so bad that day. The new gravel driveway was very welcome and the house looked so much better with the new gutters and painted roof. The verandah was now proudly welcoming them instead of leaning precariously. The outside was painted the original colours as best Dean and Mark could match and she looked happy in Danika's opinion.

Cristian turned off the security system and turned on the ducted heating. Inside was the smell of clean fresh paint and polish. There were new blinds and curtains at the windows with a new hall runner and a couple of the rugs from Hollingrove that looked perfect in this setting. The house was so much more welcoming. There was still minimal furniture until the back bedroom where there were several pieces and boxes to unpack. Danika was most excited by the instant hot water in the kitchen and bathroom. The first bedroom now had a queen-sized bed with a pile of linen to decide on. Danika suggested lunch from Ann's hamper before considering any other work, not that Cristian ate much as was normal before the change. The rain was getting heavier and loud on the tin roof despite the new insulation. They talked as they ate with the roar of the rain overhead.

Danika was so pleased and amazed what had been achieved in four weeks. The kitchen and bathroom would be a future project when the weather was more stable. She could see through the kitchen window that Rainbow had been moved but, looking out the back window, she couldn't see where she was in the sheds. Cristian found the keys to the locked shed and braved the rain rather than Danika to confirm that was where Rainbow was now that all the unwanted items had been cleaned out. He knew she wouldn't be satisfied otherwise. He was drenched when he came back in but elected to strip off most of his clothes as he would be doing that in a couple of hours anyway. He was getting hotter as a fore runner to the change. Then he was on a mission to get the bed made and furniture moved so that Danika didn't try to do it while he was gone. He knew she would follow the theme of not listening to him as in the past. Danika insisted on putting a stronger seek charm on his chain before he left. She hugged him and could feel the increased heat from his body but was still worried he would be cold and wet when he was outside.

'You could sit it out here on the verandah or in the sheds,' Danika suggested. Cristian kissed her and loved her naïve hopeful suggestion.

'I have no control over him you know that. He won't sit until later in the morning. Don't come looking when it is dawn, it's a late moon and I may not be back until full sunrise.' Cristian tried to send her strong thoughts again to stay safe for their babies and she said she would. She ran her hands over the faint lines of his fight with the wild dog, now almost completely faded except for the deepest ones. 'They will probably be gone after this change. Another perk, that's why I don't have any childhood scars.'

He sat outside on the chair on the verandah and watched the solar lights come on around the house before the change started. Danika watched from the lounge window and sent her usual love and calm vibes until he no longer could hear them.

Danika

In all his magnificence he stood on the verandah watching the rain. She spoke to him and she could see his ears move to hear her. 'Why don't you stay there until the rain ends or come back to dry you handsome boy?' She cooed at him. He turned to look straight at her and then, shaking his head, he leaped off the porch and was gone in the dark and rain. She concentrated and felt him head for the ridge.

After another snack from the hamper and a cup of tea Danika decided to curl up in the bed with a battery radio quietly playing in the background as she read a few magazines. She slept for several hours before an echo of a howl woke her. Looking at the time on her phone she realised it must be the full moon. She tried to sense where he was and it seemed as if he was close and out the back, maybe in the sheds. The solar lights had long ended as they had not had enough sunlight to charge them for a whole night. The rain had stopped and the clouds parted long enough for her to see a slight silhouette of him wandering the sheds sniffing everything.

She tried speaking to him again loudly through the window. He looked over her way. His coat looked darker and heavier so she knew he was drenched. He shook again and more water glistened in the moonlight but he ran off again. Danika was wide awake now and could feel a faint nausea so decided on a chamomile tea and plain cracker to ease her stomach. She put her head down on the table after trying to read for a short while, waking to the sound of Cristian coming in the laundry door and turning on the shower. She sleepily wandered down to see him muddy with a few scratches standing in the stream of a hot shower. She stripped off her clothes and joined him to wash his back and other parts until they were mutually satisfied and clinging to each other, laughing at the snug and slippery space.

Dressed and eating a large breakfast with coffee, Cristian checked if Danika wanted any but she shook her head and walked out of the room until her stomach settled. She sent a thought that she was alright but didn't want to push her luck. She wanted to ask how he went last night but realised the answer would be 'I don't know.'

He caught the remnants of that thought and asked her if she had tracked him at all.

'You headed up to the ridge and after moonrise you were wandering around the sheds very wet. I didn't get much more than that.'

'I think we need to get internet here so we are not so isolated and a TV as well,' Cristian suggested.

'We don't watch TV,' Danika pointed out.

'I know, but others do and I'm hoping we can have visitors here one day,' Cristian pointed out as he sent thoughts of a family gathering at some stage. The image made her smile.

'Do you mind if we stop in the village on the way home? I just want to say hi to Marge and look in that shop she mentioned.' Danika wasn't sure if she would come again next month.

'Of course but not too long. After that rain last night it may be longer to get home so we should pack quickly.' He finished his breakfast and washed the dishes so Danika didn't have to smell it. She sent him a thank you and then carried the bags out that she had packed. After they both walked through to make sure all was okay before they left, Cristian set the alarms and locked up.

Marge was happy to see them again and hear their good news of twins, plying them with a huge box of pastries to take back. In the little art and crafts gallery Danika did really like the printed silks, confirming they would feature some in their gallery if the artist agreed, which she did. They bought a dozen with a view to order more if they were successful and exchanged business cards as a polite gesture of understanding. Three hours later they were finally pulling into Hollingrove after many detours again. Ann was not offended at all by the box of pastries and looked forward to trying something she hadn't made herself when they suggested she take them home to her family for the weekend.

Cristian was finally able to check his emails and was surprised to have one from Peter under his pseudonym to say they hoped to plan a trip out to Australia as invited for September but it would be a closely guarded secret. He was going through a number of emotions at the email and Danika was by his side quickly as she felt them all. He worried of the timing and that they would need to be at Lunar Haven together which brought on excitement and trepidation almost simultaneously. To be able to run with someone else again was thrilling to Cristian but Danika sensed his worry for her safety around a different wolf. It was also the first step towards ending the curse if Peter managed to bring the artefacts needed as he intended. Danika understood the enormity of the end to the curse and now it was closer to coming true she determined to focus on the positives rather than the negatives. In her mind there were only positives.

It was still a couple of hours until dinner so a visit to Elizabeth's rooms was arranged to talk about the planned visit.

'Ingrid made a comment about wishing she could see me again after so many years but apologised that she would be visiting relatives in Canada instead,' Elizabeth told them. 'I think it may be a ruse to hide their travel plans.'

'You could be correct, Elizabeth. Our focus is now how to accommodate them. We can here easily once we refurnish all the bedrooms. At Lunar Haven though there is only two bedrooms. Do you think Ingrid would be happy to stay here with you while we go there?' Danika asked. 'How old is their son do you think he would be running also?'

'No Friedrich is only fourteen but he may be aware of the curse, I'm not sure,' Cristian answered for his mother.

'I wonder if he would be happy to sleep in Rainbow,' Danika suggested.

'I'm sure Ingrid will be fine here with me, it is unlikely that Friedrich will want to stay here with his grandmother. He is youthful enough to sleep anywhere I would think.' Elizabeth was feeling quite pleased at the thought of hosting guests, Danika could feel her emotions.

They all agreed that the visit was to be kept secret from everyone and to just push on with renovations until the last minute to advise the staff. Danika felt a bit uneasy at not trusting their secrecy but also trusted their ability to act quickly with changes. They wrote down a quick plan of action at Hollingrove and Lunar Haven to be ready for the visit on time with Elizabeth and Danika focusing on Hollingrove so Cristian could focus on Lunar Haven.

Over the next few weeks their days were very full. Elizabeth had recently assisted with charities again and did not want to relinquish that, especially with the recent floods, but was determined to support Danika in her refurbishment of all the upstairs areas. Danika kept in contact with the gallery which was still going strong. The printed silks to be a spring promotion were already showing online interest.

Cristian had travelled to Lunar Haven a few days ahead of the full moon to check progress. It was the first time they had been so far apart since imprinting and it felt like a hole in Danika's soul to not have the strong mental connection. They spoke and messaged often to fill the gap they both felt. Without saying it they knew this would be the normal for them once the curse was broken. Cristian promised to be back for her fifteen-week ultrasound.

'Cristian?' Danika asked as they spoke over the phone, trying hard to stay neutral.

'Yes?'

'I miss you so much.' Danika was glad he couldn't feel her crying.

'I miss you too darling, just a couple more days and I'll be there. Don't cry I'm fine here alone. I'll leave as soon as I am able.'

'I know, but this is the first time I know what is happening to you but can't be there and in daylight too. Please be careful, I love you.' Danika knew he couldn't control the wolf but she had to say it.

'You know I will do my best and I will call you on the other side as soon as I can. I love you.'

As Danika broke off the call she started to sob. Not because she felt any impending doom but because she couldn't feel him at all. It was like she had become addicted to the scent and sense of him and now for this short time it was ripped away. Soon with the moon and stars aligned it would be forever. He must have felt it also but said nothing. Danika understood on this deeper level how awful it had been for Elizabeth when Henry had died.

The next day seemed to go on forever to Danika. Elizabeth did her best to keep her occupied but by dinner they were both too tired to continue their efforts and each retired to their rooms. Danika laid on the bed with her phone by her side to drift off to an uneasy sleep. She dreamt of happy times and kisses until the buzz of her phone woke her. It was a text from Cristian confirming he was okay and would call later. The relief was like sunshine warming her. She looked at the time. Barely dawn, she had slept for ten hours.

Showered and dressed, Danika went down to the kitchen to get breakfast and was surprised to see Ann, Ben and Mark there. They stopped talking as she came in. She smiled at their apparent conspiratorial discussions.

'Good morning all you, wonderful day isn't it?' Straight away she could sense the relief in them. They were worried about Cristian that was quickly obvious. She could feel their love and she wanted to send them some back.

'Would you like some waffles for breakfast ma'am?' Ann asked.

'That would be lovely, thank you Ann and a cup of tea. I have a busy day ahead.' Danika was looking at Ben and Mark. 'Perhaps we can move some of that furniture back into the rooms after breakfast.'

'Well, we could ma'am, you can point and direct.' Ben was smiling back at her as he finished off his breakfast. 'Was Master Cristian going to be back this weekend?'

'I would think so. We have an appointment Monday. He plans to ring me later so I will know if it will be today or tomorrow.' Danika sipped her tea. 'Did you need him for anything?'

'There was a delivery yesterday of electronic equipment and I wasn't sure where he wanted it set up.' At Danika's look of enquiry he added, 'Big screen TV, a sound bar and gaming equipment.' All things that had been unheard of in the household until now.

'Ah that would be for the room next to yours Ben, upstairs. We have to empty it first.'

'We can bring them up to the music room then and sort from there,' Ben commented.

'I have a can of paint that was delivered in error, and credited they didn't want it back, that may suit that room. I'll bring it up for you to see,' Mark suggested.

By early afternoon Danika was getting worried. She hadn't heard from Cristian as he had promised. She was missing him more and more. Ben and Mark had kept her mind off it with their furniture rearranging and emptying what had been the spare room for Robert. They'd started on the mystery paint – a darker blue with a slight shimmer to it. It was a perfect backdrop to a media room. They were applying it just as her phone buzzed a message.

'On my way, should be home by two pm.'

It was a message, sent hours before but held up probably because of the poor connection and tower outages due to the bad weather lately. That was probably why he hadn't called. Danika walked back to her room where she shed a tear, realising how much worry she had been holding back. She washed her face before facing the men again.

'It will need another coat in a couple of hours but it is looking good I think,' Mark explained as he was covering the paint and rollers.

'Thank you both, you should go have lunch. Looks like Cristian will be back in about an hour.' Danika was looking at how different the space looked now the furniture was out.

Danika had carried the picture taken from the wall when they were emptying the room into their sitting area and looked at it propped against the desk, knowing the offending fake artefact was at the back of it. She wasn't sure what to do with it and wanted to wait until Cristian was home. Ben brought up a tray for her from Ann with sandwiches, biscuits and a fruit drink.

'Thank you Ben and please thank Ann, I am happy to relax here now for a bit.' Danika was very grateful for their sensing her needs.

After eating more than she thought she would she stood at the window and waited, hoping to get the first sense of Cristian before she saw him. At first it was like a distant memory and then a little stronger as she ramped up her power by holding the medallion. He sent her a little warning to tone it down as he was still driving. She was fine to do that now he had responded. Ten minutes later he was coming up the driveway and parking in the garage. Danika had been determined not to bombard him when he arrived as he had asked her to let him get to their rooms. It was tough though and as she felt him coming up the stairs she knew he was hiding something from her. She stood at their open door and watched him limp up the last few stairs with his hand held up to stop her running to him.

'I'm fine, I just twisted my ankle this morning. It looks worse than it is,' Cristian said and he sat on the side of the bed. Danika was not happy. In fact she was angry as she looked at him from the outside inwards.

'I'm too tired to argue with you, I needed to be with you and so I left as soon as I could. I missed your thoughts.' Cristian looked at her with dark sunken eyes that were very happy to see her. Danika's anger dissolved to concern and love. She wanted to look at him all over. She was sure he was hurt more than he was saying.

'I missed your thoughts too, let's not be separated again. I don't like it. What happened to you or was it him?' Danika wasn't there and had no idea of the timeframe for his change.

'Both. He decided to sleep in the cave because you weren't there to talk to him and that was where I woke up and had to get back with no clothes or shoes so I twisted my ankle on the climb down.' Danika was kneeling down as he spoke and carefully taking off his shoes and socks and looking at his feet. He had obviously showered but his feet were cut and bruised and his left ankle was quite swollen. She brought the first aid kit and her healing oils to deal with his injuries.

'Are you sure that was why he slept in the cave?' Danika wondered if he actually remembered the experience. She worked as carefully and quickly as she could to take away his pain.

'I don't know for sure but it felt different, like I was at a loss as what to do despite having the space and safety of the property. I thought because I left from the same spot as before he would come back there. I found this in the cave when I woke up.' Cristian handed her a dirty hair scrunchy. 'Yours, I can smell it.'

'Oh I was wearing that when we first went there all that time ago so he must have found it outside the house.' Danika realised how much the link with him had got into her soul. She needed to be there with him each time of the change and till the end, whenever that turned out to be. She did not hide those thoughts but relished sharing them. She blew on his injuries and he felt the cooling and then the pain was receding. She still taped his ankle for support. 'Any other injuries I should look at?'

'Perhaps later when I strip off completely but that was the most pressing for now. Thank you.' Cristian stood tentatively to test the soles of his feet and his ankle then he was hugging her which turned to kissing. Danika held his face and looked at him. 'What else happened while you were away? You seem so deeply tired.' Before he could answer they heard Mark and Ben coming up the stairs again.

'They are painting the media room,' Danika explained. Cristian pulled his socks and shoes back on as she went to meet them again.

Cristian soon followed to see the progress. Mark showed Cristian the electronics that had arrived and they talked briefly about where to put the TV on the wall and how the rest would fit. Cristian commented that he liked the colour for the walls. They discussed the arrangement and new furniture needed and lighting but Danika could feel his energy waning and suggested they call it a day with a day off for Sunday and that they could get back to it on Monday after their morning appointment. All agreed easily so Mark and Ben cleaned up and took all the painting gear downstairs via the back stairs.

'I think you should sleep now and we can talk later.' She pulled Cristian into their rooms. Closing the door she helped him undress before moving towards the bed to make him lay down as she was gently chanting a sleep charm over him with no argument at all. She could see the scratches all over him. There was a deep one on his chest that she worked on as he slept, the others took little to heal. She wondered if they were received before or after returning to human form. It mattered little really, more curiosity.

After cleaning away the mess and the clothes with the blood marks on them she laid down next to him with her hand on his chest to feel him breathing. She was very glad he was back but worried why he was sad. That was the sense she had – sadness – coming from him but not why. She was sure he was in a deep sleep so, with a cover over him, she made her way down to talk to Ann who she knew would be worried, taking the tray down with her.

'Thank you, ma'am, Ben could have done that.' Ann took it from her. 'How is Master Cristian?'

'Tired so I thought we could have something in our rooms later. You don't need to fuss with dinner.' She could feel Ann's worry still. 'He twisted his ankle this morning but after I taped it up it is already easier for him.' Danika could feel Ann's relief.

'Good, well I have a casserole in the fridge that you can heat as you want later with some fresh bread I made this morning. Mrs Blakesley was having dinner out with Mrs Walton I believe,' Ann mentioned.

'Oh yes I had forgotten that. Well that all works out fine then. Thank you Ann. We will be going out early on Monday for my appointment like last time,' Danika explained with a rueful smile. 'Lots of water again.'

Danika went back up to her bedroom and sat on the bed next to Cristian, watching him sleep as she researched furniture for the media room on the laptop. She was trying not to be worried about him. He was always the strength she relied on but now she felt that his confidence may have been shaken in some way and she needed to know why.

Danika felt the first stirring of his thoughts before he knew where he was or who was with him so he didn't have time to hide them. Death. That was what Danika felt. Like a premonition, not crazy dreaming. There was deep sadness there before it was hidden. So that was his fear, not his own death but hers and the babies and the deep chasm of loss that would be. She let him know she was there next to him and what she felt.

'You weren't meant to see that,' Cristian said. 'No fair reading my thoughts.'

'No fair hiding it, we agreed no secrets,' Danika countered.

'I needed to rest before I tackled that conversation with you. I guess we are having it now then.' Cristian pulled her into his arms and laid one hand on their babies. 'It happened the night before the full moon. It started as a dream of us trying to break the curse but there were so many people everywhere. Everyone we know seemed to be there so definitely a dream. The crowds cleared and the focus was on you and your mother and me all holding different artefacts. The crowd was still there all chanting words I can't remember but as I could feel I was changing I saw our babies as children standing there, a boy and a girl smiling at us. A spear went through us all and you and they were gone and I was on my own. I knew you were dead because I couldn't feel you.' Danika had seen and felt all that he said. She knew he thought it was a premonition but she did not – she would not – believe that.

'I don't think it is a premonition Cristian. I know we have both experienced the vision of the spear but it seemed more a spear of light than a tangible object and the not being able to feel each other was because we were apart. It was awful. I don't know how any imprinted couple can be apart.' She was holding his hand over their babies tight. 'But we are here now and you need to focus on that. Is that why you slept in the cave do you think?'

'Who knows I was definitely not at my best. I have woken in plenty of difficult circumstances all over the world but when I jumped down from the cave like the other time I got it wrong, hit a couple of rocks at the bottom. Lucky I have my super healer on tap.' Cristian was trying to lighten a very dark mood. 'The kitchen and bathrooms are looking great by the way. Dean and his team are magicians.'

'Yes the whole family is. Ben and Mark have powered through getting all the rooms ready. I think we should tell them we will be having guests, I don't feel right keeping it from them.' Danika was adamant they should be told this week.

'Once I know for sure from Peter we can tell them.' Cristian looked around more. 'I like the colour scheme, it's more us less dark history. I'll look around more in a while but I think I need more of nurse Danika.' Danika very briefly was worried he was still hurt until the image of her in a very skimpy nurse uniform passed between them. A couple of hours later Danika was reassessing the bruises she hadn't seen earlier and marvelled he hadn't broken any bones.

The Monday appointment was more difficult than the first one as Doctor Michael seemed to press harder and spent more time measuring each baby to check the progress. All Danika wanted to know was could he tell what gender the babies are. Cristian had a vision of a boy and a girl and they both were wondering if that would be the case. Danika thought she was going to explode and Cristian was working hard at giving her strength to continue. The doctor took many photos. He finally stopped the more intense pressure to show them some of the specific photos.

'The babies are growing as expected which is very good and I was able to get these two shots.' He brought up two photos side by side. The one was very obviously a boy making Danika cry, the other was hard to tell. 'So that one is not a boy,' Doctor Michael explained.

Danika and Cristian kissed and hugged each other, unable to be any happier than they were in that moment. Danika asked if she could make herself more comfortable and quickly slipped out of the room to change. Danika came back in as Doctor Michael explained he wanted to see her in about six weeks unless she felt she needed to see him earlier. He warned her she was likely to feel them moving around within that time. That gave her a little thrill.

In the car park they sat staring at the two photos together. This was monumental for them both. They were the first to have twins as far as Cristian was aware. For Danika the first to be having a boy also. The fact that his family had conceived females before but never carried them to term was not lost on either of them but they agreed to be positive. Now to call the mothers. This was such a big event for the two families they thought perhaps a video call with both mothers hearing it at the same time was for the best. So they sent a message to Selene that they would be calling her later to give them time to get back and set up for the call in Elizabeth's rooms away from the work happening upstairs.

Later in Elizabeth's rooms the video link to Selene showed Clay there also to support her which pleased Danika. They were able to meet Elizabeth at least by video before Danika and Cristian announced that the twins were a boy and a girl, both healthy and growing well. The call was short but very happy. Danika wanted to tell the staff about their news and the visits which Peter had confirmed would be a week before the next full moon. Danika could sense Elizabeth was worried about the female baby but she just knew all would be well and shared her positive thoughts.

In the kitchen Ben and Mark were having lunch with Ann as they walked in to tell them their happy news and about the impending visit. She explained it was still not finalised and was to be kept under wraps. The time frame was unknown but she said to assume several weeks. Danika could feel their emotions but not their thoughts. They had a slight concern that Peter and his family may be unpleasant like Robert but mostly glad Cristian and Danika seemed very pleased by the visit so that was enough for them. Danika felt Ann's concern over the photo of the baby girl, perhaps from Elizabeth's losses of the past. Ann suggested Danika a helper when the time came and that her niece had experience in that area if and when she wanted to think about it.

Of course there would be another family member available to help, Danika thought, feeling relieved to know that. 'Thank you Ann, I may meet her closer to the due date after Christmas all going well.'

14

VISITORS

DANIKA KNEW SHE was dreaming but didn't feel she could stop it, as if some other force was in her head. It felt like visions she had had before but she was more of a spectator than usual. The thought was misty, of walking towards an angel with Cristian beside her. She couldn't see him but could feel his love. They were holding artefacts and as they approached the angel she saw her mother reading from a scroll. More voices, so many voices all chanting the same words. She was holding her hands up to the angel and then a bright light, speared through them both with Cristian in his wolf form. She yelled out his name and woke but could feel the heat from his breath on her neck and the fur surrounded her. He was growling in her ear. She grasped his wrist and yelled with her thoughts and voice, 'Wake up.'

His breathing was rough and laboured as he returned to normal and his thoughts were then his again. He tried to pull away but she held him fast, sending calming thoughts and love to him as he completed the change back to human form.

She could feel that he was horrified that he had not been aware of the change and how dangerous that was to her and the babies. He tried to get up, wanting to distance himself.

'No we need to talk about this while it is fresh. We are fine, you were protecting us.' Danika thought it was logical to discuss this but Cristian wanted to walk away in disgust at his lack of control. 'What can you remember? You were dreaming.'

He really did not want to talk about this but seemed to realise her need to understand it all.

'We were walking towards the gardens carrying the artefacts. There were lots of people there. I couldn't see their faces but I knew they were friends and loved ones. I saw the moon but not the moon, it was red but I was already changing and I couldn't hear your thoughts anymore. I could hear singing or chanting, then you woke me.' He touched his face and head to make sure he was properly back. 'What about you?'

'Did you see an angel?' Danika asked him but he shook his head. 'I was not dreaming, I was channelling your dream so it was a bit misty but we were walking towards an angel that seemed to be holding something like a white box or stone. My mother was there besides all the others and she was reading from a scroll. All the others joined in then the bright spear of light seemed to go through us and I yelled your name. This is more of the puzzle and I know when it is going to happen now. The blood moon in November. We can plan but I have to get up now.' Then she was racing to the bathroom. She sent him thoughts to join her in the shower and her general happiness seemed to pull him out of his dark thoughts.

As they were dressing she asked if the dream was similar to the one he had when he was on his own.

'Yes, but I was alone in my thoughts and emotions like I had lost you that time. This time I knew you were there with me until I saw the moon in my head which obviously initiated the complete change for the first time. I'm sorry I put you at risk I don't want that to happen again.' She could feel that he was ashamed of his lack of control and tried to calm his thoughts.

'I wonder what the angel has to do with this and what was she holding?' Danika asked. 'I feel like I have seen that angel before and that it was filled with love. Did you get that?'

'The angel was familiar I guess, but I didn't get to grasp much more than that before I lost control.' Cristian was obviously still rattled and concerned more than Danika about his change.

'I think I might call Mum later and talk to her about the dream. Not about you changing,' she added to allay his concerns. 'But so we are all still on the same page. She might have an idea about the angel.'

Cristian checked his phone and emails. They had a date for Peter and his family arriving in a week's time so it was easier to make sure all the accommodation was sorted. They would arrive five days before the full moon, giving them time to become acquainted with Lunar Haven and Hollingrove as they planned to stay at least six weeks, possibly longer, to try to find a way to break the curse. Danika was sure it would be longer.

She had not been back to the apartment but Cristian had assured her it was fully renovated and available for Peter's family to stay there as long as they needed and they could enjoy the highlights of Sydney easier. Danika thought she should still go there and make sure all bad vibes were dispelled and suggested they could do that today on their way to the warehouse to view the delivery of Clay's artwork from Adelaide. Danika gathered together what she needed to cleanse the apartment if needed.

It felt strange pulling into the car park at the apartment after so long yet the wonderful memories flooded back to her. She knew it was difficult for Cristian because his last memories were very different and still he would not share them with her. As she entered the lift she felt the first glimpse of evil and started a mild chant with a plan to come back to this after the apartment. At the door Danika felt as if someone had tried to cleanse the area not just with disinfectant. 'Has someone else tried to do a spiritual cleanse here?'

'The Hong family were here besides Dean's crew, they may have done something.'

Danika nodded at how kind they were to try but the evil was still present. Inside the apartment looked completely different. The colours and furniture placement were very different. The curtains were gone, replaced by vertical blinds. It felt sterile to her but she focused on the job at hand. She set up her crystals and candles on her rug on top of the table and chanted as she went from space to space, finding the worst spots and working harder at different points. She moved to their bedroom which, like the lounge, had all new furniture and window coverings. The carpet was gone, replaced with a rug over polished wood boards. Out on the balcony there was no evil but she was not bypassing anywhere. Down the hall to her first room she worked harder again then on to the last room where she reeled from the force as she opened the door. Danika was lucky to have been prepared for the evil or it may have overwhelmed her. She asked Cristian to search the room. He looked under the bed and in the drawers and the last drawer of the tall boy was the location of the message left by one of them. It was the newspaper photo from the gallery launch with 'you will die' written across it.

'Bring it out, I can return the message.' Danika was determined they would not win this threat. She had Cristian place the message in the metal sink and then she chanted a spell as she poured her potion oils over the paper and lit it using her candle. The smoke was black as it burned a green flame. Danika turned on the exhaust fan to remove the smoke and stench as she smiled. She went back to the room to make sure nothing else remained there and informed Cristian all was now well and clear for anyone to stay there.

'You seem particularly pleased with yourself, care to share that?' Cristian asked as she packed up her things to go back down to the car.

'I asked the universe to return the message to the author by their own hand,' Danika explained without elaborating.

At the warehouse they were very pleased at how well everything had travelled and Paul showed them a large crate with the message to Danika and Cristian with love from Clay and Selene. Cristian carefully helped Paul open the crate that was taller than Cristian. Inside, once the packing was removed, stood a white angel similar style to the one in the front yard of Clay's home. This one had the Triquetra medallion in the sculpture and her hands were out in front of her as if to hold something. She was beautiful with features similar to Danika. That is her, Danika thought, sending the thought to Cristian who agreed. They knew without saying that she had to go to Hollingrove to be placed in the gardens. So Cristian helped Paul repack her ready to be transported to Hollingrove. The rest of the delivery was then to be catalogued and planned for a spring release. Danika chose the pieces to be moved to the gallery and those to be kept as replacements and those to be sold online.

Danika was keen to get back to Hollingrove to plan where the angel was to be installed and try to work out what it would be that she would hold. At the gallery Danika was pleased to catch up with Rene in person rather than phone calls and emails of late. Rene had done an excellent job of displaying the silk pieces to compliment the different pieces of Janet Wells and the last of the Walton collection. Items were selling well and a new order was soon to be placed. Clay's work would be another complimentary group to display. Rene explained there had been some interest in historical photographic pieces and wondered if they could follow up some research in that area. Danika was glad Rene and Paul were driving some of the research now as she was pleased to step back for a while until the end of the year.

Cristian was quiet on the drive back. Even his thoughts were masked until Danika could stand the silence no longer. 'Penny for your thoughts.'

'I feel like I can't protect you anymore. I missed that threat and then you just sorted it out with not a care or explanation. This morning…' He paused to concentrate on the traffic as well as gather his thoughts. 'This morning I could have harmed you with no control yet you seem so blasé about it. You are not valuing my concerns it seems.'

'I'm sorry that you feel that way. I feel so safe when you are with me, in any form which I know bothers you. I can't explain why I know he will never harm us. My spell over the threat was to return the message to the author in their own hand. The universe will decide what form that takes. But I am certain whoever wrote it will not be pleased so yes that made me smile. I feel like we are so close. All my questions are starting to be answered, we are getting shown the way we just need to understand the map.' Danika gently placed her hand over his. 'I love you but don't distance yourself because you fear your actions.'

They continued to Hollingrove in silence, each with their own thoughts it seemed rather than shared openly. As Cristian pulled into the garage Danika felt pleased to be back. She just knew this was where all would be answered. Out of the car she walked over to the gardens to view a placement for their beautiful angel trying to visualise what she had felt this morning. She held her hands out in front and tried to call to the universe to show her the way, holding her medallion and a crystal for energy. She felt compelled to stop at the fountain and stood still trying to get her bearings. Cristian came up behind her, touched her shoulder and turned her towards the fountain.

'Remember what we thought of when we were in Tasmania? The stone – that was what the angel was holding,' Cristian said as they looked at the stone his grandfather had brought from the English manor. As they shared thoughts he added, 'I'll get on to Dean to see if he can carefully remove it and replace it with another stone.'

'Of course, I don't know why we didn't deal with that when we got back. Probably because everything had to line up. Now, where to place her.' Cristian, careful to avoid the medallion, hugged Danika from behind and placed his hands on her belly to feel the babies, turning her around until they felt the pull towards the front of the house.

Danika had planned a turnaround at the front of the house and had originally thought that one of Janet Wells' statues would look nice there but now they knew it had to be the angel. Danika walked to the spot and held out her hands as the angel did then felt a flip in her stomach. 'Oh my heavens.'

Cristian put his hands over her belly again and felt the faint stir of their babies. 'They agree it has to be here.'

Elizabeth met them at the foyer as they came in holding hands and smiling.

'More landscaping plans?' Elizabeth asked.

'My mother and her partner have sent us a gift of a large angel and we thought out the front was the perfect placement for it if you agree,' Danika explained.

'Of course whatever you like.'

'We felt the babies kick so we think they agree,' Danika confessed.

'Oh that is wonderful so many things falling into place. You should call your mother, I'm sure she would want to know,' Elizabeth said.

Later after discussing with Ann about extra help Danika was running through her extensive to-do list.

'I feel very responsible for them to have a pleasant time while they are here, I've never had that responsibility before. They live different lives to us, speak a different language.' Danika was getting stressed again and Cristian felt it, making her sit down while he got her a glass of water.

'Okay spill, what is this really about? You are so capable at everything that comes your way and now you are overreacting to everything,' Cristian asked as he handed her the glass of water.

'They will be expecting me – well us – to end the curse. What if we can't? What will they think of me being the bringer of doom. Oh my heavens.' Danika was spiralling into anxiety and that was not good for her or the babies. Cristian hugged her and flooded her mind with thoughts of love, trust and calm until he felt her relaxing. He was encouraging her to take long slow deep breaths and let them out slowly. Although she confirmed she was now in control he did not let her go, instead pulling her onto his lap and, with his hand on her belly, talked to their babies to understand how much they both loved them and that they always would as long as they drew breath.

'So now you know this is about you, me and our children, no one else. As long as we are all okay everything else will follow suit.' Cristian was sending strong thoughts to her and the babies of love and trust. They kicked against his hand. 'They agree.'

'I'm sorry, that just bubbled up and I couldn't stop it. Thank you.' She looked into his eyes and then down at his hand and placed hers over the top. 'And thank you two also.' They sat like that for quite a while, discussing plans for the nursery and even discussing Christmas presents for the staff. Danika wanted to start shopping early in case she was too big to do it later.

The morning of their guests' arrival as expected there were light showers and it seemed that would be the forecast for the week. Danika was glad she had ordered in multiple pairs of rubber boots for here and at Lunar Haven. As they went down to breakfast she could feel the tension in the air, although everyone seemed on the surface to be in good spirits. The plane was not due to arrive until late morning. Peter had confirmed with Cristian they had left as planned the day before. It would be a long trip for them as they had to change their plans at the last minute he said and would explain when they arrived.

After Cristian left to go to the airport Danika felt a little at a loss so she decided to walk the gardens. Everything was dripping from the light misty overnight rain, a brief break in the clouds making it glisten. She walked past the fountain where Dean had quickly and carefully replaced the heritage stone with a white one to match the rest as if it had always been there. Their ancestral stone was waiting to be placed into the hands of the angel at the front of the house but for now it was in their sitting room cupboard with the other artefacts awaiting installation. Danika could feel the hum from them almost like a heartbeat as they were waiting for the right time to be reunited out here in the gardens. She walked over to the rotunda and sat looking out across the gardens and the pool area hoping the weather warmed enough soon for them all to enjoy the pool. She half closed her eyes and meditated to absorb the beauty of the gardens wishing their guests get through customs without problems. After what seemed just a few minutes she felt her phone buzz a message. An hour had passed since Cristian had left and he was confirming their flight was on time and they had landed, now just to get through customs. Peter had confirmed they were all fine and looking forward to stretching their legs.

Danika walked back to the house, passing the pool area to go talk to the chickens before entering the house through the back. She headed to the kitchen to see how Ann was going and yet again found Ben and Mark in there also having an early lunch before the family arrived. The men stood as she came in and Danika waved them back to their seats.

'Don't mind me, just a bit at sixes and sevens waiting for their arrival. The gardens are a picture thanks to you Mark,' Danika complimented him. 'Nice that the rain has eased today for their arrival. I think they are looking to walk around after so long cooped up for their journey.' Ann offered Danika a chai tea and a biscuit encouraging her not to go too long between meals. Danika smiled and thankfully accepted sitting at the table with the others. 'I have to thank you all for your help to get everything ready. I know you just think it is your job but you have definitely gone above and beyond for us, as have your extended family.' She could feel them getting a bit embarrassed at her assessment so she said no more.

'My niece Bethany and her son Jayden will be here after school time to help with the evening buffet meal. We can see if the boys will get on or not,' Ann said as she sat to have an early lunch herself.

'Sounds perfect Ann. I think everyone will feel a bit on edge until we get to know one another.' The babies moved, making her smile and place her hand on them.

She felt Ann and Ben's thoughts about if their guests were aware of their happy news.

'Cristian will be filling them in on our family situation on the way back here. They knew we were married but wanted to wait until they were here in person to tell them.' Danika had voiced this before she realised she was talking as if answering their silent thoughts. Yet they did not look strangely at her at all as if they expected her to know their thoughts. Danika's phone buzzed again. 'Oh they are out of customs and on their way already. That is a happy surprise so should only be an hour now.'

Cristian pulled up at the front of the house rather than in the garage now the rain had eased. Peter was sitting in the front with Cristian while Sonya, Ingrid and Friedrich sat in the back. They were all smiling which was a good sign. Danika was there with Elizabeth to meet them with Ben and Mark on hand to take their bags to the rooms. Cristian was sending Danika lots of thoughts even before he arrived that he had told them about the twins and also shown them a few photos before they left the airport so that her beautiful green eyes would not be a surprise. He had also explained to Friedrich that he had a choice of the nursery or the media room to sleep in. His choice was obvious and excited.

Without hesitation as they came out of the car they greeted and embraced each other. Danika could feel the genuine pleasure and happiness at meeting her. Their accent was strong but not harsh and mean as Robert and Karl's had been and they all spoke excellent English. They were all shown into the downstairs sitting room where drinks and light snacks were waiting for them. The drinks were welcome as it had been a few hours since they last had a chance for one. After they were keen to look around rather than going to their rooms. Ingrid however declined and went with Elizabeth to her rooms instead to put her feet up or watch them through the windows if she wanted. Danika could feel how tired Ingrid was and relieved to be here away from the threats from Robert and his cohorts. Sonya loved the garden and had said that the recent heat wave in Europe had turned much dry and brown although rains were starting again as they had left. Cristian explained that more rain was due this week but they would work around it as best they could.

Friedrich had run ahead and already found the pool. Danika asked Cristian by thoughts if Friedrich was aware of the legacy so he asked Peter now Friedrich was out of earshot.

'Yes, he knows sooner than I would have liked, but with the threats from Robert we had to explain it to him. It broke our hearts when he was shocked when I changed after that. That was six months ago so he has accepted that part of our lives now.' Danika could feel the sorrow from Peter and especially Sonya and passed it on to Cristian who could see it in their eyes anyway.

'The property I showed you in the country is where we thought it would be good to go to on Friday. There is room for you three as well as us. I thought your mother would prefer to stay here with Elizabeth, she seems tired,' Cristian explained as they continued on to the rotunda.

'Do you think Friedrich would be okay to stay in my hippie van while you are there? Or he can camp on the lounge floor? It is a bit smaller than here,' Danika asked as they sat briefly watching Friedrich running around the paths with more energy than any of them had.

'Well he was very happy to be given the option to sleep in a media room so a hippie van will be another first for him.' Sonya laughed. 'May I ask why you have a hippie van?'

'Ah well that is a long story for another day perhaps. Looks like he wants to run further, we can show him the animals and other areas if you want?' Danika said.

'Are you alright walking around?' Sonya asked as the men had walked on towards Friedrich and the pool. 'You seem a little tired.'

'I definitely should walk around more but I think I was a bit excited about your visit and didn't sleep so well last night. The babies have started to get a bit restless also.' Danika was grateful to continue sitting with Sonya.

'Twins are unknown in the family. Cristian told us that it is still a secret from Robert and the others,' Sonya said and Danika could feel her concern.

'Yes, unknown in my family also, so it is monumental and daunting at the same time. Did Cristian tell you anything else about the twins?' Danika could feel straight away he had not so she reached for Sonya's hand and looking into her eyes said, 'We are having a boy and a girl.' Danika felt the shock and fear from Sonya immediately. Sonya gripped her hand harder. 'I know about all the female pregnancies failing, the importance is not lost on us at all. I am only eighteen weeks so far, but in my family we only have girls.' Sonya was nodding and crying. Sonya wiped her eyes as Peter looked back, concerned about her. She smiled at his look to allay his fears.

'The connection with our husbands is amazing isn't it?' Danika asked.

'Yes it is the only good part of this horror that we live through,' Sonya confirmed.

'I am not sure how much Cristian has told Peter about our connection. It is a little different I believe than anyone else.' Danika felt safe talking to Sonya having felt her truth as she held her hand before. 'My family are only women and we are a long lineage of witches.' Danika sat watching for Sonya's reaction which was a mixture of surprise and now understanding at the hope to end the curse. 'If we can end the curse of which my family suffers also in a different way, the mental and emotional connections may be broken. It has only been my experience for these few months and I would miss it.'

'I have spoken with several of the family who have lost their partner and the loss of connection has sometimes broken them. This would be different though because they will still be there physically. It would still be worth it if the curse is broken.'

'That is what we believe also. It is so good to talk to you about this.

Cristian says they are over at the stables now and Friedrich has seen the gator,' Danika said without thinking.

'That is quite a connection,' said Sonya. 'What is a gator?' They heard the motor of the vehicle as it started up.

'It is an all-terrain vehicle that they use around the estate over the rough ground, a boy's toy,' Danika explained. She pointed to where they could see a glimpse of it with Cristian, Friedrich and Peter all wearing helmets as they cruised over to the other end of the estate. 'Perhaps we can just go back inside. I can show you to your rooms.'

Danika showed Sonya inside again and started up the stairs with Sonya stopping to look at the family photo wall Danika had installed on the stairwell. Danika decided to show Sonya where Friedrich was going to stay before showing her the other rooms. Sonya smiled and confirmed he would be much happier there but probably consumed by gaming. They continued on to the balcony and sitting room which Danika said they were very welcome to use anytime. Briefly she then showed Sonya her and Cristian's bedroom and the nursery still to be completed. Further on to the rooms for Sonya and Peter. Danika explained that Ingrid would be staying downstairs next to Elizabeth. Sonya agreed that it was an excellent idea as both women had lost their husbands. Though Ingrid was older than Elizabeth, they had lost their husbands at a similar time by accident, Ingrid's husband having fallen from a cliff while running with Robert. Sonya explained that the truth of the accident had never been fully discovered. Danika had not known that and was horrified.

'Peter and I only talk about Robert when we are certain we are alone. It is not fair for Friedrich to worry or have the responsibility of keeping secrets. Karl is worse than Robert and their mysterious sorcerer is strange and dangerous. We only have limited knowledge of him based on the little a like-minded family member has passed on to us at great risk.' Sonya was now sitting on the bed wringing her hands. 'Peter will probably tell Cristian later but we believe he is dabbling in black magic, perhaps searching for a way to keep the legacy from being stopped or damaged. It may have gone wrong because last week our friend told us all hell was breaking loose at the castle because Karl kept writing on photos and personal papers the words 'you will die' and yelling that he couldn't stop it for a few days like it was a curse or spell on him.' Danika was smiling broadly at the image.

'Was that you?' Sonya asked as she saw Danika smiling.

'No it was all him, I just asked the universe to send his own message back to him. I didn't know who it was,' Danika explained. She could feel that Cristian had returned to the stables and they were going to come back in to clean up as they were quite dirty. Danika reminded him to use the back stairs. 'They are on their way back, dirty and full of testosterone I think.'

The three boys came noisily upstairs and were indeed very muddy and dirty but happy. Sonya made sure Friedrich was sorted out, leaving Peter to sort his own clothes. Danika followed Cristian into their rooms.

'I'll have to show Friedrich the electronics shortly then he should be fine during his stay. He is a good kid, very polite and follows directions well. Peter was pleased to see him more at ease. I think they have all had a very hard time of late,' Cristian explained as he stripped off and got in the shower.

'Yes Sonya I think wants to talk more about what they have experienced and that they are just glad to be away from it. She said something very interesting about my little message to the universe, remember at the apartment? Apparently it must have been Karl that wrote the note and he was writing those words out all over things for days until obviously the universe was satisfied.' Danika was laughing by this time. 'Probably not funny for those having to put up with his nasty temper though.'

'Wow darling that is some return message.'

'Thank you but I really believe the universe is behind a lot of this. This curse, if I am right, is two hundred years past its use by date.'

'Peter wants to talk to us after dinner once Friedrich is otherwise occupied about the artefacts he was able to bring,' Cristian explained.

'Of course, I think Jayden will be here shortly with his mother so you could show them both the electronics, or maybe they will show you.' Danika guessed the teenagers probably had a better idea of how it all worked than the adults.

With eight of them sitting down to the buffet dinner it was a noisy and happy time. Ann certainly did them proud with the huge range of foods for every taste. Friedrich and Jayden hit it off immediately, eating quickly to be able to go set up the games upstairs. Ingrid and Elizabeth had been talking most of the afternoon with both now appearing to be getting tired. Although Peter and Sonya were also tired they were trying to stay awake as long as possible to get their bodies in tune with the southern hemisphere daytime. The older ladies said their goodnights and the teenagers raced upstairs. Cristian suggested Peter and Sonya join them in the upstairs sitting room where they could keep an ear out for the boys but still discuss their own affairs.

Peter went to his room first to bring the artefacts to the sitting room for them to see. Danika wisely gathered some protection for herself just in case. Cristian cleared a small table between the chairs near the open fire for Peter to lay out the linen wrapped pieces. Danika could feel the malevolent force immediately and so could Cristian through her. He moved to pull her back but she gave him a sign she could cope as she chanted while holding her medallion and crystals, standing away from them.

'I don't want to remove the force until we know it is not needed,' she explained to the others who could clearly see the effect it was having on her.

Peter unrolled the one linen to show the manuscript he had sent photos of. The other was a small bag with the twin to the medallion in it. It was easy for Cristian to touch as it was from his family but Danika's stomach reeled so Cristian had to close off his thoughts and emotions to her for now. He brought it over to their desk in the corner so he could clearly light it and took many photos before carefully rolling the fragile manuscript back up for Peter to remove from the room with the horse bronze also.

Danika excused herself briefly to gather her calm again and returned shortly after Peter. Cristian showed them all the zoomed in photos on his larger screened notebook. That Danika could deal with. He opened up his thoughts and emotions again as he touched Danika and kissed her lightly on the head, checking she was alright now.

'Sorry about that. To explain there was a malevolent force emanating from the pieces and so I had to protect myself. It is aimed at me and my family. It is very old as you are well aware of but it is the original thought so to speak. The one from the beginning of the curse. So it is essential we understand it rather than me just trying to neutralise its power. I'll be glad when my mother can be here also to help.' Danika thought they should understand what she had experienced.

'I've tried to read it before but it seems to be of more than one language,' Peter explained. 'There is some repetition so perhaps it was the original curse.'

Danika looked closely at the zoomed photos. 'I think some of it is Romany. It is unlikely the author – your ancestor – spoke Romany so it must be a memory he has written, filled in with English. Or maybe the curse had both anyway. Lots of maybes. We need to write this out.'

Cristian was already on to that. 'Do you read or speak Romany?' Sonya asked Danika.

'No unfortunately, but strangely if I hear it in my dreams I know what it means,' Danika answered.

'Does that mean you are related to Gypsies?' Sonya was not being rude, just curious.

'Probably, but our family history is a mystery past two hundred years ago when my ancestor was transported here on a prison ship.' Danika looked at Cristian to get his approval to explain her theory on Jessica.

'My ancestor Jessica I think imprinted with your ancestor Cristian two hundred years ago but because of her fear and the actions of Cristian's father they were separated and she was shipped to Australia. She and he were meant to break the curse back then. Well that is our theory so far anyway.' Danika could feel the emotions from each of them, the shock and deep sorrow but not anger.

'We can't control our past only our future,' Sonya said as she held Peter's hand.

'This is a lot to take in. You have found more than we could have hoped for,' Peter expressed. Danika could feel how grateful he was to be here.

'There is more that we have discovered. Perhaps a drink is in order first though,' Cristian suggested and made Peter and Sonya drinks as he was sharing thoughts with Danika to tell them everything they knew. He poured Danika a soda water also. They were sitting now on the two couches, each couple together with the wood fire seeping warmth out to them. In the background they could hear the boys playing a game and whooping or shouting their wins and losses.

'We took a short holiday to Tasmania which is south of the mainland and was the place where the convict ship my ancestor was on landed. She made a life there, hard and dangerous with her daughter and then granddaughter. We found a piece from the beginning of the story there – a rune. My family symbol is the Triquetra.' At this point she could feel Peter's thoughts that he had seen that symbol. 'It appears on my medallion.' She held it up for them to see and Peter leaned forward to look at it. 'And on some other pieces. You won't be able to touch it Peter I suspect.'

'I have been burned more than once by them,' Cristian confirmed as Peter sat back.

'How did you find it?' Peter asked.

'I get visions, sometimes as dreams, other times while connected to certain objects. The visions guide me to the next piece in the puzzle so to speak or give me warnings at times,' Danika elaborated. 'My mother Selene and I believe we need three pieces at least from the original time to create a strong enough link to attempt to break the curse.'

'Do you have three pieces?' Peter asked the big question as he held Sonya's hand.

'Yes.' Danika could feel their emotions moving from hope to relief and Sonya was tearing up as Peter squeezed her hand. 'But we still have to work out exactly what the curse was to be able to negate it. That manuscript you brought us and the twin to my medallion we think are imperative. So a very big thanks to you both.' She sensed it was a dangerous action.

'We were lucky to have had the opportunity and help to get them at great cost and risk to other family members.' Peter's emotions showed some horror.

'There are more family that want an end to this than don't want it. There is much fear in the family that they will not be able to hide much longer. There are few opportunities to purchase safe acreage where family can still conduct business and enjoy a family. The war in Ukraine and previous refugee movements has created some very dangerous and also personally horrific situations that I will not elaborate on.' Peter and Sonya's emotions ranged from horror to terror at the memories which Danika briefly shared with Cristian as Peter may want to speak to Cristian about it. 'We don't want that experience for Friedrich or any other children so whatever you need from us we will do.'

'Well for now perhaps we should check on those boys before it gets too late to calm them down from their gaming. I feel like we might be able to rest for this time zone now,' Sonya expressed but Danika could feel she was actually very keyed up from the information they had heard so far.

'Of course I can help with that,' Danika explained and winked at Sonya. They walked over to the media room where the two boys were still laughing and jumping around as they played. Friedrich spotted his mother and lowered his gaming control. Jayden did the same.

'It is getting late boys, perhaps you can resume this another time,' Danika said as Bethany came up the stairs to collect Jayden. She was pleased that neither of them argued.

The boys shook hands and Danika could feel they both wanted to play again as soon as they were allowed. Danika thanked Bethany and said her farewell to them both as they went downstairs to leave. Sonya and Danika helped Friedrich tidy the space and fold out the bed from the couch, spreading the blankets and quilt for him to sleep on. Danika then left Sonya to help him sort out his preparations for bed returning to the sitting room slowly, warning Cristian she was returning in case they were talking privately.

'We have written out what we could from the manuscript. Some of the letters, not just the words, are foreign to us and need a bit more research,' Cristian explained and sent her a thought that he would fill her in on more in private.

'Oh good something to look into tomorrow or later. I'm fairly tired and you and Sonya must be by now also,' Danika directed to Peter.

'Yes and no, lots on our minds now of course but I'll set an alarm so we rise in the early morning to try to adjust our body clocks. Cristian and I are going to run the estate,' Peter confirmed.

'That's fine, I'll just sleep in till you are back,' Danika said, smiling without really meaning it.

'The boys were so good, no problem getting them to stop gaming. It would be good if they could get together again.' Danika was sending thoughts of Friday and the weekend to Cristian for the boys to stay at Hollingrove rather than Friedrich coming to Lunar Haven.

Danika was reading the notes the men had written as Sonya came back in looking exhausted, not just from the trip and time zone change but also the extra emotions tonight. Peter and Sonya retreated together for the night. Danika suspected they needed to comfort each other after tonight.

Danika sent thoughts to Cristian that she needed to recoup on the balcony if possible as she felt drained. Out on the balcony it was damp but the rain had eased and a slight break in the clouds was showing a few stars and the waxing moon. Standing in the dark she pulled in the power from celestial bodies. She could feel the babies moving and started to hum a little tune as she continued to draw energy. They seemed to settle then she felt the hands of Cristian on the babies as he stood behind her. She leaned into him as his thoughts encouraged her to continue. They stood for a few minutes more, Danika's arms outstretched slightly glowing with Cristian behind her loosely holding her with his hands across their babies. It helped as she was so tired she almost had given up the drawing of energy until Cristian had come to support her. Now she felt fully recharged and slowly turned in his arms to kiss him and then they were both smiling as their kisses were interrupted by several well-placed kicks.

They went in to go to bed Danika asked if Peter had revealed any of the problems they had at home but Cristian said that was not something he wanted to share just now and kept those thoughts tightly closed off. Danika was careful to take off her medallion before bed but placed several crystals either side of them and tried to cast a spell of dreamless sleep over them both.

Danika sleepily realised her efforts the previous night must have worked as she woke alone and rested, sensing that Cristian was running with Peter around the estate. She could feel that Sonya was awake but that was all. Danika stretched like a sleepy cat and briefly thought about staying in bed until the babies' well-placed kicks had her rushing to the bathroom. Danika was showering and getting ready for the day as Cristian came in, hot and sweaty from his run, his clothes with muddy marks also as it was still damp and misty with fine weather not due until the weekend.

By the time breakfast was over everyone had been consulted and agreed to the plans for Friedrich to stay at Hollingrove with Jayden visiting for the weekend. When Danika was in the kitchen speaking to Bethany, Ben had mentioned that the boys may enjoy the pool on the Saturday despite being cool the water was mild under the blanket. All seemed to be coming together nicely, their family all seemed much more at ease and refreshed after their long journey. Ingrid and Elizabeth were getting along like long lost sisters and the strain Danika had felt in Ingrid had eased considerably.

The next few days were very easy indeed. Cristian and Peter ran the estate no matter the weather in the mornings. They saw some of Sydney and agreed better weather was needed to enjoy it fully. Danika and Sonya got to know one another a lot better and talked in private about their personal experiences with living with a werewolf including unplanned changes. Sonya explained that, by choice, Robert and Karl had closed off their link with their spouses, rarely spending time with them. Their spouses were stuck in an ugly unloving life with them but stayed to try to protect the rest of the family with their knowledge and observations. Danika could not imagine how dangerous and awful their lives must be.

'Do you know anything about the supposed sorcerer hanging around them?' Danika asked.

'Not a lot. Even Margrit, Robert's wife, wasn't sure of his real name, perhaps Claus but he likes people to address him as Merlin. He is quite delusional and very dangerous because he has some magic skills and Robert and Karl seem to like him. Although he couldn't stop Karl writing on all his personal items that little message you sent. When it stopped of course he claimed he had. We think he wants to be a werewolf and thinks that with his magic and Robert's help he can be. Robert has been lying to him to get what he wants. Of course Robert could change him but he would die,' Sonya explained. Danika could feel the disgust from her. 'There are only very old stories thought to be just to scare new legacy boys that if a person is bitten by one of them while they are a werewolf that they change also. But it is actually a fatal disease to others, like rabies. Merlin seems to think he can survive it.'

'I don't know if he could but he has been using dark magic, very powerful and dangerous. There is a price to pay for any magic. It is so important to know and understand that and be prepared.' Danika was trying to judge Sonya's reaction to her knowing of his actions.

'What price do you pay if you use magic?'

'I'm not sure if this makes sense but I sort of pay it forward to the universe. It seems very mystical but I try to live by helping appropriately whenever I can and then when I need help it is available to me. Sometimes though it does take all my energy and I have to draw from the universe again. Cristian gets worried then.' Danika tried to send a few thoughts to Sonya for her to understand also as they had been getting along so well. 'I don't use negative power; I protect myself and others and use positive power. Negative or dark magic will have that return result in my opinion anyway.'

'You were meant to find each other I am sure. When Robert and Karl came back from their visit here they were nastier and more brutal more than usual. Even Merlin apparently was a little scared of them. Do you think they suspect you and Cristian can break the curse?'

'Robert definitely tried to plant a false artefact with dark magic some time ago. To no effect, I might add. When they saw me it definitely rattled them. When we all stood up to them they reacted badly and were basically ordered to leave Australia by Cristian or be arrested. That is the short version of events so yes I think they are getting prepared in some way.'

The evening had been spent trying to decipher the manuscript which they had sent to Selene who was also following up the translation. Selene had agreed that the blood moon was the most powerful time to break the curse and confirmed that she had made arrangements to visit then to be there to support Danika with the magic, now only nine weeks away. They were still struggling with the Romany words as they were not just another language but very old also. Modern Romany like modern English had changed a lot.

In the morning they didn't take long to pack the large vehicle on loan from Dean that sat out the front and say their goodbyes. Mark was standing next to Friedrich talking to him and Danika knew he would be well entertained over the weekend. She could feel that Sonya and Peter were still a little concerned leaving Friedrich in a strange country after only a few days. She tried to share her love to them to allay their fears.

'You are very kind. We are fine, conserve your energy,' Sonya said, clearly more intuitive to Danika's attempt to help.

The road trip together was enjoyed immensely. Sonya and Peter commented how the layout of housing, roads and the forests were so different to Europe. Even the buildings that for Australia were old looked new to them. They commented that was a stark difference to the ancient roads and buildings they were used to. The roads are so much wider, the yards prolific, unlike inner cities and suburbs near them that basically did not have gardens and the green spaces were to share. Sonya explained that of course they lived on or near large acreage for obvious reasons but they tended to be flanked by heavily occupied or inaccessible areas.

'Yes, we are lucky to have literally wide-open spaces but it is mostly pasturing large grazing lands, not much other industry or work. I guess it is all relative to your needs. These areas have plenty of people in them, not as densely populated but not suitable to your particular situation. Lunar Haven was a unique opportunity that I believe the universe showed me. I hope you both enjoy it.'

After an hour Cristian turned off the highway on to the more winding and waterlogged areas. He was glad of the large vehicle where there were signs of water across the roads and more potholes than last time. It was a couple of months since Danika had come this way and she could see more of the water damage. Danika sent a thought that she needed a comfort stop at the next town. Despite the rain he was able to find a park close to her needs and the others decided to walk around as well.

They were all in good spirits as they continued to Lunar Haven with an overflowing bag of snacks, drinks and souvenirs. Pulling up to the gate, Peter jumped out to unlock the padlock, opening the gate so Cristian could drive through. He waited for Peter to close the gate again and get back in the car. Low cloud hid the mountain ridge as Cristian turned off the security and opened the door. They decided to put everything on the verandah first so they could take off their shoes which were wet before going inside. Danika turned on the central heating until they could sort out the wood fire. Then she went from room to room opening up the curtains and blinds with Sonya's help while the guys brought in the bags.

'This is a lovely holiday home. So cosy,' Sonya remarked.

'Yes it is. It used to be someone's home but the water and power was very minimal. They lived very frugally. We are probably a bit soft needing all these modern conveniences. I'll tell you some of our first encounters another time.' Danika had turned on the fridge and was starting to load food into it from Ann's hamper.

Peter and Cristian came in just as Danika was deciding what they could have for lunch and was told they were going to do a drive around so Peter could get his bearings. She knew tomorrow they wouldn't want to eat big so it was best to make sure they had plenty today and tonight. She was just about to open the esky when Cristian stopped her and gave her a thought of don't look at its contents. 'Leave that one love, we will deal with it when we are back.'

'I might wait till tomorrow when the rain stops to look around,' Danika said. 'But you should go with them Sonya I bet the waterfall is raging with all this rain.' She sensed Sonya was keen and made sure she had her phone with her to take pictures. They loaded up with wellington boots and rain jackets and left to look around the property and Danika was glad to be able to check that no spiders or such had come into the house. She made sure their bed was made and that Sonya had fresh linen to make up their bed and plenty of towels before she contemplated the fireplace. Cristian must have still been within range and sent her a wait till I'm back order which made her smile that he was still checking on her.

'The waterfall was raging well when we got there,' Cristian said as he came back inside after having shown Peter and Sonya around the property. 'Some of the rocks had come down which we may have to deal with once the wet weather moves on.' Cristian showed her the pictures he had taken. 'The roos were fairly calm as we went past, but if you feel like walking over there tomorrow I think Sonya would like some close ups.'

'Well the weather is meant to be better tomorrow so I would love to walk over there.' Danika smiled.

The esky in the corner of the room intrigued both Danika and Sonya so Danika sent a question to Cristian. He pointed at the esky for all their attention. 'Tomorrow night's hunt I hope and not the roos.' Danika hoped so also but knew they would have no control after the change. She didn't ask what was in the esky. Danika felt Peter and Sonya's concerned emotions regarding possibly hunting the wild kangaroos and passed it on to Cristian.

'How long has it been since you were able to run free?' Cristian asked Peter.

'Nearly a year.' He looked at his wife who was holding his hand. 'It has been a difficult time.' Danika sensed this was the horror they had hidden.

'How did you cope with the change?' Danika remembered the cell that Cristian had to stay in and wondered if they had something similar.

'Cristian has told me of the cell you have below Hollingrove. Unfortunately that was not a feature of our home so I had to install chains.' Peter was not prepared to say more but he didn't have to, the concept was clear to both Cristian and Danika.

'It was something that Robert and Karl held over me, the

permission to run at their estate, so I decided as horrible as my situation is, it was better than being beholden to them. The other options are too far away to go there every month,' Peter explained. 'We were hoping to find another living option but world events over the last two years interfered with that. That just made Robert and Karl even more powerful in their opinion.'

'How did you get the artefacts out of his clutches?' Danika was amazed if they were so intimidating and powerful.

'A few months ago during the full moon our inside informant was able to get to the safe while Merlin was distracted and replace them with replicas. They have a lot of security in the castle as they know most of the extended family is not happy with them so that had to be disconnected. As well as that damn sorcerer needed to be out of the picture for long enough to do all of this without suspecting who it was. It took a long time to set up and three people to be able to complete the plan.' Peter was clearly grateful for the risks taken. Danika and Cristian wondered if he was going to say who they were.

'Our saviours were putting their lives and others at risk of punishment or death. So far they are still unknown to Robert and Karl.' Peter took a breath and with Sonya's agreement he continued, 'They are Robert and Karl's wives and one of the maids.'

Cristian and Danika were shocked.

'How did they hide their thoughts and actions?' Cristian asked what Danika would have.

'Robert and Karl had both cut the connection with their wives some years ago but warned them if they wanted to leave it would be alone and in poverty with death as their other option. They have been our inside informants ever since at great risk. The maid was a real surprise though. She is from a Gypsy family that have had a minor connection with the family for decades perhaps longer. She seems like just a quiet worker but she knows everything and remembers everything. She has helped with our knowledge of the sorcerer. He has a sickening attraction to her which she used to distract him when needed.' Danika felt Peter's horror at what she was forced to do for them to be able to get the artefacts. 'Now it is our responsibility to get this finally over with for us all.'

Danika felt an enormous weight of responsibility for her role in this. Before today she was doing it for themselves and their future families without realising the large group of others that were relying on her actions. Cristian felt her thoughts.

'It is not just you doing this darling. We are all involved, you do not carry this burden alone.' Cristian was clear to show her they all carried the weight of these actions. He held her hand and could feel she still needed to rest. He made a suggestion that she lay down now so that she could enjoy the evening. She reluctantly agreed.

'I might go lay down for a while so I can focus clearer later,' Danika explained as she stood and was about to clear dishes until Sonya stopped her.

In her room Danika set an alarm on her phone in case she slept longer than she wanted. Pulling the cover over she briefly heard Sonya moving dishes before she went into a deep sleep.

She felt and heard the chanting and, although dreaming, it was as if her subconscious was watching. She knew this dream and yet it was different. It wasn't the chanting of their friends with Cristian standing with her, it was more distant and her own voice was loud but the others were not as clear and a roaring breaking noise seemed over the top. She was trying to memorise the chant as she was saying it at the same time as if she were two people. As the other voice got quieter she yelled louder, repeating the words as she held the medallion. From her hiding place she could see him standing at the window watching as her family was burning to death. Their voices stopped and she screamed the last of the curse as she absorbed and blasted out the last of their voices and souls across the murderers and the coward standing at the window, smashing the glass into him.

Cristian was holding her as she wept and clung to him. Between her sobs she said, 'It was Bronwyn, I could hear her.' She looked up to see Peter and Sonya quite shaken watching her. Sonya held her camera up and now turned it off.

'We heard you yelling and I suggested we film you rather than wake you because I knew it would be important to us all. You were talking Romany in a strong accent. Until you screamed.' Cristian was kissing her head and her hands. 'I'm sorry if I was wrong.'

'No you all did the right thing.' Danika's voice was croaky and Peter quickly brought her a drink.

'Did you understand what you were saying?' Cristian asked. 'Because most of it was in a different language with a strong accent.'

'I understood it as I was saying it. Give me paper and pen and I'll try to write what I remember.' Peter handed her his travel journal and pen as she sat up in bed. On the back page she jotted down what she could remember. 'So much for a peaceful sleep.'

'You have been asleep for a couple of hours, this only started a short time ago.' Cristian filled her in.

'Are you alright now?' Sonya was very worried about Danika and the toll this would take on her and the babies. Danika could feel her concerns.

'Yes, I will be fine. This is getting to be a regular experience. I am keen to watch what you filmed once I have more drink and make myself more comfortable.' Danika swung her legs off the bed and Cristian made sure she was stable as she stood up.

After tidying herself up and washing her face in the bathroom she made her way to the lounge where the fire glowed welcomingly with the other three waiting for her. Sonya handed Danika her phone so she could watch the video first. Danika watched herself and yet she looked and sounded like someone else. She realised she experienced more than what Sonya was able to capture which seemed to be just the last few minutes – the point at which her family died and Bronwyn screamed her grief and anger at the murderers and the coward whoever he was. She watched it again and jotted down a few more words and notes from her observations not just what she had said.

Then she handed the phone to Cristian to watch. He found it difficult to watch her writhing in grief and instead decided to only listen, not watch, and was able to pick up a few more words. He added them to the notes. Then he handed the phone to Peter to do the same so they each could write what they thought they heard and deciphered.

Danika lifted her legs up on to the couch and leaned against Cristian as she watched Peter and Sonya dissecting what they saw and heard.

'Now we have all written what we think we heard and saw I will tell you what I experienced. I was crouching down in a hiding, sort of way. Away from my family who I am sure were in a house that was being burned. They were all chanting the curse I believe. It was so many voices saying the same yet different as they built the curse up. I looked up and saw a man standing at a tall window in a castle like house, watching and doing nothing. There were others I could not see that were the ones burning the house my family was in. Once they could no longer chant because they were either dead or overcome by the fire, I drew in their last breaths and heartbeats and screamed them back at the murderers as a force of their souls, up to the man standing at the window. I cursed him also, the force smashing the windows.' Danika had recited her memories as she held out her hands and stared straight ahead, not looking at anything or anybody. Then she focused and Peter and Sonya were staring at her enthralled. 'I'm sure the girl I was channelling was Bronwyn. I don't know who the man was, but obviously a Blakesley.' Danika was feeling very accomplished knowing this was another missing piece of the puzzle found.

The other three sat still looking at her, Cristian sending love and pride, Peter and Sonya still partly in shock from what they had seen and the speed of finding the information needed.

'I can see that this is a lot for you both to absorb but there is more a small piece we did not tell you.' Danika shared her thoughts and Cristian agreed it was important to tell them. 'We had a DNA test of each of our families to make sure the pregnancy would continue alright with the history of miscarriages. Our families are related at some very distant time. We suspect Bronwyn and that Blakesley ancestor maybe four hundred years ago.'

'Are the babies alright though?' Sonya asked. Danika was so humbled that Sonya was more concerned for her babies than the curse. Danika sent loving thoughts to her.

'Yes, they are growing as expected at this point. Thank you for thinking of them.' Danika smiled encouragement at them both.

'You keep surprising us with your findings and experience and strength as a witch. Is it okay to call you a witch? I don't mean to offend,' Peter asked.

'It is not a term bandied about that is for sure. I'm not offended, I just have not heard it said by others. Thank you for your compliment by the way. Sometimes I wonder if I and my mother will be strong enough. When the curse was spun there were several – I don't know how many, but there were at least three – women besides Bronwyn that I heard in my vision and perhaps two men. Two hundred years ago Jessica may not have been able to break the curse anyway as there was only her I believe, but she carried the guilt.'

'What do you think you need to have and do to break the curse?' Peter asked, resolute to help in any way as he held Sonya's hand. 'And what can we do to help?'

'We must decipher the manuscript. Strange that a Blakesley wrote it out, I suspect the first one. Perhaps it was so ingrained he had to write it out, perhaps he even thought he could break it. We shall never know. But lucky that he did otherwise we are relying on my visions. We now have the rune and medallion from Bronwyn and the twin to the medallion and the third piece is a stone from the original Hollingrove manor in England. It is engraved by a PC – which is one of the Carling men I believe – with the Triquetra symbol,' Danika surmised.

'Now that we have the things we need the words and the place and time and the people,' Cristian added.

'Do you have any theories about the time and place and what people?' Sonya asked.

'My other visions have been of an angel and at first we thought a spear. But it seems it may be a spear of light that goes through Cristian and me while we are in front of an angel.' Danika was trying to remember the details without the fear.

'The angel we have. Danika believes it will be at Hollingrove here in Australia at the time of the blood moon eclipse in November. The people we both feel are all those that are important to us. So family and friends, as many as possible it seems,' Cristian said as he gave her encouragement.

'Correct me if I'm wrong, you mean we are going to be on full view through the change to everyone and you are going to participate in this ritual while you are changed?' Peter sounded worried at their plan.

'It seems so. Although none of the visions have been of Cristian in that form so perhaps the eclipse changes that whole process. It is a guess guided by the universe.' Danika sighed.

'You know as much as us now. Apart from bringing two of the most important aspects of this it is really good to share all this openly with someone else, with you specifically. So thank you.' Cristian was very genuine.

'Well that may change once we change tomorrow and run together for the first time, you know that don't you?' Peter was only half joking which had Danika looking worried as she could feel Cristian's trepidation. 'Have you run with a stranger before?'

'You're not a stranger Peter, but no, I have only run with father and that was a long time ago.' Cristian was trying to allay Danika's concerns but she could feel it from Sonya too.

'Is it likely to be an issue?' Danika asked, trying to be supportive. 'Because I can calm you both down if you have trouble getting acquainted during the change.'

'I have run with several of the family of different ages over the last twenty-five years and occasionally it does not go well to the point of fighting which is very dangerous.' Peter looked at Danika. 'Usually because the others were cocky or ruthless in the human form if you get my meaning. What do you mean you could calm us down?'

'Let's say that animals respond well to my suggestions. I can ramp that up a lot more if needed.' Danika was a little cryptic.

Cristian was nodding and added, 'Yes she can.'

Peter rose and put more wood on the fire and stoked it up, needing to think on what he had heard. Sonya also seemed to need to think and went to the kitchen and could be heard putting something in the oven before coming back with glasses and a bottle of wine and a soft drink for Danika.

Sonya poured three glasses of wine for them each and the soft drink for Danika. 'To be honest, it has been a lot to take in. I'm not sure what we expected when we came here. Something to change our lives hopefully, but this is monumental and you are both so brave and clever to have worked all this out.' Peter came over and put his arm around Sonya as he took the glass of wine she offered.

'I was a hippie moving from one simple job to another as I travelled in my camper van five months ago. Now I am married to a werewolf, going to be a mother of twins running a successful art business and apparently going to break a four-hundred-year-old curse. Not much surprises me these days.' Danika lifted her glass and cheered them. They laughed at that.

After dinner, Danika said she was going to try to build up her strength from the waxing moon now that it was getting dark that the view was amazing from the verandah.

As Danika set out her rug and candles the faintest glow was on the horizon, the sky covered in broken cloud patches. She had her crystals and runes also and wore her medallion. She started with a warming spell so she could stay there longer and sensed Sonya was curious so sent a thought to Cristian to invite them to watch if they wanted.

They all sat watching and listening as Danika thanked the universe for the help and gifts she had received. Then, with respect, she asked for help to decipher and build the remedy to the curse. When some of her chanting turned to Romany, Cristian recorded her. The moons glow lessened as the clouds became thicker and Danika wound down her chant.

Everyone felt as if they had been holding their breath. Danika had shared the warmth as best she could but now having let it end the full effect of the cold hit them. Cristian tentatively sent her a thought which she answered with a request to help her get up. She blew out the candles and Cristian helped her get up and gather all her things into the rug. They were all keen to get back into the warmth of the house.

'Thank you for letting us share that very private and personal part of your life,' Sonya said to Danika. 'We feel very privileged. You were glowing, is that usual?'

'I don't know that I do. You three are the only ones besides my grandmother many years ago when she was teaching me that have ever seen my spiritual connection,' Danika admitted.

'I wondered if it was only me that saw that until now,' Cristian explained.

'Well I can confirm I'm not selling tickets,' Danika said as she stood at the fire warming up, feeling a little embarrassed at their scrutiny and admiration.

'Did you know you were talking Romany towards the end? I recorded it,' Cristian asked.

'Yes, some were the words I had learned and some were new that I was given from the universe to understand. A bit like a dictionary,' Danika explained. 'After all, I did ask for help. So I need to write a few more notes.' Danika picked up the journal she had written in before and added a few more notes.

'Something else happened out there, the guys starting a partial change,' Sonya informed her. Peter and Cristian seemed a bit uncomfortable with her sharing that. 'Well she needs to know, it may be important. I think it felt different to other times.'

'Thank you Sonya, yes I do need to know. Different in what way? You have experienced this more than me.' Danika directed her question to Sonya. Sonya glanced to Peter before continuing.

'Peter has partially changed by accident and choice in the past. But it was very much a part of the wolf as a whole. Tonight it was more like still human but with more hair,' Sonya explained. 'When I have felt it before, the sense of being human reduces or ends completely at full change. But tonight they stayed human except for the hair. I don't know if that is significant.'

'Have you been with Peter with no barriers when he changed completely?' Danika asked.

'Yes several times. Being there helps calm him. I have never felt frightened,' Sonya confirmed.

'How did it feel for you guys?' Danika asked, hoping they would be honest and open.

'Unexpected for a start. Not as painful as usual of the hairs sprouting as if we were being shown something,' Cristian explained and Peter nodded. 'Was it your spiritual connection or the moon do you think?'

'Perhaps both. Do you think it is safe for us to be with you when you change tomorrow night?' Danika was keen to try it out. All three at the same time answered her.

'No.' The answer surprised her and deflated her plan.

Peter continued, 'Any connection spouses have is just for them. Some push the boundaries of safety because they have complete faith in their husbands but honestly the wolf has no real honour or respect for others.'

Cristian was going to send by thought but decided to say out loud, 'I have said this to you more than once. Now that you have heard it from another, will you listen to me?'

'I think you have pointed something out Peter. No honour

or respect, that was part of the curse – as in the reason for it. The Blakesley symbol of the wolf and moon, the Lleuad Blaidd, it all makes sense really.' Danika felt as if it was becoming clearer. Cristian handed her the phone to view what he had recorded. She was indeed glowing and it seemed strange to see it for herself. It was only a few seconds but enough to realise it was very fundamental Romany. 'When we get back I think I would like a white board to write out all the bits and help work out how to link them together. That way everyone can help also.'

They all thought that was a sensible idea. Cristian decided he would call early tomorrow to have one delivered there for when they get back.

Danika decided to call it an early night as she wanted to jot down more ideas and notes. Sonya agreed, both seeming to sense that the guys were keen to build a strong link so that tomorrow's full moon would not see them fighting. She did send a thought that she would like Cristian's comfort before she went to sleep tonight.

Danika looked at the notes she had written and was starting to build a mind map of all the things she could remember. She looked at the print outs of the manuscript. There appeared to be a small gap, perhaps they forgot to print one of the photos. There was plenty here to work with anyway. It was nearly midnight so she sent a thought to Cristian to see if he still wanted to stay up with Peter because she wanted to go to sleep. He said they had just finished a drink and he would make the fire safe and be in there with her. She was glad as she needed to feel the warmth and strength of him beside her as he would be out all tomorrow night with Peter.

The morning was sunny although cold and damp from the previous rain. Danika could feel the warmth of Cristian still wrapped around her. She would have stayed like that but needed to move with the pressure of the babies movements.

'They already won't let me sleep in,' she commented with love.

They all pitched in with juggling the bathroom needs and getting breakfast ready. The guys, as expected, didn't want much more than cereal and coffee, leaving the women to enjoy warm croissants with their tea. Everyone thankfully had slept well. After, they all donned boots and walked around the grounds, starting with the waterfall and ridge area in case Danika didn't want to go much further. The roo's stood up out of the scrub as they approached. Danika pointed to the mother and joey for Sonya to take photos and then talked to them as she went, getting Sonya to walk behind her. Danika kept her hands low and asked them if they could stay there and let them take a photo. They got within a few metres so Sonya took several wonderful photos. Danika thanked them and then let them move slowly away.

The guys had been looking at the fallen rocks and where they had come from, thinking getting up on the ridge would be too dangerous at present. They moved on to the forested area. Cristian pointed out the animal tracks leading into the scrub. They went a little way in but it became too thick to continue for their size, indicating it was lower smaller animals getting through.

After their walk, Peter and Cristian collected the esky to take it over to a rocky area near the forest clearing. The women stayed at the house but talked about the possible changes to the trees as the few there were blossoming and the last of the daffodils in patches flowered. They saw the men coming back with the esky and heading out the back so they walked around to meet them. They were filling a few containers of water for later. Sonya was interested in the old farming sheds that had little in them now, mostly old tools for display.

'Where is this hippie van you spoke of?' Sonya asked. Danika got the key to the enclosed shed to show her.

'This is Rainbow. Actually I should probably start her up while I'm here, it has been a while,' Danika replied.

It took some cajoling but eventually Danika was able to get Rainbow purring well enough to drive out of the shed so they could all have a better look. Danika handed Peter – who loved the idea of Rainbow – the keys and suggested he drive around the yard. Sonya sat in the passenger seat. They laughed as they got back, saying it was much fun but they couldn't imagine trying to sleep in it.

'No it is too tight a fit for two adults,' Cristian confirmed, sharing a memory with Danika who blushed.

'Friedrich could sleep in here and we could have a tent,' Peter proclaimed.

'You're serious, aren't you? Well maybe for a week but I like my hot showers. How do you cook?' Sonya asked.

Danika showed her the fridge and the cooking stove and where she stored a small table and a chair in the back under the bed. Peter was looking at the roof rack and where the water tank was and the fuel tank. He was becoming quite animated about the possibility of a trip even for a few days. 'Perhaps we can plan something after this weekend.'

'Perhaps a discussion for later that is for sure. Would you like one more drive around and then back her into the shed again?' Danika suggested to Peter who was keen and had Sonya get in again also. They were both smiling and laughing as Peter negotiated driving around the house and sheds before carefully backing in the shed with Cristian's guidance. It had been a welcome break to the serious thoughts of the day so far.

With several hours before dusk and nothing left to do outside, they all came in and viewed various photos and talked about possible short trips in Rainbow. They even played a couple of hands of gin rummy before the guys decided it was best to get ready out on the verandah. Cristian moved his ring to the chain and Peter handed his to Sonya. It was a strange time for them, filled with excitement and longing to run together, yet hoping it would nearly be their last. There was a slight sadness at a loss of some of who they were.

Out on the verandah they stood briefly as the last rays of the sun tinged the tops of the trees with gold before dipping below the line of the mountains. They could see the kangaroos moving out of the bushes to feed on the grass in the paddock. Danika knew Cristian could sense the pull to hunt. Turning to his cousin they hugged briefly and nodded to each other before taking off their clothes and folding them up on to the chairs. Sonya and Danika were both crying silently at the scene they watched through the window. Both were sending thoughts of love and encouragement. Danika was also 'talking' to Cristian and sending as many thoughts for Peter to go with Cristian as she could.

Cristian changed quickly and, Danika sensed somehow, with less pain than in the past but waited patiently for Peter, who was a stunning shining black, tinged with lighter fur on the extremities. They sniffed each other before running off the way Danika had hoped towards the forest.

Danika turned to Sonya and they each hugged and cried a little more from so many mixed emotions of pride, love and trepidation for the future, lastly resoluteness that it would be ended as soon as possible.

'They are in the forest at the moment,' Danika informed Sonya. 'I have placed a charm on Cristian's chain, it took a few goes to get it strong enough but I can track his movements as long as he is not too far away. I'm so glad you are here with me.'

'I'm glad also. It is a lonely life for us wives. I have felt guilty that I was glad to share the last few months of knowledge with Friedrich and torn by the horror he felt at the knowledge. I won't call him tonight and spoil his day. I will let him know tomorrow that we are all fine,' Sonya remarked, trying to sound positive.

'It is still an hour until full moon. We will hear them then I'm guessing. Let's have something to eat,' Danika suggested. They had just finished eating when they heard the first howl coming from a long way out the back. Danika went to the back window and they both thought it sounded high up also. She retrieved the night vision glasses. It took some time to focus but eventually she had a glimpse of movement on the side of the mountain and quickly handed them to Sonya.

'That is the first time they have been useful here, too many trees and dips to get a clear view normally,' Danika said as Sonya was transfixed watching.

'I can see them both. They are standing still now, staring this way.' Sonya handed her the glasses to view again, and then they both howled again.

'I'm going out the front, let me know if they are coming back.' Danika went out the front and stood looking at the moon and drew as much energy as she could from the moon and stars in the short time she had, repeating her thanks to the universe for any help. She could feel the warmth spreading through her.

'They are coming down Danika,' Sonya yelled from her viewing point. 'I've lost sight of them in the treetops.'

Danika was well aware how fast they could move and wisely came back inside. Sonya cleared away their dishes and made them a hot drink, insisting Danika sit and enjoy the rest as no doubt they would both not sleep well tonight. Settled in the lounge, Danika spoke of when they first got the keys to the house and how difficult it had been. Danika had Sonya laughing at the images she described of the bathing and washing attempts and Cristian's fireside cooking. Danika missed the open fire for its distraction but knew it was too dangerous to go outside for more wood to start it.

'Do you really want to go on a trip in Rainbow?' Danika asked.

'Yes and no. I understand that Peter sees it as a great adventure in a new country but I worry that he sees it as a bucket list before impending doom. Besides, it is rather small.'

'Yes it is small. I would suggest staying in caravan parks with the hot showers and camp kitchens and usually a games room. It can be much fun and Rainbow needs a decent run. The school holidays are in two weeks so probably best to think about it before or after that,' Danika suggested. 'I can feel Cristian is closer, just out the back.'

They both went to the back window again and watched as Cristian and Peter drank from the water containers. Danika spoke to them, making them look up. Sonya said a few endearments in German then Peter and Cristian shook their heads and playfully bounded off again.

'Thankfully they seem to be getting along alright so far,' Sonya remarked. 'Perhaps you should lie down for a while, I could wake you if needed. We both need to be rested for them tomorrow.'

'Yes I think I will and I'll set an alarm to make sure you get some rest also,' Danika agreed and stayed dressed under the quilt, setting an alarm for a few hours' time.

Danika woke to bumps and muffled growls and realised Peter was on the verandah, apparently enjoying a leg of meat. Sonya was asleep on the couch and she sensed Cristian was over in the rocky patch. She watched Peter and whispered a few words. He looked up but went back to his meal. Danika felt Sonya stir and held her hand up and whispered that Peter was eating on the verandah. Sonya nodded and Danika could feel she was relieved he was close.

'He came to be close to me and I spoke to him until he settled then I dosed off. That was a couple of hours ago,' Sonya filled Danika in. 'I didn't see Cristian.'

'He is in the rocky field. It's about two hours until dawn, do you want to go lay down until then?' Danika asked.

'No, I want to be awake when he changes back. I put a couple of blankets out for them to wrap up in when you went to bed and brought in their clothes,' Sonya informed her.

'That was a good idea but a little dangerous, so I am told,' Danika pointed out.

'I could hear them in the rocky field so I looked through the night vision glasses from our bedroom window and could see them chasing something small, like a rabbit. I stood on a chair to get high enough,' Sonya admitted. 'I like those glasses.'

'They will come in the laundry door so I'll make sure there are plenty of towels for them. I think I shall shower now myself.' Danika smiled at Sonya. 'You don't need to do anything.'

The women waited and, as the faintest glow started on the horizon,

Peter began the change. Danika left Sonya to talk to him in private as she tried to feel for Cristian in the rocky field but he was further away in the paddock and asleep she thought. Peter had walked around the side to come in through the laundry so Danika picked up the blanket and Cristian's sneakers, ignoring the ravaged leg of meat and walked across the dewy grass towards where the kangaroos were in a mob. She talked to them as she went so they didn't startle as she approached. In the middle of the mob was Cristian, waking as the first beam of the sun touched him.

'Good morning.' Danika smiled and sent love to him. He sat up and started to shiver. Apart from a couple of muddy smears he seemed fine. She handed him the shoes and blanket.

'Thank you darling. How is Peter?' Cristian sounded tired and his voice was a little croaky but he seemed better than he had in a long time of changes.

'He appeared okay. Sonya is with him of course. The roos seemed very at ease with you being in their paddock,' Danika pointed out and Cristian looked around as the roos were slowly loping back into the bushes. 'Peter brought the leg of meat onto the verandah to be close to Sonya she thinks.' Cristian nodded at the images Danika shared with him. Back at the house Danika left Cristian to go in the laundry alone as she went in through the front door to start breakfast. Sonya was already there, loading pans up with sausages and bacon with eggs and toast also planned. Danika started the coffee percolator. They worked well together in the kitchen.

Now clean and dressed, Peter came in and hugged his wife for some time, sharing their loving emotions and thoughts with relief. He sat and Danika gave him a steaming cup of coffee.

'Thank you.' His voice was also a little croaky. 'I think we must have yelled a lot last night.' He grinned.

Cristian came in and slapped Peter on the back before hugging Danika also. He sat with a coffee and gratefully accepted when Sonya dished them up a large protein-filled breakfast.

Danika just had toast and an egg with her tea as she watched them clear their plates.

'Did we disgrace ourselves last night?' Peter asked as he stretched. 'I hope not.'

'Not that we are aware of. Cristian was in the paddock on roo duty,' Danika said flippantly.

'You were both chasing rabbits in the rocky field,' Sonya added.

'We will do a walk around with a shovel and make sure all is okay in a little while. How were you two last night, no frights?' Cristian asked.

'We used the night vision glasses. They worked well this time, we saw you both on the side of the mountain above the forest and then in the rocky field.' Before Cristian could admonish her she added, 'We stayed inside.' Danika sent what images she could to Cristian and Peter, not sure if he could see them. Mostly everyone exuded relief.

The girls tidied and packed as the guys walked around, checking for anything that needed dealing with, including the leg on the verandah. They buried them away from the house. They were on their way home before ten so Danika let everyone know back at Hollingrove they would be there around lunchtime. It was a relatively more sedate trip back, everyone a little tired.

15

THE MANUSCRIPT

THE NEXT FEW days were a whirlwind of planning, decisions and packing. Peter and Sonya planned their family camping road trip in Rainbow with Cristian driving them to Lunar Haven. While Elizabeth and Ingrid planned to stay in the apartment in Sydney. The Norton family just got on with making sure it all went smoothly and Danika was insistent that they have the time off while everyone except her and Cristian were away, with no argument.

'All got away okay then it seems,' Ann said to Danika after everyone's successful departure. 'Ben and I wanted to have a word with you ma'am, if it was alright with you?' Ben came in from the cellar holding a bottle of wine for later.

'Of course Ann, you all should feel free to talk to me anytime.' Danika could feel they were unsure how their news would be received.

'When I was tidying up in the sitting room when you left on Friday I found a page you may have missed on the floor,' Ben explained. Straight away Danika knew which page he meant – the one she was missing of the manuscript. 'I know I should not have read it but I did and I recognised some of the Romany words. My grandmother had tried to teach me.' Danika could feel he was getting a bit embarrassed that he had overstepped his role here. 'I showed it to her. I can't explain why I did that but I knew I had to. Well she translated it and here it is with the translation.' Ben handed the page to Danika who was stunned as she looked at it as if it was the Rosetta Stone. Without hesitation she hugged him.

'Your family are from gypsies then?' Danika asked. Seeing and feeling their withdrawal from that term she added, 'Like my family. I have been able to feel a connection from you all since I arrived. Do you know what this is?' Danika held up the page and translation.

Ann and Ben looked at one another. 'Yes, it is part of a curse, my grandmother said,' answered Ben. Danika decided to take a leap of faith, trusting her gut feeling about the Nortons.

'It is a small part of a large curse that was cast four hundred years ago over the Blakesley family by my family and cursing their descendants at the same time.' Danika could feel that they were not surprised. 'But you already knew that, didn't you?'

'Not everything. Just that we had to make sure the Blakesley family remained safe and private because one day they and others were going to need us. Our family has it like a creed across the world but mostly here in Australia for this particular line,' Ann explained with pride. Danika was crying by now as the full impact became clear.

'Are you my family also from back then?' Danika was sure there was a deeper connection.

'We may have been distant relatives to your line but once the curse was known it was decided this was our role to protect the family to get to the end of the curse. Some of the meaning and understanding I think has been lost along the centuries but not the duty and service to the family,' Ann continued to explain but now had come over to hold Danika's hand, making her sit down. Danika felt the link with Ann stronger than ever.

'Do you know what the curse is?' Danika asked and held her breath.

'That Master Cristian is a werewolf. Yes we know and that you are a witch.' Ann was saying it with love and pride, not hate or disgust. Danika burst into tears of joy.

'We are proud to be the custodians of this secret and to serve you all as long as you need us. The family we have served live their life with dignity and charity to all, despite the difficulties of their lives,' Ben expressed and Danika could feel his genuine emotions.

'Just wait until Cristian is back. What an amazing turn of events. We are hoping that the curse can be broken on the blood moon. There are a lot of people who have risked much to get to this point and now your family are part of that also.' Danika wiped her eyes and Ann gave her a glass of water. 'Phew, I feel like the weight of half the world just lifted. We still have a long way to go to put all the pieces together and my mother and I have to consult to cast a charm to break the curse held over both our families but this is a big part of that answer.' Danika held up the pages again.

'I have foreseen you all helping us on the night and wondered how that was all going to work. Peter is very concerned to show himself to others. He and his family have been and are still in great danger in Europe and elsewhere until this curse is broken.' Danika added, 'I spoke with Cristian last week that we should have your mother over to visit, Ann. That was before I knew this about your family because she is the longest link to the Australian line of Blakesley. When did the Nortons come to Australia?'

'Before the Second World War. Other families were being ostracised and imprisoned in Germany in the 1930's so they sold up and moved as many of the family as possible. Some went with their respective lines of the Blakesley if they relocated away from Germany. The family in England could not move to Australia when Mr Henry's father came here, so they contacted us to take up the duty and here we are,' Ann explained.

'Are there any known witches in your family? You all seem very in tune.' Danika looked hopefully at Ann. 'I hope you don't mind me asking, it has just been a very isolating and lonely time for my family.' Danika was touching her babies.

'Not that we know specifically. But some of us do seem to have a bit of a sixth sense that we don't discount and share with the others. It is a bit of an honour to have you in the family and be able to serve and help you,' Ann expressed humbly. 'We have felt your shared love and happiness. It is quite unique.' That had Danika crying again at their kindness.

'I'm sorry I just can't seem to stop crying, I am just so overwhelmed. I asked the universe for help and well… here you have been all along, phew.' Danika blew her fringe after taking a breath to calm down. 'I think I might go up and try to gather my thoughts until Cristian is back. Thank you so much Ben and Ann, once again.'

Upstairs, Danika took the pages into the nursery to put with the other pages and ended up sitting in the nursing chair and crying more. The enormity of the task ahead for her and her mother was always there but now it was in the forefront of everything. She looked around the room at the half-finished nursery and just wanted to be a happy mother-to-be without the massive responsibility ahead of her. She was feeling very tired and anxious and the babies started to move around. She hummed a tune and gently rubbed her belly trying to calm them again. 'Sorry my little darlings, Mum is just feeling a little fragile.' She decided to go have a lie down until Cristian was home.

Cristian

Cristian had been sending thoughts to Danika as soon as he knew he was close enough. She had not answered his message that he was nearing Hollingrove now the others had gone safely on their way. He'd started to worry why she was not acknowledging his thoughts.

It seemed unusual that she would be sleeping this early in the day. He parked the car in the garage and then was nearly sprinting into the house when Ben intercepted him.

'She's fine, just tired and sleeping,' Ben said but then stood back for Cristian to continue sprinting up the stairs, his concern obvious.

Cristian saw her calm resting face, noting that it was tear streaked, and needed to know what had happened while he was gone. Gently he nudged her and pushed his thoughts for her to wake up, smiling as she stirred and seeped love towards him.

'Hello sleepyhead, what have you been up to while I was gone?' Cristian was probing her thoughts. She released them all for him to feel and see, reaching up for him to hug her. He pulled her into his arms and shared his disbelief that he had not known about the Nortons and how much love and respect he had for them. 'I'm away from you for a few hours and look, you grow a big family.' This had her laughing a little.

'I said I felt something in them but I had no idea. After this curse is sorted out I think we need to make sure they have a holiday.'

'Yes I agree with your thoughts, getting them to go has always been difficult. Remember their last three week break they spent here getting the pool, garden and renovations done,' Cristian reminded her.

'How did Peter and Sonya go? Are they excited?'

'They decided to book into a caravan park near the coast for the five days to have a base but today they are going to the Hunter Valley gardens. I told them the story of how we met and Sonya took up the romantic bait I set and insisted,' Cristian informed her.

'Very clever my darling, you know we will have to go back there one day and actually look around. We could take the babies next year perhaps.' That gave them both a warm glow.

'I need to go down and speak to the others now I have this new knowledge,' Cristian said.

'You go first, I'll just wash my face and follow you shortly.'

In the kitchen – the happy meeting space Cristian had always felt comfortable in since he was a boy – stood Ann at the counter with Ben and Mark waiting for Cristian to speak. He held his hand out to Ben to shake it and then Mark then hugged Ann. 'I feel like I am meeting you all for the first time.'

Ann had a tear in her eyes as she said, 'We have been beside you always and always will be no matter what happens Master Cristian.' Cristian nodded because he didn't trust his voice. 'I just made a bit of lunch if you and Mrs Blakesley are hungry.'

'I'd like that if we can have it in here with you so we can chat.' Cristian could feel confirmation from Danika as she was coming down.

'Of course.' Ann set the table for five and placed a large platter of sandwiches and one of fruits on the table. Ben poured sodas for them all. Over lunch Cristian explained the camping plans of Peter and Sonya. They discussed some future holiday ideas for the boys who seemed to be getting on like long-time friends. Mark had obviously taken a shine to Rick and liked to see him enjoying his time here.

That evening was the first time they had been alone for a few months in the house. It seemed bigger somehow, definitely quieter. Cristian made sure all the appropriate locks were in place before going upstairs where Danika was checking her phone. She was smiling.

Danika was pleased but faintly disappointed not to be out having fun as the remainder of their visitors and family were doing. She pulled that thought back because she was also very pleased to be alone for the weekend. He shared his thoughts of the fun they could have, making her smile as she put her phone down to go into his arms.

Their days alone were leisurely feeding animals and walking the gardens. Danika picked a few flowers and all the meals were well planned or pre-prepared by Ann. They worked on the translation of the whole curse and only had a few words that they needed help with to ask Ben's grandmother next week. Danika could already feel some of the words to break it but needed to confer with Selene once it was fully translated. She had sent photos to her mother of what they had achieved so far.

Their nights were casually enjoying each other's company quietly or with gentle loving. They even talked about baby names but really were struggling with two they both liked. Cristian wanted a strong name for their son, not necessarily a family one but he also wanted a pretty name for their daughter – the concept so alien to him it still gave him a thrill. Danika on the other hand wanted a strong name for their daughter and a peaceful name for their son. They agreed they had plenty of time to decide.

Danika relayed the messages she had been receiving from Sonya and showed Cristian more photos.

'They seem to have had plenty of experiences already, good and bad. They managed to find some family favourites at that supermarket chain I told them about with the international foods. I think they don't mind Aussie foods, they just needed a little reminder of home.' Danika was thinking about the concept of being in another country not knowing your future. 'Do they intend going back? I assume they have work, a home and other family.'

'They have visas for twelve months but I think they would like to feel safe going back to their home. Sonya has some distant family and Peter does have other distant cousins like me. I have told them they are welcome to stay as long as they need to in the apartment or here. He is in finance and has been able to juggle it so far,' Cristian advised.

Danika nodded, knowing it would be too dangerous for them to return before the blood moon. How things would be after that was unknown.

'Tonight is our last one alone together. I have really enjoyed these few days but I have to admit to missing the noise of a busy household. Next month are we all going to Lunar Haven again? It is an all-day moon.' Cristian could sense Danika's hesitation to bring it up, clearly not wanting to spoil their calm but her worry was obvious.

'We will have to. It is the safest place, especially for two of us. We 'could go alone if you are worried.' Cristian knew as he said it that Danika and Sonya would not agree to that.

'You know we have to be there darling, but Rick doesn't. He can stay here with his grandmother, and Mark will keep an eye on him.'

Cristian sensed danger suddenly and rushed to his feet, telling Danika to stay where she was. He ran downstairs and outside but felt even then as Danika moved to watch him through the security cameras. A dog ran in front of him amongst the herd of deer and, overwhelmed by the memory of the dog at Lunar Haven, Cristian felt the change rip through him.

When he came back to he was standing naked above the dog bleeding below him, a giant bite mark across it's throat. He walked to the stables and, regretting that he had to do so, he grabbed the shotgun to cover up the obvious bite wound. He kept his thoughts blocked as he grimly took care of it, but when he came back inside to clean up, Danika was waiting for him, shaking from fear but holding his clothes for him. He sent as many calming thoughts as he could. The clothes were ripped, lucky they had only been loose track pants and t-shirt, so they went in the bin. As the hot water washed over him he swore once and then composed himself.

'I have to call the police to report the discharge of a firearm and a vet to check the dog and the herd.' Cristian was trying to keep his thoughts even and not scare Danika but it was attention he did not want. 'We have to wipe some of the security camera vision if it shows me before they get here.'

'There was only one for a few seconds I think,' Danika confirmed. Cristian nodded. 'I can do that and if I can't I'll call Ben.'

'The dog had a collar so it would be looked for. I had to cover up where I killed it.' Cristian was not happy that he had to kill anything. A family dog was very distressing.

The next several hours were awful for them both. Ben came immediately when Danika called for help with the vision on the cameras, deleting and turning off the one incriminating view. The police were very helpful checking the firearm and licence and took away the collar and registration to contact the owners. The vet examined the deer as best he could at night with them so unsettled and said he would be back if they noticed anything in the light of morning. He also took away the body of the large mixed breed dog. They needed to talk but it was not possible with so many people around. Ben offered to get Ann and Mark to come also but Danika said enough people had been upset tonight already. Tomorrow would be soon enough. Looking at the clock they all seemed to realise it was after midnight. Ben made hot drinks for them both and then went about cleaning up and disposing of the ruined clothing. Cristian insisted Danika go back upstairs to rest and went with her to make sure she did before returning downstairs. To make sure all was locked up again and talk with Ben.

Finally Cristian came back upstairs and lay down next to Danika who was dosing under the cover at last. She stirred so he hugged her to him as he carefully explained what he knew had happened.

'That is the first time a change like that has happened and hopefully the last. I think I will get Mark to sell off the whole herd. It is time. We will have to check the deer. I'm not sure if the dog just harassed them or did actually bite them.' Cristian explained slowly and carefully as Danika asked in thoughts more than words for the details. 'Ben is still here. He said Ann and Mark will be in around dawn. They wanted to come straight away but I said we were fine. Are you okay?'

She wasn't. Tears flowed, she was crying for the shock, the dog and for Cristian. He knew she needed to see the deer as soon as possible. As she cried he crooned and rocked her, stroking her hair.

They lay holding each other and dosed for a couple of hours but woke as soon as Cristian heard voices downstairs at six o'clock. As they went into the kitchen, Ann held out her arms for Danika who went into the warm embrace for a minute and then Ann made her herbal tea. Cristian went with Mark outside to go look at the deer then thought showed Danika the deer who were still quite spooked so she left the kitchen to go try to calm them so they could be examined. A couple did seem to have nips on their back legs and a few may have hit the wire in their panic. They decided to separate those few for the vet to check over. It felt new but fine to use her craft in front of Mark.

It was a quiet breakfast all glad that everyone was alright but realising the problems that could arise from this event. Cristian had not said exactly what had happened. They didn't need that fear, although he suspected Mark found his tracks, larger than the dog ones. Danika confirmed she had felt that from Mark also but no fear at all. Cristian had Mark contact his agent to move the deer on in two lots, giving the injured ones a chance to recuperate.

The police had contacted the vet who passed it on to Cristian that the dog had been lost on the other side of the national park some weeks ago. It had been reported by several walkers but no one was able to find it when they searched. The rangers had found some dead small native animals in the park, also possibly as a result of a dog, with the owners offering to pay for any vet bills. Although they were grateful to have an answer it still did not make them feel any better. Cristian advised the vet that the owners had enough to worry about and he did not need them to pay for the costs of his services. Cristian just felt sorry for the dog.

Mark left to pick up Elizabeth and Ingrid in the estate car, leaving an easier space for Peter to get Rainbow into the garage again that afternoon. The house would be full and busy again in a few hours. Bethany would also be back to help Ann and Ben with anything that was needed and likely Jay would be with her; Danika thought they all needed the distraction.

Distraction was certainly what it was. Ingrid and Elizabeth were laughing at some joke Mark had made as he pulled up out the front. With Ben and Mark taking their bags inside, they made their way to the sitting room to talk about their happy days. Danika felt bad about having to dampen their spirits by telling them about the incident but it was important that they also needed to know about the support of the Nortons. Ingrid took it better than Elizabeth because she had experienced many other dangerous situations and was a great comfort to Elizabeth worrying about Cristian. An hour later when Rainbow appeared, driven by Peter, the mood was lighter again. Friedrich came bouncing in wanting to tell everyone that he had caught the biggest fish on the charter and everything else he felt he had excelled at. He couldn't wait to tell Jay and was pleased to know he would be there in a couple of hours. Cristian had met them in the garage to help guide the parking of Rainbow and let Peter and Sonya know what had happened while they were away. They, like Ingrid, took it well without minimising the effect it had on Cristian and Danika not knowing the local police and reporting requirements.

Lunch was a rowdy and happy event that Danika absorbed and shared. This was just what they needed, she agreed with Cristian who looked lovingly around at his family. Sonya said she was looking forward to a proper bed and facilities again but admitted she had enjoyed most of the experience. They were even considering hiring a mobile home to travel further and hopefully away from the wet weather in the future. Everyone laughed at the different anecdotes she told of their trip.

'So will you be staying here this week? Did you have any plans?' Danika asked.

'I think so. Maybe go to Sydney Saturday for a couple of weeks. We still need to sort out dates and so forth.' Sonya was non-committal. 'Our packing is a mess to sort out.'

Friedrich was showing everyone his photo holding the biggest fish then as soon as he was excused he rushed up to his room to try out a new game he bought. So much energy to burn, Cristian heard Danika think, followed by her imagining chasing two toddlers in the future. He reached for her hand.

Danika

'Do you need any help sorting your packing?' Danika asked Sonya, popping her head in to visit them after dinner. She could see clothes and other items strewn around the room in an out of character way. She touched Sonya's arm and the worry turned her into Danika's embrace. Danika shared her thoughts of calm and support until Sonya felt she could let go. Peter seemed at a loss.

'Thank you Danika, you are generous as always. When we left home we took a flight to go to Canada as that was the ruse we had constructed for Robert's benefit. Our family in Canada have kept up the ruse for us. But the climate literally has been a drought which has impacted everyone's ability to hide. Now Robert is getting suspicious fed by comments from the insane Merlin wannabe. Apparently they already broke in and searched our home.' Sonya was starting to shake as the fear was taking over. Danika directed her to the bed.

'Peter, I think we should discuss this with Cristian in our sitting room. I'll let him know and I'll come in with Sonya shortly,' Danika suggested to Peter who was reluctant to leave Sonya until he felt Danika's positive push.

Sitting next to Sonya amongst the pile of clothing Danika held her hand until Sonya had managed to collect herself. 'I had hoped that we could be gone from the fear here but it is still there. I worry what he will do to the other family members if he finds we tricked him.'

Danika placed her other hand over Sonya's like a hug and, with a gentle chant, pulled some of the worry away and let it go in a slight wave of her hand as she let go of Sonya. Then she encouraged her to take a few deep breaths. Strangely she felt more powerful than usual. It almost felt as if some was coming from the babies as they lay still, or maybe that was her imagination.

Danika lead Sonya out of the mess to the sitting room, telling her they would come back and sort it out afterwards. Peter and Cristian were already talking when they came in. It seems their plan had been working well with the pretend trip to the family in Canada, supported by calls to family in Europe from Peter's pretend new phone, just in case the call could be tracked. Up until they said they were extending their stay. That was when their home was broken into and searched. Their caretaker had reported it to the police but nothing was taken and it was dismissed as probably kids. Not being in Germany now it was harder for their contacts to get word and information to them of Robert and his cohorts movements and actions but they believed he was building up to some big event before the end of the year.

'Are they suggesting you should return?' Danika asked Peter.

'No, they are determined that we stay here and do whatever we can to end the curse and the tyranny of Robert. We feel responsible for their safety which we have no control over from so far away,' Peter explained.

'Unfortunately we cannot make time speed up. November blood moon will be our focus and we just need to have everything ready for then. I have asked Ann to bring her mother on Wednesday to finish the translation of the manuscript. Then I and my mother Selene will work on the spell to break the curse with the heavens help,' Danika explained.

Danika's calming influence made it easier for Sonya and Peter to refocus. In no time she had Sonya sorting everything in the room.

The night that Ann brought her mother June to Hollingrove was a tense build up for all. Now that the long-held secret was out in the open and Elizabeth had not seen her since June had retired, it was like meeting for the first time again. Cristian had brought the details of their research down to the main sitting room with a large, printed composite of the manuscript to make it easier for June to view and read. Sonya and Peter felt it best for them to go back upstairs with

Rick and Jay after dinner. Elizabeth and Ingrid also retreated to their rooms, not wanting to overwhelm June after they had all enjoyed the banter at the dinner table.

On Danika's suggestion, Ann and Ben came in with June into the sitting room to offer support. They all sat with the manuscript photo on the coffee table. Danika could feel that the Nortons felt a little out of place as they had not sat down in this room before always being the staff. Danika tried to share the feeling of calm reassurance and welcome to them all.

June placed her hand on Danika's. 'You are very generous my dear, I do feel welcome.' She let go of her hand. 'Now, let's have a better look at this curse.'

Cristian lay it out in front of June who pointed to the corner that Ben had brought her last week to translate. 'This was the piece Ben showed me. In isolation the words are correct but seeing the whole verse it is a little different.' Danika was trying to keep her excitement of this new analysis at bay. June wrote a few notes with the pen and paper Cristian gave her. 'Be careful not to say this out loud Danika. Is someone helping you with the spell to break it? They must not voice this either,' she asked.

'My mother Selene who lives in Adelaide is. She will come here for the blood moon. I'll warn her but I think she probably already knows,' Danika explained.

'Good.' June handed over her notes to Danika who could feel the pride coming from Ann and Ben.

'We have both had visions of the night of the blood moon, with you all and many others around us. Do you think that is something your family would agree to doing?' Danika asked.

'Of course. We have all been preparing and waiting for this event for many generations. Master Cristian,' June now touched Cristian's hand, 'Your family has been through so much and been so kind to our family that it would be our privilege to be part of your quest.'

'Is your family going to be able to cope with seeing Peter and myself change into our lupine form?' Danika could feel Cristian's concern not to horrify and disgust them all.

'Some of us have seen this already, the others have been taught what to expect,' June said with fondness. Danika could feel his shock and was surprised herself. 'We are a curious lot. Our family in England knew of the legacy as you call it and told us. As you can imagine we wanted to know ourselves. Your grandfather was alone in a new country with two small children and we were tasked with keeping him safe. It was inevitable we would view the legacy at some stage.'

'Have your family been watching over the Blakesley line in Europe also?' Danika could sense a bigger connection.

'As much as was possible. Wars and disease have made it difficult over the centuries, we were almost wiped out in the Second World War. The Blakesley families that moved out of the European war zone took our family with them, otherwise there may have only been the Australian line.'

Cristian was in awe of this large family keeping his family safe for so long. 'Why have you not shared this over the years?'

'Not all of your relatives and ancestors have been so welcoming or inclusive, but we still had to keep a watch on them waiting for the legacy to be broken. As a people the Gypsies and witches were horrified at the curse once it was known. There are old tales of the deaths from the newly turned not understanding the dangers. So it has been about keeping everyone as safe as possible and was going well until your uncle Robert and his family.' June almost sounded apologetic at having to mention him. 'He always resented being brought to Australia and blamed Master Henry for the death of their mother. He was not happy right up until he left to live in Germany as a teenager.' Danika could feel that June had initially felt uncomfortable to say this but was now relieved it was out in the open. Danika shared that to Cristian.

'So you protected my father from him, didn't you? He always

thought of you as his mother, I could see that.' Cristian squeezed June's hand. 'Is that why you left?'

'It was time I retired. Ann is very capable but your father's accident was a heavy blow to me. I stayed until the funeral but your uncle Robert's visit was more than I could bear so I made sure your mother had plenty of support and I left.' Danika caught some of the emotions towards Robert from June and it was mutual. She sent supporting thoughts to June who looked at her and smiled. Danika could feel how tired June was now and needed to leave.

'Thank you for all your help June, now and over the years. We are in your debt I feel,' Cristian said.

'As we are in yours, I know how often you have helped our family be successful. It is time I was going now, but I will be back when you need me.' June accepted Cristian's help to stand with Ben and Ann, helping her from the room to the car. Danika and Cristian farewelled them from the front steps. Back inside they hugged, all the emotions of the build-up and revelations of tonight shared between them.

'I think we should share this with Peter and Sonya and Friedrich also perhaps,' Danika suggested just as Bethany came from the kitchen to say she needed to take Jay home. Upstairs the boys understood that Jay needed to leave and asked if they could spend some time together over the holidays. Bethany agreed to discuss it further with his father and, of course Peter and Sonya, to work out a time the boys could enjoy one another's company. After Bethany and Jay left, Cristian and Danika shared the discussions with Peter and Sonya, leaving it to them to decide what Friedrich needed to know. They were shocked also at the revelation that the Nortons and their world-wide family connections had been watching over the Blakesley family.

'It makes more sense why the maid at Robert's castle is so involved. To take the risks she is to relay information,' Peter commented. 'I wonder if the family connections in Europe have seen the legacy of the change, I suppose they may have?'

'Very likely it seems. It is easier to protect what you understand,' Cristian confirmed.

It didn't take long for Danika to drift off to sleep that night. The anticipation of meeting June, then the revelation of the family connections, she felt as if she couldn't hold her head up anymore. Her night was not peaceful though as her dreams were constant but jumbled as if they were not her own thoughts. In her subconscious mind she could sense her babies' restlessness. The dreams became more insistent and clearer, a warning about the moon but not at night, instead in the day sky. She felt a shaking and then heard Cristian's gentle voice and felt his hand on their babies.

'Wake up Danika. You were dreaming, all of you. I think I can feel them also.'

Groggily she laid her hand over his and said, 'They were the ones that wanted me to go to bed last night and then filled my head with strange images until finally a warning, I'm sure it was channelled from them crazy as that sounds.'

'Nothing seems crazy in our lives. What was the warning?' Cristian was now hugging her to him.

'Nothing tangible, just a feeling of danger in a daytime full moon and lots of water.' Danika tried to explain. 'I've lost track, is the next one during the day?'

'Yes it is, in a couple of weeks.' Cristian had relaxed now that they were all calm now. 'Do you think we will lose this connection after the blood moon?' Cristian added.

'I don't know. It is more likely that we will if it is only connected to the legacy. Do you know if your father sensed you as a baby?' Danika had wondered this herself.

'Not that I am aware of, you could ask Mother. Perhaps it is more to do with your psychic connection than mine.'

At breakfast they broached the subject of next month's travel plans, no longer having to be careful of their audience.

'We need to talk about the next lunar cycle before you leave for

Sydney this afternoon.' Cristian started the discussion once everyone had selected their breakfasts. 'It is during the day in two weeks' time. It is too dangerous to travel on the day so Sunday I was thinking was the best option.'

Everyone listened and had their own thoughts. Danika could feel them all. Surprisingly Ingrid spoke first. 'I think you four should go to that farm of yours and Friedrich can stay here with us and his friend if he likes.' Friedrich was already nodding his head with his mouth full.

'We wouldn't be back until the Tuesday or Wednesday, depending on how we go,' Cristian explained.

'I'll be fine, Uncle Cristian. Mark has said he was going to show us some archery in the paddocks now that the deer are going. I can hang out with him when Jay is at school.' Friedrich was quick to jump in. Danika sensed he didn't want to be around his father or Cristian during the change but she kept that to herself for now.

'Okay, well we can work out the finer details closer to that weekend. I think today we are packing for our trip to Sydney for the next ten days and planning what we are doing there,' Peter interjected before the tone became solemn.

'I would like to go to the zoo and the gardens,' Sonya piped up.

'Luna Park, Jay told me we have to go there,' Friedrich said, then they were all making suggestions and laughing at some of them. Danika looked across at Cristian who was enjoying the table banter but underlying he was concerned at Danika's dreams or premonitions.

There seemed to be so much noise and laughter as Peter, Sonya and Friedrich packed and loosely planned their trip to Sydney. Ingrid also chimed in wanting to go to the markets. Danika absorbed the happiness and spread some to Cristian. It seemed the day went so fast and already they were packing the estate car that Mark was going to take them in, picking up Jay on the way. Once they were at the apartment they would use taxis when they needed them. Then they were gone and the house was quiet.

Danika called her mother to discuss her dreams. Selene answered on the second ring.

'Hello, Nika, is everything okay?'

'Hello Mum. Yes and no, not really at the same time. We are all fine and had more revelations last night with Mrs Norton which I will tell you, but I am ringing because of strange dreams I have been having. Well the babies as well I think.' Danika sighed.

'Oh okay, some of that is normal but early. I suppose I should have warned you. Normal for us anyway, it is the witch psychic connection, not normally until the third trimester,' Selene explained.

'Yes it would have been nice to know but it is only a couple of weeks early. How did it present for you?' Danika asked.

'Well you let me know when I needed to rest and if I was stressed you shared calming vibes. You liked it when I sang to you.'

'So far I have experienced all of those feelings. What about dreams?'

'I did have some strange dreams towards the end, not really actual places and people but the feel or smell of them. I guess that is all a baby has. One time, about a week before you were born, I had dark dreams that made me cry as I woke. It was the strongest emotion of fear. Later, I had to go out at night and was going to walk to a bus stop and the fear came again and instead I called a taxi. I heard later that another lady was attacked near that bus stop. I often wondered if it was a premonition but then you were born and I was too busy enjoying you to give it any more thought until now. Why, what have you experienced?'

'The dreams were intangible, like misty blobs of emotions. Happy, tired and calm but then it was clearer, yet I knew it wasn't my dream as such. I saw the full moon in the daytime and much water. Not like a lake or a river, just a lot of water bubbling. It sounds strange I know. Cristian woke me because he could feel we were all distressed. Do you think it is a premonition?' Danika answered slowly.

'Is that next full moon Nika?'

'Yes I think so. We are going up to the farm again. It really isn't safe for Cristian or Peter anywhere around here during the night these days let alone during the day. There is a small waterfall there but not much else. It's not like I'm going anywhere near that anyway if it is flowing hard,' Danika said almost as a question.

'Just be very cautious as I was. Do you know if it is just the girl baby giving you these feelings?'

'I honestly feel it is both of them but I don't know for sure. Mum, we had Mrs June Norton here last night and she translated the whole manuscript. I'll send you some notes in a while. As a continuing family group they have been watching over the Blakesley's since the curse four hundred years ago. They know about the legacy of change and have even seen it. They don't think any of them are related to us though. June said neither you nor I should say the words aloud as they are too powerful. We do need to get together to work out the chant to break the curse. When do you think you can come here for the blood moon?'

'That is a lot to take in at once Nika. I need to talk to Clay first but I know I have to be there with you. I feel like he should be also, so I am going to have to let him know everything.'

'Yes I think he needs to be here also. How is it going with you two, are you dating yet?' Danika answered.

'Well we agreed we were sort of dating for many months around the markets and such, so after your visit it got a bit more serious because we saw how happy you two are and wanted to test the waters ourselves.' Selene was being unusually non-committal.

'Test what waters? So are you a couple now with all the benefits? Why didn't you tell me?' Danika asked with surprise.

'It felt a bit strange to tell you. I feel a bit like a teenager telling her mum. You know he is only the second man I have ever been with. He is so patient and delightfully romantic.'

'Wow Mum, this is big news. You definitely have to tell him about us.' Danika was happy for her.

'Oh he already knows we are witches. He was not surprised in the slightest. I just haven't told him about Cristian and the curse and so on.'

'I am sending you those notes shortly plus my idea in a secure file. Password is Nanna's name. I love you mum, give Clay a big hug for me.' Danika ended the call and was just sitting stunned at her mother, firstly jumping at a chance to be happy but also keeping it a secret. She had heard the love in her voice when she spoke of Clay.

Cristian had stayed away, leaving Danika to talk to her mother in peace. He even tried not to listen in but some of her more intense emotions had him concerned and curious. He still tried to seem surprised when she came bouncing in to tell him her mother's news.

'You heard didn't you?' Danika accused him, not really upset though.

'You seemed upset so yes I was listening. I like Clay, he will take my truth well I think and I believe we need him as you do.'

'Yes we do need him. I think everyone will play their part in this celestial event not just with their actions but with their love.' Danika smiled.

The week went so fast despite the quieter nights with their extended family away being tourists. Danika and Cristian were busy with the gallery and some other real estate business as they tried to help Elizabeth with her charity work for those needing affordable housing. The problems seemed to be exacerbated by the recent flooding now forecast to become worse.

In the city one day, Danika searched for more items for the gallery to keep it relevant and well stocked, knowing in a couple of months she would be too busy to work at the gallery. She found Rene was getting better at finding possible pieces and collections that Danika only needed to view quickly to make a decision. Rene had an eye for more modern abstract and surreal pieces so Danika suggested Rene put together a proposal for a gallery exhibition of her style to run for the month of December. Rene was so excited and thankful, running out the back to Paul to tell him. Danika could feel their shared love and wondered how long before they moved in together.

Danika sat down and sighed knowing her babies were giving her the rest vibe. She stroked her belly and smiled as she stretched out her legs and hummed to them. Her phone buzzed a message from Cristian asking how she was. She was just about to answer when he called anyway.

'Are you okay? I sent a message an hour ago.' Cristian had worry in his voice.

'I only just received the message, this weather is playing havoc with the phones.' Danika tried to sound calm. 'I'm okay, just tired, but I am sitting down resting as ordered by the twins.'

'I think you need to step back a bit from the gallery. Let Rene and Paul do more and me of course. After all in a couple of months you will be busy with the twins.' Cristian sounded concerned.

'I know, I was talking with Rene this afternoon and I'm going to let her plan and run a new exhibition from December. Paul and Tony can help but we may need some muscle at the warehouse. People who are careful though.' Danika was now worrying about that.

'I'm on to that, I was talking to Mark who talked to Dean and so on. The Nortons have a couple of teenagers that are interested in the arts and would like to spend some time helping at the gallery after their exams finish. They are cousins of Jay, a girl and a boy. What do you think?'

'I think that is a fantastic idea. So that they can get the full going for job experience we should interview them. They could do some weekend work if they aren't cramming for exams. Rene and Paul should be part of that also.' Danika was pleased with the suggestion but then groaned.

'What, are you okay?'

'Yes, sorry, they are playing soccer with my bladder I swear, I have to go. We really need to decide on names.' Danika kissed through the phone and hung up and just got to the bathroom in time.

They were approaching the time they were supposed to be meeting Peter and Sonya for dinner in the city. Shortly after the phone call, Cristian arrived at the gallery to pick her up.

'Oh hello, I didn't expect you this early,' Danika said as she saw him coming through the back entrance. She was sitting down at the little kitchenette sipping tea.

'I thought you might prefer to go home than go out tonight, you sounded tired,' Cristian explained.

'Actually I would love to go out, but they wouldn't.' She pointed at her belly. 'It seems they are getting a bit demanding that I rest with my feet up. Heaven help us once they are born.'

Cristian leaned in and placed his hands on her belly and sent thoughts to them as he hummed. 'They like that tune I think. So I'll let Peter know we will take a rain check. It is sort of literal anyway, I'm not keen to drive you in the dark in this weather. Come on kids let's take Mum home.'

Peter and Sonya didn't mind at all not going out either. Their week had been very full, fitting in everything they each wanted to do each day and a night relaxing appealed to them all.

Back at Hollingrove Cristian insisted Danika go lay down before dinner. Although she protested that she had napped in the car most of the way home she took his advice and was surprised how good it felt to lay down at least for a few minutes. Part of her mind was trying to wake up despite having only lain down briefly, the other part was wafting marshmallow like images that seemed familiar and as they swirled from mushy mist to actual images the feeling of fear built. The image of the moon in daylight followed by a lot of water gushing, this time not over her but more past her. The fear gave way to interest and then she woke. Moving her hands around she felt the bed and the soft quilt Cristian must have pulled over her. It was getting dark, making her realise that she had slept for an hour not just a few minutes. Cristian came into the room not quite out of breath.

'I was out in the stables when I felt your thoughts, did you have another dream?' he asked, looking her over to check she was alright.

'Yes but it was much clearer this time. I'm sorry to have worried you.'

'What do you mean by clearer?'

'It's a bit difficult to explain because it is difficult for me to translate. The dreams – or premonitions – are coming from the twins. I spoke with Mum and it is a thing for us witches but normally a bit further along in the pregnancy. It's happening earlier by a few weeks maybe because there are two. They have thoughts and dreams that are based on feelings and emotions, all mushy and misty then vague shapes and views start to appear. They don't understand because they have no reference.' Danika looked at Cristian to see if he was following her explanation. 'I think they pull some of my memories to form the visions together for the premonition, so some of it scared them. If I am reading it correctly they are worried about the daylight full moon but the answer is in a large amount of water.'

'That isn't really an answer,' Cristian voiced.

'I know, but seriously these are still forming babies with psychic powers. It is pretty awesome really,' Danika commented. 'Mum said she forgot to tell me it happened to her at about the thirty-week point. Nothing like this though.'

'And I didn't think I could be surprised by anything anymore.' Cristian shook his head. 'Are you sure it is both babies?'

'No and yes. I want to believe it is both of them and if it wasn't I don't know which is which anyway.' Danika touched his arm. 'Can we please decide on names? It feels wrong talking about them and to them as anonymous beings.'

'Yes you're right. After dinner.' He quickly tidied himself and put a jacket on.

At the table Ingrid and Elizabeth were comparing some of the photos they had taken over the last week and some of Peter's also. They had spent some time in Sydney also, sharing the fun with the others when it was not too demanding.

'Oh good, we have some photos to show you,' Elizabeth said.

'Did you enjoy your time in Sydney?' Danika asked, already knowing they did by their smile.

'Yes some days pushed us a bit but the energy of those boys keep you going. They are such good friends it would be a shame when Friedrich goes home,' Elizabeth commented. 'Have you two decided on any names for the twins yet?' Elizabeth asked as if she had read their minds.

'No, not yet. We are going to try a shortlist later to see how they sound.' Danika jumped in.

'Well not that you need my input but I would recommend not using any family names. This is, after all, a very momentous event worthy of names to respect that,' Elizabeth added.

'No pressure then,' Cristian commented.

'No none at all, just a suggestion.' Elizabeth was smiling at them both.

'I agree with your mother,' Ingrid added her thoughts.

After dinner Danika and Cristian were in their sitting room with a baby name book and the laptop trying to sift through names. They laughed over a few odd ones to lighten the moment but it felt like the task and decision was beyond their ability to agree, which was at odds to how they usually worked together. Danika was feeling cramped leaning over looking at the list they were creating and crossing off just as quickly and decided to sit back with the book on her lap.

As she thumbed through the pages from the beginning yet again she could feel the twins moving around. Going through the pages as she looked until one name for the girls the kick was more deliberate. Cristian could already feel her thoughts and placed his hand on her belly as they looked at the names. Danika was pointing at one name and as they said it together she could feel contentment. So that was one name down. They decided to see if it would work for the next one and slowly turned pages into the boy's names section and had a quick response. Cristian smiled at her because it meant their son had some abilities also, in their opinion anyway. They both tried the names out loud on their own and with the surname and everyone seemed very pleased with the result. They did decide that they would keep it just between themselves though for now, to surprise the rest of the family.

16

NAOMI

Despite the previous rain the drive to Lunar Haven was uneventful. As they came to their turn onto the dirt road to their property an emergency services vehicle was about to pull out of the road instead, stopping to talk to Cristian.

'The road is closed ahead, where are you going?' the officer asked.

'Our house and property is about two kilometres ahead,' Cristian explained.

'Depending where your entrance is you may not be able to get to it, the road is washed out. There is a roadblock, don't cross it.' His two-way radio called for assistance elsewhere. 'I have to go. Don't cross any barriers please, we are getting calls for rescues in flood waters all the time.'

'Thank you for your assistance, we won't cross the barrier.' Cristian watched the emergency vehicle leave before continuing. Danika could feel that Peter and Sonya were very worried now but Danika felt calm and shared that with them all.

Cristian continued slowly and, as they turned the last bend to Lunar Haven, they saw the road closure, about a hundred metres before the entrance to the property. He pulled the car to a stop, looking up at the mountain shrouded in mist ahead. Then sideways at the fence at the corner of their property.

'That is the corner of the property, Peter. I think we can open up the fence and get in that way. I'm not going against my word to the officer. Besides, we have to assess the road ahead before taking chances there. I think I know where it would be washed out,' Cristian suggested as he got out of the car to get out the toolbox.

Danika was calming Sonya. 'It will be alright, this was part of the premonition. Just that it wasn't this clear.'

It didn't take long to open up a gap big enough for the large vehicle to get through but, just in case, Cristian had everyone get out while he manoeuvred the car through the fence and up the rocky paddock and stop so he could help the girls through and Peter to reinstate the fence as best they could. Sonya and Danika decided to walk across the rocky ground as Cristian carefully navigated it in the four-wheel drive with Peter walking along and guiding him through the best path. The girls were at the house turning off the security and unlocking the door before Cristian pulled up the last of the driveway. He looked back at the muddy wheel ruts across the paddock and was very thankful for Dean's car.

After emptying the car and getting the heating and fridge going they all decided with boots on to go have a look at the wash out. As Cristian had suspected, the waterfall and creek at the foot of the mountain had gouged a deeper path towards the roadway below. Where normally it would flow under a low bridge, instead the bridge was underwater and probably damaged judging by the landslides and road subsidence they had seen. There were no other properties close by and Cristian thought there was another road this one linked to if anyone had to get to other properties. He was confident they were going to be isolated for quite a while.

Danika realised her plans for a meditation area near the waterfall would have to be amended after seeing the power and force of the water, not that it was a high priority anyway. Back at the house the girls worked at getting rooms ready as the guys checked out the sheds and brought in firewood. Sonya had made Danika sit down with her feet up on another chair in the kitchen while she planned and prepared the roast for the evening meal. Danika sat sipping her herbal tea as she watched Sonya work.

'I know you have a visa to stay for twelve months. Do you think you will go back home before that?' Danika asked Sonya.

'I don't know. It depends how things go over the next few months.' Sonya did not want to put any pressure on Danika about the curse. 'We both – well, all of us actually Ingrid included – are loving being here. We have to work out if we can stay longer or if we have to go and come back. There is a lot to consider: work, school for Friedrich, a home I think. Peter and Cristian have talked about it a bit.'

'Do you miss home?' Danika asked as she felt Sonya's hesitation.

'A little, but Robert and his cronies had spoiled it for us long before. It has been frightening and unpleasant for quite a while. Maybe if they were not there we would be happier to return. Peter can run his business without living there and he is looking at setting up an Australian branch. I know we are on holiday but it is also so calm here compared to Europe at the present time. Do you mind us being around so much?' Sonya sounded worried and Danika could feel she was beginning to worry they may have outstayed their welcome.

'Good heavens no, it has been wonderful having you here. I have never had a girlfriend really, not even at school with my strange family background. To be able to talk and confide in you has been a revelation.' Danika felt a tear escape her eye. Just then the guys came in noisily to grab a late lunch before going back out to check the perimeters.

Cristian looked at Danika and placed a hand on her belly. 'All okay?' She nodded and shared her thoughts.

'We are going to take the gator and look around for any other landslips or areas of danger before tomorrow,' he explained to Danika and Sonya.

'Tomorrow, I thought it would be Monday?' Danika asked.

'It is a strange moon this month. It rises tomorrow, not quite full and changes in the early morning. So it can mean a two-day cycle. It happens occasionally,' Peter explained. 'Dangerous for those of us that could not hide or have a safe place to go.'

Danika looked at Cristian and had not realised all the intricacies of the curse they lived with. He was sending her loving thoughts that it was alright and they were safe here. He could feel how tired she was and suggested she nap so she could enjoy being with them all tonight. Sonya was happy to work on her photo art plans and preparations for meals so Danika agreed to lie down.

When Danika woke she could hear the guys in the laundry and bathroom with Sonya talking sternly at them so she focused on Cristian's thoughts. They were quiet immediately and he was slightly contrite as he said to Sonya, 'Danika is awake.' She wondered what the telling off was about.

As she headed for the laundry Sonya came out a little flushed and said to her, 'Don't go in there they are getting cleaned up and cleaning up their mess.' Then they heard them laughing. 'Come I'll make you a cup of tea.' She shook her head exclaiming, 'Children.'

Danika sat as Sonya poured her a cup of tea and sat with her. 'Are you going to tell me?'

'Oh they went out on the gator to inspect the property and got it bogged. They got it out with a shovel and were both covered in mud. Then wet when they cleaned up the gator which apparently turned into a hose fight then they sat drinking the strong German beer in the shed and thought they would just come dancing in to get a change of clothes.' Sonya shook her head again. 'Children!' But she was smiling, she enjoyed seeing Peter happy.

'I see. Just as well you greeted them, seems like they had fun anyway. That roast smells amazing.' Danika realised she had slept for a couple of hours. 'How did you go with your photos?'

'I'll show you my ideas, just a beginning not decided.'

After they had cleaned up, Sonya enlisted Peter to help with the dinner preparations while Cristian started the wood fire in the lounge, for aesthetics mostly as the electric heating was working well. Danika sat watching him work, humming as she laid her hands on her belly. She was feeling very content watching him work and listening to the banter between Sonya and Peter. It was more feeling their emotions than listening as they were talking in German, which was rare for them around others. Danika was sharing with Cristian and then closed the connection to give them privacy as Peter and Sonya were kissing.

'Peter thinks we can stay longer in Australia under business rules, especially as I'm thinking of working for myself also. Cristian's lawyer has been looking into it for us. We would enrol Friedrich in school next year.' Sonya had wanted to share this information all day, Danika could feel it. 'I was supposed to keep it a secret until after it was finalised but I needed to tell you.'

'I'm so glad for you all. What about Ingrid?' Danika was worried she would have to return alone.

'She is self-supporting and there are rules regarding relatives. Apparently we have plenty of time to sort it out. She doesn't want to go back either.'

'When I first met Cristian it was such a hard decision to leap into this relationship and his life but I had been so lonely, and of course the rapture was very strong also but I could have broken it. The thought of having a family was overwhelming, now I have this huge extended family and I am so happy. The more the merrier.' Danika felt her heart swelling with joy.

They stood up so they could hug one another. The twins picked that moment to give a little kick, making both Danika and Sonya laugh. Danika could feel something a little different and looked at Sonya closely. Danika grabbed her hand and looked at her more deeply then closed her eyes to focus her thoughts. Sonya stood still watching the change in Danika.

'Did you know you're pregnant?' Danika opened her eyes to look at Sonya and could feel she did not know that. Sonya's thoughts brought Peter concerned into the room. Sonya went into his arms, crying.

'Are you sure?' Peter asked.

'Pretty sure, but you definitely should take a test once you are back in Sydney.' Danika was crying also. 'Why do we cry when we are happy? Oh, you are happy I hope?'

'Nervous more than happy. We had given up because it was too stressful. I guess we forgot.' Cristian came in as Danika shared their news.

'Congratulations.' Cristian slapped Peter on the back and kissed Sonya on the cheek. Cristian brought in soft drinks for them all to toast the unexpected and momentous occasion. Danika could feel how worried Sonya was as she had lost so many pregnancies before. Danika felt this time would be different. 'Another good reason to sort out your business in Australia now,' Cristian added.

'We don't want to say anything to Friedrich at this stage until we know for sure that we can stay and know that all is healthy and good with Sonya and the baby,' Peter stressed. 'At the moment he still thinks it is a long holiday.'

'Of course, that is very wise. I think he will be pleased to stay, I've noticed his accent has changed a little already,' Danika observed and they laughed at the fact he had been practicing a few iconic Australian terms. 'Jay has been teaching him, I think the trade-off was Friedrich taught Jay how to swear in German.' They were imitating the two boys until they had tears from laughing so hard.

Danika wanted to know more about tomorrow and the next day, feeling a bit naïve to the possibilities and not wanting to spoil the light heartedness that all felt. Cristian just squeezed her hand and said, 'Ask away.' This made Sonya and Peter look at her.

'I'm pretty new to this. I had thought that the change only happened at night on the full moon until the last daytime moon, but now you are saying it could happen even earlier,' Danika asked them. Peter answered instead of Cristian.

'The moon can rise and become full as it is while it is visible, it is dependent on the sun actually shining on it. That is what will happen tomorrow. Rising late and changing in the early morning.'

'So when will the change happen?' Danika still felt murky on the details.

'The feeling will probably start at the first sign of the moon, perhaps even at dusk. Depending on the strength of the person it can probably be held off at great expense. Then it is inevitable at the full moon,' Peter continued.

'What great expense?' Danika sensed Cristian was hiding that but she could feel Peter and Sonya's emotions clearly.

'Physically it hurts everywhere, emotionally it is also damaging. It makes for an angry wolf, so not ideal,' Peter elaborated.

'Has that happened to you?' Danika asked Cristian directly and could already feel the answer was yes.

'A couple of times when I was in other countries and alone. Having support makes a big difference.' His love and gratitude towards them all was obvious.

'Okay, so when you get the feeling which is what? Will you change? I'm sorry I just need to understand.'

'The feeling is itchy and prickly besides the loss of appetite. We can speed up the change, we could go full lycan now actually, but once we do on the moon rise we will stay that way until the moon has set. At this time of year it will be a fair while,' Cristian explained and then added as Danika processed that, 'You have to stay inside the whole time.' She began to protest before Peter was saying the same to Sonya.

'How can we make sure you are safe though? During the day anyone might see you.' Danika was worried but knew it was very unlikely, especially with the road closed now.

'We have already scoped out the area behind the house and we will likely rest up there. Not that that is certain with the other brain and all,' Cristian added.

'Well if needed I can steer you both that way remember.' Danika was trying to be helpful.

'Let's just warn you not to come out and hope that you listen.' Cristian offered Peter an Irish whiskey and Danika went to make a cup of tea for Sonya and herself with Sonya following her.

'I don't know how you have coped with this for so long,' Danika said.

'It was easier when we first met seventeen years ago. During the first couple of years while I got used to the legacy and had Friedrich our land was private and the tension was not so great with Robert. But then the internet and drones opened up everyone's need to see and know everything. Then the wars in Europe and the weather changes have all taken more and more of our privacy. Plus the strain of losing so many pregnancies, just having to be in contact with doctors and so on have all taken a toll. I was on the pill to stop falling pregnant but I forgot to get more while I was here.' Sonya shrugged her shoulders and did not dare to be happy.

'Well we are going to have to think of something to do while they are roaming about besides obviously sleeping.' Danika changed the subject. 'Maybe we could get them to show us one of the video games.'

Much later after selecting games that they may like to play, Danika and Cristian were in bed when Danika allowed her emotions free and, hugging him, began to cry.

'I'm so sorry my ancestors did this to you.'

'It's okay, your hormones are getting the better of you darling. Peter and I and the others have lived with this for a long time and you are not to blame for something four hundred years ago.' Cristian hugged her tight and kissed her face.

'We have to fix it, so Sonya can have her baby and Friedrich doesn't have to go through it.' Danika was so determined.

'We will. You have been so strong and clever. What is this about?' Cristian asked, trying to read her thoughts.

'I don't know, I'm feeling a bit scared that I will fail.' Danika's tears were flowing again.

'It is not just you remember, there are lots of people invested in this now. It is not just your battle, we have an army now.' Eventually he was able to calm her and take her mind in another more happy and enjoyable direction but he had his own fears.

In the morning, Danika and Sonya made a large breakfast of which the guys only had toast and coffee, their appetites already diminished. Peter checked the esky for their 'hunt food' of lamb legs now that venison was no longer on the menu.

'Enjoy this while you can, Sonya, before the morning sickness. I had it bad for several weeks.' Danika was reading the feel of the tension and was trying to lighten the mood.

'We are going to check the perimeter in the gator to make sure we are secure,' Cristian advised the girls and then left with Peter. Danika checked Cristian's thoughts, he confirmed he was just being cautious.

After their breakfast Danika and Sonya donned boots and walked over towards the waterfall and cliff area. They could hear it before they saw it and the nice sitting area was gone, washed away exposing large boulders. All that soil had washed down to the road and it's bridge and beyond. The kangaroos were now mostly in the paddock as the grass was so deep, over waist high. Many of the bushes had been washed away or broken. The power of the water was incredible. They could hear the gator up in the back forest. Danika could also sense Cristian there. She would have to renew the charm on his ring and chain before dark.

'Are the kangaroos alright?' Sonya worriedly asked.

'They are used to the weather although it is wetter than usual. Cristian is very protective of them.' Danika tried to allay Sonya's fears.

'What did you mean by "steering them away from the road" last night?'

'I try to put the thought in their minds by pictures. Words are not much use, although I say them for my benefit to firm the thoughts,' Danika tried to explain.

'The mental connection seems to break as Peter changes, yet if I speak to him in German slowly and calmly he responds. He doesn't remember and is a bit sceptical.'

'I know what you mean. Just before you arrived we were here and I thought he was up the mountain and I slipped out to get something from my van when a serious nausea had me doubled over being sick. Next thing he was standing over me protective. He didn't believe me and was angry I put myself in danger but I never felt that.' Danika was so pleased to share this with Sonya.

'I slept with Peter during a change once, as in actual sleep,' Sonya clarified. 'I never told him, he would have been so angry at me.' Danika felt Sonya also was glad to finally confess to someone.

'Your secret is safe with me.' Danika smiled. They walked to see where the bridge was damaged and the road washed out. This was obviously going to be like this for a long time as it was not a substantial road. As they wandered back to the house they admired all the bulbs and fruit trees flowering. Danika said she was keen to plant more. They heard the gator getting closer, walking around to the sheds to meet them. In the back were a few logs and some stones Cristian had found washed out of the cliffs.

'We were checking out the storm damage and found these, I think they may be semi-precious, they look interesting anyway,' Cristian said as he handed one to Danika.

'Oh nice, how exciting. I've heard sapphires are common.' Danika was looking at the dark stone.

'We thought you may want more wood also, we just have to cut it smaller,' Peter added. 'No carrying for either of you.' Peter was still in slight shock of the baby news Danika could feel.

Danika was feeling a little tired from their walk anyway so was happy to sit and watch them work. 'How safe are the cliffs?' Danika asked.

'There are some unstable points but we found a few safe tracks. We will place the hunt meat out that way in a couple of hours,' Cristian answered.

They watched or chatted as the guys sawed and chopped the wood before taking it into the house to start the lounge fire. The sun would be setting in an hour so Peter took the meat to the cliff face and returned, stating he was feeling uncomfortable. Cristian confirmed.

'Don't hold it for us, we are fine,' Danika confirmed, now she had placed stronger charms on Cristian's ring and chain.

Without hesitation, Peter and Cristian undressed on the porch and elected to change early just as the sun set. It was so quick and Danika could feel they felt little pain when it was by choice. They were magnificent and so eager to run, jumping over each other like teenagers. Sonya and Danika had watched them from the open windows, saying their own words of love to each of their mates. As they disappeared from view they closed the windows against the cold and turned to look at each other. Without words they hugged, briefly glad to share this horrific yet wondrous phenomenon together in relative safety.

'Okay, shall we make some dinner?' Sonya suggested. The hours passed quickly once they started on the video games to build a farm, laughing at their eagerness. Danika yawned and, looking at the clock, read it as midnight. They heard Cristian and Peter howling. The moon was up and changing also. Danika concentrated and felt that they were on the mountain, higher than before. She hoped they weren't going to leave the property so she tried to call to Cristian, forgetting Sonya was watching her as she moved towards the back of the house and out the door. Sonya picked up a broom as she went following Danika outside into the cold. Danika drew energy from the moon and tried to pull them back from going to the top of the mountain and perhaps over the top where she would lose the connection. They howled again but it sounded closer but Danika still worked at pulling them back until Sonya laid a gentle hand on her shoulder to pull her back into the house.

'Come in Danika, they are safe.' Inside the exertion was now showing on Danika's face so Sonya made her sit on her bed.

'Why do you have a broom?' Danika asked.

'In case I had to warn them away,' Sonya answered.

'Good idea,' Danika said. 'Sorry I sensed they were nearly at the top of the mountain, I was worried they would go out of my mind's eye.'

'Good idea,' Sonya copied. 'But I think bed for you now.'

'Please set an alarm for dawn,' Danika insisted but promptly fell asleep as soon as she lay down.

Danika woke to an alarm. It seemed dark outside still but as she shuffled in her slippers to look out the front windows she saw a hint of a glow down the valley. Testing her senses, Cristian felt close – in the rocky paddock perhaps. Sonya came into the lounge and Danika let her know where she thought they were.

As the sun rose, they howled again, which felt strange. As the women were eating breakfast they heard them around the house, as if both were trying to give them reassurance and suggestions to lay down in their individual way. The women heard them growl. Looking through the window they watched them looking towards the road. Then they heard a truck.

Danika grabbed the keys of the 4WD out the back and quickly manoeuvred it in front of the house, telling Peter and Cristian to go to the mountain. Sonya did the same in German. They were hesitant and still growling so Danika pushed harder in her thoughts. As they appeared to be going as suggested she drove to the gate, just as the truck came to a stop on the roadway. With the window down but still sitting in the car she greeted the workmen.

'Hello, is everything okay?'

'We didn't know anyone lived here. We can move the road closed sign to here so you don't have to go through the paddock,' the worker said.

'Thank you, we didn't mind. We only use it as a holiday house.' The boys howled again up the mountain.

'Have you got a wild dog problem?' the workman asked.

'No, my malamutes are being a bit boisterous. They love the space,' Danika answered with a smile as she was trying to send thoughts to the workers to go away. One of the men put the sign out and the other turned the truck around to go. Danika waved them off and drove back up to the house. There she was met by Cristian with Peter at the house listening to Sonya's gentle words.

Danika sat looking at him and decided to chance getting out of the car. He stood watching as she walked slowly to the house past Peter, and Sonya who followed her into the house. They looked back at Cristian and Peter standing outside at the doorway as if they didn't know what to do. They both looked tired. Danika suggested they leave the back door propped open and put water in a bowl with towels on the floor. Then she tried to encourage them with thoughts and words as Sonya did also. The women went into the main house, shutting the door behind them. Danika leaned against the wall as they listened for a short while before going back to their unfinished breakfast in the kitchen.

'Well that was a bit exciting and stressful,' Sonya said after letting out a deep breath. 'What did you do when they howled while you were talking to those men?'

'My heart skipped when they did that, probably territorial. I said they were my malamutes in case they saw them.' Then she put her hand over her mouth, remembering the shiver of fear. 'The workers were moving the road closed sign. I hope the guys sleep and change soon now.'

'That was quick thinking. I think they are very tired, I hope they sleep too. It is a bit like dealing with children, really big ones.' They laughed a little about that.

The women packed away the photos in the dining area and were in the lounge playing the video game when they heard the shower running in the afternoon. Danika checked for thoughts and said to Sonya, 'That's Peter.' Sonya went to make sure he had clothes.

When Peter came out in a towel and went into their room, Danika went in with clothes and stood watching a sleeping beauty turn into her handsome man. She wanted to store that memory to share with him as hopefully it would be the last time. She used her mind to gently wake him. He woke, unsure of his surroundings briefly, until she was reassuring him that they were alone and safe. He gave her a mental hug and blew her a kiss as he walked into the shower. Danika put his clothes down on the vanity and closed the back door before picking up the grubby towels and the water bowl.

Not long after they were all sitting at the kitchen table while the guys ate and Danika and Sonya gave them a rundown of the last twenty-four hours. They listened as they ate and then Cristian said, 'Malamutes, boy that's a new one. Quick response though.'

'I was so worried they had already had a glimpse of you,' Danika elaborated.

'I actually wouldn't mind going home this afternoon, if everyone is okay with that? I don't think we need more visitors,' Cristian said as he shared his concern for a repeat visit.

They all agreed. It was a quick uneventful drive other than stopping at a chemist for Sonya to buy pregnancy test kits.

Back at Hollingrove after unpacking Danika checked all was going to be fine at the gallery with the new recruits for the week so she could focus on planning for the next lunar cycle and all that would entail.

After Sonya happily confirmed more than once that she was pregnant Danika suggested she book to see the doctor she was seeing. Peter and Sonya decided they would wait to tell Friedrich until after the next lunar cycle. Regardless of the outcome of next month's event, they had decided to stay in Australia as long as possible so had started to look for suitable properties. Peter wanted plenty of space, acreage to allow for spreading out but realised they still needed to be close to schools and other services. Sonya wanted enough rooms to accommodate Peter's mother and their growing family, plus visitors. Over the next two weeks, with Dean's guidance, they looked at several properties within a short distance of Hollingrove. Eventually they decided on a farm with enough room to accommodate their growing family.

Selene and Clay would be arriving on the day after Halloween, a week before the blood moon to get prepared for the momentous event. They would be staying at Hollingrove while Peter, Sonya and Friedrich stayed in Sydney until that day. Danika was grateful and eager to see her mother, to share the load she felt on her shoulders despite Cristian's words of encouragement that it was a shared task.

The day before Selene and Clay were due to arrive Danika was feeling anxious and emotional at the same time as she checked again for the umpteenth time that their room was in order and Ann had suitable vegan meals organised. Mark and Ben had left for the day as their family was having a Halloween gathering, while the children went trick or treating. Rick and Jay were dressed as zombies for the event. Sonya had sent a photo of them in their ghoulish costumes. This at least made her smile. Cristian had been trying to get to the bottom of her concerns as they sat in their sitting room.

'Tomorrow is the beginning of the end.' Danika was not really making sense with her words or her thoughts.

'You need to give me a bit more context sweetheart.' He placed his hands on her belly as he hugged her. 'Come on kids, help me.'

'Tomorrow Mum arrives and we have to finalise the chant to break the curse and test the artefacts for strength. Whatever we have then is all that we have to finish the curse. What if it isn't enough?' Danika was crying at the thought of the unthinkable. The loss of her babies, Sonya's baby perhaps and the horror for Friedrich.

'We will all deal with whatever happens, one thing at a time.'

Cristian was trying to give her calming thoughts and she could feel the twins doing the same.

'I'm sure something is wrong with Mum. She won't talk about herself and Clay when I ask, they are very elusive.' Danika had not shared these worries with Cristian until now.

'They probably just want their privacy.' Cristian kissed her tears away. 'Besides, they will be here tomorrow and you can see and hear for yourself how they are.'

He leaned in, kissing her belly and talking to the babies by name.

'When do you see Dr Michael again?' Cristian asked, worried for her safety.

'Next week, I'm going with Sonya for her first visit after the event.' She felt his worry about the effect of the next most important lunar event.

'I'm sure we will be fine, as you said a shared load.' Danika was feeling much more relaxed than an hour ago thanks to the love surrounding her.

The next morning Danika woke late, realising Cristian had removed her alarm to let her sleep in. Before she could get worried he was already sending her calming thoughts that they had plenty of time to get to the airport and that breakfast was just being served.

Danika quickly showered and dressed and came into the dining room, hearing laughter from Elizabeth and Ingrid. They were showing photos and explaining the antics of the children during the evening of Halloween. This was just what Danika needed and she absorbed all the happiness and energy she could, sharing it back as love and gratitude. The photos of Rick and Jay as zombies were hilarious and watching the frights of some at the decorations at Dean's house were amusing also. Eventually the conversation came around to Selene and Clay's visit. Danika agreed she was looking forward to seeing her mother after several months and that Clay was the one who made the beautiful angel statue. Cristian received a message which he glanced at and put his phone down again, smiling at Danika to share his thoughts. Clay had confirmed they were checked in at Adelaide airport and would see them in a few hours. No message from Selene.

Danika was feeling uneasy at the lack of connection with her mother, as if she was hiding something. Cristian tried to keep her from overthinking that concern. Ingrid was talking about the boys wanting to camp out to watch for the meteor shower on Saturday.

'Is that something that is useful to you Danika?' Elizabeth asked, breaking her reverie.

'Thank you for thinking of me, but no. Meteor showers or shooting stars, as pretty as they may be, are dying celestial bodies so sadness is attached to them for me. Also that particular shower takes a long time to see any. I hope the boys are patient.' Danika smiled.

'No, they aren't, but they will enjoy the camping out no doubt,' Ingrid confirmed. Ben came in to make sure everyone was finished and clear the dining room. He addressed Danika separately.

'I noticed that the herbs and new flowers are looking lovely now and wondered if you would like to cut some for your mother? I have shears in the kitchen.' So, Ben and probably Ann had picked up her unease.

'Thank you Ben, that would be nice.' Danika did not want to worry any others for her probably unfounded fears. Cristian agreed with that and checked if she would like company in the garden. Danika thought she would be fine.

Danika did enjoy the slow walk around the garden with hand shears and bucket in hand absorbing the sounds of the bees and the birds as she selected stalks of herbs and some of the many flowers. She sat briefly in the rotunda and looked out across the revitalised gardens and could hear the water feature gurgling, now fully repaired and working again. It felt like she had always lived here and yet it was only a few months. She absorbed the beauty and felt grateful for her life as it was and what she hoped it would be with her growing family. As usual, her extended family of the Nortons guessed this was what she needed to calm her mind. Back in the kitchen Danika took her bucket of finds for Ben to sort and put into vases to be placed on the landing upstairs, thanking him for his thoughtfulness.

Finally time to pick her mother and Clay up from the airport, Cristian and Danika headed off to the city. They reached the airport early as the flight was not due to arrive for another hour. Danika was pleased to be early though and was absorbing the happy feelings as people met loved ones off of flights. Cristian received a message from Clay they had landed so they made their way to the arrival gate. Danika's emotions were again running high as he held her hand and tried to calm her down.

Danika felt her mother's presence before she saw her coming from the plane, yet still there was a slight barrier. Clay was beaming and waved at them both as he spotted them waiting. As he approached them he said to Danika, 'You're looking swell.' And then laughed at his own joke, disarming her immediately.

'Yes, getting bigger every day,' Danika acknowledged as she lovingly laid her hand on her belly. Her mother dropped her bags and hugged Danika tightly, letting all the barriers down and they were both crying. Danika was so overcome she could barely let Cristian know what was happening. Then he caught the gist of the tears and could finally shake Clay's hand and congratulate them both.

'Married and going to be a father, I'm the luckiest man alive. Besides you of course mate.' Clay was beaming hard again and slapping Cristian on the back. Danika was in disbelief on top of absolute happiness.

'When? How?' she asked aloud.

'Let's get their bags and we can go talk somewhere else if you like.' Cristian and Clay went off to find their bags leaving the women to hug and cry some more.

Not far from the airport they found a quiet café to sit and talk. As they sat with their drinks, Selene filled them in as she sat holding Clay's hand.

'Well to answer your question Danika, you know very well how.

But I thought it was impossible with the prophecy and my age as well, but apparently we are both very fertile.' Clay was beaming again and his love and pride was boundless.

'I suspected I was starting menopause but felt sick rather than hot flushes, so I went to the doctor. Poor Clay was so worried about me he was waiting in the car. It took me quite a while to understand what the doctor was saying about check-ups because of my age. I was in shock.' Selene reached over to kiss Clay.

'As soon as she told me, I asked her to marry me and my darling said yes.' Clay kissed Selene back. Danika was shocked, seeing her mother so openly in love. 'We wanted to surprise you but had to keep it a secret for weeks. Getting married is not a fast process.'

'It can be if you are Cristian,' Danika confirmed and squeezed his hand. 'So when was the wedding?'

'Last week at the registry office in Adelaide. Apparently I'm about eleven weeks and due in May.' Selene had a flush of happiness in her face and then showed them her rings. A white gold Claddagh ring with small diamonds in the crown and a blue sapphire heart with a plain white gold wedding band adorned Selene's left hand. 'Clay has Irish heritage and organised this while we were waiting for permission to marry in secret. We have a couple of photos.' They admired the photos of Clay and Selene on their wedding day, photos taken by a stranger at the registry office.

'You scrub up well,' Cristian said to Clay.

'Thanks mate, but Selene was the star, such an angel.' Clay was very much in love and only had eyes for Selene.

'This is going to be quite a gathering next week. Our cousin Sonya is pregnant also, a surprise for them too. Imagine all the babies next year.' Danika loved that her family seemed to be growing by the minute.

'We have more to tell you. We are living together at the farm,' Selene said.

'Well that makes sense,' Danika said.

'Clay sold his home and moved all his pottery business to the farm into a new shed. Those builders you recommended have been fantastic. We have a new extension to the house and so much more. I can't wait for you to see it all.' Selene was more enthusiastic than Danika had ever known. The term 'a new woman' came to mind.

On their return home, Clay whistled his admiration when he saw Hollingrove as they drove up the driveway and then felt pride when he saw the angel as the centre piece to the drive. Ben and Mark came out to help with the bags. Danika introduced Ben and Mark to her mother Selene and Clay as her stepfather, feeling a thrill at the use of the word. Clay could not have been prouder to call Danika his daughter, Danika could feel this.

They all followed Ben up the front steps where Elizabeth was waiting to greet them. Cristian introduced his mother to Selene and Clay. Elizabeth did not miss a beat and said how pleased she was to finally meet them. Mark assisted Ben before moving the car back to the garage.

Elizabeth ushered them into the sitting room where Ann brought in light drinks and homemade biscuits. Danika introduced Ann also, who hesitated slightly as she shook Selene's hand. Danika caught a surprised thought from Ann and was sure she realised her mother was pregnant.

After settling everyone into rooms and taking the afternoon to relax and recuperate, dinner was filled with all at Hollingrove.

'Do you have any name ideas for your babies?' Selene asked.

'Yes, we have decided but we are keeping them to ourselves until they are born,' Cristian confirmed.

In the dining room at first Selene felt a little out of place Danika could sense but once they all started chatting she felt more at ease.

After dinner they moved to the sitting room although Selene and Danika made an excuse to go towards the kitchen. Danika knew Selene had detected Ann's intuitiveness and that she would want to pry further to discover if Ann's family had any relation to their own.

Ann was not surprised to see them, Danika could sense that. Selene did not hesitate to ask. 'Ann I feel like we are connected on a family level but I have never met you before. Do any of your family come from Adelaide?'

'The Adelaide branch of the family has been there since the seventies. My uncle Bill then a young man went that way for work in the building trade. His son and grandson have been working on your house I believe,' Ann confirmed.

'The Bartlett's? The name isn't familiar.'

'They took the name of my uncle's wife because her family were in the building trade but my uncle is a Norton. He once said his wife was the rebound wife after a lost love. He pined after an older woman named Naomi that he lost contact with after only two dates. She had told him she was travelling from interstate and he could not find where she went. He remembered her green eyes.' Selene had to sit down as the shock of this information washed over her. Danika could feel the rush of emotions and the realisation that they were most probably related to the Norton's through her grandmother.

'My mother's name was Naomi, she had green eyes, I was born in 1975. She said little about my father as is our way, only that he was a strapping younger man good with his hands. She met him in the city and afterwards never went back there.'

'Is your mother still alive?' Ann asked politely already knowing the truth through Danika.

'No unfortunately, she rejected treatment for cancer and passed many years ago. What about your uncle?' Selene asked.

'Yes he is still with us and fit. He likes to travel with his wife. They are very happy. Perhaps you may like to meet him.' Danika saw Selene withdraw at that suggestion.

'Oh no, I don't think so. It is all speculation and I am not into DNA tests or wanting to prove a connection. It was just mildly interesting.'

'Well, if you change your mind. You do, after all, live in the same state,' Ann offered but Selene was still trying to digest the information.

'Thank you. A nice gesture but best let sleeping dogs lie I think.' Selene could see too many problems of connecting with a possible other family, Danika sensed, while trying to contain her excitement at having a half cousin. As they left the kitchen Selene said she wanted to go to her room and could Danika let Clay know. Danika had felt Cristian pushing for an update of why they hadn't come back but she had kept most of it to herself.

Danika went back into the sitting room and explained that the travel had caught up with her mother who wanted to relax so she had plenty of energy tomorrow. She did not hint at the revelation discussed with Ann.

Clay finished his drink and excused himself to go check on Selene. Elizabeth also decided to retreat to her rooms, leaving Danika to explain to Cristian what they had discovered.

'If your mother is reticent about taking it further, I think you need to dial down your enthusiasm. It really is up to her, don't you think?' Cristian was trying to be supportive but honest.

'Oh I know, you're right. Believe me, this is huge for Mum. She was like me, very lonely especially when Grandma died and now she possibly has a father, a brother and who knows how many other relatives. I already considered the Nortons my family anyway.' Danika knew he was right and didn't want to pressure her Mum either. 'The universe is really giving it out in spades. I just know next week is going to be amazing.' Cristian could see her glowing and suggested she do some meditation to keep from crashing from an energy overload.

'I love you and how you know what I need, even when I don't.' Danika hugged him and they both grinned as the twins kicked him in the solar plexus. Danika's meditation worked to calm her excitement and allow her to sleep dream free. When she woke she felt Cristian had already left on his run so she slowly planned the next few days on her notebook of when to finalise the plans for the night of the blood moon and when to have a meeting of those that would be at the gathering. She was writing notes when she felt Cristian coming through the kitchen and his surprise that Ann was not there, with Bethany filling in.

Danika put aside her note taking to join Cristian in the shower. Once they were dressing they talked about it being unusual Ann not coming in, but glad she felt she could stay home if necessary. Bethany had assured him Ann was well but had family business to deal with.

At breakfast that morning Danika suggested a meeting between all the parties on Monday evening in the ballroom, which was agreed to on a provisional basis until everyone else could be contacted. Elizabeth was planning to meet with Ingrid and Jean Walton today and said she would speak to Ingrid then. Danika kept it light, not wanting to dampen the other's enthusiasm. Cristian had come in just as this was being organised and said he needed to talk with Peter today and wondered if they would all like to go to the city. This was a new sudden arrangement that Danika knew must be important, so agreed that Selene and she could work tomorrow.

Using the estate car they dropped Elizabeth off at Jean's house and parked at the apartment to see Peter and Sonya. As they sat with Selene and Clay also, Peter proceeded to fill them in on the events in Germany with Robert and the family.

'From the information we have received it appears they – as in Robert and Karl at least, and possibly his other son Eric – are planning something. He is getting less tolerant of the witch Claus, who wants to be called Merlin. Especially as they have discovered the real artefacts gone and replaced without knowing when. Our insider has had to leave but she was able to find out a bit more about Claus. She has called the police after she saw Robert and his sons leave with luggage, it appears to the airport last night.' Peter let that linger for a short while then continued.

'Apparently when she went back in, Claus had been bitten by one of them as he had requested and was trying to do a spell to survive the poison. Now the police are looking for Robert and his sons in connection with poisoning Claus who is a wanted man anyway for fraud and deception. Their wives had already left last week, fearing retribution over the artefacts. They are staying with other family but are certain Robert and his sons are coming here to Australia. The wives have told the police they believed Australia was the destination so hopefully the authorities here have been advised.'

'What if they get into Australia before the authorities know? Do you think they would try to stop the gathering?' Selene asked, her worry evident.

'They have no other reason to come to Australia but we can make sure we have plenty of people watching out for them and, if necessary, they can call the police,' Cristian said honestly.

'How many people will be at the gathering?' Clay asked.

'Not counting Peter and Cristian, at least a dozen, perhaps more. I thought we could have a meeting the night before to explain the proposed sequence of events. We will know more about numbers then,' Danika estimated.

'We have to assume they will be in Australia by tonight,' Peter surmised. 'So I don't think anyone should go anywhere alone but especially Cristian and Danika, they are the key.' Danika leaned over and grasped Selene's hand as she could feel her getting concerned.

'You have all been living this danger for a long time, we are only just catching up.' Selene grabbed Clay's hand with her other one.

'Just let me know what needs to be done and I'm in,' Clay said.

'I think protecting Selene and Danika is your priority Clay, not leaving their side so to speak,' Cristian suggested. 'There is likely to be many distractions so having someone like you with focus will be essential.' Danika could feel the pride and determination building in Clay who had struggled with confrontation since his military service.

'Will you both be in wolf form all night?' Selene asked.

'From dusk, which is moonrise. So we will be visible until the maximum eclipse which is a couple of hours. Then during the maximum full eclipse, which is about an hour and a half, we can revert to human form by choice. What happens after that is in the hands and words of you lovely ladies,' Peter answered Selene.

'Oh, I didn't know you could choose,' Danika said.

'It can be uncomfortable and problematic, depending on the circumstances. Believe me, we will change by choice,' Cristian explained. 'We are most vulnerable at that point and naked of course.'

'Yes all things to be considered,' Peter added. Sonya had been quiet through the conversation and Danika could feel her trepidation and noted her hand on her stomach. She squeezed her mother's hand who sensed her intention.

'Sonya, I think you should join Mum and I in the chant especially as we are all carrying babies.'

'Yes you are right Nika, I believe that would help the force we are creating,' Selene agreed.

'I didn't think I had much to offer. Will the babies be safe?'

'Darling, you need to be there to talk to me of course like no other can. Our baby will only be safe if this succeeds with your help.' Peter hugged her as she let a tear escape then nodded.

'What about Friedrich? Should he stay here?' Sonya asked.

'No, I'm coming with you to help.' Friedrich came into the room, clearly having been listening in.

'Yes, we need you to help with the perimeter. This weekend we will have the radio headset comms that Mark is organising, Clay you could help with that no doubt,' Cristian answered him. Danika could feel the emotions running high through everyone and was trying to share and calm all at the same time. Cristian touched her arm and sent a thank you but not to overdo it at the same time.

Friedrich came and stood next to his mother with his hand on her shoulder in a protective stance. *He really was becoming a strong young man*, Danika thought.

They naturally broke into two groups: the women making drinks and the guys with paper and pens from Friedrich drawing maps of the estate and surrounds to discuss vantage and problem points. By the time they were leaving it was decided a whole gathering meeting was best on Sunday so they had the Monday and Tuesday to sort out any issues. They would all stay at Hollingrove from then until the end. This would take a bit of creative sleeping arrangements but Danika knew Ann, Ben and the others would come through for them.

Danika sensed her mother was missing her connection with nature as she had moved out to the balcony again. 'Why don't you get a taxi to the botanic gardens for a bit? We won't be leaving for a few hours to collect Elizabeth. It would do you good. The views are stunning.' Clay came out just as he caught the conversation.

'Come on Sel, let's be tourists for a couple of hours, you will be busy tomorrow.' Clay kissed his wife.

Danika could feel her wavering and gave her a little mental push. 'Okay you two, I agree.'

Danika was pleased her mother was going to enjoy this afternoon because she felt the rest of the week would be hectic and confronting. Cristian agreed and was giving Clay a quick rundown of the area and the address to come back to as the taxi pulled up.

The rest of the day seemed to go fast and before long they were pulling into the drive at Hollingrove with all three women snoozing in the back of the car until then.

Over the next two days Danika and Selene alternated between trying the connections with the artefacts, working on the curse and chant, and meditation to regain strength. Clay and Cristian more critically assessed the dangers and pitfalls of the perimeter and security with Mark and Ben's help. All the wireless communication and some weapons had arrived. Guns and knives were out of the question, Cristian had said as they were far too dangerous and basically illegal. So cattle prods and electric fencing were the weapons of choice, all legal with their deer farming background. 'We don't want anyone to die but we do need everyone to be safe,' Cristian explained.

'I think we need to try them to understand the effect,' Mark pointed out. 'I'll go first.'

Clay nodded and suggested he run at him. So they were in the stables taking turns at being zapped when Danika arrived breathless. Cristian had forgotten to turn off their connection. He was apologising as soon as he sensed her.

Danika could see their point but still shook her head at the boy-like amusement they were having.

'It's a deterrent and distraction, not a lethal weapon,' Cristian explained to her.

'Okay, that's good. Mum and I are working on something similar for the others to use.' She held up a pouch and Cristian was backing off immediately. She came closer and he reached out and could feel the barrier. When he touched it, he felt physically ill and dropped to his knees.

'Just for werewolves,' she explained as the others looked on in shock and admiration to some extent.

She walked over to the side of the stables to put the pouch down and came back to Cristian. 'Sorry darling, I had to test it out.' As she reached down to touch his back, the nausea was abating and he stood up, nodding his head.

'That works well, I hope you're not storing it in our bedroom.' Cristian grinned to lighten the moment. He agreed mentally he should have closed his thoughts. Danika went back to her mother, picking up the pouch as she went.

By Sunday morning, Peter, Sonya, Friedrich and Ingrid were back at Hollingrove. Ann approached Danika after breakfast to share some news that may shock her mother and wanted her guidance. Danika brought her mother into the kitchen.

'My uncle Bill and his son Michael and grandson Luke will be at the meeting this afternoon. But he would like to see you both beforehand if you agree.' Ann was almost holding her breath. Danika held her mother's hand and then they both agreed they would like that.

Ben was in charge of the security cameras and allowed visitors in as they were identified. When Bill and his family arrived they were shown into the downstairs sitting room where Selene and Danika waited. The likeness between Selene and her brother Michael was unmistakable, Danika thought and was amazed she had not seen it also. Bill offered a photo strip to Selene. It was a photo booth shot of him and Naomi, both laughing then sticking their tongues out. Finally the last one was of them kissing. It was compelling truth. 'I never knew she had a baby. I never saw her again after the two days. To think she and you were just up the hill all that time.' Bill was quite amazed.

Selene held her hand out. 'Hello Dad.' Bill grasped it and Selene felt the link immediately and went into his arms.

Michael looked at Selene and said, 'Hi Sis.' Danika was crying openly now as she felt all the love surrounding her and her mother.

She looked at Luke and said, 'I guess we are cousins.' He nodded, a bit overwhelmed at the whole event.

They sat and Selene and Danika tried to explain the situation from their perspective to them, guessing Ann already had filled them in enough for them to be there.

'When Ann called me to tell me Naomi had a daughter that was a big enough shock. But this witches and werewolves part of it I never really believed, despite it being taught to us as kids,' Bill acknowledged. 'I'm sorry that I didn't take it seriously, so we are going to be on catch up.'

'It feels like we are living in a movie,' Michael admitted.

'That's understandable. You aren't alone. The curse change is not witnessed by many, Mum hasn't seen it either. We are hoping Tuesday night will be the first and last time anyone sees it,' Danika told them. 'Everyone else is probably arriving now upstairs.'

Danika showed them up to the ballroom where multiple chairs had been set up. Also on the stage was a pull-down screen and a white board. Down the side of the room were tables with equipment one end and bottles of water the other. Once everyone was seated Cristian and Danika stood on the stage together. They looked out across more than twenty faces.

'Thank you all for coming today. Some of you know and understand what has and will be happening and others do not, so we will go through a quick précis to date and the plans for Tuesday at more length. Can we leave the questions until the end? Thanks.' Cristian's booming voice carried well in the room. 'I'll hand over to Danika to start with.'

Danika explained the events as they knew them from four hundred years ago creating the curse. That the Romani Gypsies of the time vowed to watch over the Blakesley family until the curse ended. That her ancestor Jessica came to Australia two hundred years ago missing the opportunity to end the curse then and now, two hundred years on, the time is right again. Cristian then took over his family's side of the story, mainly in Europe with one section coming to Australia and one recently to Canada. He told of the misunderstanding of wealth and power attached to the curse creating a malevolent attitude to breaking the curse, despite the dangers and horrors the Blakesley men and their families have been enduring.

'Hence we have a substantial threat from one section of the Germany family. We believe my uncle Robert and his two sons Karl and Eric have left to come to Australia. We have no way of knowing if they have arrived and if they got through customs as there is likely an international police report for their arrest.' Cristian let that sink in. 'We are going to assume they got through and they intend to stop the breaking of the curse at all costs.'

Danika continued, 'My mother Selene and I have been working on a chant to break the curse. Thanks to Ann's mother June for helping us with the translation of what, we hope, was the original curse as remembered by the one of the first Blakesley's to suffer it. On Tuesday during the blood moon we, plus as many women as possible, will need to recite the chant continuously until the blood moon ends. This will take hours so it is a tall ask, hence needing as many as possible to take over as needed.'

Cristian spoke again, 'The men will be needed to maintain the perimeter to stop any unwanted persons or wolves from stopping the chant and protecting the women. Mark will explain the communications for each person and the deterrent weapons and their usage while Danika has something extra to ward off werewolves. So I'll open the floor up for questions.'

'Where will the chant take place?' Ann asked, Danika sensed, on behalf of everyone.

'Out the front at the angel. We will be using the power of three artefacts from the original event,' Danika answered.

'How many werewolves will there be and when?' Michael asked.

'Myself and Peter here now and possibly the three we are concerned about,' Cristian answered.

'How will we tell you apart?' Michael asked again.

'As this has not been an issue before we had not prepared for that contingency but we are going to trial a collar of sorts,' Cristian answered.

'If we come across these trespassers, what do we do with them?' Bill asked this time. Danika and Selene felt he wanted to stop them forever.

'If they are wolves we need to subdue them without putting yourself at risk of being bitten. As men, we would do similar, but call the police,' Cristian answered.

'What happens if anyone is bitten?' Luke asked.

'A werewolf bite is poison and anyone bitten would die, eventually,' Cristian answered. 'I think it would be a good time for Mark to go through the communications and weapons.'

Mark took the floor and showed them the Wi-Fi ear pieces that each one other than Danika and Selene and Sonya could and should be wearing. Then the cattle prod for the men predominately and the electric fence being installed at the cliff area that was not fenced from the national park.

Ann had gone to bring a few snacks out from the upstairs kitchen to place near the water.

Danika retrieved a couple of the pouches. Keeping her distance from Cristian and Peter she went back up on to the stage and got their attention.

'These little pouches are the extra Cristian was talking about. They are very potent and not to be misused. The distance at which they start to work is about two metres.' She looked at Peter who had not felt the result as Cristian had. 'Are you game?' He nodded then started to approach her. At about two metres Danika could tell the nausea was intense but he was trying to fight it. As he came closer she held it up and he dropped to his knees as Cristian had and started to heave. She backed off immediately. Ben helped him up. The audience was quiet.

'I won't hand them out until Tuesday,' Danika said. 'They are for those watching the perimeter and those not associated with Cristian and Peter.'

Danika had copies of the chant for the women and, as she handed them out, reminded them they could not say it aloud but needed to memorise it. 'We don't want a well-conceived plan to be ruined by going too early.' They each understood the gravity of her words.

'How will we know it worked?' Bethany asked.

'They won't be able to return to the wolf form by choice or at the continuing full moon,' Danika answered.

Elizabeth and Ingrid had sat quietly at the back of the room holding hands as they watched their family working hard towards the most important event of their lives. Danika could feel their pride, both wishing their husbands were here to see this. Danika approached them and gave them the slip of paper with the chant. 'You are an important part of this also.'

After another hour, everyone had tried the communications and saw how the cattle prods worked. Danika sensed that the younger boys and girls were both nervous and thrilled to be included. Friedrich had a high stake in this event. If it didn't succeed he too would succumb to the curse next year.

Danika approached Bill to ask where he was staying. 'We are being billeted with Ann's family, thanks. It has been far too long since I visited last and we have a lot of catching up to do. Perhaps once this is over we can have a quiet drink together and a chat.'

'I'd like that. What do your other grandchildren call you?' Danika said, acknowledging their connection.

'Pop or Pa. I'd be happy if you called me Will,' he replied. Danika smiled, thinking of her grandmother.

'Okay, Will, that is easy.' Danika could sense some regret from him. 'How are Michael and Luke taking all this?'

'Better than I expected. I never told them the family history and we have been so far removed from it. Even when Dean reached out to us to help Selene I knew why but didn't know how to start that conversation. Then with Ann's call this week about Naomi, I had to come,' Will explained.

Danika could feel that the others were murmuring to leave but no one wanted to be first. She sent a message to Cristian to wind it up. Cristian stood on the stage again and thanked everyone for coming.

Danika and Cristian had moved to their sitting room with Sonya and Peter, Selene and Clay. They sat quietly at first until Clay pointed out how wonderful it was to see such a large family together. 'Despite the reason this has happened and the risk it may not change, this family is now stronger for being known to each other and working together. Safety is essential.' Danika could feel them all agreeing and was pleased with Clay's comment.

Later that night, Danika was lying awake in bed listening and waiting for Cristian to check all doors and windows were locked. He left a few strategic lights on and joined her in bed, having felt her thoughts and knowing she was still awake. She snuggled up to him, her head on his chest, but they said nothing. Each had their private thoughts as he reached his hand across her burgeoning tummy to rest it on her hip. Danika could not keep the tears from spilling over.

'Are they happy tears, my love?' Cristian gently stroked her hair with his other hand.

'Yes and sort of no. What Clay said tonight was so lovely. I have a stepdad, a grandfather and so many family members I have lost count. I feel like my heart is bursting with love and gratitude but now I am worried for them all.' Danika accepted the tissues he offered her.

'I know what you mean. They are so accepting of us but that is without having seen the curse for most of them. They may change their opinion then.' Cristian was still keeping some of his thoughts closed. Danika nudged him.

'Full disclosure, what is bothering you the most?' Danika asked. He opened his thoughts. 'Ah, the risk of being bitten by any of you. They know that is a risk, I know that is a risk. We are all going to be as careful as is humanly possible.' Danika groaned and said, 'I have to move, I'm squashing one of them.' She rolled on to her back and Cristian laid his hand across their babies and felt them moving around. The wonder of it fascinated him as an elbow or knee rolled under his hand.

'Typical, they've woken up now just when I want to sleep.' Danika hummed and eventually the movement slowed and she also drifted off to sleep.

17

THE BEGINNING OF THE END

Waking to barely light Danika knew both Cristian and Peter were running. They seemed to be further away than usual though so after making herself comfortable she tried to stretch her thoughts as far as possible. Cristian pinged her back in a fashion realising she was trying to test where he was. They were in the national park zone. Danika quickly showered and dressed to greet any guests that rose early. Clay was the first coming down to get a cup of tea for Selene. Danika hugged him, needing the contact to calm her nerves.

'The guys are scoping out the hill behind us that is the boundary of the national park,' Danika explained, knowing it would mean something to Clay.

'Good. That area is a strategic black spot of sorts, difficult for us to monitor and defend.' Clay smiled as he put a biscuit on the side for Selene and took the drink upstairs.

In the kitchen Ann and Bethany were cooking up a storm of protein plus waffles and slicing fresh fruits. 'Good morning ma'am, breakfast will be along shortly.'

Danika brought a cup of herbal tea in with her to sit and watch them work. 'I'm fine Ann, just enjoying the thrum of the waking house.' She could feel Sonya stirring and the familiar question of where her mate was until realising he would be running. Selene was content with her man and her baby to focus on as she sipped her tea. Rick, Elizabeth and Ingrid were yet to stir.

'I was thinking to bring Jayden with me in the morning ma'am, thought company for young Master Friedrich, if that is alright?' Bethany asked as she placed waffles in the warming tray to go into the dining room.

'Wonderful idea Bethany, I'm sure they will follow Mark around all day helping where they can,' Danika agreed. 'Is he scared of what is going to happen tomorrow? Are you?'

'Master Friedrich apparently explained it as only a teenager could to him and he now has a mixture of awe and trepidation but completely accepting of course.' Bethany placed jams and other condiments in dishes. 'Me… well, I just want everyone to be happy and safe and I will fight anyone that prevents that.' Bethany smiled broadly at Danika. They all looked up as Peter and Cristian came noisily through the back door covered in dirt and leaves. Ann ushered them back out to brush off and take their shoes off before coming back in, then handed them a cup of coffee each to take with them to go shower.

Cristian kissed Danika and mentally said, 'Good morning gorgeous.'

'Thanks Ann, good morning everyone,' he said aloud before racing upstairs to shower.

Peter thanked Ann and continued along the corridor to Ann's rooms where he and Sonya were staying. Danika could feel that Ann loved having so many people to serve, pleased to get to share their lives. Danika knew better than to try to help with the dishes of foods and instead waited, then went into the dining room to find a place to sit and eat.

'What do we want this morning kids?' she said with her hand on her stomach, unusually deciding on bacon with her waffles and maple syrup with a side of fresh berries and perhaps an oat biscuit. She was really feeling hungry this morning.

Cristian was in the dining room just before Peter, both very hungry also and loading up their plates. Cristian raised his brows in his surprise to see how much Danika had in front of her to eat. As he poured himself another coffee and a tea for Danika he was commenting on her food choices. She was mid mouthful so answered by thoughts. 'Really hungry and actually wouldn't mind a coffee.'

Sonya came in with the others coming in behind her. The dining room now had nine people talking, serving food and eating all at once. Danika tried to focus on the emotions other than hunger to calm her babies desires down, she was humming also. The urge to keep eating was finally abating.

'I am having some crazy craving effect,' Danika whispered to Sonya.

'That happened to me around this stage of being pregnant around the full moon as well,' Sonya explained.

'Is there anything else I should know before tomorrow's full moon?'

'I'll let you know after breakfast,' Sonya whispered back. That did not ease Danika's mind although Sonya didn't seem to be worried at all.

After breakfast Sonya took Danika aside and apologised that she had forgotten that side effect from fifteen years ago. 'Tomorrow, just like Cristian, you won't want to eat much so probably some protein drinks or boosted teas to get you through.'

'I won't want to go hunt anything, will I?' Danika was getting a bit worried at what else she might crave.

'No, well I say that and I didn't, but you are much more in tune with Cristian,' Sonya admitted. 'I'll remind him to not get hungry again today.'

'I was thinking about doing a bit of a practice this afternoon at dusk, just so we know how it feels and looks. I have to discuss with Mum but are you okay with that?' Danika asked Sonya.

'Of course, I am happier to be busy. The guys went up into the park this morning and said they couldn't smell or see any tracks so were pleased,' Sonya explained.

'I wondered why they were up there. I think that area has them all worried,' Danika agreed. 'I noticed Elizabeth and Ingrid were very quiet this morning, do you think they are alright?'

'I think they are up to something actually, very conspirator like. I will try to keep an eye on them,' Sonya suggested.

The day seemed to drag for the women watching as the men were planning defensive areas, checking fences and cameras. Ben had more cameras installed along the back fence line next to the national park. He explained they weren't too sophisticated at short notice but would give them some view at least.

Danika suggested Selene and Sonya enjoy the gardens and get a feel for the entire area during the afternoon. They sat in the rotunda looking out across the gardens now bursting into full spring bloom.

'I meant to ask you what you put in those little pouches that floored Peter last night,' Sonya asked.

'Some of it is what but most of it is how,' Selene cryptically answered. 'We couldn't separate Peter and Cristian so we decided to just go with wolves. There are some herbs and a small rune in each pouch. The main herb is wolfsbane, quite poisonous to anyone if consumed. But it is mostly about the spell on the runes, basically causing the poisoning effect for any wolf-like creature.'

'That's very clever. We just have to make sure we don't get them too close to Peter and Cristian.'

'How are you going to keep Cristian and Peter from running off or any other unwanted reaction?' Selene asked Danika.

'Firstly we have hi-vis collars which I am going to place a tracking spell on. Then Sonya and I are going to talk to them. We have been practicing for a while. There isn't much else we can do as they are basically wild animals at that point. But we do know they will protect what they love. Really it is best to ignore them and let them pass,' Danika explained to her mother. 'After dinner, which will be earlier tonight, we can come out here with the artefacts to do a dry run so to speak, just on dusk so we can work out what we can see and where.'

The wait was starting to become nervy. They would all be glad for it to finally get started. At dinner Danika wasn't quite so ravenous as Cristian had tried to stay 'topped up' most of the day. She did eat more meat than usual and hoped it didn't give her a stomachache.

After dinner Clay helped Selene and Danika bring the artefacts down. Peter brought the Lleuad Blaidd bronze symbol. They could all feel the push and pull of the artefacts as they became closer. Danika felt it the most with Cristian feeling her thoughts and emotions stronger than usual. They had a small audience of Rick, Mark, Ann, Elizabeth and Ingrid watching as they worked out the best position for the artefacts and holding each piece. The stone from the original Hollingrove carved by Danika's ancestor was placed in the hands of the angel. Selene stood on one side with her hand on it, Danika on the other with Sonya between them. Danika held her medallion in the other hand and Selene held Jessica's rune, handed down from Bronwyn. As they gripped each other's hands the flow of power was obvious even to Sonya.

'This feels right. We can recite the chant as soon as Peter and Cristian change,' Danika said. 'Ann if we start to falter can you come over to add some strength?' Ann walked over and placed her hand on Danika's shoulder. 'Yes, like that would be great.'

Cristian and Peter walked up to them. 'So assuming we now have the full maximum eclipse and can change back what are we doing next besides being naked?' Peter asked.

Ingrid and Elizabeth then answered, 'We have these.' They held up long kaftan style shirts for them to throw on and slip on shoes.

'Peter, you are protecting the link with Clay until Cristian you pick up the Lleuad Blaidd and join the chant. As you join it to my medallion I'm hoping they become one.' Cristian picked the Lleuad

Blaidd up from the stone it rested on and brought it towards Danika's medallion. They could feel it being repelled like an opposite magnet so he turned it over and the force was then to attract. They didn't let them join as yet. But by Sonya stepping aside for Cristian the link was reduced. It took a few different juggling of positions before eventually realising that the Lleuad Blaidd for Cristian needed to be as a medallion also. Mark found a piece of string to hang it from. As Cristian moved closer to Danika the two medallions were attracted but they didn't let them touch.

'I think we need to improve the light out here,' Mark commented as it was getting difficult to discern one person from another in the gloom. 'It was worth doing this trial tonight.' Ben switched on all the house lights which helped but more was needed.

'I can protect you too.' Friedrich came up to his parents, wondering what his role was going to be.

'Yes you can, in case Dad cannot hold the human form you will be essential to protecting us,' Sonya told him and, after looking at Peter for approval, she added, 'We just found out you are going to be a big brother so you will be protecting your sibling also.' Sonya placed her hand on her stomach.

Danika felt his pride grow. 'I will protect you all.'

Ingrid had not known either and hugged Sonya and then Peter.

'I think if we are happy with this trial that we should go in now that it is dark and cold.' Clay had his arm around Selene to warm her up. Clay helped them bring the artefacts into the house again.

Ann had gone in ahead of the others and had Ben usher them into the sitting room where she served some hot drinks, chocolate and biscuits for everyone.

Danika was glad to sit down and rest her legs and wondered how she was going to cope standing for several hours tomorrow night. They each went their separate ways shortly after. It was a late night for Ann which worried Danika so she suggested Ann came in later tomorrow, especially if Bethany was coming to help. 'It is going to be a very long day and night tomorrow Ann and we are going to need you, so please give yourself a late wake up.'

Cristian picked Danika up in his arms and walked her upstairs, laying her on their bed and helping her take off her shoes. He suggested she lay for a while then he would help her get ready for bed. 'Your feet look a bit swollen so I think stay off them as much as possible tomorrow.' He put cool flannels on her feet as she admitted they were a little sore.

'It was a good night trying it out without pressure, I could really feel the force of the pieces, that must mean something.' Danika was fishing for confirmation as the night to end the curse of her and Cristian's families was so close.

'Yes we certainly don't want to be fumbling around when there is a time frame to work in,' Cristian agreed. 'Hopefully the threat of Robert and his sons does not eventuate. I feel strange leaving it up to others to protect us. I have been the driver of my own destiny for so long.' He helped her out of her clothes and into her night clothes, kissing her and the babies along the way and kissing her tattoo for good luck, making her giggle.

Cristian

As Danika slept, Cristian sensed and then saw a movement on the balcony. He rushed to it, realising it was Clay who jumped to see Cristian standing beside him.

'You almost gave me a heart attack mate,' Clay said.

'Sorry, I just saw a movement. Too soon to sleep also?' Cristian asked. Clay nodded. 'I feel like I need to do a perimeter run, what about you?'

'The perimeter bit, not the running bit, my leg is a bit dodgy,' Clay admitted. They made their way down the back stairs and found Peter was already out there, also not able to sleep yet.

'We could do this quicker in form,' Peter pointed out. Cristian agreed but was concerned about Clay.

'Don't let me stop you,' Clay said. They both stripped off and were in form in seconds, sniffing the air and lopping off.

After an hour, Peter and Cristian returned to the back of the house, where Clay and Mark stood waiting.

Peter and Cristian grabbed their clothes and showered in the pool area amenities. Mark and Clay said they would do a last check around the house and then pack away the comms units. When they reconvened in the kitchen, Ben was there making drinks and putting out sandwiches.

'Hello Ben, you not sleeping either? Oh thanks,' Cristian said as Ben handed him a coffee.

'Checking the new cameras, good vision. I spotted you all. Of course there are blank spots. We would need a hundred cameras. But they are covering the key areas,' Ben answered.

Cristian and Peter grabbed the rare beef sandwiches and, between mouthfuls, confirmed they had not sensed any unwanted activity around the perimeter.

'How far can you sense outside the fence?' Mark asked.

'To the top of the cliff face on the park side which is our main concern. The entrance side is murky because it is so close to other houses and walking tracks for people with dogs. It would be risky on a visual basis for them to come that way but we can't rule it out,' Cristian explained.

'So, you are sure they are coming?' Clay asked.

'Yes I heard from a contact that they were spotted coming through on a domestic flight from Perth last night. I think that was how they got through the customs and police before the international report was received. They have been in Perth for the week,' Cristian confirmed.

Everyone was silent for a few minutes. 'Well that is one question answered. What can we expect from them?' Clay asked.

'They are arrogant and brutal but very clever. We have to expect they have a plan. Robert has seen the new fencing and security but he will not expect the force of people,' Peter answered.

'Distraction is a ploy they might use. Our forces have no military or conflict experience to make those kinds of decisions,' Clay said.

'Lucky we have you then. I think coordination is your best role, Clay. We have others to protect the ladies.' Cristian had always wanted Clay in that role but knew he had to get there in his own time. Clay looked at Mark.

'Happy to hand over to your experience Clay, I'll be your second,' Mark admitted. Clay nodded his head, knowing they were right and he needed to do this to protect his family. He shook Mark's hand.

'Those comms worked well by the way, I could hear you both clearly,' Ben advised them.

It was after midnight when they finished their drinks and snacks so, trying to be quiet, they each drifted off to their own rooms to get what sleep they could.

Cristian left Danika in the morning deciding on clothes for now and later, to go down to talk to Mark. Clay was already there discussing reconnoitre of the outside of the property including the park. 'I was just coming to talk to you about that, I'm glad you were on the same wavelength.' As he finished Peter appeared with the same idea. 'I'll let Danika know we are going out, she will tell the others.' They all expected him to go but he made his way to Mark's car with them. When they looked at him confused he tapped his head. 'She knows.'

At first they drove around the local area past houses and paths looking at different access points and the dog walking tracks. They travelled on up to the road that lead into the national park and made their way to the lookout. There were already a few people there scoping out the best position to photograph the eclipse of the moon tonight despite the park being closed at night. Through binoculars they could just make out the furthest side outer fencing of the estate. The roof of the buildings was obscured by the cliff and trees.

'They could easily get here early and hide. These people obviously plan to hike here, that could be a problem,' Mark mentioned. 'I'll call the authorities about what we have observed, it may help.'

'Yes, we certainly don't need civilians caught up in our foray.' Clay was in military thought processes.

They all got out and walked around the edge of the parking area. Peter and Cristian had already been up the cliff before but looking down in human form was different.

'I'll leave that to you guys, heights aren't my thing,' Clay said.

Satisfied they had looked enough at the lookout they returned back to Hollingrove. Mark contacted the national park's authorities who confirmed they already had to monitor all lookouts tonight.

'I'm not sure they would be there the whole time but that was all I could do,' Mark advised. 'Unless you have something else for me to do I'm going to go around with the blower for a bit. Gives us a clear field to check for footprints.'

Mostly Cristian guessed Mark just needed to be doing something while they waited for time to pass. They were probably all feeling the same. Danika confirmed Selene and Sonya were helping her making potions and protection pouches in the upstairs kitchen so not to get too close, and yes she was sitting down.

'The ladies are in the upstairs kitchen but we can't go there,' Cristian informed Peter. 'Clay can though, can you bring down the field maps mate?'

'Sure can, just be a jiffy.' Clay was keen to assist and check on Selene.

They laid out the maps on the dining table. One map of the estate and more of the housing area and the park. They marked in red the concerning areas.

Sonya came down to touch base with them but stood back from

the doorway. 'I'm going for a shower to cleanse the repellent off. Danika and Selene are doing the same. The pouches are in a cooler box in the kitchen upstairs, just as a warning. We've told Danika to lay down for a bit and sip her protein drink. I'll catch up with you in a bit okay?'

They nodded until she was gone and then took a deep breath. 'Were you two holding your breath?' Clay asked. They nodded and dropped their heads.

'Powerful stuff those wives are brewing up Clay,' Peter remarked.

Ben did the rounds, letting people know there were drinks and food on rotation in the kitchen from now on.

The first family members arrived early as expected. Bethany, her husband Matt and Jayden, followed by her brothers Dean and Tony. Mark showed them the comms units and walked them around the areas needing to be monitored as Will, Michael and Luke arrived. Behind them was a surprise visitor – June was brought by her two sons Andrew and John, Mark's father. Elizabeth greeted June and brought her inside to sit in the sitting room with Ingrid.

Danika

Danika could feel the love pouring from everyone towards them. There was so much anticipation but no fear, everyone knew they would each protect each other. Ben had placed a stool strategically near the angel in case Danika needed the support. He brought the cooler box down to the front steps for Danika and Selene to hand out the pouches. They used food tongs to give one to each person to hang around their neck or put in a pocket – whatever worked best – reminding them all of the repellent around Cristian and Peter. They had plenty left over so

Elizabeth and Ingrid grabbed more when Danika moved away, taking one into June also.

Danika watched as the three older women conspired, whispering amongst themselves. Their thoughts revealed only their determination to help however they could.

The night was going to be clear with only a light breeze so at least the weather would not be an issue. Outside, the preparations were in full swing and everyone that needed them had comms and was moving into position around the estate. Clay was a master at keeping control and focus of his crew. Ben was confirming as he had sight of each person in the cameras and had switched on all the extra flood lights. Danika, Selene and Sonya were making their way to the angel with the artefacts. Cristian let Danika know it was getting hard for them to hold human form even though the moon was not visible yet. She whispered for them to come out and join them. By the angel Cristian and Peter stripped down quickly without any feeling of embarrassment as the love and respect of everyone was directed at them. They pulled the collar over their heads as Danika spoke to Cristian and Sonya to Peter. They changed but stood their ground. Selene had gasped at the speed of the change and the magnificence of their lupine form. Elizabeth, Ingrid and June had watched from the steps as they had the repellent with them still, marvelling at the beauty yet horror of the change.

'Come back my love when I call you,' Danika said as she reached up to lay her hand on Cristian's soft head. Sonya did the same with Peter, crooning in German as he brushed against her. Cristian and Peter slinked off towards the back of the house. Ben had seen this on the cameras and had let everyone know they were in wolf form and moving around.

Danika, Sonya and Selene took their positions at the angel and started the chant. Elizabeth, Ingrid and June came down to join them just as the moon glow tipped the horizon, already in the beginnings of the eclipse. Calmly but with conviction they all started the chant.

'By the will of the universe at this blood moon, we Romana and Blakesley ask the universe to end the armaya too long the torture to all. No longer the curse of the wolf at full shon, no longer the shi shugra to be denied love. Let all bearing the armaya from now live, love and prosper as humans by the will of the universe.'

They all repeated it. Ben in the comms room repeated it; those on comms chanted it between updates of position as if it was natural like breathing. As if they had waited a lifetime to say those words. It became a mantra, over and over, slowly, not rushed they each found the rhythm of the words.

The first distraction was the howling from many directions. It wasn't actual wolves but humans howling as wolves. Almost immediately the howling was followed by explosions as if the howling was the signal. Ben checked all cameras and saw people in dark clothing throwing lit fireworks around the fences and reported this over the comms. This was the sort of distraction Clay had warned of and spoke clearly and firmly for everyone to remain calm and alert. Ben kept up a commentary of the actions of the strangers, probably paid by Robert to cause the distractions. Ben could see the neighbours close to the fireworks were angry and taking photos of the nuisance, possibly reporting them also.

Clay kept the crew focused on watching for intrusions. Some reported having Cristian and Peter pass them with their luminous collars, sniffing the air and boundary and moving on. Danika wanted so much to call Cristian back but knew she had to continue the chant, not knowing the exact point at which it would break the curse. Again there was howling but it was obvious that some were people pretending and some were real now, sounding like it was above them. She heard growling and looked to see Cristian and Peter close by but looking at the cliff, growling more just as a loud bang occurred at the back of the house, then another. They raced off to see. Mark confirmed someone had thrown rocks down the cliff and some had made it to the bottom, banging into the shed and poultry pen. More fireworks exploded in unison out the back and at the gate. They could smell smoke from the fireworks but also from burning grass.

Danika could hear sirens in the background signalling the police and fire brigade. Still they maintained the chant. Ann and Bethany had been close by and heard and reported the commotion as one wolf had tried to jump from the cliff over the fence and been met with cattle prods and repellent pouches. Danika looked up to see that the moon was almost at maximum eclipse and had Ann take over briefly as she tried to call back Cristian. He appeared in human form from the gardens as Elizabeth gave him the clothes and shoes to put on. He stumbled to the angel where Danika had resumed her chant. Ann swapped for Sonya so she could call for Peter. Danika sensed Cristian and Peter were both very disoriented but determined to reach them at the angel.

Danika tried a mental connection with Cristian but it was very fuzzy, as if he was drunk. He swayed but managed to pick up the Lleuad Blaidd and started the chant himself. They could hear yells and screams of pain behind the stables. Ann relayed to them that others had caught another wolf that was reverting to human now. The police were at the gate with sirens blaring, yelling into the intercom for Ben to open the gate. Clay told Ben to stall them if he could. Clay was still trying to locate Robert.

Cristian grabbed Danika's medallion and linked it to his. As it burned his flesh he continued to chant with the others, all joining in for a last push of will. That was when Robert rushed out from the garden with a plant stake in his hand, running awkwardly towards Cristian and Danika screaming obscenities at them as if to impale them. Elizabeth, Ingrid and June intercepted him with cattle prods, forcing him to the ground then draped the repellent pouches around his neck. They stood around him, ready to prod him again as he retched from the repellent. The twin medallions were burning Cristian's hand and Danika grabbed them also. She could feel the power shooting through them all until a light pierced through them, taking their breath away. They dropped to their knees and were caught by Peter and Sonya. Ann grabbed the stool for Danika to sit as Cristian regained his balance.

Ben couldn't hold the police with the excuse of a stuck mechanism any longer and allowed them entry. Elizabeth and Clay, minus any comms, set off to meet the police in the drive and explain they were having a baby shower and these three naked men started to harass the event. Mark and Ben were directing all the others to bring the comms to the stables and grab a drink in the kitchen before coming out the front as it was a party they were portraying.

The police were shown the two brothers, yelling in German, naked in the stable enclosure. They had been throwing up from the repellent and stunk. Robert had thrown up also until the bright light, then he ripped off the pouches and was trying to complain to the police about being stabbed by the old women. He stood naked still, with the garden stake in his hand, and found it impossible to drop it as he was warned to do by the police. Danika had been waving her fingers and whispering, her mother joined in the spell directed at Robert. He couldn't drop the stake and as it was a weapon the police officer had warned him to drop it. The officer tasered him.

Robert, Eric and Karl were arrested and Elizabeth admitted to the police they knew them and that they had harassed them in the past and damaged family property. Also that she had heard that the German police may be looking for them.

Several police officers wanted to take statements of which Elizabeth asked if they could do it inside as they were cold, tired and needed to sit down. Inside on a table near the stairs were several wrapped parcels and a couple of balloons, pink and blue to complete the charade. Several people were holding cans of soft drink and a cake could be seen in the dining room. Unbeknown to Danika and Cristian, Elizabeth had been busy arranging this illusion with Ann and Ben's help. Cristian and Peter's strange attire was explained away as swim wear. Will told the police how worried he was about his daughter and granddaughter both having babies being threatened in this way.

After an hour of questioning the police decided to leave them alone and hoped the rest of the night would be okay. By that time the eclipse was out of maximum and starting to reduce. As they pulled out of the estate Danika cried and Cristian hugged her as Peter was hugging his crying wife. They were still human. Friedrich hugged his parents. Everyone cheered.

Ben handed them track pants to put on then they sat on the main stairs as Ingrid and Elizabeth handed the boxes which were actually gifts out to the three couples awaiting their babies, with Danika first. She had matching pink and blue bibs with 'Daddy's little angel' written on each. The others had similar funny captions on bibs in neutral colours. Finally they looked at the cake in the dining room iced with 'to the happy couples and their families' with lots of stars in rainbow colours.

'Thank you so much everyone for everything but especially this cake because I'm starving,' Danika said, making everyone laugh, more so as a release of the tension and excitement of the evening. Ann and Bethany deftly cut pieces of cake, handing them around to everyone.

Everyone was talking about their individual experiences tonight and the force they each felt go through them at the time that the light penetrated Cristian and Danika.

'I can't feel our mental connection,' Cristian commented to Danika. 'How are the babies?'

Danika confirmed they felt fine.

Peter and Ingrid were missing and when Elizabeth realised Danika and Cristian were looking for them said, 'They have gone to call family overseas.'

'Of course it will be a shock to them when nothing happens to them in a few hours.'

Cristian

Cristian still couldn't believe it had worked and wandered outside to look at the moon. The eclipse was still waning, yet it felt like a miracle to look at it at all. He was fifteen the last time he had looked upon it as a human. He felt his mother join him. 'I wish Father was here to see this.'

'I do too, he would be as proud of you as I am.' Elizabeth put her arm though his. Cristian turned to look at her.

'I need to say, way to go nannas! Did you three have that planned? I just caught a glimpse of your attack on Robert as he rushed at us.' Cristian was very impressed at their fast action.

'It was Ingrid's idea and June was right up for it also.' Elizabeth smiled. 'How are you feeling? It must be strange after so many years to not have that other part living within you.'

'I feel weak at the moment and I can't read Danika's thoughts which I miss, but I'll get used to it.' Cristian really just wanted to have a shower and go lay down now. 'Me too.' He spun round to look at his wife who smiled at him.

Lots of hand shaking and hugs later and the majority of the family were leaving. They agreed it would be a late breakfast, nothing fancy so that Ann didn't feel the need to rush back in the morning. Ben was the last to go, locking the gate as he went there were still people milling about as well as fire officers checking for spot fires and police interviewing neighbours.

Standing on the balcony, Danika could just see the moon before it was going out of sight behind the house. She called to the universe, thanking it for all they had been given. She continued to talk to several stars and, holding one arm across her belly, waved the other at the moon wishing health and happiness on Skye and Aiden. Cristian wrapped his arms around her and recited the same wish for health and happiness for Skye and Aiden and felt them moving beneath his arms.

'Come to bed my love, it is already tomorrow. You need to rest.' Without waiting for a reply he picked his family up as one and walked them to their bed.

The next morning where they had hoped to rest became busier than expected with phone calls from the police explaining that Robert, Karl and Eric were being extradited to Germany as soon as possible on murder charges. The police's own case of harassment and attempted assault was likely to be shelved while that was sorted out. Cristian agreed he was glad they were going to be out of the country.

Several messages of thanks and shock from family worldwide beeped on his phone and more calls from police regarding the firework hooligans looking for CCTV. Ben said he would review if anything showed up for them.

A few news journalists were trying to find out what had happened last night with several police reports and men arrested.

Peter, Sonya and Friedrich returned to the apartment in Sydney until they could move into their own home in a few weeks.

Will and his family planned a luncheon in Sydney with Selene and Clay before they returned to Adelaide on Thursday. Danika apologised she had to decline as she had a doctor's appointment later today and needed to rest also. However as soon as she could travel with the babies next year she would definitely visit.

Cristian stopped her from thinking about ordering baby things and said resting was her only option today until he took her to her appointment. He set her up on the bed with the laptop and a drink nearby while he tried to answer all the enquiries from different family members.

'We made the news,' Danika suddenly commented. 'Well the front gate did anyway.' He came in to watch a short video of one of their neighbours being interviewed about the firework hooligans throwing crackers at the gate and setting the dogs off howling. They smiled at that because it was around the other way. Then the news showed the police attending and some men being arrested, however the owners of the estate house declined to be interviewed. The camera had zoomed on to the gate and name of the estate.

'How does your hand feel?' Danika asked him. She had forgotten about it since last night when she rubbed it with her healing oil and blew on it. He showed her it was just a bit pink now.

'All good, so you still have your powers,' Cristian said, pleased that she did. 'Including sending me thoughts. Shame I can't return them.'

'I get your emotions though so when you are happy or angry I'll know.' Danika smiled as he kissed her and caught an erotic emotion. 'I'm supposed to be resting you said.' They both laughed.

After the busy and sometimes stressful build up to the event of the blood moon, the week that followed was an anti-climax. Danika had some thoughts she wanted to share for the next couple of months activities but waited until they were alone to run them by Cristian.

'Did you have any plans for your birthday?' she asked him.

'Oh, I forgot its next week, I don't do anything for my birthday since I was sixteen, bad memories etcetera,' he replied.

'Well that is all going to change, happy days from now on. I thought we could have a pool side barbeque with whoever is available.'

'Only if you let Ann and the others arrange it and do the work. Remember Peter and Sonya may be busy, they get the keys to their house just after that.' Cristian was trying to give her firm thoughts without knowing if that worked.

'Okay and I want a huge tree and lots of decorations for Christmas.' Cristian pulled a pretend face at her knowing he would give in anyway. 'Also I was wondering if we could go to the apartment for New Year's Eve to watch the fireworks after the countdown.'

'We could but I'm not sure that we should. You will only have four weeks to go by then.' Cristian laid his hand on their babies.

'Well I will be able to check with Doctor Michael before to make sure, is that okay?' Danika was adamant she needed to be there. 'I just feel like I need to do this.'

'Okay, well that is still six weeks away so let's just take a week at a time,' Cristian tentatively agreed.

'Yep, pool BBQ first,' Danika agreed. Cristian sighed and knew he would probably give in to whatever she wanted.

Another fairly calm week later Mark had made sure the pool area was perfect and Ann and Bethany had all the food ready for Ben and Mark to cook, just as Dean turned up with his boys and wife. Mark's wife and Ben's partner – who he had kept very secret until today – also came. Ben introduced Nicholas to them. Mark deferred to Nicholas to help with the BBQ as he was a chef apparently. Jay was already there and came down with Rick to go in the pool. Danika sat with her legs up on a pool lounge on Cristian's orders taking it all in.

Peter and Sonya were missing and Cristian looked around, wondering where they were. Elizabeth and Ingrid had settled also in the shade just as Peter came around the corner from the stables to announce they had a delivery of a gift from Danika for Cristian. Cristian looked puzzled from Peter to Danika who was smiling her love at him. Sonya walked around the corner holding a lead, at her side was a beautifully groomed golden retriever.

'Happy birthday darling, this is Buddy,' Danika said. Sonya handed the leash to Cristian. Buddy was looking a bit surprised at all the people and sidled up to Cristian as if he was the safe haven.

Cristian knelt down and buried his head in Buddy's fur. 'Hello Buddy.' The dog's tail wagged slightly.

'He is a rescue dog, needing a loving home and lots of attention and playtime. I thought that sounded like us,' Danika said as she wiped her tears.

Cristian's throat was thick with emotion and just nodded his head. Peter handed him a beer as he stood up with Buddy now sitting on his foot.

Between screams from the boys in the pool and tall tales from

Mark and Dean, the food and drinks flowed freely as did the laughter. Buddy was Cristian's shadow all day that he felt was the most natural thing, as if he had always been in the family. Danika had been discussing her ideas for Christmas and New Year with Sonya and their mother's in law while she watched Cristian and Buddy as they in unison looked over at different sounds and sights during the afternoon. Cristian and Peter's senses were still above average but not as keen as before the curse was lifted. Thankfully their stamina was slowly returning.

Danika

After eating, the men were discussing the plan to get Peter, Sonya and Rick into their new house next week. Danika felt a little left out as she would have to wait until they were in before she visited.

'After we get the furniture in do you think you could help pick out some art for the walls?' Sonya asked her. Danika smiled, knowing Sonya was trying to make her feel included.

'I would love to help out. I'm looking forward to seeing your new home,' Danika replied.

'It will be a little sparse until the container from Germany arrives with our heirloom pieces. Most of what we had has been sold off with the property in Germany. We didn't want to go back to it after Roberts's family invaded it,' Sonya explained. Danika held her hand and tried to reduce the pain in her words. Sonya had not expressed how she had felt about that episode until now. They both looked across at Cristian who was idly rubbing Buddy's ear as he sat next to him, chatting with the other men. Peter was looking at the interaction also.

'Peter wants to get a dog also.' Sonya changed the subject they had been on. 'He said that he had not realised that his alter ego was such a large part of his life 24/7 until it was gone. When he helped you find Buddy it stirred that feeling again. I think he is going back to the rescue home to pick one, I just said no puppies because we will have enough to do with a new home and then a baby in June. Friedrich is keen, of course.' Sonya smiled at her family as they were splashing in the pool. 'Looks like we will need one of those also.'

Before long they were gathering up dishes and cups and making plans to leave. Cristian helped Danika out of the pool lounge so she could see their guests off.

Later, when they were alone, Danika showed Cristian several dog beds for the bedroom, sitting room upstairs and downstairs, plus toys for Buddy. Danika could sense that Buddy was still trying to find his place in the family dynamic and kept a close watch on anything Cristian was doing.

'Do you miss your other self?' Danika asked Cristian as she sat on the bed.

'Yes, strangely. I didn't know that some of my actions and thoughts were driven by that side of me until it was gone. The connection with Buddy really helps. I think Peter wants a dog now also after looking after Buddy for you last night.' The dog looked up at the sound of his name. 'Mostly I miss our thought conversations, the sense of you on that other level. Thank you for my great birthday.' Cristian hugged her close to him. Buddy nuzzled them with his tail barely wagging.

'I hope that isn't jealousy Buddy,' Cristian said as he felt the dog's nose.

'No he just wants to join in, like it is a natural pack action,' Danika explained, so they included him laughing as he licked their faces. He was very gentle and stopped to look at Danika's belly and carefully laid his nose on the wriggling babies.

'I have to check a few things online and that we are locked up. Are you okay to stay here?' Cristian asked.

'Just hand me the laptop and take Buddy with you, he needs to know the lay of the house,' Danika suggested.

Cristian

Cristian grabbed the lead to put in his pocket and proceeded to show Buddy around the house inside and out. All the staff were gone, only Elizabeth was still in her rooms. The different smells were fascinating to Buddy and time passed. Cristian decided he would take him around the grounds tomorrow. He sat on the front steps with Buddy by his side, thinking about all that had happened in the time he had known Danika as he looked out at the angel where his life had changed forever. He considered himself lucky to have met her and looked up at the few stars he could see and thanked the universe.

18

NEW BEGINNINGS

IT SEEMED THAT the days rushed by. Between moving Peter, Sonya and Rick – now only called that – into their new home, then making sure Danika attended her weekly appointments, as well as making sure she rested, they stayed busy. Cristian understood her frustration at having to sit with her legs up so much on Dr Michael's orders, but the alternative would be a hospital stay. Danika was set up in the downstairs sitting room with her laptop, phone and Buddy often keeping her company. Everyone in the house checked on her between tasks. Cristian had spent several hours looking at the full moon at intervals, still in awe he could watch it. Christmas lunch was to be at Peter's this year with Ann, Ben and Mark spending the day with their own families. Danika constantly planned from the laptop the events at the gallery or ordering things. Rene's December gallery exhibition had gone well and the plan was for Sonya to exhibit her photo art works after the school holidays, about the time the twins were due. Parcels seemed to be arriving nearly every day for the nursery or secret surprise Christmas gifts.

On Christmas Eve, Danika, Cristian and Elizabeth handed out gifts to Ann, Ben and Mark. They contained small personal gifts with an extra envelope they had thought were Christmas cards until they opened them. They each were given QANTAS flight vouchers to organise their own holidays to anywhere around the world.

'It seemed the only way to make you take holidays,' Danika said to them as they sat in shock at the generous gift. They each kissed her on the cheek and shook Cristian's hand before going to the kitchen to bring out the light buffet Danika had requested, knowing the next day would be very filling. Danika noticed Cristian nod at Mark who left the room and really wished she could read his mind still. By the end of the day Danika found she was not hungry or thirsty, just very tired. She nibbled on Christmas nougat and listened to Ben and Ann discussing possible dates of holiday. Mark came back in and they all turned to look at Cristian who said he wanted to give Danika her Christmas gift early, if she didn't mind, but that it was outside. They all followed him out to the front where Mark had parked what was obviously a car under a silky green cloth. This was not what Danika would ever have expected. With a flourish, Cristian pulled the cover off to reveal a large shimmering white car.

Danika put her hand over her mouth. 'The colour is called moonstone. It seemed appropriate. Enough room for the twins and all the things you need.' He came up to help her look around it as she started to cry. 'It is automatic but very safe, even to go to Lunar Haven.'

'I think it is wonderful. Thank you so much, you kept this very secret. How did you fit it in the garage?' Danika turned to Mark who obviously had something to do with it.

'I sold Martin. Don't worry, he's still in the family,' Cristian said, motioning to Ben. Ben gave a brief wave to Danika who smiled her happiness. 'Grandfather's old car has gone to a collector with Mother's blessing. Rainbow is still there until the right time to make a decision.'

'You are all very sneaky and I love you for it, but I think I'll go back in now.' Cristian helped her back up the stairs while Mark moved the car back to the garage. It wasn't long before she decided to call it a night and the others cleared up and left with the last Christmas wishes.

Cristian came up to the bedroom to find Buddy sitting at the foot on his bed and Danika resting on the bed. He could see she was tired and getting fed up that she could not get around so well. 'When do you see Dr Michael again?'

'Wednesday morning. Hopefully he lets me have the New Year's celebration I wanted,' Danika explained.

'Well your health and the twins' come first, so we will see. You need to let us all do more for you so you can rest.' Cristian was concerned at how flushed she looked.

The next morning while still in bed, Danika handed Cristian her gift to him – a titanium medallion engraved with the Lleuad Blaidd one side and the Triquetra on the other. She explained their lovely jeweller Mr Pearce had taken a long time to get the medallions and engrave them so intricately. She showed him her own white gold one that matched his, but with a sapphire in the middle from Lunar Haven. Then she directed him to a bag that was for Buddy. Inside was a large soft toy with a squeaker and a rustle section. They made a big show of giving it to him and his reaction was better than expected, with him running around the landing and the rooms making it squeak, the most animated he had been since they got him, making them both laugh.

'We may regret this,' Cristian said as the squeaks continued. Cristian looked at his phone when it beeped. 'Peter wants us to bring Buddy to meet their new dog. Not until after eleven though. I think they are trying to make sure you rest.'

'Suits me, it will take that long to decide what to wear,' Danika replied almost painfully. She had swelled more than she expected and now had very limited clothing choices. Her swollen feet meant only beach sandals or slip-on's would fit.

'Well stay here and I'll go get you herbal tea and we can decide together.' Cristian kissed her and went downstairs. He met his mother in the kitchen where she was boiling the kettle and planning a tray of breakfast for Danika.

'Merry Christmas darling. Oh good, saves using the dumb waiter, you can carry this up for me and I will bring her gift.' Elizabeth pointed to the bed tray with a bowl of fresh berries and yoghurt and a plate of toast and honey. She topped up a little pot with boiling water, a single red rose on the tray.

Cristian picked up the tray and followed his mother upstairs to their rooms. He carefully put his head in to check she wasn't getting dressed but she was still on the bed with Buddy's head under her hand. *Good boy*, he thought. He walked in with Elizabeth behind him, carrying the parcel for Danika.

'Merry Christmas Danika,' Elizabeth said as she came in.

'Oh how lovely, thank you. Merry Christmas, Elizabeth.' Buddy moved away as Cristian put the tray on the bed beside Danika so Elizabeth could give her the gift. The parcel was large and soft. When she unwrapped it, there were some dresses for Danika. They were cleverly designed with adjustable ties and openings to make them tighter or looser in bright colours. There were also some hair slides that matched the dresses.

'These are so lovely and soft and very needed.' Danika accepted a kiss from her and continued, 'Those lovely clothes you gave me I seem to have grown out of.' She rubbed her large belly.

Buddy was playing with his new toy and they all laughed at the squeaking. Christian grabbed a box from the sideboard and handed to his mother. 'This is from us to you.' Then he gave his mother a kiss on the cheek. Inside was a compact yet powerful digital camera. 'We thought you may like to keep a record of our historical journey, first of everything in four hundred years.'

'I would be honoured and happy to practice on everybody.' Elizabeth smiled. She turned it on and pointed it at Buddy for the first shot.

Later, after getting all the gifts and Buddy into Danika's new car with Elizabeth in the back seat, Cristian offered to drive, much to Danika's relief. Peter and Sonya's new house was only fifteen minutes away which was very pleasing, as already Danika felt like she wanted to spread herself out. They were greeted in the driveway by the family, which made it a little chaotic with the two dogs getting to know one another.

Peter's dog Max was a lot more excitable as it was only a year-old kelpie cross, also from a rescue organisation. Rick kept the dogs busy with toys and fetch while the others took all the presents inside and found a comfortable chair for Danika. The dogs were safely enclosed outside in a fenced area. The next few hours were loud, busy and much fun as food and jokes flowed freely. Peter and Sonya had been trying to embrace the Australian Christmas tradition, which is a day later than for German traditions, but still sharing their own style.

Danika was on her way to the bathroom when Sonya waylaid her, saying she had a secret to share with her in a minute. Danika was excited to find out some good news, she was sure, as she could sense Sonya's happiness. They went into a private room where Sonya held Danika's hands before telling her she had been to have her ultrasound a few days before.

'We were lucky enough to be able to get a good look at the baby. We are having a little girl.' Both were crying and hugging now. 'I'm due in early June. This is all because of you and Cristian. We will never be able to thank you enough. We haven't told anyone else yet.'

'Oh how wonderful, this is going to be amazing. So many babies in the family at the same time, Mum is due in May.' They tidied up and wiped away their tears before going back out to the group in time to open presents. All were small thoughtful gifts except for the one for Rick which, Cristian was clear to explain, was for the whole family and to be shared. Now they were intrigued. Rick whooped with joy as he opened up a virtual gaming set that included several games, all sport related for exercise.

'You know we won't see him again for hours now,' Peter commented but Danika sensed Peter was keen to see it also.

'We are still getting a lot of contact from the overseas family with everyone discussing the wonderment and interesting sidelines to breaking the curse,' Peter commented after Rick had left to set up the game. 'Some retained the strong senses in different degrees, some lost them but it could possibly be age related. All suffered the lethargy. A few of the original staff from the Gypsy origins have coupled with the single Blakesley men, seems they can now express their feelings for each other. All now own pets, mostly dogs but cats and horses also. The big one is several pregnancies, so next year will be a boom year for Blakesley's it seems.'

'Any more news on Robert and his sons?' Elizabeth asked. Ingrid sat next to her and laid her hand on Elizabeth's as Peter proceeded.

'It seems now that everyone is certain they are safe, Robert, Karl and Eric's wives have been filling in the authorities on everything they were doing. They are now being charged with my father's murder as well as several counts of intimidation to acquire property. The case is likely to take some time to go to court as there is so much evidence to sift through. They are calling it a cult, Karl and Eric's sons have been arrested also.' Peter held Sonya's hand. 'I may have to go back at different points to testify. Apart from Robert's direct line, everyone is very happy though. We have been sidelined by bigger news with the war in Ukraine and the pandemic but we should all be aware that media may try to contact once they realise the connection.'

Danika had been listening and taking in all the various emotions rushing out from everyone. She was going to try to help calm those in distress but the twins were not having that and were becoming active. She started humming and laid her hands on them to assure them she was alright. Cristian realised what she was doing and looked at Peter before breaking the conversation.

'Well I think we need to move back to a festive subject like cutting the stollen,' he suggested.

'Yes I agree, I have been curious about it sitting in the middle of the table,' Elizabeth agreed.

'I made it as I do every year, so you will be getting the traditional German version,' Ingrid explained.

Sonya, Rick and Peter made hot drinks to go with the stollen and, before Ingrid cut it, she gave thanks for her family here and abroad and for their futures. It was a delicious end to a happy day but they were not surprised when Cristian said he needed to get Danika home.

At Danika's doctor appointment Dr Michael was blunt and clear that if her health did not improve he would be admitting her to hospital. Her blood pressure was up and her weight was not.

'You are not eating and drinking enough. I know you say you are not hungry or thirsty but it is a rapid decline if you do not follow my instructions. You are putting yourself and your babies at risk.' Dr Michael was not normally this harsh with her. Danika was crying now. 'You are resting but I think if your intake does not improve you will need IV fluids. The longer you can carry the twins the better but, be prepared, you may go into labour early.' Cristian had been holding her hand as she was grasping his in a tight grip.

'I was hoping to be in Sydney for New Year to see the fireworks. Is that going to be possible?' Danika asked.

'Not a priority, but at least you will be close to the hospital and I will be on call that night anyway. So you have a few days to eat, drink and rest. Watch some TV and listen to music, whatever calms you. I want to see you again on Tuesday.' Dr Michael was smiling at her now. 'Not long to go now and you will be glad you had your feet up in the last weeks.'

Once he had her settled in the car Cristian turned to look at her. 'Why are you so insistent about the fireworks?'

'Skye and Aiden have been telling me we have to be there that is all I know. They have been quieter lately, I'm getting worried.' Danika was crying again. Cristian handed her a bottle of water and instructed her to sip it while they were going home.

After a couple of days in bed watching TV – a new experience for Danika as she had not been interested before – plus eating and drinking on strict instructions and monitoring from everyone it seemed, Danika had to admit she was feeling better and the twins seemed happier also. Cristian had been very worried and, with it, a little harsh in his words for the first time, making Danika realise just how worried he was. 'I'm sorry I worried you, darling.'

'You are such an independent person and, without the mental link to keep you on track, I feel like I let you down, not keeping you and the twins safe. So I apologise if I was terse with you, you had me scared.' Cristian admitted his fears. 'Just to update you on tonight, Peter will be coming to get Mother and Buddy to take back to his house. They are going to celebrate there and make sure the dogs are safe. Ann, Ben and Mark will leave after we do and not be back until Monday. So it will be just us in Sydney. I am going down to help fit the baby capsules in your car with Mark shortly in case we need to get any other fittings for when they arrive. Oh and the apartment has plenty of food and drinks already organised.'

'I'm feeling a bit redundant at the present time, but I have to admit that I feel better than a few days ago. I've been bingeing, I think they call it, a series quite ridiculous about the devil but strangely enjoyable.' Danika was genuinely pleased at how she felt. 'Those two bags are to go in the car by the way. The big one is our stuff, the small one is my hospital bag, just in case.' Danika pointed at the bags sitting in the corner.

The traffic on the roads was intense and, with a comfort stop for Danika, took almost twice as long to finally get to the apartment in the early afternoon. Danika loved their home at Hollingrove yet the apartment held a special place in her heart as it was where they fell in love. She walked around it, telling the twins this as she went and looking out from the balcony on the scene of the bridge and Opera House, breathing in the smells and sounds of the harbour city. Cristian came out and stood behind Danika, laying a protective hug around her and the twins.

I'm so glad we are here, Danika thought.

'So am I,' Cristian answered. Danika turned to him.

'You heard me?' Danika asked.

'Yes very faintly and more feelings than words.' Cristian kissed her.

'I have been practicing a little with concentration.' He closed his eyes to send a thought message, *I love you.*

'Oh, I love you too.' Danika placed her hands on his face. 'This is wonderful.'

'Still a little blurry and may never be as accurate or intense as before, but it is a start.' Cristian kissed her soundly then looked at her belly. 'The twins seem quiet.'

'Yes but content I hope.' Danika also had noticed they were quiet today.

'It is a long time until midnight and the fireworks, so we should plan that you are going to have a rest and sleep on the bed this afternoon, no arguments,' Cristian said and tried to send firm thoughts also.

'Yes sir, no argument from me. I'm going to stretch out on the couch now though I think,' Danika said and, with Cristian's help turning the couch for a better angle to the TV, settled in with cushions and a drink and snacks within reach.

Cristian sat at the kitchen counter so he could use his laptop and watch over Danika at the same time. He was worried about how the pregnancy was affecting her health. It was never his intention to put her in harm's way. He guessed all husbands felt that way at this stage, especially where twins were concerned. Cristian continued to type out his thoughts. He had started a journal shortly after reading his father's but not handwritten on paper. The laptop was an easier option for him and kept it private. He surprised himself how much he had written about his life so far and one day would print a copy for his children to read of his family's extraordinary life. He was sure Danika had drifted to sleep and carefully lowered the sound on the TV. She gently touched his leg.

'Can you help me up? I need the bathroom and I think I'll lay on the bed for a bit,' Danika said, a little sleepily. 'The twins seem to be pressing on my back a bit more, space is tight.'

'That sounds like a good idea. Do you want me to rub your back?' Cristian asked as he helped her up from the couch.

'Yes please, and a warm wheat bag. Perhaps then I will be well rested for tonight.'

Satisfied she was comfortable with pillows and the wheat bag against her back, Cristian left Danika to sleep. He was glad he had been able to help in some small capacity, his concern getting deeper. It was dark when the first loud noises around the apartment started. Revellers and parties seemed to be all around them. It was the first time in decades that he had been in Sydney for New Year. It was certainly louder than he remembered. He thought he heard Danika and checked to see her sitting on the side of the bed wriggling her toes and trying to see them.

'How are you feeling?' Cristian could see she was tired but smiling.

'Much better thanks, it sounds like the parties have started,' Danika commented on the sounds from many directions.

'Are you hungry? I could make an omelette,' Cristian asked as he steadied her through the apartment to the couch, now over by the balcony for her to look out.

'Oh thank you for this. Actually I would like herbal tea first, then I'll let you know.' Danika tried to give him reassuring thoughts as she settled on the couch. 'I'm feeling a bit useless at the moment, I'm glad we are alone. I suppose most first-time mums feel this way. I really should have picked Sonya's brain a bit more. Oh I forgot to say, did you know they are going to be having a girl?'

'Yes, Peter told me Christmas day to keep it quiet. They want it to be a surprise for the others. He is over the moon, excuse the pun.' Cristian smiled as Danika laughed at their family joke. He handed her a cup of ginger and lemongrass tea. Danika cradled it on her belly and started to cry. Kneeling down he took it back from her and hugged her, with her arms around his neck, stroking her hair and crooning loving words to her until it passed.

'I've not been much of a wife to you lately, I'm so sorry,' Danika said between tears. He handed her tissues. 'Perhaps Dr Michael was right, I should go into hospital. I wouldn't be a burden then.'

'You are not a burden and never will be. We are into this parenting journey together. I just wish I could help more. I like having you with me to talk to and share thoughts and hug but if hospital is the safest place then yes you should be there.' Cristian lifted her face with his fingers under her chin and gently kissed her then handed the drink back to her. He opened the curtains and the sliding door to the balcony to get the breeze and waft of the scents of the sea and cooking and the smell of sparklers. Revellers yelled 'Happy New Year' as they went past, although it was still a couple of hours before midnight. Danika handed her drink back and said she felt like she needed to get up again and the pain in her back was getting worse. As he lifted her she made a little groan of pain and he knew he was going to call the doctor.

'Oh I think something is not right.' Danika looked at him in fear as the pain was getting stronger, then seemed to relax.

'I'm calling Dr Michael,' Cristian said as he helped her to stand at the kitchen counter. The call was fairly brief as the doctor was already at the hospital for another mother who had just delivered. He was sending an ambulance to get Danika as with the busy roads they would get through quicker than Cristian and also it would come to the preferred hospital where he was.

'I need my bag darling and my slip-on shoes,' Danika directed him. 'And remember the phones.'

Cristian went around closing windows and doors before making sure he had what was needed, slipping his wallet and keys in his pockets and placing Danika's hospital bag and phone at the door when he heard a siren and hoped it was for them. She leaned hard on the counter as a wave of pain came again but tried to keep it from Cristian so as not to worry him.

'It worries me when you don't share your pain,' Cristian said and tried to help her focus on him. The siren was getting closer so he said, 'I'm going to meet them. Do you think you are okay for a minute?'

She nodded as he quickly went out the door, not shutting it, and sprinted down the stairs to the car park. Cristian had to admit later that the next few hours seemed to go past in a blur when asked. He went with Danika to the hospital in the ambulance as he knew it would be difficult to get there with their car. It only took a few minutes to get to the hospital it seemed, then lots of questions were his main memory. Everyone seemed to be asking him the same questions multiple times. Nurses, doctors, anaesthetists and more nurses. He was getting the gist that they were considering a C-section. He knew Danika was getting anxious. Dr Michael explained to Cristian that even with one baby, epidural or spinal block delivery for a C-section was common now but with twins it was almost essential. He explained how it wasn't at a critical level yet but that they really shouldn't let it get to be an emergency. Better to have some choices still.

'This way Danika can still be awake to share the birth with you. The anaesthetic will take about twenty minutes. Do you agree?' Dr Michael was asking Cristian first which he thought was strange.

'Yes of course whatever is safest for Danika and the twins.' The doctor directed him to go back in with Danika so he could explain it to her.

Danika was crying and clutching Cristian's hand as Dr Michael explained slowly and in detail what he was suggesting. 'You could try to deliver naturally but with your recent high blood pressure and low sugar count I think you are putting yourself or the babies at risk. Possibly both,' Dr Michael finished.

'Let's get this done then,' Danika said. 'But I want Cristian with me all the time,' she insisted looking at him for confirmation.

'I'm not going anywhere,' he replied.

'Of course but he may have to sit out of the way occasionally.' Dr Michael smiled and then the room filled with people again.

Cristian sat on a swivel stool out of the way as they prepared Danika for the surgery. In the background he could hear the TVs in the hospital tuned into the various New Year celebrations before the countdown. Then it was his time to hold her free hand without a drip and let her know what was happening behind the short screen if she wanted to know. After all he had seen and done in his life, watching his wife being cut open was the most confronting. It seemed only a minute later Aiden was delivered healthy and soon making little noises. They weren't really cries. Aiden was shown to them before being whisked away by a team of nurses. A few minutes later there was Skye. More indignant about leaving her comfy position, she let out a full cry making them both laugh before she too was taken to be cleaned up and checked over. They could hear people yelling and laughing and realised as they looked at the clock that it was now a new year. Even through the hospital walls they could hear the faint sound of the fireworks on the bridge just finishing.

'Well, talk about fanfare. Your babies were born just a few minutes after midnight so they get greeted by fireworks,' Dr Michael said as he was still working on Danika to deliver the afterbirth and stitch her back up.

'That's what they kept telling me,' Danika whispered to Cristian.

As the doctor was finishing up, the nurses brought Aiden and Skye into Danika and Cristian to hold. Both perfect yet so different. Aiden with his black hair like his mother and Skye with blonde hair like her father settled well in their arms. Both Danika and Cristian were crying and kissing each other and the babies, the fact of the miracle before them greater than anyone else in the room would realise. The nurses explained that, although the babies were very good weights for twins and four weeks early, they needed to go into an incubator for a little while now to make sure their lungs were not stressed. The nurses assured them they were fine but wanted them to have the best start. 'You can come see them whenever you want.'

Danika was taken to a private room and settled in a new bed, still with a drip, and advised not to try to get up as the spinal block will take a while to wear off and was handed a call button. After they were left alone Cristian sat on the edge of the bed so he could hug her better.

'You were so brave. What beautiful babies you have made for us,' Cristian said as he hugged her.

'I don't know how you watched all that, I couldn't. It was very weird not feeling much other than a slight push and pull,' Danika said. 'And it took your good genes to make our beautiful babies too. We need to let our mothers know if they are awake.'

Cristian handed her the phone where she could see that Selene had been trying to call her. Two phone calls and more tears later all would now know as the mothers were asked to let everyone else know their wonderful news.

A nurse came in again to check Danika's blood pressure and pulse and suggested it would be a quicker recovery if she could rest and then be able to see the twins later in the morning.

'I think that is my cue to leave my darling. I'll be back at breakfast. Here is your phone but really you do need to sleep now.' Cristian kissed her again and left to call a taxi.

Back at the apartment, Cristian looked around and felt a bit at a loss. He definitely wasn't tired. He was moving furniture and tidying a few dishes when the intercom went. It was Peter and Mark. When they came up they slapped him on the back and congratulated him on the twins, asking how Danika was. He was very pleased to see them. Mark had driven as he was sober but said that was easy to change which made them laugh. It was a case of expert Peter, novice Cristian and yet to be a parent Mark all comparing parenting advice and how to look after their wives during this period all lubricated by some fine scotch.

Cristian was sensible to set an alarm as many hours later as he snoozed on the couch he was reminded to get ready to go see Danika by a very annoying crowing rooster. He wasn't even sure where the other two were. He found them sprawled on the single beds in the third bedroom, so left a note about coffee and breakfast in the fridge and where he was going. Then he caught a taxi back to the hospital knowing he wasn't in any shape to drive.

At the hospital Danika smiled to see her still tipsy husband as she had been warned by Sonya that Peter and Mark had decided Cristian shouldn't be alone last night.

'Hello sweetheart, how are the others?' Danika asked.

'Unconscious when I left. I think we all sorted out the problems of the world last night.' He laughed at the few animated conversations they had together and was inwardly very humbled they had thought of him.

A nurse brought in Danika's breakfast and instructed her to eat it all or she will be kept in hospital longer. 'Make sure she does eat it Mr Blakesley, she is way too thin.' Although she seemed brusque she was very caring and brought another tray for him, saying it was so he didn't eat any of hers.

'Thank you,' they said in unison.

'The nurses have said after I eat they will take me to see the twins. Have you seen them this morning?' Danika asked as she looked through the food on her tray.

'No, I was waiting for you.' Cristian compared food and between the two Danika found suitable foods and Cristian helped her out. 'Any news on when you all can come home?'

'Dr Michael will be around in a few hours and I hope we know then,' Danika explained.

After a long and joyful visit with Aiden and Skye with Danika in a wheelchair, Dr Michael took her back to her room to check how she was and talk to them both.

'The paediatrician is very pleased how Aiden and Skye are going and, if they continue to go well, they should be able to leave in a week. They are on supplementary feeding until you are able to feed them Danika but that depends on you improving also. You are too thin and were dehydrated when you arrived,' he explained. Both Danika and Cristian felt chastised for not thinking about the impacts of Danika's poor diet. 'The breast-feeding nurse will be in to see you shortly to talk you through feeding premature babies. Hopefully if you improve over the next two days you can leave, but then you will need to come back for feeds and contact with the twins. Are you staying in Sydney?'

'We can until we can all go back to Hollingrove as a family.' Cristian had been holding Danika's hand and she now squeezed his.

Now that Danika fully understood how important looking after herself was, she was determined to do and be the best for Aiden and Skye. Although slow to start she was feeding the twins after a couple of days and this helped them gain the weight needed to be discharged as hoped a week after they were born. Danika was discharged two days before but the morning and evening drives back to the hospital each day were draining and uncomfortable on her surgery recovery. They were very pleased to be loading Aiden and Skye into the car only eight days after they were born. They had few visitors in Sydney but knew they would have many more once they were back at Hollingrove.

Sonya and Peter arrived shortly after and Danika could feel how keen Sonya was to hold the babies especially Skye.

'Skye already is full of attitude. We have to make sure she isn't spoiled more because she is the first Blakesley girl in four hundred years,' Danika said as she lovingly smiled at her cherub features then handed her to Sonya to hold.

'Aiden is the thinker of the two, taking it all in,' Cristian said as he cradled his son with pride.

Elizabeth waited her turn to hold each baby, thrilled to have the family growing and laughing again in the house. Danika sensed that the others were being patient but keen to get their own look at the twins. Danika sent a thought to Cristian hoping it made sense to him. He looked at her and nodded before going out to the kitchen.

Ann had tears in her eyes as she held Skye looking at Cristian. 'She has your looks Master Cristian, including the devilish eyes.' Danika could feel the love pouring out towards them all. Danika knew that the pain and frustration of a few months would fade in her memory but this day looking around at her family never would.

CREDITS

Cover Designer

Elizabeth McCracken @lizzacreative

Internal Formatting

Alana Lambert of Coven Press
Adobe Jenson Pro/12pt/16pt Leading
Dinkus elements sourced from Canva Stock

www.ingramcontent.com/pod-product-compliance
Lightning Source LLC
Chambersburg PA
CBHW050953180726
48291CB00006B/1811